THE RISE OF RIVERSTONE

BY MANDY SCHIMELPFENIG

To my husband, XIXO. That is all.

CHAPTER 1

Not all stories end happily for the heroes and badly for the villains. However, it is an indisputable fact that the best outcomes are hard won and often require tears, heartbreak, and sacrifice. Plus, a dose of resilience and a heaping amount of willfulness. My mother reminded me I had plenty of both on a daily... er, *hourly* basis. Not to mention an unyielding temper and impertinence.

Mother. Despite our numerous disagreements I couldn't deny everyone's praise of her beauty. There were mirrors everywhere in our house providing ample opportunity to remind her that she was the epitome of femininity: flawless skin, mahogany hair cascading down her slender, straight back, and eyes shimmering blue pools. While she sat poised and graceful at her dressing table in the evenings, I brushed her hair and mused that the softness and shade matched the fur of the otters that played in the river that flowed behind our house. I once made the mistake of voicing these thoughts and she spun around and glared at me as if I had cursed, then asked that I never again compare the glory of her beauty to a rodent. I prepared to argue, but her eyes warned that my next words could end in brutal punishment, so I held my tongue and continued brushing until not a tangle could be found in the luxurious, wavy tendrils. Before I could braid the strands, Mother waved me away.

"Let Morgan do that, darling. You always make a mess of plaiting my hair." Morgan was Mother's lady's maid, a stout, middle-aged woman who had been with the family for decades. Morgan could create masterpieces of curls, plaits, and twists fit for a queen. And she had a glare that could frighten a king.

"But I've been practicing! And besides, you're only going to bed. It's not as if anyone will see it."

Mother gave me an icy glare. I could tell she was still angry about the otter comment.

"Practicing on whom? Certainly not yourself."

She wasn't wrong. My hair, no matter how I struggled to tame it, could no easier be won over than the vicious stallion my father fought valiantly to break to saddle. Where my mother's hair was fine, mine was thick and unruly. I usually allowed the unholy mass of copper locks to fly ungoverned.

I focused on the toe of my boot tracing the intricate woven patterns of the plush blue carpet and confessed, "Amore."

"The pony? Really, my dear, I don't know what I'm going to do with you." She pinched the bridge of her nose. "A lady must always look her best, even when readying for bed. Who knows if she may be called out in the middle of the night due to a raid or a fire? She could be seen."

"Yes, his majesty forbids you to look less than spectacular while you're being raped or burned to death. What would people say?"

Mother rarely allowed me to see her angry. She said it was unseemly for a lady to raise her voice or her color, and the face contorted so horridly when in a rage. My behavior often tested her resolve, and it took all her composure to restrain herself. Most of the time, her sense of propriety won, but I was nothing if not challenging.

The brush just missed my head as I ran out of the door. My mother never took the time to practice her aim because ladies didn't throw things. Such physical activity was left to the men, along with punishing the children and making decisions. The brush clattered along the floor, and my mother drew in a sharp intake of breath through her nose and calmly exhaled to collect her sensibilities. I pressed my palm to my lips to suppress the laughter threatening to burst forth. I really was a horribly behaved daughter.

If a task didn't require looking beautiful or organizing parties and household staff, the responsibility fell to my father. While my mother was lithe, dark haired, and fair skinned, my father was a heavy bear of a man who had to duck through doorways. His golden hair frosted at his temples, and his skin was tanned from toiling long hours in the fields and after years of fighting with King Llewlyn against the desert people. Our mighty king established himself as a relentless warrior when he pursued the southern invaders out of Praed and into Crif, taking his fierce knights, including Father, with him. For five years, war raged until King Tuar of Crif was defeated, but even then our battle hungry king rose to every challenge, keeping him and his faithful fighters perpetually busy. We therefore saw Father rarely and he spoke less often, and it was mostly to dole out punishment. At least in my case.

Thus, I generally avoid contact with my father. I wasn't ashamed of this because it honestly was not unusual for girls my age to keep quiet and absent when their fathers were home from war. Men like my father were restless when they weren't fighting. Energy burned behind their eyes, and the muscles in their arms and legs twitched in idleness. Not even the harvest could keep them occupied. The only cure, especially during the five long months of winter, was a heavy dose of warm equi, a potent fermented beverage consumed by only the bravest of men. In truth, my father lived in a state of profound euphoria from fall to the first month of spring. Mother despised the laziness and tried to find excuses for Father to work, but he inevitably complained that simple tasks such as mending the south wall was beneath a knight of his caliber. I mumbled the only thing beneath him at that point was the floor, and I couldn't sit for a week after. My father might be many things, but hard of hearing was not one of them.

Impossible as it may seem, even my imposing father escaped my notice when I fled my mother's room. I collided with his thick chest, nearly toppling onto my backside. He caught me swiftly, his reflexes a habit of knighthood that certainly never waned no matter the season.

"Sorry, I'm so sorry." I flushed in embarrassment, tucked a loose strand of hair behind my ear, and muttered profuse apologies before he could scold me for running. "I should have been paying attention to where I was going, and of course I shouldn't have been running in the first place. I really have no reasonable excuse for my behavior." Was it obvious this speech had been regularly rehearsed? I continued, punctuating each point with a tick off my fingers. "There is no fire, no one is bleeding--that I'm aware of--and no robbers. That I know of." I paused to take a breath and noticed Father regarding me critically and apparently paying no heed to my apology. He was more displeased than usual, one fist balled against his mouth while he critically studied my form as if he found more than my behavior lacking. His gaze lingered on the mess of ginger hair tumbling in tangled waves down my back, and I self-consciously twisted a strand in my hand and tugged.

"Father...?" I asked. "Have I done something?" I frantically reviewed my movements that day, unease settling heavily in my stomach.

He looked up, his light blue eyes narrowing, appearing more disappointed when they met mine, dull green orbs in the middle of a freckled face.

He shook his head, and a crease formed on his brow. "I just can't figure where you came from, Laria."

His confusion swept over me, tinged with resignation. As if it wasn't disappointing enough I wasn't the son he always longed for, I should have been beautiful like Mother or sweet like my little sister. It was the least I could do, ungrateful daughter that I was. I flushed with anger and wrenched my arm out of his grasp.

"I don't believe I could reasonably be blamed for my appearance, Father. Given the choice, you know I would not wish to be a discredit to you, but not everyone can be as blessed as Mother."

Father's lips twitched briefly, wistfully, as he reached out to cup my chin in his large, rough hand. "No. No one can boast a beauty that great, but you would think a daughter bred from such a lady would reflect her in some way."

"I'm glad I am nothing like her," I snarled, slapping his hand away. "I wouldn't want her feeling she has to compete for attention, nor would I wish to rely on beauty as my one virtue. I'd rather be ugly and have wit than all the beauty in the world and an empty head."

My ears still rang as I stumbled toward my own room, the smooth leather of my shoes slipping on the polished floor. I should have known better than to insult Mother, especially right to Father's face. My parents engaged in legendary arguments involving screaming and breaking glass. We still talked about the time

Mother threw a silver serving platter at Father after he called my grandmother a meddling crone. It bears the dent from his head to this day. Despite their disagreements and outward hostility, my father was infatuated with my mother, and would defend her name and honor to any who would besmirch her, even his eldest daughter.

The door to Ula's room stood open and I stopped to peek inside. She sat in the little chair upholstered with butterflies and lilies she'd had since she was very small and refused to abandon, though her bottom outgrew the seat and she perched on the very edge with her legs outstretched to keep her balance. By the light of the fire, I watched her slender fingers expertly stitch an intricate piece of embroidery. In case there is any wonder, I am terrible at needlepoint. Everything Ula does is perfect, from her accomplishment at the task she now undertook, to her musical talent and melodic voice. The most endearing thing about my little sister is regardless of her many boastful talents, she is sweet, humble, and selfless. A lesser woman would hate having a sister, especially one three years younger, who was so flawless, but I loved and adored Ula, and she was the only member of my family who loved me.

She hummed a familiar tune while she worked, smiling slightly, and I recognized the song as one our mother used to sing when tucking us in at night. I pushed open the door and joined in the song with my less than enchanting voice. That's the kind way my mother describes it, but if I'm being honest, a dying cat is more pleasant to listen to. Ula's light blue eyes brightened at the sight of me, and her voice lifted high to carry mine as the song finished. I knelt next to her chair and traced the lines of stitched colors that became wildflowers so vivid I could practically smell their perfume. The room was quiet save the gentle crackling of wood burning in the hearth. The only movement was my own as I gently caressed the perfectly crafted scene that might someday have a head placed upon it--a waste of my sister's skill if anyone cared to ask my opinion. I was unaware of Ula staring intently at my face until she tenderly touched my temple and ran a finger down my cheek.

"What offense this time, Laria?" she asked softly.

"My own fault," I said. "Nothing unusual." I covered my cheek and turned away, ashamed. I could sense Ula's pitying eyes watching me, and I forced a smile to keep my anger from flaring. I didn't like her feeling sorry for me. I could bear the worst, but not my sister thinking she had to protect and comfort me. As the eldest, it was my duty to look out for *her*.

"It's really nothing to worry about, little gem. Now show me what masterpiece you're creating here and make me envious."

While she described the needlework as her interpretation of the meadow that hid among the dense trees of the Sessyl Forest on the opposite bank of the Rhyvor, the mighty river that flowed from the high peaks on the northern border of Praed past noble estates like our own, I nestled my fingers into her thick, raven hair and stroked the silky strands, occasionally twirling a lock into a twisted knot before releasing it to fall perfectly back into place. At twelve, Ula was blossoming into a young woman, and I could hear the slight change in her voice, deepening from her once tiny squeak to a mature timbre. Soon, she would be taller than me, and her figure would be fuller. Where I was slender and wispy, Ula was starting to develop a womanly shape, complete with swaying hips. Once, I overheard my mother lamenting to Morgan how terribly awkward it was to have a daughter as flat chested as a boy. It was very disagreeable to have the ladies at court continually commiserate that some ladies were "late to bloom" and reassure her I certainly would be a credit to my family before I came of age.

Though it was embarrassing to hear Mother speak of me this way, especially to a servant, my androgynous appearance was of no concern to me. The last thing I wished for was lascivious leers from amorous men and the threat of an arranged union. The less desirable my figure, the easier it was to keep myself free from the shackles of marriage. Ula, I knew, would not be so lucky. Between her emerging beauty and her many accomplishments, I wouldn't be surprised if Father had already been approached with offers of beneficial alliances featuring Ula as the bargaining piece. Ula would accept our father's decree in such a matter with obedience and dignity, calling upon her sense of duty and honor, while I would fight against him, lock myself in my room and starve to death before I would marry some random stranger to please Father's pocketbook.

I really was an ungrateful child.

These precious moments with Ula soothed my agitation, and as the vexation eased, I realized the conflict with my parents had left me utterly exhausted. I gave Ula's hair a final pat, kissed the crown of her head, and bid her delightful dreams.

CHAPTER 2

Morning mist clung to the dew-soaked grass when I cautiously slipped from my tower room, the spiraling stone steps frigid under my bare feet. When I reached the second floor, I pressed my boots against my chest, my fingers digging into the supple leather. I squeezed my eyes and held my breath before cautiously stepping on the wood floorboards. Silence. Relieved, I took another step, avoiding the weak boards. I stopped briefly to listen to Ula's steady breathing to ensure I hadn't inadvertently wakened her with my attempts at being stealthy. One might find it difficult to believe, but grace, like every other ladylike attribute, could not be counted among my achievements. Satisfied she remained undisturbed, I continued down the corridor and another set of winding stone steps. Near the bottom, I slowed, taking shallow breaths as my heart drummed against my chest. I braced my hand against the throbbing to muffle the sound as I peered around the corner. The hallway was quiet, thankfully too early for servants to be working in this part of the house, and no sign of my parents who rose at the first crow of dawn.

I tiptoed toward the lord's rooms where my father entertained the king and his closest circle of knights. None of the ladies were allowed in those rooms, and truthfully, they held no interest for me except that beyond was the back entrance leading to the stables.

My breathing quickened in anticipation as I neared freedom, amazingly without being noticed. I froze when I heard muffled voices, afraid I'd been discovered. The voices sounded agitated, and I concluded it was probably Mother and Father in their version of a polite discussion. I inched forward on the balls of my feet, holding my breath, moving against the wall to avoid the creaking floorboards. The door to the lord's rooms was closed, but I knew from previous eavesdropping that if it was quiet enough, you could put your ear directly against the keyhole and hear entire conversations. Admittedly, there was very little worth hearing since discussions among intoxicated, bored knights usually involved politics, sport, and women. Boring, boring, and gross.

Father had obviously come here to escape her because they didn't generally choose this room for their discussions, which meant it was he and not I who was in trouble. I suppressed a satisfied snicker and pressed my ear against the cold metal keyhole.

"I've never even heard of this family! How insulting for them to presume they can challenge our king. Where are they from anyway?" My mother's voice was more annoyed than angry.

Challenges to the king's crown were not unusual in Praed. In the ninth century, a king died and left his crown to his waifish son. The public outcry inspired a knight with a strong following to seize control, and the council crowned him king. Thus was established a tradition of overthrowing a king as a right of succession if the challenger felt his cause was just. King Llewlyn relished the chance to display his bravery and prowess on the battlefield. The more eminent the family, the greater the honor of slaughtering the foolish upstart hoping to wear his crown, and the merciful proclamation of pardon of the attacking family facilitated his charitable image. It had been many years since King Llewlyn had a proper war, so I thought my mother would be pleased to have Father busy, but if the family was obscure or poor, fighting was not worth the effort.

"Ilano," my father replied with a sigh. Ilano was the neighboring country several days' journey to the east. Clearly, Father didn't feel the insult as Mother did, probably because he'd been home for months and couldn't find any more excuses to avoid the list of improvements Mother compiled to keep him occupied.

"They are of the Ebony Eagle."

I'd never heard of such a family, and if Mother hadn't either, this was highly unfortunate if they hoped to be worthy of challenging our noble king. The delicate titter of my mother's amused laugh filled the room, and I took the opportunity to slip away. If I had not heard it by illicit means, the matter they discussed would most likely never have reached my ears. Another day, another poor idiot on a crusade against our powerful ruler. I left the matter behind with Mother's laughter, never to give the conversation another moment's thought. I hastily shoved my feet into my boots and dashed toward the stables.

The stables at Riverstone were renowned throughout Praed. Built from the dark wood harvested from the Sessyl Forest, it boasted fifteen stalls, an enormous circular training arena, a large tack room, a washing stall, and rooms for servants. The hay loft stretched the length of the building, making it easy to drop food to the hungry occupants. Water pumped from the river flowed through a system of pipes to fill troughs, and during the winter fires heated water until steam released into the space under the floor. I opened the main door a fraction and peered inside. Beams of sunlight illuminated the aisleway, and the only sound was the swishing of tails and contented snorts. The comforting odor of hay and horse filled my lungs when I eased through the small gap and swiftly walked down the rows of stalls. Curious heads popped over stall doors, but I ignored all but one. Amore nickered softly and placed her velvet nose into my outstretched palm, and I smiled.

"Good morning to you, too," I whispered, my hand traveling up her face. I rubbed the white star between her eyes, my fingers turning in tight circles. She blew air out her nose, shook her head impatiently, and kicked the stall door. I cupped her jaw in my hands, enjoying the warmth of her pulse under my fingers.

"Well, then." I chuckled. "Let's see what can be done to improve your mood." I planted a brief kiss on that lovely nose, placed a halter about her head, then led her out into the emerging sunshine. It was frowned upon to leave unescorted, not because Mother worried about bandits or rogues, but propriety dictated a lady of our station should be chaperoned at the risk of damaging, perhaps severely and irreparably, our reputation. In case it wasn't yet clear, I cared very little for my reputation.

While Amore gorged on grass, I ran a brush along her wide, strong back. Her color was a deep liver chestnut, a shade nearly as dark as scorched wood, the special star on her forehead the only white from top to bottom. I groomed away dirt and dead hair until her coat shined in the sun climbing higher in the sky. Time was running out. Soon, the whole house would be stirring, and I would be expected to join the family at breakfast. I hastily ran a comb through her flaxen mane, tossed it in the general direction of the stable, and silently led her off the estate. I glanced behind to make sure we hadn't been spotted, then deftly climbed aboard. As I settled onto the solid back, I wound my hand into the long mane and tightened my thighs along her sides.

"Come on, my girl," I whispered. "Before they catch us!" A firm kick with my heels made Amore pin her ears and grind her back hooves in the earth, launching herself into a steady gallop toward the horizon.

It's impossible to describe if you've never experienced such a feeling, the thrill of becoming one with a powerful creature. The melding of bodies into a single heartbeat, communicating through subtle movements, and the implicit trust without regard to differences of species. If I believed in superstitious nonsense, I would say riding astride a horse brought me as close to ascension without the bother of actually dying. Those from Praed, a large country at the heart of the continent, understood this bond. We are of the Equus, the horse the center of our culture. They help us till our fields and carry our soldiers in battle. We drink their milk as children and ferment it into equi and the milder kumis to drown out our troubles as adults. The winter coats they shed as the snows melt upholster our seats and pillows while manes and tails provide material for sewing, brushes, fishing line, and jewelry. They are our friends, companions, and confidants. When they pass, they are mourned as beloved family members and given all the funerary rights as befitting their station. When my father's war horse fell in battle, he was honored by feasts and presented with offerings for an entire month before his bones were interred in the family crypt.

Amore had been my gentle teacher for ten years from the time I could barely pull myself by her mane to scramble on her back. She had been patient but firm even as a young horse barely broke to saddle, not moving an inch while I seated myself awkwardly and clumsily kicked her with my heels. She made me earn her trust and molded me into a confident rider. Aside from Ula, she was my best friend.

The gray stone facade of Riverstone disappeared behind a swell of prairie, the grass turning from gold to lush green in the morning sun. The land of Praed rose and fell like waves, the grasses a mix of fresh grazing fields and miles of grain crops. In the spring, wildflowers bloomed in splashes of purple, blue, yellow, and white. The fertile lands supported horse breeding families and farmers. But the closer one traveled to the Rhyvor and the White Mountain, the rockier the terrain became. Riverstone overlooked one of the widest points of the river, its banks studded with crooked trees, large boulders, and hidden gullies. When my father's ancestors built the estate, they spent generations making the land habitable for horses. The animals that resulted from their breeding program developed the hardest hooves in Praed.

I leaned forward slightly as we crested an outcropping ending in a waterfall that fed the swimming hole where I would ruin dresses when no one was watching. Ula would sit on the banks and playfully yell that my antics scared away the fish. I would splash water in her direction, and she would throw worms at me. I led Amore to the water to drink, lying across her back with my arms crossed behind my head, my eyes closed contentedly while I enjoyed the warmth of the morning. I nearly fell off when Amore shook from nose to tail. I laughed and righted myself, wrapping my arms around her neck.

"Feels good to me, too, but we'd better head home before we're missed." When we turned back, I worried the sun was a little too high and I'd been gone too long, but moments like these were worth the risk of a whipping.

And how could it possibly be wrong to do that which my family had been born to do: to ride? They might as well punish me for breathing, for both were involuntary and required for survival.

When I made my appearance at breakfast, Mother and Father were too distracted to notice my tardiness, which meant that whatever occupied their thoughts was extremely dire. I stared across the table until I caught Ula's eye then quirked my brow in question. She shook her head--she had no idea what was going on either. Maybe it had something to do with the conversation I overheard this morning? I shrugged. Whatever the matter was, it wasn't our business, otherwise our parents would warn us to be prepared. We ate in uncomfortable silence. My mother fixated on her plate, purposely avoiding my father's watchful gaze, his shoulders tense and his brow furrowed as he aggressively chewed his food. The force of his fork hitting the plate rattled the table, but Mother refused to look up. Ula looked at me worriedly. Remembering my mother's venomous dissatisfaction for the impending threat to our king, I mouthed, "It's all right. It's nothing." Ula smiled, reassured that whatever vexed our parents would pass, and that our lives would remain undisturbed.

CHAPTER 3

A fortnight has passed since that morning at the breakfast table, and I can still recall the orange yolk running from my eggs after I sliced into them with my fork and the taste of the bread I used to sop up the delicious liquid. Before I awoke on the following day, Father left to teach the challengers from Ilano no one can defeat King Llewlyn. For a week, there was no change in Mother's demeanor aside from sighing heavily when Ula asked if Father had written. Her annoyance over Father's wasted efforts waned when another week went by without a victory parade on the King's Road. Mother had been certain the threat from the Ebony Eagles would pass with a flash of King Llewlyn's sword. I wasn't sure if Father's absence or being wrong upset her more.

For the last two days, Mother insisted I join her before breakfast for comportment lessons. The afternoons had been dedicated to training me on the finer points of embroidery, music, and art since I was twelve. Now, I was expected to rise early to practice walking without slouching and given lessons on proper topics of conversation. When I asked why the sudden interest in my feminine education, I was met with icy indifference.

Mother might dictate my every movement from sunrise to sunset, but the dawn hours were for me. Before the sun had risen high enough to pass through the windows of my tower room, I was creeping down the stairs with boots in hand. I paused to listen for movement, and when I felt it was safe, I stepped into the corridor.

"Enough."

I dropped my boots and squealed in surprise. Mother stood over me with one eyebrow raised, her slender hands on her hips, and watched me retrieve my boots.

"Go back upstairs," she said. "And put on the red dress with the gold stitching."

"But it clashes with my hair," I said. I blew a strand of the ginger locks off my forehead for emphasis, but Mother crossed her arms and pursed her lips. In a huff, I turned and stomped up the stairs.

I twisted and scratched at the clinging fabric of the dress throughout breakfast, but Mother ignored me. I asked not once, not twice, but ten times why she insisted I dress so elegantly for a family breakfast, but she wouldn't respond. Even *I* was becoming annoyed with the whine in my voice. I considered "accidentally" spilling food in my lap, but I wanted answers not a beating. Even Ula refused to be drawn into our silent argument. She shook her head and her cheeks turned pink when I mouthed, "Why?" across the table, and she spent the rest of the meal absorbed in her food. She knew something. Why else would she avoid my gaze and nudges under the table?

"Ula, you are dismissed," Mother said.

Ula dropped her fork and was out of her seat before I had a chance to reach across the table to grab her sleeve. Traitor. I slowly turned to look at Mother, who was staring down her nose at me. I fidgeted with my sleeve under the table while she scrutinized my appearance, my unease growing as her eyes travelled from the top of my head to my waist. She released a slow breath from her nose and closed her eyes resignedly.

"Go upstairs and I'll summon Morgan to do your hair. Come down to the drawing room when she's finished," she said.

"But why---"

She raised a hand to halt my words. Her eyes flashed angrily, then she closed them and took another deep breath through her flared nostrils. A whistle emanated through her pursed lips, and she said, "Do as you're told and go upstairs."

I pushed away from the table, making Mother wince as my chair vibrated across the floor. The effort to keep from arguing made my teeth grind, but I didn't refrain from stomping up the stairs. I could hear my mother's headache all the way up in my room.

In the drawing room, my head ached under the tight coils of Morgan's creation. I pressed a hand against one of the braids, but Mother slapped it away.

"Don't ruin it," she said. She picked up her embroidery, but I had nothing to occupy my idle hands. I drummed my fingers against my bouncing knee and sighed every five seconds. I still didn't know why we were here.

"What are we doing?" I asked.

"Waiting," Mother said without looking up.

"Waiting for what?"

There was a light knock before the aged butler, Carik, stepped inside. I stilled, and Mother set aside her work and folded her hands in her lap.

"Brock Gefroy, my lady," the butler said.

"Thank you, Carik. Sit up straight, Laria," Mother said.

Carik bowed as low as his creaking spine would allow and moved aside. Before I could speak, a tall man with pale skin and rounded cheeks walked in, bowed, and rang his hands. While Mother asked after his family, I narrowed my eyes and studied our guest. It's happened, sooner than I thought, but Mother has commenced the introduction of suitors. His smooth skin turned a deeper and deeper pink the longer Mother spoke to him, and I swear his beady eyes glittered in admiration.

I get it. My mother is beautiful. Can you pull yourself together?

I couldn't blame him. He looked very young, too young for even a shadow of facial hair. He shifted from one spindly leg to the other, and when he answered

Mother's questions, his voice cracked several times. All these faults I could forgive, but the pristine white doublet that shimmered with tiny gems curled my lip. My family was one of the most prosperous in Praed, but we showed our pride with our horses, the cleanliness of our stables, and in our bearing. Despite our disagreements, I appreciated that Mother frowned on ostentatious displays of wealth. She said people who displayed themselves so obviously were trying too hard. To me, a shiny clean doublet signaled someone who stayed indoors too much.

"My eldest daughter, Laria, fourteenth generation Audrey of Riverstone," Mother said.

I shook myself and managed to curtsey without tipping over. The young man bowed, but I didn't hold his attention. He looked back to Mother, and she indicated that we should all sit down. I fell heavily into the chaise, and our guest seemed to need direction on what he should do next.

"Move over so Brock can sit down, Laria," Mother said.

I didn't think my annoyed sigh was loud, but Mother's glare suggested otherwise. Brock sat at a respectable distance and after situating his fine clothes, he appeared to recall the purpose of his visit.

"Miss Audrey, it is a pleasure to meet you. My father speaks very highly of your family. He served with your father in Crif," Brock said.

"Oh? Is he a knight, too?" I asked.

"Was a knight. Unfortunately, he lost a leg and was retired by the king."

"I'm sorry." Very sorry. I had hoped that his father might have some information about the current fighting with Ilano.

"Miss Audrey, um." His eyes flickered toward Mother, who appeared to be absorbed in her embroidery, but I knew by the tilt of her head she was listening. "Tales of your mother's beauty have not been exaggerated." He grinned, revealing a crooked front tooth.

"I would think not," I said.

"Um." He looked at the top of my head, then met my blank stare. "You, um, are a credit to your family."

I raised an eyebrow. A bead of sweat trickled along his temple, and he glanced back at Mother. I didn't move, knowing that she was probably offering some encouragement to this fumbling suitor. He scooted closer, and his cheeks flushed. He looked down, then clumsily reached out and placed a damp palm over my folded hands. I wrenched away, looking to Mother for the reprimand I was sure she'd give, but her eyes remained fixed on her work, a raised eyebrow the only sign she knew what was happening.

"I'm sorry to be so forward," Brock said. His voice was strained and he wouldn't look at me as he groped for my hand again.

"You don't have to do this," I said. I lowered my voice and tugged my hand free from his firm grasp. "I'm not interested in being courted at present. You don't have to pretend you want me."

His eyes widened, but he didn't let go. "It is an honor to be considered for an Audrey alliance."

"I'm sure it is." I gritted my teeth and pulled away. "But I don't even know you."

"That's why he's here." We looked up at Mother standing over us. She smiled her most engaging smile at Brock, and he melted.

"She's, um, lovely," Brock said. He threw an arm around me, but he barely allowed his skin to touch mine. Mother didn't seem convinced, so he leaned over and placed a brief, wet kiss on my cheek. I gagged, but Mother clapped her hands together in delight.

"It's just what your father and I had hoped," she said.

"Father!" I pushed Brock away and jumped to my feet. "Father isn't here. And if he was, I'm sure he wouldn't wish for his eldest daughter to be pawed at by a boy barely out of his cradle. No offense," I said with a quick glance down at the wide-eyed suitor.

"Laria," Mother said, her voice a low warning.

"He doesn't even like me! You can tell just by looking at him." I waved a hand over his sweaty brow and trembling knees. "Do you think he's going to tolerate my torn hems and wild riding? Look how clean he is! Have you ever seen *me* this clean?"

Mother looked at Brock then quickly back to me. Her cheeks were reddening, and she raised herself up to her full height.

"It's no bother," Brock said and hastily got to his feet. "It was an honor to be considered, Lady Audrey. And, um, lovely to meet you, Miss Audrey." He reached out to pat me on the shoulder, reconsidered, then excused himself.

Mother and I locked eyes as the door closed, and I shivered. Mother moved so fast I only realized she'd struck me when pain bloomed on my cheek.

"You're going to have to accept your place, Laria," Mother said. "You are our eldest daughter. We will arrange a marriage with the best advantage and all you must do is smile, stay silent, and do as you're told. Is that clear?"

I refused to answer, hiding my face behind my hand and clenching my jaw to keep from screaming.

"If you continue to defy me," she said, her voice eerily calm, "then I won't give you the courtesy of an introduction to the gentleman before the wedding." With a swish of skirts and the dainty tapping of fine shoes, she was gone.

Mother summoned me to the drawing room often in the next two weeks to meet prospective husbands, which made me suspect she anticipated I would fail to impress these young men if she had a queue prepared. She knows me well. I avoided further ire by presenting myself as the respectable elder daughter: hair coiffed, hands folded, lips sealed.

It worked for approximately five minutes.

Eager first born sons of noble lords were happy to set aside their initial distaste at my unattractive ginger hair, freckles, and lack of curves for a chance to marry into our distinguished family, but I could not overlook their repugnance. Nor could I ignore Mother's growing tension. Father had been gone for a month and aside from rumors, we'd had no news. Mother remained poised, but I could tell by the vehemence with which she stabbed her needle into the handkerchief she embroidered that she was worried. Was this the reason for the sudden interest in having me settled?

I was not content to be sold off no matter the circumstances. I fended off the advances of the suitors gently at first, shifting away when they tried to touch me and responding minimally to their conversation. But when Godfrey Elyot leaned in with his puckered lips, sparse mustache, and greasy face to fulfill his father's dream of a Riverstone alliance, I broke my promise to be an obedient daughter. From the moment Godfrey tried to kiss me to when he was clutching his face was a blur of nails and blood punctuated with Mother's shocked screams. Godfrey was bundled off back to his father with a sizable apology and a gallon of Father's equi, I was sent to my room with a sore backside, and Mother retired with a glass of wine and a pounding headache.

Throughout dinner, I shifted painfully in my seat, but Mother paid no attention. She refused to look at me, even when I tipped over a shaker of salt. I told Ula about Mother's humiliating treatment, but though she sympathized, she didn't dare speak against her. She sat across the table casting furtive glances between Mother and I while I slouched in my chair in a final attempt to force Mother to acknowledge me. Her response was to delicately dab her mouth with a napkin and call for a refill of wine.

Mother didn't speak to me for three days.

CHAPTER 4

My body was heavy, full of the languid dreaming of a child safe and secure in a preciously sheltered and spoiled life. Blankets were tucked tightly around me, my nightgown soft against my skin and my hair snug under a cap. I was not weighed down with responsibilities, but rather with a full belly. My limbs melted into the bed, owing to the goblet of kumis I surreptitiously drank over evening supper while Mother extolled the virtues of temperance, secretly laughing over the irony only I could acknowledge.

Sweet, innocent sleep held me in its sublime clutches, and I was its content prisoner unwilling to break the wonderful bonds. Amid the joyous images of sparkling waters and flying manes, a blackness seeped into the idyllic dreamscape, and then all my dreams shattered, forcing me to face the startling nightmare awaiting me outside my imagination.

I opened one eye, not quite willing to abandon my warm bed to investigate. I blamed the kumis for my inability to understand the foreign sound coming from my window. Was it that stupid cat? That damn, smelly feline that my mother insisted served us by exterminating vermin but delighted in attacking my bare feet? That stinking creature was probably screaming for a mate again. If I acted that way, my mother would have my hide, but when *the cat* made that horrible noise and waved her tail in the air, it was accepted because it meant more mouths to eat rats. Hypocrisy ran rampant in this family.

As the haze lifted from my mind, I realized the sound did not come from a cat. It sounded too agonizingly painful, too desperately afraid, and clearly human. Wailing, mournful screams pierced the night to deafen my ears. Screams of unimaginable suffering. The sound pulled me up by my stomach, tying it in knots as I listened, paralyzed with fear.

The screaming was accompanied by a roar and pulsing heat from the window overlooking the stable. Light danced across the faded tapestry like the sun reflecting off water, as if this was not an illusion but another moment along the banks of the Rhyvor. For a moment I was transfixed, twisting and fading in and out of consciousness, unable to move through the fog of my thoughts. I blinked when I realized the screaming was no longer coming from outside, but from Ula's room, and above the shrieking my mother's forceful and always composed voice demanding an explanation. I flung off the blankets and ran to the window to peer down on the scene below.

Fire and ash, the sickeningly sweet smell of burning horseflesh, a glimpse of a face I did not recognize, the features twisted in the light of the blaze. Images flickered like the flames climbing into the sky as embers drifted downward illuminating the wet ground. I thought it strange since there had been no rain for days. Then a spark ignited a haystack and with a groan, I realized the glistening was not from a storm or morning dew. I heard a squelching sound and saw massive, booted feet sink into the sodden, crimson ground.

The fire spread, and I recognized some of the shapes darting in and out of the dark. Servants I had known all my life were seized attempting to flee or dampen the flames. Swords were plunged into their bellies without hesitation. A boy who worked in the barn sweeping hay from the loft into the stalls reached for one of the iron latches to free the beast inside, though it must have blistered his tender skin. Before the bar slid free, he was grasped by the hair and his head violently forced backward as a blade glided across his throat with casual ease, as if cutting a slice of bread. The body barely touched the ground before his murderer turned away without pause. I shrank from the window and vomited the remains of my dinner.

The sounds outside my room echoed on the stairs as they drew nearer, and I hoped the footsteps were Father's, returned from war to come rescue me. A figure crashed against the door, sending it flying into the wall. A knight in tarnished black armor emblazoned with a red eagle across the chest loomed in the doorway. My heart lodged in my throat and I could not scream. He was not my father. The man swiftly reached out and grabbed my arm, dragging me wordlessly toward the door. My voice was lost, but my mind had shrugged off the last remnants of sleep and kumis. *Move, move, you fool! Outside that door is death, and fire, and blood!* A terrifying sound I didn't recognize burst from my breast and reverberated off the gray stone walls. I growled and shrieked, swinging my free arm toward the narrow eye slits of the man's helmet, though it was well out of reach. The towering figure caught my wrist mid-swing, holding it tightly, then shook me like a child. My teeth chattered and my nightcap pitched to the floor, releasing my ginger hair to obscure my view. Shockingly, my captor released his hold, in repulsion or astonishment I did not know, nor did I have time to wonder for just as quickly he grabbed me again and pulled me down the stairs, my feet scraping against the rough, cold stone as I fought against his unyielding grip. I felt the icy night breeze briefly before the heat of the flames consuming our stables engulfed my face and dried my tears. I vaguely heard Ula, though her voice sounded fuzzy, as if underwater, and I felt the presence of my mother close, but I could not look for her. Though my eyes burned, I could not turn away from the horror, could not cover my ears to the shrill screams of the dying horses, could not escape from the hands holding me steady, forcing me to watch the end of my family.

As the walls crumbled and the agonizing noises no longer pierced the air, the night became still and quiet. Until then, I had not thought to question what was happening, who had done this. And where was Father?

The light from the fire was eclipsed by an enormous man. Though shorter than the knight from my room, he was thick, his massive chest larger than my father's. He removed his blood-smeared helmet and brushed brown hair off his sweaty brow. Ash clung to his thick graying beard, and embers reflected off the black eagle boldly displayed on his breastplate.

Black eagle.

Ilano.

I shivered at his towering form, his dark eyes devoid of feeling. He stood before my mother and she stared right back, her chin raised defiantly.

Mother once told me, "Never lower *your* eyes to a lesser man." I asked how I would know the difference. She cast me a shrewd look, her eyes narrowed. "An Audrey always knows."

He addressed my mother. "Evening, madam." The man's terrifying voice was so calm and low, yet it resonated over the subsiding destruction of the stable as it fell apart. "Apologies for the late hour, but this house is now my property. Collect your children and come with me. You are being relocated."

"And just who do you think you are?" my mother hissed, and I shuddered. Whoever he was, he just suffered her no-nonsense tone that usually preceded a sound beating. I ought to know, having heard it more than anyone. "My husband and the king shall---"

"The old king is dead." He spoke with no emotion. "I am your king now."

"My husband---"

"Is also dead, I'm afraid. You should be proud, madam. He died with a sword in his hand. And in his chest."

My feet ached as we marched along the King's Road to Praed Castle. There had been no time for tears after we were told that our lives were no longer our own, nor were we allowed the simple dignity of shoes. We were bound and led in our nightdresses down the cobbled road, the rocks digging into our soles until they bled. Ula was by my side doing her best to suppress the whimpers of pain, but after hours of walking, her steps left little red footprints in the dirt, and it crushed my soul to see her suffer. My mother bore the insult well, with her head high and her back straight, and she never once glanced back at her struggling daughters. I glared at the back of her head, my eyes burning with hatred, and I wished it would set her precious hair on fire. Even now, she played the part of Lady of Riverstone, not allowing for one moment a shred of humanity to alter her appearance of composure, not even to comfort her children.

We learned that the man bearing the black eagle was Conall, and he led the procession of knights, soldiers, and prisoners proudly through the scorched landscape left in the wake of his invasion. His night raids had allowed him to push further and further into Praed, leaving no survivors behind to warn of their approach. My father and his knights were the greatest warriors of Praed, and they had fallen like wisps of burnt hay.

Inevitably, Ula stumbled, and her hands and knees were shredded as she tried to catch herself on the rough surface we trod upon. The mounted knight who held her bound hands jerked a rope, scraping her across the ground while yelling at her to get up, and my temper could be restrained no longer.

I screamed, a guttural sound made hoarse by my parched throat, and rushed at the blackguard. Before my fisted hands could connect with his thigh, my own binding was pulled backward, and I nearly fell myself. I scowled up at the knight holding me, the one who had dragged me from my room. I focused my energy toward him instead and struck out, hitting his knee, which probably hurt me more than him. I despised them all, and I would unleash my fury on this man even if it cost me my life.

Without a word, the rope binding my hands was jerked taut so my hands rested against the pommel of the saddle. I glared up at him, feet dangling above the ground and teeth gritted as my arms stretched across the horse's withers.

"Leave her alone, you monster!" I hissed, the words drowned out by the other knights' laughter. The black knight grabbed the back of my hair and leaned close to my face. The lascivious whistling that followed replaced my anger with fear as I imagined all manner of vile deeds he was planning. He drew so close I could see myself in his cerulean eyes, and he could no doubt hear my teeth chattering.

"Don't," he whispered. Without another word, he released my hair and hands and I dropped to the ground. Ula was already on her feet, her eyes full of fright.

"It's all right," I told her when I clambered back onto my feet. I moved to her side and asked, "Are you very hurt? Can you walk?" She nodded bravely, and we were once again pulled along.

My mother never looked back.

In the past when a king was overthrown, there was an unspoken understanding that the royal family was not to be harmed but instead exiled. However, it soon became evident our new king did not adhere to such pleasantries. As we travelled along the King's Road toward the White Mountain, destruction lined our path. All around, the houses of noble families that had been passed down for generations were burnt shells occupied only by wisps of smoke trailing into the hazy sky. Prized possessions were strewn along the road, and men plundered the heirlooms of the murdered knights of dead King Llewlyn. Those allowed to live fled or were forced into servitude alongside us, their faces blackened with the soot from their homes.

On a clear day with dry roads, it would take my family several hours to reach the castle, and we always arrived before dark. However, this was an army of thousands accompanied by exhausted prisoners. Though the crooked peak of the towering mountain we called "The Center of the World" signaled we were close, I worried that Ula wouldn't make it. We were given enough water to moisten our sticky mouths and rations of bread, but it barely sustained us for the arduous journey. I eventually gave Ula my share, but she still barely kept up with the knight dragging her along. Her little voice pleaded with the man to let her rest, but he ignored her, keeping his attention instead on a boisterous conversation with another knight riding beside him.

Ula started swaying, and I braced against her so she could lean into me. I whispered encouragements to urge her forward, demanding she respond. Inevitably, Ula's eyes rolled closed and her knees buckled. I tried to catch her, but I was wrenched away by the bindings connecting me to the black knight. My throat was dry and my tongue stuck to the roof of my mouth, turning my cries of protest into the squeaks of a dying mouse. Ula fainted, but her captor didn't notice and started dragging her limp body. Desperately, I planted my feet and tugged on my bindings, but the black knight ignored me. I looked back, and the sight of Ula face down in the dirt made the blood drain to my toes, then surge back up in a flush of anger.

Impulsively, I clenched my jaw, clamped a rock between my bound hands, and heaved it at the black knight's back. The toss was awkward, but the rock struck with a clang between his shoulder blades, and his horse reared with the force of the resulting jerk on the reins. I swallowed hard at the furious look he turned on me, but I managed to raise my trembling hands to point back at Ula. The anger faded when he saw her being dragged carelessly in the dirt, and he called for a halt.

The black knight issued the knight holding Ula's rope a firm reprimand for ignoring his prisoner. Faster than I could react, the knight jumped off his horse, threw Ula over the pommel, and mounted up. I ached to hold her, to brush her matted hair away from her soiled brow, but the black knight was pulling me forward at a brisk trot.

"Your Majesty," the black knight said to Conall. "The ladies need to rest for the night."

Conall cast his dark eyes on me, and his lip curled. I stared back, too exhausted to be afraid. He looked toward the mountain outlined against the setting sun.

"We're nearly there," Conall said.

"You can't present them as trophies if they're dead."

Conall met the black knight's eyes, and a heartbeat passed in tense silence. Then the edges of the big man's eyes crinkled in amusement, and he planted a hearty slap on the black knight's shoulder.

"It would be impressive to have everyone formally waiting to greet us on the steps of the castle."

The black knight nodded, and the king pronounced that we would make camp for the night. My eyes remained on Ula's pale face, even when I was led off the road and tied to a tree. I bared my teeth at the knight who deposited Ula next to me, and he raised his hand to strike me. He laughed when I flinched away, then left to attend to his duties.

I cradled Ula in my lap where she eventually regained her senses. I distractedly brushed her hair with my fingers while we silently watched soldiers erect tents and build fires. The sun dropped behind the Center of the World. In its shadow was the White Mountain, and atop it was Praed Castle. We would reach it by late morning. What would happen to us then?

Eventually, we were given water and a meager meal. I gave most of my rations to Ula, and she didn't argue, which was a testament to her debilitated condition. We huddled in each other's arms under the boughs of an ancient tree while feet away Conall's men celebrated into the night. I guarded Ula's sleeping form, but no one bothered us. My eyes fluttered closed in the dying firelight, the men gradually settling into sleep or passing out from drink. The screech of an owl penetrated the veil of sleep, sharp and high before fading into a mournful silence. Then I was completely consumed by darkness.

CHAPTER 5

Market Town sprawled at the foot of the White Mountain. The collection of stalls selling food, leather works, jewelry, and arms were always crowded whenever my family visited. Ula and I would feast on fresh pies while Mother browsed the selection of necklaces and Father discussed the crafting of new gauntlets with armor smiths. Now, the stalls were empty or destroyed, the merchants lying among the debris or picking up the pieces.

The road began to rise upward, and we passed under the arches of ancient trees. The smoke had dissipated, and the great castle towered in the distance, nestled atop the mountain that once inspired awe. But now the blood of war dripped from the tarnished stone and imposing walls that would now be our prison. Our legs trembling with exhaustion, we ended our journey at the castle threshold where unfamiliar faces glared down at us. Among the gathered crowd stood apart three people: two women, one old and one young, and a young man. Their fine clothes led me to conclude that they were likely the new royal family, and my suspicions were confirmed when the self-proclaimed new king at the head of our procession threw his arms wide and addressed the trio.

"So wonderful for you to greet us! I trust everyone has settled into our new home?" I noted that he did not embrace them, but he did take the hand of the old woman, albeit briefly.

"It smells," the young woman sneered. The king laughed, and I'm sure the whole exchange was done loudly so that we would be certain to hear.

"I've brought you presents." The king waved us forward. We were dragged in front of the assembled family like cattle and forced to kneel. My mother and Ula kept their eyes downcast, but I stared defiantly. The older woman unnervingly fixed her milky gray eyes on me. She did not smile or frown but was perfectly impassive, and though it was obvious she was completely blind, I felt she was studying me intently. I repaid the courtesy, noting upon closer inspection the shimmering gold highlights in her brown hair. Though her blindness leant her an aged appearance, there were few lines about her eyes and mouth, leading me to conclude she was nearer to Mother's age than I originally thought.

"How strange," a male voice remarked before fingers roughly inspected my hair.

"Ew, don't touch it," the young woman scolded before I could protest. She slapped the young man's hand away and looked at him disgustedly. "Would you touch a frothing dog or a pile of manure?"

"Enough, Caelyn," the king admonished, though not harshly. I suspected this quarreling was routine. "Now that you're a princess and your brother a prince, you must conduct yourselves better, especially in public and in front of servants. Besides, that's no way to speak to your new lady's maid, is it?" The princess curled her lip and looked at me with scornful dark blue eyes. The prince laughed, leaving me to surmise this assignment was a punishment for both of us. The princess grabbed her brother's hand and used it to force my head to the ground.

"I am your princess," she hissed, "therefore you will show me respect and don't look at me with your ugly, freckled face." I bit my tongue and held back a sob as she rubbed my nose in the dirt.

The prince finally freed his hand, pulling my hair in the process and unleashing the tears I had struggled to contain. I didn't want them to see, so I kept my face down, my forehead touching the ground as dust stirred from the puffs of air I exhaled. I would not permit them to hear a sound from my lips, so I clenched my teeth against my tongue. I remained that way as the king made proclamations and speeches and the crowd responded exuberantly. I listened as he declared the old king dead and the crowd clapped and cheered and called out, "Long live King Conall!" I didn't move when my mother was presented to Queen Shaeli as part of her entourage, not even for the satisfaction of witnessing her reaction to such an insult. Even when they sentenced Ula to life as a laundress, I remained still. I made a promise to myself as I breathed in the dust and regained control of my emotions that I would never let them see me wounded. So, while the people began to disperse and I could hear the tiny footsteps of Ula being led away, I kept my head pressed into the ground and closed my eyes tight. The voices of the prince and princess arguing with their father drifted away, and I still didn't move a muscle. The world began to fade, and I hoped if I stayed where I was, I could disappear with it. But then I felt someone reach under my arm and gently pull me to my feet. I opened my eyes and there was the big knight from my nightmares towering over me, blocking out the sunshine.

"Come." He led me toward the castle, and I did not resist.

What would Mother do? I lifted my chin and stepped purposefully, all sadness and anger abandoned. No words will leave my mouth, and none of theirs will reach my ears. If I'm to survive, then I must build my own walls to hide behind, and never let them inside.

The Elejick royal family provided me with a plain tunic, thin leather shoes, and a tiny closet to sleep in within eyesight of the princess' room. I was ordered to change and promptly report to the main hall where a month-long feast would commence to honor the new king. The new regime wasted no time in stripping the castle of King Llewlyn's banners and replacing them with sky-blue standards emblazoned with a diving bird of prey, talons outstretched. I later learned that all evidence of the previous family was burned, including the body of King Llewlyn's son and heir who had been slain upon the death of his father. The former queen had been spared to serve her replacement, but she chose to lacerate her jugular rather than live in disgrace. I couldn't blame her, but the suicide of a former queen made us all look weak.

I moved freely about the castle not as a statement of trust, but because I would be a fool to try and escape or attack the guards. I hastened toward the main hall, head down, and arms swinging. These corridors were familiar to me from visits to King Llewlyn with Father, but this was my first time among them as a prisoner, a slave to the current residents. Strangers passed me without a glance, and I avoided guards who sauntered by conversing jovially with goblets in their hands. The entire palace was celebrating, and the party started early for some. Echoes of laughter grew louder as I approached the main hall, and the sound became deafening when I pushed through the heavy oak door to reveal banquet tables lined with a vast feast. Smells of meats dripping with herbs and spices, fresh bread, buttered potatoes, every dessert imaginable, and mountains of cheese invaded my nose and went straight to my rumbling stomach. My mouth watered, and though I had decided to stubbornly refuse any offerings from these people, it had been hours since I last ate, and my body rebelled against my resolve in its need for sustenance.

There was barely room to move in the crowded hall. Knights sang songs with mugs raised while ladies swooned and fanned themselves. Old men clutched full bellies and bellowed until their cheeks turned red and I expected them to next grab their chests and fall over dead. Rather, I wished they would. The characters of the current court were much like the previous, but the voices were harsher and the gluttony greater. I shuffled along the back wall trying to remain inconspicuous as I neared the seat of my new mistress, Princess Caelyn. She sat at the head table at her father's left hand directing a smug smile at her brother, Prince Brannon, who was calling and waving after a young woman. The princess laughed when he nearly fell off his chair, and he snarled some curse before drinking deeply from a goblet, amber liquid dripping down his chin. My stomach lurched in disgust, but I kept my face neutral as I stepped behind the princess, at the ready to tend to her needs. Later, in my little room, I would be fed a meager meal, but as a servant, I was there to work.

The princess ignores me for most of the evening, occasionally peering over her shoulder and looking displeased when she sees me.

I'm obviously not a fitting example of a regal attendant, but she resigns herself to my presence and wordlessly lifts her glass for me to fill. As she prattles on with her friends, my eyes scan the faces that I must now familiarize myself with. They blur together in a whirl of crude voices, lips glistening with grease. Large men threw bones to growling dogs, and the women are just as boisterous. Knights pound each other on the back and congratulate themselves as they tell stories from the battlefield, and I can't stand listening to the tales of blood and glory. Everyone is talking, each person louder and louder as they compete to be heard. I wanted nothing more than to cover my ears and drown out the noise, but I had vowed to remain deaf to the chaos.

I continued to survey the crowd, noticing one person remaining as silent as me sitting in a place of honor at the king's table. It was the knight from my bedroom, in the shadow of the king's immense frame, staring at me. Though he no longer wore armor, he nevertheless dressed completely in black. Even his hair and neatly trimmed beard were black. Candlelight flickered across his angled jaw and straight nose, and the flame reflecting in his blue eyes made me shiver. I narrowed my eyes and glared back--consequences be damned. He didn't break his gaze or yell at me to avert mine. He just sat there, blank faced and unwavering, obviously trying to intimidate me. It worked.

A crash reverberated above the roar of noise and broken glass splintered across the floor toward the royal slipper of the princess. She jumped to her feet and fixed murderous eyes on an enfeebled servant who had collapsed under the weight of an overloaded tray of wine-laden goblets.

"You clumsy imbecile!" she screamed, and the room silenced as the old man shakily regained his feet. No one came to his aid. Not one of these people would be kind enough, and the servants were too afraid.

"I'm sorry, my lady," the man apologized, and I suddenly recognized him. I'm ashamed to say I couldn't recall his name, but he had served King Llewlyn faithfully for decades. He was always kind to the children, sneaking us sweets when our parents weren't looking. He had held a place of distinction in the previous court, and now he was reduced to the lowliest station, serving drunkards.

"Sorry?" she repeated incredulously. She turned to her father, appalled. "He's 'sorry,' Father. His incompetence nearly spilled royal blood and all he can say is 'sorry.' What are you going to do about it?" I tried not to reveal my emotions as I waited desperately for his answer. What sort of man would this new king be? His response, I knew, would expose his true character, and set a precedence for the time to come.

The king quietly regarded his daughter, the pair locked in a battle only they could comprehend. The room waited with me, watching the exchange and throbbing with anticipation. Finally, the king directed his attention on the old man trembling in fear, his chest heaving as he struggled to catch his breath. Could they see what I saw? He wasn't just afraid; he was in pain.

I never believed in *unspeak*, the ability to send your thoughts to people and have them hear you, but I concentrated every ounce of strength toward that poor man, willing him to see me, to feel my sympathy. When the king began to speak, the old man's eyes met mine, and I pushed all my compassion into my eyes, leaving my face blank. The king proclaimed that an act of violence against his family, even unintended, was a threat against the king himself. With my thoughts I told this man whom I had known nearly my whole life, "I am here. They can't hurt us. We're stronger than they are."

In the next breath, King Conall sentenced an old man to death for breaking a glass, and I told that man, "You are better than this king, and you will die with honor." And the old man whose name I could not remember smiled as he was led to the dungeon.

Later that night I was forced to scrub my hands in scalding hot water until my knuckles bled and my skin began to peel. The princess insisted this routine be performed any time I was expected to touch her whether to brush her hair or help her dress. And I thought Mother was critical.

My sore hands shook as I brushed the princess's long, dark hair that nearly reached her waist. Even with Mother I had never been so careful. If I accidentally pulled Mother's hair, the worst that could happen was a beating. In this situation, I was certain one error could mean my life. Or at the very least dismemberment.

As I carefully plaited the princess's perfectly smooth hair, the door to her bedchamber was thrown open and the prince walked briskly into the room, threw himself onto the bed, and huffed dramatically. The princess ignored him, and I watched her reflection in the mirror while she twisted a ribbon around her finger, deliberately focusing her attention on anything but her brother. I followed her example and did not acknowledge his presence either, concentrating hard on making her braids even.

"How much longer is she going to take?" Prince Brannon sighed.

"As long as I wish," Princess Caelyn replied, still not meeting his eyes. "There's nothing else going on. Why does it matter?"

"Are we to have no privacy now that Father has conquered these savages?" The princess finally turned to face him, and I nearly lost my place.

"If they're such savages I wonder why you worry about talking in front of them. Besides, this one belongs to me, so we can trust her silence."

"Can we?" His eyes narrowed as he studied me, his gaze roaming up and down my body.

"Of course. She may be stupid, but I'm sure she knows the punishment for betrayal. Also," the princess smiled wickedly, "I'm fairly certain she's deaf or mute. Or both."

The prince smiled, "Oh? Well, in that case she should know her father died a coward crying for his mummy and pissing his breeches."

The princess laughed and watched my face. I remained impassive, as if they hadn't spoken a word.

"Also," he continued, "I heard our father became extremely aroused when he saw her bitch of a mother and plans to show her what a real king can do between a woman's legs."

I felt nauseous, but I did not respond. A part of me knew he spoke such filth to antagonize me, but I feared he used the truth as torture.

"See?" the princess gloated. "If the thought of her father in disgrace and her mother's perfect face ruined doesn't move her tongue, nothing will."

The prince, seemingly satisfied that any words spoken between him and his sister would not be repeated, flopped back among the goose down pillows. He watched me complete one long braid and begin the next, his fingers intertwined and his head cocked at an angle as if contemplating a puzzle.

"I do wonder at her strange appearance," he said.

The princess' attention had drifted to the adornments on her nightstand and barely mustered the slightest, "Hm?"

"The younger one plainly favors the mother, but this one," he said. "No resemblance to Lady Audrey whatsoever. And she certainly doesn't favor her father. What do you think? Is she even his?"

"Wouldn't surprise me if she wasn't." The princess continued as if discussing the harvest and not the question of my lineage. "From what I understand, Sir Maccus Audrey was away at war quite often and his wife, great beauty that she is, must have been lonely. Women have needs, too."

"So I hear…"

The princess abruptly abandoned her task, turned to her brother, and snapped, "You would know better than I."

He chuckled. "Relax, dear sister."

She continued to glare at him, and my fingers worked faster to finish so I could be excused.

"Well," the prince continued, unfazed by his sister's anger. "Here we are. Father has really done it, hasn't he?"

"Mother said he would." Her face showed no sign of softening. The tension was becoming unbearable.

"Yes, but you know I don't believe in her nonsense."

"You're a fool," she said decidedly, her manner relaxing. "You always have been, even when the truth is right in front of you."

"Do you think she's right about everything?"

"We can hope." The princess turned and stared at her reflection, and at me tucking her completed plaits into her nightcap. "I refuse to live this way for longer than absolutely necessary."

"Patience was never one of your virtues."

"I do have patience," she said, "but not when others are in control of my fate. I can be very patient when it comes to executing my own plans. Like a hawk circling its prey."

"More like a spider in a web, I'd say."

"You just do your part, Brannon. Let me handle the rest."

"Of course." The prince rose from the bed to leave. "Hard work was never one of *my* virtues."

As the door clicked shut, I stepped away from the princess, head bowed and hands clasped, and waited for her to excuse me.

"It will have to do," she decided after inspecting my work. "At least until you can be taught how to properly tend to a princess." Mother would be furious with her assessment, not for the insult toward me, but because my inability to style hair reflected poorly on my upbringing. Although she might secretly feel vindicated in her admonishments for my deplorable grooming habits. I continued to silently wait, knowing if I walked out at this moment, she would use it as an excuse to dismiss me from her service in a permanent fashion. I had only known her one day, but I had learned enough to know that if I wished to see a lifetime, I must not provoke her.

Silence reigned for several seconds, and my face grew hot as I sensed her regarding me, her fingers tapping the nightstand in irritation.

"What sort of creature are you really?" she mused.

Princess Caelyn rose to stand before me and took my chin in her hand. She forced me to look her in the eye, and I was struck by how tall she was, at least a head above mine.

"I'm not convinced you cannot hear me, but if nothing else, can you at least read my lips?" I nodded. "Then understand this: what is said in these rooms will not be repeated. Not to anyone. You have no friends here…" she faltered, annoyed, "whatever your name is. No one will believe you, and if I hear you spreading gossip, I will punish you like that old man downstairs. Are we clear?" I nodded again, hiding the fear behind an expressionless stare. "Good," she released me and moved toward her bed, dropping her robe to the floor. I stooped to pick it up and laid it on the back of a chair, her eyes watching me closely.

"Leave me," she commanded when I met her gaze. I needed no further encouragement.

That night I was lying on the narrow, thin mattress in my tiny room, listening to the fading sounds of the remaining revelers retreating to their rooms or passing out in the corridors. There was no lock on my door, and I feared that someone might mistake my room for theirs and stumble in to find me huddled under the covers. Or worse, they know I'm here and purposefully invade my space for reasons I don't want to contemplate.

To my relief, I remained undisturbed, and I fell into an exhausted slumber replete with nightmares fraught with flames, black smoke, screaming horses, and men, always men, dictating how the world shall spin.

CHAPTER 6

The days stretched into arduous weeks as King Conall established his iron rule. The fires receded, but the number of dead or missing increased as the population was cleansed of King Llewlyn loyalists clinging to hope of an uprising. The king's soldiers raided estates, forced the residents to kneel to their new king, and confiscated lands. Those who refused were arrested, stripped, and paraded down the King's Road supporting weighted beams across their shoulders. Once they reached the castle, the king ordered them into the courtyard where they stood for three days without food or water. Some bent to his authority, and their deaths were merciful--an axe to the neck. Those who refused were publicly humiliated. It amused King Conall to have the prisoners chained and fed rotten meat, and they would crawl in the resulting filth for days. Soldiers were encouraged to toss bones to the starving men, then release their hounds. The prisoners and dogs fought over the scraps, and the men, including the king, would laugh until their faces turned red.

Eventually, King Conall ordered their deaths, and the Praed-born servants were forced to watch dozens of men be hanged, disemboweled, and quartered. The bodies were left in the sun for days before King Conall made us clean the courtyard until not a drop of blood remained. I tasted bile and smelled putrid flesh for a week afterward.

I managed to convince the royal family that I was deaf after practicing for hours to still my expressions, especially my eyes. A flinch at a loud noise could be my undoing, so I trained them on the floor, and focused on something small until my vision blurred and sounds faded. It helped that no one cared to look at me. It was easier to pretend to be mute. I had a lot I wanted to say, but it would end with my body rotting in the sun.

As the reality of the new regime became undeniable, everyone settled into their new roles. My routine began in the early hours with instructions to the kitchens regarding the princess' chosen meal to break her fast, followed by the preparations of her bath and laying out her gown with associated accoutrements. Half the time, her highness would inevitably rise late and change her mind and make me rush to fix everything before she finished her toilette. Most mornings, she chose to eat in her rooms while she poured over her correspondence, which I pretended not to be able to read. She left behind many friends in Ilano, and they wrote to her often detailing the news only interesting to one who grew up there. Amid the updates of engagements, gossip, and death notices, the letters were filled with exaltations of jealousy and envy of Caelyn's current position, and I knew she relished these passages the best.

Every afternoon, Prince Brannon would barge in unannounced into the princess' rooms and whine about every defect he found with Praed. One day the bread was too doughy and the next too dry. His pillows were never soft enough. The smell from the stables was too strong, and he had his rooms changed several times to avoid unpleasant odors. I found the prince to be annoying and childish, and I was glad he ignored my presence. The princess seemed not to mind, but the longer I served her, the more I noticed how irritating she also found him. She never responded to his criticisms, her nostrils would flare, and her ears took on a rosy hue as he prattled on, unaware of her rising ire. Finally, she would suggest a walk to the mews to ease his discomfort.

I hated the mews. The structures were promptly built when King Conall took possession of the castle using the shells of the vacant extra stabling that the previous king had filled with his prized saddle horses. I never had the nerve to find out what happened to those beautiful animals, but in their place were the terrifying birds that were the cornerstone of the Ilano culture.

We walked around the northern wall of the castle, low rows of buildings lining either side of the track that once led to a magnificent outdoor arena where knights displayed their skill at arms. Wire mesh windows offered the only protection from the devils housed inside. I tugged anxiously at a lock of my hair when I passed and suppressed a squeal when the birds screeched and flapped at the mesh. The beasts surely sensed how much I feared and loathed them. The princess stopped at one mew and laid her hand against the wire, slipping a piece of raw meat to the waiting beak inside. This was her "darling," as she called it, a dark gray falcon with ash white feet and black eyes. It made tiny chirping noises as she cooed to it, and I resisted the urge to roll my eyes.

Inevitably, Prince Brannon grew impatient and steered her down the path where annual tournaments had been held on King Llewlyn's birthday. The seats where the crowds had cheered were gone, replaced by thirty large boxes with barred windows, and the arena was now home to arched stands where fearsome birds perched in the afternoon sunshine. In Praed, birds of prey were common, and they were close in size to the falcons. But the eagles were twice as big, some half as tall as a man. Men milled about cleaning mews and feeding the large, black birds with talons the size of my fingers. Every time we ventured toward them, the blood drained from my face and my knees shook. A week ago, I had watched the prince show off to one of the ladies of Queen Shaeli's entourage by flying an eagle over the jagged rocks to snatch a mountain goat kid off a ledge with ease then, at the prince's command, drop it. The bleating as the kid plummeted to the ground echoed against the stony cliffs, and the eagle returned dutifully to the prince's arm. What a pair of cruel monsters they made. Ever since, I never looked on those birds with anything less than abhorrence.

Prince Brannon walked up to his precious murderer now, sitting there on its perch with dead eyes, and stroked the feathers along the back of its head.

"I think he's grown a little since we've been here," Prince Brannon observed. His eagle was not as large as some of the others, and the prince took this personally.

"He'll never be really big. He is a male after all," Princess Caelyn said in a deliberate attempt to upset him. If he was so bothered by how small his stupid bird was, why didn't he just get a different one?

"Don't listen to her, Verix," the prince told the bird, trailing his fingers down the massive wings. "You're perfectly capable of being more than you are. She'll see." I closed my eyes and inhaled deeply to keep from gagging.

After touring the mews, the prince left us for whatever task perpetually bored princes did to occupy themselves, and I was stuck sitting with Princess Caelyn while she embroidered, wrote letters, practiced singing, and generally performed those accomplishments which I had always avoided in my previous life. Now I was an observer, proving there were indeed worse things than improving oneself. Damn Mother for being right.

As stimulating as these late afternoons were, I would gladly sit and count stitches any day rather than be subjected to the weekly visits to Queen Shaeli. An intimate gathering met in her anteroom furnished with plush chairs arranged in a circle around a small table covered with assorted refreshments. You couldn't accuse this family of neglecting their guests.

There had never been a reason to explore the queen's rooms in my past trips to the palace, so I could not compare the decor. However, nothing I had seen came close to the taste of the current monarch. The windows were draped with heavy, black velvet curtains, blocking out all sunlight. Mirrors shined on all the walls, which I found strangest of all since Queen Shaeli was blind. The image of all the people reflecting off their surfaces created the illusion that hundreds of attendants were amassed inside. The chairs were colored deep burgundy and wide enough to hold two people each. The room smelled of burning grass and a musky odor that reminded me of angry skunks. Between the closely grouped people and enormous fire blazing in the hearth, the air quickly became stifling, and I felt droplets of sweat inching down my back. The worst part about the queen's rooms were the people in her attendance, namely one person: my mother.

My mother and I had not spoken in weeks, but we saw each other whenever the princess attended these private sessions. At first, I had tried to catch her attention, but she resolutely avoided my gaze. Once, I tried to pass her a note enquiring after Ula, but she tossed it into the fire just as quickly as I placed it against her palm. Whatever her reasons, her behavior effectively ceased my attempts to communicate with her. While the ladies waited for the queen, I observed my mother briefly, noting any changes since the last time I saw her. Her features had aged drastically since leaving Riverstone. Lines ran like tributaries from the corners of her eyes and mouth. Gray hairs marred her once flawless locks, so many that she couldn't possibly pluck them all out, as I'm certain she tried. Once the perfect example of feminine physique, her body was now thin, and her clothing no longer flattered her small waist and full bosom. Despite her appearance, she still retained her stately composure: chin raised, back straight, and hands folded neatly in her lap.

Queen Shaeli entered, and the conversations quieted as she smoothly traversed the room and placed herself in one of the chairs without guidance. Her thin form was draped in layers of gauzy fabrics in muted green hues that complimented her flawless olive complexion. A crown nestled in her thick, intricately plaited hair, jewels glittering in the candlelight. She elegantly gestured toward the other seats and everyone, save the few servants like me, nestled into the cushions and waited for the spectacle to begin.

Travelling gypsies often broke their journeys to entertain us at Riverstone. They juggled, told stories, and played instruments in exchange for a meal and a warm place to rest. Our favorites were those who told our fortunes by reading cards or gazing into a glass ball. We laughed at their predictions of handsome admirers and plentiful harvests, knowing full well the whole act was a game the gypsies played for extra coin. My parents did not believe in seers and had encouraged Ula and me to control our own destinies and not rely on magical fantasies as an easy way to a prosperous life. Therefore, we always thought of people who claimed the power of the third eye in the same vein as troubadours or charlatans trying to extort money. The woman before me might dress elegantly and have a royal title, but I considered her performance on the level of those gypsies who would dance in the Riverstone picture gallery.

There was much about these people that made no sense, but what happened in the queen's rooms was ridiculous superstition, and the absurdity was the most perplexing aspect of the Elejicks as a whole. When the room was silent, the queen would close her eyes and lower her head while one of her ladies waved leaves emitting a thick white smoke around her body. The queen whispered inaudibly, and then slowly raised her head and stared ahead in a trance-like state while everyone leaned intently on the edge of their seats. The only person in the room unimpressed was my mother, who never moved, and me, trying not to roll my eyes and laugh. The queen would then declare she was ready, and one by one the people in the room would ask questions about deceased loved ones, if they would find happiness, the location of family treasure, and to reveal long buried family secrets. The queen would answer their questions calmly and often vaguely, convincing me she was playing a trick for her own amusement. Though she listened raptly, the princess didn't make any inquiries herself, and she always left looking disappointed, like she was waiting for a revelation that never came.

After a lengthy discussion on the faithlessness of Lady Brines' husband (though why she was shocked was surprising--the man was a shameless philanderer), Queen Shaeli announced the session was over by yawning audibly. The Senior Lady-in-Waiting, Mistress Alisai of Neve, dismissed the attendants so the queen could rest. Everyone reluctantly shuffled out, some wondering aloud if they would be invited next week. The queen's ladies remained behind waiting patiently for the final attendant, Princess Caelyn, to leave.

"Caelyn, wait," the queen called.

"Mother? Do you have news?" Caelyn's voice was etched with concern. She knelt at her mother's side, her fingers trembling on the arm of the chair. The princess had rarely shown such blatant emotions, so it was disarming to see the flash of excitement in her steely blue eyes and flush on her cheeks. She grasped her mother's hand, her chest heaving as she waited.

"There's a haze over our future, my dear. Someone is coming, or is already here, that will disrupt the course."

"Can you see this person?" Princess Caelyn snarled.

"No. My eyes burn when I try to see. But they do not know the threat they pose. Their path shall not cross ours for many years."

"Then we have time to prepare! Fear not, Mother. I will not let this person ruin everything we have worked for." She hastily kissed the queen's hand and left the room. I followed close behind, but not before searching out Mother's eyes to observe her reaction. For the first time in weeks, her expression was no longer passive, but showed confusion and interest, and she finally met my eye and regarded me. My heart swelled with a sentiment I had not felt for weeks, like a small child reunited with mama after a long absence. Until that moment, I didn't realize how much I missed my family, even my perfect, critical mother. I blinked, and the link was severed, replaced with the indifference that had become as commonplace as cruelty.

I could barely keep pace with Princess Caelyn as she hastened to her rooms, threw open her door, and purposefully sat at her writing table. I took hold of the door to prevent it from slamming against the wall while the princess scratched out a letter.

"You!" she called over her shoulder and waved me close. I latched the door and stood before her, waiting.

"I need you to find His Highness, Prince Brannon." She spoke slowly, deliberately, so that I was sure to understand the movement of her lips since I was deaf and intolerantly stupid. "Give him this," she said and handed me a quickly scrawled note. "Make sure he reads it immediately. He'll want to speak to me after. Bring him here." I nodded, then gestured to the note, looked pointedly around the room, and shrugged my shoulders questioningly.

"I don't know where he is!" she exclaimed. We had found a sort of pantomime language so I could communicate when necessary using hand gestures and body language. Writing was out of the question due to my feigned illiteracy. "I'm sure you can skitter around and find him. Go!" She pushed me toward the door and without another word began frantically writing once more.

The dark passages of Praed Castle were not completely unknown to me. Since girlhood, we had visited on numerous occasions owing to Father's place of distinction in King Llewlyn's close circle of knights. It was more convenient for Mother that Ula and I stay out of the way, so we occupied ourselves by exploring the castle in search of hidden rooms and secret passages. We never found anything noteworthy, but we spent many hours losing ourselves among these halls. For the first time in weeks, I was not pressed for time and was allowed to roam alone. This small freedom lifted my mood, and I considered it may take me several hours to find the prince in such a big castle with so many confusing twists and turns. The thought made me smile, and before I could resist, a laugh escaped my lips.

"Something amusing?" a low voice emanated from the darkness.

I choked in fear. Around me, tall monoliths and the smell of timber closed in, and my vision struggled to adjust in the dim light. The voice did not return, and gradually I could make out shapes, and recognized where I was. Without realizing, my feet brought me to my favorite room in the castle: the library. I ran my hand along the nearest bookcase, feeling the worn leather bindings as I guided myself further into the room, listening. Had I imagined the voice? Or is this place haunted, as Ula always feared? The aged floorboards creaked, then heavy boots struck the floor, and I froze. A small shaft of sunlight from a narrow slit in the castle wall and a flicker of candlelight revealed a looming figure. I turned to flee, but in a few broad steps the figure was upon me and had grabbed my arm. I flailed and kicked, but he was so much larger than me I doubt it made a difference.

"Enough!" he commanded. "There will be plenty of opportunity for you to defend yourself. Now isn't one of those times." He released me, and I was startled to discover it was the knight that still filled my dreams with terror. Once again he was dressed in black from his doublet to his boots, and I wondered if he was in mourning or simply couldn't see colors. He had never spoken more than a word to me, and none since the day I arrived. I had seen him briefly as I trailed after the princess, but he didn't break his stride to speak to her.

"You shouldn't be wandering around alone," he said.

I didn't respond.

"Are you lost?" he continued, but I remained silent, and stared blankly back.

"I suppose you wouldn't be. You've been here before, I think." His voice was less harsh, almost sympathetic if I could believe for one second that he had feelings.

"There's no point in persisting in the fabrication that you're mute," he said.

I continued to be silent.

"Remember, I've heard you speak before. Quite forcefully."

I did remember the words I spoke when I tried to protect Ula. My eyes misted thinking of her, wondering if she was all right, if she was safe. Well, safe enough.

"She's unharmed," he said, as if reading my thoughts. "In case you didn't know." He watched me, and if he was expecting a thank you, he was in for a long wait.

"I'm looking for the prince," I blurted out. "I mean, His Royal Highness, Prince Brannon. His sister, Princess Caelyn, has a message I'm to deliver to him."

He nodded, but didn't reply, his lips pursed in indecision.

"Have you seen him recently?" I asked irritably.

"Yes."

Oh, fabulous. He was back to being taciturn.

"Well, can you take me to him?" Not only was he being useless, but because of him, my few hours of freedom had vanished.

"Perhaps it would be better if *I* delivered the message." He held out his hand, and I instinctively stepped back.

"No," I protested. "I was given very strict instructions to deliver the message myself. There are penalties when Her Highness's wishes are ignored."

The black knight sighed and nodded, resigned. "Come then," he said. "But don't forget I offered to leave you out of it."

"I have a perfect memory," I retorted as I glared at him darkly. Without another word, he led me from the library, and I followed a few paces behind. He stopped abruptly and I nearly ran into him.

"What?" I asked, annoyed.

"You don't have to do that."

"Do what? Exist?"

"Walk behind me. You're not my servant."

"I'm below everyone in this castle," I said. "Even you."

He faced me and the corner of his mouth quirked in amusement. I wanted to claw that smirk off.

"I won't tell anyone," he said.

You know what? Fine. But he should be walking behind me! I moved to his side, several feet of space between us, and together we continued down the hall past portraits of people I didn't recognize and unfamiliar trinkets. I stopped to inspect a bronze sculpture of an eagle perched atop a cradle. I could just imagine in the next instant that terrifying bird was going to swallow the infant.

"It's Amyl and Artur," the knight informed me, though I didn't ask nor care.

"Did that awful bird eat that poor baby?"

"No," he said, sounding both cross and wounded at my question. "Many hundreds of years ago, a battle was fought between my people and the jungle warriors of Vyt from across the steppes. Vyt had been a prosperous people, but a drought left the jungle barren, and starvation impelled them toward Ilano in search of land and food. Artur's father was the Lord Protector then, and had Vyt come with honor, he may have traded and dealt with them peacefully. However, at that stage of desperation, the warriors were crazed, and attacked without provocation. They murdered women and children, destroyed villages and plundered storehouses. His Lordship amassed an army, but the Vyt warriors were already at his doorstep, swarming into houses and leaving no one unmolested."

"I can picture it," I murmured and stared at him accusingly. He ignored me and continued, putting a hand on the eagle.

"As the Lord Protector fought for his people, his child lay in his cradle. The Vyt pushed through the line of protection outside, and as they flooded into his home, a great black eagle flew through an open window and landed atop the sleeping babe, daring any man to approach. Many did, and one by one she sank her talons into them and saved the life of the child. She was the first eagle to become devoted to an Ilano. As Artur grew, the eagle, Amyl, did not leave his side. Thus began the relationship between man and eagle, woman and falcon."

"A pretty story. What happened to the Vyt?"

He dropped his hand from the statue and held my gaze.

"What always happens to people who pick a fight they cannot win." He turned and strode down the hall but said nothing when I joined him.

We passed rooms and ventured down hallways, remaining silent, until I realized we were heading toward the Trophy Room. Like the gentleman's room at Riverstone, this was a place that women did not enter. I faltered briefly then resolutely moved forward, hoping the black-hearted monster at my side didn't notice. He did.

"You don't have to go in. I can deliver the message just as easily." He paused at the door, his hand on the handle.

"No. I can do this," I insisted, watching his hand. But he did not move to open the door.

"I'm Risteard," he said unexpectedly, as if I cared for an introduction. My eyes fixed boldly on his and burned with hatred.

"Good for you," I spat. After the words left my mouth, he promptly threw open the door and led me inside.

The Trophy Room wasn't called as such simply because the walls were adorned with antlers and miscellany taxidermy from centuries of hunts. Here, a man could display not only plunder from battle, but conquests of beauty. No high borne lady crossed the threshold of the Trophy Room, only those painted to slake the lust of lonely and bored lords. Mother didn't talk about what went on in the

Trophy Room and I never witnessed Father going inside, but Ula and I overheard rumors on occasion that were enough to make us disgusted with the male gender. Our theories of what happened here were grossly under-exaggerated. We weren't completely ignorant of what went on between a man and woman after marriage, but the dry, scholarly version we heard from Mother did not prepare me for what my eyes now witnessed.

Anger hung about my features as I stepped past men tipping goblets over a naked young woman and lapping the liquid off her flesh, loud voices sang horridly, and everywhere hands touched body parts I'd never seen before. I kept close to the black knight, remaining unnoticed by the raucous gathering, so different from the quiet set of ladies I'd been with earlier. Past a dented suit of glimmering red armor with large leather gloves draped across the shoulder reclined the prince on a luxuriously blanketed chaise lounge, his shirt unbuttoned and his jerkin on the floor. A woman lay along his body, kissing his naked chest. His head was tipped back, and his expression fluctuated from smiling to pained. Sweat dripped from his temples. The woman squirmed oddly on top of him, rubbing her hands up and down his legs, and I couldn't tell by the prince's reaction if she was being helpful or hurtful.

"Your Highness," the black knight whispered over the prince's face. His eyes fluttered open and focused briefly before shutting again.

"What do you want, Risteard? Can't you see this lovely creature is about to put my cock in her mouth?"

His what in her what?

The knight angrily glanced at me and then roughly shook Prince Brannon's shoulder.

"Your Highness has a message from Princess Caelyn brought expressly by this young woman." The prince's eyes opened fully, first in irritation, then surprise when he finally noticed me standing there. He quickly sat up, propelling the lady off his lap as he did so. The woman retreated to the end of the chaise and pouted, arms crossed like a petulant child. Men in the immediate vicinity quieted and watched, though they weren't about to exile their companions.

"Well, well, I suppose you find this all very curious." The prince leered and didn't bother to make himself presentable. His chest remained bare and his breeches gaped open. He reached for a goblet and drained its contents before asking the purpose of the interruption. I nervously handed him the note from Princess Caelyn. He rolled his eyes and scanned the lines, clearly not expecting anything important. Apparently, he found the contents quite interesting, for he turned to me wide-eyed. I gestured for him to follow, pointing at the letter to indicate the author wished to speak to him in person. The prince swung his legs off the chaise and hastily laced his boots.

"Sorry, sweet thing," he said in the direction of the woman on the chaise. "Princely duties call." He leaned over and gave her the most disturbing kiss I'd ever seen, if you could call it that. I could barely hide my distaste as their faces squished together and their tongues darted in and out of their mouths, hands roughly grabbing and squeezing and pinching. Right then, I wished the Vyt would burst in and put me out of my misery. Once the prince was satiated, he casually pushed the woman aside and called out to the room, "Have an available one here, lads! Unsoiled!" He winked at the black knight to the sound of clapping and cheering, then leaned so close to my face I could smell wine and perfume.

"Lead on, then. We don't want to keep my sister waiting." To my horror, he grabbed my arm and nearly dragged me from the room. I didn't bother to struggle. Honestly, I wanted out so desperately I would have allowed the prince to escort me by my hair.

The prince released me as we entered the hallway so I could walk behind him as my station demanded. I rubbed my arm and followed, the black knight at my side. The prince soon noticed we weren't alone and stopped.

"I'm sure your services are required elsewhere, Risteard. I know my way around." The knight looked at me and the prince continued. "Don't worry about her. She's very loyal to the princess and wouldn't dare threaten me. Besides," he stepped toward me, and I flinched. "I think I can easily overpower her if she tries anything." The black knight nodded and stepped aside, allowing us to proceed. The prince strode down the hall so absorbed in himself that he didn't observe the black knight move out of the shadows and follow, disappearing when we reached the princess' rooms.

The prince entered her room without knocking, threw himself onto the bed, and sighed dramatically. The princess was standing by the window, and when she saw her brother, her shoulders relaxed.

"Finally!" she exclaimed. She turned to me. "I thought I would have to send someone to find you, too!"

"What is this nonsense?" the prince interrupted, waving the message I handed him. "You'd better explain yourself, Caelyn, because I was very busy when your little pet fetched me."

"I'm sure you were," she said dryly. "Mother received some news today. She said someone was coming to ruin our plans. They may even be among us now."

"Is that all? You worry too much."

"You don't worry enough!"

"Caelyn." He rose from the bed to stand before her. "I'm being perfectly serious. If you're anxious, everyone will see and suspect something's wrong. If we're confident and carefree, then everyone will relax and let their guards down. Mother can't see everything. If anyone tries to get in our way, we'll take care of it." He placed his hands on her shoulders and massaged them until she visibly calmed.

"Remember, sister," Prince Brannon said darkly. "No one stands between an Elejick and power. It's you and me. Nothing else matters."

Princess Caelyn smiled wickedly. "You're right. No one stands between an Elejick and power."

CHAPTER 7

The next day the king announced the royal family and entourage would parade through Praed to ingratiate themselves with the populace. This sent the princess into a tantrum as she possessed "nothing suitable to wear." She spent the morning tossing gowns on the floor and rummaging through chests attempting to find something "royal enough" to impress the crowd, which I found particularly humorous considering her general disdain for her subjects. After emptying her dressers of every article of clothing she owned, she stood in the middle of the room, tapping her foot, hands on her hips, and consternation on her face. She looked at me briefly then stalked to her writing desk and scrawled a note.

"Here," she thrust the paper at me. "These are instructions for a gown suited to my specifications with my measurements. Take it to the castle dressmaker immediately." My heart pounded as I took the note and dashed out of the room. I had never been so eager to run an errand because conducting business with the dressmaker meant a consultation with her seamstresses. And sewing was the main duty of Ula.

Disregarding propriety and my goal of remaining invisible, I raced through the castle, dodging ladies and hiding from knights and lords. I skidded to a stop at the top of the stairs descending into the workrooms where castle staff mended tapestries, polished boots and armor, laundered, and created the wardrobe for the inhabitants. I steadied my breathing and collected myself before hurrying down and entering the spacious room where women were working. There were dozens of them hunched over tables and yards of fabric, sewing in a dance of needles and thread. Having never met the dressmaker, I wasn't sure whom to approach, but a white-haired woman wearing an apron full of pins and ribbon fluttered by inspecting the other women's work, adjusting, and giving orders. I took a chance that she was the lady I sought and stepped forward.

For an old woman, she was hard to catch moving about the crowded space, but I finally came close enough to grab her sleeve and tug. She spun around, a stern look on her face and a reprimand on her lips, but her attitude shifted when she discovered I wasn't one of her underlings.

"Whatcho want, young lady?" I tried to convey who I was, pointing to myself and bowing to an invisible royal, but she interrupted. "I know who you work for. State your business quickly. I've much to do." I offered the note, and she snatched it from my hand. I noticed our exchange had drawn the attention of the other ladies, so while she read the note, I searched the faces, and there, right behind the old woman, was Ula. It took all Mother's training to restrain myself from launching into her arms. We stared at each other, unmoving, while the old woman mumbled and ranted.

"Are you listening?" she demanded, her face inches from mine. "What is the meaning of this? She thinks she can make such impossible requests? Of course, she does. She's the princess." The last was muttered under her breath. "A new trousseau in under a week. Well..." she crushed the note in her hand, pulled out a small notebook, and wrote for several seconds while I continued to stare at Ula. When she finished, she pointed it at Ula and ordered, "Bring me all these things from the storeroom. Have the lady here help you so the princess appreciates how dedicated we are to serving her needs."

"Yes, ma'am," Ula said in her soft, sweet voice as she dropped a curtsey then gestured for me to follow.

Approximately two seconds after we were out of sight, I pulled Ula into my arms and clutched her to me as if she were the only solid ground in a stormy sea. I held her until she was forced to extricate herself in order to breathe. When I looked down at her, there were tears trailing down her flushed cheeks.

"Laria!" she cried. "I was so scared I'd never see you again! How have they been treating you? Are they kind to you?"

I laughed and brushed away her tears. "I'm well enough. What about you? Are you eating enough?"

"Yes," she pulled away and started gathering the supplies on her list. "We don't have much time."

"You're right. Something is going on. I can't figure it out quite yet, but I think the princess is up to something. She keeps talking about a plan with the queen and the prince, and I don't think it involves gowns."

Ula paused, her face drained of color. "Be careful what you say, Laria. There are spies everywhere."

"She thinks I'm illiterate, deaf, and mute."

Ula laughed.

"How have you managed to fool them this long? You've never been able to hold your tongue for five minutes."

We laughed companionably, and suddenly we were back at Riverstone, huddled under my down covers during a thunderstorm while I told funny stories to prevent Ula from being afraid. The precious moment of nostalgia was not to last.

"In all seriousness, Laria, be careful."

"I will. You know me. I'm no revolutionary."

"Not in the least," she smirked. She handed me a few yards of cloth and simultaneously we steeled our features, strangers once again.

The morning of the procession, Princess Caelyn was resplendent in an emerald gown with gold stitching and strings of pearls woven into her luxurious brown hair. The color perfectly complimented her ivory skin, or so she pointed out every few minutes. I was just happy that I didn't stick her with a pin. Her hair was thick and a chore to style. She especially demanded compliments from King Conall, which he was happy to bestow on his jewel of a daughter.

"In all of my travels, I've never seen a treasure that could compare to your beauty, my dear," King Conall proclaimed. How trite. She stiffened when he pinched her cheek then ran his fingers along her jawline. His brown eyes narrowed, then he shook his head and shoved her face aside. The princess did not move as the king exited the castle, his massive arms swinging and his footsteps heavy. I shifted uneasily, and the princess blinked and followed, chin high and hands fisted at her sides.

The entire royal family, including the queen, the king's most trusted knights, and all their attendants were gathered in their finery in preparation for this ridiculous display. Every lady glittered in jewels and fine gowns. Knights shined to perfection in formal armor etched with intricate designs. Banners bearing family crests fluttered in the breeze. The colors varied, but they all depicted the form of a bird in some fashion. It didn't matter how pretty they looked; the people of Praed would never forgive this family. I ignored them, my attention keenly focused elsewhere.

Months had passed since I had been near horses. Grooms held them steady while ladies were assisted into side-saddles and knights mounted their steeds clad in matching finery. Princess Caelyn's horse was a stout gray mare approaching middle age judging by the sway of her back. I volunteered to hold her steady as a groom lifted the princess into the saddle, and I stroked the whiskered nose and inhaled the mixture of hay and distinctly earthy scent. The princess gathered her reins and waved me away, and I was led toward my own horse, a gray-muzzled bay gelding. I ran my hand along the white star on his brow and nearly wept thinking of Amore.

"Do you need a leg up?" said a deep voice behind me. I hastily rubbed my eyes before shaking my head resolutely, not bothering to face the man whose voice I recognized. I moved toward the horse's side, running my hand along the neck and gripping the reins as I did. The horse was tall, several hands taller than Amore, and I could barely reach my foot into the stirrup. Taking firm hold of the pommel, I bounced once, twice, and a third time trying in vain to propel myself into the saddle. On my next effort, hands grasped my right calf and swung it over the top of the horse. I seated myself onto the fine leather, relaxing with a sigh at the familiar feeling. I turned to the man several feet below me.

Risteard was adjusting my stirrups and checking the girth. I didn't ask nor thank him for his assistance, but I didn't say anything disparaging--I felt such bliss at that moment. I ran my fingers through the black mane and studied the other riders. I straightened in my saddle when I noticed something curious. Excluding the princess and the queen, I was the only female riding alone, and not in a side saddle. The king shortly thereafter called for the parade to begin, and there was no time to contemplate this interesting observation.

Riding through Praed like conquering heroes was a most humiliating spectacle. Everyone came out to greet the king, clearly on pain of death. I took in the stiff and stolid faces and noted the lack of waves or cheers. Women didn't bring forth their babies for kisses. From my vantage point, it was obvious no one was impressed. The king didn't seem to mind as he waved and made promises and ordered trinkets and coins tossed to the waiting crowd. Clearly, he thought he could throw money at the people and they would forget how their homes were torched and loved ones murdered in the streets. I squeezed the reins, wishing I could dig my heels into my horse's sides and gallop back to Riverstone. Everyone was so engrossed in making fools of themselves they probably wouldn't notice I was gone until it was time for the princess to brush her hair.

"Does he suit?" a familiar voice asked from nearby.

"What?" I blurted out before I could check that no one would hear me speak and betray my charade. Luckily, my horse had slowed and we were out of earshot. I relaxed and patted his neck.

"I know he's quite old, but he's strong and quick on his feet if given the chance."

"I don't think he'll have much of a chance today," I said. "He has a kind eye, though. And well-muscled for a horse of his years. Someone must ride him regularly."

"Quite regularly."

"Not by the likes of her." I indicated the princess swaying and jerking on that rocking horse of a mare. Surprising she didn't fall out of bed more often.

"No." Risteard's mouth formed a hint of a grin. "By me. He's mine."

A shiver ran down my spine to settle in my nauseated stomach. I looked down at that beautiful animal, polluted by association with the black-hearted villain. It wasn't fair. For the first time in months I felt the tiniest pleasure and in an instant it was ruined. Once again, this man crashes into my world and shatters my dreams.

"Don't blame him for your hatred of me," he said flatly. "It's a discredit to him and beneath you." I glowered at him, wondering why he engaged me in conversation and why I rode one of his mounts.

"Every third step is off," I blurted out.

"What do you mean?" He glanced at the horse's legs.

"It's subtle," I said, "but I think he's experiencing some pain in his left hind. Maybe just a bruised hoof, but I wouldn't rule out arthritis at his age. Was he worked vigorously recently?"

"We went for a long ride yesterday."

"Did he stumble? Perhaps misstep?"

Risteard shook his head. "Not once. He's always been surefooted."

"It's probably nothing then. Sore joints most likely."

"I wonder if he should be ridden." His eyes swept over me--probably debating whether he should make me walk.

"We're hardly galloping over mountains," I said. "If we continue to travel at this pace, he'll be fine. He should be well rested when he's returned to the stables. A massage would be beneficial."

"How would I do that?"

I finally made eye contact and my jaw dropped. "You don't know? What's the point in owning such a creature if you don't know how to care for it?" His eyes darkened and I shrank back.

"Same reasons as you, if the stories are to be believed. Work, transport, companionship…"

"What do you know about it?" A small corner of my mind screamed for me to be silent. I was being entirely too free with my opinions and ran the risk of being overheard.

"More than you give me credit for."

We had reached the edge of the stalled procession, and I knew his next words would be the last spoken between us.

"You're not the only person who's ever lost someone."

I flushed with anger. How dare he try and humble me--as if *he* wasn't the reason I felt hollow and afraid? I could not speak in the crowd, so I projected all the pent-up resentment and humiliation through my verdant eyes. He appeared somewhat abashed but offered no apology. The line in front of us resumed its journey along the marred cobblestones displaced by the turmoil the new monarchy was encouraging the people to forget. I waited, allowing the distance to grow before giving my charge a gentle nudge. The black knight kept pace, remaining quiet for several minutes.

"Will you show me?" he asked.

"What?"

"How to take care of him." He directed his gaze at the animal below me, the same look I used to give Amore, and my barely mended heart broke again.

"Yes," I agreed without allowing myself time to consider. I turned my face away, pretending to focus on the crowd, and surreptitiously brushed off a traitorous tear.

The ridiculous parade marched on, past frantically erected replacements for the buildings razed in the conquest of Praed. Families struggling to piece together some semblance of existence gawked at us, and I was ashamed to be there, looking down at their dusty faces, the pain etched across their features, and knowing there was nothing I could do. I couldn't even commiserate with these people. We passed a mother and her three small children, and I wondered what they would be doing had their lives not been torn apart. Would she be baking bread while the children played around her skirts? A father was nowhere to be seen. Had he been slain, as so many fathers, husbands, and sons? I rode closer, noting one of the children was missing an arm and the wound seeped through a dirty cloth. I could no longer stomach their plight and lurched over the side of the saddle and vomited in the dirt next to the black knight. Once my stomach was empty, I righted myself and leaned into the horse's mane, breathing in the soothing scent to settle my nerves. After re-establishing my inner poise, I continued without acknowledging the shadow accompanying me, and nothing more was said for the duration of the parade.

Back at the stables, I dismounted before anyone could offer me assistance and led the black knight's horse into a stall to be untacked. The princess was nearby, her voice loud over the bustle of ladies and gentlemen congratulating the king on a successful cavalcade. I heard her complaining about the dust clinging to her new gown and the smell of the filthy people who littered the highway and why did she have to waste a perfectly good afternoon? For all her complaining, I knew she enjoyed displaying herself as much as any lady. The prince had abandoned his charge to a groom so he could sidle close to a young woman and gallantly proffer his arm because she surely would have fallen over walking into the castle unassisted. I had no patience for either of them, and since the princess was currently busy entertaining a circle of young lords, they clearly had no use for me.

Private moments to myself were a foreign concept since I had been taken from Riverstone. As the weeks turned into months, the noose was loosened in increments, but the small freedoms of wandering the halls under the direction of Princess Caelyn were fleeting, and her grip was absolute. Standing in that stall, I was able to block out the rest of the world, leaving just me and the horse in an enchantment I hadn't experienced since I last felt Amore's soft coat under my hands. I pulled the saddle from his back and slung it over the stall door, then stripped off the ceremonial blankets and bridle. The horse shook off loose hair and dirt and snorted contentedly. I laughed softly, running my hands down the broad neck and back, watching the sweat evaporate off his back. I listened to the grinding teeth as he munched hay while I meticulously groomed the gray flecked coat, a process that I would indulge in for hours with Amore until she shined.

Footsteps approached and stopped outside the stall, and I hastened to finish brushing. The stall door opened, and I froze, thinking how stupid I was to let my guard down in this enclosed space where I found myself trapped. My breath hitched as I turned toward the source of the footsteps--the black knight. My shoulders slumped, in both relief and annoyance.

"What now?" I asked.

"I've come for my lesson in proper horse management," he said dryly. He scanned the array of grooming implements I had assembled. "How many brushes does it take to groom a horse?"

"Depends on how thorough you wish to be. Whether brush, comb, or curry, each tool has a purpose."

"Which is the most important?"

"This one." I held up my hand.

The side of his mouth twitched briefly, and he nodded, striding closer.

"You said you'd show me how to tend to his leg."

I set the brushes down and bent over the horse's hind leg, grasped it just below the hock, and demonstrated how to apply steady pressure along the tendon that bulged below the skin.

"It doesn't feel hot," I noted. "So, I don't think there's an infection, but if you have liniment, that will soothe the tendon even more."

"Where did you learn all this?"

I couldn't meet his eyes. "My father. Horses are an important part of my people's culture."

He didn't reply.

"They give much of themselves to us and in return we are responsible for their comfort."

Still he said nothing.

"You can never understand the gravity of what you did to us."

"I expect not. But you will never understand what you don't bother to learn. Not everything is as simple as you think."

"So I'm being willfully ignorant?" My voice rose to a shrill pitch. I inhaled sharply to calm myself.

"You make quick judgements without asking questions. Your opinions remain muddled, and you've done nothing to remedy that."

"Forced servitude will do that to a person," I said. "Besides, if I ask questions, they'll know I'm not a brainless mute, and then I'll be in danger."

"Fair, though what more could you possibly fear if they knew?"

I wasn't angry enough to expose my intentions of using my supposed disabilities to garner information, though what I would do if I learned anything useful, I had yet to determine.

"Right now, I'm ignored," I said. "If it was known that I could speak, or worse, that I have a thought in my head, they'd notice. The last thing I want is to attract attention."

After a minute he said, "Your secret is not mine to share. It's safe with me."

"No one is safe with you." I rose hastily and slipped out of the stall.

I untangled the wind-blown knots from the princess's hair while she ranted about the grimy country she begrudgingly lived in. I found myself considering the black knight's words. While I despised him to my core, I wondered at his assessment of how I came to be here. In my estimation, the Elejicks challenged and brutally attacked King Llewlyn's kingdom, destroyed the city, murdered my father and countless innocents, burned the Riverstone stables, and forced scores of people into servitude. I accepted this as fact, based on what I had witnessed, and never entertained the possibility that there was more to the story. I remained in contemplation until Prince Brannon strolled in unannounced but clearly not unexpected.

"So glad to get that dull waste of a day over with," he sighed and dropped onto the bed. "What did you make of it?"

"The people are broken but not defeated," Princess Caelyn replied. "They've obviously started to rebuild, which means they're determined to stay."

"Have you had a report from Arlen and Crane?"

Who? I hesitated for the briefest of moments before resuming my task and listened intently.

"They told me the people clearly hate Father. To them, he's the root of all their problems."

"Just as we want him to be," the prince said. "They were surely impressed with the expensive gowns you ladies wore," the prince continued. "The silver pommels glistened, and the queen's jewels sparkled. A very impressive display of excessive wealth. If only Father hadn't insisted on handing out coins."

"On the contrary, I think it worked in our favor. Did you notice the coins remained in the dirt? The people must have seen the charity for what it was: a bribe. They left the money untouched, at least while we were looking."

"They must have been quite insulted."

"Grievously disrespected," the princess smirked. "Just as we want them to be."

"I admit I doubted the loyalty of your spies, but they've been quite useful."

The princess stared blankly ahead and idly fingered an intricately carved apple-shaped pomander.

"When Father first talked about invading Praed and extending Ilano's power, I thought it would take years for the people to realize his true nature. He can be so fatherly when he wants to be."

"Yes." The word barely brushed past Princess Caelyn's lips.

The prince sat up and noticed the princess' downturned face. With a sigh, he pushed off the bed, nudged me aside, and leaned over the princess, her back cradled between his arms.

"Look at me," he said. She met his eyes in the mirror, and her nostrils flared.

"I can no longer be ruled by him," she said.

"If all goes as planned, you won't have to."

The prince left the room, and I hesitantly raised the brush to finish combing out her hair. A snap pierced the silence, and I looked at the princess' fuming reflection. Slowly, she opened her fist, and the pieces of the crushed pomander rattled across the vanity.

Alone in my dark, cramped space, I considered the conversation between the prince and princess. There was no question they had a clandestine purpose, and I was willing to wager Queen Shaeli knew something of the future, or she claimed, but really was using her sight to plot and scheme herself. But to what end? They had everything they could possibly want: royal titles, riches beyond compare, and a secure future. Something was missing, and there was no way for me to discover the truth. Not here in this tiny room. For months I've lived as a slave because that's what I am, outwardly and in my mind. Without realizing, I allowed my circumstances to pigeonhole me into exactly what they wanted, and my safe, alternate persona made me forget who I really was. Laria Audrey rarely took the straightforward course. If I was doomed to a confined life, I would work within the boundaries to find the truth, to use my invisibility to listen, watch, and wait for my moment to act. The violence of the princess' temper made this risky were she to discover my secret, but I would risk death itself to set Ula free.

CHAPTER 8

During the afternoons when the princess was occupied by her letters, embroidery, and other solitary accomplishments, I decided to take the chance she didn't require me constantly hovering over her and started politely excusing myself with a raised brow and gesture toward the door. She preferred not to be in my presence anyway since my appearance disgusted her. She forced me to wear a cap to hide my ginger hair, but she couldn't cover up my lineage.

"Don't dawdle," she would say without asking exactly what I was up to. "I don't want to come find you if I need anything."

By this time, the sight of me in the corridors was commonplace and the household was aware of my perceived shortcomings and paid little mind to a dumb, odd-looking servant to the princess. Instead of the mundane errands they assumed I was carrying out, I only had one desired destination.

The library door creaked with the effort of aged wood as I slowly peered inside to confirm it was unoccupied. In the days of King Llewlyn, I inevitably encountered a few scholars pouring over ancient texts or young ladies hiding in corners with romance novels. Now, only cobwebs and dust occupied the once bustling chamber, and I could count on at least an hour of solitude before being missed. I slipped inside and carefully shut the door before searching the shelves. In my prior life, I spent many hours reading fairy tales and fantastical stories of faraway places. I pored over histories of the horse, including a text written by a physician who spent most of his life studying horse anatomy and physiology. In short, I read what interested me and ignored other subjects. Now, I intended to learn everything I needed about Ilano to understand how I came to be here and how I was going to leave.

There was little to find about Ilano, only a short mention in the journal of an explorer who passed through the steppes on a pilgrimage. He described the landscape as lushly carpeted with bluegrass and rows of trees stretching to the horizon. The air was pungent with the scent of fruit and ominous black birds circled overhead.

Nothing was written of the people or the city, I expect because he didn't linger. In contrast, volumes written about Praed were crammed into several bookcases, overflowing with the descriptions of the beauty of the prairies, the turbulent history, and the prosperity of the people. Most were about King Llewlyn, and every word was embellished with praise of his righteousness of rule. Even for me, the language was extravagant, and I reluctantly decided I would find nothing useful within these pages. Still, I scoured through one tome after another, gleaning as much as possible in the time available. And every afternoon I left unsatisfied, feeling more and more that something was amiss, the answers just out of reach.

One afternoon, I entered the library as usual to find it empty. But next to the only window on a small table lay an open book. I glanced around to confirm I was alone, then hesitantly picked it up. The leather was soft, and the pages made from fine paper. Placing my thumb inside to hold the place, I turned the book to read the spine. The title was *Unmasked*. The author was unknown to me and unpronounceable. I began to read.

The author wrote of the Ilano tradition of falconry, how the birds were trained for hunting small game and performing skillful aerobatic maneuvers. Falcons were the choice for women, smaller but no less fearsome than the black eagles trained by Ilano knights for centuries. Much like fine horses, black eagles were bred for desirable qualities over generations.

I slammed the book shut. In my hands I held what I had been searching for after weeks of failure: insight into the people and culture of Ilano. Where did this come from? There was no time to speculate. I settled into the armchair near the hearth and continued to read.

The book told of Amyl, the legend of the first black eagle. It was as--what was his name?--Risteard had described. I learned when young Ilano men turn twelve, they enter the eagle yard and are chosen as a companion by the bird rather than the other way around. The pair remain together for life. I paused over one passage before re-reading it several times:

> *This author spoke to an aging Ilano knight who said, 'It is not a matter of choosing the largest, fiercest, or strongest bird. There is a bond neither of you knew existed until you come together in the yard and see each other for the first time. It is like finding a long-lost twin, a part of your soul torn away and brought back to make you whole again.'*

My mind's eye drifted to the dancing flames as I remembered Amore and the friendship we shared. When I was a little girl, I travelled with Father to a neighboring farm where an impressive mare was soon to give birth to a foal my father had promised to his eldest daughter on her fifth birthday, the first possession that would be completely and solely mine. I vibrated with excitement and followed them into the barn where the grunting of a mare in labor echoed along the corridors. At her stall, my father lifted me so I could see, and there in the straw lay a large, red chestnut with flaring nostrils and damp flanks. My father and the other man spoke in hushed tones, but I only had eyes for her. The two men entered the stall, and to my horror, Father reached inside the mare. He locked eyes with the farmer and gave him a disparaging look, and then turned to me, my eyes wide and hopeful. His jaw clenched. He gritted his teeth, stretched his body along the ground, and used his free hand to brace against the mare's rump. Each time her muscles tensed, Father pulled, sweat dripping from his forehead. The passage of time was marked by the mare's shrieking and Father's arm inching out of her, until I could see two tiny hooves and then a dark nose. The foal was born very quickly after, her head and shoulders emerging. The mare clambered to her feet and she fell to the ground in a wet heap. Father and the farmer rubbed the little filly's limp body dry. To revive her, Father wiped her mouth clean, held her muzzle, and breathed into her nose. Once, twice, many times he gave his breath to her and with each I crept closer until I was kneeling beside him. Father lay the small head on the straw, exhausted, the foal unresponsive. In a daze, I reached out and ran my fingers down the white star on her head, whispering, "She's the most beautiful thing I've ever seen, and she's mine." Before my father could speak, the foal's eyes opened. She lifted her head, and the mare began to nuzzle and lick her clean. My father and the farmer were in awe, but I knew that despite all their efforts they lacked the one thing that would bring the foal to life. Love.

The day Amore came into the world I found the other half of my soul. I'd held onto the conviction that the people who destroyed Riverstone were not capable of feeling deeply, could not understand the connection between man and beast. I had ignored the affection the prince and princess showed for their birds and regarded it as something ugly, but now I understood. This revelation did not make me hate them less, but it softened my attitude towards the birds.

Every afternoon I read a passage from the small book and replaced it on the table, and the next time I returned it was open to another section. After the fourth time this happened, I started believing in Ula's ghost. The only people I could conceivably suppose were responsible were Ula and my mother. However, Ula was essentially confined to the lower floors and Mother showed little initiative in helping me. I concluded that her apparent disinterest was a front, much like my own, and that she was sneaking information out of the queen's rooms.

The princess was in a sour mood when I removed the ribbons that had been in place while she slept, creating cascades of wavy locks that flowed down her back.

"Make sure the hair covers my neck. It's getting cold. I nearly froze to death last night," she said.

Winters were harsh in Praed, especially in the mountains where the icy winds blew. Ilano experienced rain and the occasional frost, but rarely snow. As children, when the river pool froze, Ula and I attached skates to our boots and spent hours trying to carve our names on the glassy surface. Our noses turned red and our fingers grew numb before we came home to thaw ourselves by the fire, telling stories and drinking warm milk that Morgan mulled with cinnamon.

Father taught us how to break through the ice along the banks of the Rhyvor and drop in our fishing lines to entice the dormant creatures underneath.

The princess was wholly unprepared for the winter she was about to experience, and it was sadly my responsibility to help her.

After plaiting part of her hair in a crown and allowing the rest to flow freely, a task I was becoming more proficient at, I held up two heavy gowns.

"Those are so bulky!" she complained. I set them back down and rubbed my arms, indicating they would keep her warm. She rolled her eyes and chose the blue one. "How long is winter going to last?" Oh, dear princess, it has barely begun. I held up one hand, fingers spread, then swept the hand along the sky in an arch.

"That better mean five weeks." She narrowed her eyes, and I shook my head. "Months?"

I nodded.

"Tell me you can at least get letters through."

I shrugged, moving my hands to indicate uncertainty.

I expected her to throw herself on the bed and declare she would sleep until spring, but she pressed her fingers to the bridge of her nose and took a deep breath. I was as proud as a mother bird kicking her chick out of the nest to fly on her own.

She grabbed several letters off her writing desk. "Take these then," she ordered. "I don't want them to get lost in a snowbank...wait, does it snow here?" I nodded. "A lot?"

Yes, yes, I nodded again.

"Then I'll be requiring a new wardrobe. After you post those, give my instructions to the dressmaker."

As you command, my lady.

Before placing the letters in the hands of the page, I figured if I want to be a spy, I may as well act like one. The letters were all sealed with the royal Elejick stamp: an eagle holding a scepter in one claw and some type of fruit in another. I didn't want to risk damaging the seal, so I left it alone and read the addressee. I recognized a few names from letters she had sent and received as friends and acquaintances in Ilano. One letter was addressed to an unknown male, Jervell Kade, and I wondered that she didn't speak his name before. I delivered the letters to the page, filed the name away in my brain in case it would be important later, and then swiftly made my way to the lower realms of the castle. When the dressmaker saw me, her face immediately stormed over, and she placed her fisted hands on her hips.

"What now?" I rubbed my arms and pulled at my frock to indicate the princess desired cold weather clothes. Thankfully, she understood the message. "Her Highness feeling the frost, is she? She's in for a surprise! You." She pointed a bony finger at Ula. "Take her to the storehouse and have her pick out some fabrics to suit her highness's taste. And fetch some hides for the fur lining."

I could barely suppress a smile as we walked together, the stone walls echoing with our footsteps. The air had already begun to chill in the castle depths, and I took Ula's hand to check its temperature.

"Your fingers are frozen!" I exclaimed. "They need to give you gloves if they expect you to work under these conditions. Are you wearing layers?"

"Yes." She giggled as I opened her threadbare sweater and tickled under her arms. "Gloves do tend to get in the way of the sewing, though," she said.

"So, make some that only cover your hands. At least that would be something."

"You mean, gloves without fingers?"

"Why not? You could always knit anything. While you're at it, knit yourself a woolen hat. Your ears are red." We reached the storeroom and gathered supplies fit for a princess. Ula was sorting through furs of all colors and textures, and I was tempted to have her pick out the coarsest ones out of spite. However, I would be the one having to listen to the princess complain, so I resisted.

"Have you seen Mother?" Ula inquired.

"Yes, often. She doesn't talk to me or acknowledge my presence, though. She's serving Queen Shaeli."

"I know, I just thought maybe you'd spoken. Can you give her a message?"

"I could try. No promises I'd have a chance to deliver one."

"I just want her to know I'm all right."

"She must know," I said softly and laid a hand on her shoulder. "I'm sure she asked the queen. You're her favorite after all."

"Oh, Laria, stop!" she said. "Do you think it will be like this forever?"

"No, not if I can help it."

"What do you mean?"

"I think Mother has been trying to help us. I've found a book in the library I've never seen before. Someone keeps leaving it out for me to find."

"What's the book about?"

"Ilano. I've read about their crazy obsession with eagles, their export of textiles and produce, the weather...I even read about these public pools where everyone visits and bathes *together!* I'm learning so much about them, Ula, and I know we can use this to our advantage."

"And you think Mother left it for you?"

"Who else but Mother would do such a thing? Who else would have access to books from Ilano?"

"Someone from Ilano...?"

"Very well, let me rephrase that: who else in this rotten castle would want to help us get away from them but Mother?"

"Shh!" Ula placed a finger to her lips and looked around the empty room.

"Sorry," I whispered. With our arms loaded, we started back to the workroom.

"Don't worry," I said. "I can feel I'm close to something useful. We're going to get out of here. I promise."

When I returned to the princess, she was in the music room practicing on a stringed instrument that sounded like a wailing phantom. The queen insisted she become proficient in playing, but I didn't detect any improvement in the last few weeks. Based on the dissatisfied appearance of the queen, she wasn't impressed either.

"Enough, enough!" Queen Shaeli commanded as she struck the floor repeatedly with her jeweled walking stick.

"I told you this was a waste of time!" Caelyn said.

"Only because you are not applying yourself. Your lack of enthusiasm is expressed in your hideous playing."

"Who exactly do you wish for me to impress, Mother?"

"The people, Caelyn."

"Breathing through my nose should be enough to impress these people."

"Need I remind you that no matter what your personal opinion, the people of Praed must follow you if you wish to accomplish our ends."

"I know," the princess sighed. She raised her bow and began playing again with a little more concentration.

The king took a few minutes out of his busy schedule to settle his bulk into a chaise and listen. The feasting was starting to turn his muscular frame soft. The queen inclined her head in his direction, but the princess ignored him and played on. After a few moments of drumming his fingers and bouncing his knee, the king declared the princess remarkable and left. The reserved exchange was typical of the family in private.

"Again," the queen directed after the piece was over. When the princess started playing, I slipped out of the room, calculating I had at least twenty minutes--thirty if there was an argument--before the princess was finished practicing for the day. I headed straight for the library, my pulse throbbing in anticipation of what I might find.

I was not disappointed. The book sat on the table with its pages exposed. I took it to my usual spot and began to read.

Ilano's roots were in a fiefdom ruled by a Lord Protector rather than a proper kingdom. A cadre of local knights was raised to defend the Lord's manor and the region at large, each knight rewarded with a holding of their own. Ilano's population was peaceful, occupied year-long with production of their famous apple cider and pumpkin cider at the harvest festival. The history was quite dull, except for one notable military engagement two decades ago.

The desert people, under the rule of King Tuar, began expanding their territory across Crif and threatened the northern countries. Lord Protector Davian sent a message to King Tuar asking for peace. It was nearing the rainy season, and the Crif were ill equipped to handle the terrain. King Tuar ignored this plea, instead sending the severed head of the messenger by way of reply. Sensing an impending war, Lord Protector Davian entreated the help of a neighboring country but was denied. The desert people of Crif attacked, ripping people from their beds before the knights were able to mount a defense. Soon the sky was black with war eagles. King Tuar, unprepared for the heavy rains and uneven ground, was driven back to Crif, where he would heal and plot his revenge.

Lord Davian was crippled and unable to walk thereafter. His younger son, Conall, sustained a traumatic head wound but recovered. Lord Davian's elder son and Ilano's strongest knight, Alyx, was killed. He was survived by his wife and son.

I slammed the book shut with a resounding *thwack*. Someone wanted me to know about this battle. What was Mother trying to tell me? The mention of King Conall gave me chills. He must have been a young man when this happened. And the head injury explained quite a bit, frankly. I rose from my seat and tossed the book back on the table. I wanted no more of this.

That night I tried to fall asleep in my tiny hole-in-the-wall but couldn't stop thinking about what I had read. I felt for the innocent people who lost their lives like I did for the people of Praed. King Conall must have been irreparably damaged, not only physically but emotionally, by the loss of his brother and disfigurement of his father. It may explain why he was here now, but not completely. Events may have prompted him to strike out in anger, or lunacy, but why Praed? Was it because our king was graying and perceived as weak? Did he simply want to expand Ilano's territory and crown himself king? It was very confusing, and I had more questions than answers and felt no closer to freedom.

Over the next couple of weeks, the prince and princess became increasingly concerned about their birds' exposure to the decreasing temperatures. The birds themselves appeared nonplussed, but the pair whipped themselves into such a frenzy that one morning the three of us found ourselves amid the mews with frost clinging to our noses and our breaths visible. We inspected every board and crevice for weaknesses and drafts. We used straw mixed with manure to plug up any holes and ordered extra bales of straw to bed down the interiors. While the prince and princess supervised these improvements, I wandered away to peer into the cages and study the birds I despised. If I stripped away the resentment I felt for their masters, I had to admit the birds themselves were quite elegant with their shiny black feathers and stark orange beaks. The royal voices faded as I drifted further along the row. Much had been on my mind these past weeks, and I had not returned to the library since reading that last passage.

A loud knocking sound drew my attention and I paused to discover the source. The noise grew louder as I approached one of the mews and stood on tiptoe to peer through the barred window to see inside. I nearly lost my grip when the inhabitant let out harsh, yelping calls and flapped immense wings against the walls. My eyes widened at the sight of the largest bird I had ever seen--bigger than any other eagle. If I stood next to it, I estimated it would reach my waist. The bird settled suddenly, folded its wings, and uttered a lyrical *keee-up*, *keee-up* tipping its head from side to side.

"You're a strange creature," I said. "Can't make up your mind to be angry or content, can you? I know the feeling." The bird continued to mutter quietly, its dark eyes blinking curiously at me. "Are you the king's--what do they call it? Soulmate?"

"No," a deep voice resounded behind me. "She's mine." Startled, I fell from the side of the building and fearfully looked up. Standing over me with a suppressed grin was Sir What's-His-Name who enjoys making me miserable. I scrambled to my feet to brush off my skirts and glared at him with unconcealed malice.

"Did you want to meet her?" he said.

My eyes darted toward the mew where the occupant excitedly flapped her wings and vocalized. Without waiting for an answer, Risteard unlatched the side door and stepped inside. I watched through the window as he approached the bird confidently, spoke softly, and ran a gloved hand down the feathered chest. He held his forearm out and the giant bird stepped up, the long talons encircling his arm. I dropped back to the ground as the pair emerged but kept their distance. I watched warily as the knight attached leather jesses around each of the bird's legs, and then beckoned me closer.

"You're perfectly safe. She won't harm you," he said.

I took a few steps forward and stopped an arm's length away, eyeing the pair distrustfully. Risteard returned his focus to the bird, feeding it morsels of meat and conversing with it like an old friend. It suddenly occurred to me that here was the only person who could possibly answer the questions plaguing me for days, however abhorrent I found the idea of saying more than necessary to him. I glanced around to make sure we were alone.

"I've been doing some reading," I began.

"Naturally," he responded.

"About Ilano."

"To better understand your enemy?"

"Something like that…" The eagle stared at me with its blank eyes, and I imagined the eerie twinge in my stomach must be what its prey experiences. "There was a battle many years ago, against the desert people?"

Risteard hesitated briefly in his ministrations and finally met my eye.

"I had not yet reached my tenth year, but I remember."

"King Conall was there?"

"As were many others." His expression was blank, so I couldn't decide if he was angry. I figured I better be as diplomatic as possible, otherwise he might have me flogged or worse.

"It must have been awful," I said. "Being injured and having to take on so much responsibility. The stress alone would be more than most people could handle."

The knight remained silent.

"Ilano seemed so peaceful," I continued. "But now, here we are. The conqueror and conquered."

"Did you have a question?" He seemed irritated.

"What changed? It happened so long ago, and suddenly he decides to attack *us* without provocation? It doesn't make sense."

"Because you're not asking the right question," he said.

I bit my lip, thinking, and my eyes drifted back to the massive bird still focused intently on me.

"What's her name?"

"Aquila."

"Why does she keep staring at me?"

"She's never seen ginger hair before either."

"Either?" I tucked a loose strand back into my cap.

"It's not a common shade in Ilano. Is it here?"

I avoided his gaze. "No."

He turned the eagle to face away from me.

"Since she's making you uncomfortable."

Seeing her expansive, solid black body shining in the sunlight drew me, and my hand subconsciously reached out to touch her, but I pulled back, afraid.

"It's all right," Risteard whispered calmly.

Before I could reconsider, I put my hand on the eagle's back. Stroking her dark feathers, I was amazed at how soft she was, like goose down. She didn't flap or react in any way to frighten me as I continued to run one hand, then both, along her body, learning every curve and contour.

"Is she heavy?" I asked, regretting how stupid it sounded.

"She is, even for a female."

"I understand you have to train a long time to be able to carry one."

"Yes. You still aren't asking the right question."

I stopped petting Aquila and looked up at him, his face once again unreadable but not intimidating.

"Why did Ilano attack Praed?" I whispered hoarsely.

"A better question would be, 'Who turned their back on Ilano when they desperately needed help?'"

I heard the exasperated voice of the princess in the distance, probably because she was looking for me. Yet I didn't break away from the knight's intense gaze despite the growing tension.

"Was it Praed?" I whispered weakly.

The princess stormed toward us. "There she is! You there! Oh, damn, the stupid thing can't hear me...Risteard! Get that girl's attention, would you?" An annoyed grimace flashed across the knight's features briefly before becoming stone once more. He pointed past my shoulder, though he knew I needed no help detecting the princess's presence. She strode up to us and grabbed my shoulder, turning me around.

"I've been looking for you," she yelled, enunciating each word. "I have an additional task for you to complete every day. You've had far too much time on your hands, and you know what they say about idleness."

She directed her attention at Risteard. "Don't pay this one any mind. She's strange, but harmless. You needn't protect me from her. Come on." She took my arm. "We're going to show you how to clean and bed down the mews. You should have no trouble with your vast experience mucking stalls." As she towed me along, I glanced over my shoulder. Aquila remained still, her eyes fixed on me while I was pulled away. She pierced the air with a mournful call, and I felt the urge to run to her, just as I had for Amore the night she turned to ash.

CHAPTER 9

I rubbed my fingers vigorously and cupped my hands over my mouth, breathing warm air across my frigid skin, then spread my hands wide over the welcoming heat of the fire, my teeth chattering, my body wracked by shivers. The last few hours had been spent raking straw, disposing of soiled bedding, and pitching bales, but unlike my experience with horses, these duties were performed for raptors. The stable at Riverstone was warmed by steam released under the floors, providing comfort to the horses and stable hands during the early morning hours. Here I labored in the ice and snow wearing meager clothing, running between each mew as quickly as possible for what warmth they offered. At least I wasn't forced to feed the beasts. I don't think I could stomach hauling scraps of meat, chiseling each piece off the pile before tossing it into waiting talons and preventing entrails from getting on my frock. The only addition to my sparse wardrobe when the cold became abusive was a thin leather greatcoat that was several sizes too large. Ula knit me a woolen cap to fit under my usual headpiece that hid my offensive hair, but she had not yet completed a pair of matching mittens.

My days had become very busy in the past month, starting early with the usual directions toward the kitchens and preparing a proper winter wardrobe for the princess. After ensuring she was suitable for company, I was permitted a small breakfast of two slices of warmed bread, a portion of butter, and brown, bitter tea, then I would bundle into my coat and brace myself for the outdoors. The white ground crunched as I trudged across the snow toward the mews I was tasked to clean. Other laborers nodded as I passed, all of us comrades in dissatisfaction with our circumstances. I crammed my numb fingers under my arms and my worn shoes were soaked through. It took me several hours to clean the mews, dispose of the waste, and spread a fresh layer of straw. Mostly, the birds left me alone since they were fed quite early and content. I soon learned that some birds, despite a full stomach, would test my patience with their mischief and some were downright vicious. I once tried to convey my fears to the princess, but she pretended she couldn't understand. A small part of my mind whispered she was purposely trying to endanger me.

I had several minutes between finishing up chores and preparing lunch for the princess when I could warm myself and ensure a decent appearance. Once, I came straight from chores thinking it would please her to arrive so promptly. She found my wet clothing, dripping nose, and stench so abominable she took to bed the whole afternoon with a headache. She instructed me that henceforth I was not to approach her until making myself presentable. So, in accordance with her wishes, I retreated to the library where a blaze always roared in the hearth. I shrugged off my overcoat and boots and laid them on the floor to dry while my limbs and muscles revived.

When my fingers and toes were once again pink and flexible, I removed my caps and laid them next to my coat, unbound my hair, and allowed the unruly tangles to fall over my face. The outer layers were damp, but the thickness prevented the moisture from reaching my scalp, protecting my head from the chill. I ran my fingers through the mess and tried to dry the ends without making the knots worse, which mostly worked. The ritual was cathartic, and it cleared my mind of the stress and anger that perpetually plagued my life. These private minutes were the only ones I would have all day, and I relished them, savoring the time like I did the sweet treats we used to receive at our birthday celebrations. I refused to think about Ula laboring in the bowels of the castle or Mother's continued indifference, or the hard slab I slept on every night, or the pieces of straw I stuffed in my boots to insulate my freezing feet. And I certainly paid no attention to the book lying ominously on the table, open to pages unread and ignored.

Since learning of the history of Ilano and Praed, I had avoided reading further, afraid of what I might discover. Ilano had been in danger and Praed had refused them help. Why? Was there more history between the two, unknown even to the author? I spent the last several months experiencing the wickedness of Ilano so I never bothered to learn the motivation behind the attack. It wouldn't make their actions justified, but at least I'd stop living in an ignorant, depressed haze.

Through the strands of my hair I peered at the book, existing innocently like the bright yellow fruit of the solpan bush that grows beneath the mammoth trees of the Sessyl Forest. The fruit appears deceptively sweet, but if eaten results in profuse vomiting and diarrhea. Without understanding why, I rose and plodded over to the book to run my hand over the pages. The familiar feeling made my fingers tingle, and I laid my palm against the words as if to absorb knowledge through my skin. I thirsted for information, and I was parched.

Reverently, I took the book in my hands and saw what appeared to be a complex family tree scrawled across the pages. Before I could really study the names and relationships, I heard the doorknob rattle and footsteps enter the library. Frightened, I tossed the book back on the table, scooped up my clothing, and retreated into the shadows.

"Don't worry about being interrupted. No one comes to this moldy place." I recognized the voice of Prince Brannon and shrank back against the bookcase.

"Why the secrecy…Your Highness?" I was shocked to hear Risteard, his tone irritated as usual.

"Come on, no need for that. It's just you and me after all." The prince paced in front of the hearth and stopped. Holding my breath, I inched around the edge of the bookcase. I could see the prince in the light of the fire, his arms outstretched toward the flames. Risteard strode up behind him, arms crossed, and stared down impatiently.

"You asked to see me?" Risteard asked.

"I just wanted to check in and make sure everyone is happy, you know, in their roles."

"You're wanting to know if there is any dissent?"

"You always have a way of getting straight to the point, Risteard."

"And you of avoiding it."

The prince chuckled softly. Admittedly I bit my tongue to keep from giggling myself.

"Yes, yes, I've always been the scatterbrained one, but that doesn't make me stupid." The prince's voice dropped menacingly. "I want you to inform me immediately if you hear any talk, even a whisper, of mutiny."

"I don't expect anything of the kind."

The prince twisted his mouth into a strained smile and placed his hands on Risteard's shoulders. Though I couldn't see his expression, Risteard tensed visibly at the prince's touch.

"I know this must be terribly difficult for you," the prince said, kneading the knight's muscular shoulders. "But I know I can count on your cooperation, can't I?"

Risteard stepped out of the prince's reach. "Do you insult me by questioning my loyalty, Your Highness?" The hairs on the back of my neck and arms rose at the dark tone of his voice.

"No, no, no!" The prince made a placating gesture and sounded afraid. "No one would accuse you of all people of betraying Ilano."

"Has Your Highness been listening to rumors again? You know you can't trust the closet talk of bored and uneducated people."

"I know, but if the people talk behind my back, then they don't respect me. And without respect, there cannot be loyalty. How can the people follow me if they're not loyal?

"You mean follow the king?"

"Yes, of course." The prince turned away from Risteard to stare at the fire. "But I am the prince, and therefore an extension of His Majesty's rule. Someday, I may venture out to expand the kingdom and I will require subjects to vow fealty to me."

"Your Highness can be assured that any dissent will be addressed and threats to the crown treated swiftly and without prejudice."

"Meaning?"

"Traitors will be thrown into the dungeon and a sword plunged into the hearts of conspirators and assaulters of the king."

"Now you're speaking my language. I do enjoy your murderous rage, Risteard."

"No one knows it as well as you, Brannon." The prince shifted uncomfortably and brushed a hand along the side of his face but did not correct the lapse in formality.

"I must say, your ideas for trade relations in the east are brilliant. I'm sure the king can be persuaded to see reason once he feels more secure."

Risteard's voice darkened. "He's been beyond persuasion before."

"Well." The prince straightened and, shockingly, bowed to Risteard. "I'm glad we've had this talk and understand each other." The prince nearly tripped as he hurriedly exited the library.

Risteard leaned against the mantle, his face buried in the crook of his elbow for several seconds while I watched, breathlessly. Suddenly, he balled his hand into a fist and struck the smooth stone of the hearth, growling a curse as he did. Once again, I had to clutch my hand around my mouth to keep from crying out.

"I know you're there," he grunted through clenched teeth. "And you can come out now. I'm sure you're due to serve the princess in whatever senseless task she has assigned today."

Angrily, I emerged from the shadows and stood as close to his face as my diminutive size allowed. "If I wasn't afraid someone would hear me," I snarled, "I would scream curses in your face."

"Is fear of discovery holding you back or is it because swearing is so unladylike?" he said.

"I'm no lady, sir," I said, my jaw clenched. Out of the corner of my eye, I was certain I glimpsed a snake slithering down the stones of the fireplace, but when I focused my full attention on the dark ribbon tracing down the mantle, I realized it was a trail of blood running from his fist still pressed against the stones.

"Congratulations, hero. You've protected us all from the threat of centuries old rock and mortar. Was it plotting against the prince behind his back?"

Risteard did not appreciate the joke, at least his face did not betray any emotion besides rage. He drew his hand away, and it hung at his side dripping blood on the once pristine polished floor.

"You could at least have a little respect for the poor servant who has to clean up after you," I said. I reached for his hand and inspected the wounds for broken bones. I pulled a finger or two, eliciting a sharp intake of breath but felt no grinding.

"It's not broken." I tore a strip off my frock for a bandage. "But not for lack of effort. What was that all about?" I bound the wound tightly to stem the flow of blood.

"Nothing that concerns you," he said.

"Fine." I finished wrapping the bandage, knotting it a little rougher than necessary. "How did you know I was here?"

"I heard a book close before you scurried into the dark leaving a trail of dripping water. You're lucky the prince is too self-absorbed to notice."

"Still, it could have been anyone."

"Who else would be here reading after morning chores?"

"Fair." I stepped back and stood once more before the warmth of the fire.

"Doesn't the princess provide you with suitable clothing?" I looked down at the simple frock clinging to my damp skin. A surprised gasp escaped my lips, and I hugged my arms around my body and dashed behind the bookcase to retrieve my belongings. I re-emerged to his muffled laughter, his eyes averted politely.

"A gentleman would have said something sooner!"

"I am no gentleman," he said in a low, husky voice, his eyes burning into mine. I wrapped my overcoat tighter and clumsily stuffed my hair safely into my cap.

"Um...thanks," he mumbled while inspecting his bandaged hand.

"That's the kindest thing anyone has said since I was dragged into this nightmare. You're welcome, I suppose."

His focus was neither on his hand nor my face but directed at the floor. I followed his gaze and was embarrassed to realize he was staring at my worn boots. I shifted uncomfortably, using the toe of my right foot to cover a hole on the left.

"Well," I broke the silence loudly, trying to detract attention from my attire. "Princess Caelyn will be requiring my services. I should go." I moved to leave, but he blocked my path.

"I'll speak to the king," he said. "No one representing the royal family should be clothed so disgracefully, even a servant."

"You don't have to do that." I shook my head fearfully. If he spoke to the king on my behalf, the princess would certainly hear of it and make my life more miserable.

"Surely the princess can appreciate that if you become ill, you will not be able to perform your duties. At least the thought of having to bathe and dress herself will be enough to secure you a decent pair of boots."

I resisted the urge to smile when he finally let me hurry off. Some young ladies dream of handsome men or pretty dresses, but this one had a spring in her step with thoughts of dry feet.

While the prince and princess sated themselves with sweet meats and loudly sipped tea, their forks and spoons screeched against plates in a rhythm that made my eyes twitch and hair stand on end. Yet I stood in the corner with a tiny, secretive smile playing about my lips as I imagined warm toes snuggled in new boots. Even if Risteard did not follow through, I had something to dwell on other than my dreary day-to-day misery.

"I've had a letter from Jervell," the princess mumbled around the scone in her mouth. My ears perked at the name I recognized but could not place.

The prince didn't look up from his papers. "Oh? What news does that vermin have?"

The princess slammed her teacup onto the saucer, spilling the contents and capturing her brother's attention. "I would hold my tongue if I were you. We wouldn't want Jervell to think we don't appreciate his support."

"Helpful or not, you cannot deny the man is slimy. And his face resembles a rat."

"Disfigurement aside, he says there are some in Ilano who wish to stick with the old ways and remain isolated. Apparently, some find the expansion of our borders undesirable and we should all return."

"Some people lack ambition and despise wealth, I suppose. Jervell can change their minds, or they can leave."

"If we're going to have a kingdom, idiot, we need the people! They need to see the world as it can be and know their families will be safe. If the people are content, then they will be compliant. We need the people to trust us."

"And how do you propose we earn their trust? Some people weren't exactly thrilled with Father's decision to come here."

"They need to see Ilano is not forgotten. Jervell says we need to consider uniting the kingdoms through marriage."

"You mean marrying someone from Praed?"

"No!" The princess curled her lip in disgust at the thought. "By choosing a bride from one of the primary families in Ilano and crowning her in Praed, we will effectively form an alliance between the two."

"Bride? So, I'm the one to be sold off in this plan."

"Please." The princess rolled her eyes and took another bite of scone. "As if you would object to a woman legally required to join you in bed."

"That's not what distresses me. It's the thought of sharing it with the same woman for the rest of my life."

"I didn't think faithfulness was something you believed in, Brannon."

"I also didn't anticipate being forced into wedlock, but here we are."

"We all have to make sacrifices."

"What have you sacrificed, Caelyn? From where I sit, no one has forced you to do anything you don't want to do. You're Father's favorite after all."

Princess Caelyn screamed and hurled her teacup at Prince Brannon's head. He ducked before it struck him, and the porcelain shattered against the wall. It was fortunate I was used to her outbursts and only betrayed myself with a sudden tension of my shoulders. Neither noticed.

"If you ever say that again, I'll expose you as a traitor myself," she said. Her face was red, her breathing rapid, and there was malice in her eyes. The prince nodded, and she closed her eyes to calm herself.

"Every day I'm stuck here being waited on by that aberration over there." She gestured toward me standing in the corner pretending not to understand. "It's an interminable prison sentence."

"Oh, it's not as bad as you insist it has to be." Prince Brannon rose from the table and sauntered over to me. He gripped my chin and jerked my head up to look at him. "She's just a child, after all." He released me and ripped the cap off my head, pulling several strands of hair in the process. I flinched but made no sound. He grasped a strand of hair that had fallen free. "Even this you could get used to in time. You may even be able to boast of such an unusual creature in your entourage, like an exotic animal."

"Animal being the operative word. No one will admire a disabled mute." The prince released my hair and laughed as he took a seat. I retrieved my cap from the floor and hastily replaced it on my head, biting the inside of my cheek to keep the tears at bay while I hid my offensive red hair. Whatever pleasure I had indulged in earlier was gone, replaced by the constant suffering at the hands of these vile, selfish brats who in no way deserved their royal titles.

"You will do what Jervell says, won't you?" Princess Caelyn said.

"And when shall this blessed event take place?"

"He says we should allow things to settle, ensure Praed is stable, and he will approach some council members about the possibility of an advantageous marriage for their daughters."

"It sounds as if Jervell has everything in hand."

"Yes. All you need to do is enter into an engagement with the lady of our choosing."

He frowned. "Don't I get a say in the matter?"

"We both know making decisions isn't your strong suit, especially when it comes to women. We need to think with what's above our necks, not below our belts."

I listened motionless in the corner trying to disregard the ugly banter and concentrate on the conversation. If there were arrangements being made for marriages and alliances, why were this pair and a man I remembered was the princess' correspondent in charge of the plans and not the king? It seemed quite unorthodox, even for them. And where did this Jervell person fit into all this? The mounting questions were frustrating and I had no way of answering them. Even though I kept telling myself to let it go, I couldn't stop asking.

The assembly room at Praed Castle hosted balls that created enough gossip to fuel wagging tongues for months. The arched alcoves that lined the vast room were perfect for couples stealing moments alone, and dance partners glided across the polished floors. But it wasn't the flowing gowns nor the magnificent chandelier that made the room a topic of interest. Stained glass windows depicting the history of Praed stretched to the vaulted ceiling, and when the sun set, rainbows illuminated the room.

Today, the royal court was gathered in the assembly room to admire one another, complain about the weather, and kiss His Majesty's...ring. The king announced the people of Praed were welcome to the castle so he could hear their requests and magnanimously solve their problems. The gathered people erupted in gasps and whispered conversation, and my heart thundered at the thought of seeing people I knew. I stepped away from the wall where I was close enough to the princess to refill her cider but far away enough not to embarrass her with my presence. When the doors opened, the crowd parted to form a path where the king sat on the throne, Queen Shaeli to his left and Risteard standing at his right. The prince and princess took their places on either side of the dais looking bored as usual. I wandered closer to the throne and held my breath as a figure stepped over the threshold and approached the king.

I had no idea who he was because he was from Ilano and had emigrated shortly after the battle. The next man was also from Ilano, as was the next and the one after. Being stuck in the castle, I didn't know so many outsiders settled here, moving into the homes passed down in Praed families for generations. Their complaints were trivial and mostly revolved around the unfamiliar snow. My shoulders sagged and I left my place in the crowd to retreat into obscurity, when I heard a familiar voice addressing the king.

"Your Majesty," the voice began. "My crops were destroyed by your soldiers and did not recover before the first snows. My storerooms were raided, and therefore we have no food to support us through the winter. What will Your Majesty do to secure the survival of my family, who are now your responsibility?"

As she spoke, I pushed through the throng to confirm her identity. I nearly cried when I saw her, so pale and thin, her clothing tattered and soiled. She was Telva Blu, and her estate of Ashforde bordered Riverstone, our families neighbors for centuries. As a child I had admired her grace when she rode her gray mare across the rocky hills and marveled how she danced without restraint during King Llewlyn's birthday celebrations. Her children were younger than Ula and me, and they would hold hands behind her in a chain when they walked through town. During harvest, she baked cobblers and pies that made my mouth water weeks in advance just thinking about how the juicy berries burst between my teeth. She was a sweet, loving mother, who showed an affection for her children I never experienced from my own mother. She doted on them, showering them with kisses and hugs I longed to receive. Her husband was a knight like my father. If he was not here today, then he, too, must be dead.

"I have heard your pleas," King Conall said, his hand covering his heart. "From one parent to another." The prince and princess turned away to hide their amusement. "How many children do you have, ma'am?"

"Five."

"Well, perhaps one or two could come to work in the palace? That would ease your burden."

"It's not the children who are a burden, Your Majesty."

"I see. Well, you've lived many winters here, I gather. You should have been more prepared." The king's knee started bouncing and a flush creeped up his neck.

"We weren't prepared for invading soldiers to act dishonorably and leave us with nothing, Your Majesty. This is the fault of your men. How are you going to make amends?"

The king's face reddened, and the crowd stirred uncomfortably, waiting for his anger to burst at this poor woman. Before he could open his mouth, the queen placed a hand over his and leaned forward to whisper in his ear. His fingers dug into his chair, but the movement of his leg slowed. The room was silent, waiting anxiously for the king's decision.

Once the queen drew away he said, "There is no way to know which men stole from you, my lady. In any case, they cannot be blamed for the actions carried out during war. However," he raised his hand to cease the protest on her lips, "I will provide for the people of Praed, not as an apology, but as a promise. I am your king! As such you can call me your father, and you will find I am generous to my loyal children." He waved at Telva in dismissal.

"When may I expect your token of generosity, Your Majesty?"

"By the end of the week, provisions will be delivered to your storerooms. Now go."

Telva bowed gracefully and walked with deliberate poise while the crowd watched. I sneaked away, sliding out the door and down the corridor, and hiding behind a pillar in the foyer. When the footfalls drew near, I peeked around my hiding spot, and made sure we were alone.

"Lady Blu!" I whispered. She turned toward my voice, and I beckoned, hoping she wouldn't think I was a villain lying in wait.

"Who's there?" She came closer.

I grabbed her sleeve and pulled her close, throwing my arms around her waist and hugging her. She pushed me away.

"Wait!" I pleaded as she turned to flee. "It's me!"

She looked at me, confusion masking her face. I removed my cap and her eyes widened.

"Laria?" She touched my cheek. Her blue eyes were still bright, but her brown hair had grayed considerably and lines creased her skin.

"You've grown." She smiled and took my face in both her hands. "Thank goodness you're alive. We feared what may have happened to you. What about your mother? Does she live?"

"Yes," I said. "But she's...different."

"We all are, my dear. And Ula?"

"Alive. She works in the lower castle sewing and mending."

She closed her eyes and sighed in relief.

"What about the children?" I asked. "How are they?"

"Well enough, Laria. I haven't lost everything to those monsters."

"And…" I couldn't bring myself to ask about her husband.

"Sir Blu was slain." A tear dripped off her long lashes.

"My father was, too."

She took a deep breath and wiped her eyes. "Laria, I have to go, but I want you to know, many people will be overjoyed to know you're alive. The news will bring great comfort. And hope."

"Because of me? Why? I'm nothing."

"You're a daughter of Riverstone, Laria. No matter what these people do to you, don't ever forget."

"I haven't. I won't."

She pressed a kiss to my forehead and was gone.

I slumped against the pillar and buried my face in my hands, crying as I did the day I arrived: unrestrained and hidden from view. Fearing my absence would eventually be noticed, I allowed myself one more minute to mourn the life that had been ripped from me, and then I wiped my face and replaced the cap on my head. I stared blankly ahead, entering the assembly room once again, no longer caring to see another familiar face. One by one, people approached the king and were treated mercifully. I remained in the background.

How could an illiterate, deaf-mute servant girl give hope to Praed?

The princess was charged with distributing the goods the king promised to show the people Ilano was not their enemy. This order sent her into a hysteria I had yet to encounter. She insisted on overseeing everything, from the carriage decor to the arrangement of items in the delivery wagon, from her wardrobe and that of those accompanying her. Nothing was to be done that did not meet her approval. Of course, she didn't lift a finger herself. After my normal chores, I ran all over the castle sending messages and helping with ridiculous last-minute changes. The princess was long asleep in her bed before I was able to fall onto my hard mattress and rest for a few hours.

After one of these grueling days, I stumbled into my room, half conscious from fatigue and aching from my toes to the roots of my hair. I dropped my coat to the floor, followed by my cap, not bothering to place them on the only chair in the room. The one candle I was allowed sputtered when I set it on the small chest next to my bed. There, in the flickering candlelight, in the middle of the narrow bed, stood a pair of tall, shining brown, leather boots. I picked one up and ran my fingers along the seams, reveling in the unmarred surface that so contrasted the pair currently on my feet. Grinning excitedly, I sat on the bed, pulled the old boots off, and flung them aside, spilling straw as they bounced across the stone floor. My eyes slipped shut as I slid my feet into the new boots luxuriously lined with thick, soft fur, then walked around the cramped space. The fit was perfect.

I'm not ashamed to admit I fell asleep with a peaceful smile on my face, clutching those boots to my chest.

CHAPTER 10

I swayed to the gentle rhythm of the wagon rambling along the roads leading to the estates and small farms dotting the landscape of Praed. Homes destroyed and rebuilt rose over fields blanketed with freshly fallen snow, and people rushed around busy with chores and family needs. Watching from a distance, I felt a longing for the comforts of home, a yearning to give anything to have Mother yelling at me to drag my lazy self out of bed on cold mornings, telling me the horses can't feed themselves.

In the carriage ahead of me, Princess Caelyn sat bundled in furs and hot stones, waving to the people and handing out goods with great condescension. She put forth an extra effort to ingratiate herself to the people by engaging in polite conversation and patting the heads of small children. I picked up snippets here and there of the people's impressions, and they were surprisingly favorable. The princess's kindness was appreciated, but I heard nothing agreeable about the king himself.

"She's nice, Mama," said a little girl, her voice muffled through a woolen scarf wrapped around her face and neck.

"Yes, she is, my dear," her mother said. A man worked next to her, loading supplies on a fuzzy, sway backed mule. She leaned toward him, scowling, and mumbled something about the king.

"Shhh," the man admonished. "It's by his grace that we'll be able to last the winter."

"Hmpf. It's by his grace that we're in this situation."

The crowd ignored me, too absorbed in receiving the much-needed aid. Some I recognized, though understandably they had aged considerably in recent months. I made no attempt to communicate, choosing to remain invisible in case one of them exposed my secret.

We travelled at a comfortable pace, the snowcapped trees passing by quickly. I settled into my seat, wrapping the one blanket I was provided tightly around my shoulders. I wiggled my toes in my new, warm boots, drawing my attention to the person responsible for the gift. Risteard rode alongside the carriage, protecting the princess from bandits and wolves should she be set upon by either. While the caravan trekked down the road, I amused myself by imagining a pack of snarling wolves surrounding the carriage, the knight's sword swinging wildly as he tried to fight them off but failing, and the princess being carried off to the wolf den to be devoured. Admittedly, this was a terrible thought, and I felt guilty picturing the demise of the princess. Maybe the pack would simply run off with her furs to warm their pups and leave her to catch a chill, and I delighted in the vision of her red, swollen nose.

Since discovering the boots, I hadn't thanked Risteard, and this distressed me. Whatever his reasons, the gift represented the only kindness I'd received since coming to the castle, and I appreciated it regardless of its source. The last thing I wanted was to be indebted to anyone, especially the man who dragged me from my room and forced me to watch my life go up in flames. But here I was, and the longer it took to express my thanks the more time he had to think about repayment of his generosity. If I wait too long a simple 'thank you' might not satisfy.

"So grateful, Your Highness. So very grateful." The loud, exaggerated praise came from a thin woman bowing over Princess Caelyn's hand. She elbowed her younger companion, who repeated the sentiment.

"I am honored to serve you," the princess said.

I coughed to cover the laugh that escaped my throat and organized the supplies. The pair wandered toward me speaking in low tones, but I didn't miss the mention of a familiar name.

"You'll end up just like Lady Blu if you're not careful," the woman said.

"Unspeakable," the girl said. She crossed her arms and spit onto the ground.

The woman reached out when I handed her a crate of winter produce. "When a king offers kindness then does the opposite, he's sayin' he's not to be trifled with."

I froze, my fingers clutching the coarse wood beneath my fingers, and the woman narrowed her eyes and tugged at the crate when I wouldn't let go. I released it with a meek smile, and she tucked it under one arm and draped the other across the girl's shoulders.

"The poor girls," the woman said. For the first time, I wished I wasn't pretending to be mute so I could call out to them and find out what happened. But I remained silent. I leaned over the side of the wagon to try and hear more, but the wind carried their voices away before they disappeared into the house.

The caravan halted at the last stop and two people stepped forward wrapped completely in thick, woolen garb, only their eyes visible. The princess bestowed a few words while I climbed into the back of the wagon to hand out the designated goods. One of the figures came toward me and I held out a bag of flour. Their hands brushed mine, and they paused. I looked up and they just stared. I motioned the bag into the person's hands, indicating they should take it. I was unprepared for what happened next.

"Laria?" the trembling voice spoke. "Is that you?" I met the eyes in surprise. The wool scarf was pulled down, and I nearly fell off the wagon. It was Morgan, lady's maid to my mother and trusted member of our household since before I was born.

"Do you recognize me?" she asked. Like so many others, her face had aged, but those amber brown eyes had not changed. They were as clear and sharp as the day she caught me tying Mother's finest ribbons into Amore's mane. I clutched her hand, squeezing it tightly so she could feel how I wanted to embrace her but could not. The bag of flour fell to the snow at her feet as she took both my hands and kissed them, tears tracing the lines on her tired face.

"Thank the stars above," she said. "After they took you away, I never heard what happened to you. What about your mother? Does she live?" I nodded. "And sweet little Ula? They didn't harm her?" I shook my head. She closed her eyes and whispered a silent thanks. She examined my face and clothes. "You're so thin, Laria. Those monsters. Don't they feed you?" I smiled. No sense worrying her about my meager rations. A voice called out, Morgan's husband. She waved and turned back to me, gave my hands a last squeeze, and retrieved the bag of flour.

"You don't know what this means to me, Laria." She turned to walk away, but before she could take two steps, I grabbed her sleeve.

"Does Riverstone still stand?" I spoke without ensuring we were alone. It was dangerous, but I needed to know.

"It does." She beamed with pride before walking away.

I pressed my palms to my eyes and breathed sharply through my nose to keep the emotions at bay. When in control again, I uncovered my face, and there he was, watching me from atop his horse with a characteristically void expression.

"I knew her," I said quietly. "*Know* her, actually." I don't know why I felt the need to explain--I owed him nothing. He continued to stare, and I glanced around to see if anyone was close enough to hear.

"Thank you--for the boots I mean."

"I hope they're sufficient."

"They more than suffice. They're perfect."

A smile briefly played on his lips. "You're welcome."

"I still despise you."

"Understandable." He tugged the reins to direct the horse back toward the princess's carriage.

"Wait!" I called out. "I still have questions."

"Naturally."

"I don't suppose you could be bothered to answer any of them?"

"I could. Meet me in the library tonight after Her Highness is asleep."

"Should I arm myself with a weapon?"

"Only this one." He pointed to his temple.

Princess Caelyn, after a long day in the elements, was convinced she would develop a severe illness and insisted I do everything possible to prevent it. I drew her a hot bath laced with lavender oil and peppermint leaves and then drained it because the smell of the herbs was too harsh for her delicate sensibilities. In its place, a new bath was prepared with rose petals, which she deemed acceptable. While she soaked, I served green tea with lemon and honey, but the sweet and sour combination was upsetting to her palate. Tea was for the daytime, she insisted, and wasn't possibly strong enough to help her sleep after such a stressful day. A kitchen maid delivered a strong concoction of hot cider and something called 'brandy' in response to my silent plea for help. Once the princess was warmed through by a combination of bath and drink, she languidly melted into a fleece nightgown and poured herself into a bed warmed with pans of hot coals. Moments from sleep, she motioned me over and directed me to put one or two more furs at her feet and stoke the fire. Three seconds after placing another log on the hearth, she was snoring.

I stood at the library door, knees trembling, thinking the late hour meant Risteard probably gave up and left. It wasn't clear which I dreaded more--that he was inside or that he had gone. I told myself if he wanted to harm me, he had several chances to do so without luring me into the library. Before I could analyze the situation further, I pushed open the door and slipped inside.

The room was dark and silent save for the faint crackle of flames. I maneuvered myself along the bookcases until I saw a figure sitting in a leather chair bent over a large tome. I crept closer, so close I could see the lines on the page. Just as I was about to peer over his left shoulder, Risteard spun around, each of us startling the other.

"Either I'm getting sneakier," I said, "or you're going deaf."

He chuckled softly--the first time I'd heard such a sound from him.

"Neither." He shook his head. "It was a lack of observation. I was so absorbed in the impressive history of King Llewlyn I blocked out everything else."

"Yes," I agreed, taking the book from him. "King Llewlyn proved himself worthy to the people by winning the Tournament of Kings. No other man was able to withstand the feats of strength, cunning, and prowess. He ruled for many years and Praed was prosperous under his leadership. He had many successful campaigns, several of which my father participated in and fought by his side."

"The very definition of the conquering hero."

I slammed the heavy volume shut between my hands. "You would know."

He gestured toward the chair opposite him.

"You're the one who wants answers," he said, "so it might be in your best interest to refrain from antagonizing me."

"Well." I tucked the book next to me and sank into the plush leather. "Give me a reason to act differently. As far as I'm concerned, you're the man who destroyed my family and burned our stables to the ground. How would you feel if I did the same to the mews?"

His face darkened and a nauseous knot formed in my stomach. Perhaps I had gone too far.

"Fair," he responded hoarsely. "I know it wouldn't matter if I told you I wasn't responsible for your father's death, or for the destruction of your stables and loss of your horses."

"They were more than just horses!" I cried, tears instantly blurring my vision. "The other half of my soul was in her stall when you callously set a torch to it."

"It wasn't me," he growled, his fists digging into the arms of the chair.

"You may not have lit the spark, but you were a part of it. You allowed it to happen. And you made me watch. I'll hate you forever for that." He had the decency at least to appear ashamed.

"I couldn't stop him," he said. "But you're right." He held my gaze, his eyes burning cerulean lightning in the reflection of the flames. "I should have."

Brushing the back of my hand across my face, I turned away and watched the fire dance among the logs in the hearth. Before, fire had signaled warmth, comfort, a hot meal. Now, it meant screaming, and fear, and death.

He spoke quietly. "Whatever you want to know I'll tell you."

I couldn't look at him. "Why did you murder our horses?"

"Strategy," he answered shortly. "King Conall knew how much they meant to you. He knew without them your family would be broken and he could control you."

"How perceptive of him. He killed my father?"

"Yes. Do you want to hear about it?"

"No." I wasn't interested in the glory of a soldier's death.

"He didn't suffer."

"Small blessings, I suppose."

"Did I hurt you?"

"What do you mean?" I asked, my voice sounding distant.

"When I... removed you from your room."

I'm certain my expression as I faced him matched my thoughts: *Are you crazy?*

"Despite the impression I have given thus far," he said. "I'm not a monster."

"Time will tell."

"You said you had questions." He sat back in his chair, looking annoyed, and I had the urge to throw the book at my side straight at his thick head.

"Yes." I inhaled deeply and brushed away thoughts of Amore. "Since I've been alive, King Llewlyn has never resisted the chance to fight. Why would he deny Lord...what was his name?"

"Davian."

"Right. Lord Davian asked for help and King Llewlyn's refusal makes no sense."

"Perhaps he thought the books written about him were too thick already."

"That's ridiculous! Much more has been written about him since. Enough to fill a library!"

The corner of Risteard's mouth curved up. "Maybe it was personal."

"You mean King Llewlyn had a history with Lord Davian and didn't help out of spite? What could possibly have happened to make King Llewlyn dislike him so much he refused a call to battle?"

"What usually causes turmoil and strife between two men?"

"Money?"

"Ilano and Praed hardly relied on each other for prosperity. What else?"

"I don't know."

"A testament to how young you are."

I scowled.

He continued. "It was of course that timeless impediment that makes enemies of friends and entices men to dispatch one other. That one thing that can make fools of kings."

"What?" I asked impatiently.

"A woman," he said matter-of-factly.

"Oh, please." I rolled my eyes. "It's not a woman's fault all those people died."

"No, of course not! But a woman came between King Llewlyn and Lord Davian."

"How?"

"They wanted the same woman. She chose Lord Davian, and King Llewlyn never forgave either of them."

"How would they have known the same woman if they lived so separately?"

"She travelled as an emissary to King Llewlyn's court to represent Ilano. You will not read about her in his history books. She came before his marriage, when he was young and newly kinged. Her name was Beja, and she was renowned throughout Ilano as a great beauty and diplomat. When she arrived in Praed, King Llewlyn was infatuated, and lavished her with gifts so precious there was no doubt of his intentions. However, she sent them back because her heart was promised to another. The king demanded to know who the man was, and she told him. Davian, though he was not yet a lord. The king was furious and ordered her to leave the palace. In Ilano it was said Beja broke many hearts, but none so completely as that of the King of Praed."

"I've never heard this story," I breathed.

"You wouldn't have. How would it look to have such an exalted king rejected by a foreigner?"

"So when Lord Davian asked the king for help, the memory of his broken heart kept him from acting honorably?"

"Worse things have been done for the sake of a woman."

"Men are so stupid." I wrapped my arms around my knees and made a gagging motion. "So, King Conall attacked Praed for revenge?"

"That's the simplest explanation."

"It doesn't seem simple at all." I picked up the book and flipped through the pages. "Ilano is hardly mentioned in any history books. Praed has dealt with other countries, some through war and others trade, but never Ilano. Is that why Beja was here? To establish a relationship between our two countries?"

"No. To strengthen it."

My hands numbed and the blood drained from my face.

"You don't know?" His voice was quiet. He tilted his head to the side and regarded me, and I couldn't bear to meet his gaze.

"Ilano and Praed signed a peace treaty three hundred years before King Llewlyn was crowned. He broke it when he ignored Lord Davian's plea for aide."

I riffled the pages again, searching for any mention of our neighbors to the east.

"History is controlled by those who write it," he said.

Slowly, I closed the book and ran a finger over the leather binding. The seal of the royal printing press established by King Llewlyn was stamped in gold on the cover.

As this new revelation swirled in my head, I tried to suppress a yawn. The hour was late, and my mind and body had been pushed beyond their limits.

"Enough for tonight." Risteard rose to stand before me. "Once you have digested these new truths, come again to have more revealed. I'll be waiting." He held out a hand to assist me, but I ignored it, brushing it away as one would a fly.

CHAPTER 11

Over the next several days I avoided the library because I was absorbed in a more pressing matter: Ula's birthday. The date was only a few weeks away, and I was at a loss on how to mark the occasion. Though it was the least of my worries, focusing on Ula's birthday was an escape from the rigors of everyday life. In the past, I surprised Ula with special treats hidden around the house in the days leading up to her birthday and spent hours entertaining her with stories, rides to hidden glens, and midnight stargazing sessions. Our current lack of freedom filled me with melancholy over the realization that we could not celebrate Ula's birthday for the first time in thirteen years. My moping did not go unnoticed.

"What's wrong with you?" The princess grabbed and shook my arm after I'd brushed the same strands of hair for the past ten minutes. Wordlessly, I moved on, numbly brushing as I would be for the rest of eternity.

Prince Brannon burst into the room in his usual way, but I heard none of their conversation. They could have been discussing the violent death of my mother and it wouldn't have registered. Our livelihood had been stripped away and I held no illusions that I would see Riverstone again, let alone live there. But if I could preserve any traditions, it would be to maintain our family bond, a welcome distraction from such tasks as preparing rose water basins for Her Highness' toilette.

I pinned the last braid around Princess Caelyn's head.

"When is your friend scheduled to join us?" Prince Brannon asked her.

She inspected my work in the mirror. "Uh...next week. Father wanted a report in person."

"How very kind of Father to ask Jervell to inconvenience himself by forcing him to travel in this weather."

My eyes widened and my heart quickened at the sound of that name. They had spoken it before, and I knew there was some scheme between the three the king may not be aware of. Now, this man was coming to Praed. Who was he? What business did he have with the king? I should have been paying closer attention.

"Go away now," the princess said as she flicked her hand toward the door. The perfunctory dismissal meant she was satisfied with her appearance, and it was time to clean the mews. At least there was enough on my mind to distract me from *that* arduous task.

Several inches of freshly fallen snow blanketed the path to the mews, making my trek more difficult as I trudged through the packed layers of ice and powder.

My legs above my boots were already numb by the time I made it to the shed to gather tools, and my frozen fingers fumbled with the implements as I waddled toward the first mew. Winters in Praed were harsh, but I couldn't remember a colder one than this. I'm sure my lack of appropriate apparel skewed my perception, however.

Snow piled up against the doors had to be shoveled clear before I could enter the buildings. The yard was quiet, sounds muffled into the enveloping softness of the wintry landscape, and the only interruption of the stillness was the scraping of the shovel blade and my panting. While I raked out soiled straw and avoided flapping wings and striking beaks, my thoughts turned to Ula. If I told her my concerns, she would tell me not to worry, that her birthday was trivial in the grand scheme. I would promptly instruct her to shut her mouth, she would pout, I'd apologize, and round and round we'd go arguing about the importance of marking family occasions.

The crunching of snow outside the mew I occupied interrupted my thoughts. I stopped to listen for someone to pass, but the sound ceased at the doorway. The hair on my arms and back of my neck stood on end. Aside from the prince and princess, no one troubled me since arriving here, but I lived in perpetual fear of being bullied. Someone knocked at the door. My breath whooshed out and I nearly jumped out of my boots. Obviously, I couldn't call out for the person to leave me alone, so wielding the rake as a weapon, I inched to the door, opening it imperceptibly, and peered out at the intruder. Risteard. I sighed in relief and flung the door wide, stepping back into the mew to finish my chores.

"What do you want?" I groaned with more irritation than I felt. Risteard stepped into the mew and briefly stroked the eagle's feathers before answering.

"It's been a long time since we've spoken." He stepped to the window and scanned our surroundings.

"And what? You've missed me and my random questions?"

"I certainly didn't miss your tendency for exaggeration."

I snarled at his back. "Did you need something or were you simply honoring me with your presence? Because I have a lot of work to do."

He spun around angrily. "You're in a particularly unpleasant mood."

"I didn't realize your people concerned yourself with pleasantries." I didn't look at him. I concentrated on cleaning the mew quickly so I could leave.

"What happened?"

"Where should I start?"

"Enough!" He pulled the rake from my hands and threw it in the corner, upsetting the eagle nearby. He held a hand up, as I would to calm a raging stallion. The bird settled, folded its wings, and watched us curiously.

"You're being evasive, and more onerous than usual." He was calmer, but anger burned in his eyes. "Has something happened? Has someone...hurt you?"

"Not recently," I said.

Risteard sighed and ran a hand through his thick, black hair.

"Listen," he said. "I'm not in the habit of entertaining blatant rudeness, especially from children."

My face flushed hotly. I may be a servant, but I didn't have to 'listen' to the insults of one of the castle residents. I tried to push past him, but he blocked my way with an outstretched arm.

"I have work to do!" I shouted. "Why keep me here if it means having to talk to a child?" Reluctantly, he removed his arm. I retrieved my rake and finished cleaning out the mew while he watched silently. I wished he would leave me in peace, but at least he stayed out of my way and kept his mouth shut. Fueled by my anger and frustration, I completed the task in record time. As I was spreading fresh straw, the serenity was shattered.

"I should not have called you a child, despite the technicality of your age."

"Especially considering your feelings toward antagonism." I glared sideways at him.

"Yes." The corner of his mouth twitched. "I allowed my indignation to overrule my judgment. My apologies."

My ire abated, I sank into the straw, emotionally fatigued. I sniffed quietly. "You were right," I whispered. "I'm not well. It wasn't fair to take it out on you."

"Regardless of how much I deserve it?" I looked up at him, shocked, but he was smiling.

"Well, some of it perhaps." I smirked, brushing my nose across my sleeve.

"If someone has injured you, I can speak to the king on your behalf."

I shook my head. "No one's hurt me."

"Then what's troubling you?"

"You'll think it's stupid."

"Only if it is."

I started to laugh, but the sadness of my predicament overcame me, so what escaped my lips was more of a tortured sob. Embarrassed, I buried my face in my hands. I felt Risteard sit in the straw nearby.

"It's my sister, Ula. Her birthday is soon and I have nothing to give her. I used to spend so much time planning and picking out the perfect gift. I know we have other things to worry about, but this will be the first time in thirteen years she won't have a celebration."

"That isn't stupid," he said gently. "But you're being too hard on yourself. She'll understand, I'm sure, that under the circumstances, a birthday like she's had in the past is no longer possible."

"I know that!" I wailed, much to my shame. "But now more than ever, she deserves a gift, an afternoon to herself, anything to mark the day. And I can't give that to her. I have nothing."

Risteard's brow furrowed and he looked around the mew. I took the opportunity to fix my disheveled appearance. I stood abruptly and walked toward the door, mumbling that I had to get back to work. He followed me out to the debris pile where I dumped the last load, then into the next mew. Before I could start raking, he held out his hand and searched through the straw.

"When I was a child," he said, "my mother used to pass the time by using the feathers of my father's eagle to create beautiful pieces of art. The primaries were best for quills, but the secondaries and tall feathers of the body she used to paint intricate portraits and detailed landscapes." He found what he had been hunting for, a wide, black feather.

"How's your artistic skill?" He held the feather out to me.

"Sorely lacking."

"I don't think she'll mind." He placed the feather in my hand. "I'll let you get back to work."

"Wait!" I called out. "I don't have any paints or brushes."

"Everything you'll need will be in the library tonight." He disappeared into the wintry morning.

Risteard was true to his word. That night, I found paints, brushes, a palette, and a cup of water for cleaning on the small table. Smiling, I gathered the supplies in my arms to take back to my room, when I spotted the now familiar book pushed to the side, still closed since I last read its pages. It was tempting to take the book with me as well, but I feared the repercussions if the owner decided to take it back. So I left it behind and retreated to the safety of my hole in the wall.

For a moment I stared at the supplies and feather, feeling dismay over my pitiful artistic talents. But unless an alternative presented itself, this was my only option for a gift for Ula. In the dwindling candlelight, I thought about my sister and the memories we made at Riverstone. In the summer months after foals were birthed, they would lie in the sun, and we gathered purple and blue prairie flowers and weaved them into crowns while lying across their soft, warm bellies. The palette came alive as I mixed the colors of my memories, and the brush danced across the feather that was my canvas. I paid little attention to the strokes, imagining the yellowed grass that scratched roughly against our cheeks when we rolled down the hills, laughing, our loose hair catching on branches. The wind blew tears from our eyes as we flew saddleless across the terrain astride our favorite ponies, our feet bare and our hands full of mane. The brush painted while I reminisced, and I allowed the bristles to interpret my thoughts. After several minutes, I laid it aside and inspected my work.

A wave of yellowish brown swept over the feather like the prairie landscape, dotted with flecks of purple and blue. A ribbon of dark gray-blue the hue of the spring-swollen river bordered the prairie and above the scene a crude rendition of a horse's head set against a hunter's moon. Ula would have created a masterpiece of the painting, but it was the best work in my personal portfolio. I tucked the feather under my bed to dry, cleaned the brush, and packed the supplies into the barren chest. My joints popped when I climbed into bed and my eyes burned with exhaustion. But with relief, I slipped into a dreamless sleep with thoughts of Ula's birthday present and the look of happiness I hoped to see on her face.

CHAPTER 12

For the first time in months, I smiled as I went about my duties in service to the princess. I stepped brightly when I visited the kitchens, and my grin spread from ear to ear as I roused Her Highness from sleep. The fact this annoyed her made my smile even broader.

"What do you have to be so happy about?" she mumbled. "I'm about to have someone dress me and attend to my bathwater and you'll soon be drowning in bird feces."

Her foulness didn't alter my mood. She could have sentenced me to a decade of cleaning her chamber pot and I would have borne it because I had something made with my own hands for Ula's birthday. My nails dug into my palms when I recalled the day I reached thirteen years. It had been particularly cold that spring day, and Mother was upset the frost would spoil her periwinkle roses. In her hysteria, she forgot my birthday. Father was occupied with work in the fields-- not to mention a local farmer had also cracked a barrel of freshly aged equi--so the only person to notice was Ula. When evening came and nothing had been said about the significance of the date, Ula spoke with the kitchen staff and arranged for my favorite meal and my favorite dessert of cream custard with orinberries sweetened from the frost. Mother bristled at the change of menu, but Ula clapped her hands excitedly and wished me a happy new year. Mother realized her mistake, gave me a half-hearted smile, and squeezed my hand briefly.

"This is an important day for you, Laria," she said. "Now is the time to put aside childish notions and concentrate on becoming a lady." Thanks for the heart-to-heart, Mother.

The princess continued to scowl as I plaited her hair. My obvious happiness clearly soured her demeanor, evidenced by the fact that she had me re-do her hairstyle three times before she decided it was acceptable. When I finally turned to leave, she grabbed my arm and forced me to look her in the face so I could read her lips.

"I don't know what's come over you today but trust me when I say this. If there is any way for me to destroy this perfect attitude you've developed, I will." My features darkened at the threat, and I hastily left the room, more willing to brave the bitter cold than suffer the icy blackness of Princess Caelyn.

On my way to the servant's stairs, a figure emerged from the landing leading to the king's chambers. A pale and disheveled young woman clutched her clothing to her chest. Her movements were frantic, like a spooked horse, and she jumped when she noticed me standing in the hallway. I held up my hands in a calming gesture, but she trembled so violently when she saw me I feared she would fall down the stairs. I put a finger to my lips and shook my head, then smiled. She made a mewling noise and brushed her unkempt hair off her tear-stained face. I clapped a hand over my mouth to keep from gasping aloud.

Her name was Joan, the eldest daughter of Telva Blu. She was older than me, though barely eighteen when Praed was invaded. She was a graceful, sweet, dark-haired beauty, but this frightened shell before me held no resemblance to that girl. I stepped forward, drawing a hand around my face, hoping she would recognize me. She flinched and shuffled backward. I pulled a lock of hair out of my cap, and for the first time, her dead eyes focused.

She drew close and pinched the tip of my hair between her fingers. I noticed the hollowness of her cheeks and red circles around her eyes. Her shift was torn at the neckline, revealing a bruise on her collarbone. Even if I wanted to risk it, my throat was so tight I couldn't speak to comfort her.

"L-l-l," she stuttered. She swallowed hard, then tried again. "L-laria?"

I nodded and covered her hand with mine.

"Mother told us you were alive," she said. She dropped her hand and stared at the floor, and I recalled overhearing gossip about Lady Blu. A tear struck the floor, and I tipped up Joan's chin and raised a questioning eyebrow. She shook her head, and the pain in her face told me everything.

A thud came from the king's room, and before I could stop her, Joan disappeared down the stairs. I didn't chase after her, but I wouldn't allow her mistreatment to go unpunished either. I took a few steps toward the king's stairway and had a foot on the first step before I remembered I was only a servant. I pursed my lips into a thin line and peered into the darkness. Laughter filtered down the stairs, a strange, low laughter devoid of mirth. Carefully, I lifted my foot off the stair and inched backwards, then dashed after Joan.

The poor girls.

The woman who had lamented over the fate of Telva Blu had said, "The poor girls." Lady Blu had three daughters--Joan, the eldest, Murelle, and Posy. Posy was only ten years old, but Murelle was sixteen, old enough to serve in a castle. I looked for her in the corridors, in the kitchens, in the Great Hall, but to no avail. Joan became a staple at the king's table, always at his side dressed in lovely gowns and jewels. Neither the princess nor the queen paid attention to her, but in private, Joan was the subject of bitter gossip.

"I don't know what he could be thinking bestowing favor on such a skinny little Praed savage," Princess Caelyn said. She stabbed herself with her needle in her ire and cursed.

"Savage, indeed," Queen Shaeli said. Her fingers danced along the strings of a small harp so expertly I forgot she was blind. "You know why he does it."

"I thought he wanted to endear himself to the people not threaten them," the princess said.

"They won't see it as a threat. They'll see the girl serving his majesty as an honor."

"I wouldn't consider her form of serving honorable."

"Look past your anger, Caelyn. He could have done worse."

"It would have been more tolerable if he had burned their house to the ground. At least we wouldn't have the embarrassment of watching him put his whore on display."

The queen stopped playing and the princess looked up from her embroidery.

"She's no more a whore than you are, Caelyn," the queen said.

The ensuing silence was broken by the sound of the princess ripping her handkerchief in half and stomping out of the room. I followed, but not before glancing over my shoulder at the queen. She remained stoically seated, but her ladies had gathered around her and were watching us leave, their eyes full of pity.

The feather for Ula remained safely tucked within the folds of my frock for the next week to protect it from Princess Caelyn, and I deliberately formed my features into a permanent frown to disguise my delight. As Ula's birthday drew closer, I relaxed and imagined the look I'd see on her face. I was so consumed with the precious parcel that the impending arrival of the infamous Jervell Kade escaped my notice until the princess instructed me to dress her with particular attention one morning.

"We're expecting an important guest this afternoon," she said proudly. "I must impress upon him the significance of my station."

Several tedious hours later Princess Caelyn declared herself presentable enough to meet with her distinguished guest. Drained from the exertion of bathing, dressing, redressing, and styling the long, dark locks to strict specifications, I could barely drag myself through the knee-deep snow. My muscles ached as I stripped and cleaned the mews, and my mind was so sluggish it wasn't until I discarded my last load that I considered the implications of Princess Caelyn's visitor. There was no possibility of getting information about him beyond the scant conversations I'd overheard between the prince and princess. I heard no whispers in the corridors or during the sessions with Queen Shaeli, which continued to leave me in a state of perpetual ennui. The only person I could speak to was Risteard since he was the only castle inhabitant besides Ula and Mother who knew I wasn't deaf and mute. If I made a habit of soliciting his assistance, I feared he might ask for something in return.

I shuffled along the corridor toward the library, my head lolled in exhaustion, rubbing my frigid hands together. I was so distracted I neglected to check I was alone before stumbling into a chair to warm myself by the blaze roaring in the hearth. I scanned my surroundings, noting the room was empty. I fanned out my hands and my fingers danced before the flames. I wondered why, when this place remained unused, was there always a fire? But that was a question for another day. I didn't have the strength to solve more than one mystery today.

I stood to warm my backside and glanced at the little table by the window. There, as if fixed in time, was the book I hadn't opened in weeks. It had been my sole source of information about Ilano, besides what had been revealed by Risteard. Hoping to discover something of our esteemed guest, I sifted through the pages. Expecting the history to be chronological, I skipped to the back and searched for the name Jervell Kade. Once again, I found the genealogical chart, but only gave it a cursory study before moving to a section written many years before the conquest of Praed.

Page after page described the life and death of Lord Protector Davian, who lost his son and faculties during the battle with King Tuar. Mourning the loss, His Lordship fell into a profound depression and passed away. He was survived by his son, Conall, Conall's wife, and three grandchildren.

Three grandchildren? I browsed the last several pages, but this was the last section in the book. Recalling the part about the battle with the desert people, I searched until I found the passage about King Conall's fallen brother, Alyx, and noted the mention of a son. Could Jervell Kade be that son? The close connection might explain the princess's reliance on him for information and the trust she placed in arranging a marriage for the prince. Curious, I looked for the family tree I had previously ignored, but before I could find it, footsteps sounded outside the library door. I threw the book on the table and retreated to the shadows of the bookcases.

"Don't worry, old friend," I heard the prince say. "We'll be quite undisturbed in here."

Cautiously, I inched my head around the bookcase just enough to see the prince and a short, thin man standing by the hearth. It was difficult to study the stranger in the dark, but he was several inches shorter than the prince and had stringy hair poking out of his woolen cap. Unlike the tunics most men in the castle wore that reached mid-thigh, the stranger's flowed to the ground. The firelight reflected the fine, gold stitching along the hems, and the fabric billowed softly when he moved.

"It's damned cold here," the smaller man complained in an unnaturally high voice that scratched across my spine and made me shiver.

"Intolerably so. It's one of the many reasons I want out of this place."

"Does Caelyn, pardon, *Her Highness*, know you're meeting me here?"

"This is between you and me, old man." The prince clapped the small man's shoulder, making him collapse slightly.

"What service can I render, Your Highness?" the stranger snarled.

"This marriage business Caelyn mentioned. How serious is it?"

"Not yet ready to commit yourself, hmm?"

"Not in the least bit interested. I've only been crowned prince for less than a year. It seems terribly unfair to be so quickly married and tied down."

"Marriage never stopped any nobleman from satiating his appetites." The lecherous tone turned my stomach.

"No, I would expect not," the prince said. "But ladies are so funny, you know. There's a certain class that has standards, and a married man is beyond their interests. If a woman of this caliber believes she has a chance of a crown, she is much more easily conquered."

"I see...well, the princess will not be pleased to wait."

"I can handle my sister as long as you advise her that waiting would be more prudent than rushing into matrimony."

"She'll smell your influence in this decision, especially if Queen Shaeli has one of her 'visions' and informs the princess of your meddling."

"My mother is the least of my problems."

"Indeed." The little man bowed and left the prince to watch the flames crackle in the hearth.

I held my breath and waited for him to leave, hoping he wouldn't detect my presence as Risteard had before.

"Whatever you're playing at Caelyn," the prince said to himself. "You will not get the best of me."

A side of him that had yet to be seen, I snickered to myself. Before leaving the library, he kicked the stone hearth, swore mightily, and then whimpered as he limped away. I left my hiding place and returned to my daily tasks, knowing for sure the little weaselly man I saw with the prince was Jervell Kade.

That afternoon, Jervell Kade was formally presented to King Conall amid a crowd of finely garbed Ilano nobles. Clearly, the man was someone of great importance to be received with such splendor and deference. I felt certain when the gathered attendants parted and bowed at the passing man that he must be related to the royal family in some way, especially when the king approached his prostrate form with open arms.

"Now, now, Jervell," the king said. "No need for such formality. Come and embrace me, dear friend." The little man smiled, revealing sharp white teeth. He was quite old, I saw now, much older than the king. The top of his balding head gave way to thin white hairs sprouting like roots from the side of a cliff, trailing down to his shoulders and plastered with grease against his scalp. He stood proudly, his movements deliberate and graceful, surprising for such a crooked form. The darkness of the library had obscured the twisted back that gave him a sloped appearance and added a subtle limp to his walk. He dressed in formal green robes adorned with a shock of red cloth across his chest. He accepted the king's affectionate greeting with dignity, embracing him long enough to establish the closeness of the relationship without crossing the lines of propriety.

"Ladies and gentlemen," the king addressed the assembled, holding the visitor at arm's length. "I am proud to present my trusted friend and Lord Protector of Ilano, Jervell Kade."

The mixed response of enthusiastic cheers and polite clapping was drowned out by the ringing in my ears. The Lord Protector, I had learned from my reading, was an extremely prestigious position in Ilano. This explained the power he held over the lives of the prince and princess as well as the king's welcoming disposition. I heard nothing of the accolades recited by the king because I concentrated on the princess. Her expression was blank, and she sat motionless except to inspect her manicured cuticles. I learned enough about her to know, like me, the princess wore a mask for the public. She wasn't merely bored. She was biding her time.

Hidden behind the king among a throng of ladies was Joan. In the days since I discovered her coming from the king's chamber, I'd seen her several times in public at the king's side. She was thinner, not surprisingly since I rarely saw her eat, and I longed to help her. I squeezed her hand and smiled when no one was looking, but these gestures brought her no comfort. When she first arrived, I overheard the ladies making nasty comments behind her back, but now they pitied her as much as I did. Maybe, if I could somehow persuade the ladies at court to speak to the king, he could be persuaded to let her go.

And maybe I would sprout wings and fly.

After the king finished his speech, the crowd dispersed into small groups and milled around the assembly room talking amongst themselves. The princess glided to the king's side and curtseyed to the guest. I moved close to the royal cluster around the Lord Protector to eavesdrop on their conversation. I was sorely disappointed. The king was apologizing for the frigid temperatures, blaming the desolation of the mountain for the inconvenience of having to wear multiple layers of clothing. However, I could hear him assuring the guest, the valley boasted some excellent game and vast tracts of land the king was keen to reward. The Lord Protector raised a bony hand to dismiss the apologies. He spoke quietly, and I stepped closer and strained to hear his words. The prince had interrupted, asking about a woman acquaintance. The king laughed, and I could just detect the Lord Protector reporting the lady's good health, when the princess slipped something into his robe--likely a note. She quickly stepped away as if nothing happened. The thought of the princess showing affection for anyone was beyond all comprehension but based on the physique and age of the Lord Protector, I was certain Princess Caelyn wasn't passing a love note. I was fixed in place and blinked, once, twice, three times, sluggishly recognizing I had witnessed political intrigue.

"What is this intriguing creature?" an eerily soft, low voice asked. I noted the stiff posture of the princess's back as she cocked her head toward the sound.

"Oh, that's Caelyn's little pet," Prince Brannon said. I met the eyes of the elderly Jervell Kade. His face was lined with age, but his gray eyes were bright and sharply intelligent. He smiled, his thin lips twitching slightly as they split his face into creases.

"She's something of an oddity." The princess' voice was close behind, and I felt the hair on my arms stand up. "Just look," she tittered before ripping the cap from my head, sending my ginger hair tumbling around my shoulders. The blood drained from my face and I instantly became nauseated. Silence fell around us.

"Interesting indeed," the old man whispered. He reached his elongated fingers with thick, untrimmed nails toward my head and trailed them through my uniquely colored hair. He inspected a strand in his twisted hand. "Where does she come from?" My knees shook and I balled my hands into fists to restrain myself from slapping him away and scratching his eyes out.

"Her father served the former king of Praed," Princess Caelyn said with disinterest. "Father thought she could be useful to me. She's suitable enough for a deaf-mute."

"Truly?" the Lord Protector's thin eyebrows rose, and I swallowed bile as he brought my hair to his nose and inhaled deeply.

"A shame she's so hideous," Prince Brannon said. "Otherwise her condition would be quite advantageous, if you understand my meaning, Jervell."

"Acutely, Your Highness," the Lord Protector said.

"You must join us in my rooms this week, Your Lordship," Queen Shaeli said, much to everyone's surprise. She rarely spoke outside the rituals she performed, and the public invitation was highly out of character. The Lord Protector bowed graciously, finally releasing my hair in the process. While he praised her majesty and expressed his gratitude for the offer, I shuffled backwards, hoping to escape without notice.

Someone abruptly pulled me backward into the crowd, spun me around, and grabbed my wrist, weaving me awkwardly between the swirls of fabric and shifting bodies. I relaxed and took a deep, settling breath when I recognized my rescuer. I focused on the leather stretched across the back of Risteard's black doublet, listening to the chatter of the royal family and their distinguished guest fading behind me. The darkness of the hidden alcoves closed around us, and I tried to break his grip on my wrist.

"Don't," he said.

"You're the last person I expected to feel gratitude for."

Risteard held onto my wrist, watching the people, his eyes darting from face to face while I retreated behind him.

"What's the matter?"

"You need to be more careful." His eyes still roamed the crowd.

"More than usual?" He looked at me sharply, his blue eyes flashing.

"This isn't a joke."

"I'm not laughing," I whispered.

"I'm sorry." He let go of my arm. "But I saw what you were doing, and you were being careless."

"What do you mean?"

"Please." He turned back to the crowd. "I'm no fool. You were quite obviously trying to eavesdrop. I'm not sure what you were hoping to learn, but you would be wise to keep your distance from Lord Protector Kade."

"You'll have no argument from me on that score." I tucked my hair behind my ears, shocked when I touched my bare head.

"Oh, no!" I gasped.

"What?"

"My cap. The princess must still have it."

"Is that all?"

"Isn't that enough? My hair will be exposed, and I'll have to fend off curious onlookers."

"Yes, I see. Wait here." He headed toward the group clustered around King Conall and his family. I retreated further toward the exit, ducking behind pillars and couples so absorbed in each other that they ignored everyone else. Freedom was in view, and I dashed past servants and narrowly avoided spilling drinks. Two steps from the doorway, stood Risteard, my cap dangling in his hand. Wordlessly, I took it and placed it on my head.

"You have questions?" he asked.

"I always do."

He nodded and gestured toward the door. Once in the library, I rushed into my favorite chair to warm my chilled bones by the fire. The encounter with Jervell Kade left me feeling nervous, uncomfortable, and strange, as if I'd just done something to be ashamed of. Risteard sat opposite me and remained silent, but I could feel him watching.

"So," I said, rubbing my hands together. "That was the most esteemed Lord Protector of Ilano."

"Yes."

"He's delightful." The stillness in the room was heavy but not oppressive, and I sank further into the leather chair while the roaring from the hearth filled the void of unspoken words. But my time was not my own, and soon the princess would require my services in preparation for the afternoon's activities.

"Is he a relation to the king?" I asked.

"No, but he has served the family for many years."

"Why is he here?"

"On official business."

"I suppose it's none of mine?"

"He's the Lord Protector of Ilano reporting to the King of Praed on the current state of his country. That isn't something most ladies find of great interest."

"No, most ladies wouldn't."

"It's clear you're not thinking with the same insight as usual. When you've organized your thoughts, I'll be waiting." He stood, his words barely registering in my scattered brain.

It wasn't the lack of curiosity that had rendered me incoherent, but rather the sheer number of questions swirling in my mind and sticking in my throat. However, I couldn't allow him to leave without explaining one puzzling enigma.

"How did Queen Shaeli become blind?"

Risteard paused and sat back down.

"There was a third pregnancy---"

"The prince and princess have another sibling?" My eyes met his in shock.

"No," he said irritably. "I didn't say there was a *child*. I said there was a *pregnancy*. May I continue without interruption?"

"Fine." I crossed my arms.

"Unfortunately, the child did not survive. It is said she became blinded by her intense grief. The queen, however, claims she traded her sight for the visions she receives through her communion with the dead babe."

"That's nonsense," I scoffed. "Do you believe that she can see the future in the form of messages from beyond the veil?"

"Whether her predictions come from a stillborn child or vigilant spies, I have never known the queen to be wrong." Once again, he rose and stood before me. "You'll be missed if you don't return to the princess soon."

Reluctantly, I untangled my legs and stood. I locked eyes with him, holding his gaze with a challenging stare. "Why are you helping me?"

"Should I not?"

"If King Conall knew, wouldn't you be punished? We are enemies after all."

"As you keep insisting. Although, your opinion continues to influence your perception."

"It's hardly a matter of opinion. Your people killed my father."

"And *your* people killed mine!" he roared, frightening me so much that I expected him to strike me as he stormed toward the door. I trembled so violently I fell back onto the chair clutching my hand to my chest. I drew in several shuddering breaths before I trusted myself to regain my feet and leave the library. I carried with me a terror I had not felt since the night Risteard had ripped me from my home.

CHAPTER 13

The princess was resplendent in a velvet, form-fitting indigo gown trimmed with the furs of ermine that gave their lives for royal fashion. She bade me to pay special attention to styling her hair into a coiffed tower of curls adorned with tiny sprigs of handcrafted faux berries featured in her family's famous cider recipe. She admired herself in the mirror, inspecting each inch of her primped body while I stood by waiting to escort her to dinner. Behind me, the door opened and closed, and I expected the prince to make another inappropriate comment. Instead, Jervell Kade's reflection joined Princess Caelyn's in the mirror, and I became uneasy.

"Lovely," he said as his decrepit hand clasped the princess's shoulder. His eyes shifted, and he noticed me in the corner. "Oh!" he said, stepping away from the princess and turning toward me. "I didn't realize we had company."

"Oh, her?" the princess said, continuing to inspect her attire. "Pay no attention to her, Jervell. Remember, she's completely deaf and sadly quite stupid."

My gaze remained fixed on my feet while Jervell's eyes roamed up and down my body like a horse trader scrutinizing a prime stallion.

He took my cap and dragged it from my head and across my shoulder with deliberate care. Addressing the princess, he said, "If I may suggest, Your Highness. You shouldn't hide this extraordinary hair."

Caelyn sneered. "Really? It's so repulsive! I can't bear to look at it."

"Not many ladies can boast such a creature in their entourage. If I were you, I would take her with me everywhere, like a fantastical animal."

The princess chose not to respond, diplomatically choosing to resume perusal of her dress, but I could tell she was considering his suggestion. Jervell joined her, my cap in his hand.

"Your brother is reluctant to follow through with the plan," he said.

"Which part?"

"Which do you think?"

"Amyl's feathers!" She sighed with exasperation. "He's always thinking with the little head between his legs and not the fat one wobbling on his neck."

"He wishes for me to postpone the engagement."

"For how long?"

"Long enough to sow the noble ladies of Praed."

"What do the others think?"

"They're men. They understand the prince's feelings and are willing to be patient."

"Fine," she snapped. "Let him have his fun for now. When the time comes, he's either with us or against us."

"How dramatically final, Your Highness."

"And the negotiations with her father? How are they progressing?"

"Favorably. I would expect no less with the prospect of a prince for a son-in-law."

"They'll have to be satisfied with anticipation for the time being it seems." Caelyn glanced in the mirror one last time and stalked out the door. A chill shivered down my spine as I met Jervell Kade's eye. He smiled but this gesture did nothing to put me at ease, instead plowing a dark hole in my stomach. With a flick of his wrist, he tossed my cap into the flames of Princess Caelyn's fire and followed her to dinner, leaving me in a state of dreadful foreboding.

As I feared, the evening unfolded into a progressively awful nightmare beginning with my entrance to the Great Hall sans cap. Whispers escorted me to my place behind the princess, and heat radiated up my neck and face as I struggled to ignore the stares and unabashed pointing in my direction. The princess glared at Jervell Kade's smug expression, bristling at the unwanted attention. I couldn't decide if it was embarrassment or envy that moved her to proceed as she did that night, but the result was a disaster.

Elegant dishes of succulent meats and bright, fresh fruits were served with great distinction by formally attired servants, dressed to impress the king's honored guest. No longer distracted by my disturbingly red hair, the curious eagerly shifted attention to the feast, washing it down with goblet after goblet of the king's personal cider. Jervell Kade ignored Princess Caelyn's icy stare and conversed with the king, taking dainty bites and wiping his dry mouth each time with a white handkerchief. Prince Brannon arrived late and drunk, stumbling his way through the bustle and plopping in his seat reeking of perfume and equi, eager to join in the gluttony. He spotted me out of the corner of his eye.

"Well, then!" he shouted in a volume beyond his control. "I see you've unveiled your pet, Caelyn. But she's so hidden back there. She should be on display for all to enjoy!"

"Yes," Jervell Kade said. "Please, young lady, let the assembled indulge their eyes as well as their stomachs." He held out his hand to me and I kept my eyes averted, pretending not to understand.

The back of the princess's neck flushed red, but she played along, taking my wrist and pulling me to the center of the room.

"If it pleases your lordship." Her words dripped with sarcasm. "You may gaze upon my freakish lady as long as you wish, providing it doesn't upset your digestion." Laughter rippled through the crowd. I stood frozen, eyes downcast, while the smacking of lips and clinking of glasses echoed around me. My father once told me that when sensing danger, a rabbit will freeze to blend in with its surroundings. I had nowhere to hide, but I remained transfixed, hoping that if I made no movement, my enemies would grow bored and tire of the chase. It worked. For a time.

"Does the little vixen know any tricks?" Prince Brannon called to his sister, pointing his goblet at me.

"Let's find out," the princess said. She approached me and the room quieted. She raised my chin so I could read her lips. "Don't move." She carefully balanced a goblet on my head. "If you move," she threatened loud enough for all to hear. "Not only will you clean the mess you've made, but you'll be on your hands and knees scrubbing this hall. By yourself."

The prince chuckled. "I'm sure I can think of something better she can do from her hands and knees."

"Now, Brannon," the king said with a dark grin. "She's only a child."

I kept my breathing shallow and blinked slowly, willing my muscles still. I stared blankly ahead, but I couldn't hide the burning hatred in my eyes. I wished for fantastical powers like the queen claimed to set fire to them all with the intensity of my gaze.

For several minutes, the goblet remained in place while the diners seemingly forgot about me. I relaxed thinking I could survive. Just then something struck me, stinging my cheek. Again, nearly hitting my eye, then another on the forehead. Laughter filtered into my ears. The prince held out his hand, palm open, and flicked a piece of bone, hitting my nose. I squeezed my eyes shut, wishing I was anywhere else, stubbornly refusing to let the goblet spill.

"Enough!" Princess Caelyn yelled, slamming her hands on the table and rising from her seat. The prince quieted, and she marched toward me, grabbed the goblet, and poured it over my head.

"There," she said, tossing the goblet to the ground. "You've had your entertainment." She returned to her meal and didn't give me a second glance.

Later, while scrubbing the floor, I heard slow, deliberate footsteps approach. The toe of a black boot rested on my hand, ceasing my movements, and I looked up at Jervell Kade, his white teeth bared in a menacing grin.

"I've heard of your father, little girl. I understand he was a great warrior. How ashamed would he be of his eldest daughter, a servant to the man who killed him? If indeed you are his daughter at all." He laughed, a hollow terrifying sound, and spit a thick, brown sludge onto the floor at my fingertips.

Hours passed, and the voices of the full and happy people faded into the castle. As if the enveloping silence was a signal, one by one servants snuck into the hall and wordlessly helped me finish the momentous task of cleaning. When she was close enough, a woman I recognized but could not name clutched my hand and smiled before going about her business.

That night, I sat shivering in the glow of the library fire, rivulets of amber liquid trailing down my back and dripping from my forehead to puddle on the floor.

I rolled my shoulders and massaged my neck, sore from hours hunched over a bucket and brush. I twisted my hair to release the remaining liquid, willing it to dry so I could finally sleep. I wanted to forget this night. I turned my thoughts to Ula, whose birthday was days away. The feather was well-protected in my frock, and I touched it briefly to assure myself it was unharmed from the cider that soaked my shoulders and the top part of my chest.

Exhausted and stupidly distracted in my humiliation, I didn't hear the door. The floorboards creaked, and I instinctively leapt toward the safety of the darkness. A hand clamped on my forearm and pulled me back to the fire's warmth.

Risteard whispered, "It's only me." I blame what happened next on my vulnerability from the night's disgrace, my spent body and mind, and relief that the man crouched next to me was not Jervell Kade. I wept without restraint, pressing my face against my folded knees. I cried until my sobs became snatched breaths. Quiet and still, Risteard watched the dancing flames. Soon, I was also focused on the intricate mix of yellows and oranges twisting above the glowing embers.

"There's rarely anyone here but myself," I mused. "And yet there's always a fresh fire."

"Yes," Risteard said, his voice rather hoarse.

"I've often wondered why that is. No one else cares to be here, especially the prince and princess. Why bother wasting logs for a fire?"

"Because I ordered it to be done," Risteard said without turning away from the fire. I stared at him, my mouth agape.

"But *why*?" I asked.

"Why do you think?" he answered, meeting my gaze.

"Why do you help me?"

"Because I'm nice?"

"No, you're not." I shook my head and let slip a smile.

"Fair. Perhaps I believe you can help me in return."

"Me?" I was incredulous. "What could I possibly do? I'm nothing. Besides, you're not exactly first on the list of people I would help."

"Understandable. But no one else in this castle has bothered to assist you. I'm the closest to an ally you have right now."

"How depressing." I groaned and tugged on a lock of hair. He was right.

CHAPTER 14

Aside from performing my usual duties, I spent my time avoiding Jervell Kade. Thankfully, he spent hours behind closed doors consulting with King Conall, probably distributing Praed lands to Ilano vermin. He rarely met with Princess Caelyn alone, and never spoke more than three sentences of pleasantries when the occasion arose. If he paid any attention to me, I wasn't aware because I refused to make eye contact. Since the feast, the castle residents giggle when I walk by, because seeing a poor girl humiliated is the most hilarious event in their miserable, tiny lives. The servants regarded me with sympathy, and some reassured me by discretely pressing my hand when we passed in the hallways. I wasn't quite as alone as I had previously believed.

The morning of Ula's birthday, Princess Caelyn could have plunged me in a barrel of cider, and I would have borne it happily. I cracked the ice in the small bowl I was permitted for washing, scrubbed my face with the frigid water, and dressed, tucking the precious gift into the folds of my woolen tunic. I bit the inside of my lip to contain my excitement and prevent a pique of Princess Caelyn's temper. I had not forgotten her threatening words.

My plan was to attend to the princess's morning routine as usual, then sneak away to see Ula before cleaning the mews. As the princess soaked in her bathwater, I thought about an excuse for being in the underbelly of the castle were I to be caught. The easiest would be to infer an errand for Her Highness, but if any messages were sent to her, I would be foiled. I was willing to take the chance.

The princess waved a sponge in my face. I took it and began washing her back with the scented soap she liked when she was in a foul mood. Consequently, I prepared myself for the arrival of her monthly courses by ensuring she was served plenty of hot cider and sweet treats.

"Well, isn't this a pretty sight," a voice from the doorway observed, alarming me to such a degree I nearly screamed. Thankfully, I kept my grip on the sponge and didn't betray my secret. The princess appeared more irritated than frightened, an unexpected reaction considering the intruder was an old, twisted, and unsettling Jervell.

"Jervell, do you have any notion of privacy?" the princess said. She may have considered the situation casual, but I was angry, and instinctively tried to cover her and motion frantically for him to leave.

"What a fierce little protector you have," Jervell said, ignoring my silent pleas and stepping around me to face the princess.

"She serves me well, at times. My virtue is, after all, still intact." The princess gestured for her robe, and I retrieved it, holding it to block Jervell's view.

"You know I have no interest in your virtue."

"Nor any other woman's for that matter." I led the princess behind a screen to dress, unable to hide my disdain as I glared at the grinning old man. "What do you want?" she called out to him.

"I've heard from Sir Derville. He wasn't pleased to wait but agreed to postpone the engagement."

"On what terms?"

"An engagement must be announced within the next two years, before the lady reaches an unmarriageable age."

"Yes, at twenty, a woman is positively haggard," Caelyn grumbled as she took her seat at the vanity. Jervell pulled a chair close to where I stood brushing the princess's shining hair. The overpowering smell of cologne and eggs wafted off his body, making it difficult for me to concentrate. While he and the princess plotted the prince's nuptials, I thought of Ula to keep from gagging.

"You seem rather pleased with yourself this morning." It was several seconds before I realized he was addressing me. I met the princess's eye in the mirror, noting the smile playing on my lips. I immediately dropped all expressions.

"She's been doing that lately." Her eyes narrowed as she scrutinized my face.

"Maybe it's not *your* virtue we should be worrying about."

"Don't be disgusting." She held up a hand to stop his speculation, a topic I, too, was glad to abandon. "Hurry up there," she commanded.

"My time to leave this desolate place is drawing near," he said. "There are certain things we must arrange before then."

"I wish I could leave with you," she said. "I'm tired of this place."

"In time, my dear."

"Our time has been extended thanks to my stupid brother. Everything must be rearranged due to his whims."

"It matters not. You'll simply have more time to gain the trust and admiration of the people."

What was the princess planning? What required the friendship of the people of Praed, whom she regarded as nothing more than animals? And how did the prince's marriage factor into this scheme? Again, I was left with more questions than answers.

My toe tapped with impatience as I pinned the last of her plaits into place before stepping back for her to inspect my work. Satisfied, she waved me away to attend to my morning chores. I had one foot in the corridor when I curtsied, ignoring Jervell Kade's stare as he shut the door in my face.

I stared at the closed door, then glanced from side to side to see if anyone was watching. I pressed my ear to the keyhole and heard Princess Caelyn rant more about her brother. This wasn't anything new. Disappointed, I started to rise.

"Did Crane tell you about Ulster's outburst in council yesterday?" Jervell said.

I paused, remembering I'd heard Crane's name before. I recognized some of the names of the councilmembers, but the princess attended so rarely I couldn't picture their faces.

"He sent me a brief note about it. Ulster couldn't hold his tongue any longer?" she said.

"He gently suggested the king make good on his promise to take care of the people."

"Does he not remember how I travelled to houses in the snow to distribute goods?"

"A few bags of flour hardly makes up for their losses. At least, that's what Ulster argued."

The princess' voice held a dark undertone. "How did the king respond?"

"Ulster was absent from council today. No one can find him."

The princess was silent. My palms dampened. Footsteps echoed down the corridor, coming closer. I was running out of time.

"Ulster and Father have been friends since childhood." I had to press my ear harder against the door to hear her quiet voice. "He's getting worse."

I pushed away just before a soldier patrolling the halls rounded the corner. I kept my eyes down and stepped aside for him to pass, thankful to be ignored.

It was impossible with my unique hair to travel the corridors unobserved. So, in order to be discreet, I pulled my overcoat above my head and tossed the sleeves over my shoulder, hunched over, and tried my best to look like an old woman using the wall for support. I felt like an idiot, but it worked to some extent. People still noticed, but avoided me more than anything, probably thinking I was a beggar.

The thudding of my boots reverberated off the stone walls as I hastened down to the workroom where ladies toiled for the fashion and comfort of those above. No one looked up from their work. I inched along the outer wall, drawing closer to Ula's project alcove. She was so close I could see the furrow of her brow and the tip of her tongue peeking out while she concentrated. Suddenly, I was grabbed and my overcoat was shoved off my head.

"Whatcho doin' there?" the dressmaker accused angrily. "Oh, it's you. You have something from Her Highness?" She held her free hand out but continued to hold my arm, her grip surprisingly strong. My mouth opened and closed silently, my carefully laid plan falling apart. Movement behind her caught my eye and I saw Ula watching worriedly. I clenched my jaw, raised my chin, and looked the dressmaker in the eye. I pointed at Ula, staring at the old woman in defiance. *I'm here to see my sister*, I said with my eyes. The old woman looked at Ula, then at me, her expression unreadable. She released my arm, nodded, and stepped away.

"Are you mad?" Ula whispered once we were in her workspace.

"Today? Yes, completely. But I have a good reason to be." I reached into my frock. "Hold out your hands." She did, and I proudly laid the feather on her upturned palms. "Happy birthday, little gem."

Ula gaped at the gift, not moving or speaking. Unease rippled down my spine. Did she not like it?

A tear trailed down her cheek. "Laria," she said, "It's beautiful." Without regard to anyone watching, she threw her arms about my neck and we embraced until a soft clearing of the throat interrupted our tender moment.

"You better be off now," the old dressmaker said. I nodded, kissed the top of Ula's head--which now reached the crook of my arm--and retreated from the room. I raced up the stairs, smiling over my shoulder at the sweet look on Ula's face. I reached the landing and froze. Waiting there stood Jervell Kade, looking very pleased with himself.

"What's this now?" He stepped forward. "I don't believe the princess sent you on any business to the workroom. I blinked dumbly, trying to appear innocent. He wasn't fooled.

"You're up to something," he snarled, looming over me, his sour breath blanketing my face. Shaking my head, I curtseyed, and shuffled against the wall sideways to escape. He placed his arm across my path, blocking my retreat. He leaned in, his nose nearly brushing mine.

"Feebleminded or not, I'll be watching you," he said before dropping his arm for me to pass.

I spent very little time in the library that afternoon because I didn't want to remain alone in one place for too long in case Jervell Kade looked for me. Cleaning the mews, I kept a paranoid watch, jumping at every sound despite how hard I practiced being still. My repulsive appearance usually left me undisturbed and I'd never felt the need to be so vigilant. Even Risteard had been absent the last few days, doubtless occupied with such knightly duties as stabbing things and guzzling cider. I resented his freedom, his ability to confidently go about without being accosted by a nasty old man.

To my relief, I did not see the Lord Protector for the rest of the day, and at dinner I was ignored. The prince was too preoccupied with his latest obsession, and the rest of the court had grown bored with the ginger-haired girl. Relieved, I focused on the princess, filling her glass the requisite three times and no more, clearing her dish before she finished--a lady always leaves something on her plate--and placing a napkin between her and the prince when he sloshed his drink. If this is what having a child was like I was glad to forego the experience.

In the lull between the last course and before dessert, I happened to glance around the table. The chair at the king's right hand was empty. My brow furrowed. Where had Jervell Kade gone? Was his absence innocent? I searched the room, feeling a rising panic, but he was nowhere in sight. I was certain something nefarious was afoot, and my stomach churned with nerves. I tipped forward and grabbed the back of the princess' chair. She sneered at me, no doubt worried that I would be ill and ruin her gown. I stepped back, breathing hard, my heart tight against my chest. Dessert came and went and still Jervell Kade was absent. The king seemed unconcerned. He drank and stuffed tarts into his gaping maw, spitting crumbs and laughing with the prince. Joan had been relegated farther down the table, but there was no relief from her torment. The king may have cast her aside, but other men were there to take his place.

At the end of the meal, King Conall thanked the ladies for their company, a signal that all persons of that sex were dismissed, releasing the men from their civilities. Princess Caelyn took Queen Shaeli's arm to escort her from the room, and my eyes darted from face to face searching for the Lord Protector. People crowded around me, milling leisurely toward the door. I fingered a lock of my hair and tugged it in frustration.

Risteard's barely audible voice spoke behind me. "What's wrong?"

He must have been watching me to appear so suddenly, but the thought strangely wasn't unnerving.

"He's gone," I whispered through clenched teeth, staring straight ahead with a neutral expression. "The Lord Protector." Out of the corner of my eye, I saw Risteard search the room.

"He's there." I looked in the direction of his nod, and there he was, deep in conversation with the king, as if he'd been there the whole time.

"I swear he was not here after the last course."

"I believe you. Now go." I hurried after the princess, hoping she hadn't noticed my absence.

When I caught up to the princess and the queen, their heads were close together, and I heard the queen asking if the Lord Protector would join the session this week.

"He would be a fool to miss it," the princess said. "Even Father would acknowledge the insult, and Jervell wouldn't dream of making that mistake."

"I know he has tested your patience, but I hope he hasn't tested your fortitude."

"Never," the princess hissed. "Nothing will stand in our way, Mother. I promised you the day Father announced his plans to invade Praed and you revealed the truth of our fates that I would not hesitate or stray. No man can move a mountain."

"Wind and water can cut through a mountain, Caelyn."

Princess Caelyn snorted and threw her free hand in the air. "Stop philosophizing, Mother. I'm trying to make a point." She marched Queen Shaeli to her room, the older woman tripping over her gown when pulled off balance by her enthusiastic daughter. I quickened my pace to keep up, glancing over my shoulder.

My maternal instincts were tested as I tucked the princess into bed that night, fighting her attempts to kick the thick down comforter and insisting she wasn't tired. Earlier, she had overindulged in the queen's syrupy dessert port, and I dared a thrashing by extricating the glass from her hand and directing her to her room. In her current incoherent state, I knew she would neither remember nor care if I forced her to bed, so I pressed my hands to her shoulders and held her to the plush mattress as she struggled. She finally relented, and shortly began to snore. The princess was usually careful about alcohol consumption and rarely drank to excess, but when stressed, she used the queen's special reserves to ease her nerves. Finger by finger, I lifted my hands away, and when she didn't stir, I crept backwards, avoiding every creaking floorboard. The door clicked quietly behind me, and I nearly collapsed in relief. The hour was late, the moon high and bright. It seemed impossible that it was only this morning I presented Ula with her present. I smiled a tired, yet satisfied grin as I shuffled toward my room down the hall, longing for sleep.

I pushed against the door, but it would not open more than a crack. Confused, I pushed harder, feeling something scrape across the floor. Something was wrong. My knees trembled and my hands shook, rattling the door. I debated the wisdom of continuing or running away. Taking a deep breath, I closed my eyes and stepped inside. Something skittered across the room, and I fled blindly down the hallway until I was out of breath. I leaned against the wall, palms flat against the cool stone, my chest heaving.

Once my breathing was under control, I pushed away from the wall and looked back down the hallway. No sound of footsteps. In the distance was the faintest echo of the last servants finishing up for the evening, then silence. Determined not to be afraid, I grabbed a candle from a nearby sconce and walked back to my room, my legs shaking with each step. At the door, I raised the candle, the flame flickering as my hand trembled.

I knocked against the doorframe. No answer. I listened, and hearing nothing, placed one foot forward. I nearly slipped on a moist, sticky substance. I lowered the candle and saw red. I clasped my hand to my mouth to muffle a scream and moved the light around the floor.

Yellow, green, a shard of pottery. I opened the door fully and surveyed the chaos.

My room was destroyed. The meager contents of the little chest had been tossed haphazardly--paints spilled, brushes snapped in half, the small cup shattered. The few pieces of clothing I possessed were stained and torn. The bedsheets were ripped in half, and straw pulled from the mattress. Fear was replaced by seething anger. Someone had defiled the only place in the castle that was truly mine, and I knew which monster was responsible.

After spending an hour cleaning the mess and repairing my mattress, I decided the last thing I wanted was to sleep there. Taking with me the largest piece of my torn blanket, I went to the library, the only sanctuary I had left, curled into my favorite chair, and instantly fell asleep.

The next morning, my eyes felt heavy and my bones ached as I dragged myself around the castle. If anyone noticed my haggard appearance, they kept it to themselves. Except the princess, who wasn't looking so great herself.

"What did you get up to last night?" She moaned and pressed her forehead. "Have the cook make me a tonic. I have a headache." She studied me through squinted eyes. "You better not have stolen any glasses of port. I'll have you beaten."

Hours before breakfast and already I could tell the day was going to be interminable.

While I cleared snow and raked mews, I fantasized all the ways I could exact revenge on Jervell Kade. Poison was always an option, but I didn't have access to any, nor would I have been able to get close enough to administer it. If I got my hands on a dagger, I could simply slit his throat. However, even if I managed without witnesses, there would be an awful mess, and I would hate for some poor servant to have to clean that up. I needed to be clever and hurt him in a way that wouldn't trace back to me.

I remembered Risteard hinting he wanted my help in some way. If he was serious, this could be the leverage I needed for my revenge. Chances were he would refuse. After all, he was a knight of Ilano and served King Conall, but it was worth a try--assuming he wouldn't have me thrown in the dungeon. The question was how to send him a message. Historically, he had simply appeared, seemingly out of nowhere, and usually unexpected. Now that I needed him, I was at a loss as to how to find him. I supposed I could face the freezing cold and wait in his eagle's mew until he showed up to exercise her. I certainly wasn't about to wander the castle searching through every room--especially not the Trophy Room, which I refused to enter. Servants knew everything happening behind closed doors. If I could put a note in one's hands, they'd know where to go.

I returned all my tools to storage and thought of a fake message that wouldn't raise the suspicion of a curious servant should they decide to play nosy and read it. I snuck into the princess's empty room, snatched a quill and scrap of parchment from her writing desk, and jotted a quick note to Risteard. I wrote it in a close imitation of Caelyn's hand, but the cryptic content would hint at the actual writer. I gave it to the nearest footman and pointed to Risteard's name. The moment his back was turned, I dashed to the library to wait.

Back and forth I paced before the fire. Every minute that passed left me feeling more foolish. Whenever we'd spoken, it had been on his terms. I don't know why I thought he would come when I asked. He was obviously very busy and important.

I'd decided to leave when heavy footfalls entered the library, and Risteard appeared, looking uneasy.

"What's wrong?" we said in unison. He deferred to me.

"You look worried. Have you heard something about Ula?" I asked, my hands clutched against my chest.

"No. You've never sent for me before. I thought something happened."

"Something has happened." His jaw clenched and I continued. "Someone trashed my room last night. Paint and broken brushes strewn everywhere, plus my bed was torn to shreds."

"Did you see them? Did they hurt you?"

"They were already gone. I wasn't there when it happened, but I have an idea of who's responsible."

"As do I." He moved past me and stared into the fire, his hands curled into fists at his side. He stood eerily still, his eyes dark and unblinking. I had seen him furiously break through my bedroom door and heard him yell in frustration, but the quiet anger I witnessed now was more frightening. Nervously, I stepped back to give him space.

"You...you said that you might need my help," I began. "I'm not sure what I could do, but if you prevent Jervell Kade from bothering me again, I'll do what I can--within the boundaries of propriety, of course."

The corner of his mouth twitched, but he did not respond.

I continued. "In a perfect world, I'd love to make him pay, but I also know I cannot reasonably ask you to threaten the Lord Protector of Ilano, no matter how much he deserves it."

The prolonged silence made me uneasy, and I was preparing myself for refusal when Risteard turned to me.

"I cannot make a public accusation, but if I lodge a complaint privately to the king, he will listen."

"Are you sure?" I was skeptical.

"Absolutely certain."

"He meets privately with the princess, in her rooms."

"For what purpose?"

"They talk about the prince. Something about an arranged marriage, and a plan that's not fully clear."

"A marriage to whom?"

"I don't know. He may have mentioned a name, but I can't remember. I'm sure it's a lady from Ilano, though."

"You'll have to improve your observational skills if you're going to be a spy."

I grinned. "Will you teach me?"

"You seem to grasp the basic concept. Listen without being seen, remember names, and don't get caught."

I put my fisted hands against my hips and puffed out my chest in satisfaction. "So, it appears it's you and me then, old man! I challenge anyone to find a more unlikely team."

"Old man? I'm not yet twenty-five!"

"Sorry," I shrugged. "It must be the beard."

His hand moved to his chin, and he stroked the dark hairs thoughtfully.

"I had better return to my duties. The princess is already in a mood today, and I don't want to make it worse by being late." I hurried to the door but stopped and asked.

"How do I know I can trust you? How can I be sure you're not going to expose me to the king?"

"You know because everyone still thinks you're a deaf-mute."

"Fair…" I mused with a twinge of uncertainty.

"Ask yourself what I have to gain by betraying a poor servant girl."

I straightened my posture, thrusting my shoulders back. "I am no poor servant, sir. I am Laria Audrey of Riverstone. And I am a lady!" Chin raised, I stepped proudly through the door.

CHAPTER 15

Much to Princess Caelyn's satisfaction, Jervell Kade attended Queen Shaeli's next session. He was honorably seated next to the queen, and I stayed as far away as possible, avoiding the smirk I wanted to slap off his face. Before the queen arrived, he commented to the princess I appeared to have neglected to change my frock. She flushed and insisted I improve my personal hygiene. My blood boiled and I plunged murderous daggers into his flesh with my eyes while Jervell smugly endeared himself to the assembled ladies.

The queen's session progressed with the usual questions, but instead of drifting off with my own thoughts, I listened and observed. I learned Lady Renua had a secret lover her husband knew about and he planned to divorce her. The young Miss Meena wanted to know if she would marry soon since she was nearing the age of spinsterhood. Just to be clear, Miss Meena is only two years older than me and an exceptional beauty with very high standards, which meant she'd rejected every previous proposal. The queen assured her a marriage was imminent if she kept an open mind and did not hesitate to act. In other words, quit being so picky and accept the next offer.

Jervell Kade listened with little interest. These stories were nothing new to a man who spent years in the service of nobles. Whether in Ilano or Praed, the rich were all the same, with their petty problems and flair for indulgence. He studied the jeweled ring on his finger intently, ignoring those seated around him, but the princess appeared neither concerned nor embarrassed by his lack of attention. I watched them both, waiting for a look or a sign that they were up to something. But Princess Caelyn had eyes and ears only for Queen Shaeli, her body drawn forward to receive her every word.

In the middle of Lady Serough's inquiry as to whether her lazy son would ever make something of himself, the queen raised a hand, effectively silencing the inane question.

She turned to Jervell Kade. "A message has come through for you."

He straightened in his chair and nodded courteously. "Which is?"

"Someone knows what you have done, and that person will set out to ruin you."

Jervell's smile faltered. "Oh? And what am I supposed to have done?"

"Beware," Queen Shaeli said. "You are being watched." I sensed his eyes on me, but I remained motionless, my eyes on the floor.

He tried to appear nonchalant. "Well, if that's the case, I will have to destroy them first."

The queen frowned. "I fear, Your Lordship, that this would be a dangerous course."

"Perhaps we should post guards to your room and person for your protection," the princess suggested. "The Lord Protector of Ilano shall not be harmed while in Praed."

"That may be wise," the queen said.

The princess nodded. "I shall speak to His Majesty, my lord."

"You are too kind, Princess Caelyn." Jervell spent the rest of the session sulking in his chair.

The moment the queen excused herself, he cornered the princess.

"What was that all about?" he demanded.

"I don't know," she whispered. "It seems we must be vigilant."

"How well can you trust your staff?" He glared at me.

She followed his gaze. "Some more than others. You have my word that no injury shall befall you. I'll go directly to the king this instant to ensure your safety." Jervell bowed and stepped aside for her, but when I tried to pass, a hand blocked my path, and Jervell leaned close to my ear.

"If you can hear me, as I am beginning to suspect you can," he whispered. "Know that you're no match for me, little girl. If you stand in my way, I'll do to your face what I did to your room." His hand dropped, and I hurried away, certain this was no idle threat.

The council chamber was a large room with a vaulted ceiling and red stone floor. A U-shaped table where the king and his trusted advisors balanced budgets, planned invasions, and counted taxes dominated the space. During trials, the king and queen sat on a raised dais, behind which were three stained glass windows. I was never permitted to enter this room, but I was always curious about what men talked about there. I recalled long ago, on a visit to the palace with Father, I sneaked in after him, and for a boring hour listened while they discussed figures and crops. I fell asleep under a table and never went inside again.

Princess Caelyn burst through the door without knocking, startling the assembled men. Recognizing the visitor, they stood at attention and bowed amid murmurs of "Your Highness."

"Caelyn! What is the meaning of this intrusion?" the king bellowed.

"I have something very important to discuss with you, Father," she said.

"It can wait, I'm sure. I'm in the middle of something, as you can see." He gestured toward the nobles and lords from the king's inner circle including Risteard, who looked at me intently, no doubt noticing the pallor of my skin and the fear in my eyes. The prince was curiously absent. He obviously had more important matters to attend to rather than learning how to run a country.

"It cannot!" She stomped her foot for emphasis.

King Conall sighed. "Gentleman, please excuse us. Help yourself to a draught."

The king took his place at the head of the table in a high-backed, dark blue velvet cushioned chair with silver rivets reflecting the waning sunlight streaming through stained-glass windows. Risteard took his place at the king's right hand, and once we were alone, the princess wasted no time unleashing her concerns.

"Father, Lord Protector Kade has had a threat upon his person."

"What?" The king sat up.

"Yes! He must have some protection."

"Who has threatened him?"

"I..." she hesitated. "I don't have a name. Mother had a vision."

"I see. And your mother is never wrong." His eyes darted around the room, so wide the whites showed. "Very well, Caelyn. Risteard," the king turned to the First Knight. "You will select a few of your men and post them to the Lord Protector's rooms and then choose your most trusted knight to follow him wherever he goes, day and night. A threat to the Lord Protector is a threat to Ilano!"

"I will personally ensure the Lord Protector never leaves my sight, Your Majesty." Risteard met my eye, and the side of my mouth quirked in a mischievous grin. The princess, pleased to have her way, about-faced without another word and strode out the door. I curtseyed low to the king and followed but lingered to listen at the door to practice those sleuthing skills.

"You will report back if you notice anything amiss, Risteard? We've only just begun to build a new world. I cannot afford to have some traitor ruin everything."

"I assure you if I observe anything untoward, you will be informed immediately."

"Good man. You know, I rely on your support, Risteard. I wouldn't be here if not for you." My jaw dropped. The knight may have played a greater part in the fall of Praed than I thought.

"You underestimate my importance, Your Majesty. This victory is yours alone."

"Enough false modesty. I would never have gained the support I needed without you."

"Not me, Your Majesty." I strained to hear as Risteard's voice quieted. "They followed the memory of my father."

"May he rest eternally at peace."

I rushed from the door, my ears burning and mind racing. I gritted my teeth so hard my jaw ached. What did the king mean? I glanced over my shoulder, wondering if I should have risked staying to hear more. But the princess was in a demanding mood, and I didn't dare fall behind.

After having his every move shadowed by Risteard for the last week, Jervell Kade's irritation was palpable. He clearly found the knight's presence an inconvenience, and his irritability occasionally became unrestrainable. It took all my self control not to cover my ears when his high-pitched complaints echoed through the castle. He had not been able to visit the princess' rooms, so the lady found herself torn between relief that the Lord Protector was safe, and annoyance at the lack of privacy.

Such feelings were rampant in the castle. For me, confusion tinged the betrayal I felt overhearing a conversation inferring the part Risteard played in the utter destruction of the life I knew. I don't know what I expected or why I was surprised. After all, this was the terrifying First Knight of King Conall, destroyer of Praed. Yet, even when I tell myself to stop being so irrational, I harbor resentment and anger. I ignore Risteard as if he were invisible. I avoid the library, a sacrifice to my resolve to never speak to him again. When he tries to make eye contact, I pretend not to notice. I have experienced nothing but heartache and disappointment since coming to the castle and feared the trend would continue. Regrettably, I learned I couldn't trust anyone, especially a man who masquerades as an ally and then plunges a knife in your heart when you let your guard down.

Snow continued to fall in the bitter cold, paving my path to the mews in thick ice. The birds had begun to suffer in the unfamiliar temperatures, and many were off their food, choosing instead to slip into a torpor that troubled their owners. Tapestries were hung upon the walls to insulate the buildings, and fires were placed around the yard to warm the eagles resting on their perches. The effect was a temperate oasis in the desolate coldness of the mountain, and I would pause at every pyre to regain feeling in my fingers before moving on to the next mew.

Extra hands saw to the comfort of the birds, some I recognized and others clearly experts from Ilano directing everyone. I paid no attention to these people, preferring my anonymity, and they respected the distance placed between us. One painfully cold morning the wind blew from the north and pierced my skin with tiny icicles, bringing tears to my eyes. My fingers turned blue at the nail beds even before I entered the yard. A hooded figure was hunched over a pile of wood, stacking the pieces and interlacing straw into the gaps. He stopped working and stood tall when I walked by. I ignored him, even when he followed. I increased my pace, and the crunching of the snow quickened and drew closer. I reached for the shed door, but a hand grabbed the back of my coat and pulled me backwards. I stumbled but was caught and my mouth covered in one smooth motion. I flailed, my arms striking their head several times with no effect.

"Stop, my lady, please!" A voice once strong and powerful pleaded. The hood was pushed back, revealing a man with graying blonde hair and amber eyes. He placed a finger to his lips, glanced around the yard, and carefully removed his hand from my mouth.

"You probably don't remember me," he whispered, "but I'm Fin Kinsley, and I served with your father."

My pulse quickened as I stared at the man in shock. Sir Kinsley was a well-admired knight from my father's inner circle. He was boisterous, courageous, and according to my mother a great prospect for a young lady. He had aged considerably. The once perfectly groomed face was gaunt and bristled with gray, his muscular build thinned with disuse.

"Why do you live while my father is dead?" I accused before I could reconsider. For Praedan knights, dying in battle was considered the highest honor. If one man fell while his friend lived, it was considered disgraceful.

He looked stricken and stepped away.

"Not by choice, Lady Audrey. I would have died with him given the chance, but I was spared to live in servitude, my punishment the dishonor of being denied a soldier's death."

"Stop calling me *lady*," I ordered. "Lady Audrey is my mother."

"Then she lives?" He sighed in relief. "I have been serving the house of one of the new lords and have heard nothing of her."

"She serves the queen. Like you, her punishment is survival."

"You don't know what it means to see you alive, Miss Audrey. I hope you are treated well?"

"Not as well as I'm used to, but I don't starve, if that means anything."

"If ever you have need of me, I would be honored to serve you. There are others who would feel the same."

"And what can you do? What can any of us do?"

He smiled, a sad, wistful smile. "We can hope."

"That word again," I groaned, rolling my eyes. "I have seen nothing here that gives me hope, Sir Kinsley. You're wasting your time believing in it."

"Better to hope for something other than death, Miss Audrey. Is it not?"

"Death is the only certainty in this world."

"Then why waste time hoping for something that's sure to come? For months, I grieved and wished for an end to my suffering. Then one day, I chose to live. I couldn't explain my change of heart, I just climbed from my black hole and faced the morning with a renewed sense of purpose. What that purpose was, I did not know. Until today, when I recognized you, and my heart was filled with joy. I served King Llewlyn, I served Maccus Audrey, and now I serve you, Laria Audrey." He bowed formally and rose proudly.

Servants started coming into view. "You can't tell anyone we've spoken," I said hastily. "Everyone here believes I'm mute, and I'd like to keep it that way."

He nodded in agreement, and I dismissed him with a wave. I didn't ask how I would find him, because honestly, I didn't think there would ever be an occasion to. However, knowing Sir Kinsley was alive in Praed and standing beside my family made me feel I wasn't so alone in this world of enemies, darkness, and betrayal.

CHAPTER 16

The snow drifted high against the walls of Praed Castle when Jervell Kade suggested the princess be removed to a more comfortable location. He reasoned the palace had become too confining for the young woman, and he feared the strain was affecting her bloom. The king, initially shocked and appalled at the idea, eventually agreed Princess Caelyn shouldn't be allowed to suffer. This was the secondhand information I overheard from the kitchen maids one morning. They thought the princess too delicate to travel in the middle of a Praed winter, but they were happy to be rid of her, even at the risk of her freezing to death. I didn't believe for a second the princess would agree to such a plan. She complained of the cold enough from the confines of her sweltering room with its blazing hearth, hot water bottles, and piles of furs. Nothing on earth could convince her to leave, not even an order from King Conall. I wondered at Jervell Kade's motive. Did he think he could resume his plotting with the princess if she was removed from the castle? Did he hope to intercept her when he left for Ilano?

His goal became clear when the princess was summoned to the king's rooms later that day. The princess never met with her father here, so this was my first glimpse into the king's private world. The ante-room was lavishly decorated in shades of red from plush carpet to overstuffed chaises. Red velvet curtains draped over the windows and an archway that led to his bedchamber. A shield with a diving black eagle was displayed above the hearth. The fire was so large the room felt like an oven, and it wasn't long before sweat glistened on my brow. An ornate table covered with generous helpings of food and surrounded by tall-backed chairs dominated the room. Gathered there were King Conall, Queen Shaeli, the Lord Protector, and Risteard, who had continued to plague Jervell Kade to distraction.

"To what do I owe this honor, Your Majesty?" the princess asked, her voice laced with sarcasm.

"My dear daughter, how keenly you must feel this harsh climate. You have borne it most bravely. I feel I have been selfish in keeping you here for the comfort of having my family so near."

The princess' eyes narrowed.

"What are you saying, Father?"

"I'm saying our most observant Lord Protector has advised me that you be allowed a sabbatical."

Her eyes widened. "You're sending me away?"

"Consider it a release from obligation. A brief holiday."

"Oh, Father! To be in Ilano again, even for a short time, would mean everything to me! I cannot thank you enough!"

I'd never seen the princess happy, and the sight was sobering. For once, I saw her not as an overlord, but as a woman who missed her home as much as I missed mine.

The king raised his hand. "Calm yourself, child. I said nothing of Ilano. You will be removed from the castle, but you will remain in Praed."

Her features fell into confusion and anger. "What?" she snapped. "Just where are you sending me?"

"Into the valley," Jervell Kade interrupted. "Here in the mountains, the air is thin and cold, but down in the lower regions, the temperatures are more forgiving. You will be much more comfortable there."

She turned to Jervell. "So this was your idea?"

"It was. Your Highness' well-being is always my first concern."

She narrowed her eyes, assessing. Then she casually turned away and said, "Very well. If it is my father's wish."

"Of course, with the princess leaving the castle, her safety should be our priority. Wouldn't you agree, Your Majesty?"

"Yes, of course!" said the king.

"So, it stands to reason Your Majesty should send the best men to protect her."

"No one but the very best. You're quite right, Jervell. I will personally ensure my strongest soldiers accompany you on your journey, Caelyn."

"Which should include your First Knight." Jervell gestured toward Risteard. "I have appreciated his protection, but I cannot ask for his services if the princess needs him more, Your Majesty. I insist he be released from his duty to me and beg that he keep Her Highness safe."

So here was the reason for this nonsensical scheme. If the princess were to travel under the guardianship of Risteard, the Lord Protector would be free to resume his scheming.

"Well said, Jervell. Your service to my family is truly honorable. Risteard," he turned to the black-garbed man standing stoically beside him. "You are charged with the security of our most precious treasure. If you allow any harm to befall her, your swift and immediate death will follow."

For the first time in weeks, I met Risteard's eyes, but they were blank. Not an eyelash twitched at the king's threat.

Preparing the princess for travel was as arduous as the journey itself. She inspected my choices as I packed suitable gowns into her large trunk. I listened without response to her constant stream of complaints on the inconvenience of travelling in such bleak weather. She chose accessories, placing necklaces and jewels in an already overburdened case. I'm not sure whom she was expecting to entertain while in, as she described it, 'exile,' but she would certainly impress them.

The prince barged in and observed the disarray. "Well, looks as if you're preparing to move out permanently!"

"I wish I was," the princess muttered.

"I admit I envy you."

"Really? That makes this whole nonsense worth it then."

"You'd rather be stuck here than venturing somewhere else? Seeing new views?"

"There are people here, entertainments, amusements. Where I'm going, the only person to amuse me will be her." She threw a thumb over her shoulder toward me.

"She knows a few tricks, I'm sure." The prince grinned and sauntered toward me. "Even ones that could please a woman like you."

"Get out!" she hissed. "Go please yourself!"

"Gladly, dear sister!" He laughed and dodged a cushion she hurled at him. "Safe journey!"

During the ensuing bustle for Princess Caelyn's departure, I found time to escape to the library. Since I'd been avoiding Risteard, I missed the security of the dusty room with its ancient tomes and hidden corners. I walked with hurried steps, knowing I didn't have much time to say goodbye to the last safe place in the castle. The door creaked heavily, but I knew no one else would be here, and I could enjoy a few last private minutes. The hearth was black, cold, and empty. I kneeled closer, stretching forth my hands as I had many times before, imagining the hot flames that once resided there. Disappointed, I dropped my hands, then my head, and mourned one more loss.

"You stopped coming," a voice spoke from the shadows. I stood and turned toward the sound and saw Risteard sitting in the darkness amid the books, watching me. He came forward into the sliver of light from the small window.

"Shouldn't you be tailing a weasel?" I sneered when he stepped beside me and stared into the vacant hearth.

"I have been released from that task, as you are well aware." I kept my back to him, my arms crossed, annoyed at his intrusion.

"Have I done something to offend you?" he asked.

"You have some nerve asking me that!"

"I thought we'd put the past behind us and agreed to move on."

"Things changed. I discovered the past cannot be so easily forgotten. Or forgiven. Especially when I find out you've been lying to me. Although, I can't say I'm surprised." I watched him over my shoulder, confusion and incredulity marring his expression.

"I've never once lied to you!" he said.

"You've omitted truths!" I shouted back. "Isn't that the same thing?"

He turned away, his jaw clenching. "What have you heard?"

"You played a greater part in this war than you let me believe. I'd begun to think I could trust you. I was a fool," my voice dropped. "I regret ever having listened to you, and for starting to consider you a…friend." A tear trickled down my face and fell to the floor. I shut my eyes to block it out and rushed from the room before he could stop me. He didn't follow, but I felt uneasy, feeling he was watching me from the doorway. *Don't look back*, I repeated to myself, and I kept my eyes forward, never turning to face what lurked behind.

The horses' thick winter coats billowed in the slight breeze as they trudged through the deep snow. The streets inside the city at the base of the mountain were cleared, but the outlying roads were neglected since the overthrow of King Llewlyn, prolonging the journey when the carriage wheels became trapped in drifts. Servants dug out the carriage on multiple occasions, the princess complaining at the lateness of the hour with each setback. She was in no position to complain, swathed as she was in piles of furs and blankets, a pan of coals at her feet. I was fortunate myself, having been allowed to ride inside, without such comforts but nevertheless warm in the carriage.

The carriage jerked to stop, then rocked violently when the coachman whipped the horses. The coachman shouted, the horses snorted and dug their hooves into the ground, but we remained stuck. I turned toward the window to distract myself from the princess' grumblings. I brushed away the frost for a better look and squinted through the fogged glass. I studied the white landscape and recognized the curve of the hills and slopes of the valley. We were travelling along the Rhyvor, I was certain, though I couldn't see its rocky banks. The carriage jolted forward, and our journey resumed. My breath quickened when I recognized familiar outcroppings and finally saw the river cutting through the valley. I sat back in my seat, unwilling to accept what my heart knew to be true.

The carriage stopped for the last time at the entrance of Riverstone. Reverently, I exited the carriage, looking up at the familiar stone facade without regard to the princess waiting expectantly for my help.

A footman extended his hand to the princess. "Your Highness."

"Finally." She stepped out of the carriage and joined me in the inspection of the house, silently studying the structure while behind us servants busied themselves unloading her many trunks.

"Impressive stonework," the princess said. "I understand it was the seat of your family for many generations. A shame your father was responsible for losing it." She glanced sideways at me, then rolled her eyes. "Sometimes I wish you could understand me. That was a very clever insult wasted."

The princess strode forward as the heavy timber doors leading to the front hall opened to receive us. Tentatively, I placed a hand on the stone, running my fingers over the cold rock dredged from the Rhyvor hundreds of years ago, stacked and mortared with expert care to erect this magnificent structure. My home. I followed the rest of the party inside, brushing my fingers against the wall like a child. I stepped over the threshold and breathed in the scent of aged trees. The smell of baking and fresh flowers was gone, the sounds of a bustling household nothing but a memory, but the house was still intact.

When I looked closer, it became apparent Riverstone did not escape plundering. Tapestries were torn and family heirlooms were missing. The polished mahogany floor was scratched and dull, and dust floated on the air to become trapped in cobwebs. Mother would be furious to see the house in such a state. The princess was likewise unimpressed.

"What a dark, dusty place!" she said.

A line of servants was paraded out, and a man wearing a long, light blue fur-lined tunic came forward to address the princess.

He bowed, brushed back an errant strand of dark brown hair, and smiled all the way to his chestnut eyes. His tawny skin was unblemished, unshaven, and glowing with charm. "Your Highness. Allow me to present myself as the caretaker of this house as well as your butler, Eugen. I apologize for the current state of things, but I assure you the staff will be working diligently to restore the place to its former glory."

"I trust you've started lighting the fires?"

"Of course, Your Highness! You will find a hearth lit in every room, the hottest being the one in your room. If you will allow me to escort you."

My eyes roamed the halls as we were led to the princess' rooms, noting more items missing, furniture broken, and family portraits ripped asunder.

"The rooms once occupied by the lord of the manor are the grandest, but the style is too masculine. We thought Your Highness would appreciate the femininity of her ladyship's former rooms instead."

My ears rang as we climbed the grand spiral stairs off the entrance hall and walked down the hallway to my mother's rooms. Eugen opened the door to the sitting room, and I hesitated before crossing the threshold. A fire roared in the hearth, but Mother's lush, yet tasteful furniture was gone, replaced with overstuffed yellow couches. Housemaids scurried around unpacking trunks into the dressers once containing my mother's possessions. I walked around the half wall separating the sitting room from her bed chamber. The bed she'd slept in was tidied with new coverings in the style of Ilano. The butler launched into a lecture on the improvements intended for her rooms and the rest of the house. Not wanting to listen to such depressing talk, I slipped from the room and ventured along the corridors.

Father's rooms consisted of a bedroom with an enormous iron framed bed, a gaming room where he entertained close family and friends, and a breakfast room where he ate slabs of ham and drank thick, black coffee laced with equi every morning. This was the only room I was allowed in because he would sometimes invite the family to join him to view the sunrise. Feeling a sense of wickedness, I peered into his bedchamber. The bed had been dismantled, the iron likely melted down to make horseshoes for the invaders. I ventured further and entered the adjacent room, and it was also torn apart. Trophies were gone or smashed, leather was torn from the chairs, and pages from books littered the floor. I shuffled through the rubble, searching for anything worth saving. Glass crunched under my foot, and I bent to free a small frame lodged under the rug, a portrait of Mother, painted when she was very young. I clutched it to my heart and left the room, unable to look upon the emptiness of the depressing place. Holding the picture close, I hastened to Ula's room.

Ula grew up in that room from the time she left the nursery. Surely invading soldiers would find nothing of value inside and leave it untouched. I crossed the threshold and discovered I was mistaken. Like Father's, I found Ula's room in shambles. The frame of her wooden bed was chopped down to splinters, the remnants probably burning in someone's fireplace. Her toys were broken and flung about the room. The tiny embroidered chair by the hearth was smashed, wool spewing from the tears in the fabric. I knelt next to the remains and felt the threads, remembering the last days spent in this room. I ripped a piece free and wrapped Mother's portrait inside.

Before I ventured to the next floor, I crept silently past my mother's rooms, checking that the butler was still prattling on and the princess was thoroughly occupied with the arrangement of her things. My room was in the turret, and at the top of the spiral stairs, the door stood ajar on the hinges. Books covered the floor, and the tapestry of the Rhyvor was gone. I pictured it lying across a knight's table, a spoil of war. The bedclothes were also missing, as were my gowns. I rummaged through the drawers of my nightstand, but they were empty of the treasures I'd kept there. I went to the window and stared down at the skeletal remains of the stables buried beneath a fresh layer of snow. If I closed my eyes, I could almost hear Amore whinnying for her grain.

Boots clomped on the stairs and Risteard entered, stepping over novels and worthless mementos of a lost childhood. He examined the cluttered space, the bare walls, and empty bed.

"Do you remember this room?" I asked calmly.

"This is where we met," he said without meeting my eye.

"*Met* is hardly the word I would use. It wasn't exactly a mutual decision."

"I didn't know we were coming here. I would have prepared you."

"I'm not unsettled. I'm home. But it isn't mine anymore, is it?" I didn't require a response, and he offered none. I gazed back outside, wishing I could see the grooms watering the horses and throwing spent grain to waiting chickens.

"Have you been listening to rumors? Or eavesdropping?" he asked.

"Pardon?" I didn't take my eyes off the window, imagining memories of a lost childhood dancing among the debris.

"You've changed your attitude toward me. I want to know why."

"You're mistaken," I turned to him, my gaze steady and chin raised. "I am ever constant. My heart is *cold* to *you*." He flinched but did not leave as I intended.

"I have to know what you heard." His words were fractured, his voice broken.

"I heard you, speaking to the king, extolling your glorious deeds."

His eyes narrowed. "You overheard the king and me speaking in private?"

"Yes," I whispered, returning to the window.

"Was this in reference to my father? After I was assigned to 'protect' Jervell Kade?"

I nodded. "You told me to practice my observational skills. You were right. They were most informative."

"And completely useless taken out of context!"

"What?"

"I once accused you of being a child. I was right."

I wheeled on him in surprise, prepared to fight back, but he continued.

"You only hear what you want to justify your own opinions. If you really cared about the truth, you would have asked me or looked for answers in the book. Instead, you've been looking for reasons to hate me, and now you've decided you've found one."

I blinked. "Wait, what book?"

"The book on Ilano. It sits on the little table in the library."

"You know about that?" I didn't think I'd mentioned the book to him. Had I? No. I thought it was from Mother and didn't want to betray her.

He came closer, his face red.

"Who do you think put it there?"

My jaw dropped. "Why?" I whispered.

"How better to understand your enemy?"

"I don't believe you," I sneered.

He looked past my shoulder out the window.

"Maybe," he said. "I thought if you learned our history, you wouldn't think so cruelly of us."

I gazed down at the burnt shell below us. "How can I look upon your people with anything but hatred when you've behaved so viciously."

We remained silent for several seconds.

"What was your horse's name?" His voice was calm with no trace of his previous anger.

"Amore," I smiled. "She was a beautiful liver chestnut. She would do anything I asked, even jump across the Rhyvor or gallop over hot coals! She could be willful and stubborn at times, though."

"Like her mistress." His mouth quirked in a half smile. "You didn't come to me then to ask for an explanation," he went on. "But I'm here now. No secrets. Whatever question you ask, I will answer."

"If the king did not have your support, would he have invaded Praed?"

"Yes, but he would have failed. By publicly supporting Conall, many followed, giving him the numbers needed for a successful campaign."

"All those people joined the war in memory of your father? That's quite a risk. What if you were a terrible fighter?"

He crossed his arms and his face flushed. "I have my own merits."

"Which have yet to be seen."

He opened his mouth to protest, but a small smile played at my lips, and he turned away muttering something about sass.

I continued. "You said my people killed your father."

"In a sense, yes. Praed was responsible for my father's death. As you're aware, that's not an easy thing to forgive."

"So, you came here seeking revenge?"

"That's the simplest explanation."

I glanced at the wreckage on the floor. "I suppose we've both been blinded by grief."

"I can't imagine how difficult it must be for you to be back here, under Princess Caelyn's command and rule over your own home."

"She's going to be using my mother's rooms."

"I'm sorry."

"They *are* the most elegant."

Risteard shifted closer but did not dare to comfort me by physical touch.

"I've decided not to be terribly upset about it," I went on. "Rather, I intend to help the princess feel as welcome here as anywhere else in Praed. She may wish to spend the rest of the winter here, in fact. The snow doesn't fall as thick here in the valley compared to the mountain." I risked a glance at him, and saw he was smiling all the way to his cerulean eyes.

"The princess will be glad for the hospitality of a lady of Riverstone."

The welcome Princess Caelyn encountered at Riverstone was unparalleled. The stores of preserves and dried meats in the pantry had been plundered, but the secret cache below the cellar remained undiscovered. From here came aged cheeses, jerked venison, Father's famous kumis, and Mother's orinberry jam. The princess devoured them all and became quite content to remain at Riverstone in an alcoholic, full-bellied haze.

Word came to Risteard that Jervell Kade was leaving Praed. I worried that he would route his journey here, a fear that was not unfounded. Within the week, a guest was announced, and Jervell Kade slithered his way into the salon where the princess was perfecting her embroidery.

She gestured for him to sit beside her. "It has been too long."

I remained focused on my own frightful needlework, which the princess insisted I perfect if I were to be her only companion.

"What news?" she asked. "Any developments?"

He took her hands in his. "Nothing to disrupt our plans. The king is planning a tour of the country once the snow has melted. This may be our only chance."

"Won't it be too soon? Brannon isn't even engaged yet."

"One must act when the opportunity presents itself."

The princess nodded in agreement.

"I trust you'll make all the arrangements?"

"Of course, my lady." I pricked my finger and stuck it in my mouth to suppress a curse. The movement caught his attention. "Oh! I see you are teaching your pet some tricks."

"She's not very accomplished. Shocking, considering her heritage." Jervell approached me, leaned over my chair so his nose practically touched mine, and breathed heavily on my face. I ignored him and concentrated intently on my embroidery. His rancid breath wafted over me, and I swallowed with an audible gulp to subdue the rising bile.

"I hope I'm not disturbing you," he whispered.

I didn't move, though I wanted to punch his crooked nose.

"If I didn't know any better," the princess observed, "I would think you're infatuated with that freckled freak."

He chuckled, a low, disturbing sound. "Just amusing myself, Highness."

"Amuse yourself somewhere else. Your attention to her is upsetting my stomach."

Yours and mine, Princess, I thought.

The Lord Protector chose to remain at Riverstone for a further three days, tainting the reunion between me and my beloved home. Released from the binds of the castle, Jervell felt free to converse with the princess at his whim, going in and out of her rooms as he pleased while the servants whispered behind their backs. I'd never witnessed anything to suggest a relationship, but that didn't stop the swirling rumors. Once they reached Risteard's ears, he resumed his role as tireless protector, posting himself at the princess' door and escorting her throughout the manor. The constant presence of the knight vexed her acutely, until one day she stomped her foot and demanded to know why he persisted in following her.

"For the safety of Your Highness," he said. "And to preserve my own life. For the king decreed if any injury befalls you, my death will result."

"Knights," the princess muttered, throwing up her hands in resignation.

The Lord Protector left Riverstone the next day.

CHAPTER 17

To my immense delight, we remained at Riverstone for the next few months. In part this was due to my diligent attention to the princess' needs and the generous store of delicious provisions. So by default, I became her devoted companion, sitting with her for hours sewing, listening to her play and sing, and watching her read. Makeshift mews were constructed for the few eagles that accompanied us, but thankfully I was not made to clean them. Though I was often bored out of my skull, my days at Riverstone passed in warmth and comfort. The princess continued to write her letters, but the post was delayed so severely she eventually gave this up. She taught me to play a card game popular in Ilano, and in return I tried to teach her one of ours, but she failed to grasp the intricacies and threw the cards away in frustration. Servants restored the piano in the drawing room and the princess entreated me to play, quickly discovering how poorly I performed.

"Your mother must have been absolutely disgraced to have you for a daughter. Are you good at anything?"

All I could boast about was my riding ability, but I couldn't show her that, nor could I read out loud using different voices as I did for Ula. My younger sister could show off many talents, but the princess was stuck with me, and I was sadly lacking. I shook my head at the princess, lowering my eyes in shame.

"Can you dance?"

I shrugged.

"Hm. You couldn't hear the music anyway."

I thought of one thing. It was ridiculous, but it was something. I raised my finger for the princess to wait there and retreated to the kitchens, then returned with three small apples. The princess crossed her arms, waiting. My face flushed with embarrassment, but I proceeded. I balanced the fruits in my hands, then tossed them in the air and juggled. Ula used to love watching me juggle, especially when the fruits reached the ceiling. If I concentrated and timed things just right, I could even toss one under my leg. When I finished, I caught the apples with a flourish and bowed comically. Silence. I looked up at the princess. Her mouth was agape, her eyebrows raised.

"Really?" she said. "Is that how people in Praed pass away the long winters? How childish." She quit the room, rolling her eyes and muttering about uncivilized heathens.

"I enjoyed the performance," Risteard said from the doorway. I bowed in his direction, and he approached the piano in the corner of the room.

"Surely you don't mean my tragic musical performance?"

"You never took the time to practice, I gather," he said.

I shook my head. "I confess I didn't have the patience for it, nor the talent. Not like Ula. She could look at any instrument and play as if she were born to it."

Risteard ran his fingers along the shining keys, smiling to himself. "My mother used to say talent and practice without passion could not make one a master."

"Did she play well?"

"Yes." He dropped his hands from the keys, pulled out the bench, sat down, and made room for me to join him. "Come," he beckoned. Reluctantly, I took a seat.

"Play something for me." He gestured toward the keys.

"No, trust me. I'm terrible!"

"Please. I insist."

"You asked for it." My fingers stumbled over the keys, missing notes, and clumsily pounded away. I expected him to cover his ears and beg me to stop, but he listened until the song finished.

"You don't play well because you're focused on getting to the end and rushing through to get it over with."

"Obviously."

"Because you've always felt forced to play?"

"Yes. Mother insisted. But I was always terrible. I knew as soon as the song was over or if I played horribly enough, she'd end the lesson and I could do as I pleased. Eventually, she stopped pestering me to practice."

"Did you approach riding in the same manner?"

"No! I rode for hours."

"And when you fell off, did you give up?"

"No, I tried harder. I can see where this is going, but it's not the same. Riding is something I actually enjoy."

"Do you think you would enjoy playing if your mother had not forced you?"

I sat quietly for a moment, contemplating the newly polished keys. Risteard placed his hands on their surface, and to my surprise played a low, beautiful melody. His fingers danced expertly across the keys, entrancing me as I followed their movements, listening to the beautiful music echoing from the depths of the instrument. The sound was sweet and sad all at once, filling me with joy and leaving my eyes brimming with unshed tears. I'd never heard a sound like it before. He swayed in tune with the music, his eyes closed. I felt like an intruder catching someone in a private moment. The music quickened, and he leaned over the keys as his fingers performed the final notes, the sound drifting away in a receding tide. His hands remained on the silent keys, my breathing the only noise.

For the first time, I looked at Risteard as more than a menacing figure, a knight, or a fellow conspirator. He'd shown me kindness, protectiveness, and respect. Now, he'd revealed a softness I didn't know a man could possess. My eyes unabashedly travelled up from his strong, long-fingered hands. He'd rolled up his sleeves, revealing muscular, dark-haired forearms. Past his shoulders clad in black--always in black--to his sharp, bearded jawline, until I met his cerulean eyes. Embarrassment spread like wildfire from my neck to my hairline.

"Where did you learn to play like that?" I whispered.

"My mother."

"Can you teach me?"

"If you're willing to learn." I placed my hands alongside his.

"If you have the patience. I'm an aggravating student."

"So, I've noticed. If you promise to really try, I can teach you."

I nodded, and the lessons began.

The snow ceased to fall, and slowly the ice melted, gradually revealing the landscape around Riverstone. By the position of the sun and the warming temperature, I knew spring was drawing near, and with it my birthday. The princess was eager to leave the manor, having grown restless in the confining atmosphere. With a series of gestures, I indicated the weather was conducive to walking and hinted she take a turn outside. For lack of anything else to do, she bundled herself into several layers and trudged outside with me, Risteard, and three servants carrying extra coats. I led the party on what I felt was a short stroll, but the princess quickly tired and decided to sit in the sun. I gestured, asking for permission to continue by myself.

"Fine. Don't go too far, though. Risteard, make sure she doesn't run away."

"I don't believe she'd be foolish enough to do so."

"You can't be too careful. She's not very bright after all."

"As Your Highness wishes," he bowed. "Remain with the princess," he told the servants, one of whom stared at me intently. When she caught my eye, she smiled and inclined her head. I hurried away, hoping the princess hadn't noticed. Riverstone retained several servants who had worked under my family, and I avoided them to protect my feigned disability. I was also embarrassed by how far I'd fallen.

I walked to the river, climbing over boulders and tree roots with ease until I reached the banks. In another month or two, the river would be overflowing, the flood rising over my head. For now, the level was only a hint of the torrent to come. I closed my eyes and listened as the water meandered along the banks, tripping over smooth stones. Rocks shifted behind me, and I recognized Risteard's footfalls. I scooted over to make room when he sat next to me.

I inclined my head toward him and said, "If you close your eyes, you can almost hear the river whispering, telling you the secrets of the forest."

"What sort of secrets?"

"Close your eyes and try listening for yourself."

He complied with a great show of reluctance. I waved a hand in his face, concluded he wasn't peeking, then slowly leaned toward the river. Keeping watch on his still form, I scooped up a handful of the frigid water and flung it at his face. His eyes flew open and he gasped in shock, and while he sputtered, I sprang to my feet and ran.

I heard his roar of frustration behind me as I raced through the sloshing snow. I leapt for a tree branch and pulled myself up. I must have grown since the last time I climbed the ancient tree because it was easier to reach the branches. Risteard uttered curses below me as I climbed higher. Twigs snapped under his weight as he pursued me. I may be taller than before and well acquainted with the climb, but Risteard was strong and fast. His hand clamped around my ankle, and he demanded I stop. I kicked, and his grip tightened. I lowered myself onto a thick branch and looked down between my knees. He climbed up and perched across from me, not looking nearly as amused as I felt. His face was crimson and sweat trickled from his temples, his breathing rapid.

"Out of shape?" I asked innocently.

"What exactly were you trying to do?"

I said nothing, my lips clamping shut to hold back a smirk.

"I thought you were smart enough not to try and escape," he said.

"Oh, I considered it, but then I thought, 'Where would I go? And in this outfit?' I decided the look on your face when that cold water hit would be worth it whether I got away or not."

The veins bulged in his neck, his face was scarlet, and his eyes pierced me like a sword, but I couldn't contain myself any longer. I laughed so hard I nearly fell out of the tree.

"Stop," he grumbled and began to descend. He didn't smile, but the amusement in his eyes told me I wasn't about to be murdered.

As we walked back to the house, I thrust my arms forward and noted how high the sleeves stopped. I looked down and the bottom of my dress was above my ankles. My body still resembled a boy's, but at least I'd no longer be so short. The princess would have to agree to a new frock, or soon the hem would be to my knees.

The morning of my birthday, the princess received a letter from the king summoning her back to the castle. My disappointment was acute, but I hid my emotions as always and prepared for her departure.

"I want to leave as soon as possible," she declared. "I don't want to spend another night here if I can help it." By the afternoon, the princess was fully packed, and she took a break from shouting orders to have tea and biscuits with my mother's jam. Leaving her to satisfy her hunger, I returned to her rooms to arrange for the final departure, when an elderly woman from the kitchen approached me.

She gave a kind, grandmotherly smile and curtseyed.

"My lady." She placed a small package wrapped in cloth in my hands. "Well wishes for your birthday." She shuffled away and I darted toward the library.

Once a magnificent collection of novels, texts, and scrolls, the library at Riverstone had been reduced to piles of rubble and nearly bare shelves, marble busts shattered, and any item of value stolen. Still, the library remained my favorite place, and I made it my room since being at Riverstone, refusing to sleep in a family room. The princess did not object, and I assembled a makeshift cot near the hearth. I managed to find a few books in the debris and began to fill the shelves. Risteard was the only person with my permission to enter, and he was there now, glancing up from his papers as I rushed inside and slammed the door. I brought my package to a table and gently unwrapped it while Risteard approached curiously.

"What is it?" he asked.

"Ahh!" I said as the gift was revealed. "A custard."

My favorite dessert, a delicious orinberry custard, sat before me along with a small wooden spoon. I salivated, imagining the creamy texture on my tongue. White custard with bright orange topping--so beautiful it was almost a shame to eat. Slowly, I spooned a generous portion in my mouth, savoring the first taste. I closed my eyes blissfully and sighed in pleasure as the flavor coated my tongue.

Risteard swallowed audibly. "Good?"

"Very," I sighed, my eyes still closed. "It's my favorite. Mother didn't allow it often. She said it was too sweet. But every year on my birthday she made an exception." I took another bite. "A woman from the kitchen gave it to me. She's made bread and pastries here for years. Want to try?" I tipped the custard toward him, selfishly hoping he'd refuse. He took the spoon from me and took a--thankfully--small bite.

"It's very good," he agreed. I devoured the rest before he could ask for seconds. I even licked the container clean without shame.

"Did you say it's your birthday?"

"Hmm? Yes," I dropped the spoon into the container and pushed it aside. "I'd better get back to work if we're leaving today." I hastened from the library without a second glance, struggling to hold back tears. Today was my sixteenth birthday, and instead of celebrating with my family, I was once again being forced from my home. It was unbearable, and I couldn't stand for Risteard to feel sorry for me. I avoided him for the rest of the day, as I always did when life became difficult.

The princess was content to leave the minute the last trunk latched shut, but she met resistance from Eugen, the butler.

"Many apologies, Your Highness, but the hour is late, and it will be dark soon," he said.

"We have lanterns!" she argued. Eugen wrung his hands nervously.

"Would Your Highness prefer to greet your journey well rested and be received with celebrations? I could have a message delivered to the king to announce your arrival. He would be certain to greet you with the pomp and circumstance you deserve."

"I appreciate your thoughtfulness, but I am quite determined."

Despite this statement, I could sense her resolve waning. Behind her back, I waved a hand, and when I had Eugen's attention, I pulled my bottom eyelids down. He got the message.

"Of course, Princess Caelyn. I'll set your ladies to work on powdering and rouging your face immediately." Oh, he was good.

"What do you mean by that?"

"It's just Your Highness has worked hard all day and it's left your eyes rimmed in purple and, well, I'm certain we can return the glow to your cheeks." The princess put a hand to her face and inspected herself in a nearby mirror.

"On second thought," she said, turning to face the butler. "I think travelling at this hour would be detrimental to my health, and I'm astonished you would suggest such a thing!"

"Apologies again, highness." Eugen bowed.

The princess could be a cunning, intelligent woman, but her vanity was a great weakness. After storming off to her room and calling out orders of what she would like served for dinner, I looked at the butler, my hands and expression questioning the reason for the exchange.

"In truth, the king demanded she remain tonight. According to the knight, there were rumors of bandits on the roads. I thought it best not to frighten the princess with this information. I thank you for your assistance."

Bandits? The roads of Praed were very safe, at least they were before King Conall. Who knows what sort of thieves and scoundrels followed him from Ilano.

Later, I prepared as usual to go to bed in the library, but I was intercepted by another familiar face: a laundress not much older than me. She curtseyed and addressed me formally.

"Pardon, miss, but your room's been especially made up tonight." I cocked my head in confusion. "Come." She held out her hand, and I followed her up the spiral stairs to the second floor. When she continued up the tower, I steadied myself against the wall to keep from falling backwards. She was taking me to my old room. She stopped at the door and curtseyed again, bidding me goodnight, and left. I slowly opened the door.

Candles flickered on the nightstand, the mantlepiece, and a chest of drawers. A new bed dominated the space, adorned with soft pillows and warm furs. I didn't waste time asking questions. I fell onto the plush surface, feeling like I'd come home for the first time in a year. I drifted into a deep, satisfying sleep, free of the worries I would face in the morning, and thankful for the privilege of living another year.

The road was soggy from the melting snow, but the journey was easier than when we set out for Riverstone. I insisted on walking the last few miles, choosing to luxuriate in the radiant sunshine and crisp air. The princess gave no objection and warned me not to complain in five minutes when I'd had enough. I kept several paces behind the carriage, allowing the distance to give me a sense of independence. Water dripped from low, sodden branches, and green grass emerged from the receding snow. Life teemed amid the rocks, and I paused to watch a squirrel dart through crevices looking for seeds. The carriage was farther away now, and I mused that if I ran, I'd be able to hide in the bracken until the princess returned to the castle. But Risteard halted his horse and watched me. I gazed longingly in the direction of freedom, sighed resignedly, and sloshed through the rutted road.

"I was worried you were going to run," Risteard said.

"Thought about it."

"What changed your mind?"

"Didn't want to ruin my dress." I held the hems out to the sides and curtseyed low. He chuckled and kicked his horse forward, but I grabbed the reins to stop him.

"Wait, I wanted to thank you."

"For?"

"I assume it was you who… transformed… my room. My old room, I mean." His silence confirmed my suspicions. "I really wish you wouldn't do thoughtful things for me. It makes it difficult to dislike you."

"Happy new year to you." A smile flickered at his lips, then he rode away.

Upon returning to the castle, our reception was extravagant. The road was lined with banners and people waved flags and ribbons. The princess was greeted as a conquering hero, showered with adoration and cheers of "welcome home." She had only been a few miles away for crying out loud.

The princess appeared duly honored by the celebration. She waved, blew kisses, and placed a coin or two in the hands of children. She stopped once to lay a hand on a crooked old woman and another time to admire a newborn baby. Whatever her flaws, she was brilliant at manipulating the crowd. The royal family met her on the steps of the castle, and my stomach twisted at the memories. The king and queen embraced their daughter as if they'd been apart for years, and the king announced a feast to commemorate her return. A feast. My favorite.

In the Great Hall, King Conall gave no less than five speeches over the span of a dozen courses welcoming his daughter home, promising a prosperous future, and toasting the greatness of Ilano and the addition of Praed to his kingdom. This was the first time he'd mentioned the union of Ilano and Praed, and I studied the room for the popular response. Heads nodded, some looked confused, others angry. If the king hoped to unite the countries, he'd better prepare for a fight. The people of Praed were beaten, but they were proud patriots, and nothing would convince them to call themselves Ilanos.

The celebration lasted into the night, and by the time the princess was ready for bed, I could barely keep my eyes open. The prince made a brief appearance to welcome her back, but I was too exhausted to note the conversation. The only snippet I heard was the prince saying, "What would Jervell want with all those books?"

"What do you mean?" the princess asked, emerging in her nightgown from behind a screen.

"More than once I saw him moving crates of them. You think he's up to something or just being eccentric?"

"I certainly hope he's not developing dementia. What a strange thing to do." The blood drained from my face. The princess received this news with her usual flippancy, but it filled me with dread. Nothing Jervell Kade did was without a malevolent, twisted purpose.

Seconds after the princess dismissed me, I was hurrying down the hallway to the library. I threw open the door and felt emptiness seep into every crevice of my soul. The shelves were bare, stripped of their precious contents. I trailed my fingers along the empty cases, searching for any book left behind and finding none. My footsteps echoed the lonely beat of my heart when I reached the spot where my favorite chair once sat. The little table was shattered against a far wall, the book of Ilano gone forever. I sank to my knees by the window, tears flowing down my hot cheeks. I curled into a ball on the floor, shaking with anger and cursing the cruelness of men.

The moon glowed full, its light beaming through the window and slanting across the stained floor. I watched the movement as the night stretched on until it illuminated the bottom corner of a shelf some feet away. Curious, I crawled toward it, thinking the shape strange. Upon closer inspection, I realized something was stuck underneath, and I pulled free a familiar tome. I pressed the history of Ilano to my chest and wept in relief. I flipped through the pages to make sure none were missing and once again found the sketch of a family tree. For the first time, I took a moment to study the names, tracing down the line until I recognized one: Lord Davian Elejick. A line connected his name to Beja, and their union produced Alyx and Conall. Conall was connected by marriage to Shaeli, below them the names Brannon, Caelyn, and simply 'stillborn child.' Alyx, I remembered, was the son killed in battle, and presumably the father of the unknown third grandchild. His wife was Eyrin, and my pulse quickened as I traced the line of their union to their progeny. My head spun and I nearly fainted when I read the name of their single child, the son I had been so anxious to discover.

Risteard.

CHAPTER 18

In times of stress, the mind can disconnect, leaving a person numb and eerily calm. In other cases, persons in emotional turmoil break and explode in anger. I did not know which route I would take when I learned the truth about Risteard. I squeezed my eyes shut and resisted the urge to throw the book across the room. I imagined my mother's voice telling me I wasn't a child anymore. I just turned sixteen and pitching a tantrum would be unbecoming. The time had come to think and be rational if I hoped to find a way out of this situation. I told myself to take a breath and think rationally.

Risteard left the book here intending I read it instead of admitting the facts himself. At any point I could have stumbled on the family tree. He never gave any indication of his true lineage. The familiarity between him and the royal family was evident enough, but nothing that suggested a blood bond. Maybe he thought I already knew, having left the book for me months ago. It's possible he was waiting for me to say something and was probably shocked I hadn't. The conversation between Risteard and the king made sense now and I understood why the people of Ilano were so eager to follow the king with the knight's support. If I remembered correctly, Risteard's father, the king's brother, was beloved by the people of Ilano. And that great knight was killed in battle because *my* people ignored their cries for help. His motivation for wanting to attack Praed was abundantly clear. I wanted to be angry with him, to pound my fists against his chest and scream in his face, but I found I couldn't blame him, either. I hated King Conall for murdering my father. What made him so different from me?

What troubled me further was wondering what Risteard's game was now. His uncle was on the throne and Risteard was his right hand. What more could he possibly want? And what role was I to play?

When I'd been angry with Risteard before, I would ignore him for days, pout, or be blatantly hostile. We'd have a nasty fight, but in the end come to a reluctant understanding. I was done wasting time. I decided to skip the fight and come directly to the understanding.

Released from the confines of Riverstone, Princess Caelyn no longer required my services as a companion. Once again, my routine became the mundane ritual I had become accustomed to during the winter, and after sending the princess into the world with perfectly coiffed hair, I was headed to the mews. Snow still clung to the highest points in Praed, and the track to the mew was muddy, but the sun rose high over the mountain, bathing the yard in warmth. I closed my eyes to bask in the morning sunshine and breathe in the fresh spring air. In the distance were faint voices, servants busying themselves with a little more eagerness with the change of seasons. Nobles made their way to the stables to saddle their horses for a long overdue ride. I envied their freedom and wished I could blaze a trail through the frosted grass. Before I grew too emotional with longing, I walked to the mews and set myself to task, dodging men mingling in the yard and exercising their eagles. Great wings stretched in the sun, and the giant birds barely missed my head as they flew past, diving and soaring at the command of their masters.

Aquila's mew was empty. Without regard to my chores, I put my rake aside and searched for Risteard in the yard. When I didn't find him there, I wandered beyond the boundaries of the rows of mews toward a stand of trees. On the other side, a rocky outcropping gave way to sheer, plummeting cliffs. The view of Praed from that precipice was breathtaking in every sense of the word.

The ground was thickly carpeted with tiny brown leaves crackling and crunching underfoot as I walked through the trees, my hands gliding over the rough bark as I passed. There was no sense concealing my movements. If Risteard was there, he would hear me regardless, and if not, it didn't matter. The moment I emerged from the shade of the trees, a black shape slammed against my chest, knocking me backwards onto the hard ground. A rock pushed painfully against my spine, surely paralyzing me for life. Well, perhaps not, but the pain was excruciating.

"Are you all right?" a voice called frantically. I opened one eye and felt pain pulsing across the back of my head. I pressed my hand to the knot already forming there and squeezed my eyes shut. The voice muttered angrily, and I caught the word "clumsy."

"It wasn't my fault!" I protested.

"I wasn't blaming you!"

My eyes flew open when I recognized Risteard's voice.

"I'm sorry," he continued. "We were practicing aerial maneuvers and she banked sharply. You came out of the woods at an inopportune time, but it wasn't your fault. It was an accident. At least it better have been." Risteard shot a glare at the large eagle perched close by studying us with its black, shining eyes. He reached down and pulled me to my feet. My back ached and my head throbbed, but otherwise I was unscathed.

"No permanent damage, I trust?"

"No," I confirmed, rubbing my head one last time for good measure. "I was looking for you. There's something we need to discuss."

"Go on."

"First of all, do you know about the library?"

He lowered his head and nodded.

"You know who's responsible?"

"I can guess," he said.

"Well, there's nothing to be done about that." He cocked his head and his brow furrowed.

"You've accepted the loss rather quickly."

"I was devastated," I admitted. "But sitting around crying won't solve anything, will it?"

"No," he smiled.

"He missed one book." I reached into the folds of my frock where I had secured the history of Ilano and drew it forth. Risteard took it reverently, smiling as he ran a finger over the binding.

"Thank Artur it's not lost."

"You left that book for me to find, so I could learn about your people."

"Yes." He remained focused on the object in his hands.

"So, it can be reasonably assumed you intended for me to learn everything. All the secrets it contained."

He met my eyes but didn't respond.

"I learned something very important last night, something that changed everything I thought I knew… about you. About who you really are."

Risteard remained silent.

My vision blurred, and I pursed my lips to keep them from quivering. "Why didn't you tell me?"

"Tell you what?"

"You know."

"I need to hear you say it," he said, "so I know there will be no misunderstanding."

"Why didn't you tell me you were the king's nephew?"

He closed his eyes briefly, as if he were relieved to have the truth revealed.

"I honestly wasn't sure if you'd found out or not. But then you hadn't indicated you had in the form of an angry outburst or a clandestine poisoning."

"No more secrets," I said. "I don't care if I'm behind the rest of the day. We will not leave this place until I know everything."

He nodded and motioned for me to sit on an obliging boulder roughly the size of a horse. He sat across from me on a much smaller stone so that I looked down at him, an interesting perspective. The eagle resumed her perch on his arm and was rewarded with a piece of meat.

"Try a stunt like that again," Risteard muttered to her, "and you'll be the one served up on a platter." The great bird ruffled her feathers, and if she had eyebrows, they would be raised in shock.

"Do you think she understands what you're saying?"

He looked at the bird. "Perhaps not the words, but the tone is clear enough." He turned to me. "Ask your questions."

"Why didn't you tell me who you were?"

"I don't believe familial connections define oneself, do you?"

"No," I said. "But they're important all the same."

"If you knew I was King Conall's nephew, would you have accepted any help from me?"

I lowered my gaze. "No."

"I wanted my actions to speak for themselves, without being tainted by association."

"If you're the king's nephew and cousin to the prince and princess, why would you help me in the first place? Am I not your enemy? My people killed your father, though indirectly."

"I wanted revenge, yes," he said. "But after it was over, I looked around and saw nothing that filled the hole in my soul. I believed in what we were doing, but I wasn't prepared for Conall's ruthlessness. I agreed to him killing the former king to usurp the throne and add Praed to Ilano's fold. But Conall wouldn't stop there. He insisted on removing any threat to his rule, real or imaginary. That night, when he forced us to attack Riverstone, murder innocent people and drag a family from their beds to watch their livelihood burn to the ground, I understood how bloodthirsty he was, and in the following days, I feared he had become unstable."

I listened in silence, studying him as he spoke without meeting my eyes. He looked at me then, his eyes clear as a summer sky. "On his deathbed, my grandfather warned me that Conall had become unpredictable after the injuries he sustained fighting the desert people. He also feared what might happen should he obtain power. I saw the result as we led you into Praed, and I was ashamed to be a part of it." He focused once more on his boots, shuffling them in the dirt while the eagle stretched her wings and yawned.

I reached out and touched her long wings with my fingertips, marveling at their strength and softness.

"What will you do now?" I asked.

"What I failed to do then: stop him." His jaw was set, and his eyes blazed.

"What can I do?"

"I will need the support of the people of Praed. I've seen them. They respect you. They will follow you."

"So, like the king, you will use me to garner the support of the people in your plan to wage war?"

"With your permission."

I inhaled deeply, closing my eyes and blocking out the world so I could think. True, I wanted King Conall off the throne, but I doubted my support would be instrumental in accomplishing that goal, whatever Risteard believed. My head swam and my throat tightened. I was a Lady of Riverstone, yes, but I was still a child, despite my assertions to the contrary. In addition, I was playing a mute.

How could I raise an army when I couldn't even speak? Before I could stop it, a tear trickled its way down my cheek.

"Ask me," he said firmly. "Ask me why I chose you."

"Why?" Another tear joined the first. "Why me?"

"Because even though you're much smaller than I am, even though I'm certain you knew how much stronger I was than you, when I came to take you from your room that night, you fought back. And when a soldier threatened your sister, even with your own hands bound, you came to her defense. I saw a fierce strength in you, and I thought, 'Here is a woman the people will admire and follow.' This past year getting to know you has only solidified that certainty."

"I don't know how to raise an army."

"I'm not asking you to. All you need to do is let the people know you're alive. Caelyn is very clever. She will endear herself to the people. You need to remind them, by your very presence, her family is an enemy of Praed."

"You're a part of her family," I pointed out.

He straightened and regarded me silently. "Now that you know, do you no longer trust me?"

"Who said I did before?"

He narrowed his eyes and the side of his mouth curved upward. He regarded me with an ironic smile, and my cheeks flushed when the silence stretched between us. I pursed my lips, unwilling to concede to the point he was trying to make with his wry expression. His eyebrows rose and he looked at me expectantly, waiting for me to admit that my own actions proved I trusted Risteard. I wouldn't be sitting here if I didn't.

"Fair," I said, rolling my eyes.

My gaze shifted over his head, out over the mountain to the valley stretching beyond. Below, the people of Praed struggled to regain their footing. Many were gone after the conquest. How many more had been lost to the winter? How much longer could they survive under a king whose only concern was himself?

"Tell me about your father." I spoke in the barest whisper carried on the wind, nearly drowned out by the shuffle of leaves and ruffle of feathers, but Risteard's keen hearing picked it up.

"He rarely made a wrong move in his life. He knew when to fight and when to be diplomatic. And even in battle, he was merciful. The people respected him, but what's more, they loved him."

"He doesn't sound real," I said, surveying the landscape. "Can such a perfect man really exist?"

"He was by no means perfect. What made him so respectable was his ability to admit defeat, to change his opinion, and to see things from another's perspective. My grandfather said he should have been Lord Protector."

"An impressive resume. My father was also well regarded, trusted by the king, and many knights emulated his bravery."

"And the people will remember and follow you, his daughter."

"If only they knew what sort of man he was at home." I held Risteard's gaze, my tears drying on my burning cheeks. "He kept a prosperous home, to be sure, and was faithful to my mother--at least I think he was. But as a father, he was disappointing, especially as I grew. He told me once Mother lost a child after I was born, a son. He said if a child had to have been lost, he wished it had been me."

Risteard's eyes darkened and his nostrils flared, reminding me of a horse spooked by a snake.

"Men can often live two lives," I continued. "The life people see, and the one that's real. What sort of man was your father at home?"

His expression softened. "He rarely raised his voice and was always kind to the servants. Mother said he yelled so often in battle and at court that he cherished the peace at home. He adored my mother." Risteard smiled, remembering. "They had been sweethearts since childhood. She mourned his loss for the rest of her life."

I almost placed a comforting hand on his shoulder but thought better of it.

"He taught me to fight, about when to take up the sword and when to use words. How to bring a man to his knees with a single blow, whether to knock him unconscious or end his life. He was patient and strict, but he could be playful. I was a young boy when he died, but I still recall the sound of his laughter."

"I'm sorry," I said, and I meant it, from one human being who had experienced loss to another. I slid from my rocky perch, and he rose, towering above me with that enormous bird on his arm.

"I do not wish for any more children to lose their parents," I said calmly.

"Nor do I."

I nodded and walked back through the trees, striding to the other side with purpose. Though it meant treason, I would dedicate my time to spreading hope to Praed, to show them they were not alone. I still had friends among the people, and I would send word that Laria of Riverstone was alive and fighting.

Deprived of the library for our meeting place, Risteard suggested we use the study attached to his room. He read the doubt on my face.

"Unless you feel your room would be more appropriate?"

"And by 'room' you mean the tiny hole in the wall barely large enough for me to sleep in?"

"It would be confining, for certain, but I'm willing to squeeze in if it pleases you."

In the end, we decided Risteard's study would best suit our needs.

The room was cramped, even before it had been stuffed with furniture. A large desk dominated the farthest wall and barely any light filtered through the sole window. Bookcases crammed with books, scrolls, papers, and ornaments covered two other walls, and a low settee stood just inside the door, though there was no space left to sit on. I stepped closer to examine the titles on the shelves. History, geography, botany, biology, and, surprisingly, collections of folk tales and legends predominated. Jars containing strange specimens and framed plants were interspersed between books and scrolls. I carefully inspected a jar containing the largest beetle I'd ever seen. A colorful sheen radiated across its ebony shell.

"Where did this come from?" I asked.

"My father brought it back from his travels in the southern continent. He collected all of these." He waved a hand over the jars and frames.

I replaced the jar on the shelf and turned toward the ornately carved desk. The top was dark, almost black, but the front was faced with red wood carved to resemble flames projected from the mouths of strange, horned beasts whose tails tapered to the floor and became the legs of the piece. Papers were scattered across the desk's surface with no discernable organization, a map at its center. My eyes swept the room, and I inhaled the distinct odor of old paper, dust, aged wood, ink, and leather. Risteard waited while I took in my surroundings, watching for my reaction.

"For some reason I expected more sharp objects. Swords, daggers, and the like."

"Because I'm a brute?"

"Naturally." I sat in the chair opposite his position on the far side of the desk.

"Well," I said. "Shall we begin?"

He nodded and slid several blank sheets of paper, an inkwell, and quill across the table.

Incredibly, I had not written a letter in over a year, but I trusted my fingers would remember the movements. I dipped the large primary feather in the ink and hovered over my first page, a black spot forming where a drop of ink dripped onto the paper.

"You don't have to if you've changed your mind," Risteard said.

I shook my head. "I'm only trying to decide whom to write first."

For the next several hours, the only sound to intrude on the silent room was the scratch of quill on paper, and the occasional rustle of turning pages.

CHAPTER 19

The snows were a memory in the sweltering summer sunshine illuminating my ginger hair as I stood overlooking the plains, shielding my eyes from the sun's glare. Beside me, the princess surveyed the procession of men exercising horses amid blooms of purple and blue dotting the green landscape. In celebration of Prince Brannon's birthday, the king announced a parade through Praed followed by twenty days of feasts and games, one day to mark each year of the prince's life. The princess in her typical self-centered fashion wished to present herself on the finest mount in the king's stables. She didn't seem impressed with her selection.

"Are these truly the best horses we have?" she asked the stable master.

"My lady," he bowed. "These horses are specially bred to carry a woman and are very well tempered."

"Don't you have something finer boned? These all look fat."

"Full bodied, Your Highness," he said. "Though certainly not as well muscled after the winter."

The princess turned to me and hesitated to speak, then shrugged and pressed on. "Your people know a little about horses, I believe. Would you consider any of those animals worthy enough to carry a princess?"

It was the first time the princess had asked my opinion about anything, and admittedly, I was flattered. I watched the horses gallop and canter, now with a critical rather than envious eye. They moved quite well after a winter respite, though the stable master was correct in pointing out their lack of muscle definition. I saw no signs of lameness nor missteps in any of the dozen or so horses. I indicated to the princess that I required a closer look, and she signaled for the men to bring their mounts forward. They stood in a line, some horses standing quietly while others pawed the ground impatiently. I had some idea of what the princess was searching for--a horse both easy to handle and pretty to look at. I walked down the line and stopped before a golden mare with a kind eye. She was tall and had strong legs but was finer boned than the stocky horses the Ilano women preferred. I turned to the princess and patted the mare's neck, indicating she was my choice for her parade mount.

"A fine choice," the stable master agreed. "Not too young or too old and very even tempered. And a very smooth ride if I do say so."

The princess examined the mare critically, and my heart sank as the time passed before she spoke.

"No." She shook her head and waved the horse away. "Not flashy enough. I want to stand out."

"Forgive me, Your Highness, but is it not the prince's birthday celebration? Shouldn't *he* be the center of attention?"

Oh, no. That was a mistake.

The princess glared at the stable master. "You speak too freely, old man. Take care I don't retire you along with these nags."

The stable master's eyes widened, and his throat bobbed comically.

"Now," she said. "Take me to the stables and show me the other horses."

To his credit, the man said nothing. He nodded and led us to the stable.

While the princess scrutinized the horses filling the stalls of the king's stables, I enjoyed the scent of hay, sweat, and even the musty odor of manure, conjuring memories of long mornings mucking stalls at Riverstone. A few curious faces stared at us from over their stall doors, flicking their ears and sampling our smells with flared nostrils. A hoof stomped the ground, and several nickered for extra rations. The princess passed by them all, apparently not finding whatever she was looking for. I stroked the nose of every horse I passed, relishing in the velvety smoothness. Finally, the princess halted, and stood before a stall with a restless occupant. I could hear the pacing of hooves and snorting before I saw the animal within, it's dark coat glistening with perspiration.

"This one," the princess said. "He's tall and refined and full of spirit."

Too much spirit for the princess, in my opinion. I'd seen her ride--an unpleasant sight.

"A magnificent animal, to be sure," the stable master said, a tremble in his voice. "However, he's quite young and still in training. I fear he may be too unruly for Your Highness."

"Are you implying I couldn't handle this animal?"

"I have no intention of casting aspersions on your abilities, Your Highness. I am simply expressing concern for your safety."

"My father, the king, would never allow a dangerous horse in his stables."

"He doesn't belong to the king, Your Highness."

"If he's in the king's stables, he's the king's horse! I'm certain whomever this animal belongs to would agree."

"Your Highness, I implore you---"

"Have him saddled and brought to the arena for me to try out." Without waiting for an answer, she about-faced and stalked outside.

The stable master and I locked eyes momentarily, and I'm sure my concern reflected his own, but we both knew he had no choice but to comply.

With a resigned sigh, the stable master retrieved a halter and reluctantly approached the stall while the horse inside pounded the walls with its hooves. I hurried after the princess, unsure how to remedy a situation I feared would turn out poorly.

The princess was waiting in the middle of the arena when the stable master led the fidgeting beast outside. It tossed its head and whinnied, and the stable master was barely able to restrain the animal as it threw its well-muscled body from side to side. I recognized the signs of a horse bursting with pent-up energy, and I worried without a proper warmup he would throw the princess.

I waved my hands to convey that she shouldn't ride and pointed to the stable master. I held up one finger, as if to say 'he should go first,' but she waved me away.

"Mind your own business. Go stand over there." She pointed to the fence, and I obeyed. I watched nervously as the stable master held the agitated horse steady for the princess to mount. A groom came forward to assist, and between the two of them, the princess finally settled in the saddle. She took up the reins and waved the two men away, which took some convincing.

"Go on!" the princess insisted. "Give me some room!" The men backed away, their hands raised, ready to grab the reins. The princess squeezed her heels against the horse's sides, and the animal stepped out at a quick pace. The princess bounced awkwardly in the saddle. The horse's shoulders tensed, and his jaw clenched in irritation. She yanked on the reins to bring the horse to a halt, and then urged him on again, stopped him, and then kicked again. I tugged at a loose strand of hair, my heart pounding. What was she trying to prove?

"You see?" the princess called as she passed the stable master. "He's not too much for me to handle." As if to contradict her, the massive horse bolted. The princess clung to his mane and screamed while the groom and stable master called out to pull back on the reins. I ran into the arena as the horse began to buck and toss his head. Time dragged as the horse dropped his head and kicked his back legs hard, sending the princess headfirst into the ground. The crazed animal reared high into the air, and I feared he would smash his hooves down on the princess' back. Without a second thought, I threw myself between the horse and the princess, my arms raised.

The beast's hooves struck the ground inches from my feet. He tossed his head and snorted. I stood firm, making a low shushing noise, and lowered my hands level with his face. The princess scrambled away to safety, but I remained motionless, staring into the horse's frantic eyes. The voices that were once overwhelming now faded into nothing as the horse and I regarded each other, face to face, quietly assessing. After several minutes, I dropped my hands, turned my back to him, and waited. Within moments, I felt a warm breath at my neck and a nuzzle at my shoulder. Without turning around, I reached up and took hold of the reins, and calmly walked the horse out of the arena without a glance at the princess wailing curses at us.

"What happened?" Risteard's familiar stern voice asked when I reached the gate. He took in the scene: the princess shouting at the stable master, rubbing her arm, and the animal dancing in my grip.

"That horse nearly killed me!" the princess cried.

"Why were you riding him in the first place?" Risteard asked.

"Apologies, sir," the stable master said. "I indulged the princess in her search for the perfect mount for the celebratory procession."

"You didn't tell me the horse was wild!"

"You had no business riding him," Risteard said, his tone dangerously low. "He's not ready to carry inexperienced riders."

"He shouldn't be carrying any riders! He's dangerous and should be destroyed!"

I clutched at the horse's muzzle when I saw the veins throb in Risteard's neck. Based on his reaction, this horse must belong to him.

"You wouldn't rely on an infant to teach another infant how to walk, Your Highness, just as you wouldn't trust a beginner rider to take a young horse under saddle."

The princess' eyes flashed angrily.

"He requires a confident rider," Risteard said.

"I challenge you to find a rider other than yourself who can tame him. In the meantime, my father shall hear of this! He'll be glue before the week is out!"

"I'll find a rider who can put him through his paces, and you leave him in peace. Fair?"

"As I said, anyone but you. A horse beholden to one man is worthless."

"I have your word?"

"Fine." The princess rolled her eyes.

"Her," he said, pointing directly at me. The princess' eyes widened, and she asked Risteard to repeat himself, certain she heard incorrectly.

"If you have no objections," he said to me. I blinked several times, aware the princess was staring at me in shock. Mutely, I nodded, and Risteard led the horse to the center of the arena.

"If you give him a firm hand and gentle leg, he'll respond well," Risteard whispered. There may have been more words, but I heard none of them. My full attention was on the dark bay horse pawing the ground impatiently. I ran my hand up his muzzle to his forehead and rubbed gentle circles between his eyes, then blew softly in his nose. The pawing ceased, and his ears pricked forward while his nostrils flared. My hands trailed down his neck and took up the reins, and for a moment I worried he was too tall for me, but my foot reached the stirrup, and I bounced up into the saddle. Risteard waited as I settled in, getting the feel of the animal beneath me. When I was ready, I gave Risteard a slight nod, and he let go of the reins and stepped away.

With a slight squeeze of my calves, the horse stepped out briskly, and we circled the arena at an easy walk. Months had passed since I'd been on the back of a horse, and longer still since I'd enjoyed a decent ride. I relished this moment, knowing at any time the princess could decide I would no longer be indulged.

With that in mind, I urged the horse into a trot, and then a floating canter so lovely I felt I was perched on a cloud drifting across the sky. I pulled the horse to a halt and patted his neck when he complied, feeling our time would soon be over. One more time around, I decided, and I gave a little heel. My body moved with the rise and fall of the mighty hooves, and the world became a blur, the shapes of the people watching fading into an echo of humanity, leaving only the two of us as we flew around the arena. As we came around the last corner, there stood the princess, the stable master, the groom, and Risteard near the arena entrance. With a secretive smile, Risteard threw open the gate, and without a second thought I kicked the horse into a gallop, and we raced through, leaving their stunned faces behind.

The pounding of hooves and the whistle of the wind were the only sounds as we flew across the prairie studded with wildflowers. My hair blew freely as I leaned over the neck of the beast, tears streaming down my face as the wind whipped by. The freedom I experienced was the closest I'd felt to home since the last time I rode Amore. The horse's neck soon began to froth and his breathing grew harsh. Reluctantly, I pulled back on the reins and slowed him to a stop. As he caught his breath, I stroked and patted his damp neck and praised him for his obedience. I turned in the saddle and looked back toward the castle, then at what lay ahead. If we kept riding, we could be miles away before a proper search party was launched. But then no one would be there to look after Ula, and Risteard was depending on my help to remove King Conall from power, a goal I also wished to see realized. Risteard had given me a chance to run. Was this a test of my loyalty? Or was he sincerely giving me the choice to leave or stay?

Based on the princess' expression, she hadn't expected to see me again. Risteard might not have either, but his face was blank. We strolled into the arena, and I dismounted before handing the reins to the groom.

"Give him an extra ration of oats after his rub down," Risteard ordered. The groom bowed and flashed me a smile indicating his admiration of my riding ability. My own face beamed with a grin no stern look from Princess Caelyn could vanquish.

"That was a foolish stunt you pulled," the princess said, glaring at me and enunciating every word carefully so I wouldn't miss her full meaning. "That's the last time you're allowed to ride unattended. I'll warn you this once, but next time, I'll have you flogged." She marched away, her nose in the air and a slight limp on her left side.

"I fear my actions have caused you trouble," Risteard whispered.

"It was worth it," I replied. "Thank you." I followed the princess back to the castle and made no attempt to hide my pleasure.

Two mornings later, I finished styling Princess Caelyn's hair, and before she dismissed me, she grabbed my arm to get my attention.

"I told the king about what happened in the arena the other day," she said ominously. My color drained and my palms moistened. "He wasn't pleased. He ordered that horse destroyed, and I was informed he was dispatched last night." My jaw dropped and tears blurred my vision. She studied me quietly for a minute, then released my arm. "Don't think you can make a fool of me and get away with it." She turned away so I could not read her lips. "Risteard will learn this lesson, too, if he knows what's good for him."

CHAPTER 20

Prince Brannon's birthday celebration drew nearer, and with it grew the number of tasks to complete so that Princess Caelyn was suitably resplendent for the occasion. I visited Ula in the seamstress' workroom many times to arrange a proper wardrobe, and though I welcomed the opportunity to see my sister, the princess' demands left me exhausted. The old woman who presided over the ladies no longer bothered to acknowledge me and allowed me to deliver directions straight to Ula.

Since her birthday, Ula had grown in height and beauty, which was masked by the garb of a lowly seamstress: plain dress, apron, and a cap that kept her midnight black hair tucked neatly away. Her pale skin remained flawless, whereas mine at that age was pocked with freckles and red spots. On one of my many visits, I complimented her burgeoning figure.

"I might say the same to you, Laria. You're taller."

"Perhaps," I said. "But I believe you will develop a womanly figure before I do." Ula blushed fiercely and I laughed, both of us secretly acknowledging my observation was all too true.

My heart ached for the loss of the magnificent animal that carried me over the valley almost a week ago. I hadn't spoken to Risteard since the princess revealed what she'd done. I couldn't begin to imagine how he was feeling, and I was at a loss how to comfort him. Our friendship was developing slowly, and I didn't yet feel close enough to offer condolences. Even if I wanted to, the castle was in such a frenzy with the approaching celebration that it was madness to think we would have an opportunity to speak alone.

Dignitaries from Ilano began descending upon Praed Castle a few days before the parade through the city that would begin the prince's birthday festivities. New faces swirled around me as I rushed to complete my duties, some staring as I passed and others avoiding all contact. The prince reveled in the attention and bestowed favors on all his attendants, gave flowery speeches at dinner, and luxuriated in the gifts and pampering. I shuddered to think how dreadful it would be when it was Princess Caelyn's turn to celebrate.

On the morning of the parade, there were so many people gathered to participate I could barely breathe. Ilano nobles crowded every hallway, and servants bustled about frantically in service of their masters. More than once I was shoved aside, and my toes were crushed by a tempestuous looking individual burdened with the weight of heavy ornamental armor, probably destined for a noble who had never seen battle. With a slight limp, I entered the princess' rooms to find the lady in a whirlwind frenzy, ribbons and pieces of wardrobe strewn about the room, a poor maid picking up the items and making no progress in tidying up. The princess was half dressed, her hair hanging loosely, her face flushed. When she saw me, she threw her hands in the air and demanded to know where I'd been. In response, I held out the new riding pelisse she had commissioned for the occasion. She snatched it from my hands and tossed it onto the bed.

"That's well and good, but completely useless if I haven't a gown to wear under it!" I cocked my head in confusion. She chose her outfit for this morning days ago. I glanced around the room and found the piece--an ivory gown with flowing bell sleeves and boldly jeweled neckline. I held it out and looked at the princess questioningly.

"I've changed my mind!" she declared, chin in the air. "Besides, I understand Meena will be wearing the same color, and it would be unfair to have her compared to my beauty." In other words, the princess wanted no attention drawn from herself. An idea struck me, and I raised a finger indicating the princess should wait a minute, then hurried from the room.

Ula had been working on a gown of her own design, though she wouldn't say who it was for. When I explained my predicament and that I hoped she would allow the princess to have it, Ula crossed her arms indignantly.

"It's not for her," she insisted.

"Whether it is or not, she's the princess. Everything in this castle belongs to her if she desires it. Please, Ula. If she doesn't find anything to meet her expectations, she will take her anger out on me. Do this for me if not for her?"

"It isn't finished," she said, though I could tell I was winning her over. "There are no sleeves yet."

"She has a pelisse to wear over it," I affirmed. "She won't be disgraced."

"Very well," Ula said as she removed the dress from its form. "Though it will pain me to imagine it on her." I received it gratefully, admiring the craftsmanship, wondering aloud who it was originally intended for.

"It was for you." She stared at the dress. "I know it's too late for your birthday, but I wasn't able to finish in time."

"Oh." I ran my fingers over the soft fabric. "It's very beautiful, but I never would have an occasion to wear it. It's more suited to royalty. I'm certain the princess will be pleased." Ula nodded, and I left before my guilt could overwhelm me.

The princess was sitting before her vanity tapping her toe impatiently when I presented her with the stunning blue gown. The bodice was form-fitting and adorned with expertly embroidered silver leaves bordering the neckline and fell gracefully down to the waist where the gown billowed out in flowing layers of sheer fabric in several shades of blue, creating the illusion of flowing water. The princess said nothing as she inspected the dress, which I knew was a good sign. Her hand trailed down its length, her fingers twirling in the fabric.

Finally, she stepped back and haughtily complained. "There are no sleeves. The king would be most displeased to have my body on display like a common…" She waved her hands in frustration. "Well, it won't do in any case." I reached behind me and held up the pelisse, folding over one side of the dress to indicate how her arms would be covered.

"I suppose it will have to do." She motioned me to dress her in the gown made for a servant.

The princess attracted the attention she so craved in Ula's dress, and even Prince Brannon complimented her.

"Very bold, sister," he said, indicating the low neckline. The dress clearly was tailored for a less endowed woman. "Not your usual style, but it suits you. You should reveal this side of you more often."

The princess pushed him away.

"Go enjoy your parade," she snapped.

The last time I was forced to ride through Praed behind the new royal family, I felt self-conscious and embarrassed. There were far more people today. Though I expected no notice, I vowed to ride proudly so the people of Praed could see me, perhaps recognize me, and know I wasn't beaten. Mounted on caparisoned horses, we rode from the castle with banners flying, knights glittering in the sun, and smiling faces cheering the name of Prince Brannon. Wagons followed behind to bestow gifts of drink and food on the populace. Ladies-in-waiting and servants followed, and after us came the grooms and falconers.

Crowds lined the main road. Children sat atop their parents' shoulders waving ribbons, men raised goblets, and women threw flowers. Some people were obviously pretending to be excited while others appeared genuinely happy. I wondered if the consumption of alcohol played a part.

As we passed by the throngs, I made eye contact with as many as possible. It was difficult. As a servant, I was below consideration, but I had the advantage of a very distinct hair color. Even if I couldn't name each person I saw, many clearly knew me, and I rode on ripples of whispers and finger pointing. The procession paused to allow the prince to bestow his blessing on a deserving peasant--most likely a pretty woman. An old woman separated herself from the crowd and approached me, her hand outstretched. I reached down and clasped her hand in mine, the fingers thin and skin fragile yet warm. She smiled, her face thick with lines, and I was ashamed I didn't know her because she certainly knew me.

"I attended many parties at Riverstone," she said. "I loved to watch your mother dance. She was so graceful. I thought she might have done for my son once, but Maccus suited her better." At the mention of my father, I felt heat rise in my cheeks, and I bit the inside of my lip to maintain my composure. "Those were good days." Her head bobbed slightly, and her gray-blue eyes misted.

I squeezed her trembling hand. Beside me, ladies rode by gossiping loudly. When they passed, I leaned close.

"Those days shall return," I promised, holding her gaze. Her eyes widened, confusion flickering across her dull brown eyes. I could see fear and pain in the depths of her aged face. I squeezed her hand tighter, smiled conspiratorially, and let go before we were seen. She smiled and nodded, understanding. The line in front of me moved, and I watched the old woman fade into the distance.

That night would be the first of many to feature entertainers from Ilano to please the prince. Players enacted favorite scenes from Ilano literature while attendees dined on lavish dishes and decadent desserts. Cider flowed freely, turning the cheerful noise into a roar of raucous laughter. The play was enjoyable and well acted, but I could barely watch since I was busy making sure the princess kept Ula's dress clean.

After dinner, the king invited everyone outside to the inner courtyard where musicians and dancing awaited. The castle was well decorated and the entertainment delightful, but I couldn't imagine another nineteen days of the same.

The sun had set, but the evening was still warm, and the inner courtyard glowed with torches around the perimeter. Footmen carried candelabras in one hand and drink trays in the other. The fragrance of flowers was overshadowed by stifling perfumes and powdered bodies. The musicians were gathered on a raised platform, and the king signaled them to begin. The first notes were lively, and clearly a popular Ilano dance as couples eagerly twirled and stepped to the fast tempo. Prince Brannon danced among them, but the princess showed no inclination, choosing instead to mingle with the guests and make polite conversation. Despite the swirl of activity, I was dreadfully bored. Mother hosted grand events at Riverstone and expected me to participate, but I much preferred to hide in the library or sneak away on Amore. The crowds made me nervous and I was terrible at small talk, and I would inevitably end up embarrassing Mother by telling gruesome stories and spilling ill-gotten kumis on my dress in my enthusiasm. It made her angry when I disappeared from her parties, but honestly, I think my attendance bothered her more.

My goal for this party was to keep a close watch on the princess yet remain inconspicuous. At the moment, she was debating with a noble lord from Ilano about which apple was best for summer cider, a discussion I expected to last for some time. I sought a dark corner where I could observe her in peace and found a convenient hedge, tucking myself beneath the branches to watch. Voices drew near and I shuffled further into the darkness. They were close now, and I saw a pair of huddled figures. I detected one male and one female voice, but beyond this I couldn't understand their words until they were almost in front of me.

"We mustn't," I heard the female voice say. "He'll notice I'm gone."

"Just one kiss, please!" the male voice insisted.

"Only one, and then I must go." What followed was a series of wet sounds and groans. I peeked between the branches and saw them embrace, one of the man's hands against the woman's back and the other down the front of her dress. I couldn't bear another second. I rattled the branches around me to alert them they were not alone, but they were too absorbed to notice. I burst out of the hedge, sending branches and leaves flying at the couple. My frock snagged, sending me face-first in the dirt at the man's feet. Startled, he pulled away and held the woman at arm's length as if they had only just been discussing the weather and not engaged in some reproachful activity.

The man sighed in relief. "Oh. It's only a servant."

"I know that girl," the woman said, squinting in the low light. "She's an attendant to Princess Caelyn!"

I recognized the woman now. She had attended several sittings with Queen Shaeli. Elegant, very rich, and very married. Her husband, however, was not the young man before me, staring darkly.

"You better keep your mouth shut about this!" he hissed.

"Don't worry," the woman placed a restraining hand on his arm. "She's completely deaf and speaks not a word."

"But she has eyes, and they see well enough. If she were as blind as the queen it wouldn't matter, but even a deaf girl can find ways to communicate." He stepped close, hovering menacingly. I stood my ground and stared up at him blankly. His hand shot out, grabbed me around the neck, and pulled me inches from his face.

"You saw nothing," he said. The sweet smell of cider wafted over me, and my knees trembled. "Tell no one, especially not Her Highness." The hand around my neck squeezed incrementally with each word, his fingers digging painfully into my skin. Vaguely, I heard the woman beg him to let me go, then her footsteps hurrying away accompanied by mutterings. Behind me, there was a metallic scrape of steel, and a blade appeared, its edge pressed against the man's throat.

"I don't believe Prince Brannon would appreciate this behavior at his birthday celebration, Lord Worum." I choked on a cry when I recognized Risteard's voice. The man paled and instantly pushed me away, propelling me into the hedge.

"A small matter," Lord Worum mumbled as he looked around, no doubt wondering where his companion had gone. "Just a servant needing to be reminded of her place. Nothing to worry the prince over."

"Undoubtedly," Risteard said coldly, sheathing his sword in its scabbard.

Lord Worum wiped his hands down his breeches. "I'll just return to the festivities," he said, gesturing toward the crowd.

Once he was gone, I extricated myself from clinging branches and wiped leaves and dirt from my frock. I touched the tender skin of my neck and repressed fear overcame me. I sank to my knees and wrapped my arms around my shaking shoulders. Risteard remained quiet and made no move to comfort me. He must be angry with me, blaming me for the death of his horse.

"I'm so sorry," I whispered.

"For what?" His voice was distant and devoid of emotion.

"It was my fault."

"Were you being reckless again? I told you to be careful. Lord Worum is not a man to be trifled with."

"No!" I cried. I looked up at him, and he was staring, his face blank but his eyes ablaze. "I'm sorry the princess killed that poor horse. It was my fault."

A flicker of remorse and pain crossed his stony countenance. He stepped forward and knelt so we could speak face to face.

"It wasn't your fault," he said. "It was mine."

"Why haven't you spoken to me since?"

"I've been busy."

I turned away, feeling foolish.

"And," he continued. "I thought you would be angry with me."

"Why?"

"I placed you in a difficult position and the princess punished us both for it. I know what she did to me, I couldn't imagine how she exacted her revenge on you. I was afraid of having your temper unleashed upon me in retribution."

"Can't imagine why you'd think that." I wiped a hand across my face to hide. "I believe she felt the death of that poor animal punishment enough."

"I'm relieved." He stood and offered me a hand. I took it and rose to my feet.

"Are you going to tell me what that was about?" He tipped his head in Lord Worum's direction.

"I caught him in an indelicate position with a lady." I blushed and my gaze fell to my boots. "They were making a disgusting scene and I couldn't bear it! I didn't know how to make it stop."

"I see."

Risteard said no more, and I tentatively raised my eyes to see him regarding me silently. I blinked, once, twice, before realizing there was something different about him.

"You shaved your beard!" Thankfully no one was close enough to hear my outburst.

"How kind of you to notice." The corner of his mouth quirked in a half-smile.

"What made you decide to do that?"

"It's been hot."

"Really? Not because someone said it made you look old?"

"No."

He was not very convincing, and I grinned knowingly.

"It doesn't look bad." It was the closest to a compliment I'd ever genuinely given him.

He cleared his throat and changed the subject. "You should be wary of dark corners during these celebrations. That is, if you find public displays of affection so abhorrent."

"There is a difference between affection and what I saw here--all that groping and moaning and... wetness." I shuddered.

"Well," Risteard shifted and adjusted his belt. "I better return to the prince. His Majesty has ordered that I keep the boy safe. Mostly from himself."

"Good luck!"

"Yes." He hesitated and I waited, my eyebrows raised expectantly. "Goodnight." He turned abruptly and left me confused in the shadows.

Two more days of frivolity left me feeling drained of energy. I couldn't believe the guests were able to function so well after celebrating long into the evenings. On the fifth night, the stress was beginning to show in the dark circles weighing down their eyes, and two nights later the princess was barely able to function after sleeping well into the late morning. She shuffled to her mirror, her eyes half closed. I could barely keep from yawning myself.

"My brother is mad if he thinks we can continue this way for a fortnight," she mumbled.

Yet every night the castle came alive with music and the guests summoned their merry moods for more food, drink, and dancing. I watched with little interest, keeping vigilant and swaying with fatigue. With each passing night, the princess retired earlier and earlier for which I was thankful.

On the tenth night, while nobles danced and laughed, I stood apart, resting my eyes. I felt a presence draw close and nudge my shoulder. My eyes flew open to see Risteard beside me, staring ahead.

"Come to my study tonight after the princess retires. I have something for you."

"That may be quite late," I said. "What is it?"

"I'll wait." He walked away before we were noticed.

For the rest of the evening, my mind was ablaze wondering what Risteard could mean, and I glared resentfully at the princess while she socialized well past midnight. When she could barely stand, I steered her toward the castle, fighting against her when she tried to rejoin the party. She gave up by the time we made it to her room. She fell into bed with an exhausted sigh and was asleep before I finished undressing her. I set off for Risteard's study in the gloomiest hour of the night, when the moon began to wane, yet the darkness had not relinquished its hold. I rushed, worried he'd given up on me. I saw the barest light shining from beneath the door, and I knocked softly before entering. Risteard stood and beckoned me inside.

"Sorry I'm so late," I whispered and carefully closed the door. I came forward, and from across the desk Risteard handed me a folded piece of paper. My heart pounded as I took it, the paper rustling in my quivering hand. A name was written elegantly across the top, and a shuddering breath escaped my lips to see Laria Audrey spelled out in ink after so long. I turned the letter over and broke the wax seal.

Miss Laria Audrey, formerly of Riverstone,

My dear girl, it was with great shock and pleasure that I received your letter, and I confess I had no idea how to respond. The last year has been very trying for us, as I'm certain I need not tell you. I was terribly sorry to hear of your father's death and your subsequent capture, and beyond relieved to hear you survived. Many to whom I passed on the news were equally as delighted and send their blessings to your mother.

Now to the purpose--your call for support should the need arise. My first instinct was to laugh at such nonsense, I'm sorry to say. King Conall has made such a strong showing, and circumstances being what they are, I cannot imagine how a young woman could hope to organize a revolution. My intention was to write and convince you to abandon such a goal and keep safe. Upon further consideration, and with much debate among friends, I thought to myself, we can sit here and wish for change, but none will come without action. You, brave Laria, I see as the inspiration we need to initiate the change we so desire.

We gave your father our full and unwavering support, and in return we were rewarded with lands and titles. What's more, we garnered respect, from others and ourselves, and with it the ability to hold our heads high. And now that Maccus' daughter has taken up the reins, who are we to doubt her?

When the time comes, we shall heed your call.

Lord and Lady Grissen, et al. of Alluvale

The letter dropped from my hands, and my jaw fell. I had written his Lordship Grissen on a whim, never dreaming he would reply. He and my father had been close, it's true, but he was a conservative man, a true diplomat. Though he followed my father into battle on numerous occasions, if an alternative existed, he was always the first to suggest it. Plus, he was notoriously misogynistic, and the idea of his supporting a woman whose major goal wasn't making a delicious meat pie was the biggest, and most welcome, surprise.

"What is it?" Risteard asked

I put my hands on the desk and beamed a satisfied smile. "The beginning of our army."

More letters poured in over the next several days, from the obscure nobleman I met once to the closest family servants, all pledging their support should the time come to rise. I made no promises in my letters that I would be successful, and truthfully I wasn't holding my breath that this scheme would work, but to know so many people stood behind me and my family was worth the effort.

With renewed energy, I faced the remaining seven days of Prince Brannon's birthday celebration without resentment and irritation. In the small hours of the night, Risteard and I would meet and catalogue the families from Praed whom I had enlisted with those of Ilano certain to follow Risteard. At first glance, it seemed an impressive list, but Risteard maintained that we err on the side of caution and gather as many supporters as possible before considering an uprising.

"Politics is such a tricky business," I noted.

"True, but I believe what we're doing might be considered the opposite. Some might call it treason."

"Oh, I don't know. Intrigue, secrets, manipulation, deception...seems like a typical monarchy to me." He laughed--an unfamiliar, yet not unpleasant sound-- and I returned to the list of families and potential supporters, checking off those I had written to and deciding whom to write next.

"Remember what you saw in the Trophy Room?" Risteard asked suddenly.

I laughed. "How could I forget?"

Risteard remained focused on the sheets in front of him. "And the first night of celebrations, in the hedgerows, you said you found what you'd witnessed disgusting?"

"Yes," I said quietly, setting my pen aside.

"It's not always like that."

I shifted uncomfortably. "Oh. You mean it's less moist and noisy and disgusting?" He smiled and met my eye.

"It's like, when you're angry and your face is twisted and ugly---"

"We're speaking hypothetically, right?"

"Of course! Anyway, what you saw then, that was the dark side. That's only lust and satisfying needs. It's not always like that for everyone. It can be beautiful if you're in love."

"Are you speaking hypothetically or...from experience?"

"You mean have I ever been in love? No. I've never been in love. But my mother was in love."

"And you saw her..."

"No! Never. But she and my father embraced, held hands, kissed sweetly…so, I just don't want you to allow those experiences to taint your perception."

"My father was infatuated with my mother, but we never saw any softness between them. In the elite circles of Praed, marriages are arranged. I'm not casting doubt on your claims, but from what I've seen, most relationships are devoid of feeling, whether they're conducted in the drawing room or in the shadows."

"You may find someone who'll change your mind."

"You mean fall in love?"

"Yes. Perhaps. I understand it happens from time to time."

"Not to me. If love means letting someone stick their tongue down your throat, then I'll pass. I have no desire to do any of that." Risteard sighed and shrugged his shoulders, then stretched his arms back, eliciting a creaking noise from his tightened muscles and joints.

"It's late," he said and stood.

I nodded, and without meeting his eye, left the room.

I expected to fall asleep the second my head hit the pillow, but I lay awake wondering what Risteard meant by all the talk about love and kissing. Was he simply preparing me for growing up or did he know something? My worst thought was the princess was planning a match for me, though in this life I was a mere servant and not an eligible maiden from Riverstone. Perhaps her intentions were more nefarious. Maybe I was to be used as the women in the Trophy Room, passed around to whomever she chose. I squeezed my eyes and willed myself to abandon these thoughts. I turned to the day ahead, how I might style the princess' hair, whom I would write to next, and the dress Ula made for me but worn by the princess before being tossed in a heap, to rough hands groping my body…

Growling in frustration, I tossed and turned, burying my face in the pillow. As sleep gradually overtook me, I knew the dreams that awaited would tarnish the day to come and convince me no man was worth the trouble of nightmares.

CHAPTER 21

With only two more nights of celebrations to go, I wasn't sure whether I or the princess was more relieved. As the days wore on, she became more irritated that the castle had been reduced to a drunken stupor, leaving all rationality at the bottom of a glass. True, the princess cared little about the politics of running a country, but when the actions of those around her interfered with her personal plans, her patience evaporated. Like me, she had an ulterior agenda, the details of which had yet to be revealed. And with the prince indisposed, she could only wait to resume their dealings. Even Queen Shaeli's sittings were postponed since most of her followers couldn't muster the strength to attend. The princess considered this the epitome of rudeness.

During the evening entertainment, Princess Caelyn moved through the crowd with a permanent scowl that kept everyone at a distance. I gave her space as well, only stepping forward to fill her glass and remove unwanted dishes. More than once she snapped at me for neglecting to notice a hair out of place, and even blamed me for a gentleman stepping on the train of her dress. In my irritation, I would have ripped the extra length off had I not feared this would lead to my death.

She walked confidently through the throngs, nodding at some while ignoring others, avoiding the revelers and declining offers to dance. When the way parted before us, there stood the last man I ever wished to see. Jervell Kade.

He bowed, greeting us in his high, raspy voice. "Your Highness."

The princess smiled for the first time that night. "Your Lordship Kade. I didn't expect to see you so soon after your last visit."

"Prince Brannon's birthday celebration was not to be missed, Your Highness. I'm only sorry I was not able to attend the full range of festivities."

"Don't be." The princess rolled her eyes. Jervell held out his arm, and the princess took it readily. The pair walked through the crowd, speaking low, their heads inches apart. I followed closely but was unable to hear. They stopped and watched the dancers, Prince Brannon among them, gliding and spinning to the upbeat music.

"I wonder that you do not dance, Princess Caelyn," Jervell said.

"You know I don't care for dancing--especially this sort--with these people." She wrinkled her nose and swept a disdainful glance over the crowd.

"You do a great disservice denying them the pleasure of seeing you move so gracefully."

"Stop trying to flatter me, Jervell." Though her tone suggested annoyance, I knew she was anything but by her demure smile and the gleam in her eye.

"I see you still have your little shadow," he said darkly.

My chest tightened and I held my breath. I bit the inside of my lip and dug my nails into my palms to drown out his voice, willing myself to show no sign I understood. I could feel him staring at me, but I resisted giving in to the urge to shift away.

"Yes. She has her uses," the princess said.

"Why not allow her to dance? This is a celebration, is it not?"

She looked at him as if he had lost his mind.

"She's not here to enjoy herself, she's here to serve me!"

And for once I was glad of it.

"Oh, Caelyn, how can you be so cruel?" His bottom lip thrust forward in a pout. "The poor creature has so little joy in her life, I'm sure. This one night, for the prince's birthday, can she not partake in the celebration?"

"I don't know why it matters to you. No one will want to dance with her anyway."

"I'm sure we can find someone." Jervell searched the crowd.

She eyed him suspiciously. "What is your game, Jervell? Why do you insist on singling her out?"

"Amusement, dear Caelyn. You have yours, and I have mine."

I trembled while they spoke, and I could barely pretend I didn't understand a word of their discussion. I inched away, slowly, hoping they wouldn't notice, wanting to disappear into the thick mass of people.

A hand seized my arm and pulled. Jervell Kade's voice called, "Prince Brannon! Happiest of birthdays to you, Your Highness!" A lazy smile stretched across the prince's mouth, then he waved and swaggered toward us.

"Lord Kade! So glad you could join us at last!" Prince Brannon said. He noticed Jervell holding on to me and looked curiously at the man. "Kade? Has the little waif upset you?"

"Your sister does not feel she should have her share in the amusements."

The prince threw back his head and laughed.

"Her share? She's a servant!"

"That's what I told him!" Princess Caelyn said.

"I think it would be a sign of Your Highness' benevolence to dance with a poor servant, especially one with such a distinguished heritage."

"And such a distinct appearance. I'll be a laughingstock." The prince sneered.

"They may laugh at *her*, but never at Your Highness. Don't you think it would be amusing?"

The prince didn't look convinced. His lip curled as his eyes studied the outline of my body, and my cheeks burned when he lingered on my chest. He snorted and shook his head in disapproval.

"Have you noticed," Jervell continued, his eyes roaming over my person. "How much taller she's become? And I do believe she's developed a flare to her hips. It would please me to watch her dance. Indulge an old man, Prince Brannon? For I am too infirm to partake in the pleasure myself."

Hot bile rose in my throat. I swallowed several times, but I couldn't overcome the waves of nausea.

"If you insist, old man," the prince relented. He grabbed my hand and pulled me to the set of dancers forming a line in the center of the courtyard. Jervell chuckled and Princess Caelyn sighed in exasperation as I was dragged forward. I tried to resist, pulling against the prince and planting my feet.

"Stop!" he growled and crushed my hand. "I don't like it either. I find this whole business repulsive, but he wouldn't have ceased his inane pleading and I cannot abide hearing the old man beg. Now come along!"

He pulled me so roughly I nearly toppled to the ground, but I kept my feet and reluctantly followed. I tugged on his sleeve, and he glanced back. I shook my head and gestured toward the musicians, trying to convey that I didn't know the dance, but he kept going, telling me, "Just follow my lead and try not to make me look a fool."

Whispers circulated in the hush that fell when we joined the set. The prince waved over a footman, and he drank a proffered goblet of cider in one swallow. I tried not to take offense at the prince's need to be intoxicated to suffer through this dance. Honestly, I felt the same, and wished I could summon a beverage, too.

The music started, and I did my best to follow the prince's movements. I trained my eyes on his feet, resulting in my colliding into his chest more than once. His groans of displeasure turned into irritated growls when I switched to concentrating on his face and stepped on his toes. Thankfully, the couples around us took pity on me and helped guide me through the steps. The prince, to my relief, was so embarrassed he barely acknowledged my presence, and touched me only minimally, as if excessive contact might turn him into a toad. I was completely satisfied with this arrangement because I wanted nothing to do with him either.

"Brannon!" a man called out, and the prince acknowledged one of his companions dancing close by. "Any chance I could have a turn with the little ginger girl? If you don't have plans for her after this, of course." He smiled wickedly.

Confirming our mutual disgust, the prince said, "No! You may have her for the next dance, and all the ones after if you wish."

I didn't wish, but it made no difference as I was passed from one of Prince Brannon's cronies to another, each becoming progressively more obnoxious. Their sweaty hands drenched my frock as they pressed them to my back, and I had to duck away to keep those hands from roving. Body odor and alcohol blended in my nose, and the stench of meat and cheese blew hot on my face, creating an aroma that turned my stomach. A particularly exuberant man I recognized as a knight had me effectively trapped, his grip tight at my waist and his other hand holding mine while he twirled me in time to the music. His complexion was ruddy, his eyes glazed, and a lazy smile spread across his features.

"You're pretty," he whispered in a slur. "For a servant, that is. More so if you covered the hair. Your face isn't bad, though." The hairs on my neck prickled as he leaned closer. His brow glistened with sweat, and his tongue lolled out to moisten his lips. If there was ever a time I wanted to be rescued, it was now.

As if summoned by unspeak, a steady hand took mine and smoothly extricated me from the looming knight. I watched the man disappear behind the twirling couples, craning my neck to see if he was coming after me. I was led down the line of dancers, becoming one with the music as the set progressed, until I faced Risteard. I blinked in surprise, but I clamped my mouth shut, aware I couldn't speak without attracting attention. I twirled, guided by Risteard's sure movements, his quick reflexes catching me when I stumbled. The final notes receded, and the people clapped appreciatively for the musicians and their partners. I glanced over my shoulder as Risteard escorted me away from the dancers, but I could not see the other knight.

"Won't he be angry?"

"In a few hours, he won't remember his own name," Risteard said.

"Thank you," I breathed. "He was awful."

"What were you doing out there?"

"It wasn't by choice. Jervell Kade made the prince dance with me, and it went downhill from there."

"I see."

"Did you know he was here?"

"No. The king mentioned Jervell would try and attend but made no promises."

"I don't like him. He never does anything without some hidden agenda."

"I agree," Risteard said, studying my face. "It appears he has some plan for you."

I shuddered. "He seems intent on making me miserable. Do you think he suspects I'm up to no good?"

"He's very astute, but you were plotting nothing when he was last here, and he was cruel to you then."

"That's true. I don't understand. Why does he torment me, Risteard?"

He blinked, looked away, and said nothing for several seconds. "I don't know. But I won't let him hurt you. I promise." The earnestness in his voice unexpectedly stirred an instinct to comfort him. An odd reaction considering it wasn't *him* who was just manhandled.

"He's never acted violently," I said. It was the same tone I used to calm a fidgeting horse. "He just tries to embarrass me and make me uncomfortable."

"Still," Risteard met my eye. "I wouldn't discount the possibility."

"I'll be careful," I promised.

I left him and rejoined the princess, who was in a much better mood with the return of Jervell, her confidant. The pair remained close together for the rest of the night and into the early morning hours until the princess retired, the dawn poised to climb over the horizon.

The next morning, I expected the princess to sleep late, but she was already at her vanity when I entered her room.

"It's about time," she said while I prepared her bath. "Today is the final day of the prince's celebrations, and the Lord Protector wants a tour of Praed now the snow has melted. Lay out my riding habit and tell the stable master to ready the horses." I held up my hands and started extending fingers as if counting. "It shall be a small party," she said, grasping my meaning. "The prince, myself, the Lord Protector, and a few attendants."

Once the princess was settled in the steaming rosewater, I reported to the kitchens and then made my way to Risteard's study. I knocked, but there was no answer. I opened the door a crack and peered inside, but the room was empty. I hurried inside and scrawled a quick note informing him of the princess' plan and asking if he might be available to accompany us, then found the nearest footman and mimed the note was from the king by imitating a crown on my head. By the look on his face and the haste at which he left, I was sure he understood.

The princess was emerging from the water when I returned from the stables, and her breakfast was served shortly thereafter. I fretted while she ate wondering if Risteard would receive my message in time, if at all. I was so absorbed in my worries I jumped when the door was thrown open against the wall. Thankfully, the princess didn't notice as her brother sauntered inside and perched himself on the edge of the nightstand.

"Glad to see you were able to rouse yourself for our outing," the princess said.

"Barely." He yawned, illustrating his point. "Remind me again the purpose of this plan?"

"Jervell wishes to see Praed."

"And you wish to see Jervell away from prying eyes."

She scowled. "You've been too absorbed in yourself lately, brother. You've lost sight of our goals. Jervell has not."

"I haven't!" the prince insisted. "But you can't deny me a little fun."

"A little?" she yelled as she spun around to face him. "Twenty days of excessive drinking, overeating, musicians, dancing, and debauchery is a *little* fun in your estimation?"

"Twenty-one days would be excessive. Twenty is a perfectly respectable amount of days to celebrate a crowned prince, I feel."

"You would." The princess turned back to the mirror and allowed me to secure her hair so no strands would blow free during the ride across Praed.

"Your birthday will be upon us soon, sister. How do you wish us to celebrate when the time comes?"

"I want nothing so elaborate. If Father was merciful, he would allow me to return to Ilano for the occasion."

"You know he will not permit you to leave. Perhaps some of your friends might travel here?"

"You would like that, wouldn't you?"

"Above anything."

"Have you sown your wildness sufficiently enough to consent to taking a bride?"

The prince frowned. "No. And thank you for bringing up such an abhorrent subject."

Princess Caelyn held his gaze calmly while he fumed.

"Very well," she said. "I will ask Father if I might have a few close friends join us in Praed for my birthday."

His face lit up. "Might I make a few suggestions?"

"No," she said firmly. "Now go ready yourself for this morning's ride."

With every step toward the stable I became more anxious that Risteard had not received my note or was too busy to join us. I shuddered when Jervell Kade met the princess outside and walked with her hand in the crook of his arm. My nerves were on edge when I saw the prince waiting for the groom to produce his horse, and my insides twisted as the princess was helped into her saddle. I worried I might faint, until Risteard appeared leading his horse, and Aquila circled overhead. Risteard gave me a reassuring smile as he passed, and I gratefully took the reins of a horse offered by a stable hand.

"Why have you brought Aquila?" Prince Brannon asked.

"For the safety and protection of Your Highnesses," Risteard replied.

Prince Brannon shrugged and mounted his own horse.

"At least keep a respectable distance," Princess Caelyn asked, glaring down at him.

"I will keep whatever distance necessary to ensure your well-being," he said.

The princess set her jaw, pulled the reins across her horse's neck, and kicked the poor animal roughly.

"She didn't like that," I said as she trotted away.

A glimmer of mischief flickered in Risteard's cerulean eyes before all expression disappeared from his face. "Do you need a leg up?"

"No, thank you." I quickly lifted myself into the saddle. Risteard followed suit, and then held out his arm for Aquila to land on. The great bird spread her wings and shook her head, the feathers of her body ruffling.

"What does that mean?" I asked.

"She's happy to be out."

"Me, too. I'm glad you're here. I don't trust those three alone together."

His mouth twitched, but he did not smile.

"Come." He gestured toward the group. "Before they get too far ahead."

"Race you?"

"I don't think that would be wise."

"Because you know I'll win?" I smirked.

"Because they'll see you having fun, and you know how much they'll loathe it."

"Fair." My face fell, and I nudged the bay horse into an easy canter.

Near the foot of the mountain, Prince Brannon pointed out a notable house to Jervell Kade. The structure, he explained, was built on the confiscated lands of a former resident who served the usurped king. The house had been destroyed and another erected in its place for a prominent Ilano noble. I listened, my spirits sinking with each word. I knew those lands and the family that had occupied them. A knight by the name of Sir Nils Syvestry lived there with his wife and children. He was a kind man, a gentle giant with a balding head and bushy brown beard. Ula and I were frightened of him initially, but we quickly discovered he hid treats in that mass of a beard, and his children were our constant playmates when we visited the castle.

"What became of the former owner?" Jervell Kade inquired.

"Same thing that happened to all the knights of King Llewlyn," Prince Brannon said as he slid a finger from one ear to the other.

"Does the family still reside in Praed?" Risteard asked.

The prince turned in his saddle and looked at Risteard like was an idiot. "How should I know?"

The prince kicked his horse, and the group proceeded down the mountain. I watched them, silently hating their callousness, and logged the name Lady Syvestry as a future contact.

"Are you all right?" Risteard asked.

I nodded mutely, and he straightened in his saddle. He lifted his arm and spoke quietly to the eagle perched there. She spread her wings, and he propelled her into the air, her talons curling as she gained altitude. The great bird circled higher, then soared with the breeze coming down off the mountain, casting her shadow on the valley below.

"Will she follow you?" I asked, my jaw agape as I watched her rise and fall on the currents of air brushing against my face.

"To the ends of the earth, if I asked her to." He clicked at his horse, and we made our way toward the city.

"If only people were that loyal," I said.

"You don't think they can be?"

I shrugged.

"Even after all those letters you've received?"

"Just words. Time will tell if they're truly meant." I paused as we grew closer to the group ahead. "They do bring me comfort, however, and for that I'm grateful."

"I don't like to see you in such a dark humor."

"I knew those people," I said quietly, jutting my chin forward. "On that estate. They were good people. I suppose good people suffer the worst in a war, don't they?"

"Yes," he said, his voice low and hoarse.

The prince chatted incessantly through Market Town, pointing out the best purveyors of goods to Jervell. The princess held a scented cloth to her nose to block the odor of poverty wafting from the gaunt faces of farmers selling their wares to their destitute customers. It was easy to distinguish the Ilano from the Praed among the people. While the Ilano were garbed in fine clothing and bartering relentlessly, the Praed gave in to every demand, selling their wares at ridiculously low prices. I jerked my horse to a stop in front of one of the stalls and watched an Ilano leer at a young woman and ask if they might come to an arrangement. The proprietor wrapped an arm across the girl's shoulders, looked down at the meager offerings of his trade, and solemnly asked what he had in mind. I fumed, clenching the reins, and wondered if there was any humanity left in the world.

"That won't be necessary." Coins rained down on the tabletop, and I held back a gasp. "If his lordship is short of funds, I'm duty bound to help."

The Ilano man glared at Risteard, but he was smart enough to accept the charity. He snatched the finest piece on offer and stalked away with a quick nod.

The craftsman bobbed gratefully at Risteard's back, and I bit my lip to stop myself from grinning. My eyes fell on the young woman saved by his chivalrous act. She was smiling, too, but with glittering eyes and parted lips. I frowned and followed her gaze. She was looking at Risteard. I positioned myself to block her view and trotted after him, throwing a frosty glance over my shoulder at the girl's flushed face.

Galloping hoofbeats thundered behind us, startling everyone. We turned to see, Risteard placing himself between our party and the riders. I tried to steer around him for a better view, but he held his arm out to stop me. Frustrated, I stood up in my stirrups, and saw several men headed straight for us, the king at their head.

"Father!" Princess Caelyn called out. "How fortunate for us to meet on such a fine morning." King Conall reined in his horse and raised his hand in greeting.

"A fine thing, Caelyn, Brannon, Risteard," he nodded as he acknowledged them. "And Lord Protector Kade! I hope you're being treated to a splendid ride?"

"I am, Your Majesty," Jervell bowed. "The prince and princess were just giving me a tour."

While the group exchanged pleasantries, I studied the king's countenance. His cheeks were hollow and there were dark circles under his eyes. The gray at his temples had spread, aging him considerably. Apparently, the last few weeks had been a strain on His Majesty as well as the rest of us.

"Shall I join you?" the king offered.

After an almost imperceptible hesitation, the princess said, "Of course."

The party was now doubled in size with the arrival of the king's entourage, and I relaxed. Surely his presence would mean an end to the princess' intrigues. I allowed my horse to drop back, and in the growing distance, I felt more at ease. For a moment, I could pretend I wasn't a servant. I imagined I was once again the daughter of Sir and Lady Audrey. Me. I raised my chin and breathed.

The moment was shattered. My eyes drifted shut, and I pressed my hand against the ache in my chest. The familiar smells of the market--fresh bread, perfume, flowers--had been replaced by the odor of unwashed bodies, rotting meat, and despair. I gritted my teeth and took in the disreputable state of the once bustling market. The king was a fool if he thought he could maintain the luxury he'd become accustomed to without a prosperous people.

I felt a tug on the hem of my dress. Startled, I wrenched away, fear coursing through me, but a tiny gasp made me pause. I looked down and my whole body sagged. A little girl, probably around nine or ten, stood with her hand outstretched, grimacing. Her face was clean, but her clothing was threadbare. I looked at my own dress. It certainly wasn't the standard of a Lady of Riverstone or a proper lady-in-waiting, but it was well made and--mostly--clean. When I didn't move, the little girl's hand reached forward, and she gingerly ran her fingers over the fabric. I smiled, and she shyly smiled back. Were I Laria Audrey of Riverstone, I could place a stack of coins in her hands. But I had nothing to offer. I *owned* nothing.

I glanced up at the group, but they were yards away and not paying attention. My eyes flickered over the horse and settled on the breast collar. With trembling fingers, I unhooked it from the saddle and held it out the girl. Her eyes widened at the silver accents glinting in the sun then shifted to me. I lowered it, pleading with my eyes for her to take it. She glanced around then snatched the treasure and ran, disappearing behind a row of patched up houses. I would be punished severely when the collar was discovered missing, but it was worth it. I could write letters all day long for years and it wouldn't bring me the warmth and pride of actually *doing* something.

Several minutes into the ride, I could hear snippets of an argument drifting from the front. I gave my horse a quick kick and inched forward to listen. The king and the prince were in animated debate while the princess and Jervell Kade gazed with indifference at the passing scenery. Suddenly, the king pulled up his horse and halted.

"There is no time!" King Conall shouted at Prince Brannon. "A procession takes days to organize. If you wanted one on the last day of your birthday celebration, you should have said so before now!"

"It doesn't have to be a large affair," the prince said. "A smaller gathering. You know, show the people how close we are as a family."

The king eyed Prince Brannon dubiously.

"Just the people here now," the prince continued, waving his arm to encompass the group. "Including Mother, of course."

"If Your Majesty is truly considering this suggestion," Risteard interjected. "Then I would have to insist on more knights."

"You worry too much, Risteard," the prince said.

"No, he's right, Brannon." The king's remark made the prince scowl. "Your safety is our top priority."

"How would it look, Father," Princess Caelyn said. "To have such a threatening presence during a family procession? It will certainly convey a distrust of the people if we feel a need for such security."

Risteard's teeth clenched. "The people will understand the need for protection."

"Now, now, Risteard, Caelyn has a point."

At the king's words, I saw Risteard's pulse throb at his temple and neck, the skin reddening. The king was an intimidating man, but his daughter was adept at manipulating him. I backed up my horse, preparing for an outburst.

Risteard barely restrained his anger. "Your Majesty." His tone sent a shiver down my spine. "You tasked me with the protection of your family. If you do not allow me to perform my duties, then why am I here?"

"There is no need for that," the king said, his palm raised. "Of course, I'm grateful for your service to the crown, but some situations require diplomacy."

"Diplomacy?" Risteard tilted his head and his eyes narrowed.

Even the prince and princess moved away. I wished I could diffuse this heated encounter, but being mute, I was powerless. I could always feign illness and fall off my horse, but it was a long way to the ground and I would probably break my arm.

"The people of Praed must trust my rule, and to gain their trust I must show mine. What better way than to ride through the city with minimal guard? It's been almost a year and a half since we arrived. Certainly, we've been forgiven. There would have been a revolt by now if we had not."

My eyes flicked from Risteard to the king and back again. Risteard wore a stony mask while the king smiled, baring all his teeth. When the silence stretched into several minutes, King Conall chuckled nervously.

"I'll take your silence as obedience." He gave Risteard's shoulder a hearty clap.

I held my breath, expecting a reaction, but Risteard didn't move. The king motioned for the group to continue its progress, and plans were made for the evening parade. I moved beside Risteard, and saw his knuckles were white on the reins. He looked about to embark on a murderous rage.

I waited, afraid to speak. He looked sideways at me, and my brows rose questioningly.

His eyes flashed. "Do I look all right?"

My lips barely moved. "Should I hasten away at a gallop? I'm too young to die."

He didn't laugh as I'd hoped.

"He's a fool."

"Sounds like treason."

"I'm not in the mood for jests."

"Sorry, but why does it matter if someone seizes the opportunity to attack him? You wanted him off the throne anyway."

"Not at the cost of anyone's life!"

"Then you're the one living in a fantasy. You wanted an uprising. What made you think that could happen without bloodshed?"

He looked at me thoughtfully. "I believe a strong show of force can accomplish just as much. Besides, I don't wish to harm Caelyn and Brannon. They're imbeciles, but they don't deserve to die."

"Perhaps not. And a random murder certainly won't further our cause."

"Exactly."

"Then you'd better be on your guard tonight. You may have to throw yourself onto an assassin's blade."

He kicked his horse forward, and I watched him until his horse's pounding hooves cloaked him in dust.

Risteard's stormy expression accompanied us when we gathered by torchlight for the parade. Musicians preceded us, drawing crowds and cheers as people danced in the street and children played with the trinkets Prince Brannon tossed to their waiting hands. The royal family were attended by a few knights, ladies, and valets, and I could tell Risteard was on edge keeping his eye on them. I rode in the middle of the group, looking for citizens I knew. The ride was becoming monotonous, and my mind drifted as we ventured on, passing shops and houses with people hanging out of windows and lounging on doorsteps.

I daydreamed I was astride Amore galloping over the grassy hills outside Riverstone. Beside us, the Rhyvor trickled lazily in the sunshine, the light twinkling on the surface like stars. The water bubbled as it trickled over stones and otters played and fished on the banks. The scent of wildflowers filled my nose, and with the sweet scent the memories of our family table adorned with bouquets. Birds sang from the boughs of the quivering trees as they gathered seeds and built nests. The pitch of their twittering calls rose and fell on the wind stirring the grass. The sound grew louder, and the chirping became whistles, then shrieks, and my ears rang when screams penetrated my skull.

I awoke from my daydream, my horse pacing, wails erupting all around me. I patted his neck to calm him. People frantically ran for cover, and a riderless horse sprinted toward the castle. I regained control of my horse and turned toward the royal family. One knight was leading the queen's horse back to the castle, her fear evident as she clung to the saddle. A few knights were clustered around the king, who was clutching his arm. The princess shrieked wildly, and the prince's eyes bulged. Risteard rode up to his men and shouted for them to escort the three to safety. They moved as one while Risteard systematically scanned the crowd.

Time moved sluggishly, and my breathing became ragged in my tightened throat. Most of the servants had retreated to the castle, and the prince and princess galloped wildly with knights in tow. The king was covered by a knight who looked younger than me, and Risteard followed behind to secure their retreat. I should have galloped away then, but I couldn't take my eyes off the unfolding scene. I don't know how, but Risteard must have sensed another attack, for he reined his horse in front of the king. An arrow whizzed through the air, striking Risteard just below his right shoulder. A scream stuck in my throat when he dropped from his horse. A man emerged from the shadows, another arrow nocked.

From the sky came a high-pitched, bouncing trill and a black mass descended on the man, blanketing him in darkness. I leaped from my horse and ran toward the heap, recognizing the sharp call of Aquila. She lifted her head in Risteard's direction as he approached the pair and hopped off the man. The knight stood before the would-be assassin, said some words I couldn't distinguish, and the man responded by spitting at his feet. I covered my eyes when Risteard raised his sword, not wishing to witness the man's execution. I peeked through my fingers in time to see the headless corpse slump forward, and Risteard turned away, his sword dragging on the ground. Before I could take two steps, he collapsed in the dirt.

My knees scraped on gravel as I slid to the ground by his side. He lay face down, and I cried out with the effort to roll him over. His eyes opened to mere slits in his ashen face, his lips moving wordlessly. The shaft of the arrow protruded from the wound in his shoulder, and without knowing what else to do, I broke the end off and covered the flow of blood with my hands. The warm liquid seeped through my fingers, and I pressed harder despite Risteard's groans.

"Don't you dare die," I said.

His eyes drifted shut, and I was once again left utterly alone.

CHAPTER 22

I stood alone in the late afternoon sunshine, my only companions the resting dead. Markers dotted the burial grounds on the west side of the mountain, where residents of Praed were laid for their eternal slumber. Dust billowed around me with each metallic scrape of a shovel against earth. I looked into the deep hole at my feet and watched the plain wooden box within gradually disappear beneath a layer of dirt. Two men toiled in the heat, sweat beading on their foreheads. They were silent and unmoved, so used to being near death. I waited until the grave was fully filled, and then approached the mound of earth left to mark the recently interred resident.

"Good riddance." I kicked the dirt with the toe of my boot, sending a fresh plume of dust into the air. I turned on my heel and strode back to the castle, never glancing back toward the humbly marked grave.

"They buried him today," I said. "He must not have been very popular. No one else showed up."

Risteard settled back in his chair, his right arm bound close to his body in a sling.

"I've made inquiries," he said. "No one knows him. At least they're not admitting they do. I'm certain he was procured for his services miles away."

I sat across from him, the vast space of his desk piled with paper. I considered the man I just witnessed being laid to rest in the Praed cemetery. Several days earlier, Risteard had sliced the man's head from his shoulders after an attempt on the king's life, which left the intended target with a flesh wound to his upper arm. The arrow that found its mark in Risteard's body had pierced an area just below his collarbone. King Conall declared Risteard a hero and had his injury treated by the king's personal surgeon. The surgeon explained the arrow missed vital vessels and tendons, however, the arrowhead had become lodged in his scapula and it took a great amount of skill to remove it. The injury would require months to heal before Risteard would be healthy enough to resume his duties as First Knight. I could already tell the confinement would be more painful than the injury from an assassin's bow.

I crossed my arms and kicked the side of the desk. "So we'll never discover who hired him."

"*He* certainly wasn't forthcoming with any information."

"What does King Conall say about it?"

"Very little, aside that he feels fortunate to be alive, and his constant praise of my 'bravery.'"

"Was it bravery or purely luck?" I jested.

"At the moment I'm mostly feeling the latter."

"I'll leave you to your misery, then." I'd neglected my chores all morning in favor of sleuthing, and feared I'd suffer Princess Caelyn's wrath before day's end. At the door, I paused and turned back to Risteard staring morosely at a piece of paper crushed in his left hand.

"Joking aside, I know the king's praises annoy you, but he's right. Not many people would have acted as selflessly as you did."

His gaze flickered in my direction, but he remained silent.

I glanced away, suddenly self-conscious. "I know it's not my place to say, especially since I didn't know him personally, but I think your father would be proud of you."

The shuddering intake of Risteard's breath was the only response I received as I retreated from the room.

Princess Caelyn's birthday succeeded Prince Brannon's by only a month, and the king had agreed to allow five of her closest friends from Ilano to visit, a modest request considering the twenty-day extravagance for Prince Brannon. The princess' mood alternated between delightful anticipation and agitation that all would be prepared to her satisfaction.

"I want their rooms lavishly adorned," she instructed the chamberlain. "I wish to ensure their stay here is comfortable and impressive."

"Their attendants may have to share accommodations, Your Highness. I fear we have not the room for them all," the chamberlain said.

"This is a castle, is it not?" Princess Caelyn bristled. "Make room!"

The princess decided my appearance was too disgraceful for her distinguished friends, so she resolved to 'clean me up' so that I might be looked upon as a favorable addition to her station and not a punishment. Putting aside the disparaging motivations, I was grateful to be measured for several new frocks and a new headdress to hide the embarrassing color of my hair.

"They may still notice," the princess said as she tucked a loose strand into the light turquoise scarf intricately woven around my head. "But at least you look more like the trophy I expect Father meant you to be." She inspected me closely, her eyes moving slowly from the top of my head to my feet. She shook her head.

"You're what? Sixteen? Seventeen?" It was the first time she'd asked a personal question.

I held up all ten of my fingers, closed my hands, then held up another six.

She shook her head again. "At your age I already had a womanly figure. It's just as well you don't, I suppose. It's not as if you'll be wanting for a suitor. Ever."

Memories of pawing boys flashed in my mind, and I curled my lip, unable to hide my distaste. The princess laughed and sat at her vanity so I could style her hair for the evening.

After several minutes of thoughtful silence, the princess tapped my arm. When she had my attention, she said, "I'm glad you find talk of men so unpleasant. Not that any man would find your current lack of womanly physique desirable. I'll not fear you bringing me disgrace by ruining your reputation. Your conduct reflects on me, and I would be most seriously displeased if you acted the flirt, or worse."

I nodded, knowing for certain that in this case I would have no problem heeding the princess' orders.

Prince Brannon entered the room with his usual buoyancy and reclined in a plush settee near the hearth, crossing his arms behind his head and propping his feet up.

He sported the most pleasing smile I'd ever seen on him. "Well, I'm honored you chose my idea to celebrate your birthday."

"Father told you, no doubt?"

"Most certainly. The news has brightened many faces."

"All of them your nasty comrades, I'm sure."

"Now, now, Caelyn," he said. He rose and knelt by her knee. "We're simply excited to have visitors from Ilano. Yes, the fact those visitors are female increases our excitement, but you mustn't take offense or expect any untoward behavior."

The princess eyed her brother dubiously. "I'll believe you're capable of conducting yourself as a gentleman when I see it."

The prince sighed and returned to his seat. "Whom do we have the pleasure of receiving, dear sister?"

She huffed and counted them off on her fingers as she spoke. "Sonisa Murchad, Mwiryn Derville, Mora and Nela Shaw, and Eveene Cruith."

"All very fine ladies of high birth."

"Yes." She feigned innocence.

"How very clever of you," the prince said, annoyed. He took his leave, the door slamming behind him.

A wicked smile formed on Princess Caelyn's lips.

"If you were any sort of gentleman, you'd do as you're told."

Once, I had lived idly, spending my days as I wished between lessons Mother insisted on to 'improve my chances of a good match.' All her efforts were as in vain then as now with my days filled with endless, exhausting chores. However much I lamented this change, I had to admit keeping busy was a welcome distraction from thoughts of what was and what might have been. And my new cause filled me with purpose, giving meaning to the otherwise dreary reality of my life. I was used for labor, but I also felt *useful.*

Risteard, in contrast, was miserable in his current inert state. Deprived of the use of his right arm for the last month, his mood deteriorated. I tried to lift his spirits with news of each supporter and regale him with anecdotes from my day with the princess, but he remained unmoved. I understood how he felt, having your freedom stripped away, but my sympathy wore thin as he became more and more reticent and crotchety. The extended periods of silence during our recent meetings left me frustrated, until one day the distance between us made me snap.

We'd been sitting across from one another for hours with only rustling paper breaking the stillness. I gave up on trying to pry a response from him, and it had been days since we exchanged words. For several seconds I watched his resentful expression as he shuffled papers with his left hand. Stubble darkened his face, and his disheveled appearance was unsettling. Without thinking, I slammed my hands onto the desk, and abruptly rose, sending my chair careening across the room.

"What was that for?" he thundered.

"I'm *done,*" I said. "Let me know when you're finished feeling sorry for yourself."

"I beg your pardon?" he called to my retreating back.

I spun around, incensed. "You're so preoccupied with your injury you've forgotten how to act like a human being. You want everyone to feel sorry for you? Do you want to be coddled? You want to wallow in your misery? If it's isolation you want, you've certainly achieved that goal. I'm leaving!"

"Wait!"

My hand was on the doorknob when he came around the desk to stand before me. He avoided my steely gaze, studying the floor, his fingers as they wiggled against his chest, the bookcases. I crossed my arms and tapped my toe impatiently.

"What?" I asked sharply.

He mumbled incoherently.

"I couldn't quite catch that," I said irritably.

"I'm sorry." He met my eyes. "I *have* been feeling sorry for myself and I'm taking it out on you. That isn't fair. Forgive me?"

He reminded me of a dog repenting after chewing his master's boots. The anger drained out of me. I couldn't stay mad at someone so pathetic.

"You have nothing to feel sorry about," I said gently. "You saved the life of the king. You should be reveling in the honors he's been trying to bestow on you."

"Would you accept such accolades from someone you're trying to usurp?"

"Regardless of your feelings toward your uncle you saved his life and he's grateful. You could be the toast of every man and turn the heads of every lady if you wanted. You might even get your own holiday."

"I'm sure you know me well enough now to know these are honors that hold no interest for me."

"Yes, but the feasts alone should make the time pass more agreeably."

"I have no patience for such attention," he sighed. He turned and walked back toward the desk and fell heavily into his chair. I followed and stood over him while he fidgeted with the corner of a map.

"Look at me," I commanded.

He complied, with much hesitation, and I continued.

"I don't care how you feel about what you've done or how King Conall wishes to reward you. I don't even care about the man whose life you took. I know you're frustrated and bored. You're not the only one." He tried to speak, but I held up a hand to stop him. "If there's one thing I've learned, it's that one must find a way to overcome one's limitations to find purpose and meaning in life. A good man taught me that." Risteard's eyes fluttered and he averted his gaze. "But this," I waved my hand in his direction. "Is not that man."

He swallowed audibly and his jaw clenched, the muscles of his face flexing. He still would not meet my eye as he said, "I never wanted to disappoint you."

"You will only disappoint me if you continue to alienate me. Please talk to me."

"I didn't want to say anything I may regret."

"I don't understand..."

"I've been... distracted."

"By?"

"The pain." Our eyes met, and I saw the dark circles weighing heavy under his eyes and a dullness clouding his once steady gaze.

"Didn't the surgeon give you something for relief?"

"Yes, but it dulls my mind."

"So, you've been content to suffer and not heed his advice?"

"If I cannot think clearly, I have nothing."

"So, you have stubbornly chosen to withstand the pain to have your thoughts intact, effectively distracting you from focusing on our work?"

To his credit, Risteard did not answer. I huffed in exasperation and moved behind him.

"Where does it hurt?" I laid my hands on his shoulder. I had tended many injuries in my time at Riverstone. True, my charges had been of the equine persuasion, however, there was little distinction between the two species.

He tensed at my touch, then relaxed and gestured to where his neck met his shoulder. Using the tips of my fingers, I kneaded the muscles, gently at first, then with increasing pressure. I concentrated on the bundle of knots and pressed my thumbs into them, moving in tight circles downward until they disappeared. Gradually, the tightness in his shoulders receded and he leaned into my ministrations. The tip of my tongue stuck out slightly at the side of my mouth as I concentrated, focusing as if he were a horse and not a man. A sound came from deep in his chest, and I froze.

"Did I hurt you?"

"No. Please don't stop."

His voice held a strange undertone that made my stomach flutter. I remained still, confused, my cheeks aflame. Risteard shrugged against my hands, and I shook my head. I trembled but continued, more aware of each plane of muscle against my fingers. I massaged farther down his back, until he hissed sharply and pulled away.

"I'm sorry!" I stepped back, hands raised.

"It's all right," he panted.

"There are no rewards for those who suffer yet refuse offered relief," I said quietly. I laid my hand on his back where the arrow had lodged. He nodded, still catching his breath. I squeezed his shoulder and moved to leave, but he grabbed my hand to stop me.

"Thank you," he said hoarsely. "I know I've been difficult. I appreciate your unwavering friendship despite my behavior."

I leaned close to his ear. "You've been a nightmare," I whispered. "*I'm* the one who deserves a reward." I left, accompanied by the first laugh I'd heard from him in a month.

CHAPTER 23

We gathered outside on the steps of Praed Castle, presenting an impressive picture of resplendent finery. Precious gems adorning the king and queen glittered in the afternoon sunlight, the reflections of blues, yellows, reds, and white surrounding them in a magical dance of color. The prince wore his finest dark blue velvet doublet, his black boots polished to perfection, and the intricately crafted hilt of his sword glittered at his hip. The princess was equally stunning in a long green gown embroidered with tiny pearls at the neckline and golden threads trailing down the billowing sleeves. Her hair was plaited elaborately and interwoven with ribbon matching the green of her dress. Risteard was also suitably attired, though based on his expression this had happened under strict orders. He was almost completely in black, from the sleeves of his linen shirt to his tall boots, and the surcoat draped over his muscular frame. His family crest was emblazoned on either side of his chest: a red eagle with an apple blossom in one talon and a sword clutched in the other. He wore no bandage, but a sling held his right arm close to his body. I was given a new frock and scarf to hide my hair for the occasion.

The prince bounced impatiently on the balls of his feet, but everyone else was poised when a line of carriages crested the hill and approached the castle entrance. One by one they stopped, and footmen rushed to assist the occupants.

The first ladies to emerge were clearly sisters, if not twins, based on their matching high cheekbones, chestnut eyes, and wavy brown hair. They moved forward as one and clasped Princess Caelyn's hands.

"Mora! Nela!" the princess greeted, kissing the cheeks of each. "I trust your journey was smooth and uneventful."

"Dreadfully so," one of the ladies said. The giggle that followed was a sound not meant for human ears. The princess laughed, and the ladies moved away to pay their respects to the rest of the royal family.

Another lady stepped out of her carriage, her large blue eyes scanning her surroundings curiously. Her mousy-blonde hair was straight, and a few strands framed her oval face.

The princess greeted her with less warmth than the previous pair. "Sonisa."

"Caelyn, what splendor," the lady curtseyed stiffly, as if she was made of wood.

"It is truly impressive," another lady added. This one was tall and lithe, her eyes almost as dark as her ebony hair. She nearly pushed the other woman out of the way to clasp Princess Caelyn's hands and kiss the air around her cheeks.

"Eveene, how well you look, as always." The princess grinned as if they shared a secret.

Eveene's mouth curled in a half smile as she searched the faces around her, and an eyebrow rose when she found who she was looking for.

"Riss-tearrd," she purred.

I swear his name came out as if she was a cat who'd caught a mouse.

"What a pleasure to see you again."

Correction. Her demeanor was of a cat preparing to pounce. I glanced at Risteard to see the effects of her attention, but he stared blankly ahead. This didn't appear to faze the woman. Her smile didn't fade as she greeted the king and queen.

The last carriage came forward, and the loveliest woman I'd ever seen placed a delicate hand in the footman's and alighted gracefully. Her pale blue eyes were wide when she beheld the castle. Her golden hair shimmered in the sunshine, and her milky-white skin was flawless. The princess gave her the warmest greeting, stepping forward to meet the young woman hands outstretched.

"Thank you so much for inviting me, Caelyn. Or should I be calling you Your Highness?" The young woman's voice was as sweet as her face. For some reason I resented her instantly.

"Call me Caelyn, of course, Mwiryn. I'm so glad you could come." The princess tucked the woman's hand into the crook of her arm and led her to the king and queen.

"You are all welcome!" King Conall said. "Come and enjoy the castle as if it was your home. Once you are all settled, we have some games planned for your entertainment." Everyone filed in behind the king and queen, and I watched the prince nearly trip over himself to escort one of them. I turned to see if Risteard would offer his arm to his admirer, but he had disappeared.

I stood a respectable distance from the six elegant ladies gathered behind the castle. Once the guests had changed and rinsed their faces, the princess took them on a tour, which ended outside at the mews.

"They look very well tended," Sonisa observed.

"It's true these buildings are nothing to those in Ilano, but we do what we can with limited resources," the princess said.

"What do you do here all day?" Mora asked. "Everything is so desolate."

I dug my nails into my palms to keep my wits.

"Parties and feasts, mostly," the princess said. "Exercising the birds, of course, games, music. We live very idly I'm afraid."

"Sounds relaxing," Mwiryn said softly. "A pleasant change from working in the orchards."

"What of the locals?" Eveene asked. "What sort of people are they?"

The princess rolled her eyes. "Savages."

"Isn't your girl from Praed?" Mwiryn asked, and all turned to look at me.

"Yes, from a very prominent family, in fact. You mustn't bother yourself about her. She doesn't speak and is quite deaf."

"Poor thing." Mwiryn regarded me sadly.

I wanted to slap the pity off her perfect face.

Eveene draped her arm through the princess' elbow. "Caelyn, what happened to Risteard? His arm appeared injured."

"A wound he suffered protecting the king," the princess said.

Mwiryn gasped. "How brave!"

"Ever the hero, just like his father," Eveene smiled.

"You didn't even know his father," the princess said.

"Tell me," Eveene said. "Has he yet taken a wife?"

Mora threw up her hands and rolled her eyes. "Oh, here she goes again!"

I felt a flush creep up my neck listening to their conversation.

"No," the princess said. "And please save me the pain of watching you flirt shamelessly with him. Your charms had little effect the last time, and I would hate to see you disgrace yourself further."

"You don't think," Nela whispered shyly, her eyes darting around nervously, "he prefers the company of…men?" Her cheeks turned scarlet, and she clutched her sister's arm as if the very thought would send her into a faint.

"No." The princess' lip curled. "Despite his self-imposed celibacy these last few years, I can say with absolute certainty Risteard prefers women."

"Small blessings." Eveene smiled wickedly.

"I don't know why you waste your time on such a brute," Princess Caelyn lamented, shaking her head. "You could do much better."

I narrowed my eyes and glared at her. How dare she insult my friend!

"I suppose his greatest attraction is his seemingly disinterested attitude toward me," Eveene said. "Though, I do love a challenge."

"I wonder that you would bother with a man who doesn't want you, Eveene," Sonisa said absently. "Especially when so many would gladly welcome your attentions."

"As I said," Eveene waved her hand. "There is no fun in a chase when the prey is all too willing."

"It has nothing to do with his parentage and that his uncle is the king?" Sonisa asked.

"She started making a fool of herself long before then." Mora giggled.

"Enough!" Princess Caelyn said. "I am sick of this talk."

The feeling is mutual, Princess.

To my relief, the conversation turned to mundane topics, and the group meandered along the mews to inspect the yard. Their words held no interest, so I turned inwardly, wondering at the dark beauty fixated on making Risteard her own. I didn't begrudge him companionship, especially if he returned her affections, but based on his reaction to seeing her and the tone of the conversation regarding him just now, Miss Eveene considered Risteard a possession, a trophy to display her prowess. I had no patience for such people, and she was in for a fight if she thought to ensnare *my* friend.

After a relatively quiet dinner consisting of the princess' favorite dishes, the party convened in the courtyard where musicians played a lovely melody, and performers danced an intricate ballet in the flickering firelight. It was a welcome change from the boisterous affairs in celebration of the prince. I remained close to the princess and her friends, until each was claimed for a dance. Princess Caelyn moved, perhaps not gracefully, but expertly enough, dance after dance. At the conclusion of each song, the princess would thrust another of her friends into the arms of her brother. I realized, as the prince had suspected, that her guestlist meant to lure him into a choice for a future bride, and she was determined not to be subtle.

"What have you managed to find so amusing?" Risteard asked, appearing at my side as if by magic.

"The princess." I stifled a laugh. "She's decided Prince Brannon must marry one of these ladies."

"I see." We observed them together silently for a moment, then Risteard said, "What do you think of them?"

My amusement evaporated. "The ladies from Ilano?" I frowned. "Very elegant, and I'm sure very well situated." I watched them dance, their movements the epitome of grace, their womanly figures supple and pleasing as they swayed to the music. "They're so beautiful," I whispered, and prickles of tension worked up my cheeks to my eyes. Growing up, I never resented my mother's beauty, nor did I lament falling behind the other girls as they developed into women. Until that moment. For some inexplicable reason, I was jealous of those lovely Ilano women. I averted my face so Risteard couldn't see, and out of the corner of my eye I saw him open his mouth to speak, but before he could utter a word, he was interrupted.

"Risteard, where have you been hiding?" It was Eveene Cruith in a deep burgundy gown that hugged tightly to her form.

Risteard inclined his head but gave no answer.

"You are looking well," she said, undeterred.

"As are you, Miss Cruith, which I'm sure you're well aware."

She laughed, apparently unfamiliar with sarcasm.

"Will you not dance with me?" she asked boldly.

He indicated his right arm. "Unfortunately, I am unable to in my current condition."

"Oh, yes," she breathed and lightly placed the tips of her fingers on his arm. "Such a valiant thing you did for His Majesty."

My eyes widened and darted to Risteard's face. His jaw was clenched, and he moved imperceptibly backward so he was just out of reach. It occurred to me then I failed to notice something obvious: Risteard did not like to be touched. I had never seen him shake a man's hand, nor kiss the ring of the queen. He flinched whenever anyone put their hands on him, even a jesting slap on the back. He stood slightly apart from everyone to avoid any inadvertent contact, and aside from the one time he rescued me from a drunken knight, he never danced.

Eveene Cruith did not seem to take offense, if indeed she noticed his retreat. She raised an eyebrow, waiting for him to speak. I shifted uncomfortably, and she suddenly realized I was standing there.

"Oh!" she exclaimed in surprise. "I didn't see you there." She squinted in the low light, and her eyes widened in recognition. "You're the little girl that attends Caelyn!"

I bristled at the word 'little' and nearly lost my temper.

Her head cocked to the side. "What's this?" she asked as she reached out and grasped a lock of hair that had fallen out of my scarf. It took all my inner strength to keep from slapping her well-manicured hand away as she inspected it intently.

"It's her hair." Risteard spoke with an edge to his voice.

"What an extraordinary color," she marveled. "I had no idea such a thing existed in nature. It's not fake?"

"Why would she cover fake hair?"

"Really, Risteard, you're such a tease." She laughed, finally releasing my hair.

I shoved it back under my scarf before she could touch it again.

"Well, you may not be able to dance, but perhaps you might take a turn with me?" In the short span before Risteard answered, I sensed him wrestling with the urge to say no and his obligation as the king's nephew.

In the end, he had no choice. He held his hand out indicating she should lead on, but she shook her head.

"Aren't you going to give me your arm?"

"Of course," he said, but instead of offering his elbow, he held his arm straight out, close fisted. She placed her hand on his, and they walked away. He looked over his shoulder at me, and I shrugged. *You're on your own there, friend.*

The next afternoon, the princess and her friends were scheduled to take a riding tour of Praed I was forbidden to attend. With the freedom of the afternoon open to me, I sat across from Risteard in his study, writing as he dictated his own letters since he was still unable to write himself. He paused in thought, considering his next words, and I took the opportunity to broach a subject nagging at me all night.

"Do you like Miss Cruith?" I asked. He looked up, startled. His brow furrowed as he considered my question.

"I think of her no more than any other lady," he said, very diplomatically.

"She seems to like you a great deal."

"No," he shook his head. "She does not."

"Then why else would she pursue you?"

"What makes you believe she is?"

I reddened and suddenly found my fingernails very fascinating.

"Well," I started, "she said something about it talking with the other ladies. I got the impression she's made advances toward you before."

It was his turn to look uncomfortable. "Yes, she made her intentions known. But that doesn't mean she has any particular feelings for me."

"I don't understand. Why would she pursue you if she doesn't care for you?"

"Sometimes I forget how young you are. And I don't mean that to be insulting." He held his hand out to stop the protest at the tip of my tongue. "Some people simply play these games for their own amusement."

"She called you prey," I said angrily.

"Exactly. I just happen to currently pique her interest. It will pass."

"Would you like me to slip castor oil in her tea?"

He laughed heartily until there were tears in his eyes. He wiped them away with a shake of his head. "No," he finally said when he was able to speak. "I think that would be dangerous. And think of the poor servant attending to her."

"I would feel bad about that. Also, don't forget you're only nine years older than me, Oh Wise One."

I studied Risteard as his laughter faded and feeling bold, broached another subject. "I didn't realize until last night you don't like to be touched. Has that always been the case?"

He stilled, his laughter dying on his lips. "Yes. I've never been comfortable being touched, except by those very close to me."

"But I've seen you look pained even when the king pats you on the back and he's your uncle."

"Yes, but we don't have a close relationship. Regardless, I don't welcome physical contact as a rule."

"I feel I owe you an apology then. Several in fact." I shifted in my seat. "Well, maybe one or two pokes in the ribs you deserved, but I'm sorry if I made you feel uncomfortable, especially the other night."

"You didn't," he said softly.

"I promise it won't happen again."

"No apology is necessary, and you are under no obligation to make such a promise."

I concentrated on the quill in my hands, my brow furrowed as I tried to make sense of what he'd said. Another matter occurred to me then, plucked from the myriad of thoughts circulating in my mind.

"Who exercises Aquila when you're unable?" I asked curiously.

Risteard blinked several times and looked at me quizzically. "You certainly have a penchant for jumping from subject to subject."

"Mother used to call me a scatterbrained child."

He smiled. "No one else looks after her. She's trained to my command and would not follow anyone else."

"Maybe I could help?" I offered tentatively.

"I appreciate that, but no. You're too small."

My mouth tightened.

"I don't mean because you're a woman. Most *men* cannot handle a bird her size."

"There must be something you can do. Can't you use your left arm?"

"It's weaker than my right, the arm I trained with." He gestured to the unfinished letter in front me. "Let's continue. The princess and her entourage will return soon, and I'm sure she has some important hair brushing or corset tightening for you to do when she does." He ducked as I pitched a crumpled piece of paper at his face.

CHAPTER 24

The rains arrived early the next morning, pelting the windows and dampening the spirits of the princess and her friends, who had planned an outing with a falconry demonstration.

"I'm sure the clouds will lift by afternoon," the princess assured her friends. They lounged on chairs and settees in the music room, amusing themselves with charades until Eveene Cruith sat at the piano and played a lively tune. The other ladies rose and paired off to dance, twirling and laughing like schoolgirls.

As the last notes faded and the laughter receded, Miss Cruith rose and implored the next lady to exhibit her talents. Mora Shaw volunteered, and her playing brought my inexperienced pounding to mind. Her sister joined in to rescue her and save the song from disgrace. The other ladies laughed behind their hands, and I understood why Mother insisted I be able to play.

A hand gently touched my shoulder, and I turned to see Eveene Cruith smiling down at me. The smile unsettled me, as it did not reach her eyes.

"Does *she* know any songs to entertain us with?" Miss Cruith asked Princess Caelyn.

"Not at all," the princess said. "She's worse than Mora." The assembled ladies laughed, all except Mora, who smiled good naturedly.

"We could all stand a good laugh," Nela Shaw said. "Let her play and we will point out all the flaws she cannot hear!"

"That doesn't seem very fair," Mwiryn Derville said quietly. She was overruled.

Miss Cruith led me to the piano bench and gestured toward the keys, inviting me to play. I looked at all the expectant faces eagerly waiting for me to make a fool of myself for their own amusement. I took a deep breath, placed my hands on the keys, and remembered the lessons Risteard taught me at Riverstone. I only knew the first half of one song, but I resolved to play it with all my heart and prove to these conceited ladies that even a lowly servant can produce something beautiful.

My fingers began to move, and the first somber notes emanated from the instrument. One by one, each lady's mouth dropped open, and the princess listened in stunned silence while I played. I pictured how Risteard moved with the notes and imitated his style. For the first time, I performed with passion, and though I didn't relish the audience, I didn't mind the attention.

My eyes slid shut as the song progressed, playing the notes by memory, when suddenly the lid slammed shut on my fingers. A cry stuck in my throat and my eyes flew open. The princess was standing over me, the angriest expression I'd ever seen on her face.

"Where did you learn to play?" she demanded. I breathed heavily, massaging my swelling fingers.

"Caelyn," Miss Derville said quietly behind her. "What's the matter? That was beautiful."

"The last time I heard her play, it was disgraceful. Are you trying to embarrass me?" she studied my face, but I gave no indication I understood her. "Get out," she seethed. "And see to your chores."

The slight drizzle had become a torrential downpour by the time I slogged through the mud to the mews. I stumbled several times slipping in puddles, and I almost fell face-first when my wheelbarrow became stuck. My frock was soaked through before I was half finished, and my hair was waterlogged. Rivulets trickled down my back and dripped off the tip of my nose, and my fingers were wrinkled and pale. Shivering, my teeth chattering, I stepped into Aquila's mew prepared to clean, and there Risteard sat, speaking softly and feeding small morsels of meat to the waiting orange beak.

"Oh, I'm sorry if I've disturbed you."

"It's not as if I didn't hear you coming." He continued to tend his eagle.

"Funny," I mumbled. I raked around him, moving briskly to keep blood circulating in my cold fingers. I clamped my mouth shut to keep from shivering, but a shudder ran up my spine and my teeth chattered loudly in the small space. Risteard turned around, took in my soggy appearance, and rose to shrug out of his greatcoat.

"Whh-what are y-y-y-you doing?"

"You're drenched," he said, struggling awkwardly with the coat.

"S-s-s-stop!"

He ignored me and finally removed the heavy coat and slung it over my shoulders.

"Your lips are turning blue," he said, as if this was all the justification he required.

"What about you?"

"I'm dry."

"Fine," I rolled my eyes, not willing to admit the garment brought me instant warmth. "I'll wear it long enough to finish."

Risteard kept me company while I cleaned the last of the mews, and though I'm certain he also became soaked, he didn't complain nor ask for his coat back. Chivalry is a code not yet forgotten it seems. Knights.

"You may warm yourself by my fire if you wish," he said.

"I shouldn't take the time. Princess Caelyn was quite angry with me when I left."

"What for?"

"She thinks I made a fool out of her."

"How?"

"I played the piano piece you taught me for her and her friends. I didn't want to, but they insisted I perform to entertain them. They're very bored today."

"Were they displeased with your performance?"

"The opposite actually. I guess I have you to thank for my first successful exhibition," I laughed.

"I wish I could have heard it, but why should this make the princess displeased?"

"Because the last time she heard me play, dogs howled. She thinks I played her false."

"Did you tell her it was I who taught you?"

"No," I affirmed as we reached the servant's entrance of the castle. "And I won't. It will be our secret."

"One among many."

I removed Risteard's coat, shook free the droplets of water, and handed it back to him. He took it, somewhat reluctantly, and I thanked him before hurrying through the door. I twisted my hair as I walked back upstairs, leaving a trail of water in my wake. I rounded the corner to Princess Caelyn's rooms, but a tall figure blocked my path so abruptly my shoes skidded and I nearly fell to keep from running into Eveene Cruith.

Her smooth voice cooed, "I'm so sorry if I frightened you, poor creature."

I tried to go around her, but she stepped in front of me, and I knew it was no accident she suddenly appeared. I stared up at her, my face devoid of emotion.

"Your face is so pale." She touched my chin. "You must be freezing after working in the rain. Why don't you come to my room and warm yourself?"

I shook my head and pointed down the hallway.

"I'm sure Caelyn would not wish you to fall ill. You couldn't possibly tend to her needs if you're sick in bed."

I tried again to leave, but her fingers pinched my skin.

"I insist," she commanded, her tone no longer friendly.

My stomach sank as she led me to her rooms, and I stood awkwardly while she moved about, placing another log on the fire and then removing a kettle from the coals. She poured hot water into a basin, dipped a cloth inside, and then beckoned to me.

I shuffled a few feet closer and glanced behind me toward the door.

"Don't be afraid, little one. I won't harm you." She enunciated her words loudly and distinctly. Obviously, she had observed how the princess communicated with me. When I was within arm's reach, she pulled me close and began dabbing my face with the cloth.

"Your skin is like ice." She spoke so I could watch her lips.

The cloth moved lower, down my cheeks and neck. When she reached the collar of my thin coat, she began unbuttoning the garment. I grabbed her hands and shook my head furiously, but she brushed my hands away.

"Now, now," she scolded. "Enough false modesty. You're only a child after all." My knees trembled as she removed my coat, then my frock, until I stood clad only in my undergarments. She resumed her ministrations, wiping away the cold raindrops with the warm cloth before the blazing hearth.

"It must be such a comfort," she mused as she moved behind my back. "To have a deaf-mute servant girl. What secrets one can tell in your presence without fear of discovery." She moved in front of me once more and ran the cloth down my arms. When she met my uncertain gaze, her eyes narrowed.

"I saw you with Risteard outside. What sort of secrets did he share with you, knowing you could not repeat them?" She waited, and I was unsure how to respond.

"Does Risteard ever talk to you as I am now, so you can understand?"

I nodded nervously, fearing repercussions.

"Has he spoken of any ladies?" she asked.

I shook my head.

"None at all? He's never mentioned any names?"

Again, I shook my head.

She dropped her gaze. "How disappointing." She moved me toward the fire, and steam rolled off my chilled flesh and wet clothing. Her hands rested against my waist briefly before she pulled away, a confused expression on her face. She grabbed my chin and turned my head so that I could read her lips.

"How old are you?" she asked.

I indicated my age with my fingers.

"No more a child, yet not quite a woman."

She turned away, absorbed in her thoughts, and I took the opportunity to retrieve my belongings and hastily leave the room without bothering to put them back on. I ran down the hallway and ducked into a doorway. I cautiously peered around the corner, listening for the click-clack of boot heels, but the hallway remained empty.

I began to shake, not with cold, but with a troubling fear. Sobs fell unbidden from my mouth, and I was so discomfited I could hardly dress myself. I heard a click behind me, and a door opened inward, throwing me off balance. A voice cried out in surprise, and hands braced my back to keep me from falling. I spun around, clutching my coat to my chest, no doubt with a crazed expression on my face.

"It's all right," a sweet voice belonging to Mwiryn Derville spoke, her hands raised non-threateningly in front of her.

My breath came in sharp gasps, and I struggled to regain my composure.

"You poor thing," she said, taking in my appearance. "You're so cold you can barely catch your breath! Would you like to warm yourself by my fire?"

I frantically shook my head and backed away, but before I could retreat further, she whispered desperately for me to wait.

Hesitantly, I stepped back into the doorway, but did not cross the threshold into her room. She disappeared inside briefly and came back with a heavy robe.

"Here." She draped it around my shoulders. "I hope it brings you comfort." She smiled, a sweet, innocent smile, and I couldn't help but reciprocate. My impression of Mwiryn Derville thus far had been favorable, and she seemed like a nice enough lady. I frowned as I repeated her name in my mind. I had heard it before, I was certain. Without expressing my thanks, I slowly walked away, lost in my fractured memories.

A day later, the princess and her friends gathered in the rooms of Queen Shaeli, all of them eager to hear a prediction of their futures. Mora and Nela Shaw asked the usual, boring question: am I to marry soon? The queen predicted another year would pass before they would walk the aisle. I'm not sure who was disappointed more, the ladies or the princess. Sonisa Murchad was more practical, asking about the upcoming crops and their profitability. I lost interest before the queen answered.

I looked at each young lady in the room, all leaning eagerly toward the queen in anticipation of a favorable prediction. The only face I skipped over was Eveene Cruith's, sitting poised with a small smile. My eyes swept over her shoulder to my mother, who focused on a piece of embroidery in her lap. She was masterful when it came to embroidery, and her work graced the homes of many Praed nobles. Her intricate designs resembled paintings when completed. I used to watch her for hours, sitting at her knee, while the colored threads wove a picture from her mind. Ula's talent mirrored hers, but mine was predictably lacking.

While the ladies were occupied by the queen's readings, I inched slowly toward my mother. I'm not sure what possessed me to risk such a venture, but as I neared her seat, I felt a sense of peace. Her hands froze when I finally stood beside her, but she did not speak. My heart clenched as the uncomfortable silence stretched into minutes. Quietly, she excused herself, though neither the queen nor her senior lady-in-waiting granted her leave. They didn't acknowledge her absence, and I followed hesitantly, my eyes trained on the princess.

When I reached the antechamber, she roughly grabbed my arm.

"What?" she hissed.

"Nothing," I said.

"You moved my way as if you had something to say. I told you not to speak to me. It's dangerous!"

"Mother," I sighed. "It's been a long time since the war."

"Have you forgotten Riverstone so soon?"

"I have not," I said with equal ferocity. "I am fighting for Riverstone while you sit and cross-stitch." I moved toward the door, but she laid a hand over mine to stop me.

"What do you mean fighting?"

I turned to her, exhibiting more poise than I ever did at home.

"I'm no longer the little girl who watched her stables burn," I said.

"Laria, be sensible---"

"We do not have the luxury of sensibility, Mother." I turned back toward the door, but Mother gripped my shoulder tightly.

"Laria," she pleaded, her voice wavering. "Please, listen. We have no friends here. Whatever you hope to accomplish, you cannot do it alone."

"Agreed. And I assure you I am not alone." Before she could respond, I stepped through the door and rejoined the gathering.

"Have you any visions for the good health of our Lord Prince?" Princess Caelyn inquired. It seemed I had returned just in time.

The queen gazed into nothingness until the tension became unbearable. I feared the princess would scream.

"The picture is not clear, but there is something… Prince Brannon will choose a lady to take as a wife, but not for many months. Perhaps even a year."

"Who is she?" the princess asked impatiently without regard to the ladies gathered around her.

"I cannot see," the queen said. She slowly closed her eyes and rested her chin on her chest. Her senior lady-in-waiting rose, and the ladies followed suit, exiting the room so the queen could rest.

The instant the door shut behind them, the ladies began whispering about Queen Shaeli's predictions.

"Who will be the man I marry?" Mora Shaw wondered.

"Better yet, who do you think Prince Brannon will marry?" Nela asked. "Caelyn, have you any idea?"

"No," Princess Caelyn snapped.

"Well, there is no need to rush into such things," Eveene Cruith said in her characteristically cool tone. "As the queen said, it may be a year before he's wed."

"A year is too long!" Princess Caelyn yelled. The ladies stared in shock at her outburst. The princess collected herself, straightening her gown and brushing back a stray curl. "I apologize," she said. "My brother's happiness is so important to me." She sniffed and dabbed at the corner of one eye. She was a terrible actress, but her friends seem to believe her.

"It's important to all of us, Caelyn," Mwiryn Derville said. She laid a comforting hand on the princess' shoulder, and she took it and held on tightly.

"I'm all right now." Princess Caelyn smiled. "Come ladies. I just remembered my brother invited us to play cards after the gathering."

Nela Shaw clapped her hands excitedly, and the group fluttered down the hallway, their gowns swishing in time with the tapping of their heels. I trailed behind, intrigued by Princess Caelyn's distress regarding Prince Brannon. If it hadn't been apparent before, it was now abundantly clear that whatever they planned hinged on his marriage. I felt sorry for the poor woman who would be his choice.

While the ladies tittered and laughed playing cards with Prince Brannon and his cronies, I pouted in the corner, a kerchief in my lap. I was under strict instructions by the princess to improve my skills, unless, as she said earlier, "I was secretly a master embroiderer as well as pianist." The sting was even more painful having just come from watching Mother expertly work her craft. I stitched a clumsy floral pattern that was supposed to resemble wildflowers, but it came out looking like something Mother's cat vomited up. I considered escaping and bringing the cloth to Ula to finish, but I feared this would anger the princess more than please her. Giving up after the fifth or sixth time I accidentally knotted the middle of my thread, I focused my attention on the card tables.

Miss Cruith laughed readily at every joke and did not miss an opportunity to lay a hand on an arm or shoulder. Seated between two boisterous men, she seemed very much in her element. Miss Derville sat meekly between the prince and princess, and every so often I noticed Princess Caelyn nudge her and indicate her brother, and the lady responded by engaging him in conversation.

"Oh, Caelyn, did I tell you? Remember Jylan Pite? She's the youngest daughter of the milliner?" Miss Cruith prompted.

"How could I forget," Princess Caelyn said. "She was always trailing after us."

"Her father has recently announced her engagement," Miss Cruith said with a sly smile.

"How wonderful for her," Miss Derville said.

"I recall her well enough," the prince added. "We used to call her 'Jyl the Pits.'"

The table erupted in laughter.

"Her elder sister held all the attraction, I'm afraid," he continued. "Her father was wise to marry her off before her eighteenth birthday."

"When might we be so fortunate as to celebrate *your* marriage, Your Highness?" Miss Cruith asked.

I nearly choked at her boldness, and the princess fixed a murderous look upon her. The rest of the table fell silent, waiting for the prince's response to the impertinent question.

"I have no plans to marry as yet." He turned toward Princess Caelyn with a dark look. "Perhaps we might ask my sister the same question?"

"I shall perform my duty whenever the king asks it of me," she said coolly.

The rest of the game passed less dramatically, and I returned to my embroidery out of sheer boredom. The princess reached for the piece as we left the room, and her disappointment was mixed with satisfaction upon finding my skills as dreadful as she remembered.

Risteard stretched his right forearm across the desk, testing the limits of his pain tolerance. According to the surgeon, he could start using the arm. Within reason. Knowing Risteard, he would push himself hard to regain his strength and mobility, and I was not looking forward to the aftermath. I feared it would be up to me to rein him in, a nearly impossible task. He picked up his pen and wrote in careful strokes.

I looked up from my own letters. "Would you like to hear the latest prediction from Queen Shaeli's theatrical?"

"I assume something aside from the usual gossip? Otherwise you wouldn't bother to tell me."

"She had a 'vision' the prince would be married within the year. The princess was not pleased to wait so long. Why is she so eager to marry him off?"

"It would secure his place on the throne, assuring his succession as the eldest male heir."

"Always the eldest *male* heir," I mumbled. "Why can't a woman inherit the throne?"

"It's not impossible should the king declare so as his final decree."

"But when does that ever happen?"

"Not often," he admitted.

"What would happen if the king passed and the prince was not married? Would he still gain the throne?"

"Yes. But having a queen by his side shows strength, stability--a deterrent for those seeking to attack when the regime is vulnerable. People support a king whose line is certain to be secured through marriage, especially a politically advantageous marriage."

"So, it's in the prince's interest to form an alliance. So why is he so resistant?"

"How would you like to have your sister force you to marry before you're ready? The prince is still a young man, and the king is in good health. He sees no reason for haste."

I tapped my fingers on the desk, then rose and paced the room. "Then why is the princess in a hurry?"

"You've intimated in the past that you feel the princess has some hidden agenda. Have you learned anything recently?"

"Nothing that makes sense. She's fixated on the prince and securing a marriage for him, but I don't know what's behind it. If I hear anything, I'll let you know."

Risteard resumed writing, and I listened to the painfully slow strokes of his pen. To keep myself from grabbing the quill out of his hand and demanding he dictate, I crossed my arms and studied a glass case containing a yellow insect as long as my finger, its black-spotted wings spread wide.

"Praed has a history of men seizing the throne if the king fails his people."

The writing continued while I mused.

I covered the insect with my hand. "Some kings fell in battle. Others died from illness. But a Praed king has rarely died of old age." I ran my hand over the other glass cases and tried to read the tags, but I didn't know the language.

Risteard grunted in reply.

"Ilano has never had a king. Are they making up the rules as they go?"

"A Lord Protector acts in much the same way, including the line of succession. The council has advised the king from the beginning."

"Does he listen?"

He hesitated. "Sometimes."

"If one had a spy in the council, could they influence the king?"

"Unlikely. Unless he first persuaded the rest of the council. The king could hardly ignore the majority."

"Months ago, Prince Brannon mentioned Princess Caelyn's 'spies.' I thought he was talking about Jervell Kade, but now I'm not so sure."

The pen clattered to the desk. "Why didn't you tell me?"

I ignored the edge in his voice. "Like I said, I thought I had it figured out. I wasn't purposely keeping it from you."

He huffed, and I stifled a smile before facing him. His arms were crossed and his neck red. Calmly, I returned to my seat, picked up my pen, and deliberately refused to acknowledge his anger.

He sighed and cracked his knuckles. "In the future, tell me everything. We can't work together if there are secrets between us."

My head shot up. Heat spread over my face, and I squeezed the pen in my hand until it snapped.

"I told you. I wasn't keeping a secret. I simply forgot. I've never. Once. Lied."

"I know that. Forgive me." His tone was gentler, so I relaxed, dropping the broken pen. Silently, he slid another across the desk.

"Did she mention any names?"

"I'm trying to remember. It was a long time ago," I said.

"It would make sense for them to have allies in the council," he said. "I'll listen and watch for any signs of discontent."

"And I'll pay closer attention." I managed a half-hearted smile. I hated failing when I had vowed to gather information helpful to our cause. It pained me especially to fail Risteard. He had placed his trust and confidence in me, and the last thing I wanted was for him to reconsider giving me a chance.

The rains abated enough so the ladies could venture outside and the prince was invited to demonstrate the latest tricks he'd taught his eagle, Verix. I distanced myself from the crowd, not wishing to witness whatever cruelty Prince Brannon would have the bird perform.

"I'm in need of a volunteer," he announced. The ladies glanced at each other, but no one stepped forward.

"Here," Princess Caelyn said as she grabbed my sleeve and pulled me toward the prince. "Use her. That way we can all watch." I shook my head, but it was useless since I had no choice.

Prince Brannon dragged me to the middle of the yard, told me to hold still, and placed a fresh piece of meat on top of my head.

He pointed a finger at me. "Remember, don't move!"

My eyes shifted to the eager faces of the assembled ladies. I recalled the time not long ago, when a goblet rested on my head and how humiliating that turned out. My knees trembled. A trickle of sweat inched its way down my forehead, and I resisted the urge to wipe it away.

Behind me, I heard the prince call out followed by a flap of wings. The ladies' expressions brightened in awe, their eyes tracing the path of something I could not see. A sudden heaviness settled on my head, and I realized it was Verix, sinking his talons into the meat. The edges of the long, black claws scraped my skin as he rose into the air taking the meat and my scarf with him, not to mention several strands of my hair. My legs were no longer able to bear my weight, and I slumped to the ground.

The ladies stopped applauding, froze, and stared.

"Is she all right?" one of them asked.

"Oh, she's fine," the princess said. "I am sorry her fine headdress was ruined, Brannon."

He waved her off. "Have another one made!"

Nela's high pitched voice called, "I've never seen that color of hair before!"

Before anyone could comment, the princess asked her brother if he had any other tricks to show them. He bid them to follow, walking toward the cliff face so the ladies could watch the bird's graceful flight patterns. I stayed behind, kneeling in the dirt, my arms wrapped around my body to stop myself from shaking. I felt a tickle at my temple, and when I swiped at the spot with my fingers, they came away streaked with blood. Gently, I placed my hand on top of my head and flinched when I touched a painful scratch. Not a very impressive trick after all if Prince Brannon could not teach his eagle to recover the bait without harming the 'volunteer.' What would Princess Caelyn have said if it had been one of her friends?

Later, I lay in bed staring at the dark ceiling trying to recall any details that might explain Princess Caelyn's motives. She clearly invited these ladies as acceptable choices for a bride, but the prince didn't seem to prefer any of them. The princess didn't seem to care who he chose either, except she placed Mwiryn Derville close to him on more than one occasion and encouraged them to interact socially. *Mwiryn!* I bolted upright in bed, remembering where I'd heard the name before.

Months ago, in the princess' chambers, Jervell Kade mentioned the name 'Derville' in reference to a marriage negotiation. What could Jervell Kade have to gain by the prince marrying, and why Mwiryn Derville? Did the lady herself know she was being served up as a potential bride?

I threw off the bedclothes and slipped on my frock and boots, hoping Risteard might still be awake so we could discuss the situation. I crept out of my room and listened, but no one roamed the halls at this time of night. I made my way quietly to Risteard's study, but just before the door, a candle flashed in front of my face.

"What do you think you're doing stalking the halls at this hour? Not up to mischief, I trust?" It was Eveene Cruith, and I wondered the same about her. She stepped closer, shining the light across my face. I didn't move, not even an eyelash. "I apologize if I frightened you the other night. I thought you were much younger and when I noticed the swell of your hips... well, it surprised me." She looked toward the door when I failed to answer. "Whose room is this?"

I turned to leave, but she clutched a handful of my frock and would not let go. She leaned close, the candlelight casting eerie shadows on her face.

"I have no interest in the prince as a husband."

My eyes grew wide, and she continued.

"Of course, I know why we're here. I'm no fool. I have no intention of marrying anyone. I'm only here for one purpose."

The study door opened, interrupting her, and I inched toward the protective presence of Risteard standing behind me. Miss Cruith instantly released her grip on my frock and smiled at him.

"Risteard! I had no idea this was your room!" She narrowed her eyes and glared down at me suspiciously. "I found this girl creeping around your door, no doubt searching for trouble. You cannot be too careful with servants."

"Thank you for your concern, but I don't think it wise to accuse the princess' attendant of thievery." His voice held an undertone of warning.

Her smile wavered and she pursed her lips. Risteard tapped me on the shoulder, and when I met his eyes, he motioned me off to bed. As I retreated, he suggested the same to Miss Cruith, then slammed his door in her face.

CHAPTER 25

By the last day of the ladies' visit, I could officially declare I despised Eveene Cruith. After catching me in the hallway that night, all pretense of politeness evaporated, and she continued to regard me with suspicion. This turned into an unmasked hostility following a conversation she'd had with Risteard after overhearing him ask me about my missing scarf.

She sauntered to his side and told him about Prince Brannon's demonstration. "This girl was brave enough to volunteer to have the bird fly over and swipe a piece of meat right off her head. Quite exciting."

Risteard was furious, and Miss Cruith's smile faltered when his eyes darkened, and his face flushed.

"He did *what?*"

The lady stepped backwards, cowed by his tone.

"She wasn't harmed," Miss Cruith insisted. "It was all in good fun." She looked at me desperately to support her claim. Risteard turned his thunderous gaze on me, and I paled.

"Were you injured?" he asked, his tone gentler. Slowly, I raised my hand to the top of my head and crooked a finger to resemble a talon, then dragged it along the margins of the wound. Risteard inspected it himself, parting my hair and searching for any other scratches. He released my head and said he'd speak to the prince about the incident and promptly left.

"You're fond of her," Miss Cruith whispered incredulously to herself as he walked away.

I looked away and focused on tidying the room, pretending not to notice her stunned expression. She grabbed my chin roughly and turned me to face her.

"I would not have believed it had I not witnessed it with my own eyes," she hissed. "I don't know what magical hold you have on him, but if you stand in the way of my pleasure, you'll be sorry."

She pushed me away, and ever since I kept as much distance between us as possible.

Based on the lady's permanent scowl she wore as the festivities continued, Risteard had resolved to do the same.

I kept out of her path, busying myself filling glasses and removing soiled dishes. The princess and the other four ladies danced every set while Miss Cruith refused every offer. She skulked around the party, casting daggers in my direction and searching for Risteard, who remained absent.

"What are you doing?" the princess asked her toward the end of the evening. "You haven't danced once, not even with my brother."

"I have no interest in dancing tonight," she said. "Unless Risteard asks me." The princess threw her hands in the air and rejoined the other ladies.

Risteard finally made an appearance, probably because the princess insisted. He no longer kept his arm in a sling, but he still held it protectively next to his body. Miss Cruith spotted him at the same time I did and promptly made her way through the crowd toward him. I tried not to laugh when he noticed her coming and moved off in the other direction.

By the time the master of ceremonies announced the last dance, I had retreated to the shadows. I was absorbed in the music and perfect movements of the dancers and did not acknowledge the person I sensed by my side, assuming it to be Risteard. The person spoke, but instead of the low timbre I expected, the tone was decidedly feminine.

"What an enchanting night," Miss Cruith said.

I stiffened and held my breath. She laid a gentle hand on my shoulder, and I looked into her dark, friendly eyes.

"I must apologize for my behavior the other day. You must allow a woman one outburst now and then, especially when she's not feeling her best." She touched her fingertips to her forehead. "I was suffering from a headache."

Her eyes drifted toward the crowd and she straightened, her grip tightening. "I knew it," she whispered. "If I found you, he would soon appear."

I followed her gaze and saw Risteard walking toward us. He hesitated when he noticed Miss Cruith, then strode purposefully forward.

"Miss Cruith." His voice was cold, but her smile didn't fade.

"Risteard," she curtseyed. "I was telling this sweet girl how ill I've felt lately. I think this damp weather has me out of spirits."

He continued to stare but did not respond.

"I'm much more myself tonight, you'll be happy to hear." She edged closer to him, testing his reaction. When he didn't move, she took this for encouragement and pressed on. "I see you no longer wear a sling. Does this mean you will be more inclined to dance?" She smiled in a strange manner I could not describe. "Unless..." she tugged my sleeve, drawing me into the conversation, "you would prefer the company of this young lady?"

His gaze flickered to me briefly then returned to Miss Cruith. She drew closer to Risteard, her face tilted up, her lips nearly touching his.

"Risteard," she whispered. "I can give you a night of pleasure you can't even imagine. Can she say the same? Oh, I forgot." She laughed softly. "She can't say anything at all." Her eyes drifted shut, her lips moving closer. I wished for a chasm to open for me to drop into.

He stepped away from her and angled his body sideways. She blinked in surprise when she opened her eyes and found herself kissing the air.

"Miss Cruith," he said. "I have been polite in refusing your attentions in the past. I thought I had made it clear without insulting your pride that your advances were unwelcome. I have acted indifferently and avoided contact to spare your feelings. Now, I have no other recourse but to state in the plainest terms that your efforts are not appreciated, and I request that you desist immediately." He extended his hand toward the festivities. "I encourage you to press yourself against a more willing partner."

A sharp intake of air rushed through her nostrils, and the color rose in her cheeks. Without warning, she grabbed a handful of my hair, and seethed, "You would choose a servant over me? Do you have any idea how many men have been here before you?"

"Release her," he commanded through gritted teeth. "Or I shall inform your father of your behavior here."

"Gladly," she said, then she shoved me into his chest. "Take your whore. You'll regret choosing mediocrity over a high borne Ilano woman. Don't bother coming to me when she's unable to satisfy your appetites." I kept my face buried in Risteard's doublet as she stomped away, taking her self-importance with her.

Risteard placed a gentle hand on my shoulder and eased me away. He stooped down so we were face to face and asked, "Are you all right? Did she hurt you?" I shook my head and smoothed back my hair. He stood beside me, and together we watched the couples dance in the waning music.

"I've never been called that before," I whispered. "Do you think she really thinks I'm... what she said?"

"She didn't say it to hurt you. She said it to anger me."

"Why? Why would she say something so awful about me when she was mad at you?"

"Because you're my friend," he said quietly. "And it was an easy and tasteless way for her to unleash her temper."

"Why are people so cruel to me?" I asked, my voice strained.

"They're threatened by you."

"By a servant?" I asked incredulously.

"You're so much more than a servant and they know it, whether they're aware of it or not."

My chest swelled with pride. "Thank you. For being my friend."

Without taking his eyes off the festivities, he lightly intertwined his fingers with mine and gave my hand a brief, reassuring squeeze. I relaxed with a heavy sigh.

The inhumanity I'd witnessed since King Conall conquered Praed left a void in my soul. Meeting Eveene Cruith strengthened my determination to cut Ilano out of my life forever.

After the ladies journeyed home, I was relieved to have the castle to ourselves again, though the princess felt their loss as a reminder that she was exiled in Praed without friends. The noble daughters the king hand-picked to serve as companions were a poor substitute for Ilanis.

In the study, I briefed Risteard on Jervell Kade's involvement in arranging the marriage between the prince and Mwiryn Derville. I quietly studied his face as he pondered the details. His chin rested against his closed fist, and his eyes darted from side to side as if he were reading. A lock of hair fell over his creased brow, softening his otherwise pensive expression.

"The Dervilles are a very prestigious family," he said. "But they are not a political one. There must be a reason Kade feels an alliance would be beneficial."

"Maybe he owes them a favor?" I suggested.

One side of Risteard's mouth curved upward. "Now you're thinking like a politician."

"I can't imagine Jervell Kade doing anything that would indebt him to anyone."

"Neither can I," Risteard said. "He does nothing without some benefit to himself. Aligning with the Dervilles is not negotiated for Brannon's best interest, and certainly not for the lady's."

"That poor woman would be better off marrying a diseased badger."

"Indeed," Risteard said, too absorbed to appreciate my humor.

"She is a kind lady," I said in all seriousness. "I would hate to see her used in this way. Have she and the princess been friends for a long time?"

"Yes, many years. Miss Derville and Caelyn were schoolmates."

"Do you think she knows about their plans?"

"If she does, she won't object. Miss Derville has always done what Caelyn tells her, and if her father has entered into negotiations, she will do her duty."

"Always duty!" I pounded my fist on the desk. "No woman's life is her own." I pushed away from the desk and paced around the study. "Rich or poor or a princess, she must do what she's told. 'Wear this gown that flatters your figure. Learn twelve languages and build a house using a hairpin. Marry a man you've never met because it's convenient and will make your family wealthier yet bring you no happiness.' It isn't fair." My voice cracked with emotion, and I crossed my arms to keep from shaking. I leaned my head against the cool glass of the narrow window.

"It's an unfortunate reality for many women," Risteard said. "We cannot change all of their fates, but perhaps we can change one."

I took a deep breath and exhaled slowly before returning to my seat. I met Risteard's eye and held it steadily.

"Tell me about Jervell Kade," I said, my voice calmer than I felt.

"His history is not one fit for a young woman's ears."

"I have seen and heard many things no human being should endure. Nothing you can say will disturb me more than watching my stables burn to the ground while an evil man tells you your father is dead."

Risteard nodded. "I trust you know your own limits and can stop me if you can bear no more."

I nodded.

"Very well," he sighed. "Jervell Kade was born to a very prominent Ilano family, but he spent little time there as a young man. He travelled auspiciously to the outer borders of the continent promoting trade between Ilano and spice caravans. After the death of Kade's father, Lord Protector Davian employed him as an advisor and relied on his connections to form relationships with neighboring countries. He performed his job well, but my grandfather never fully trusted him despite his elegant words. He formed a special connection with Caelyn. King Conall once said Kade called her the daughter he never had."

"What was your opinion of him?"

"He was a skilled diplomat and my family relied on his advice for many years."

I smiled slyly. "In other words, you despised him?"

He smiled. "Have I become so transparent to you?"

"Continue," I said.

His smile faded, and he struggled on how to proceed.

"There were rumors regarding Kade's unusual…appetites." He glanced at me to ascertain my understanding of his word choice. I nodded, feeling the blood drain from my face. "My grandfather ignored them. Having no proof, he did not wish to condemn a potentially innocent man based on gossip. But an incident occurred. It was almost twenty years ago, but for those involved, time will never erase the scars." He wrung his hands, and his agitation was disconcerting. "A young woman was found unconscious, attacked behind the capitol building. She had been severely beaten. A thorough examination at an infirmary determined that in addition to her injuries from the beating, she had been savagely raped. The surgeons feared she would not survive, and if she did, she would be unable to produce children. She was fourteen years old."

My eyes stung with unshed tears. Never had I imagined such evil lived in the world, and I mourned the stolen innocence of that poor young girl.

"Did she die?" My voice quivered.

"She was strong. She survived." I sighed with relief, and he continued. "A witness stated he'd seen the young woman with Jervell Kade prior to her discovery, and when she regained consciousness, she corroborated this account, and testified to my grandfather that it was Kade who had attacked her. Do you want me to stop?"

I shook my head. The roiling in my stomach bubbled up my throat, but I had to hear the rest.

"Kade remained calm and denied the claims, but the girl's family demanded justice for their defiled daughter, and my grandfather was all too eager to comply."

"He believed the girl over his advisor?"

"He had no reason not to believe her. Her injuries spoke volumes."

"I'm surprised Jervell Kade didn't pay her family off."

"No price was high enough to regain their daughter's tarnished reputation and ruined life. They wanted Kade punished. After a trial of his peers, Kade was sentenced to a decade in a laborer's prison. Before that," Risteard looked away, "Lord Davian ordered Jervell Kade to be castrated, and he was forced to consume a tincture of mint leaves and flax during his internment."

"What does that mean?"

"It means certain portions of his anatomy were removed."

"Which parts?"

Risteard shifted and still would not meet my eye. "Those parts that made him capable of reproduction." He arched an eyebrow.

"Oh! You mean he was gelded." I sat back, feeling queasy. "What did the tonic do?"

"Ensure his desires would diminish following the procedure."

"Why wasn't he executed?" My jaw hurt from clenching my teeth.

"My grandfather pushed for a death sentence, but the council voted against it."

I huffed in disbelief.

"The girl's family might not have been open to bribes but those peers I mentioned were."

"Disgusting."

"Out of respect to his family Kade was allowed to remain in Ilano after serving his sentence, but he was no longer permitted to serve publicly until the death of my grandfather. Conall appointed him Lord Protector, a position he obtained in part thanks to his friendship with Caelyn."

"Considering his crimes, it's shocking the king would allow such a friendship."

"Yes." His voice was so quiet I had to lean forward to hear him. He fidgeted with the corner of a book, then folded his hands. He stared at his whitened knuckles and chewed on the inside of his cheek. I became uneasy in the tense silence. I could tell he was hiding something.

"What happened to the girl?"

"She lived quietly in isolation for many years. My grandfather offered her a position in his household, but she could not escape the stares and whispers. The people had sympathy for her, but she wished to move forward, and their pity kept the wound fresh."

"Did you know her personally?"

"Only in passing since I was merely five or six at the time. I remember she always looked very sad."

"Go on." My voice reflected my anguish. Risteard dragged his chair from his side of the desk and set it in front of me. He sat forward, elbows resting on his knees until I faced him, my cheeks streaked with tears.

"There are not many people, whether man or woman, who can recover from such tragic circumstances. It takes a significant amount of fortitude. That young girl tried to summon the courage to continue with her life despite what she'd endured, but in the end, she could not escape the damage Kade had wrought. She withdrew from society, and a few months later took her own life."

"No!" I gasped. "That poor girl. That man is a monster."

"He is indeed."

"You warned me," my voice came out very small. "But I had no idea. I didn't know there were people capable of such vileness."

He sat back in his chair. "Riverstone may've been idyllic, but surely on visits to the castle you witnessed some of men's cruelties?"

I hugged myself and focused on the papers scattered over the desk. "Mother kept us close. Sometimes Ula and I were able to wander on our own, but not for long. Mother was particularly protective of *her*."

"But she told you why? Warned you?"

I shook my head and a flush of anger crept over my skin. The more time passed, the more I learned how ignorant I was about things Mother should have told me. I wasn't a complete fool. I knew about the marriage bed--basically. I knew not to talk to strangers or go anywhere alone. But if I asked why, Mother accused me of insolence and backhanded me across the face.

"I wish we lived in a world where this was not a lesson one has to learn, but I would rather you hear it from me."

I took several deep, cleansing breaths while he waited quietly for me to compose myself.

"How often do you think he'll come here?" I finally asked.

"A few times a year, perhaps, to make reports to the king."

I narrowed my eyes and fixed Risteard with a determined stare. "Once the king is removed from the throne, how long until Jervell Kade is stripped of his title as Lord Protector?"

"Lord Protector Kade is an intelligent and ruthless man. If you declare war on him, there is no turning back."

"How many other women do you think suffered at his hand before he was, um, unmanned?"

"I have no way of knowing, but I'm certain this girl was not the first."

"An unknown number of women, nameless, living in shame or dying alone, while he lives in comfort with the power to control a princess and influence a king. I cannot allow this to continue, for the sake of those women, and for the sake of Miss Derville. Whatever he has planned for her cannot be good."

"Agreed," he said. "But it will take patience. We have a long road ahead already with the king."

"I can be patient."

His eyebrows rose and the barest of smiles flickered over his lips. "I have yet to see evidence of this."

I kicked him lightly in the shin.

"I'm tired," I said as I languidly rose from my seat and stretched my arms. I looked down at Risteard staring thoughtfully at his hands folded in his lap.

"I hope I never have to be alone with him," I said to the top of his head. I turned to leave, but his abrupt rise made me stop.

"You won't have to worry about that," he said. "I promise no harm shall come to you."

"You can't watch over me, or any other innocent girl in this castle, all the time," I said quietly.

He lowered his eyes and stepped behind his desk.

"Perhaps not, but I *can* offer you protection." He took something from a drawer and came back to stand before me. Wordlessly, he held his hand out, a sheathed dagger on his open palm. I stared at the silver pommel and wrapped leather grip, my throat dry.

"What's this?" I whispered.

"Keep it hidden in your frock."

"I don't think---"

"As you said, I can't be everywhere at once. I believe you're capable of defending yourself if the need arises."

"I'm not!' I insisted. "I don't know how to use that."

"Your father was the First Knight and trusted friend of the former king. Did he teach you nothing?"

"Why would he?" I asked through clenched teeth, the heat rising in my cheeks. "I'm a girl."

"Boy or girl, I see no difference in training a child to defend themself."

"My father did, and he left our education to my mother. She dedicated herself to ensuring we made eligible matches, as our gender dictated."

"Nonsense."

Resentment washed over me, and I pursed my lips and snatched the dagger out of his hand.

"How hard can it be? If he threatens me, I drive the pointed end into his guts, right?"

"Essentially." He indicated the door, and I moved purposefully as he opened it for me to leave. "Tomorrow I'll start teaching you how to use it efficiently, so when you do stab him in the stomach you cause damage and don't just make him angry. If you'll permit me."

Often, I had wished harm on my enemies, especially those who had caused so much heartache. I had even imagined inflicting injury myself, but those thoughts had been driven deep into my imagination. Never had I considered that I might physically wield the weapon that would exact my fury. It was terrifying to hold such a deadly implement in my hands, let alone use one on another human being.

"I don't know." I took a deep breath. "You know how impatient I am as a student."

"If I can teach you how to perform a musical piece for the princess, I can show you how to slit a man's throat before he realizes you've left your chair."

I held his gaze, my blank expression matching his. But I wasn't as practiced as him at concealing emotions, and eventually the corner of my mouth turned up slightly.

"I never expected when we decided to take up arms that I would quite literally be taking up arms."

"You're the one who said an uprising could not be successful without bloodshed."

"True." I turned the dagger in my hands. "I just never imagined any blood would be shed by me."

"I would never force you to do something you're uncomfortable with. Sleep tonight and give me your decision tomorrow."

I lay awake for hours listening to thunder rumble across the sky and the plummeting rain. After leaving Risteard's study, I expected to fall asleep immediately, but I couldn't forget the dagger resting on my chest, nor the thought of plunging it into another human being. Once again, I considered how drastically my life had changed, and I travelled back to the girl I used to be, idling away my privileged hours at Riverstone. Even with an overbearing mother and tempestuous father, I never experienced real fear. But now, as a servant of Praed Castle, my daily routine was laced with uncertainty. I've been frightened of the princess, but I took for granted how truly dangerous it was to live in the castle. I thought of the young woman whose tale Risteard shared. I had no frame of reference to imagine what she endured, to be so close to death only to survive and live every day in a waking nightmare, sinking further and further into despair. If a man attacked me in the same manner, what would I have done? What if the girl had been Ula? Until Risteard placed that dagger in my hands, I didn't realize how defenseless I had been. My eyes drifted shut at last, but vivid dreams haunted my sleep. I awoke several times feeling pressure on my chest, as if a man were pressing me down and I was powerless to fight back. My screams were lost in my tightening throat, and I would lose consciousness, blanketed in darkness.

I awoke at dawn and dressed myself in a mindless stupor of exhaustion. But tucked in the folds of my frock was the means to reclaim control of my destiny beyond a list of names and pieces of paper with promises scratched in ink. As I went about my usual routines, my thoughts drifted to the leather sheath pressed against my hip, the weapon inside, and the man whose chest I would gladly plunge it into should he dare lay his hands on me.

After the princess settled into her breakfast, I escaped to Risteard's study and knocked lightly with no response. I continued to the mews, hoping to find him there. The rain had faded to a drizzle, but the wind blew cold over the mountain, chilling me to the core before I finished cleaning the first few mews. The already low temperatures of the rainy season promised a frigid winter ahead.

"It's certainly a good day to stay indoors," I murmured to one bird. It lifted its head lazily in response, shifted slightly, and settled back to sleep. I wished I could do the same.

In the entire yard, only Risteard's mew was empty. I cleaned it and went searching, passing through the dense stand of trees to the cliffside. A shaft of sunlight emerged from the gray clouds, and Aquila spread her wings to absorb the warmth. She perched on Risteard's right arm, which he supported with his left, working to regain his strength. The giant eagle looked over her shoulder at me and made a chirping noise, which I hoped was welcoming. She watched me curiously, her orange beak cocked to the side. I reached out and touched my fingertips to her chest. When she continued to watch without making a move to bite me, I laid my palm fully against her breast and stroked her soft feathers.

"She used to frighten me," I said quietly so I wouldn't disturb her. "But she's not vicious, is she?"

"None of the eagles are inherently dangerous. They're trained to attack on command and to protect their masters."

"Some of them hiss at me and act like they're going to fly at me when I'm cleaning."

"It's a show of defending their territory, a bluff. If any of them were seriously aggressive, you would not have been tasked with cleaning the mews."

"You seriously believe the princess is concerned with my safety?"

"I know she has made you uncomfortable and participated in cruel acts, but I believe she would never place you in any serious danger."

"If she does, I want to be ready for it. Will you train me to use the dagger you gave me last night?"

He met my eye steadily over the top of Aquila's head. "I will."

"When can we start?"

"Tonight. Meet me in the undercroft. We should not be observed there."

I ran my hand along Aquila's chest once more, then retreated to the trees. A high-pitched trill sounded behind me in the mist, followed by a flap of wings. I glanced back at Risteard's vacant arm and the black shape ascending into the gray sky.

CHAPTER 26

Little moonlight filtered into the dreary space of the undercroft where casks of cider were stored alongside barrels of flour, sugar, salt, and the queen's syrupy wine. The thick stone walls were smooth with age, and the ceiling arched low over our heads. The air was dry and still, and every step echoed in the cramped space. I sat on a wooden crate, my arms wrapped around my knees to stave off the chill. Risteard stood before me next to a dummy made of canvas and stuffed with straw, a dagger sheathed at his hip. My lessons in wielding a weapon were about to commence, and I bounced my legs in anticipation and nervousness.

Risteard began bluntly. "Before showing you any specific tactics, I want to teach you the most vulnerable and lethal places to stab a man."

I sucked a sharp breath through my teeth. "That escalated quickly."

"Would you rather we discuss the weather first before coming to the point?"

"No," I shook my head. "I appreciate your directness. Show me how to bleed a man to death."

He didn't seem to catch my humor.

"Death is no laughing matter, especially if a life is taken by your hands."

"Of course." I shrank back, ashamed.

"Sorry," he sighed. "That wasn't fair. I want you to be able to defend yourself, but I hope you never have to know how it feels to take a man's life."

"Do you ever recover?"

"Never. But as time passes, you're able to pass a day or two without picturing their faces every second."

"Are there many faces?" I whispered, my lower lip trembling slightly.

Risteard's jaw clenched, and he looked away.

"Let's focus so you can get some sleep." He directed my attention to the dummy.

I listened and watched while Risteard illustrated the vulnerable areas of a man's body. He was coolly dispassionate describing the course of blood through the body and where arteries lie closest to the surface of the skin of the neck, under the arm, and the inner thigh. I cringed when he gripped his dagger, blade facing inward, and hooked around the dummy's 'knee' and sliced upward, explaining a man will lose blood very rapidly from a wound sustained there. Next, he demonstrated where to slide a dagger between the ribs to damage vital organs, cautioning me to avoid hitting the bones themselves as the blade may become stuck or break.

"It would turn a dangerous situation into a depressing one," he explained. "I really like that dagger."

I blurted out a laugh. "Sorry. That was an overwhelming amount of information."

"I'm not finished," he said. "There's one place on the human body that can cause almost instantaneous death. But it requires precise skill and strength." He turned the dummy around and placed the dagger against the back of the 'neck.' "At the back of the head where the skull meets the spine. The blade must be angled so it slides between the bones and is driven forcefully to sever the spinal cord."

"I don't know if I have the stomach for this." My voice wavered and the blood drained from my face.

Risteard sheathed his dagger. "We don't have to continue."

"I just don't think if the situation arises I would be capable of hurting anyone, let alone killing them."

"It's amazing what a person can do when threatened with bodily harm."

"Or when putting a king on a throne?" I realized how offensive that sounded as soon as the words crossed my lips, but all I could do was wish them unsaid and wait for the backlash. I hoped the dim light made it impossible for him to see how red my cheeks were. He straightened and the look on his face confirmed the effect of my words.

"I thought we'd moved past this." The disappointment dripped from his every word.

The shame left a knot in my throat.

"I'm sorry, that was uncalled for. Please forgive me, Risteard. I didn't mean that. I can't imagine what you had to go through, and I know you have regrets and are trying to make amends. It was inconsiderate and my only excuse is nervous humor."

I hid my embarrassment behind my hands while he stood silently over me. I felt so miserable thinking I had carelessly driven away my only friend with a thoughtless comment.

He took a step forward and knelt in front of me, but I couldn't bear to meet his eyes, afraid of the anger I might find there.

"Look at me," he commanded, his voice low, yet devoid of the hostility I expected. I peeked through a tiny crack in my fingers. He sighed, pulled my hands away from my face, and pressed them in my lap to keep me from hiding again.

"I accept your apology," he said gently. "And offer one for myself. I spoke to you like a soldier. It was dishonorable for me to be so graphic and expect you not to feel the effects. You defended yourself the only way you know how--with your irascible wit." He pulled me to my feet. I wiped my face, still embarrassed.

"Go to bed," he said. "Tomorrow, we'll start afresh."

I tried to leave, but he put a hand on my elbow and turned me to face him. His eyes were soft, and his brows lifted slightly.

"Can we let the sun go down on this quarrel?" he asked.

I glanced sideways out the tiny windows where a sliver of the moon was visible.

"I believe it has set hours ago," I said, the corner of my mouth lifting a fraction.

"Good," he smiled. "Go on then."

"I do want to continue," I assured him. "I can handle it without resorting to tears or snark from now on. I promise."

"It's perfectly acceptable to have sympathy and compassion for human life. You're less likely to take it for granted and act impulsively. If you're comfortable learning more, then I'll teach you until you call an end to it. Agreed?"

"Agreed." My fortitude would be challenged, but I was determined not to disappoint him again. Moreover, I resolved not to fail myself, and to become the symbol of resilience that Praed deserved.

Torches cast an eerie glow across the cold floor of the undercroft, leaving the edges of the room in darkness. Grimacing, I bent my knees slightly and closed my eyes to concentrate. In a flash, I flung my arm across my chest, and then swung the blade hard, stabbing the inner thigh of my enemy in the hope of finding the artery that bled profusely when severed. I turned to examine my handiwork and discovered I had plunged my dagger between the dummy's legs. Risteard leaned against a barrel with his arms crossed, his eyebrows raised in surprise.

"Sorry," I said sheepishly. "I missed."

"Perhaps not where you meant to attack, but almost as effective." I wrenched the dagger free and stifled a laugh when Risteard shifted uncomfortably. For the last few weeks, he and I had rotated between our political maneuverings and tactical training. Admittedly, I found more excitement in learning the dagger. The weight of it in my hand was tangible, the way signatures on a piece of paper could never be.

"Again," he ordered.

I closed my eyes and imagined a scene like I always did before initiating an attack. I pictured myself wandering the riverbanks, my attention distracted by the fish travelling upstream to spawn. The air is crisp, my breath coming out in wisps around my face. The only sound is the rocks shifting under my feet. I kneel to run my fingers through the water, the cold turning my skin white. Unbeknownst to me, a dark figure is watching my every move, and now that I'm prone, the villain creeps closer. Just as I realize I'm not alone, hands clamp down on my shoulders. Back in reality, I drop to my haunches, shift slightly right, and swing my body backward with my arm extended, dragging the edge of my blade across the back of the dummy's 'knee.' Before the dagger completely clears the canvas, I twist and pull to slice the leg to the bone.

"Who was he?"

"No one in particular." I climbed to my feet and leaned against a crate to catch my breath.

"You have a good technique, but in the time it took you to make your attack, you could have been thwarted."

"How?"

"Where were you?"

"The river's edge. Leaning toward the water," I said. He gestured to the ground, and I knelt as if back in the fantasy.

"How does he attack you?"

"From behind. He grabs my shoulders."

As I lean over pretending to trail my fingers in the river, Risteard put his hands on my shoulders. Like before, I drew my dagger and aimed for the back of the knee. Risteard threw his arm down to block mine, and then pushed it across my chest, using his free hand to wrench the dagger from my grip before I could blink.

"Always hold the lethal points I showed you in the back of your mind, but don't discount any other vulnerabilities offhand because you're focused on a few places. And the closest target may not be the easiest."

"What would you have done?" I asked.

He set the dagger aside and picked up a scrap of wood before kneeling as I had done. I attacked him in the same manner, but when my hands grasped his shoulders, he unexpectedly clutched my left wrist and pulled me forward and over his back while raising the wood to my neck, essentially using my own momentum to cut my throat. An impressive move.

He helped me up before I fell on my head. "If you do something he won't expect, with little effort, the advantage is yours."

From the tone of his voice, I sensed the lesson was nearly over. He handed me the dagger, and without thinking, I pressed it to the throbbing pulse at his neck.

"What if someone comes at you like this?" I challenged.

His face remained impassive as he quickly used one hand to pull mine away while hitting the inside of my elbow with the other, bringing the blade close to my own face.

"What if your arms are pinned?" I asked quietly.

"And you're on the ground?" he asked.

I nodded.

He lay on his back, arms above his head. "In that situation," he explained, "you may not be able to reach your weapon, so you'll have to buy yourself a few seconds. Your legs and hips are your strongest assets, and you'll use them to push him off long enough to free a hand." He bent his leg and twisted his body. "Throw him off balance by shoving your hip into his side, then bring your knees up. He'll come after you in a rage, but your legs will protect you long enough for you to retrieve your dagger." He mimed the actions as he spoke. "Push hard and he'll tumble off you."

"Can I try? It's difficult to understand just watching your side." He sat up and gave me an odd look, and I couldn't decide if he was angry or confused. I sheathed my dagger and lay beside him.

"Don't be too easy on me," I said. "I want to make sure I can do this right."

"I can't," he protested. "It wouldn't be gentlemanly."

"You just pretended to stab me in the throat."

"We weren't in such a compromising position."

"Tell that to my throat!"

When he made no move to comply, I sighed. "I think it's important that I know how to extricate myself from such a situation, don't you?"

I saw that annoyed look--the look that said I was right, but he didn't want to admit it. I knew he would give in. He positioned himself so that he was balanced precariously over me, his legs barely touching my thighs and his hands on my wrists--tight, but not enough to frighten me. It wasn't an entirely realistic scenario, but I appreciated his delicacy.

"Now bring your knee up and use it to brace yourself, then pivot your hip hard into my side to throw me off balance," he instructed.

I gritted my teeth and imagined Jervell Kade assaulting that poor girl. I twisted sideways and slammed into Risteard. He teetered off me, releasing one of my hands. I unsheathed my dagger and wielded it proudly, pointing it at the level of his heart when he fell onto my knees.

"Good," he smiled, still balanced against my legs. "Now, if you were really ambitious, you could release the pressure and impale your attacker with his own weight."

"How?"

His cheeks reddened, but he didn't answer, which only served to pique my curiosity.

"Rist-earrrd," I said in a sing-song voice. "Tell meeeee."

His eyes darkened. "Part your legs."

Now it was my turn to blush. Impudent bastard. With the dagger still pointed up, I moved my knees apart a fraction. Risteard's eyes widened and he threw his arms out for balance.

"Gotcha!" I laughed.

"Must you turn everything into a joke?" he asked before rolling off me. I could tell he wasn't angry, but he wasn't very amused either.

"If I didn't find the humor in my situation, I think I'd go mad."

"You sure you haven't already?"

I stuck out my tongue and crossed my eyes, a trick I hadn't done for years. Risteard turned away to hide his grin.

I noted the dark circles under his eyes and his lack of a clean-shaven face. "You're looking tired, old man."

"We've had many late nights."

"We have. Perhaps we should take tomorrow off. I'm pretty exhausted myself." As if to prove my point, I yawned audibly.

"A wise decision." He indicated the exit and I preceded him out of the undercroft. We emerged from the gloomy space into the castle proper, silently walking the corridors to my room. As I stepped through the door, he tapped my shoulder.

"You weren't really going to impale me on your dagger, right?"

I raised one eyebrow, gave a mysterious smile, and closed the door on his troubled expression. I buried my face in the pillow to quiet my laughter.

CHAPTER 27

The effects of several weeks of late nights were not lost on the princess since I could not conceal the dark bags under my eyes, my disheveled hair, and the shuffling pace of my feet. She arched an eyebrow and observed me closely, but reserved her comments, until one afternoon during a reading with Queen Shaeli.

The queen's voice droned on, answering some inane questions about the upcoming winter and if the roads would be suitable for travel abroad. I swayed on my feet, feeling the strain of a few hours of sleep after training with Risteard. He had disarmed me multiple times, while I had yet to succeed. I usually ended up on my backside when I tried. I felt the strain in my body, and my eyelids were heavy with exhaustion. I would close them in brief intervals, trying to snatch a few seconds rest here and there.

The room faded and the voices congealed into a lump of incoherent sound. Faces blurred and wilted. Darkness clouded my vision, and my limbs sank into the ground.

Out of the haze came the sound of the river and the smell of spring grass. The afternoon sun was blinding. I raised my hand to block the rays, and a horse appeared from behind some boulders lining the channel where a waterfall dropped into a clear emerald pool. The animal raised its head, and I heard its call not in my ears but in my soul. Each step was like trudging through deep snow, and I looked down to see chains wrapped around my ankles. I waved my arms over my head to get the horse's attention, and it fixed a steady gaze on me before dashing across the valley at a gallop. I tried to run, but the weight of my feet was too much. If I could only take one more step, I would be free of these restraints.

I jerked awake with the resounding stomp of my foot. Everyone turned to look at me with a mix of confusion and annoyance. The princess' face glowed red with embarrassment and I knew she would spend the rest of the session devising a punishment for me.

Most women would be delighted to be right, but righteousness was overrated. The minute the princess and I returned to her room, she savagely grabbed my hair and pulled me close.

"What have you been up to?" she snarled. I shook my head, denying any wrongdoing, but she persisted. "You've looked like death every morning for weeks. Don't think for a moment you're too clever to conceal it from me. You're not spending your nights in debauchery, are you?" Again, I shook my head vehemently. "Whatever it is, it ends now. You've insulted the queen and embarrassed me!" She threw me to the ground and pinned my face to the floor with her foot. "If it's humiliation you seek, you shall have it." She brought her face to mine, ordered me not to move, then disappeared.

I lay on the hard, polished floor, time unrolling like a flowering bud, slow and inevitable. Every intake of breath burned my chest. A sharp pain accompanied every swallow, and my head throbbed as I waited. Finally, I heard the rapid trot of the princess' footsteps, followed by several heavier ones. The door opened, and the princess walked in with two guards.

"Take her to the courtyard," she ordered. Without hesitation, they lifted me under the arms and practically carried me from the room. I nearly tripped on the stairs then slipped on the wet grass of the inner courtyard. Rain fell heavily, but the guards strode forward, stopping at a post. The princess had not followed, staying dry under the eaves. Her eyes drifted upwards, and I traced her gaze to the castle walls. Staring down at me was the entire company of Ilano nobles, including the king and queen. Princess Caelyn had organized this spectacle.

Leather bindings secured my hands, and I was lifted off the ground by my wrists, my back to the crowd. The king made a stirring speech about respect and that every servant in his household, whether a scullery maid or lady-in-waiting, must adhere to the same standards of propriety. For the grievous offense of falling asleep during the queen's sitting, I was sentenced to five lashings with a thin cane. My damp hair fell over my face, and my clothing was soaked, chilling me through until my teeth chattered. Vaguely, I heard the rise and fall of voices in argument, and I turned my head toward the crowd, peering through strands of wet hair. I was not surprised to see Risteard speaking to the king and Princess Caelyn, no doubt appealing for my release. It was comforting to have him plead my case, but I feared if he intervened, if I allowed him to publicly protect me, it would cause too much suspicion in an already tenuous situation. I willed him to look at me, to stop arguing, and finally he met my eye.

Don't, I mouthed silently, shaking my head in a silent plea. His neck reddened and his jaw clenched, but he said no more.

The first lash struck my back before I could prepare. I inhaled sharply in surprise, my brain barely able to comprehend the pain before the cane sliced once again. In my childhood, I had experienced corporal punishment from my father on numerous occasions, and I had believed in those painful and humiliating moments that nothing could compare to the feeling of his belt across my backside. But as the cane came down a third and fourth time, knocking the wind from my lungs and tears from my eyes, I felt an immeasurable agony. The skin of my back was peeling away, I was sure of it, and the cane cut straight to my spine. My damp frock produced a sting like a thousand hornets. I struggled for air, and the scream that clawed at my throat. By the fifth blow, the only recourse was to shut down, and I slumped against the post, hanging limply by my pale arms. My back was warm, and I pictured the blood flowing down it to mix with the rain pooling below me. Two men lifted me enough to release my bonds, and my boneless arms fell useless at my side. They half carried, half dragged me back into the castle, and propped me against the wall. The princess appeared, arms crossed.

"Well," she said. "I hope you've learned an important lesson today."

It took all my remaining strength to nod.

"Good. Now go change into a dry frock, and then come to my rooms to dress me for dinner."

Using the wall for balance, I shuffled back to my room. My knees trembled so violently I had to stop several times to keep from falling, and it wasn't until I reached my door that my fingers stopped tingling and I could feel them again. I collapsed into the room, catching myself on the edge of the bed, and weakly dragged myself to my chest. My head throbbed, and a fire burned behind my eyes. I feared it would take me years to undress myself, let alone pull a dry frock over my damp skin. My fingers shook now, not in pain but in fear of how the princess might retaliate if I'm late.

A soft knock startled me out of my skin, and I placed a hand over the rapid beating of my heart. I tried to muffle the chattering of my teeth and listened. The knock came again, followed by a low voice.

"Are you there?" It was Risteard. I pressed my body against the door and whispered that I was. "Can I come in?" I could hear the tremor of worry.

I turned my back against the door, then immediately regretted it. Pain flared down my back and a sharp breath seethed through my teeth. I pressed my shoulder to the aged wood, sliding down the frame until I sat on the floor. Tears flowed down my hot cheeks, and I curled into a tight ball, half dressed, humiliated and sore.

Risteard knocked again, imploring me to let him in. I could not. It wasn't the disorder of my dress or the gashes striping my back. I could not let him see me in such a wretched state. True, he had probably seen me in worse predicaments, but now we were essentially allies in rebellion, I could not stomach the thought of him towering over me, a pathetic puddle, and deciding I wasn't strong enough to help him.

"Go away," I whispered. "Please leave me alone." Silence on the other side of the door, then footsteps retreating down the hall.

Astonishingly, I dressed in an amount of time suitable to spare me any further ire from the princess. I had her prepared for dinner within minutes. I limped through the evening. The throbbing in my head evolved into a pounding ache, and my chest heaved painfully with each breath. I longed for sleep, to fall exhausted into my bed, and put this awful day behind me.

Risteard kept his distance throughout dinner and the evening's activities, giving me the space I required to collect myself emotionally. I tried to conceal the pain from each step I took, but I'm certain he knew, and I was grateful he didn't say anything.

The evening was at a close, and the princess was taking her leave as I cleared away the cards and drinkware. I removed the princess' glass, and a folded piece of paper appeared underneath. I glanced around, and confirming no one was paying attention to me, I snatched it and tucked it into my frock. I continued as usual, assisting the princess into her bedclothes and brushing out her long hair, enduring the intrusion of the prince when he barged in to talk about nothing. All the while the note lay buried in the folds of my clothes, my thoughts only on what it contained. Could it be a secret note to the princess? Or perhaps she wished to pass it to someone else?

Once she dismissed me from her chamber, I wasted no time in unfolding the note. Until the moment I read the words, it never entered my mind the message was intended for me.

Meet me in the undercroft tonight. Please.

The short note was clearly written in Risteard's hand, and if it wasn't meant for me, we were both in for a shock. I headed straight for the undercroft, still wary of allowing him to see how I struggled. Carefully, I inched my way down the smooth steps, my hand pressed against the wall. At the bottom, I gave my eyes time to adjust to the dim light, and slowly stepped around barrels. I wondered if I preceded him, but as I moved into the room, I could hear him pacing in the dusky silence. He stopped when I coughed lightly and stepped forward to tower over me as I composed myself.

"How is the pain?" he asked, getting straight to the point as usual.

"Tolerable enough," I rasped.

His eyes narrowed, and he placed a finger to my chin and raised my face. He studied me critically, then pressed the back of his hand to my forehead.

"You're feverish," he said.

"I'm fine," I said, but my body betrayed me with a coughing fit that left me feeling lightheaded.

He frowned. "You're ill. And no wonder considering how you've been treated." He turned me back to the stairs and led me out of the undercroft. He ushered me into my room and made me lie down. I complied without hesitation.

"Sleep," he said. "I'll have a physician dispatched."

"Please don't," my voice was barely a squeak in my throat. "I don't want to cause trouble. More than I have at any rate."

"Even the princess can appreciate that an ill servant requires medical attention. We aren't barbarians, though we sometimes act like it." The last was mumbled angrily under his breath.

I tried to argue further but experienced another fit of coughing so fierce I felt the pain in my back was inconsequential.

"I'm having a physician come up immediately," he said. "Give me the dagger. I don't want him to find it on you."

I nodded and he turned around to give me privacy. I removed my frock, then unbuckled the sheath. I was astonished it wasn't detected this afternoon. I lay the sheath at the foot of the bed before covering myself with a blanket.

"All right," I said.

He retrieved the weapon, then left the room, promising to return with a doctor. With a sigh, I lay against the pillow, and immediately drifted into a weary and fitful sleep.

The heat on my face was so intense I felt my skin should melt away and my hair ignite in a plume of red. The dark smoke billowing around me limited visibility, and I lowered myself to the ground to escape the taste of it in my mouth. Failing wood creaked amid the roar of flames, and I crawled forward on my hands and knees, my skin marked with burns from smoldering embers. Beams crashed to the ground as the building gave way. I heard screaming, muffled by the smoke and flames and the pounding of the blood in my ears. I recognized the shrieks of dying horses being burned to death in their stalls. It grew louder as I inched forward. I called out for Amore and moved toward her stall, her screams rising in pitch. Sweat dripped into my eyes, the heat overwhelming, my palms raw and my dress torn and singed. The whole structure could collapse at any moment, but I had failed Amore once and I could not again. I reached her stall and slid my hand along the door until I felt the latch. Her hooves pounded against the stall, her cries frantic. I grasped the hot iron tightly, a wisp of smoke trailing from my burning skin. I pulled hard, and the instant the latch came free, the noise from inside the stall ceased. Frantically, I slid open the door and crawled inside. Amore was not there. I rubbed away the tears streaking my face and searched the piles of straw. I felt something solid, and I brushed away the straw, crying as huge timbers crashed to the ground. I recoiled when I felt human skin-- a face in the straw, burned but recognizable. Ula. I screamed louder than the roaring blaze consuming the stable, disintegrating into rubble and ash.

I awoke from the nightmare, my eyes flying open and my arms flailing at the face hovering over me. A pair of hands gently took my wrists and a voice calmly explained I had a dream, that I was safe, and he was there to help. I froze, inhaling gasps of clean air, clearing my vision from the haze of sleep. In the dim candlelight, I made out the face of a middle-aged man, smiling kindly. He put down my hands and explained he was a physician sent to examine me. In the corner stood a young woman, perhaps my age, holding a black satchel. She began removing items from the bag. The physician explained she was his niece, his 'little nurse.'

"She hopes to be a midwife someday," he said. I settled into the bed, and he began his examination. He felt my throat, under my arms, and my belly, asking if anything hurt. I pointed to my throat and my back.

"Lie on your stomach," he said. I rolled over, and he worked the shoulders of my nightgown downward. I flew out of bed and fixed him with a nasty glare. He held up his hands, saying he needed to examine me fully and meant no harm. He asked if I would feel more comfortable if Seline, the young woman, undressed me instead. I looked at the woman. She smiled. Reluctantly, I returned to the bed and submitted to a full examination, allowing the physician to closely study the wounds on my back, press his ear to several areas, and then apply a dressing that instantly soothed the pain. Seline wrapped me in a bandage to keep the medicine in place and then helped me turn over so the physician could listen to my heart. As he lay his ear against my chest, I began to cough violently, and I'm certain I dislodged a piece of lung.

"Take this." He handed me a small vial. "It will help you sleep peacefully. And you must stay in bed." He looked around the small room. "No hearth, so you'll need extra blankets to keep warm and smother out the fever. I'll give the cook medicine to make a broth." He rose from the bed, and I grasped his arm to stop him. I placed my hands on my head in the shape of a crown and made a motion to brush my hair. The physician cocked his head quizzically, and I continued to mime anything to indicate the princess, but he clearly didn't understand.

"Uncle." The young woman tugged his sleeve. "I believe she's worried about the princess."

"Ah," he said. "You serve Her Highness?"

I nodded.

"Don't worry. She would rather you be healthy." They gathered their things and left the room. Beyond the door I heard him address someone outside.

"She will live," he said, "but I insist she remain in bed, at least until the fever breaks. I will have my niece visit her over the next several days to monitor her. It would be in the girl's best interest to avoid the outdoors for the remainder of the rainy season, perhaps even the winter. She's a servant to the princess I understand?"

"Yes," came Risteard's distinctly low tone.

"She was wise to have me summoned. If the girl had remained in her current condition, the outcome may have been grave. She must be fed good broth with this medicine and kept warm. The fever is high, but not dangerously so, and the congestion in the lungs is not fixed and can be broken up and expelled. I have applied a poultice that will ease the pain of the wounds on her back. They will not scar. Please let the princess know she may well have saved the girl's life."

"I will."

"Fetch me if there is a change for the worse."

"I will."

"I bid you good evening then."

The physician and his niece's footsteps faded, and for several seconds silence permeated the room.

I sat up, staring at the vial with a clear, thick liquid in my hands. I sensed Risteard lingering outside the door, but he did not knock or speak. I knew he would wait all night until I invited him inside or told him to leave.

"Come in." The words came out in a tiny squeak. I'd genuinely lost my voice. I swallowed, mustering all my energy, and the strain to produce the words once more was almost too much to bear, but they were loud enough for Risteard's keen ears. He came inside and sat on the edge of the bed.

"You look terrible," he said with a small grin.

I stuck my tongue out at him, and his smile broadened.

"I think I may enjoy your inability to actually speak. Your silence is refreshing."

I punched him in the shoulder.

"You're lucky you took the dagger," I croaked.

"The physician says you'll heal with plenty of rest. And well deserved."

"I can't!" I squeaked. "The princess!"

"I'll handle the princess. If I make her out to be the hero who saved the life of her lady-in-waiting, she'll be so absorbed basking in the praise she won't even notice you're gone. A temporary replacement will be sent, and her hair will remain free of tangles in your absence."

My eyes narrowed. "You know that's not all I do."

"Of course. No more talking. Did the physician give you something to sleep?" I held up the vial. "Good. Take it."

I eyed the liquid suspiciously, concluded I was not important enough to poison, and tipped the contents into my mouth. A warm sensation travelled down my throat, and my eyes drifted shut when my head settled on the pillow. I hoped Risteard could see himself out. I was quite indisposed and did not intend to regain consciousness for some time. In a perfect state of dreamy euphoria, I would not have cared to awaken ever again.

CHAPTER 28

Princess Caelyn deigned to visit me once during my convalescence to bestow her best wishes for a quick recovery and magnanimously release me from my outdoor duties.

"At least until the snows melt," she amended. "But I do expect you to resume your work within the castle walls before the first sign of winter." Winter, I knew based on the drop in temperature, was not far off.

Seline, the young woman whom the physician referred to as his nurse, visited me in the castle several days a week to bring fresh medicines and observe my progress. I was feeling better. My coughing had turned from a dry hack to a wet, sloppy mess that produced all manner of expectorant, which she assured me was a good sign. My muscles ached, and my appetite had waned, but I was able to keep the broth in my stomach. However, when she introduced bread, I vomited. She watched me with concern, cleaned my face, and felt my skin. My temperature fluctuated from chilled to inferno hot, and I struggled to sleep. She left several vials of the sleeping draught with instructions not to drink more than one per night and promised to return with her uncle within a few days.

Aside from Seline, my only visitor was Risteard, who checked on me often throughout the day until I ordered him to stop. His constant attention was a mark of dereliction of duty and an annoyance.

"How do you expect me to get any sleep," I croaked, "when you keep barging in at all hours?"

"If I bother you to such an extent," he said with a tinge of insult, "then I will cease to disturb you with my cares about your welfare."

"I'm not saying you shouldn't care. Just not so often."

He stayed away for an entire day after that, but I only felt slightly guilty. In truth, I was enjoying a break from the everyday toils, even if I was spending the time miserably ill.

The violence of my coughing fits eventually faded to a tolerable level, but my fever had yet to break. Seline returned with her uncle, whose troubled expression was not lost on me.

"We will have to bleed her," he told his niece. "The fever is not behaving as I had hoped. If it becomes dangerously high, it may travel to her brain. Uncover her feet." Seline did as told and began rubbing my soles.

"They are very warm," she said.

"Fetch a basin of cold water. We must wrap her feet in wet cloths to draw the heat away from her head."

After Seline left the room, the physician took a small basin and black case from his bag. He opened the case, and from it withdrew a shining silver instrument ending in a sharp blade. My breath quickened as he laid the scalpel on a strip of linen near my head and began to roll up my sleeve. Instinctively, I pulled my arm away, but he held it firm, saying this was necessary to draw the toxins from my body and break my fever. I grew frantic, fearing I would bleed to death, and in desperation, I struck the physician in the face with my fist. In my weakened state it only startled him into letting me go. I retreated to the corner of the room and reached into my nightgown for the dagger that wasn't there. I'd forgotten Risteard had taken it, and I growled in frustration. This man might not even *be* a physician for all I knew. No doubt this had been a ploy to leave me vulnerable, to weaken me so he could slice an artery or two.

I grabbed the nearest heavy object, a candlestick, and raised it over my head just as Seline returned carrying a basin of water. She gasped, nearly dropping it. The physician held out his hand to quiet her and said, "She's delirious. We must be careful and act quickly."

She set the basin aside and approached me with her hands raised imploringly.

"It's going to be all right," she said softly. "We're trying to help you. Just put the candlestick down before someone gets hurt."

The only one who'll get hurt around here is you, lady, I thought. I swung the makeshift weapon wildly in her direction. Her sweetness couldn't fool me.

She jumped back and looked at her uncle. "What do we do?"

"We need someone strong to overpower her. In this state, even though she's small, her body will believe it's capable of fighting both of us. She'll end up hurting herself if we don't subdue her quickly."

"Should I find a guard?"

"Yes." He placed a finger to his lips and then pointed it at his niece. "Who was that knight who summoned me? He should be quite capable of helping."

"I've seen him," she nodded. "I'll bring him back straightaway!" Their voices were muddled and slow, as if they spoke from behind a thick door after being out in the icy cold. I watched Seline leave, then turned my burning gaze on the physician. He smiled and held his hands up.

"I won't hurt you," he said, though I could barely understand him. His next words were a jumbled mess, and I was sure he was speaking an unknown language. A spy, no doubt.

My arm began to feel the strain from holding the heavy candlestick, but I would not relent. I was finished being a victim, finished allowing others to use me as they wished, to damage my body, and to poison my mind. Minutes ticked by and it remained just the two of us. I began to think that if I struck quickly, I could eliminate this man before he had a chance to blink. I focused on the top of his head where the butt of the candlestick would crack his skull, steadied my breathing, and prepared to leap.

The door flew open and Risteard strode purposefully inside, pausing by the physician and taking in my appearance. His expression was characteristically blank. "What's going on?" Risteard asked the physician without taking his eyes off me.

"She's become mad with the fever," the physician said. "We must begin treatment immediately, but as you can see, she has gone wild. We need you to help subdue her."

Risteard flinched and took a step toward me.

I gritted my teeth and gripped the candlestick tighter, widening my stance. He took another step, his gaze darting over me, and another until he stood within arm's reach.

"Put it down," he ordered.

In that moment, I knew with absolute certainty he was responsible for everything: the attack on Praed, the death of my father, every awful thing between then and now. Even this illness which weakened my body. It was all his fault. He played me for a fool, but now my eyes were wide open, and I would exact revenge for my family's honor. I raised the candlestick higher, and when his eyes caught the movement, I balled my other fist and drove it hard toward the vital parts of his anatomy.

Before my fist could strike, he caught it in his own, denying me the satisfaction of bringing the First Knight of King Conall to his knees. I swung the candlestick toward the side of his head, but he anticipated and grabbed my wrist, squeezing until I dropped it at his feet. He drew me close and whispered in my ear.

"You forget. I know all your moves."

I fought against his grip but was no match for him even at my best. I struggled valiantly, kicking his shins while he dragged me to the bed and threw me down, pinning my arms. Seline grabbed my ankles and held my legs firm as the physician laid a cloth over my mouth and nose. I breathed in a sickly pungent odor, and fog spread over my mind and heaviness weighed on my limbs. Before the darkness claimed me, I locked eyes with Risteard, tears rolling down my face. My eyes closed and the only words I could speak were to myself, asking why he would do this to me. And I knew I would never get the chance to ask him out loud.

A flash of white, more brilliant than lightning, slashed across my vision. Whispers echoed in my ears, and I felt light as the whiteness spread, beckoning me closer. My mind was calm, and my body was enveloped in a warmth that spread from my head to my feet. The heat rose until I felt I was boiling in hot oil, and then suddenly the heat dissipated, and the light faded. I opened my eyes a fraction. Faces hovered over me, blurry and distorted, and muffled voices swirled and congealed in my ears. I closed my eyes again and faded like the light.

My eyes blinked open again, and the room was quiet. I turned my head, but my vision was too blurry to recognize the person sitting asleep in the chair next to the bed. I shook my head to clear my thoughts and instantly regretted it as pain radiated across my skull. I pressed my hands against my head, and the movement drew the attention of the person next to me.

"Hey, there," a soft, feminine voice spoke quietly. I lowered my hands, rubbed my eyes, and looked at the face hovering over me. I recognized Seline. She dabbed my forehead with a cool cloth and said, "You had us worried for a while, but the fever finally broke last night, thank goodness."

I spread my hands then made a motion of the setting sun--my way of asking how long I had been asleep.

Seline gave a half smile. "No need to pretend. You talked quite a bit during your fever dreams. Don't worry," she assured me after panic crossed my features. "I won't say anything, and my uncle is sworn to secrecy by his professional oath. And...because that big knight threatened his life if he talked."

Risteard. Listening to Seline, I remembered the horrible things I had done and said and thought, not only regarding him, but her and her uncle.

"I'm sorry," I whispered.

"There's no need for that," she said. "The fever made you say and do those things, not you. I've seen it before. The sickness poisons your mind with all your deepest fears."

"I need to apologize to the knight," I said. "I fear I may have hurt him. Can you find him?"

"That shouldn't be difficult," she smiled. "He stays close to your room. That's a good friend you have there."

"I know," I said quietly as I faced the wall.

"I'm going to have a supper prepared for you. You need to start eating solid foods as soon as possible to build up your strength."

"All right," I whispered. She left the room, closing the door quietly behind her. I dreaded the look on Risteard's face when I saw him again. I know what I thought and what I did--I couldn't imagine what I said while delirious with fever. Did I believe Risteard was using me or betrayed me? Instinctively I thought *no*, but an inkling of doubt crept into my mind.

Minutes later, the door opened and Risteard rushed into the room. He pulled the lone chair close, and I felt a sob building in my chest and bit the inside of my cheek to quell it.

"Seline said you were awake." He couldn't keep the excitement from his voice.

"How long was I asleep?"

"Three days. Doctor Bayl and his niece have been here night and day to break your fever."

"They saved my life?"

"Yes." His tone was strange.

I finally turned and faced him. His blue eyes were dull, and he looked like he hadn't slept in days.

"You look terrible," I whispered.

"You should look in a mirror."

"I suppose the princess expects me to return to my duties soon."

"She heard of your dire condition and has been milking sympathy from everyone."

"Typical." I stared at the ceiling, too embarrassed to offer the apology Risteard deserved.

"I'll let you rest." He rose to leave.

"There is a possibility I may have spoken out of sickness, but the fears are real," I said. "You're not pretending to be my friend with the intention to betray me, are you?" I shook, and my voice trembled. He said nothing. I turned to look at him, and his usual blank expression was gone, replaced by a flash of anger that gave way to emotional anguish.

"I will try not to take your doubts personally," he said. "I only wish to regain your trust. I hope you take my word as truth." He reached into his tunic, pulled out my dagger, and tucked it halfway under my pillow. He held my gaze for a moment, then turned away.

My eyes settled on the dagger. "Risteard, *stop!*" I propped myself up and angled toward him. He was halfway out the door. "I'm sorry." I doubled over and sobbed. He closed the door and knelt by the bed.

"I know you didn't mean it," he said. "But I don't blame you for thinking it. I can only say that it would bring me no honor to deceive and betray an innocent young woman." I buried my face in the blankets, ashamed of my words and thoughts, and he continued saying, "I enlisted you to work toward the same cause because we both wish for the same outcome, but I'm your friend because I want to be." He grasped my shoulder and squeezed it lightly, and I uncovered my face, sniffled, and took several deep breaths. Finally, I met Risteard's eye, and he smiled reassuringly. Impulsively, I leaned forward and touched my forehead to his, breathing deeply one last cleansing sigh.

"Rest," he said.

I slid under the blankets and watched him leave. Before the door latch engaged, I'd fallen into a dreamless sleep.

CHAPTER 29

In accordance with the princess' wishes, I resumed my duties before the first snowflakes fell. My sore and weakened state made my movements slow, which perturbed the princess since it made her late to breakfast. To expedite my return to normalcy, she heeded the physician's order for meals including red meat at least three times weekly. I was more than happy to comply and enjoyed choice cuts of beef and jerked venison for several weeks until my strength returned. I even boasted extra body fat that would insulate me over the winter.

While I recovered, Risteard and I shelved our combat training in favor of political intrigue. We had amassed an impressive list of people who pledged to stand behind us, and Risteard began planning the strategy for a revolt.

"It would be beneficial to strike when the kingdom is most vulnerable," he explained. "And attack at its weakest point."

"Winter is a vulnerable time," I said.

"True, but it's difficult to move a massive army in the snow. An economic downfall would suffice, such as a poor crop season. Or perhaps an emotionally turbulent time."

"Like a death in the family?"

"Yes, though such a thing is hard to predict when everyone is otherwise healthy. I'm thinking of a less dire situation. Something that might occupy everyone's attention. A marriage perhaps?" He smiled slyly.

"A marriage of one of the king's children would absorb much of his resources as well. He would be very distracted," I agreed.

"We must find out more about this arranged marriage Caelyn has planned. Has she said anything recently?"

"No, and she hasn't received any letters from Jervell Kade in months."

"I'll start dropping hints to the king that an advantageous marriage should be considered to secure the throne for his children. If he believes his crown is in danger, he'll be persuaded to act."

"What do you want me to do?"

"Listen. Pay attention to correspondence." He paused thoughtfully. "Caelyn is very anxious to marry off her brother. We should give her reason to feel additional pressure."

"What do you mean?"

"If she believes Brannon has affection for a woman who she deems unsuitable, she'll act quickly to secure him the marriage she prefers."

"What might lead her to believe the prince feels such affection?"

"Evidence of an affair," he stated matter-of-factly.

"I don't think she would be shocked at his having casual…*relations*…with assorted women."

"She would not. What she might find alarming is him paying regular attention to a particular woman."

"What sort of evidence might this require?"

"Tokens of affection: a letter, a lock of hair, a handkerchief…little things women give their suitors."

"I have no idea what such things would be."

"I'm sure you've had suitors. Didn't they try to win you over with gifts?"

"I don't know why you'd presume that." I curled my lip, remembering the string of spoiled boys Mother paraded into Riverstone. It wasn't a subject I cared to discuss.

"You're the daughter of a noble house."

Obviously. Girls were of prime marrying age starting at fifteen. The fact that Risteard considered me marriageable made my cheeks burn.

One of his eyebrows rose and he tilted his head, intrigued. "Not a pleasant subject?"

"Let's just say nobody won."

He rolled his eyes. "All right. What might a man give you that would accurately convey his intentions to your satisfaction?"

I shrugged. "It depends on his intentions."

"You know what I mean!" Risteard threw his hands in the air. "If you loved a man, what might you give *him* to indicate your affections?"

I focused on the scattered papers on the desk and truly considered his question. I loved so few and even fewer loved me. I knew how to show my love to Ula and Amore, but a man? The little experience I had with suitors in addition to the actions of the men at the palace didn't exactly inspire romantic imaginings. I looked up at Risteard and he raised a questioning brow. Firelight from the hearth emphasized his straight nose and strong chin. He ran a hand through his black hair and a lock fell onto his forehead while another stuck out at an angle. I expected him to fix it, but he didn't. I bit the inside of my lip to keep from smiling at his untidy appearance.

"Well," I began, "if we're speculating hypothetically, I suppose I would accept the attentions of a man who gifted me a horse and promised never to come near me unless I asked him to."

He chuckled. "I guess that's fair. Good luck to the poor man who chooses to court you."

"I don't think I'll have to worry about that. Between my position as a servant and the fact that I'm utterly horrible to get along with, I'll end my days a spinster."

"Well, at least you have a realistic view of yourself." He ducked when I tossed an apple core at his head. His reflexes were aggravatingly acute.

I never imagined I would miss cleaning the mews in the icy coldness of a Praed morning, but after spending several weeks inside the castle without a taste of fresh air, I was ready to claw through the walls for a few precious seconds of cool breeze on my skin. The princess now called the outside time "accomplishment improving," and it wasn't *my* accomplishments that were the focus. Apparently, she had moved past the embarrassment she felt being shown up by my piano playing and was eager to have me teach her the piece. I didn't know how to teach like Risteard with patience, diligence, and repeated practice. So, I mimed the notes so she could mimic them. This strategy worked to some extent, but without passion, the melody was lifeless. Still, she was content with her progress, and eventually performed for Queen Shaeli, who dutifully praised her daughter's talent.

"I haven't heard that piece," the queen noted. "Where does it come from?"

"Oh, some local piece I thought I'd learn to entertain the people of Praed at the winter celebration."

Winter celebration? What was she talking about?

"Ah, well it is quite beautiful, but perhaps not appropriate for an uplifting celebration."

"Nonsense, Mother." She waved away the comment. "If there is anything these people know, it's depression. This is me relating to the natives."

"Careful, my dear," the queen said. "I have not yet seen who stands in the way of our victory. It may be a person of Praed."

"Please," the princess laughed. "The only thing the people of Praed know how to do is lose their country."

I'd learned to see past Princess Caelyn's callous words to the information hidden in what seemed an innocuous conversation. I presumed the king was planning an event that included the people of Praed--most likely to curry favor with nobles and endear himself to lowly farmers. Would I see people I knew there? Inevitably. Might I have opportunities to speak with them? If I was careful. Could this celebration signal the onset of an affair between the prince and an unknown lady? If my devious skills served me well.

The rest of the day, I fidgeted restlessly wondering how I could mingle with the Praed visitors, let them see me and feel my resolve, and set the final act of this dangerous play in motion. I couldn't wait to tell Risteard what I heard, although he probably knew the king's plans already. I rushed through the preparations for the princess' evening beauty regimen and had her at the dinner table faster than ever.

"It's high time you dedicate yourself to your obligations with such haste," she said.

The king and queen took their places, followed by Prince Brannon, characteristically late. Risteard joined the table occupied by the king's inner circle and most valued knights, but I couldn't draw his attention before the first course arrived.

Platters were passed and the clinking of utensils and goblets overcame the voices quieted by the anticipation of filling mouths with food instead of words. King Conall rose from his ornate, high-backed, banquet chair and raised his hand for attention. The din receded, and the king's loud voice boomed.

"Friends," he began, an unsettling smile on his face. "Your devotion over the last year has been truly humbling, and I wish for nothing more than to reward you for your loyalty." He raised his hand for quiet again when the crowd pounded the tables enthusiastically. "The time has come to officially unite the kingdoms by bringing Praed into Ilano's fold."

A noble stood, and the king gave him permission to speak.

"You have been very generous, Your Majesty. Many of us in this room have been granted lands and houses in Praed, and though the climate has proven difficult for some, I believe I speak for many that we have made a good home here." The man paused while people around him murmured and nodded. "I would be interested to hear what more Your Majesty has planned to further our cause."

"I'm very glad you asked, Lord Suidh." The king grinned darkly. "The people of Praed admittedly have impressed me with their resilience. However, I think we can all agree that a conquered people must be reminded of their place lest they entertain certain ideas of revolt."

My stomach twisted. Did the king know what Risteard and I had been up to? I sought out Risteard, but he did not meet my eye nor give any indication he was troubled by the king's words.

"In a few weeks' time, we will enter the heart of winter, at which point I will hold a celebration. We will have dancing, a grand feast, winter ale, and the worthiest people of Praed will be invited as our guests." The king continued amid the confusion. "We will show great kindness, as a father would to his children, and in turn they must oblige us with obedience. You may not agree with my proposal, you may find my decision insulting, and you may return to Ilano in anger. Know this, if you defy my decree and flee, your lands will return to the crown." He waited, building the anticipation.

"We will bring the people of Praed into the castle and into our households. Not only as servants, but as spouses. This is the business of ruling a kingdom, and the ultimate end to a conquered people." Voices blended into a cacophony of confused and angry conversations at the shocking decree. The king sat back, a satisfied grin on his face, and ate as if nothing had happened.

Princess Caelyn barely contained her anger. "Father, you cannot be serious. You don't honestly expect a decent Ilano nobleman to take a Praed in marriage."

The king set down his fork. "Now, what's wrong with Praed women that they cannot make decent wives? Many beauties were spared, and many from honorable descent."

"Honorable or not, it would tarnish their Ilano lineage!"

"Look around you, Caelyn," the king whispered. "Many Ilano nobles you see here were not doing well at home. They are not exactly the elite of Ilano. At least not anymore. If they expect to continue to live in the manner to which they have become accustomed, they will heed my words."

"What about me or Brannon?" Caelyn demanded, her cheeks crimson. "Do you expect *us* to marry Praed natives?"

"Of course not." King Conall looked insulted at the thought. "You and your brother are royalty. You are held to higher standards."

Princess Caelyn met Prince Brannon's eyes across the table, and the pair engaged in a silent conversation. The prince drank the entire contents of his goblet, and I wished that I, too, could escape into an intoxicated haze.

The princess barely took two steps into her room when the prince joined her, his face pale as he paced. He perched himself on the edge of the settee by the hearth, his leg bouncing rapidly and his hands wringing nervously.

Caelyn sat at the vanity. "What are you so worried about?"

"You heard what Father said!" The prince exploded, getting to his feet again. "He means to raise the people of Praed to our level."

"Is that what he's doing? Or is he alienating all the men who brought him the throne?"

His brow furrowed, considering her words. "You think this will benefit our cause?"

"I don't care what he says," the princess sneered while I unpinned her tight curls. "No decent Ilano man will find comfort in the arms of a Praed woman. We are two different species."

"With all the same parts in my experience."

"It's one thing to take one as a lover. Marriage is an entirely different matter. Giving a Praedan woman the run of an Ilano household is insulting."

"You're such a snob."

"I have taste and high standards. If that makes me a snob, then I'm proud to be one."

"Do you think many will return to Ilano?"

"It doesn't matter if ten men or one leave. If any return, they will spread the news of what he's done here. And though the people of Praed may be grateful for an evening of free food and drink, when they realize they're being put on display and potentially forced into marriages, they will also spread dissent. Father has made a grave error indeed."

The prince smiled, a wicked thing.

"Don't do anything foolish before you're properly engaged," the princess warned.

"Such as pledge myself to a Praedan woman?"

"Exactly."

"There's no need to worry on that score. As you said, they make perfectly acceptable lovers, but marriage would be despicable."

"It might be in your best interest to curb your appetites in that direction. You never know when an Ilano noble may have intentions toward the lady you wish to bed."

The prince sighed. "You demand much of me, Caelyn."

"You're a grown man, Brannon. Show some restraint. Not only for your own benefit, but for the woman who may stand next to you someday."

"Father doesn't appear troubled by such considerations. Neither does Mother."

"Father is discrete," she pointed out. "And you are a fool if you do not believe his infidelities affect Mother. But as a queen, she is poised and indifferent. Those women are nothing and shall never hold her place at his side."

"Why can I not have the same arrangement?"

"Because you're an idiot who displays his manhood for any woman to mount. Your lack of discrimination and public indecency would insult any wife's sensibilities."

"We cannot all live our lives in pious celibacy as you have, Caelyn."

Much to my astonishment, the princess laughed.

"I wouldn't have chosen those particular words for my brand of celibacy. I am a lady and am therefore chaste until marriage as my station dictates."

"A pretty turn of phrase, I grant you."

"I believe 'pious celibacy' is better applied to Risteard, don't you agree?" She turned to the prince with a raised eyebrow and a sly smile. My hands did not hesitate as I pulled a brush through her thick hair, but my mind whirled at this strange exchange.

"He really can be a terrible bore," said the prince. "I was only having a bit of fun, and no harm came to the lady."

"Which is more than can be said for yourself."

He touched the side of his nose. "I still maintain my nose remains slightly crooked to this day. He has no sense of fun and has a beastly temper."

I betrayed no smile, but secretly I delighted picturing Risteard hitting Prince Brannon squarely in the nose, defending a poor lady. I imagined the prince on the floor, blood pouring down his face, him wailing in agony and indignation while Risteard stands over him, glaring with hostility. In general, I abhorred violence, but when justified, the prospect was satisfying indeed.

CHAPTER 30

Risteard agreed the winter celebration presented a good opportunity to further our plans, and when the date drew near, I became jittery. I had made a point to avoid anyone from Praed out of pride, embarrassment, and fear. Now, I relished in the anticipation of secret exchanges under the king's nose. I had to be careful not to be noticed for one overheard word could ruin my deaf-mute disguise. I prepared some notes to pass surreptitiously to supporters in advance and scouted some hidden places to talk in private. Keeping the princess occupied was a priority. I planned to keep her glass of cider full, but Risteard went further. He hinted to several nobles that the king was considering a match for her, and he anticipated they would trip over themselves vying for her attention.

"That's pretty devious," I said. I feigned disapproval at his underhanded deception, but a grin twitched at the corners of my mouth.

"There's no harm in it. She loves being the center of attention," he said.

She proved that statement later. She swept through the corridor resplendent in a flowing indigo gown, her hair glittering with jewels. Daughters of Ilano nobles fawned over her, and their giggles reached such a pitch it was a struggle to keep from flinching. The princess accepted their compliments with pleasure, but I could tell she found no joy in their company. These ladies were not her trusted Ilano friends but substitutes meant to bolster her ego and relieve boredom. I tried to remember their names, but the princess had them on a rotating schedule and it was hard to keep track.

"Father was so angry when the king declared Ilani men should take Praedan women as wives. He was arranging an alliance between my brother and a nice Ilano girl, but now he has to start over," one lady said.

"That girl was me," another said, glaring.

The ladies came to a stop and stared. The princess raised an eyebrow and the first lady's eyes widened.

"I'm sorry," she said.

"The king should have considered what would happen to us 'nice Ilano girls' when he ordered the men to marry Praeds." She gave an accusatory glare to the princess before hurrying down the corridor. The other ladies shifted nervously and looked to her for guidance.

"Go on," the princess said. "I'll follow shortly."

She watched the ladies with pursed lips, hands clasped tightly before her. I waited, head bowed. That girl wouldn't be joining the princess' entourage again.

"Are you there?" the princess whispered.

The hairs on the back of my neck raised. Was she talking to me?

"I'm here," a voice said. "Meet me in the gentlemen's drawing room. It's empty."

She grabbed my arm and dragged me down the hall. A man dressed in a red velvet robe lined with fur met us outside the room. I recognized the clothing of a high councilman. He wasn't very tall, but that didn't stop him from looking down his snub nose at me. His eyes were like doll's eyes--black and lifeless.

"You received my note?" the princess said.

"Yes." He lazily turned toward her and the corner of his mouth inched upward. "Shall we?" He extended a hand toward the open door. It was small, delicate, like a lady's hand. There was a thin silver band on the little finger. A signet ring perhaps.

She turned me to look at her and said, "Keep watch." She emphasized her words by pointing at her eyes and then out into the hall. "Knock if anyone comes near." She rushed inside, but her companion was less eager. He casually swaggered after her, casting a smile over his shoulder before closing the door.

I dropped to my knees so hard pain shot up my legs. I pressed my ear to the keyhole and listened.

"I can guess what this is about." His voice lilted, mockingly, and he punctuated his words with a giggle.

"Why is Father forcing intermarriage? I know it isn't to 'unite our countries' as he so tritely claims," she said. I could hear her agitated pacing.

"My dear princess, you know why. Praed is full of dirty blood. The king wishes to cleanse the people."

She stopped with a stomp. "The council is behind him?"

"There was no arguing against it. He's already arranged marriages."

"Even for you?"

There was silence for several moments. I glanced around to make sure no one was coming, then closed my eyes. I heard the princess' toe tapping, and I could picture her waiting impatiently for a reply.

"Perhaps," he said.

"Are you prepared to marry? Did the cure work for you?"

"Did it work for you?"

Her pacing resumed.

"There is no speaking against him." His voice was so soft I had to cover my other ear to hear better. "He wouldn't listen then, and he won't listen now."

"This doesn't change anything. It will only serve to persuade others to join our side. The plan still stands."

"What an inspiration you are."

"We should only speak through messages from now on. We can't risk being overheard."

"Don't you trust your lady to sound the alarm?"

"She's an idiot. She might wander off and we'll get caught."

"Suit yourself, dearie." His voice was closer, and I straightened just before the door started opening.

"Watch yourself, Crane." She stalked down the hall, and he snickered at our backs.

My hands shook and my skin prickled. I knew that name. The prince had spoken it referring to a co-conspirator. I stifled a smile. I was right. The royal siblings had a spy in the council.

Ever alert and eager for public display, the princess drew up instructions for a new set of gowns and sent me to deliver them to the dressmaker. I hadn't spoken to Ula since my birthday, and I planned to take advantage of the opportunity. Once the princess' gown specifications were in the dressmaker's hands, she waved me away and I hurried to Ula's station.

We embraced and I said, "Will you ever stop growing?"

"You're looking well yourself, Laria." She inspected my figure. "You don't appear nearly as thin as when I last saw you."

"I have been given extra rations until recently," I told her. "I was ill for a while and quite weak, but I'm better now." I said nothing more for fear of deepening the concern I read on Ula's sweet face.

"What else has been happening?" she asked. "I feel very ignorant being stuck in this corner."

"Well, I'm sure you're aware of the winter celebration. The king is using it to entice his fellow countrymen to take Praed brides."

"Why?" Ula asked, her jaw agape.

"Why else? To unite the countries."

She looked skeptical. "Do you really believe that?"

"No. I think he means to breed us out."

"No respectable Praedan woman will marry a man from Ilano."

"She might not have a choice. Times are desperate. Faced with starvation or a roof over her head, a woman may choose the lesser of two evils."

Ula's shoulders sagged and her bottom lip trembled. "Everything's falling apart," she whispered, her eyes misting with tears.

I put my arm around her shoulders. "Don't worry, little gem. I'll keep you safe."

"I don't worry for myself. I worry for you, Laria. Down here, I'm out of the way. Hidden. But you're up there among them. How are you staying safe?"

I glanced around to ensure no one was watching, then opened my frock slightly to show Ula the dagger.

Her eyes widened. "Laria!' she whispered. "Where did you get that?"

"Never you mind." I folded the weapon back into the fabric.

"Do you know how to use it?"

"Yes, so there's no need to concern yourself with my welfare."

"I don't like this," she said nervously.

"I'm not thrilled about the prospect of having to use it, but I cannot go on as a helpless waif."

Ula regarded me as if seeing me for the first time.

"Does Mother know?" she asked quietly.

"No," I shot back, a little too loud. "Mother has been no help to me, and I don't need her approval nor her permission. She sits passively with her embroidery while the queen drones on. She makes no attempt to show the strength of character she prided herself on and wallows in the past and anger." Ula lowered her eyes, and I realized I'd crushed her hope that Mother would somehow orchestrate a rescue. I hugged her tightly, whispered my love, and rushed from the room.

It was hard to fathom that this time last year I was fretting over what to give Ula for her birthday, and now I worked toward giving her a lifetime free of servitude. People flooded into the Great Hall, more people than I had ever seen assembled there. Familiar faces gaped at the finery on display, shocked at how different the castle looked. Many appeared in good health while others clearly reflected the hardships of the new regime. There were only a few I did not recognize, and many were on my list. I took a deep breath to calm my nerves. Everyone finally settled for the feast while dancers dressed in bright reds, greens, and yellows entertained them with graceful prowess. Every movement glittered in the candlelight, accompanied by the strum of lutes and the ringing of bells.

Course after course of meats dripping with sauces were served, along with seasonal vegetables roasted, spiced, and drenched with butter. A light selection of fruit compotes and freshly baked pies followed. Wine and ale flowed freely, and no glass or goblet went long unfilled. Between the warmth of the fires, the full bellies, and the loose atmosphere of intoxication, every face in the room wore a smile. Except, of course, Risteard with his perpetual serious expression. For his own sake, I wished he could for once relax and enjoy the jovial atmosphere, even if we intended to use this opportunity to work. On further thought, I don't believe I'd ever seen Risteard intoxicated, and the very thought made me cover my mouth to stifle a giggle.

Elejick banners draped from floor to ceiling in the alcoves between pillars wrapped in green velvet trimmed with gold lace. Iron chandeliers crafted to resemble tree branches glowed above our heads, and twinkling candelabras filled the room with dancing light. Liveried servants stood ready to attend every need of the guests, filling crystal flutes with sparkling cider and delivering delectable treats to guests. Musicians tuned their instruments on a raised platform, and the swish of skirts mingled with the rhythmic tap of boots and murmured conversations. But beyond the finery and awestruck faces, the satisfied bellies and fuzzy heads, lay the inevitable truth that this was but a fantasy, and tomorrow all would face their normal lives--some in poverty, others in prosperity. But tonight, all accepted the dream as reality.

Until that evening, the princess insisted I don a simple frock consisting of a long-sleeved shift, a shapeless, ankle-length woolen tunic, and an apron. Tonight, the princess wished to exhibit her generosity by ensuring all the servants were properly dressed and presentable. For me, this meant for the first time I was outfitted in a proper gown, fit for a lady-in-waiting. The soft fabric was cut modestly just below my neck and was the color of the river at twilight. The sleeves were a shade darker and hugged my arms down to the wrist. There was no pattern stitched across the bodice or train, but the simplicity suited my taste for understated elegance. A new scarf wrapped my head to cover my hair, but when the princess wasn't looking, I tugged out a strand to hang down my back as a signal to my friends. Glimpsing my reflection, I was pleased I had begun to slightly resemble a woman.

The musicians began a traditional dance of Praed and it turned my stomach to hear the familiar melody, knowing it played to patronize the people and manipulate their trust. Men and women I recognized filled in the set with wistful expressions, many with tears gleaming in their eyes. I couldn't bear to watch, and I retreated to the shadows behind a pillar, wishing I could drown out the noise that brought memories of a forgotten past.

A deep voice spoke from the darkness behind me. "How refreshing to see you formally dressed as a lady-in-waiting."

I startled, my hand flying to my chest. "You scared the living soul out of me, Risteard. What are you doing hiding back here?"

"I should ask the same of you," he countered. "Aren't you supposed to be mingling with your fellow countrymen?"

"Most of them are dancing."

"It's a song of your people?"

"Yes." My voice dropped to a whisper. "We used to play it in the spring, when newborn foals brought hope to the upcoming year, and every noble house would take turns holding banquets to show their appreciation to the laborers and raise glasses of kumis to toast good wishes for a bountiful harvest. My mother danced so beautifully to this music. Everyone from lords and ladies to hired hands said so, and they loved watching her. My father could not have been prouder." I pursed my lips, resentment rising like bile in my throat.

"Did you enjoy dancing, too?"

"Oh, no." I laughed. "I was much too awkward and clumsy. Mother made me sit silent and smiling politely while the music played. Ula dances very well, though. I wish she was here." I stepped around the edge of the pillar and watched the dancers, remembering the movements I could rarely practice myself.

"Laria? Laria Audrey of Riverstone?" I turned around at the sound of my full name, which I hadn't heard spoken for many months. A man stood there, regarding me with wonder.

"It's really you isn't it?" the man stepped closer, the candlelight illuminating his face. I felt Risteard tense at my side, and his hand moved to the hilt of his sword.

"Thom?" I whispered, my lips barely moving. I recognized him as Thomlyn Wyrwyk, whom I had known almost my entire life. He'd grown up the son of a noble lord on an estate northwest of Riverstone called Thistledon, and his family raised prized ebony stallions whose bloodlines were coveted throughout the country. He was not much older than I, yet his dark brown hair was already gray at the temples. The mischievous gleam in his dark brown eyes had faded, his face lined with worry. I stepped toward him, clasping the hands of the boy I knew to give comfort to the man before me.

"It's Lord Wyrwyk now," he said.

"I'm sorry. Your father was a good man."

"Yes," he whispered, blinking back tears. "As was yours. My family mourned his loss."

"Thank you," I lowered my eyes and released his hands. "I wrote to your father not knowing of his passing."

"Yes, I know. As Lord of Thistledon, the letter was placed in my hands. I couldn't believe what I read and thought it might be a trick."

"No trick," I held his gaze. "We may have lost Praed, but the war is not over. Many have pledged to stand together when the time comes. Will you?"

Lord Wyrwyk hesitated, then looked over my head.

"Will you dance with me, Laria? And we can speak more of this."

"I can't. You know what a clumsy oaf I am! Besides, these people think I'm mute. If I talk to you so publicly, I'll be ruined."

"How ever have you managed to fool them this long?"

I punched him solidly in the upper arm.

"Ouch! Just the dance then. It will give me time to think."

My eyes flickered briefly to Risteard standing like a statue.

"If you insist on being disgraced," I said. "Then I'll dance with you. But your toes might never forgive you."

Lord Wyrwyk smiled, took my hand, and led me to the set of dancers moving perfectly in time to the music. I felt eyes on me, and more than one person whispered behind their hands. I knew it was important to be seen, but I dreaded being on display, unlike Mother who relished attention. I played through the steps in my head, trying to remember their order when Lord Wyrwyk grabbed my hand and led me in sync with the others. I tripped and missed several steps. His smile did not fade, and I began to trust his lead and relax into the movements. Even when I collided with another lady, I smiled, and the ripple of ease spread to the other dancers. Our hardships faded, and we were once again among friends, dancing together in the palace of King Llewlyn, our families and homes restored.

The music ended and the dream with it. I stared at my feet and pretended not to hear the clapping. Then Lord Wyrwyk led me off the floor to a private alcove. If the princess saw, she did not ruin the moment by ordering me to fetch her a sweet treat or fill her glass.

"That was wonderful," Lord Wyrwyk said after ensuring we were alone.

I was breathless. "I haven't danced in years!"

"It shows!"

"Very funny, *Lord* Wyrwyk."

"Please call me *Thom*. No one else does since Father died, and I rather miss it."

"If you like. Have you thought about my letter?"

"You don't waste time with small talk, do you?"

"There's no time for small talk. Besides, I've always been terrible at it, you know that."

"Others have pledged their word to serve you?"

"I wouldn't say 'serve' me. But many have said they would support me and raise arms should I ask."

"I never thought you of all people would play such a risky game."

"Why not? I never did what I was told and defied my parents every chance I could."

"Yes, but always for your own ends."

"Are you saying I'm selfish?"

"Back then, yes. But now, I find you changed."

"Haven't we all?" We turned toward the crowd gathered in the ballroom.

"My family has been fortunate to have an estate secluded enough to escape confiscation. If I publicly support you, I could lose my home."

I wiped a hand across my brow to hide behind my sleeve. "You've already lost your home," I said. "You've simply retained a building."

"Oh?" he turned on me sharply. "And if you still had Riverstone and weren't made to be a servant, would you be entertaining this ridiculous notion?"

I opened my mouth to argue but paused to think. *Would* I stand up against King Conall if I had been allowed to live at home with my family? I would have felt the loss of my father and the injustice of a new king, but I would have been comfortable. Would I have noticed the suffering of the people? I wouldn't have personal knowledge of the royal family and how horrible they were. Perhaps we could have lived a semblance of a normal life, not as happy as we were, but content enough. That is, until the king decreed that Ilano men should take Praed ladies as their brides and force them into marriages to weaken her people.

I bowed my head. "I cannot deny I would think very differently if I still lived at Riverstone," I said. "However, though my days might pass in comfort, my mind would be filled with fear. For what might stop the king from seizing our lands or burning it to the ground? I do not wish to live in a world where a black-hearted villain controls my destiny."

"You're determined?"

"There is nothing I want more in this world than to see the Elejick royal family crumble into dust," I whispered.

"You've become quite fierce, Laria. I'm almost frightened of you myself. I cannot imagine the look on those blackguards' faces when this crashes around them."

"Does that mean you're with me?" I asked hopefully.

"I fear what you may do if I say no, so I heartily say yes."

I grinned and it took all my self-restraint to keep from hugging him. I settled for pressing his hand and thanking him sincerely.

"I can't make any promises that we will be successful if I call upon you, but if we stand together, we will show King Conall he has underestimated our people."

"I find you much changed, Laria," he said, a warm glow in his eyes. "And all for the better from what I've seen."

"I must return to my duties," I said. "There are many other people I must speak with tonight."

"I will spread the word myself and say Laria of Riverstone is not a woman to trifle with."

I gave my old friend a knowing smile and disappeared into the crowd. I found the princess feigning interest while the elderly Kaylein Sergia prattled about her father's farm, a fine manor house built with only a large stone and his bare hands to hear her tell it. She hesitated when meeting my eyes, then continued discussing the fireplace stone carved from the Cliffs of Kreeg. The princess drank the last of her wine and said she needed another.

I moved to get one for her.

The princess grabbed my arm. "No. I'll get it myself."

The old woman and I stared at each other silently until the princess was out of earshot. I nodded toward an alcove, and we retreated to the shadows to speak privately.

Once we were alone she said, "I received your letter."

"And I received your reply. I thank you for your confidence."

Kaylein Sergia may be an incredible bore at times, but she was a proud and intelligent woman. Ula and I enjoyed her stories of living in the Rhyvor valley before estates dotted the banks and the central city was a village hamlet. She married young to a leather merchant and lived a prosperous life until his death many years ago. Her children had grown and moved on, so she was alone in a large house with only her maids. Mother made us visit her every week, and Ula naturally became her favorite. She tolerated my presence until I grew impatient with her stories, and she would send me outside to help tend the horses. I spent so little time in the house, she diplomatically informed my mother one day that perhaps I should stay home. That was a few years before the conquest, and I admittedly regretted my behavior. Writing her had been nerve-wracking and I never expected it to bear fruit. Yet here she stood, regal in her straight-backed grace, her light blue eyes still retaining that spark of wisdom. Her hair had gone from gray to completely white. She kept it uncovered and styled with curls studded with tiny pink flowers that complimented the color of her muslin gown.

"I was surprised--nay, shocked, to have such a letter from you. You could never concentrate on anything for more than two seconds unless it was horses." She smiled, a sweet, grandmotherly gesture.

"I hope you will find me changed for the better, regardless of what has happened here."

"From the style and tone of your letter, I expected to find you petulant and indignant. But I can see you are a young woman seizing control of her own life. I sense great potential in you to be a strong leader, Laria Audrey. Whatever you ask of me, I am willing to follow."

"There is something," I smiled mischievously. "If you would indulge me in involving you in a little intrigue?"

She smiled back, a twinkle in her eye. "Go on."

"Might I have a token? Something you might give to a young man?"

One eyebrow arched. "I am many years beyond such offerings."

"But if you were not, what would you give a man to indicate a level of intimacy, something that might signal a relationship perhaps?"

She thought for a moment, then removed her white lace gloves and handed one to me.

"They are very dear to me," she said. "If I were to give one to a man, it would be a declaration of love."

"It's beautiful," I said as I turned the glove over in my hands, marveling at the craftsmanship in the intricate details of the woven threads. "Might I borrow it?"

"If my glove plays a part in bringing an end to this nightmare, then I am honored to give it to you."

I resisted the urge to throw my arms about her neck and curtseyed instead. She inclined her head, then moved away with a rise of her chin and slight grin playing at her lips. I tucked the glove into my frock and began searching for my next contact.

Sir Fin Kinsley, the former knight who approached me almost a year ago, attended the party in service to an Ilano lord. There was little chance of having a decent conversation, but I wanted him to know I remembered him, and the hope he placed in me was not unfounded. I maneuvered through the throng of people toward him. His eyes were fixed at his feet, and he dozed for a few stolen seconds before he was recalled to service again. I brushed against him, shoved a note into his hand, and kept walking. I ducked behind a pillar to watch his reaction. He stared at his hand for so long I thought he'd fallen asleep. Slowly, he opened the note, then his head shot up and he scanned the room. His eyes found mine, bright and hopeful, and he smiled. I inclined my head, placed my hand over my heart, and mouthed the words, "I will not fail you."

I disappeared into the crowd with a swell of pride and searched for the next contact. Heads turned in my wake, followed by whispering when they saw the lock of ginger hair trailing down my back. The musicians struck the first notes of another Praed favorite when I caught sight of a shock of black hair with flecks of gray. I approached slowly and pressed a note into the tall man's hand, glancing briefly over my shoulder at the regally attired lord. He narrowed his eyes curiously as he read the missive. His eyebrows rose in surprise, and he followed me to the outskirts of the crowd.

"I would never have believed it had I not seen that flash of red hair," Lord Grissen said. "Laria Audrey, as I live and breathe."

I motioned him to silence and whispered, "We must be careful." I glanced from side to side to ensure no one was listening.

"You're looking very grown up, Laria," his lordship whispered, his eyes flickering over my figure.

I wrapped my arms around my chest and shifted awkwardly.

"Lord Grissen, I want you to know you're not alone in your support, which is very much appreciated."

"I'm glad to hear it, my dear," he smiled. "Come," he extended his hand. "Dance this one with me."

I hesitated briefly, then laid my hand in his and allowed him to lead me to the set. He swung me lazily, holding my hands longer than necessary and pressing himself against me when he circled around my back. The conversation was mundane, and he wasn't bothered by my lack of response. I curtseyed and turned to leave as the last notes faded, but Lord Grissen grabbed my elbow and leaned close to my ear.

"A great surprise to see you, Miss Audrey. You have made this a most agreeable evening," he said.

"I hope you were earnest in the support you promised, Lord Grissen. I treasure your generosity." My lips barely moved when I spoke, and my brow dampened with sweat. I feared if we weren't careful, someone would see us conversing.

"I cannot express how gratifying it would be to bring Praed back to the prosperity it once knew. To have a child of Maccus Audrey leading the charge brings joy to my heart."

I steered him toward a private alcove. "You're not alone in your thoughts, my lord."

"If you would indulge me, my dear," he laid a hand on mine. "What exactly is your plan?"

"I cannot reveal all, my lord, and I cannot tell you if or when I will call you to action, but I promise I will not sit idly by and watch our country crumble into dust."

"You speak brave words," he mumbled, and by the way his body swayed, I knew he'd had several glasses of cider. I grasped his shoulder to steady him as he tipped forward and pressed his hand against the wall for balance.

"My Lord Grissen," I whispered sharply. "I hope you have enjoyed your evening at the palace. We have been most honored to receive you and hope that you return home safely to consider your role in bringing about change in this trying time."

"I am grateful for you, Laria of Riverstone," he slurred. I propped him up with my shoulder, but he was far heavier than my small frame could support, and my knees buckled.

"There you are, my dear!" a familiar voice called over Lord Grissen's shoulder. I peered behind him on tiptoe and saw his wife approach, then hesitate when she noticed me trying to keep him upright.

"My lady," I whispered. "I fear His Majesty's cider has quite outdone his Lordship. May I have your carriage called for?"

Lady Grissen signaled her attendant, who hurried to take the burden of his master.

"I would be much obliged to you…Lady Audrey," Lady Grissen said, arching an eyebrow in uncertainty.

"It's only Miss Audrey, my lady." I darted away to summon the carriage.

It was disappointing that Lord Grissen was too drunk to have a meaningful conversation since he was such an important figure in my father's life. I would have wished to reminisce about better days. I moped for an hour afterward, barely acknowledging another former knight and his lady beyond dropping notes into their pockets. I found myself poised over a sideboard that was momentarily unattended. Impulsively, I drank a large goblet of the queen's reserve wine and walked away before I realized it was a mistake.

The king tired of Joan Blu and abandoned her months ago to a councilman whose grim expression suggested their recent marriage was forced. Her figure was fuller, but she remained pale and withdrawn. I regarded her sympathetically and hoped in time she'd find peace. She noticed me staring and a ghostly smile crossed her lips before she raised a glass and inclined her head. I returned the greeting and the room tipped with me. I nearly toppled over. I threw out my hands for balance and made my way to a pillar, hugging it like a long-lost friend. I never imbibed the queen's wine, though I'd witnessed the results of the princess' overindulging. One glass practically knocked me on my backside, and I worried about drawing attention to my drunkenness. I needed help, and the only person I could count on was Risteard. But when I scanned the faces, the features blurred into one another, and I could not distinguish one man from the next. I decided on a different approach and closed my eyes, moved along the wall, and listened for his distinct voice. I collided with a few confused guests, but by that time, many people were intoxicated, so they paid me little attention. A thought struck me that Risteard was probably hiding in a corner when I heard a deep rumble that was clearly his voice. My eyes flew open, and only a few feet away Risteard stood with his back to me, talking to someone whose face I could not see. I strode up to him as naturally as possible and, acting with zero restraint, tugged firmly on his sleeve. He spun around, stepping backward to escape my touch, his body tense and expression alarmed. He relaxed when he saw it was only me, and I grinned, showing all my teeth like an idiot.

"That's Princess Caelyn's lady-in-waiting is it not?" a young man asked.

By his posture, I guessed he was a soldier, but he didn't look a day over twenty. That might have been because a stray lock of curly blonde hair had fallen over his forehead and would not be tamed no matter how much he tried to brush it back. When he smiled a small dimple appeared on one cheek.

Risteard turned toward the young man and said, "Yes, it is. Thank you, Olim. That will be all."

The man bowed respectfully and left.

"Who's that?" I whispered loudly.

"A young man training for the knighthood." Risteard's eyes narrowed.

"He looks very young," I observed. "Can he even lift a sword?"

Without answering, Risteard grabbed my elbow and led me out of the ballroom, past couples talking and otherwise behaving less than appropriately in the hallway.

"Have you been drinking?" he asked when I was tucked into a sitting room.

"No!" I said indignantly. "I drank...well, one glass to be precise."

"Of what?"

"It was red. And tasted like fresh fruit."

"The queen's wine?"

"Maybe..." I said evasively, suddenly finding the wood paneling very interesting.

"Have you ever had alcohol before?"

"Yes! Of course. I'm not a child."

"But not very much based on your intolerance of one glass of wine."

"All right, maybe I wasn't allowed alcohol. But once or twice I sneaked some."

"Like tonight?" A smile twitched at his lips.

I sighed dramatically. "You don't understand. I was feeling absolutely desolate after a disagreeable encounter with a benefactor who chose to trifle with me on the dance floor instead of holding a respectable conversation."

He crossed his arms and stared down at me. "What do you mean 'trifle'?"

"Oh," I waved him off. "Nothing important. He just touched me a little more than necessary during the dance. He was shockingly drunk. Don't clench your jaw at me!"

He shifted and pursed his lips. "He touched you inappropriately?"

"No!" I rolled my eyes. "You don't have to rescue me from everyone. I *can* take care of myself sometimes."

"So I'm learning," he smiled. "What did you do with Lord Dalliance?"

"Gave him back to his wife and called his carriage."

"Good girl."

"Well." I swayed off balance and fell against Risteard's chest. He gripped my arms to steady me and laughed when I tripped over my hem.

"This stupid dress," I muttered.

"I wouldn't say that," he murmured. "It suits you."

"A saddle would suit me better." I straightened up.

"Yes," he agreed. "You should get back before the princess notices you're gone."

"Because I'm very important." I raised my chin and marched toward the ballroom.

"Wait." He stepped beside me and leaned close. "Drink some water and avoid the wine."

"There you go again being the noble knight." My smile faded and I laid a hand on Risteard's shoulder to stop him. He looked at me expectantly, and I felt the alcohol loosening my thoughts.

"If I may be serious for a moment," I began. "I want to tell you that your friendship has been one of the most important in my life." A softness I had never seen came over Risteard's features, and he started to speak, but before the words came out, I bent over and retched violently, emptying the contents of my stomach onto his boots. I clasped my hand over my mouth and flushed red in embarrassment, muttering incoherent apologies as I looked for something to clean my mess.

"Don't trouble yourself," he said. "Go back into the ballroom, drink several glasses of water, and make it through the rest of the evening without making a spectacle of yourself."

Tears welled in my eyes as I continued to lament what I had done, but Risteard brushed off my concerns and directed me back into the busy ballroom guests were thankfully beginning to exit. I rubbed my eyes, collected myself, and sought out the princess, vowing to never touch a drop of alcohol ever again.

CHAPTER 31

The morning after the winter celebration, my head was throbbing, and my stomach churned at the mere thought of breakfast. Every footstep on the wooden floor, every bang of pot or pan in the kitchen sent my mind spinning. I threw open the curtains to the outside shining with a fresh dusting of snow, then hastily pressed a hand to my forehead and squeezed my eyes shut to block out the brightness. The princess stretched languidly in bed, unaffected by the food and alcohol she'd consumed the night before. Clearly, she was more practiced at this life than I was. She wrapped herself in a robe and moved to the window beside me, silently observing the winter landscape.

She wasn't impressed. "I hate this time of year." She sat down at her vanity, and I dutifully began untying ribbons and untangled her thick, dark hair. She inspected her hands, and a slight crease formed at her brow when she observed a crack in one of the perfectly manicured nails.

"I should not have accepted a dance from a native," she muttered. She huffed and looked in the mirror, then tapped my hand to get my attention. Our eyes met in the glass, and she said, "You appeared to enjoy yourself."

I froze, nodded briefly, and shrugged indifferently. She was not convinced.

"I believe I saw you dance once or twice, and not unwillingly. Don't worry. You're not in trouble. Just don't think because your people were treated to one night of spoils that anything will change." She narrowed her eyes and asked, "Those men you danced with, are they important?"

I shook my head.

"I don't suppose you could tell me if they harbored any traitorous ideas?"

Another shake of my head coupled with an innocent look.

She returned her attention to her damaged cuticles, and I breathed a sigh of relief.

Once she was settled at her breakfast table she dismissed me, instructing me to report to the housekeeper in case I was needed to help clean up last night's celebration. Since the physician gave the princess strict orders to keep me indoors for the winter, she delighted in finding menial tasks for me. There were only a few servants in the ballroom, and they clearly had worked all night to restore order. One woman looked particularly exhausted and pressed her hands to her straining back. Her little round belly protruded, and I hurried to her side when my brain sluggishly registered what the fullness meant.

"You don't have to do that," she said hastily when I took a mop from her hands. I smiled, pointed at her, and then put a hand to my face as if I was falling asleep. She understood my meaning and appeared worried. "I'll get in trouble," she whispered fearfully. I shook my head and pointed to myself then wrapped my arms across my chest, hoping she would understand I intended to protect her. By her smile, I believe she felt my meaning. She took my hand and introduced herself as Ailis, assured me she knew who I was when I tried to explain, and then left the ballroom.

I turned my eyes to the floor and began to mop, but a tingle ran up my spine and the hairs at the back of my neck raised. Slowly, I lifted my gaze and saw faces watching me from all parts of the room. Servants paused in their work to watch our exchange and now regarded me with a mix of curiosity and compassion. I ignored them and went about my business. They returned to their duties, small smiles playing on their tired faces.

An older woman moved toward me, eyes trained on the tables she wiped. When we were close, she laid a hand on my arm. I looked up, and her smile told me she was pleased, but tears glistened in her eyes. She mouthed the words 'thank you,' and I acknowledged her with a quick bob of my head. She nodded toward the pregnant girl and whispered, "That young woman is my daughter. I worry about her working so hard." The old woman gave my arm a squeeze and returned to her chores.

My thoughts turned to Ailis several times that day. Her face was familiar, but I knew nothing about her. For all the time I lived in this castle, I'd never bothered to form relationships with my fellow servants. I'd been blind to their stories, and I vowed to reach out and listen, starting with the woman I met toiling in the ballroom.

Later, while the ladies played cards and the men retired to drown in cider and self-importance, I slipped from the drawing room to search for Ailis, checking rooms for cleaning staff. Most were empty at this time of day. I inched open the door of a noblewoman and found Ailis inside making the bed with freshly pressed blankets. I stepped inside, closing the door quietly behind me. She looked startled but relaxed when she recognized me.

A worried look crossed her face. "What is it? Am I in trouble?"

I shook my head and without prompting, helped her finish piling lush comforters on the bed. She thanked me, then began laying a fire in the hearth. She moved with quiet grace, and I wondered where she had come from and what sort of life she lived before. Was she the daughter of a knight, like me? Her golden hair was tied tightly around her head in a single braid. Her pale skin showed lines of wear about the eyes and her hands were rough from work. I estimated she was around the princess' age, nineteen. I watched her for a few moments, wondering about the child's lineage, before my curiosity won over propriety.

I reached out and pressed my palm to her swollen belly, then indicated the tiny timepiece dangling from her waist.

"Oh." She laughed. "The baby won't be here for another four months." I looked at her hand, saw no commitment band, and impulsively ran a finger over the spot one would be if she had a husband. She pulled back, and a blush crept into her cheeks. I thought perhaps her husband was too poor to give her a ring, so I smiled reassuringly, shaking my head and rubbing my fingertips together.

"It's not about money," she said sharply before resuming her work. "I have no man to give me a ring."

My face fell, and I looked away ashamed. Her husband was dead, and I obviously opened a fresh wound. I placed a hand on my chest to convey my sympathy. I mimicked a veil being drawn over my face and pointed to the timepiece again.

She looked confused, then she realized what I was asking. Her features darkened.

"He didn't die," she said flatly.

The confusion was now mine, and I suspected I shouldn't continue to pry. I prepared to leave, but she caught my hand and apologized for her brashness. I perched myself on the stone floor, wrapped my arms around my legs, and waited. She sighed heavily and returned her attention to the hearth, laying the last logs and lighting the tinder. Flames gradually spread upwards, and we watched the play of oranges and yellows silently.

"He's a knight," she whispered. "No one of real consequence, though he certainly believes himself to be." I put my hands over my heart and raised an eyebrow.

"No," she said. "I have no affection for him, nor does he for me. This child was not conceived in love. It was not even conceived with my consent."

My heartbeat quickened when the gravity of her words struck me, and it angered me that everywhere I turned men were taking liberties with vulnerable young women, using them and tossing them aside.

"Who is he?" I asked with a menacingly dark undertone.

Her eyes widened in shock. "You *can* speak!" she cried.

"A fact which does not leave this room if you hope to receive any help from me," I said.

"Of course, I will not breathe a word of it, not even to Mama."

"I'll do what I can to make this right if you tell me his name."

"If I had it, I would give it to you. I only know him by his face. He approached me while I worked a few times and spoke to me, but I ignored him. The last time, he would not let me walk away." She lowered her gaze.

"Does he know about the child?"

"Yes," she sniffed. "I sought him out after the second month of no monthly courses. He laughed in my face and told me if I ever tried to extort a marriage from him, he would have my mother sent away and have me punished for promiscuity."

"I hate men," I said.

"I want nothing from him." She raised her chin. "I certainly don't want marriage."

"But he should take responsibility for the child! At least he could support you with money."

"I want nothing from him," she repeated. "If I took one coin, I would be relying on him, and he would hold that over me for the rest of my life."

I respected her resolve, but I still wasn't convinced she wasn't due compensation.

I stood up. "I won't keep you from your work."

She followed, using the edge of the fireplace to keep her balance.

"Thank you," Ailis said at the door. "I know you want to help. It's not necessary, but I appreciate it nonetheless."

I left her, convinced there was no mercy in the world and that kind, decent men were virtually nonexistent. Every day I discovered more and more proof that monsters were real, and that they wore fancy clothes, drove elegant carriages, and lived in Praed Castle.

The princess was not pleased by my tardiness.

"Where were you?" she demanded.

I knelt and mimicked cleaning the floor.

"Well, you certainly weren't doing it in here," she sneered. "I can't be late for dinner. I'll forgive you this one time, but don't make it a habit or you'll be punished accordingly."

I performed my usual routine, my thoughts on Ailis and her unborn baby. I worried about the struggles she would face as an unwed mother. No honorable man would marry a soiled woman, especially if it meant raising another man's child. Any chance at a normal life was gone along with her innocence. If I learned one thing about men, it was that they were only concerned with their own needs without regard to consequences.

An angry scowl accompanied me to the Great Hall and did not fade. My eyes roamed the room, seeing men shovel mounds of food into their maws and downing glass after glass of cider, arrogantly basking in their greatness. I studied the face of every knight, wondering which had treated Ailis so abominably. The prince and the king disgusted me with a loud tale of some large-bosomed woman they saw in town. The lewd acts they described were so vile I almost betrayed myself by covering my ears. I wished a chandelier would fall on their heads.

My sour mood continued throughout the night, and even the princess remarked I looked unwell. I tried to keep a neutral expression, but I was boiling. I turned down the princess' bed with little thought to neatness and proceeded to brush her hair, perhaps a bit roughly. After pulling her hair painfully one too many times, she grabbed the hairbrush and struck me in the side of the head.

"Get out!" she demanded. "Tomorrow you better have an improved temper, or I'll have you whipped and replaced!"

I was too angry to show remorse, so I did as I was told and left, resisting the urge to slam the door.

I was not two steps from the princess' door when I heard Risteard's voice. "Feeling the effects of last night's overindulgence, I see." I brushed past him without responding and stormed off toward my room.

"It's nothing to be ashamed of," he continued, following me. "You're not the only one suffering today."

"I'm not ashamed of anything," I snapped without slowing.

"Why are you so angry? What happened?"

"Why? Are you going to fix it? You're not a knight from a storybook. You can't fix everything!"

He took two long strides forward and blocked my path with his arm.

"What's gotten into you?"

"You!" I hissed as I thrust a finger into his chest.

"Me? What have I done?"

"You men are all the same. Walking around doing whatever you please thinking you're all magnificent heroes and you're owed whatever you can take from a woman."

His eyes darkened, and he grabbed my arm and turned me toward his study.

I didn't make the task easy. I planted my feet and hit him repeatedly with my free hand, and he practically threw me into the room where I stubbornly refused to look him in the eye.

"Enough," he said. "Speak plainly. Has someone 'taken' something from *you*?"

"No," I said in a low voice. "Not from me. From a young woman working in this castle. She carries a child she was forced to conceive."

"I see." His voice softened, and he came closer. "So from this you conclude all men are evil monsters?"

"I have seen nothing to suggest otherwise." I crossed my arms and stared at the flames in the hearth.

"I should be insulted. I know I have not always acted nobly, but I never considered myself a monster. Nor did I ever think you would claim friendship with one."

My shoulders sagged, and I regretted unleashing my anger on him when he'd showed me nothing but friendly concern. "I'm sorry," I sighed heavily. "It wasn't fair of me to be angry at you for something you weren't responsible for."

"Who is responsible?" he asked, leaning against the mantle. "Did she give you a name?"

"She doesn't know his name, only his face. He's one of your knights."

"I can make inquiries. What's her name?"

"Ailis," I said. "And she wants nothing from the man who did this to her."

"Admirable, but he has not acted by the honorable code to which any knight of my command must follow. If he has committed rape and abandoned a child, he must be punished."

I met his dark gaze with an unwavering one of my own.

"Next time you're all practicing drills in the courtyard, I'll have her point him out to me."

"I'll call for a surprise inspection in the morning."

I nodded, and we both turned our attention back to the dancing flames, absorbed in our own thoughts.

"How are you feeling," he asked quietly. "After last night?"

"Better. I don't understand people who drink to excess on a regular basis. I was miserable for most of the day."

"Eventually one builds up a tolerance, but yes, many will drink until they are as ill as you were. They think only of how it feels at the time. Many consider the price of the morning after worth the enjoyment."

"Those people are crazy. I'm never drinking that much again."

"Did you enjoy yourself up until that point?"

"Yes. I almost felt normal again, like I was at home entertaining Mother's guests."

"You looked content," he hesitated. "Happy."

"I suppose I did feel a spark of happiness once or twice. Don't tell the princess."

"You have my word as a magnificent hero."

"Sorry," I said sheepishly.

"You mustn't think harshly of all men. Think of your friend, Lord Wyrwyk. Is he not a good example of an honest man?"

"You're right," I agreed. "I allowed a few bad seeds to taint my perception. Thom would never act so despicably. Nor would many others. And you," I turned to face him, "are also a good example of how a man should behave. I shouldn't have lost my temper with you."

"Thank you," he said. "Now, you should get some sleep."

"Promise not to stop me?" I grinned.

"I promise."

My smile faded. "See you in the morning then."

Risteard was true to his word, and the knights and men-at-arms were summoned to the inner courtyard early to await inspection. I rushed from room to room searching for Ailis, and when I finally found her delivering soiled bedding to the laundress, I grabbed her hand and pulled her behind me without explanation. She protested and tried to retrieve the dropped items, but I would not relent. A puzzled laundress picked up the blankets and watched us disappear outside.

We emerged along the outer walls of the courtyard to see disciplined lines of men standing at attention, boots and buttons polished and not a thread out of place.

"Which one." I gasped for breath. "Which was the man who fathered your child?"

Ailis' brows creased, and she held her belly, her face flushed with exertion. She looked down at the men gathered beneath us, then back at me, shaking her head.

"I can't," she said. "I told you I don't want anything from him."

"What about justice?"

She chewed her bottom lip, considering my words.

"He won't know it was me who told you?"

"Not if you don't want him to," I promised.

The men were clad in distinguishing surcoats, each bearing the color and coat of arms of their rank and family. It would take me weeks to sort them, but without hesitation Ailis pointed at a man amid the swarm of knights. Like his companions, his eyes faced forward, stiffly at attention while Risteard moved along the ranks, his eyes occasionally drifting upwards to us. He saw Ailis pointing and followed the direction she indicated to a muscular knight with curly brown hair, brown eyes, and light stubble covering his square jaw. Risteard stood in front of the man and ordered everyone to leave. Worry shadowed the man's face when Risteard spoke, and I strained to hear. Ailis turned to leave, but I caught her arm.

"Don't you want to see what happens?"

"I don't want to look at him a moment longer," she said.

I apologized instantly. I'd been so preoccupied with bringing her justice I didn't stop to consider her mental anguish.

"You've been very brave," I assured her. "You may return to your duties." When I turned back to the courtyard, it was empty.

Later that afternoon, the entire castle, including the royal family and the contingency of knights and soldiers, gathered in the courtyard. The knight was on display, appearing greatly diminished from the angelic specimen he presented earlier. His hands were bound, his face streaked with dirt, and his hair in disarray.

"Risteard," King Conall addressed his First Knight standing close to the bound man. "Accusations have been made regarding the honorability of this man,

Sir Kian Luca. How does he answer for the crime of seduction and rape of an innocent?"

"Not guilty, Your Majesty." He held his head proudly. "Where is the evidence? Where is the girl who accuses me?"

"For her own safety," Risteard said, "she does not wish to be named, but His Majesty has been apprised of the circumstances, and it does you a further disservice to deny these charges."

"This is madness!" Sir Luca cried. "How can you trust the word of a woman against mine, Sir Risteard?"

"The lady has not sought any monetary compensation and wishes to remain anonymous. She has no reason to lie."

"Your Majesty, how can you be sure the lady didn't seduce me and then imagined this scheme out of regret and scorn that I would not marry her?"

"Sir Luca," said the king. "Taking a young woman's innocence and refusing to marry her is not how I wish my knights to behave."

"This is nonsense! How many men here have taken a woman to bed and haven't married her? Why are they not on trial?"

"Next time," the king said. "Be more discrete."

"Next time," Risteard said through gritted teeth. "Find a more willing partner. You are not on trial because you bedded a woman. You're on trial for *raping* one."

Sir Luca's face paled and his fellow knights cast sympathetic looks in his direction, but no man moved to support or defend him.

"Your Majesty," Sir Luca pleaded. "This is a case of one man's word over another's. Without the lady to testify, how can you choose?"

"I trust Risteard's word above any man's," King Conall said. Many heads nodded agreement. "At his alone, I would grant him permission to carry out the punishment fitting your crime. However..."

With that one word, mouths gaped and Risteard stared at the king in shock.

"I wish to be a king who does not convict a man on mere circumstantial evidence, and therefore I will reduce the severity of your punishment. You shall be flogged but spend no time in the dungeon."

Murmurs filled the courtyard, and Risteard was clearly furious.

"Your Majesty," Risteard's voice boomed over everyone's voices, halting all conversation. "This is not only a matter of the law, but of honor. As First Knight of Your Majesty's Army, I reserve the right to carry out the punishment I see fit."

"You are not above the king, Risteard," King Conall replied calmly. "Carry out his punishment."

Two guards stepped forward and took Sir Luca by the arms. Risteard strode toward him, and if he were a lesser man, I believe Sir Luca would have urinated on himself at seeing the murderous look in his commander's eye. Risteard grabbed a fistful of Sir Luca's tunic and leaned in close to speak in his ear. The color drained from his face and his knees buckled. The tunic was ripped from his body. The guards spun him around and held fast, steadying the knight between them. Another guard handed Risteard a whip unlike any I'd ever seen. The handle was short, and from it dangled several braided leather cords knotted on the ends. Sir Luca's bare skin was slick with a sheen of sweat, but to his credit, he stood still and braced himself for his punishment.

Risteard planted his feet, and with quick, strong movements, he swung his arm and struck once, twice, three times in succession, leaving the skin raw and red. After sustaining a total of fifteen lashes, rivulets of blood dripped down Sir Luca's back, and the knight could no longer support his own weight. The guards dragged him into the castle, and Risteard followed, sending a burning glare in the king's direction.

I offered to give Ailis the details of Sir Luca's punishment, but she declined, saying the thought of him standing humiliated in front of the entire castle was enough for her peace of mind. She told me she feared retribution. But I allayed those fears, remembering Sir Luca's face when Risteard spoke in his ear. He would be a fool to harm anyone under the protection of the First Knight of His Majesty's army.

CHAPTER 32

For the first time Ula's birthday passed without even a small token to mark the occasion, and though she assured me it didn't matter, I still felt guilty for being so absorbed in my own dealings I couldn't be bothered to patch something together. Several times, I lamented letting her down, and each time she reminded me we no longer had the luxury of planning birthday parties. In the end, I made it up to her by stealing a sweet treat from Princess Caelyn's discarded dinner plate.

Since I told Risteard about Councilman Crane, he started observing the man's movement's. More importantly, he kept his ears open for discontent and noted anyone who might be sympathetic to our cause. It helped he started making his own opinions known in council, which was the greatest strain on his taciturn disposition. I placed a hand over my heart and gushed over how proud I was of him and he didn't speak to me for hours. He could be such a baby sometimes.

We passed the next few wintry months in the rituals of work and sleep, and in between I nurtured the friendship between me and Ailis. I grew concerned as the strain of work increased her discomfort, and I entertained thoughts of smuggling her out of the castle for her confinement.

Ailis had a particularly trying day, rising early to light fires throughout the castle and taking few breaks to rest her swollen feet or eat. When I visited her in the afternoon, I feared she would faint. She was pale and sweat beaded at her forehead. She complained of dizziness, and I insisted she lie on a nearby settee. When I was satisfied she was comfortable, I hurried to Risteard's study and threw open the door without bothering to knock. He sat at his desk, book open in front of him, his eyebrows arched in surprise. I braced my hands on the cluttered wooden surface and fixed him with a determined stare.

"Yes?" he prompted.

"I need your help," I said.

"For...?" he asked as he closed his book.

"Ailis, the woman who carries Sir Luca's child?"

"I remember."

"She's not well. She works so hard, and it cannot be good for her or the child. I want her removed from the castle and placed somewhere safe."

Risteard leaned back in his chair, an amused expression playing along the edges of his mouth.

"That sounded like a command," he said.

I straightened and averted my eyes. "Sorry," I said nervously. "I didn't mean for it to come out that way."

"I'm not offended."

"I do wish for her to leave. I fear for her health."

"I'll see what I can do, but I can't make any promises."

I could have hugged him--if he'd allow it--and I was so excited to return to Ailis that I completely forgot to thank him. When I came upon her, she was sleeping soundly, and I was loath to disturb her few minutes of solitude. So I left her to resume my duties to the princess.

Hours passed. I was standing behind the princess at dinner when I saw Ailis' mother surreptitiously moving closer to me. I stepped backwards to widen the distance between myself and the table and met the older woman's eyes. She seemed upset, and she wrung her hands to keep them from trembling.

"Please," she whispered. "Have you seen my daughter?"

The blood drained from my face, and I nodded. I indicated the princess and then mimed drinking from a small glass. Basically saying I'd help once the princess retires to the drawing room. She agreed, and then resumed clearing dirty dishes and filling glasses. I felt queasy for the remainder of dinner, and I couldn't wait for it to end. The princess was barely out of her seat before I hastened her from the room and found her a place at a card table. She looked at me as if I had gone mad, but I placed a glass of port wine in her hand and she forgot about me all together.

Ailis' mother was waiting when I left the room, and I led her to where I had left the young woman earlier. I found it difficult to believe Risteard had not only found a place for her, but that she had left already. Where could she have gone?

I opened the door to the small parlor where I had last seen her, and my heart sank--Ailis was still sleeping on the settee. Her mother rushed forward and shook her shoulders, but she would not be roused.

"Ailis?" her mother called. "Ailis wake up!" She turned to me. "She is so pale, and her skin feels cold."

I slogged along the floor as if dragging chains, and it felt the closer I came, the farther she was from me. I reached out and touched my fingers to her forehead. She was damp with sweat and chilled, but the shallow rise and fall of her chest told me she was alive. I took her mother's hand and held it to Ailis' chest so she could feel her daughter's heartbeat.

"She's alive! I must fetch a doctor!" I stopped her, pointed at myself, and indicated she should stay with her daughter. Then I rushed from the room and back to the princess, where I frantically began motioning for help.

"What is wrong with you?" she demanded. I placed the back of my hand against my forehead, felt my pulse, pretended to take medicine, anything to convey what I desperately needed. The others at the table stared at me as if I'd grown another head, which embarrassed the princess.

"Are you losing your mind?" the princess yelled. "Do I need to call for a doctor?" I nodded with relief, and she motioned a man over and instructed him to summon the physician immediately.

I waited at the servant's entrance for the doctor, pacing the length of the floor and biting my lip to hold back the tears. The latch clicked and I nearly toppled the poor man when I embraced him. I grabbed his hand and led him to the parlor. Seline accompanied him, asking questions. I let the woman's condition speak for itself when I presented them to her lying on the settee.

Doctor Bayl turned to Ailis' mother. "How far along is her pregnancy?"

"She still has two months," the woman said. "What's wrong with her, doctor?"

"Exhaustion, I suspect, coupled with malnourishment. The child is not as large as it should be." He waved a vial under Ailis' nose, and the young woman's eyes fluttered open. She gazed at the faces hovering around her.

"Let's get her to bed. I'll prepare a draught and instructions for meals. She must not leave her bed until the child is born."

"That's going to be difficult," her mother said. "She's a servant. Her absence will be noticed." I laid a hand on the old woman's arm and smiled reassuringly, placed a hand against my chest, then placed it upon Ailis' to convey that I would take care of her, even if it meant doing her chores myself. The old woman took my hand and mouthed 'thank you.'

Seline and I helped Ailis to her feet, and though weak, she was able to walk with assistance. At the door, she cried out and clutched her stomach. We looked down, and to our horror a plume of red streamed from below the swell of the babe and spread down the front of her dress.

"Pick her up!" Doctor Bayl ordered. "We need a bed now." Seline wrapped her arms across Ailis' chest and I took her legs, and together we carried her to the closest safe place--my room.

The four of us crammed into the small space and placed Ailis on the narrow bed. I stepped aside, offering what comfort I could to her mother. Ailis wailed in pain, twisting her body and bracing one hand on the wall and the other against her belly. Doctor Bayl lifted her dress and examined her, then asked for his bag. Seline pulled out several instruments and left to fetch water.

"The child is coming," Doctor Bayl said.

"It's too soon!" Ailis' mother wailed.

"I will do what I can, but you must prepare yourself." He looked at the old woman pointedly, and she collapsed to her knees. I held her close, rocking her and staring ahead.

The physician was speaking to Ailis, but whether she heard his words or comprehended them, I do not know. Seline returned and placed herself at Ailis' head, encouraging her to push the child out. For a while, Ailis complied, bearing down with each ripple of pain, but soon her strength was lost, and Seline had to push for her, pressing on her belly when her uncle instructed. After what felt like hours, Ailis lay quiet, and the child emerged from her womb. Her mother held her breath in hopeful anticipation, but the child remained silent. Doctor Bayl handed it to Seline, and she rubbed its back, slapped its bottom, flicked its feet, and even puffed air into its nose and mouth. But the child did not cry, and its color was a dull gray. Doctor Bayl looked up from under Ailis' dress, and Seline shook her head. She wrapped the child in a length of cloth and held it close while Ailis' mother sobbed, no longer able to hold herself together. My eyes were trained on the physician working diligently to save Ailis, whose eyes were closed behind dark lids, and whose skin matched the shade of her stillborn child.

They carried her out with the child in her arms, pressed tightly to her breast, wrapped in a simple sheet. The ground was too frozen to dig a grave, so at her mother's request, Ailis and her child were cremated together on a funeral pyre at the base of the mountain. Their ashes would be saved until spring, then thrown into the Rhyvor so they could flow to the sea and be free.

I had not moved from the floor since she was taken away, my eyes fixed on the blood that stained my bedding. Seline tried to talk to me, but I was in a daze. Doctor Bayl squeezed my shoulder, then he left me alone. I have known people who have died and been close to death more than any person should. I had even been near enough to watch souls leave the body. But this was not a death brought about by old age or illness or even war. I had never seen a tragic death resulting from an event that was supposed to be the most beautiful in a woman's life. What hurt more than anything was this was not Ailis' choice. She did not choose to conceive a child, and the child had taken her life. I wished Sir Luca could see the large pool of blood, could smell the sickly sweet stench of death, could have witnessed the limp child being pulled from her body, and could have seen Ailis' poor mother weep over her daughter's lifeless corpse.

There was a knock on my door, but I didn't realize it until Risteard entered and sat on the floor beside me.

"Seline came and found me," he said. "She told me what happened."

"The child came too soon," I said in a small voice. "It was too small to survive. Doctor Bayl tried to save Ailis, but she was bleeding so much... It isn't fair. She didn't even want a child!"

"Did she make it clothes?"

"What?" I met his eyes in confusion.

"Did she make the child clothes? Knit blankets? Give it a name?"

"Yes," I said slowly. "She didn't have a name picked out yet, but she had many she liked. And the child had more clothes than I do."

"She certainly did not choose to have a child," Risteard said softly. "But she wanted it."

The tears came then, like a river after a thaw. Risteard's arm came around me, and I leaned into his shoulder, crying without restraint.

"Why did this have to happen?" I wailed.

"I don't know," he whispered. "Childbirth can be dangerous, even for a healthy woman."

"But she wasn't healthy! She was overworked, and the doctor said she looked malnourished!"

"She should have been better provided for. You're right."

Risteard offered no more words of comfort. He sat quietly, allowing me to grieve the loss of a friend. I was convinced that if Ailis had been cared for properly during her pregnancy, this would not have happened. The king had known she was heavy with child, and yet still expected her to work just as hard and eat just as little. If I didn't hate King Conall before, I certainly did now. I wanted him off the throne by whatever means necessary.

I still had the glove Kaylein Sergia gave me at the winter festival, waiting for the opportunity to play a part. I began carrying it with me, always ready for a chance to implicate the prince. As the snow began to melt and the date of my seventeenth birthday drew near, I became impatient. The prince had taken the king's declaration of mixing with the Praed inhabitants to heart and had been visiting farms and manors endearing himself to the locals. The princess scoffed at his efforts, calling him a toady, but he assured her his intentions were noble.

"Bollocks," the princess spat. "You want the people to like *you* better than Father."

"Doesn't that suit our needs?"

She rolled her eyes and wouldn't speak with him for several days. I never cared for the prince, but their growing distance did not suit *my* plans at all.

A few days before my birthday, I was summoned to the dressmaker's workroom, ostensibly to consult with a design of a gown recently commissioned for Her Highness' twentieth birthday, two months away. When I arrived, the old woman pointed her bony finger at the corner, and I followed her directions to Ula's workspace. My sister brought out a form with the beginnings of a pink muslin gown.

"It's lovely," I told Ula. "Though I didn't expect that she would have chosen pink. It's too bright and happy."

Ula laughed behind her hand, and I noted her voice had deepened with the passage of another year, and she had grown another inch.

"There's something I wanted to give you." Ula ducked behind a screen and returned with a long nightgown of fine linen, dyed a light blue that reminded me of the sky on a summer's day.

"It's for me?" I asked reverently.

"Well, last year the princess ended up with *your* gown, and you said you couldn't wear it anyway. So I thought, what could I make you that you could actually wear? As far as I know, you still sleep, right?"

I ran a hand down the soft fabric and felt tears prickle my eyes.

"It's beautiful, Ula." I hugged her tightly.

"I hope it fits," she said. "I haven't taken your measurements in so long."

"My body hasn't changed much, I'm sure." I laughed.

"Haven't you looked at yourself lately?"

"Not if I can help it."

"Your frocks are not flattering to your shape." She grabbed a handful of fabric at my back and pulled it tight. "You're blossoming into a woman under this burlap sack. You should let me take this in."

"Why?" I shrugged out of her grasp.

"To feel pretty."

"I'll settle for feeling pretty while I sleep." I took the nightgown and folded it neatly.

Before bed, I stripped out of my scratchy wool frock and slipped the nightgown over my head. The cool linen felt luxurious. I ran my hands from the collar to the hem. The sleeves were long, but Ula had underestimated the length of my arms, so the fabric stopped above my wrist. I was shocked at the low neckline, but more at the swell of bust that finally decided to appear. I twirled in my small room, laughing and picturing Mother's approval observing my long-delayed womanly shape. If we were still at Riverstone, she'd undoubtedly double her efforts at securing me a husband, and my pleasure at thwarting her attempt would be equally great.

The next morning, I placed my frocks in Ula's hands to be altered.

The prince's birthday was fast approaching, but the extravagance last year would not be repeated. The king stretched the treasury thin, and now took a more active interest in the production of crops in Praed. He told Prince Brannon this year would be a lesson in frugality. The prince was not pleased and took to moping around, trying to guilt his father into relenting. The king would not be moved, feeling the strain of running the kingdom with such demanding children.

The prince threw open Princess Caelyn's door after weeks of silence, surprising even her. He fell back dramatically onto her bed, his arm covering his face, and sighed heavily.

"Typical," Princess Caelyn said irritably. "First time we've spoken in weeks and it's because you're pouting over your birthday. Is it possible for you to think of anyone but yourself, Brannon?"

"No," he huffed, like a child defying his mother. "It isn't fair! I'm the prince! I deserve a birthday celebration!"

"You had such a big celebration last year you should be satisfied for a lifetime."

"Exactly!' he exclaimed. "Last year was spectacular, so it stands to reason I should outdo myself this year."

"If you attempt it," the princess cautioned. "Some may collapse from exhaustion or die of alcohol consumption. That would certainly make your birthday memorable, though perhaps not as you would wish."

"I suppose you have a point," he grumbled. "Maybe I should hold a celebration that includes the natives, as Father did this winter."

"If you wish to further impress them."

"It would be in our best interest, would it not?"

"As long as you don't get attached to anyone in particular."

The prince was silent, and I looked at him out of the corner of my eye. He was staring, lost in thought, and I felt this hesitation was the opportunity I'd been waiting for. The princess noticed his lack of response and glared at him suspiciously.

"Brannon," she said with a note of challenge in her tone. "You're not thinking of anyone, right?"

The prince shook off his dreamy thoughts. "No," he said. He rose and left the room without a backward glance. The princess brushed off his strange behavior and inspected her hair. She dismissed me with a wave once she was satisfied, and I nervously moved past the bed on the way to the door. I paused, pretended to spot something, and withdrew the lady's glove from my apron. The princess was applying the finishing touches to her outfit, and I tapped her on the shoulder to get her attention.

"What?" she snapped. I held up the glove and indicated I'd found it on the bed. She took the glove from me and said it wasn't hers and was about to give it back when the implications dawned on her. She looked closer, confirmed I indeed found it where Prince Brannon sat, and then dismissed me again. I complied, a mischievous grin on my face as I closed the door behind me.

The glove sent the princess into a panic. Convinced her brother had designs for a Praed woman, she sent for reinforcements to persuade him he was making a grievous mistake. None other than Jervell Kade came to her aid. He arrived the morning of Prince Brannon's birthday, presumably as a surprise guest for the feast planned that night. I was dressing the princess for the occasion when the weasel came in uninvited and unannounced for a private audience. The princess rushed to take his hands when she saw him, and he patted her head like a child. I turned away in disgust, afraid I could not hide my revulsion.

"I'm so relieved you're here," Princess Caelyn said. They sat together on the settee, and I moved into the shadows to listen and watch.

"Your letter sounded desperate." The sound of his voice brought bile to my throat.

"Brannon left this behind in my room." She showed him the glove. "It is not mine, and no one else in the castle will claim it."

Jervell inspected the glove. "It's lovely. The fabric appears aged, but not worn. A poor lady did not own this. She would be a woman of taste and leisure. This is perhaps a family heirloom."

"Does it come from an Ilano craftsman?"

"No. I do not recognize the work. It must be of Praed origin."

"That's what I was afraid of." The princess crossed her arms and fell back into the cushions.

"This does present a problem," Jervell agreed. "If it means anything at all. It could simply be a token a lady presented His Highness in passing."

"If that were the case, he would not have kept it on his person."

"I will speak to him." He tucked the glove into his coat. He looked past the princess, saw me, and smiled wickedly. "Your lady-in-waiting is growing into a proper woman."

The princess glanced at me. "Hmm. She's no longer a disgrace to that dress, I suppose." She waved a hand in dismissal.

"You don't think she might be the object of Prince Brannon's affections, do you?"

I'm not sure who was more offended at this prospect.

"My brother might be many things, Jervell, but he is not sentimental. He would never plant his affections in such poor soil." She looked at me as if I were an insect.

"If you're certain," Jervell said. A smile spread across his face, and he left shortly. A chill ran down my spine, and I feared the devilish deeds that monster was plotting.

During Prince Brannon's feast, I kept a close eye on Jervell Kade. I was disappointed the Lord Protector came alone without an Ilani lady to tempt the prince into marriage. He remained close to the prince throughout the evening, whispering in his ear and monopolizing his time. I imagined him lecturing the prince, pointing out the faults of Praedan women, and telling him a Praed bride would disgrace Ilano. The prince seemed distracted and rarely paid attention. But halfway through the main course the prince leaned intently toward the older man, his brow furrowed. Whatever he was hearing seemed to hold great interest. I surmised Jervell was setting the stage, planting the seeds of betrothal before presenting him with a favorable choice.

During dessert, I caught the prince staring at me oddly, torn between confusion and surprise. Jervell was in his ear again, whispering who knows what. He was probably telling the prince all manner of lies about me. I felt certain the clever Lord Protector knew I was up to something. Once the last plate was cleared, the party moved to the courtyard, where the prince continued to fix me with his puzzling stare. I ignored him and feigned innocence, following the princess and engaging with no one. He shed the burden of the Lord Protector once or twice, dancing with several ladies and drinking heavily with his friends, but like a pox, Jervell Kade would reappear to whisper in his ear.

I met Risteard's eyes across the crowd of revelers, but I did not dare leave the princess' side. The last thing we needed was for Jervell to suspect the two of us. If he already distrusted me, I couldn't bear to bring Risteard down with me, so I avoided him all night.

The pair approached the princess and me, the prince with his usual swagger and the old man with his sly grin. The princess acknowledged them with a slight bow, but otherwise said nothing. They watched the dancers quietly.

The high voice of the Lord Protector pierced the silence. "You have not danced tonight, Princess Caelyn."

"You know I don't care for it."

"It's your brother's birthday celebration. For his sake if not for mine, indulge us with your grace and elegance this next set."

Flattery was the easiest way to get anything from the princess, especially if coupled with an opportunity to put herself on display.

"If you wish, my lord." She curtseyed and sought out a partner whom she twice rejected earlier, leaving me alone with the two men. I stared blankly ahead, still as a statue, hoping they would also leave. I was not so fortunate.

"Every time I see you," Jervell said so I could see his face. "You grow more and more into a fine woman." He appraised my figure, slowly roaming his eyes over my body. "What do you think, Prince Brannon? Is she a loyal servant to the crown?"

"She's never given any indication otherwise." The prince also studied me. "Besides, I don't think she's smarter than a dog, and they are the most loyal creatures that walk the earth."

"True, she may be simple, deaf, and mute," Jervell mused while taking my chin between his clammy fingers.

I itched for the blade hidden in my frock and silently dared him to make a wrong move.

"But she has become more enjoyable to look at."

"As long as that awful hair is covered," the prince said.

"Such an innocent little thing," Jervell continued. "A precious girl becoming a woman at last. She must be a treasure to someone, don't you think?"

"Doubtful. Caelyn wouldn't allow it."

"An unspoiled beauty like this is a rarity indeed. The man who claims it… now that man would be lucky indeed to boast such a conquest." Jervell finally released me and left me alone, taking the prince with him. The breath I had been holding exploded from my mouth. The vision of a woman lying in a dark alley flashed through my brain, and I shuddered. Jervell Kade may be a gelding, but his evil tendencies had not vanished with his manhood. If he wished to intimidate me, he was sorely mistaken to think a few words would distract me from my path. If it was a fight he wanted, I was prepared to parry his blows and deliver a few of my own.

CHAPTER 33

Jervell Kade chose to stay an entire month in Praed, spending much of his time close to Prince Brannon. Since this meant he was away from the castle inspecting crops and visiting tenants, I was overjoyed with the arrangement. He did not meet with the princess in her rooms, nor attend the queen's meetings, so I only saw him at the evening meals. As much as I appreciated the distance, I began to grow suspicious that Jervell and the prince were up to something other than matrimonial proposals. The prince was elusive, less boisterous than usual, and he also stayed away from the princess' rooms. How the lady herself felt about this I couldn't say, as she remained as constant as ever: wholly preoccupied with her own affairs.

Letters poured from the princess' pen, all addressed to Ilano. Some names I recognized as her friends and didn't bother to pry, but an increasing number were sent to people I didn't know. I did my best to read over her shoulder without drawing suspicion. In them, she detailed her routine, the weather, and praise of "our glorious king." Risteard suspected she was feeding information to allies.

I was skeptical. "You think they care what she had for dinner?"

"No, but they would care about the state of the roads, what time the king retires, and the proclamations he's made," he said.

I looked down at the notes I'd taken. They seemed so mundane, but now I saw that everything she wrote had hidden meaning. Plotting rebellion was a sneaky business. I kept track of the names for Risteard. He hoped to undermine the princess and steal support for us.

The letters she sent were easy to spot, but the secret messages she passed within the castle walls were harder to intercept. She was careful to appear above reproach. She associated only with ladies and spoke to gentlemen only in company. I watched her closely, but she never touched anyone, even briefly. Not even Jervell Kade. And she didn't meet with Councilman Crane again.

The princess' birthday was days away, and the gown Ula created was ready. I held it proudly before Her Highness, the layers of fabric draping softly over my arm and billowing to the ground. She took a piece in her hand and ran it through her fingers, then picked at a stray thread.

"It will do," she said, which for her was the closest to a compliment I could hope for.

For her birthday, the princess had planned a traditional Ilano performance of birds wherein each handler would train their falcon or eagle to perform new tricks and aerobatics. This was common in Ilano, and people travelled for miles to show off their skills as trainers. The princess planned to display her own falcon,

Gyonessa, and practiced daily to teach her an aerial dive that ended with a perfect landing and a bow. I was loath to admit it, but Princess Caelyn was a patient and skilled trainer, and she showed more affection for that creature than for any human being.

The prince also planned on showing off his eagle, Verix, though not with the trick he'd played on me. At least, not with a person. His new trick was to place a morsel of meat on the back of his horse, thus not only showing the precision of his eagle, but the steadiness of his mount. The bird had nearly been kicked several times.

I asked Risteard one afternoon if he planned on performing as well. His scowl was all the answer I needed.

"Are you nervous about having an audience?" I teased.

He lifted his chin haughtily. "I simply don't think it's fair to upstage their royal highnesses."

Touché.

The morning of the celebration, several servants and I were tasked with preparing the space for the performance. The large perches in the yard were moved to clear a space for displays, and rows of chairs and tables for refreshments were placed around the periphery. The mews were cleaned with extra care, with walls and perches scrubbed of waste and dried blood and fresh straw piled high. The birds seemed to sense the extra air of excitement and stretched their wings, called, and flapped animatedly. Aquila watched me curiously, her head turning from side to side, and chattered as if to ask what all the fuss was about.

"It's a lot of work for a lot of nonsense," I muttered in reply. She ruffled her feathers, making her appear twice as big. "I'm not sure what that means," I smiled. She shook her head and wiggled her tail, and I laughed at how cute and ridiculous she looked.

The sun reached its zenith when Princess Caelyn led the procession of ladies and nobles to the yard, falcons and eagles held proudly aloft. The king and queen stood beside their daughter, and King Conall made a moving speech about the princess being the jewel of Ilano and that it was their children who would keep their traditions alive. The speech ended with him sending his own eagle flying into the bright sky, a parcel tied to its legs. Once it had reached a considerable distance, the king pulled on a cord, and colored paper fluttered to the ground. The crowd applauded generously then took their seats in anticipation of the start of the performance.

Princess Caelyn naturally put her own bird on display first, and she did remarkably well. I had never seen such a performance. The only time I'd watched the falcons and eagles do anything other than hunt was Prince Brannon showing off how cruel he can be. As each bird dove, flipped, and somersaulted, I became entranced by the intricate relationship between bird and master. I found myself applauding along with everyone else when a bird did a particularly difficult move. Even Jervell Kade ceased his whispering and concentrated on the spectacle.

I felt a tug on my sleeve, and I looked down at the princess. Her eyes were glossy, and she swayed slightly.

"Gyonessa is getting agitated and needs her hood. It's back at her mew. Go get it."

I nodded, took one last look at the magnificent eagle executing a spiraling dive, and ran up the hill toward the falcon mews.

The sounds of the cheering crowd faded, replaced by the rustling breeze. I paused to enjoy the heat from the summer sun, feeling the warmth wrap my body like a blanket. I inhaled the fresh smell of earth and freshly sprouted greenery covering the mountain, then opened my eyes and marveled at the cerulean sky. With a sigh, I walked behind Gyonessa's mew and opened a small door containing leashes, jesses, hoods, and other training equipment, and I chose a hood with a tassel of feathers the princess would find acceptable for such an occasion. I turned around and stopped short in surprise. The prince was standing a few feet away, watching me. I curtseyed and moved to return to the princess, but he blocked my path. I looked past his shoulder, but the rows of mews concealed us from the crowd.

"I've found myself becoming quite curious about you," the prince said, and my heart sank into my stomach. Jervell must have been filling the prince's head with lies. I shook my head, not knowing what else to do.

He stepped forward, and I stepped back and kept backing up until I was up against the side of the mew. Hesitantly, he touched a hand to my face and caressed my cheek, then down my neck, and as his fingertips reached the top of my frock, I bolted sideways.

I thought I was fast and had the advantage of being small, but the prince was faster. He grabbed me, clamped a hand over my mouth, and wrapped his arm around my chest. I fought hard, pulling at his hands and kicking back against his legs as he dragged me behind a mew. I finally clutched the hand covering my mouth, yanked it downward, then bit hard into the fleshy portion between thumb and forefinger. He cried out and loosened his grip briefly, then tugged me back and slammed his fist into my stomach. I collapsed to my knees, struggling for air, unable to scream. The prince grabbed a handful of hair and leaned inches from my face.

"I'm not in the habit of working this hard to get what I want, but I do admire your fighting spirit." He threw me to the ground and laid on top of me. I pounded against his chest, still breathless from the blow he had delivered.

"Stop!" he hissed as he pinned my hands above my head. His lower body pressed into mine, the hilt of his sword grinding into my hip. "I don't know if you *can* scream, but if you do, I'll make this hurt so bad you won't walk for a week." Fear paralyzed me, keeping my arms still when he let them go.

"I've never had a virgin before." He ripped open the front of my frock, exposing my skin to the warm afternoon breeze.

Feeling returned to my arms and I frantically tried to squirm out from under him, but he took my wrists firmly in one of his hands and gripped them tightly above my head. Tears poured down my face, and my throat tightened when I tried to scream. He trailed wet kisses across my face and ran his tongue down my throat. When he roughly grabbed and squeezed my exposed breast, my mind became a black void.

I had been injured before. Growing up on the back of a horse came with such consequences. I endured the breaks and bruises as battle scars, lessons to be learned and laughed about. No number of falls ever brought me so low that I quit riding, nor did I ever believe I could not brave whatever might befall me. In the moments I felt the prince's knee against my thigh to spread my legs, I knew I had to make the choice to remain in the darkness until this was over, or to defend my body.

He released my breast and reached for the front of his breeches. While he was thus distracted, I brought my knee up and threw my hip against him with all my strength, a guttural growl escaping from my throat as he fell sideways in shock. Panting, I climbed to my feet, groping for the dagger hidden in my frock. I brought the blade up just as the prince was about to overtake me again, and he backed away, hands raised.

"Where did you get that?" he demanded.

I lunged toward him.

He took several steps back. "I am the crown prince of Praed, and you have just made a threat on my life. I'll see you hanged for this."

I lowered the dagger. As much as I wanted to bury the blade into his soft belly, I didn't consider him worth dying for. Without turning my back on him, I began to circle my way toward the yard, toward people, to safety. He made no move to stop me, and I turned to run.

Something struck my back. Pain split across my spine and drove me face-first into the ground. I rolled over, my back throbbing. The prince tossed aside a long, thick bird perch and stalked toward me, his face set in an angry sneer. The dagger had been thrown out of my reach. I crawled backward in the dirt, certain he would next draw his sword and run me through. I glanced down at his belt and was puzzled to see the weapon wasn't there. The prince straddled me and struck me against the side of the face with the back of his hand, the ring on his last finger leaving a red scratch along my cheek. My eyes widened as he wrapped his hands around my throat and squeezed, not enough for me to lose my breath, but just enough to frighten me into lying still.

"No servant has the right to deny me," he said darkly. "Just lie there like a good girl, open your legs, and let me take what I want."

"Your Highness, apologies for the interruption."

I nearly wept with joy when I heard Risteard's voice. The prince paled, and a tremor shook his hands around my neck. He released me and scrambled to his feet. My legs felt boneless as I struggled to stand and pull the torn ends of my frock together.

"What is the meaning of this?" The prince put his hands on his hips and spoke as though Risteard was the one caught committing a crime.

"Your presence is required by the king. I'm sorry, young lady, but the prince can no longer see you. You are the lady-in-waiting to Her Highness and therefore quite off limits." I dared to look up at Risteard, and his features were characteristically blank as he steadily held the prince's gaze.

"Yes." The prince straightened his rumpled tunic and looked at me over his shoulder. "Sorry, old girl. You'll have to find someone else to entertain you. Thank you, Risteard." The prince hurried away, his dignity intact. I looked down at Risteard's white-knuckled fists and shuddered. He'd also made a choice between bloodshed and prudence.

We stared at each other while the prince's footsteps receded. When I could no longer hear them, my legs gave way, and I collapsed. Risteard knelt close, arms outstretched, not touching me.

"Are you very injured?" he asked. I shook my head.

I choked out a response between tears. "You know---you know I didn't want it---right? You just said that to make him leave?"

"Yes." The word rushed over me, heavy with emotion. "I know. Of course I know."

I made an incoherent noise I hoped he would interpret as an apology, but I was beyond the ability to speak. I couldn't hold back the flood of tears and swell of emotions breaking me apart. Sobs racked my body as I fell forward onto his chest. His arms wrapped around me, and I cried without restraint, soaking his tunic with my tears. He offered no comforting words or platitudes. He simply held on, stroking my hair silently.

Gradually, the tears ran dry. I moved away and shyly met his eye. There was no judgement there, only concern. Carefully, he touched a finger to the bruise forming on my cheek, and traced the red line left by the prince's ring. His expression darkened, and he squeezed his eyes and shook away whatever troubling thoughts resided there.

"Come." Risteard helped me to my feet. I crossed my arms protectively over my chest, flushing red in embarrassment. "Go change," he said. "I'll make your excuses."

"The hood," I said. "The princess needs it." I pointed a shaking finger in the direction of Gyonessa's mew where I dropped the hood.

"I'll take care of it," he said. "Go."

Shame washed over me. Had I done something to provoke the prince? If so, I could not fathom what it was, how I brought this upon myself. I walked the corridors of the castle, my eyes fixed at my feet, keeping close to the wall for fear of bumping into anyone. When I reached my room, I shut the door and braced myself against it in case I was being followed. When several minutes passed without a knock, I wrenched off the torn dress and threw it across the room, resolving to burn it later. Even though the temperature was quite high, I put my coat on over a new frock and buttoned it to my chin, not wishing to expose a single inch of skin. I tidied my hair, opened the door with trembling hands, and prepared to face the crowds as if nothing happened. Every day of my life, I wore a mask to protect myself, to go unnoticed as the unassuming deaf-mute servant not worth bothering about. That mask had failed, and now I was forced to face the world stripped bare, vulnerable, and raw.

When I rejoined the princess' side, I could feel with each glance that everyone knew what happened. Everyone was staring, wondering what the prince could have possibly been thinking to want a woman like me. Perhaps, like the prince, they were also curious and now saw me as fair game. I clutched my coat collar tighter and kept my eyes to the ground, watching the movement of my shadow. Sweat flowed down my temples and trickled down my back. When the princess rose from her seat to return to the castle, she eyed me with curiosity at my change in attire but made no comment.

Using my long hair to cover my face, I managed to keep the princess from noticing the bruise blossoming on my cheek until I was preparing her for the evening feast. She narrowly observed the change in my demeanor, the way I curled into myself and hid my face, the extra layers I wore despite the heat. She said nothing until she was seated at her vanity and able to see my face in the mirror.

She tapped my hand, and I met her eyes in the glass, carefully avoiding raising my head. She motioned for me to put my hair back, but I would not. She asked where my scarf was, and I did not answer. Frustrated, she rose, and before I could react, she used both hands to pull my hair back from my face. Her fingers dug into my scalp when she saw my exposed cheek.

"Did you suffer a fall?" she asked.

I nodded, thankful for the plausible explanation.

She eyed me suspiciously and leaned closer. "That's quite a scratch, and that bruise will last for a while. What shall I do with you? Do you have injuries anywhere else?"

I shook my head.

"Odd that you fell hard enough to cause such an injury to one spot on your face but nowhere else."

I remembered the stick, and I pointed to my back.

"You fell and hit the side of your face and your back at the same time? Doesn't seem possible. In fact, I would say that's *im*possible."

I lowered my eyes and felt tears welling. My face flushed in shame, and my hands trembled.

She grabbed my chin to force me to meet her eye. "Did someone do this to you?" she demanded.

My lack of response confirmed her suspicions.

"Who was it? Do you know his name?"

I shook my head, afraid to tell her the truth.

"There's no sense in protecting him. You are my property, and an attack on you is a personal offense to me. Now I demand to know! Is he a servant?"

I shook my head.

"A noble?"

I remained still.

She appeared disturbed, as if the very thought of a person of her own station doing this to me was insulting on a personal level. She began naming nobles, and I responded by shaking my head to each. Her frustration mounted as I declined every suggestion, until she was at a loss.

Suddenly, her face flushed and she gritted her teeth. Speaking in a low, menacing tone she asked, "Was it Prince Brannon?"

My chin trembled and I blinked to hold back tears. She cursed, and I expected her to accuse me of lying, but instead she asked, "Are you still a maid?"

I nodded hastily, and she sighed in relief.

"Thank goodness for that at least. The fool." She turned away and paced around her room, muttering that he was getting worse and "we" needed to act before he did something very stupid. When she had collected herself, she instructed me to keep the incident to myself. She didn't have to tell me twice. The last thing I wanted was to spread the news of what Prince Brannon had done.

After I brushed and styled the princess' hair for dinner, she surprised me by seating me in her vacated chair. Then she spent several minutes powdering my cheek to conceal the bruise. Whether this was out of kindness to me or to avoid any embarrassment for herself, I didn't care. I looked at myself in the mirror and noticed my face almost appeared normal. She then braided and pinned my hair and covered it with one of her own headdresses. She stepped back to examine her work, then motioned me to stand. I tried to resist when she reached for my coat, but I could hardly fight with the princess. She tossed the garment aside, and I felt instant relief shedding the warm layer.

"You should not have to hide because some idiot couldn't control his impulses," she said. "No woman deserves such abhorrent treatment, even a servant."

My shock was eclipsed by a wave of relief. Though I was fathoms below Princess Caelyn in social standing, she still felt a sense of camaraderie with me as a woman. It was as close to compassion I'd seen from her, and I almost felt guilty for conspiring against her.

"I suppose you shouldn't be left alone with him," she said. "If you no longer have the body of a child, you probably aren't as innocent as one either, and the allure of the attention of a prince may prove too difficult to resist after a time. It could potentially spoil his prospects if he were to become involved with a Praed servant."

The warm feeling dissipated, replaced by a renewed determination to have my revenge on the entire Elejick royal family.

CHAPTER 34

I continued through my normal routines like a ghost. I tried to put the incident in the past by pretending it never happened, by shutting off my emotions, the feelings of fear and shame and others too complex to name. Risteard asked how I was only once, and though his concern was appreciated, I made no answer except to glare. He said no more. The princess immediately sent Jervell Kade back to Ilano. I assumed he was expected to return with a potential bride for Prince Brannon. She seemed to consider the attack evidence of uncontrollable urges, and her solution was to have him securely married before he did something truly regrettable. What he had done to me was forgivable.

I wished I *had* stabbed him. At least I would be swinging by a rope and not listening to Princess Caelyn's nonsense or seeing the prince nonchalantly going about his business. I resented the casual ease at which he went about his life, unaffected by what he'd done, while I wallowed in a living nightmare expecting to be molested at any moment. Risteard retrieved my dagger from the yard, and I made it more accessible by cutting slits into my frocks. I practiced with the dagger every night before bed and became so proficient at drawing the blade I silently dared the prince to try and touch me again.

As the weeks passed, I became more withdrawn, barely slept, and performed my duties in a mindless haze. My appetite decreased until the taste of food was repulsive. I lost the extra pounds I gained from the healthy diet following my illness and then some, thinning my body to sharp points of hips and ribs. The color of my hair dulled, and I found loose strands on my pillow every morning. The only person who acknowledged my transformation was Risteard. His worry was so palpable he couldn't maintain a neutral expression around me. I decided to relieve his stress by staying away from him as much as possible.

In due course Jervell Kade returned to Praed, much to the surprise and delight of King Conall. With him came the kind, beautiful, and well-bred Mwiryn Derville. The princess whisked her away to converse conspiratorially while the Lord Protector resumed his place at Prince Brannon's side.

Princess Caelyn settled her friend on a plush settee. "You must be exhausted from your journey."

"Not so terribly," Miss Derville replied in her sweet voice. "I was so happy to be invited to Praed again, Caelyn. I have missed you."

"And I you, my friend," the princess smiled. "But I am not the only one."

"Oh?"

"Indeed," the princess said. "My brother has spoken of little else but you since your departure. You made quite an impression it seems. I couldn't bear to hear his laments any longer."

It was a bald-faced lie. Prince Brannon had done no such thing and persuading this poor woman that selfish monster had feelings for her was cruel. I wished there was a way to warn her, but my heart froze remembering that a royal marriage was just what Risteard and I had been waiting for--a distraction that would make our plans possible. Miss Derville had always been kind to me, but she was still an Ilano, and I would have to tolerate her part in this scheme without interfering.

At dinner, Miss Derville was seated beside Prince Brannon, and he dutifully attended to her, though with little of the enthusiasm the princess claimed he possessed. Afterward the prince accompanied her at the piano while his sister and the Lord Protector lurked in the corner watching their every move. I felt sorry for Miss Derville, who basked shyly in the prince's warm smile. I had to look away when bile rose in my throat at the memory of those eyes staring down at *me* while he pinned me to the ground.

Risteard maintained a respectable distance, waiting for me to span the chasm between us. It was not fear or anger keeping us apart, rather my detachment from all feelings that left me apathetic and unwilling to reach out and rekindle our friendship. A part of me knew this was unfair, but I was too distracted by the struggle over the injustice of what the prince had done to me to care about the morality of distressing my friend.

I did not stir when Jervell Kade stood beside me to watch the prince interact with Miss Derville with a smug smile on his weaselly face. I shifted away, trying to appear as if I was casually adjusting my stance, but Kade was no fool. He inched closer, and I could smell the cider and musk on him.

"Such a lovely pair they make," he whispered in my ear. I made no indication I understood, but he persisted in speaking. "She's a delightful creature. Rich, beautiful, from a respectable Ilano family. Obedient. She will do whatever her father asks for the honor of her family and whatever her husband demands as a dutiful wife. The perfect woman, if you ask me." I continued to ignore him, which he seemed to find amusing rather than irritating. He eventually grew bored with my inattention and moved near the prince so he could peer at the lovely woman whose life was not her own.

Princess Caelyn devoted every waking hour to arranging activities so Prince Brannon and Miss Derville could spend time together. One day the prince entertained the ladies with a new trick for next year's falconry games, and on another day, Queen Shaeli gave them all a lesson in watercolors. I'm still trying to wrap my brain around that. Miss Derville suggested an afternoon ride and picnic, and the princess readily agreed. Princess Caelyn knew it would be difficult to enjoy an intimate picnic with a retinue of guards, so she requested a minimal escort. This met staunch resistance from the king.

"I would not feel safe having the three of you out on your own without protection, especially after the attempt on my life," the king said.

"That was a year ago, Father," the princess argued. "There have been no threats since."

"None that I make you aware of," he said. His eyes darted from side to side and his nails dug into the armrests.

The princess cocked her head and raised an eyebrow. "Have I reason to fear, Father? Have there been threats to your person?" Her tone did not suggest concern at the prospect of such threats, but anticipation. The king did not appear to notice the concealed pleasure in her eyes.

"I have been made aware of some treacherous developments," he answered cryptically, wiping his brow, and the blood froze in my veins.

The princess was firm. "I will consent to a small contingent of guards, but they must maintain their distance. We wish to have privacy."

The king stared into the distance, his expression blank. After several confusing moments, he nodded slowly. "They must be within sight and able to hear should you call for help."

"Of course, Father." She bowed, a grin playing at her lips.

I was permitted to accompany the party because *someone* had to serve the picnickers. A handful of knights would escort us, including Risteard and the young man I saw at the winter celebration. Olim was eager for a break from drills and the confines of the castle. His energetic stride was uplifting but did not melt the ice around my heart. My spirits had plummeted so low even the prospect of riding did little to improve my mood.

A groom brought a horse to me, and I laid my palm on the soft nose, slid it over the muzzle and head, and caressed the strong neck before I took up the reins. A twitch at the corner of my mouth grew into a small smile as I placed my foot in the stirrup and tried to bounce into the saddle. My strength left me in the weeks since I stopped sleeping and eating properly, and I trembled and slipped down for another try.

"Allow me." Risteard's deep voice spoke from behind me. I hadn't noticed him approach. I leaned my forehead against the saddle and took a cleansing breath. I wanted to say no, to wave him away, and scream to be left alone, but I could not get into this saddle on my own. I stepped back, and he cupped his hands to help me up.

He stared up at me while I settled into the saddle, adjusting my stirrups and finding a firm grip on the reins. I nodded, indicating he could go, but he continued to study me critically.

"You've become quite thin," he said. "Have you been ill?"

I shook my head and avoided his gaze. He inhaled sharply before walking away, but I did not look up.

The comforting motion of a horse beneath me gave me the first moment of peace I'd experienced in weeks. I closed my eyes as the rocking motion eased my aching bones and tired thoughts. The party traversed the side of the mountain and entered the valley. The midsummer sun was high overhead, and I shielded my eyes from the intense glare off the white rock of the mountain while I surveyed the town below. Workers had finally repaired damage from the war, and life was returning to a semblance of normality.

The crunching of rocks under hooves ceased when we left the road for the lush green grass dotted with colorful wildflowers. I inhaled their fragrance, the sweet perfumes calming my nerves and relaxing my senses. The prince and princess rode ahead with Miss Derville and found a suitable spot below a drooping sallow tree, whose chartreuse leaves cast cooling shade over a patch of flat ground. They spread a blanket over the grass while I carefully lowered myself to the ground, feeling instantly sore. I hobbled to a pack horse and started unloading baskets. I could barely carry one, and I was ashamed at how weak I allowed myself to become. Risteard and Olim unpacked the rest and carried them over as I unloaded dishware and appetizers.

"That will be all, Risteard," Princess Caelyn said, waving him away. "You and the other knights can go perch on that hill over there and watch for marauders." Risteard gave her a perturbed glance before shifting his gaze to me. I met his eyes blankly, and I sensed he wanted to talk, but I could not bear to hear what he had to say. The last thing I wanted was a heart-to-heart about how fractious I was and advice on how to move on.

I set out fruit and bread while the pampered nobles lay against cushions and commented about the lovely weather. When each had a glass of honeyed cider in their hands, their conversation turned to more interesting topics.

"Did you hear?" Miss Derville asked. "Eveene is engaged!"

My ears perked up at this. I hadn't heard that name for a year, and I hoped to never see her again. An engagement meant perhaps she'd have no reason to come back to Praed to torment Risteard and me.

"It's about time," the princess said. "She'd become much too free with herself."

"I don't know who will be more pleased--Eveene's father or Risteard," the prince said between bites.

"She made such a fool out of herself with him," the princess added. "Too much effort for someone not worth the trouble, if you want my opinion."

"I recall you bestowing it upon her on several occasions," the prince said.

"Perhaps she didn't give up because she had true feelings for Risteard?" Miss Derville suggested.

The princess clasped her friend's hand. "You're so sweet to think so."

The prince swirled the cider in his glass, a lazy smile on his face. "The only 'feeling' Eveene had in regard to Risteard had nothing to do with the heart and everything to do with what's under his tunic."

I turned away to dish up lunch and hide my embarrassment.

"Gross, Brannon," the princess said. "Hold your tongue in front of Miss Derville, if you please."

"The view up here is so lovely," Miss Derville said. "Your Highness, what is the name of that estate over there? The one with the red rock walls?"

"Please, Mwiryn, you must call me Brannon when we're alone," the prince said sweetly.

She glanced away and blushed.

I practically shoved dishes into their hands to stop the idiocy. The princess gave me a dirty glare, but I ignored her. Miss Derville smiled and thanked me, and the prince nodded without meeting my eye. Coward.

Once they were served and eating amid more pleasant conversation, I sat in the sun a safe distance away. The warmth soothed my aches and the tension in my shoulders relaxed. I stretched my back, feeling my joints pop when I pressed my fists into my spine. I looked over the valley to the house Miss Derville pointed out. The layers of red, yellow, and dark gray stones of the outer walls were mined from the valley floor. Before the invasion, the place belonged to Ardt and Elifa Bromley. Ardt built the manor with his own hands, cleared the land, planted the crops, married his young wife, Elifa, and raised their five children in that house. Their children grew up and moved on by the time Ula and I met them, and they were delighted to have our laughter echo off those lonely walls. During my letter writing campaign, I learned Elifa died during the conquest, her heart unable to handle the stress. Ardt held out to keep his home, but he was forced out by an Ilano noble. He died that winter of starvation. Not a pretty story for a woman you're trying to court.

My gaze drifted up the hill to the small contingent of knights. Their horses were hobbled and unbridled, grazing contentedly on fresh green grass. Three of the knights lounged in the grass, their laughter carrying across the valley on the breeze. The young knight, Olim, kept busy checking harnesses, glancing down the hill at the three people sitting under the tree, and then back at Risteard. I had the distinct impression he desperately wanted to impress his commander. The black knight himself was on his guard, standing firm while his companions relaxed. I'd only seen Risteard anywhere near relaxed once or twice. Did he actually sleep? I wasn't sure.

Risteard wasn't simply watching the valley for danger or keeping an eye on the three nobles behind me. I realized his stare was fixed on me. I couldn't read his expression from this distance, but I could tell his gaze had not shifted since mine settled on him. He'd been very patient these last few weeks. He had seen me at my most vulnerable, and it tore me apart. For him to see me so weak was humiliating, and it certainly was not a desirable trait in a co-conspirator. I turned away when Olim moved up beside him and chattered excitedly.

After the last sweet treats were eaten and the cider was gone, Miss Derville proposed a walk to settle their stomachs. The princess agreed and glared at the prince until he acquiesced. Without shame, Princess Caelyn took Miss Derville's hand and tucked it into her brother's elbow, and the three of them wandered down the valley. Instantly, four guards scurried to tail them, and I was left to clean up the mess by myself. Risteard appeared beside me, clearing dishes and placing them in baskets. We worked silently, the only sounds the rustling of leaves and the distant snorting of horses.

"There's some bread left here," Risteard said quietly. "You should eat some while they're gone."

"I'm not hungry, thank you." I spoke hurriedly without meeting his eye.

He sighed. "I wish you wouldn't push me away. I only wish to help you."

"I know." My throat tightened. I knew, I truly did, but I was broken, and it pained me for him to see it.

"Please." He reached out a hand to still my movements and then quickly pulled away. By his own admission, he did not like physical contact, but our close friendship seemed to make him comfortable enough to extend comfort when needed. I imagined he was probably disgusted and couldn't bear to touch my tainted skin. He was my friend, and if *he* didn't want to touch me, what would be my family's response? Would I be shunned? I'd never entertained thoughts of marriage, but there was certainly no point now. No man would have a polluted woman.

I cried freely, the dark thoughts flowing with my tears. All the anger and resentment, shame and hatred, all the suspicions surrounding Prince Brannon's motives and the fear the king would discover how I'd pulled a dagger on him, all the emotions I buried bubbled to the surface. The longer Risteard kept silent, the more wretched I felt, believing with every fallen tear I was incrementally losing his respect. I sensed him shift and expected him to leave in disgust. But I felt his forehead gently touch mine. My tears ceased instantly, and my breath came in quick gasps. I took a deep breath and released it slowly.

"I'm sorry," I whispered.

"All you have to be sorry for is this wasted bread. You need to take care of yourself." He sat up and offered the bread. I wiped my face dry and began nibbling at the soft insides. My stomach welcomed it. I devoured the remainder of the bread, followed by some stray pieces of fruit and a slice of pheasant the princess thought too fatty.

"That's better." Risteard watched with a satisfied smile as I dabbed the grease from my lips with the hem of my apron.

A few hundred yards down the valley, I saw the four knights, the prince, princess, and Miss Derville near a trickle of a stream that apparently held some interest. I closed my eyes, and a warm breeze caressed my face, bringing with it the scent of wildflowers and a hint of horses. I turned my attention to the beasts on the hill. They were still grazing, their tails swishing across their bodies. The sun glinted off their saddles and coats, and I had an urge to climb on one and ride away.

"I'll cover for you if you want to ride," Risteard said.

"Am I so transparent?" I asked with the barest of smiles.

"Sometimes."

"I can't," I said. "It'll get us both in trouble." I sighed and returned my attention to the vastness of the valley. "Sitting up here, without being confined to the castle and to my duties to the princess, I feel almost normal. As if I'm my own person again, beholden to no one."

"I promise you'll feel that way again."

"Will I? I don't think so. We're all beholden to someone, even as children, though we don't feel its effects as acutely. No, I'll never get back what I felt as a child growing up at Riverstone. But you know what?" I met his intense stare. "That's all right. I can't live in the past forever."

"You may not be able to recapture your childhood at Riverstone, but you can be happy again."

I focused on my feet, unable to reply.

"Please don't let Brannon take that away from you. He's not worth it."

"Do you think my family will forgive me?"

"There's nothing to forgive!" he shouted, then looked to make sure he was not overheard. The group had left the stream and were slowly meandering back toward us. "You've done nothing wrong."

"I feel like I have." I rose hastily and finished clearing the picnic.

"The only thing you should regret is that you didn't stab the idiot when you had the chance," he muttered.

"I didn't think he was worth being hanged for."

"If he isn't worth dying for, then why are you killing yourself?"

I stared at him in shocked silence, my mouth agape. The nobles returned before I could respond, and Risteard wore a thunderous expression all the way back to the castle.

After dinner, Miss Derville reclined on the settee in Princess Caelyn's room while I brushed the princess' hair. They bantered and exchanged minor pleasantries, nothing worth noting, and I ignored them to concentrate on my own tangled thoughts.

Risteard had been angry with me, not because of what happened, but because of my response. How could I possibly control that? I'd been through a terrible ordeal, one that some women never recover from. I suppose I was lucky he rescued me in time to save my virtue. But I didn't feel saved. Mother, I knew, would not see a distinction between 'raped' and 'almost raped.' Any intimate contact between a man and woman was reserved for the marriage bed. For a fraction of a second I wondered, why did I care what my mother thought? She ceased any interest in my affairs since the day we arrived here. Why was I giving her feelings precedence over mine? The only person whose opinion I really cared about was Ula's, and I knew she would simply show me the affection of a concerned sister.

Well, it wasn't entirely true that Ula's was the only opinion I cared about. Risteard's had become increasingly important, and he made it clear nothing had changed between us. Though, he may never forgive me for hesitating to kill Prince Brannon.

"I was so pleased to see you enjoy yourself today, Mwiryn," Princess Caelyn said. "You looked exceptionally lovely in your yellow dress. Like a wildflower."

"Thank you," Miss Derville said. "Caelyn...um, I'm not sure about this."

"About what? Enjoying yourself on a beautiful day?"

"You know what I mean. His Highness has been kind to me, but---"

"He's shown you a great deal more than civility, Mwiryn. I've never seen him so attentive."

The woman flushed a deep red and concentrated on her perfectly manicured fingernails. The princess joined her on the settee.

She took one of Miss Derville's hands and in a soothing tone said, "Don't worry, Mwiryn. You're performing splendidly."

"You've persuaded me that Prince Brannon's marrying an Ilano noblewoman is what's best for the kingdom, but I don't think I'm worthy of such an honor. And..." her voice dropped, and she looked away. "I'm not sure marriage to His Highness would be in *my* best interest."

"I know these feelings you're struggling with, dear friend," Caelyn soothed while rubbing Miss Derville's back. "And it does you great credit to overcome them. You must not despair. Marriage to my brother means security, comfort, wealth, and eventually a crown. Not to mention having me as a sister-in-law." The princess smiled.

"You're right of course." Miss Derville sighed, placing her hand over Princess Caelyn's. "Thank you. I may not appear grateful for what you're doing, but I promise I am. My father, too. He has high hopes for this visit."

The princess' smile dropped. "Let's not disappoint him then."

CHAPTER 35

Princess Caelyn continued to throw Miss Derville in her brother's path at every opportunity. Jervell Kade was the master painter, and she was the brush bringing his visions to life. Their shared dream of a marriage for Prince Brannon seemed a foregone conclusion, and they reveled in their genius while the relationship blossomed. When satisfied he was leaving the couple in capable hands, Jervell Kade announced a departure date, and the king naturally held a farewell feast.

Prince Brannon was surprisingly reluctant to see the Lord Protector leave. During dinner, the prince directed all his attention to him, fairly ignoring his potential future bride. Jervell listened and nodded, patting the prince on head or hand as if he were a child. I couldn't hear what they were saying, but the prince was clearly disturbed. He whispered urgently in the older man's ear, gesticulating for emphasis, and avoided eye contact with the princess sitting across from him. The Lord Protector had no such qualms, and his eyes casually drifted in her direction and then past her shoulder to rest on me. I kept my expression neutral but cringed inwardly when a slow smile spread across the Lord Protector's face.

I tried to avoid Kade for the remainder of the evening, but it was difficult in the confines of the music room. Between the royal family, Miss Derville, Jervell Kade, a smattering of knights, nobles, and their attendants, I could barely turn around without bumping into someone. Miss Derville relinquished the piano bench to the princess, but before she took two steps, the Lord Protector held out a hand to stop her and extended his other hand toward where I hid in the shadows.

"I understand from Miss Derville that your lady-in-waiting is a hidden talent," he said in his high-pitched, grating tone. I paled, and the princess gave me a sharp look.

"I'm fairly certain she knows only one song," the princess said. "And since we've heard it, there's no sense in putting her on display."

"*I* have not had the pleasure," he said. He grabbed my wrist and pulled me toward the piano. I searched the crowd with a silent plea, and thankfully Risteard stepped forward and spoke into Caelyn's ear. She pursed her lips and strode toward the Lord Protector.

"I insist you release her," she hissed. "You embarrass me treating my lady-in-waiting in such a manner."

Jervell released my arm, and for the first time I saw his evil glare directed at the princess. She stared right back. "You may find amusement in tormenting her.

But you cannot do so when such pursuits detract from what we're trying to accomplish here."

"All eyes will be watching this young woman," Jervell argued. "This will allow you to secret the prince and Miss Derville away from prying eyes." The princess glanced at me and considered his words.

I begged her with my eyes to let me go in peace, but her desire to see her brother married overwhelmed all reason. She nodded and gestured for me to sit at the piano. Jervell smiled triumphantly and assisted me to the bench, and I jerked away when he reached past me to shift the pages of the music.

"Can you read the notes?" he asked.

I shrugged.

"Well, then just play this song I've heard so much about." He gestured for me to play, and I looked around at the faces watching expectantly. Risteard had moved closer to the piano and stood protectively just behind my right shoulder while Jervell Kade hovered at my left. I closed my eyes, placed my fingers on the keys, and began.

A general expression of shock and amazement permeated the room as the notes poured from the piano. The king's brows knit in confusion, and the queen had an understanding look about her. Jervell Kade was speechless, his hand clutching his bony chest. I was secretly pleased. As the last echoes of the notes receded, I peered at Risteard and basked in the gratification of playing flawlessly and being rewarded with his smile.

I retreated into the shadows to escape the stares. Another woman took my place, and I was quickly and thankfully forgotten. When Jervell Kade engaged the king in conversation, Risteard took the opportunity to join me in my hiding spot.

"You played very well," he said in a low voice.

"Thank you." I smiled. "I'm glad you were able to hear how well you taught me."

"Do you think your mother would approve?"

"If you weren't a knight already, I believe she'd dub you based solely on your bravery for taking me on as a student."

"Kade was quite insistent that you play," Risteard noted.

"He saw it as an opportunity to distract everyone so Miss Derville and Prince Brannon could sneak away. I don't see either of them, or the princess."

"She's very intent on securing an engagement."

"Which is what we wanted, right? A marriage to distract the king?"

"Yes. Has Miss Derville indicated she would accept a proposal?"

"She will do her duty," I said dryly. "Like a good, obedient girl."

"Not everyone can afford to be willful."

"Funny. If there weren't so many people around, I'd show you how willful I can be."

"Would it involve your elbow in my ribs?"

"For starters," I said with a half-smile.

The crowd applauded enthusiastically at the conclusion of the piece, and another young lady rose to exhibit herself. I scanned the room, but the conspirators were still missing.

"It's been too long," I whispered. "I'm worried. What if something has happened? What if they've cornered Miss Derville somewhere?"

"I don't think Caelyn would orchestrate an attack on her friend."

"How do you know? She's capable of great cruelty. And she's determined to have Miss Derville as a sister-in-law."

"Trust me. She will not place Miss Derville in danger. But if it will ease your mind, I'll go and find them."

"It would, thank you." He bowed as if I had issued a command and left. I shook my head, annoyed at his jest.

Unfortunately, his absence meant I was alone when Jervell Kade slithered next to me. He touched my face to turn me toward him so I could understand his words, and I nearly smacked his hand away in disgust. It took every ounce of strength to maintain my composure.

"You surprised me with your playing. I didn't think I would have such an experience at my age. When you're as old as me and have seen much of the world, little amazes you. You, however, continue to intrigue me. How far you've fallen, and yet there's something so steady, so unbreakable about you. I can see a fire in your eyes, and no matter what I try, I can't seem to put it out."

I shivered and took a step back, which seemed to please him.

"It's such a pure emotion, fear. You can be the strongest knight or even a king, and we all have it. And you cannot hide it no matter how well-trained you are. The eyes always give you away. Tell me, young lady, how afraid were you when the prince laid on top of you?"

My nostrils flared and I felt the blood rush to my face. If I remained there and listened to his words, I knew I would do something I would regret. I took two steps forward, but he grabbed my arm in his surprisingly strong grip and pulled me backward so he could whisper in my ear.

"Never send a boy to do a man's work," he said, his breath hot against my skin. He laughed, a low, gleefully evil laugh, his fingers digging into my skin. I wrenched my arm free, his nails leaving trails of red scratches in their wake, and I calmly walked among the dwindling crowd. Risteard had not returned, and I decided to look for him.

I strode down the corridor looking in doorways, listening at keyholes, and peering around dark corners searching for Risteard and the princess. I started to panic after minutes passed without seeing them. I held my breath when slow, deliberate footsteps echoed behind me, daring me to look. I turned around casually, finding Jervell Kade in the middle of the corridor, staring at me with his dead eyes and crooked smile. I held my head high and confidently marched toward him and tried to pass. He slid sideways to block me, and when I tried to move the other way, he followed. My hands twitched, and I resisted the urge to push him aside. I doubted I could avoid punishment for attacking the Lord Protector. I gave him my best authoritative look and waved my hand to indicate he move aside.

"You are no longer the lady of the manor, my dear," he chuckled, a sound emerging from deep in his chest that still retained the high tone of his voice. "You still need to learn your place." He grabbed me again, but this time I did not hesitate. When his hand locked around my wrist, I clasped him so our arms were wrapped together, pulled him forward to throw him off balance, and drove my knee into his stomach. While he was bent over gasping, I ran.

My feet pounded against the hardwood floor, while behind me Jervell cursed and shuffled after me. My room did not have a lock, so there was no point hiding there. The nearest door I could reach led into the kitchens, so I ducked inside and waited, listening. He must have seen me because seconds later the door handle rattled. I bolted through the room before the door flew open and Jervell shouted. There were only a few servants left working, and they watched curiously as I dashed toward the back door. None moved to help, but I couldn't blame them.

The sky glowed orange, and I could see perfectly as I ran down the hill past the mews, not stopping even when my ankle twisted. I didn't know how close Jervell was, or if he was still in pursuit. I passed the last of the eagle mews, crashed through the small copse of trees, and skidded to a stop at the top of the cliff. I bent over, bracing my hands on my knees, my legs trembling from exertion and my breathing harsh and painful.

My heart thudded so forcefully I feared it might burst through my chest. I eased my breathing with shallow breaths. He's an old man. I can outrun him. If I do, he'll leave me alone. I looked around, but there was nowhere to hide. At the edge of the cliff, I dropped to one knee, clutching at the rock. I closed my eyes, visualizing a scene like I did in the undercroft. A twig snapped, and I froze. I knew if he saw me vulnerable, he'd get cocky. If he grabs me, I'll fling him over my shoulder. Just in case, I unsheathed my dagger and hid my hand in the folds of my frock.

I could tell by his careful steps he was trying to be stealthy, but the wind carried his stench, and rocks skittered downhill. I gripped the hilt and tensed, waiting for him to attack. I panted, hoping he would think my loud breathing would cover his footfalls. He inched closer, quieter than I expected, but I knew every stone of this cliffside. My fingers clenched, scraping my nails to the quick. He was right behind me, so close I could sense him reaching toward me. Instead of grabbing my arm or shoulder, his hand curled around my throat in that surprisingly tight grip. Another took a fistful of my hair and forced my head backward. I clawed at the hand at my throat, gasping for air, and Jervell Kade lowered his face to mine, grinning from ear to ear.

"You've been caught, little vixen," he whispered. "I'm looking forward to experimenting with you. I assure you I've been practicing, and the results may prove satisfactory. For me." His lips pulled back over his crooked teeth and he straightened, finally releasing my throat. I gulped lungsful of air as he dragged me toward himself, his waist at eye level. He still held my hair tightly, and with his other hand he started unfastening his belt.

While he was distracted, I removed the dagger from its hiding place, and in a flash of movement, I sliced the blade across the back of his knee. The force was not as strong as I wished but judging by the torrent of blood oozing down his leg, I found the artery. Jervell released me, dropped to his knees, and screamed.

It is quite incredible how hours compress into a few seconds. The moment the wails of agony flew from his mouth, I panicked. If someone heard him and found us like this, it wouldn't matter what I said or what he tried to do. I am a servant, and the man on his knees is the Lord Protector of Ilano. Right then I knew it was his life or my own. No time for a conscious choice. I had to act to preserve myself. The world around me blurred as I focused on Jervell's pale, gaunt face. The skin was stretched over his gaping mouth, and a tear traced its way down a crease to settle on his lower lip. His eyelids opened, and his piercing gaze met mine. I raised the dagger numbly, feeling like a puppet, and plunged it into his eye with a *pop*, burying the blade to the hilt. The screaming instantly ceased, and the body of Jervell Kade slumped backward, silent and still, never to rise again.

I stood over him as blood dripped from the dagger--one drop, two, three. I wiped it clean on his tunic. I gripped his ankles and dragged him to the side of the cliff, and with a growl pushed him over the side. I watched the body fall, striking rocky outcroppings, his limbs bouncing wildly, until he landed in a broken heap of flesh and bone at the bottom.

My hands shook, and I looked down at the blood on my right hand smeared up to my elbow. I used the underside of my hem to wipe it clean, shivering despite the lingering warmth. I wrapped my arms about my shoulders, turned toward the castle, and never looked back.

The sky was blood red by the time I returned to the music room, staring blankly ahead. The princess stalked up to me, demanding to know where I'd been. I tried to explain I had been looking for her, but she did not appreciate this explanation.

"I wish to retire immediately," she said. "I'll devise an appropriate punishment for you."

Punish me all you wish, Princess, for now I cannot feel anything but emptiness.

CHAPTER 36

The sudden disappearance of Jervell Kade was whispered about throughout the castle, though it was speculated he simply returned to Ilano early. Risteard knew something was wrong, but I could not reveal the truth. In fact, I couldn't say anything. For two days, I was truly mute, even to him. Then one evening, the king announced Jervell Kade was discovered at the bottom of the mountain. His body was badly mutilated by the fall and predation by wild animals, so it was difficult to determine the cause of death. It was theorized he was taking in the view and fell, either tripping on the treacherous rock or losing balance due to his age. Murder had been ruled out, for who would dare harm the Lord Protector at King Conall's doorstep? I felt Risteard's eyes on me when the announcement was made, but I stared resolutely ahead. The princess was inconsolable, and I ushered her back to her room so she could mourn privately. Miss Derville accompanied us to soothe the princess, wiping away her tears and comforting her while she sobbed on the settee. I'd never seen the princess display such honest emotion before, let alone cry.

I was not two steps out of the princess' chambers when Risteard stepped in my path, locked eyes with me, then turned and walked to his study. I followed without a word and barely sat in my chair when he asked what happened in a tone that brooked no argument. I shivered violently, wrung my hands, and my teeth chattered. Risteard fed more logs on the fire then wrapped his greatcoat around my shoulders. He crouched in front of me and took my frigid hands between his and rubbed vigorously.

"Let us speak honestly," he said. "Do you know what happened to Kade?"

"Y-y-y-yes." I clamped a hand over my trembling lips. He rose and poured a glass of dark liquid.

"Drink this," he instructed. I took a sip and the liquid burned down my throat. I coughed, but he urged me to empty the glass. I complied, and the warmth eased my tension as it spread through me.

"He'd been tormenting me the entire night," I said. "Whispering such vile things in my ear. I tried to avoid him, but he was relentless. I left to find you and the princess, and he followed. He wouldn't let me pass, and I was afraid---" I swallowed, remembering. I closed my eyes and hugged myself tightly. "It was Jervell Kade who put the idea to attack me in Prince Brannon's head. He said as much that night." I heard the scrape of Risteard's chair dragging across the floor, and I opened my eyes lazily as he sat before me. He leaned forward to hear my every word, his features tightly controlled, and when he didn't say anything, I continued.

"I ran. And he chased me. I didn't think an old man could run so fast or so long. I ran outside, past the mews and the trees to the cliffside. I never thought he might possibly follow, but he did." I shivered once more at the memory and closed my eyes, unable to look at Risteard when I told him the truth. "He came up behind me and grabbed my hair. I didn't understand what he was saying, but his meaning was clear. He pulled my face toward him and he started unbuckling his belt. I panicked," my voice broke and a soft sob escaped my lips. "I couldn't go through that again, so I pulled out my dagger and cut the back of his knee. He started screaming. It was like I wasn't even in control of my body. I just acted." The words rushed out of me like the tears running down my face.

"I killed him!" I cried. "He was kneeling there screaming and I just wanted it to stop, and I knew I wouldn't survive if he lived, so I stabbed him. Right in the eye! And I pushed him off the mountain! I'm sorry!" I was crying hysterically now as I rocked back and forth.

Risteard quietly removed the glass from my grip and covered my quivering hands with his own.

"I'm proud of you," he said simply.

I stopped crying and slowly opened my eyes. Risteard was looking at me sympathetically and without anger.

"You're not angry?" I asked cautiously.

"Why would I be angry? You were defending yourself."

"He's the Lord Protector."

"And if he were an honorable man, he would have acted as such. You've done everyone a service in ridding the world of that monster."

"I can still see his face when I close my eyes."

"That will pass." He squeezed my hands.

"I'm not sad he's dead, but I wish it wasn't me that killed him."

"I'm sorry you were placed in a position to make that choice, but it was the right one."

I nodded, smiling slightly in appreciation.

"You should get some sleep," he said.

"I'm too frightened." There was a tremor in my voice.

"Think of something pleasant before you close your eyes. Like riding your horse."

"Will it help?"

"It can. If nothing else, you can distract yourself until the memory fades."

"Is that what you do?"

"Yes." He led me to the door and opened it for me to leave.

"What do you think about?" I asked.

"It's late," he said evasively. "Goodnight."

"Goodnight," I said. "And thank you."

I lay awake for several hours trying to recapture the memory of riding Amore along the Rhyvor on a warm summer day. I could hear the rushing of the water and the shifting of rocks underneath her hooves as we rode along the dry banks. A gentle breeze swept across my face, and I inhaled the earthy scent of horse sweat and foliage. I laid a hand against Amore's neck and felt the heat from her damp flesh. She snorted contentedly when I let her grab a mouthful of grass, and as she munched, I surveyed my surroundings. The top turret of Riverstone that housed my bedchamber loomed in the distance. I shielded my eyes from the bright sun and squinted. A figure appeared at the window, cloaked in darkness. I reined Amore around and raced toward home, fear filling my heart. I reached the threshold, dismounted, and looked upward. The figure was gone. I burst through the front door and stepped inside, nearly slipping in something wet and sticky. I looked down and a trail of blood led further into the house. I followed the red streaks, my heart pounding and stomach churning. Up the stairs and down the hall to Ula's room where it ran under her door. I pushed it open with shaking hands. The walls were covered with splatters of blood. On the bed lay a crumpled blood-soaked body, the dark figure hovering over it. I screamed, and the figure turned and smiled, its mouth full of white jagged teeth. It pointed a bony finger at me, and in a high-pitched voice it said, "You're next, little vixen."

I awoke drenched in sweat and calling Ula's name in the dark confines of my tiny room. The nightgown she gifted me clung to my body and my hair was matted to my forehead. I was breathing hard, and it took several breaths before my heart returned to a normal rhythm. My pulse throbbed at my temple, and I shook with fear. I lay back and tucked under my blanket, but I could not stop the shaking that rattled my teeth. I closed my eyes and tried to picture something happy--Ula's sweet face (covered in blood), riding Amore (burned to ash), an orinberry tart (rotten). It was no use. I was wide awake now, but too terrified to stay in bed. I threw off the bedclothes and felt around in the dark for my coat but touched the fine wool of Risteard's greatcoat I forgot to return before I left his study. I draped it over my shoulders and crept out of the room.

I had no plan. I only thought if I wandered around the castle for a while, I might grow weary enough to fall asleep. However, the more I walked, the more alert I became, and my imagination played tricks until I became too nervous to peek around corners. The castle was quiet, as though the building itself was resting for the night. Every creak of wood and call of a nighthawk startled me out of my skin. I was ready to return to bed, tired or not, but I meandered for so long the prospect was terrifying. I tiptoed down the hall, jumping at every candle flicker and rustle of tapestry. Eventually, I convinced myself the ghost of Jervell Kade was stalking me.

I came to the door of Risteard's study. If he was still awake at this hour, surely, he would indulge me by escorting me to my room. I knocked quietly, but there was no answer. I moved down to the next door, which if logic served led to his bedchamber. I felt uneasy disturbing his sleep but fear ultimately won over good sense and I knocked rapidly before whispering it was me. I heard rustling from within, a muffled curse, and then the door opened to Risteard in his nightshirt pulling on his breeches.

"What's happened? Are you hurt?" he asked, his voice rough from sleep. His black hair was disheveled, and I would have laughed at the way it stuck out at odd angles if not for my fear and his honest concerns.

"I had a nightmare and couldn't sleep," I said. "I've spooked myself, and now I'm too afraid to go back to my room. I'm sorry to wake you for such a stupid reason, but can you walk me to my room?" If I hadn't been so earnest, he probably would have been angry, but he relaxed and looked at me sympathetically.

"Did you try to think of a happy memory?" he asked.

I shook my head. "It didn't work." A floorboard creaked, and I jumped three feet in the air and clamped my hand around my mouth to keep from screaming.

"Do you need something to help you sleep?"

"I'm fine," I said, not even fooling myself. "Can you please take me to my room now?"

He studied me for a few moments, trying to make up his mind about something, then looked up and down the hallway before stepping aside and gesturing me inside.

I hesitated, unsure of the wisdom of such an action.

"It's all right," he assured me. "Come in." I took a few steps inside and he closed and latched the door.

I pulled the collar of the greatcoat tight while I watched him turn down the bedclothes and drag a settee to the side of the bed.

"So you don't have to be alone tonight. I'll stay awake until you fall asleep."

"I can't," I said, shaking my head. "It wouldn't be proper."

"It's only improper if someone sees you."

The large bed looked inviting with its plush feather pillows and thick blanket, but I was wary of sleeping in a man's bed and made no move to climb under the covers.

"Do you trust me?"

I met his steely blue gaze. "Yes." The temptation of comfort won out over propriety. "Turn around." He complied, and I shed the greatcoat and placed it at the foot of the bed, then slid under the covers still warm from his body. My head fell against the soft pillow, and I pulled the comforter snuggly over myself. I had not slept in a real bed for over two years, and I felt as if I had tucked myself into a cloud.

"All right," I said when I was modestly covered. Risteard turned around, retrieved the greatcoat, then stretched his long form on the settee before covering himself with it. My eyes began to drift open and shut in contentment, but Risteard's were wide awake and fixated on his feet.

"I didn't mean to take your bed out from under you," I said drowsily.

"It's no trouble." He turned to me. "Get some sleep."

"Will you sleep once I'm asleep?" I slurred, my eyes no longer open.

"Yes," he whispered.

"What if I have another nightmare?"

"I'll wake you. Sleep now."

"You're a good friend," I whispered before sleep overtook me, and I was enveloped in blissful darkness.

When I awoke the next morning, the settee was vacant, the only evidence Risteard slept there the greatcoat draped over the back. Sunlight shone orange-red through the windows, and I left the bed to see the view. The morning was still new, the sun barely gaining the horizon, illuminating the lush valley below the mountain and turning the white stone bright pink.

"You're awake," Risteard said. He approached, fastening the last buckle of his jerkin, then he abruptly stopped, and his cheeks reddened. He turned his back to me. My brow furrowed in confusion before I followed his gaze down my body. It was my turn to flush in embarrassment when I remembered I was scandalously clad in the revealing nightgown Ula had made for me. I retrieved the greatcoat and wrapped it around my body.

"Thank you again." I unlatched the door, cracked it open to check no was around, and hurried back to my room. Thankfully, I encountered no one at this early hour, and returned without causing a stir. I leaned against my door after closing it and thanked my luck that I wasn't seen. I shed the greatcoat and prepared for my day. I felt irreparably changed, and I feared the princess would ask questions. Donned in the simple frock that dictated my station, I left my tiny room no longer the naïve seventeen-year-old I'd been only a few days ago. I took a life, came to terms with the fact, and now faced the future with the certainty I would do anything to secure peace in Praed.

CHAPTER 37

Princess Caelyn refused another dish and dabbed her eye with a handkerchief. The Great Hall was crowded with nobles feasting in Jervell Kade's honor. His body was being prepared for burial, and I'll admit I was curious to witness an Ilano funeral. In Praed, we took a reverent approach to death. Clad in black, the family of the deceased led a procession along the King's Road. Mourners would pay respects and join them until hundreds of people followed the hearse. The body was then buried on the estate, oftentimes with a favorite horse, or cremated if the ground was frozen. For three months, the household would eat a meager meal only at dawn and dusk. Obviously, it would take more to subdue Ilanos than the death of the Lord Protector.

The only concession to modesty was the exchange of bright colored clothing for shades of brown. Even King Conall's tunic was the color of freshly tilled earth with gold threading. The prince had a goblet in front of him, but I'd only seen him take a few sips. The king patted him on the shoulder, but the gesture held little affection.

After dessert, the king rose and soberly walked out of the hall with the queen on his arm. I followed the prince and princess and glanced back to see the rest of the nobles lining up behind us. Risteard walked beside me, but we didn't risk speaking.

Dusk had yet to settle, but the courtyard was already lit by torches. Rain drizzled, but the air was warm and sweat broke out on my brow. To my horror, Jervell Kade's silk-wrapped body was on display in the middle of the courtyard. One by one, nobles approached the corpse and left offerings. The king placed a hand on his head and wished him safe journey beyond the veil. I peered at the queen and wrinkled my nose. I wondered if she would use Kade's ghost as a source of her 'visions.'

The princess stepped forward and stumbled. I caught her, and she clung to me, not letting go when she approached the body. I tried to break free, but she gripped my arm. One look at her red cheeks and sallow eyes and I knew she would fall over if I didn't stay.

"Jervell," she croaked. "Why did you leave me?" She pressed a handkerchief to her mouth. "I promise I won't forget our plan." She swallowed and set her jaw. She reached for the wrappings covering his face and worked them free. I clamped a hand over my mouth when his mutilated face was revealed. It was wiped clean, but slashes cut across his face and animals had eaten the softer parts.

"He'll pay for what he's done." She placed a kiss on a patch of unmarred skin, and I had to swallow bile.

I escorted her back to the crowd without looking back at Jervell Kade's horrifying face.

For two days, Kade's body remained in the courtyard. And for two days, the castle feasted in his memory. I remained close to the princess in case she revealed details of their plan, but even in mourning, she was vague. Her devotion to the twisted old man was clear, but I still couldn't explain why.

At dusk, the mourners gathered once more and listened to King Conall give one last elegy to Jervell Kade. He described the deceased as a worldly man, devoted to his country, loyal to the crown, and a faithful servant of Ilano. I didn't know whether to laugh or gag.

After this stirring speech, the body was placed in a litter and paraded down the mountain. The princess used me for support, and I wondered if her attitude toward me would change after relying on me so much. Native Praeds waited at the foot of the mountain. I knew by their wary glances they showed respect because the king commanded it. They followed us to the cemetery, but a grave had not been dug. An elaborate pyre was illuminated by a ring of torches, and Kade's body was carefully placed upon it.

The prince extended a hand toward the princess, and she reached for it unsteadily. He led her to the pyre, and they lowered their heads. The queen asked for everyone to clear their thoughts and help Kade find his way through the veil. I looked around and saw all the Ilanis closing their eyes. I looked back at the Praedans, and their heads were bowed. My mouth curved when I saw one lady bite her lip to stifle a smile.

I sensed someone stand next to me, and I shifted toward Risteard's familiar presence.

He whispered in my ear, "My study tonight?" I looked around to make sure no one noticed. But everyone's eyes were still closed.

Our eyes met briefly, and I nodded. He turned his attention to the ceremony, but he stayed by my side. The royal family were handed torches, and as one they stuck them into the pyre. Flames licked the edges of Kade's body, and in moments he was completely engulfed. I watched him burn to ashes, my relief falling away like embers. An enemy was gone, and I had killed him. I proved I was strong enough to fight for Praed, whatever the cost.

Princess Caelyn was snoring before I left her room. I'd never seen her so exhausted, even after twenty days of Prince Brannon's birthday celebrations.

I lounged before the hearth in Risteard's study while he sat beside me sipping brandy and stretching the aches in his neck. He offered me a glass, but I declined, choosing the fire to warm me instead.

"That was my first Ilano funeral. It was more festive than I was expecting," I said.

"We like to think of it more as a celebration of life rather than focusing on death," he said.

"What'll happen with his ashes?"

"They'll be sent to Ilano and interred in the capital." He shifted and cleared his throat.

I narrowed my eyes. "What?"

"Caelyn requested an urn pendant so she could carry some of his ashes with her."

"Ew."

"The king felt the same way, but the queen overruled him."

I wiggled my fingers and spoke in a high tone. "Probably because she hoped he would commune with her from beyond the veil."

He chuckled, but I noticed he didn't contradict me.

"I was relieved but also surprised the king didn't suspect murder."

"He did. He raged at the council, convinced there's a conspiracy and he's next. He accused council members of concealing information and ordered a guard detail to accompany him everywhere. He was angrier than I've ever seen him, even in battle. No one could reason with him."

"Then why has there been no investigation?"

He ran a hand through his hair. "I may have pledged on my honor there was no evidence of murder, and if there was, I would have arrested the murderer myself."

"You...lied?"

"I used his trust in me to calm him. He believed me and settled down. Then it was easy to convince him no one would be foolish enough to murder the Lord Protector knowing he was under the protection of such a venerable king."

"Clever." I felt overwarm and scooted away from the fire. Risteard had lied for me, in council, to the king. If anyone found out, our alliance would unravel. I didn't want to think about how he would be punished. I tucked my knees to my chest and wrapped my arms around them.

"Thank you for covering for me."

He looked at me incredulously. "What else would I have done?"

I hid a smile behind my knees.

"The princess seemed dependent on Jervell Kade's council," I said. "Do you think her plans will fall apart without him?"

"What do you think?"

I shook my head. "She's very determined. She promised his dead body she'll go on. Something really awful must have happened for her to plot against her own father."

He stared into the flames. A minute passed. Two. Unease rippled over me when the silence dragged on.

"Risteard?"

"I don't know anything for certain, but several years ago, Caelyn was sent away. The family didn't say why. Admittedly, I didn't care. I had my own problems to occupy me."

I nodded knowingly. "Puberty?"

He turned slowly, deliberately, and glared darkly.

"It's all right." I patted him on the arm. "We've all been there. Continue."

"She was gone for months. Before she left, she was reserved but happy. Kind even. When she came back, she transformed into this bitter, angry young woman. She alienated all but a few loyal friends. She fought with her father constantly."

"Did you ask her what happened?"

"Once. My mother didn't care for Conall. After my father died, we stayed away from him, so we were never close. But after Caelyn returned from her...trip, Brannon asked me to talk to her."

"He must have been desperate if he asked *you*."

"Terrified. He told me he caught her trying to poison herself."

My hand flew to my chest. What happened to her?

"What did she say?"

"Not much. Like I said, we've never been close. She considered my asking an intrusion. But after she threw a bottle and screamed to leave her alone, she did say one intriguing thing. She called me lucky."

"Lucky?"

"She said I was lucky my family didn't hate me. She wouldn't elaborate."

"They seem on fairly good terms now. At least, she's forgiven the queen and doesn't have qualms plotting with her brother."

"All against the king."

I sighed. "I don't have any solid proof yet. They're careful. And I can't exactly blab to the king."

"And now Kade is dead, she's lost a contact whose letters we can intercept."

I leaned back with a huff. "We're back to waiting for the prince to propose."

We watched the flames in comfortable silence until my eyelids started drooping. I stretched, yawned, and bid Risteard goodnight.

"My mother was dying."

My hand slipped off the doorknob at Risteard's words. He hadn't moved, but his hands gripped the armrests. I returned to my chair and resisted the urge to cover his hand with mine.

"Care to elaborate?" I asked gently.

"That's why I didn't care when Caelyn left. My mother had been ill for a long time. Physicians kept her alive with herbal treatments, but by then only opium gave her relief."

"I'm sorry." I recalled how I'd teased him, and my cheeks reddened. "I'm so sorry. I shouldn't have opened my big mouth."

"If you didn't have your humor, you wouldn't have anything." He half-smiled, but it didn't reach his eyes.

"I can't imagine what it must have been like for you. You've been on your own a long time."

He met my sympathetic gaze but didn't reply.

"Do you prefer it that way?" My heart clenched and my stomach knotted waiting for his reply. He said he was my friend, but what about when this was over? I tugged a strand of hair and bit the inside of my lip.

"I did."

I waited for him to continue and silently cursed his taciturn nature when he said no more.

When he remained silent, I told him not to stay up too late and headed to my room. I pressed my face into the pillow and screamed in frustration. I was such a clumsy-lipped dunce sometimes. No wonder Risteard considered me a child.

CHAPTER 38

Summer gave way to the rainy season, and after the tumultuous events of the last few months, I was anticipating the next to pass quietly. But like so many other aspects of my life, I was soon to find myself sorely mistaken.

Miss Derville continued in Praed to further her relationship with the prince, which had thus far not borne fruit no matter how much encouragement he received. In frustration, the princess decided to call for reinforcements and fired off letters to friends who might offer support. I found myself becoming just as anxious because the marriage of Prince Brannon meant the possibility of a well-timed uprising. If I knew what form the princess' help came in, I'd have been satisfied to wait.

Miss Derville sat with perfect posture on the settee watching me plait and style Princess Caelyn's hair one morning. A comfortable silence permeated the air accompanied by the swish of a brush through the princess' thick, dark hair and the occasional contented sigh from her friend. Outside, rain fell in slow, evenly timed drops as if asking permission to moisten the dry earth.

"Oh, I almost forgot to tell you," the princess said, breaking the glorious stillness. "Eveene will be joining us soon with her new husband."

"Husband?" Miss Derville asked in confusion. "But they were betrothed only a few months ago."

"Apparently she pressed for a quick engagement," Princess Caelyn smirked. "Can't blame her for it, I suppose. There's no sense in dragging out such things unless you mean to change your mind."

"She must truly love her husband, I think, to have wanted to marry him so quickly."

"You think that, Mwiryn, if it comforts you."

"Stranger things have happened than a woman marrying for love," Miss Derville said quietly.

I felt a twinge of regret that I hoped for her to marry the despicable Prince Brannon. It seemed all women somehow were doomed to be a pawn in someone else's game.

"Marriage for love is a fairy tale, Mwiryn," the princess said matter-of-factly. "You must look at marriage as a means of establishing yourself socially, for comfort and wealth, for producing children if you must. If you cannot meet your need for love from your husband, you can find it elsewhere."

"Caelyn!" Miss Derville's mouth gaped in shock. "What a scandalous thing to say."

"My dear friend, you mustn't live in a fantasy. This is the way things are. As women, we cannot stand by and allow men to dictate how our lives are lived."

"And I appreciate your strength and empowerment, but I don't think as you do." Miss Derville shifted uncomfortably, which the beautiful young woman managed gracefully. She wore a simple three-quarter sleeve light pink gown as elegantly as a ballgown. Her golden hair was intricately braided, not a strand out of place. The only flaw in her ivory skin was the slight blush of embarrassment. The princess took a seat beside her and wrapped a comforting arm around her shoulders.

"I know you do not, you sweet girl."

"I wish to be faithful to my husband no matter what sort of man he may be."

I had to admire her tenacity, but the princess had a strong will I feared would overwhelm such a fragile resolve.

"A noble endeavor, and I wish for you to uphold those standards and live contentedly. My only concern is for your happiness."

I nearly choked. The last thing the princess concerned herself with was other people's feelings.

"How can it make me happy to deceive my husband?"

"Mwiryn, I thought we had an understanding." The princess' tone was cold. She pulled away from Miss Derville.

My brow furrowed at this exchange, and I speculated there was yet another hidden agenda between the princess and her seemingly innocent friend. I expected it of the princess, but what sort of scheme would Miss Derville agree to?

"I'm sorry, Caelyn. I'm not regretting my decisions, I swear. I guess I simply never thought about the repercussions."

"Are you worried about my brother's feelings? Because I promise you once you're married and he grows tired of you, he will not hesitate to find excitement elsewhere. Once the newness of a situation wears off, he's bored."

I was shocked at the princess' candid comments about Prince Brannon made to the woman she wanted him to marry, the woman she brought here expressly to entice him. The woman she plied with lies and exaggerations to convince the prince cared for her. Her long standing friend. What possible motive could Princess Caelyn have?

"Please don't, Caelyn," Miss Derville pleaded. She dabbed a tear away with a dainty white handkerchief. "This isn't easy. When I came here, I was so sure, and now that nothing has come of it, I'm starting to wonder if I've made a mistake."

"A mistake?" Princess Caelyn said quietly.

"Not everything." Miss Derville covered the princess' hand with her own. "I'm being silly, I know." She shook her head. "I'm finished. I promise I will be stronger in the future."

"I didn't mean to paint such a bleak picture of your future," the princess said. "You know how blunt I can be."

Miss Derville smiled. "Yes, though you might not be very tactful, I do appreciate your honesty. I'm not a fool. I know Prince Brannon isn't the most honorable of men."

That's an understatement.

"But perhaps, with the right woman, he may change."

"I harbor no such hope, but if anyone can make Brannon a good man, you can."

The princess seemed sincere. She obviously cared about her friend, but she still insisted on condemning her to a lifetime of servitude.

"It's going to be an awfully dreary day," the princess said. "So, the queen promised a special sitting. I'm hoping she'll see good things in your future."

"*Our* future." Miss Derville's eyes sparkled.

I held back a sigh of exasperation over the new treachery to be rooted out.

I cleaned the mews in the rain, and my frock clung to my body and rivulets of water trickled down my back when I stood in the queen's private rooms for a special reading limited to the princess and Miss Derville. The princess was in such a hurry to attend the session I wasn't permitted to change, so I was condemned to stand shivering and dripping behind the princess while the queen burned herbs to reach behind the veil and predict an uncertain future. The queen's senior lady-in-waiting, the Mistress of Neve, and my mother were also in attendance, though I gave up trying to engage Mother in any conversation. She clearly felt the same way based on her lofty attitude.

The princess and Miss Derville perched on the edge of their seats, their eyes wide. The queen lowered her head to inhale smoke from pungent herbs. Then she raised her eyes slowly and told the princess to ask her questions.

"Will Prince Brannon announce his engagement before the winter?"

"The prince is torn," the queen said. "Between duty and desire."

"Typical," the princess muttered.

"A young woman has a claim upon him," the queen announced.

"What sort of claim?" the princess demanded as Miss Derville paled.

"It is unclear," the queen said. She shook her head to focus her thoughts. "But the prince will certainly marry. And then…"

"Then *what?*" the princess asked urgently.

"The marriage will not last. A death will sever the tie."

"How awful!" Miss Derville gasped, her hand flying to her mouth.

"But who shall he marry?" the princess repeated.

"You should ask *him,*" the queen said, her voice edged with exhaustion.

"Mother," the princess said, and I could sense desperation in her voice. "Please, can you see anything about our plans? Are they in danger from my brother?"

Miss Derville asked timidly, "Do you see anything about me, Your Majesty?"

The queen turned her hazy gray eyes on Miss Derville's hopeful face.

I shivered and waited for the pronouncement.

The queen spoke with motherly compassion. "My dear, I see disappointment, but not forever. You have a great capacity for love, Miss Derville. Just be sure you don't place your faith in the wrong hands." The queen bowed her head, signaling the end of the session.

Before following the ladies out, I glanced back at Mother. She stared blankly ahead, and I didn't bother trying to get her attention. I had nothing to say.

The princess was fuming at the suggestion that Prince Brannon had his attentions engaged elsewhere. The moment we left the queen's rooms, she whisked Miss Derville to her room and began writing a note. I knew I would not be changing into a dry frock any time soon.

"Insufferable!" Princess Caelyn scratched quill to paper.

"What does it mean?" Miss Derville asked.

"It means my brother has forgotten his duty." She folded the note and placed it in my hand. "Take this to the prince. They'll be in council right now. I don't care if the king complains, you will deliver it into the prince's hands immediately."

I turned to leave, but the princess caught my arm and made me face her.

Her eyes narrowed, studying me, then she asked, "Has the prince made any further advances toward you?"

I shook my head emphatically.

"Good. Now go!"

I rushed down the corridors, water dripping off my hair and hem leaving a trail to the doors of the council chambers. They loomed dark and heavy, and I rubbed my arms to regain some warmth. An interruption of the king's council must be a matter of great import to warrant the intrusion, and I knew the princess' distress would not be viewed so by the king. I stood a moment weighing the situation, trying to decide whom I'd rather anger more: King Conall or Princess Caelyn.

I pounded a fist on the door and entered before I could lose my nerve. The king paused mid-speech and his entire council looked at me in confusion. I curtseyed low, and the king's irritation was evident when he slammed a fistful of papers on the table.

"What is the meaning of this?" the king roared.

I raised a trembling hand and presented the letter, then pointed it at Prince Brannon. The king, red-faced, stormed across the room. He grabbed me by the scruff and pulled me toward the prince.

"Deliver your note, then," the king said.

I thrust it in the prince's hand as if it contained a contagious disease. While the prince read, the king twisted my dress until the fabric dug into my skin. I winced and turned toward the councilmen. Most looked annoyed, others uneasy. My eyes fell on Risteard. He was eerily still, but I could sense he was primed to reach for his sword. While I appreciated his protectiveness, it wouldn't help our cause if he defended me against the king in front of the council. I gave him a warning glare, and I swear he pouted.

"What vital information warranted this interruption, Brannon?" the king demanded.

The prince's face flushed red, then he refolded the note and slipped it into his jerkin.

"It's from Caelyn," Prince Brannon said. "She urgently requires a meeting with me."

Muffled laughter rippled through the room, and even the king seemed amused, though he was clearly in no mood to indulge his daughter.

"She can wait," a noble said.

"Can she?" another jested.

"Now, now, gentlemen," the king said. "The princess engages in important matters of state as well. Let's not belittle her contributions to our prosperity."

The laughter could no longer be contained, and the room erupted into a raucous cacophony. Though I felt the princess' behavior just as ridiculous, I was loath to side with a room full of men laughing at a woman's expense. Risteard apparently felt the same. He rose from his chair deliberately, meeting the eyes of every man until the laughter faded, and the room became silent.

"Whether we agree with her or not, the princess believed the matter was important enough to call the prince away during a council meeting. Who are we to pass judgement on something we do not understand?" Risteard said, and to their credit the nobles looked abashed.

"Find out what she wants, Brannon," the king said tiredly. He released me and pushed me toward the door. "Return as soon as you can."

The prince looked every bit as guilty as the rest. He rose and preceded me to the door but paused at the threshold. He stood awkwardly aside and gestured for me to go first. I eyed him suspiciously but complied. We walked in silence to the princess' chambers, my eyes fixed ahead in a hard stare while he darted a glance at me every few seconds. As I reached to open the princess' door, the prince tugged at my sleeve. I wrenched my arm away, my hand itching for the knife at my hip. The prince raised his hands, and he pleaded for me to listen. I cocked my head to the side and allowed the words to sink in. He shook his head, called himself a fool under his breath, and rubbed his temples.

"Of course, I don't mean 'listen.' I only ask you to give me a chance to speak."

The harsh glare did not leave my eyes, but I eased my hand away from my hip.

He relaxed and lowered his own hands. "I only wanted to say… what happened… Kade had me very confused. He would not stop talking about you, saying how much a prize a young virgin's body would be. I admit I lost control, and I'm not pleased with my behavior."

I waited for an apology, but not surprisingly none was forthcoming.

"I don't suppose the princess knows?" he asked.

I nodded. "Well," he continued, "I'll agree to say nothing at present about your secret weapon under your skirts if whatever question I ask of you in front of the princess, you indicate *yes*. Deal?"

The implication of siding with the prince was frightening, but the prospect of a hangman's noose was worse. Once again, I chose life. Reluctantly, I nodded.

"Good girl," he said with relief.

We entered the room together and were immediately approached by an angry princess. Miss Derville sat quietly chewing her bottom lip. I stood by to play whatever part the prince required.

"Answer me truthfully," the princess demanded. "Who is she?"

"You'll have to be more specific, Caelyn," the prince replied nonchalantly. He bowed slightly to Miss Derville and added, "Perhaps if we speak privately you can elaborate."

"It's too late for that," the princess asserted. "Everything is in the open now. Mother told us about your indiscretion."

The prince's gaze shifted to me briefly before returning innocently to the princess.

"Which indiscretion would that be, dear sister?"

"Don't play coy, Brannon," the princess waved off his evasion. "Tell me who the woman is that you're using to play Miss Derville the fool."

"Don't be so dramatic." The prince sat at the end of the princess' bed as far from Miss Derville as possible.

"Brannon," the princess began, her voice gentler. "Have you formed an attachment to someone?"

He didn't answer, and he wouldn't look the princess in the eye.

"Do you… care for her?"

Still no answer, but he finally met her steady and seemingly sympathetic stare.

"Please tell me. Perhaps we may salvage this situation."

"All you ever think about is yourself, Caelyn. Every move we've made has been dictated by you because of some vague vision of Mother's. Have you ever stopped to wonder what I want?"

"I know what you want. Ultimately, it's what we both want. All we have to do is follow a few simple steps."

"*Your* steps!" Prince Brannon shouted. "Can't I have a say in any of this? It's *my* marriage!"

The princess paled. "Who is she?"

"She's a high-born lady," he said firmly. "From a good family. Young, beautiful, and a sweet-tempered creature."

"You've described Mwiryn perfectly." The princess gestured toward her friend.

"I've enjoyed every moment with you, Miss Derville," the prince said. "But I've found myself tied to another."

"What do you mean: tied?"

"I've made… promises," he said, eyes falling to the floor.

The princess narrowed her eyes. "What promises? Have you entered into an engagement?"

"Not officially."

She shook her head in exasperation. "Brannon…"

"There's a custom in Praed." Here Prince Brannon looked at me. "Where a man gives a woman a ring as a promise of commitment."

The princess' eyes turned to me, and I nodded my assent that this was true. "It doesn't mean you're engaged, but an engagement often follows." I nodded again.

"Can the promise be broken?" Princess Caelyn directed this at me.

I made a face indicating it could but would be regarded very poorly.

Confused, the princess asked him, "Why would you make such a promise?"

He looked away sheepishly. "It was an exchange."

"And what did you get in return?" the princess asked.

The prince didn't answer, which was all the princess required to confirm her suspicions.

"If for once you thought with the head above your neck and not the one below your belt you wouldn't find yourself in so much trouble!" She seethed, her tone rising as she spoke. She threw her arms above her head and pulled her hair in frustration. She glanced at her friend, whose eyes brimmed with tears.

"Wait," the princess said. She turned back to Prince Brannon. "Why would you use a Praed tradition on an Ilano woman?"

"I never said she was from Ilano," the prince said.

The princess screamed and threw a bottle of perfume at him. He ducked, and it shattered against the wall over the headboard.

"Father himself said we should intermarry with Praed women," he argued.

"That was for *lesser* nobles. Not for us. We are better than that."

"If I'm pledged to a Praed woman, will that not gain the respect of the locals and encourage them to follow us?"

"Who cares about the locals! We aren't here for them! You're ruining everything!" The princess stormed past the prince into the hall. I followed, the prince close behind. Miss Derville sat frozen at her place on the settee, perhaps in shock at what she just witnessed. Without knocking, the princess pushed open the doors of the council chambers, and for the second time that afternoon the king's meeting was interrupted.

"Caelyn!" King Conall's voice thundered. "What is the meaning of this nonsense?"

"We need to speak privately," the princess replied, crossing her arms and staring pointedly at him.

"Later," the king responded. "I'm in the middle of a council meeting as you can see."

"This is more important than how many inches of rain to expect this season," she sneered. "This is a family matter that cannot wait."

The king sighed, and I swear several strands of his hair became gray in that moment. "Gentleman," he said apologetically. "If you will indulge my daughter for a few brief minutes, I would greatly appreciate it."

As one, the men rose and filed out of the room, casting sympathetic looks toward the king and the unruly Princess Caelyn. I paid close attention to secret signals as they passed her. Crane flipped his head in her direction but didn't so much as wink. One other man's gaze lingered on her. He was tall and slender with long curly brown hair and pale green eyes. She didn't speak to him but nodded subtly.

"Remain here, if you please, Risteard." The king sat heavily in his chair.

"Why does he have to be here?" the princess demanded.

"You said it was a family matter," the king responded flatly.

The princess rolled her eyes but didn't argue.

"Do you wish for me to disturb your mother and have her summoned for this nonsense?" the king asked.

"I'll acquaint her with the details later," she said. She proceeded to launch into an angry diatribe on the prince's ruination of all her well-laid plans.

"Would you please explain to him the importance of maintaining a respectable lineage through a proper marriage?" She stabbed a finger in the prince's direction.

"What do you mean?" the king asked.

"Tell him," the princess ordered her brother.

"Caelyn's upset because I don't want to marry the woman she chose for me." His arms crossed his chest in consternation.

Risteard glanced at me, and I raised an eyebrow. Just wait for the big reveal.

"You led her to believe a proposal was imminent!" the princess yelled. "You've acted very dishonorably toward Miss Derville."

"Is this true, Brannon?" The king's face flushed with anger.

The prince's confidence wavered. He cast his eyes downward before answering, "Perhaps to some degree, but if she believed I was sure to propose, then it's Caelyn's fault for raising her hopes."

"Miss Derville is a fine choice for you, Brannon," the king said. "She comes from a distinguished line of Ilano nobles, her father is well regarded and holds great tracts of land, and her dowry is substantial. Furthermore, she is beautiful, graceful, and meek. What possible objection could you have to entering into an engagement to such a woman?"

"Yes, Brannon," the princess sneered. "Tell him what possible impediment there could be."

"I---," the prince hesitated, choking on the words. He swallowed, looked at me out of the corner of his eye, then continued. "I have made a commitment to another lady."

"Who?" The king's eyes sharpened, and his voice dropped low.

"Well, she's from a prosperous family," the prince said in a rush. "Very wealthy and well regarded. There could be a great political advantage aligning myself with her."

"What family does she come from?"

"It would be better to ask 'where' she comes from," the princess interjected.

"Enough of this evasion," the king insisted. "Caelyn, if you have something to say, say it and be done."

"Brannon has pledged himself to a Praed woman," she said smugly. She crossed her arms and waited for the explosion of anger that was sure to follow. She was not disappointed.

"You've done *what?*" the king roared. He pounded his fists on the table and kicked his chair to the floor as he stood. "Explain yourself, Brannon!"

"She will secure the support of the people," Prince Brannon said. "You yourself worried about the possibility of rebellion. If we accept a Praed bride for a princess, wouldn't that send the message we truly embrace Praed as a part of our kingdom?"

"Giving the people handouts and marrying them to lower nobles is one thing. Crowning some nobody as a princess is quite another. I thought even you would have been smart enough to know the difference."

"She's not a nobody to Praed," the prince said.

"No doubt her father put her up to entrapping you, Brannon. You should be more careful."

"She has no father. He's dead."

"How did she do it, Brannon? Did she make promises?" King Conall shook his head. "You can have a woman without coercion. She must have had something truly impressive to offer if you made such a foolish mistake to procure it. No doubt, you were not her first. She must be a very learned and experienced woman."

"She is neither," the prince said, anger rising in his voice. "She *was* a virgin. The only persuasion was on my part, and my motives were not merely to have the first claim on her."

"Do you have affection for this woman?" the king asked.

"I have… feelings… for her."

"Father," Princess Caelyn interjected, her lower lip quivering. "If he's permitted to marry this woman, it will be the disgrace of Ilano. Furthermore, we'll lose the support of the Dervilles. And they will tell all their friends about how cruelly their daughter was used. Would you allow loyal Ilanos to be insulted and alienated to indulge Brannon's whims?"

"And what of the Praed families that will be insulted if I withdraw my promise from the lady?" Prince Brannon asked.

"Who cares?" Princess Caelyn yelled. "We need to focus on pleasing our own people. These Praedans are not our equals, Brannon. They are meant to follow and obey. We do what we please."

The king raised a hand to stop the princess' rant.

"Who is she?" the king asked in a chilling tone.

The prince seemed to understand the dark implication and hesitated.

The king's unrelenting stare was more persuasive than angry words.

"Noraa," the prince finally said. "Of Thistledon."

The blood drained from my face and my knees quaked. I felt Risteard staring, and I dared to meet his eyes. I had known Noraa my whole life. She was my age, seventeen, but taller with fair skin and raven black hair. She was always very shy, hardly leaving the house because interactions with people terrified her so acutely. Mother made me sit with Noraa and practice embroidery at the request of her mother in the hopes social interaction would bring her out of her shell. Once the meetings began, however, I believe the lady regretted her decision. Aside from my horrid skills in embroidery, I was much too outspoken for the respectable young lady. Inevitably, I would grow bored sitting indoors with a girl who never responded to my conversation. I often abandoned her to play with her more entertaining older brother, Thomlyn, now Lord Wyrwyk. Clearly, Thom felt the need to plan for all possible outcomes by putting his lot in with me and attaching his sister to the royal family. I couldn't believe for a second this was Noraa's idea. The timid girl could barely utter a 'thank you' much less orchestrate a marriage.

"You will make your apologies to the young lady and her family," King Conall said calmly. "We will make restitution for besmirching her reputation and arrange an eligible marriage to a respectable Ilano noble whom we can pay handsomely for his assistance. You will then cease all contact with the lady and become engaged to Miss Derville."

The prince stared defiantly at King Conall, and for a moment, I was sure he was going to refuse. For that, I felt an ounce of respect for the prince. I loathed him a miniscule amount less for standing by Noraa and preparing to marry her.

"If I break my promise, it will reflect very badly on all of us." The resignation in his voice convinced me he was not as upset about this as he appeared.

"It's not *her* family you should be concerning yourself with," Princess Caelyn said.

"Do you have a true affection for the lady," Risteard asked suddenly, "Or are you reluctant to part with her because you've made an agreement that serves your own purpose?" All eyes turned to the black knight, then back to the prince.

"Answer him!" the king demanded.

The prince scowled at Risteard and said, "Risteard thinks very poorly of me no doubt and suspects treachery at every turn, even from his own family. But he's incorrect in assuming this has anything to do with me and everything to do with furthering our influence in Praed."

"Stop it!" Princess Caelyn screamed. "No one believes you! For once in your life just shut up and do what you're told before you ruin everything."

"Brannon," the king said with a low, eerie calm. "You will end your association with this woman. If you insist on continuing to defy me, you will find yourself without a crown."

It was a threat no one in the room doubted. The prince clenched his jaw to restrain his anger, and I wondered if he would choose Noraa over a crown. It would be a true declaration of love if he had, but Prince Brannon was nothing if not selfishly driven. He nodded shortly, and the king sighed in relief.

"A good king puts the needs of his people first, Brannon. You've made the right decision," the king said as he placed a hand on the prince's shoulder.

The princess turned on her heel and dashed out of the room without another word, the door flinging against the wall. I left behind her, Risteard's heavy footfalls following.

I rounded the corner and ducked into the shadows. Risteard glanced around to see we were alone before speaking in a low voice.

"Who is she?" he asked. I explained who Noraa Wyrwyk was, at least when I had known her, including her connection to the young man he had watched me dance with at the winter celebration.

"Noraa was always a very obedient girl," I told him. "And dedicated to her family. She would not have come up with this plan on her own."

"You think your friend was instrumental in this plot?"

"I would not have guessed it of Thom, but he has a lordship to defend now."

"You believe he has no faith in you?"

"I think his actions are less personal and more strategic. If he aligns with me and then engages his sister to the prince, he wins no matter what happens."

Risteard was silent while he thought, and I could tell he was chewing on the inside of his lip.

Impatience got the better of me. "What?"

"If Brannon cared nothing for this girl, he would have taken what he wanted and abandoned her without a second thought. The king would have known nothing about it, nor would he have threatened to disinherit him."

"The prince doesn't have feelings," I insisted.

"Not historically," Risteard agreed. "But a man doesn't always know what he's capable of until faced with an unfamiliar situation."

"So, you think he became enchanted by a woman who is not even close to the type he's found attractive in the past and fell in love with her?" I shook my head violently.

"You may be personally averse to love," he said irritably. "But not everyone shares your distaste. Even spoiled scoundrels like Brannon have the capacity to be stirred by love if given the chance."

"I have nothing against love," I grumbled, looking down the corridor. "I'm just skeptical that any man is capable of the sentiment." I turned back and shrank at Risteard's narrowed eyes and curled lip.

I shrugged one shoulder, trying to shake off my unease. "What?"

He opened his mouth, then shut it abruptly. Unable to maintain eye contact, I checked the halls again, and when they were empty, I hurried back to the princess' room.

One thing I had to admit about life in the castle, every day brought fresh surprises. From hidden plots to secret agendas, there was always something to keep me on my toes. Today was no exception, but I was mistaken if I believed the day's revelations to be over.

Low voices belonging to the princess and Miss Derville were barely audible on the other side of the princess' door. I felt for the poor girl and the humiliation and heartache she went through that morning. Wishing not to disturb the quiet tete-a-tete, I eased the door open without making a sound. The open door revealed a puzzling scene. The princess and her friend stood by the hearth in close confidence, their heads nearly touching. I closed the door silently and watched the princess raise a hand to Miss Derville's face and brush away her tears. I stepped toward them and heard their hushed words.

"I promised we would be together," the princess was saying. "I will not allow my brother to keep us apart with his stupidity."

"He doesn't care for me," Miss Derville lamented through her tears. "How can he marry me if he doesn't want me?"

"He's a fool to treat you this way, but when you are queen, it will make no difference. And you will be queen. I always keep my promises."

To emphasize her statement, Princess Caelyn pressed her mouth fervently to Miss Derville's in a desperate kiss. My jaw dropped, but astonishingly Miss Derville did not pull away. On the contrary, she returned the kiss with equal fervor. I stared transfixed for several moments before sliding backwards toward the door, opening it, and then shutting it firmly behind me. The noise startled them apart, and I nonchalantly strode forward. The princess resumed her seat at the vanity while Miss Derville became engrossed in the dancing flames in the hearth, both pretending with practiced ease that nothing untoward had transpired.

"King Conall will fix everything," Princess Caelyn said casually over her shoulder. "Do not despair. You shall be a bride before the first day of summer. I promise."

CHAPTER 39

In due haste Eveene Cruith arrived with her new husband to expedite the engagement of Miss Derville and Prince Brannon. Though I welcomed the assistance for my own selfish motives, I was not looking forward to the way that help would take shape. I did not like Eveene, and I feared she blamed me for her failed attempt to seduce Risteard. For my own sake as well as Risteard's, I hoped her marriage meant she was beyond any remaining anger.

The guests were received with the fanfare their important positions deserved, for Miss Cruith, now Lady Sharp, was the wife of Lord Martyn Sharp of Ilano. From conversations between the princess and her companions I gathered Lord Sharp came from a line of wealthy landowners and held tracts of orchards. His late wife died several years earlier without providing him an heir. He required a young wife, and Miss Cruith was only happy to oblige in exchange for a title and heavy purse. The couple arrived in an enormous black carriage pulled by four dappled grays and lined with plush blue velvet. I chewed at my bottom lip while I waited for them to alight, picturing Lord Sharp as a tall, dark-haired, striking man based on her obsession with Risteard. What emerged was an older, short man with gray and thinning hair. He was not what I would consider portly, but he clearly spent more time drinking cider than harvesting and manufacturing it. His eyes roamed over us with barely concealed distaste. He extended a gloved hand toward the carriage, and Lady Sharp allowed herself to be assisted to the ground. Her beauty had not faded, but rather had become luminous with jewels at her throat and luxurious satin adorning her shape. She smiled sweetly and reached out toward Princess Caelyn and Miss Derville when they stepped forward to greet her.

"How desolating to only see each other once a year," Lady Sharp said to the princess. "But I'm so happy to be here with his Lordship." She gestured toward her husband who was bowing obsequiously to the king and queen. His stiff posture was either due to extremely proper form or arthritis, and I had to bite the inside of my cheek to keep from giggling.

"We need you now more than ever," Princess Caelyn said. She weaved her arm through Lady Sharp's elbow and led her into the castle.

"Yes, I heard about the difficulties you've been having," Lady Sharp cooed and squeezed Miss Derville's hand. "Not to worry. Between Caelyn and myself, we will secure an engagement before winter."

"How was your journey?" Miss Derville asked.

"A mess," Lady Sharp said in exasperation. "It rained the entire time, and the roads were a disgrace."

The three ladies prattled on about the wretched state of the roads and the inconvenience of travelling during the rainy season while ahead of us the king with the queen on his arm boisterously congratulated Lord Sharp on his recent nuptials and declared a celebratory feast would be held in their honor that evening. Shocking. Really, King Conall would hold a feast for a dog.

Risteard's familiar footfalls came up behind me, and I studied his reaction. He appeared as unaffected as I was.

"I'm so happy for your marriage," Miss Derville told Lady Sharp with great sincerity. "You look positively radiant, Eveene."

"You're the sweetest soul, Mwiryn," Lady Sharp said, sweeping a hand across the jewels at her neck. "Yes, becoming Lady Sharp has contributed greatly to my happiness."

"He's not who I would have expected for you," Princess Caelyn pointed out.

"Why not?" Lady Sharp asked innocently.

"He's old," the princess said bluntly.

"What does age signify?"

"Nothing, I suppose, if there's a great sum of money that goes along with it."

Lady Sharp laughed, a high-pitched titter that grated on my nerves. Miss Derville flushed in embarrassment, and I secretly agreed with the assessment.

"I will admit," Lady Sharp said in a conspiratorial tone. "He's not the most attractive of men, and his lack of youth certainly is a downside, but these are nothing to the attributes he does possess."

"A large house, substantial acreage, and a fortune?" the princess prompted.

"Exactly," Lady Sharp confirmed with a sly smile, eliciting a snicker from the princess and a reluctant grin from Miss Derville.

"I understand his first wife failed to produce an heir. Is he even capable of breeding children at his age?" Princess Caelyn asked.

"Don't remind me of that unpleasant duty," Lady Sharp said with a twist of her features.

"Which part do you find most abhorrent? The man you must produce children with or the children themselves?"

"Hopefully the term 'children' will not enter into the marriage at all. With any luck, he'll produce a boy by me promptly and there will be no need to trouble ourselves further."

"I never thought you of all people would be troubled by the marriage bed."

"What happens in the marriage bed is tedious and only a means to conceive an heir. What happens with a lover, on the other hand, is much more pleasing and exciting."

"Doesn't the same thing happen in both?" Miss Derville asked innocently, a touch of pink on her cheeks.

Lady Sharp laughed into her palm. "Oh, Mwiryn, how naïve you are! No woman enjoys her husband the way she does her lover."

"Especially when her husband is twice her age," the princess said.

"Enough about my marriage," Lady Sharp said, though I was sure the subject would arise several times throughout her visit. "What of Mwiryn? His Highness has not yet proposed?"

"And doesn't appear inclined to," Miss Derville added sadly. "He spoke of affection for another woman."

The princess hastened to assure Lady Sharp the unfortunate affair had been dealt with.

"All connection to this other woman is severed? You're certain?" Lady Sharp asked.

"Definitely," the princess said. "If he values his future, he will speak to that lady no more."

"But what of his feelings for her?" Miss Derville said. "Surely he cannot forget them so easily."

"My brother's feelings are fleeting. Once a few days go by without seeing her, the allure will dissipate, and he will forget he ever preferred her."

"I just have a difficult time reconciling myself as an alternative, as second place."

"Mwiryn, you mustn't see it that way. You should have been his first choice, but some upstart girl thought she would steal herself a throne. Luckily, he has been saved from ruination, and in time he will see you as his savior," Lady Sharp said.

"I only wish I knew how this all happened," Princess Caelyn said. "Where did this girl come from? How did he meet her? I'd like to have a few words with her."

"And I'm certain they would do you no credit," Lady Sharp said. "Put her out of your mind, Caelyn. As you said, she's been dealt with."

The princess did not appear completely convinced, but she let the matter drop and focused on developing a strategy to convince the prince the best course for both his family and the kingdom would be to marry Miss Derville.

"The only chance Brannon has at salvaging his relationship with Father would be to marry Mwiryn," the princess said. "Despite Brannon's promises, Father is still wary, and his distrust could cost Brannon the crown if he's not careful."

"All summer you spent cultivating a relationship with parties and outings. All of that time wasted," Lady Sharp said. "Now we must be direct. A threat would be too dramatic. Prince Brannon must see marrying Mwiryn as his only choice, and he must come to this conclusion himself. The more you lecture him, Caelyn, the more resistant he'll become. No man wants the woman his sister insists he marry, no matter how lovely she may be."

"What do you suggest?" Princess Caelyn asked.

"Men are heavily influenced by each other. I will inform my husband what must be done, and he will work on the prince. As one of his peers, he may be more successful manipulating the prince than we women."

"And if Lord Sharp states such opinions," the princess said, "Brannon's cronies will be sure to agree and convince him to heed his Lordship's advice."

"Men are so simple," Lady Sharp said. "And they say women are the weaker sex. No one is more malleable than a man."

"What should *I* do?" Miss Derville asked.

"Just continue to be yourself," Lady Sharp said. "The prince will come around once he sees how constant you are." Their perfect plan in place, the three ladies turned to the crowd to observe the poor simple men in their natural habitat.

Lady Sharp noticed me lurking in the shadows.

"I see your little ginger pet still follows you around," she said.

"Her? Yes, I still find her moderately useful," Princess Caelyn said.

Lady Sharp floated toward me with all the grace and distinction of her new title, and her eyes flitted over my still form.

"My, my," she said. She placed a finger under my chin and raised my face to hers, presumably so I could read her lips. Our height discrepancy diminished in the last year and a half I noted as she inspected me thoroughly. "You've grown into a woman at last. Are you still a maid?" My brows furrowed angrily, and I replied with one decisive nod. She leaned forward, her nose nearly touching mine, and whispered, "How long do I loom over you menacingly until he comes running to rescue you?"

Calmly, I stepped out of her reach, my chin held high. She came toward me again, and once more I moved away without emotion. I raised an eyebrow and crossed my arms, trying to convey I needed no rescuing and was perfectly capable of taking care of myself. Whether she understood or not I wasn't sure, but the absence of fear or uncertainty which she expected to produce proved frustrating for Lady Sharp, and without the satisfaction of eliciting the desired emotions, she left me to return to her friends. I pursed my lips to contain the smile threatening to spread as I watched her retreat and felt a swelling of pride at the victory of this small battle I won against such a dangerous adversary.

My fist trembled in anticipation when I knocked on Risteard's study door. Since catching the princess and Miss Derville in a scandalous position, I had been bursting to tell him and to discuss the implications of such a discovery. I pictured his reaction many times, the mixture of surprise and horror that was sure to be elicited from such news. I bounced on the balls of my feet, impatiently waiting for his reply, and I nearly pushed him over when he opened the door.

"You will not believe what I have to tell you," I began without preamble. Calmly, Risteard closed the door and moved around his desk to take a seat, indicating for me to do the same.

"Go on," he said.

"I would not have believed it myself had I not seen it with my own eyes."

"What's that?"

"Princess Caelyn kissing Miss Derville!" I sat back, my mouth agape, anxiously awaiting his response.

"Explain," he said.

My eyes narrowed. He wasn't cooperating as I imagined for this exchange.

"After the princess found out about Prince Brannon's lady and fought with him over it with the king, remember? She retreated to her room in such an agitated state I was sure she'd reveal her reason for hurrying the marriage. I crept into the room unobserved. She was talking to Miss Derville very intimately. She promised they would be together and she would make sure Miss Derville would be queen. And then, much to my shock, she kissed Miss Derville. Not like a friend on the hand or cheek, but full on the mouth. And not a quick kiss, but a long one, like lovers."

"And you've seen enough kisses between lovers to know the difference?"

"You don't seem excited about this news." I crossed my arms and waited for an explanation.

Risteard sighed and leaned back in his chair.

"Caelyn's preference for her own sex is a closely guarded family secret. It's never been substantiated."

"Meaning?"

"Her family has always suspected she liked women over men, but she's never admitted it, nor will anyone ask her directly."

"Why does everyone suspect?"

"Certain aspects of her behavior. She's never run after boys nor showed any interest in them as her peers have. Her father caught her holding hands with a girl once. She's always preferred the company of her own sex to the flirtatious games her friends played."

"She does seem to find that sort of behavior repulsive," I said. "She can't seem to stomach it when the ladies talk of men."

"What you observed is merely a confirmation of everyone's suspicions."

"What would happen to her if they all knew?"

"Miss Derville would be sent away to keep her from temptation, I'm certain. If their relationship became public knowledge, Miss Derville would be blamed as the instigator and punished to save face."

"How awful," I said.

"A hasty marriage would follow for the princess to erase any memory of the incident."

"And if she refused?"

"Caelyn is no fool. Regardless of her true nature, she will do her duty to the crown."

"As we all must do it seems. Duty must always be obeyed over desire."

"You feel sorry for her?"

"I've never liked the princess. That's no secret. In the simplest terms, she's selfish and cruel. She never does anything without an ulterior motive, and she plays with people as if they were puppets. But I still sympathize with her situation as one human being to another. She forces others to play a part, and yet she's also an actor in her own life."

"Not unlike yourself."

"True. No one should be forced to be something they're not."

"And you are no servant."

"No. I'm only playing at one until I find out who I really am."

"You don't know?"

"I used to know. I was Laria Audrey of Riverstone. But now, the time I had at Riverstone is gone, and I'm stuck wandering through life here until I find my place again."

"This time it will be one of your own making."

I regarded Risteard silently from across the vastness of the cluttered desk. I didn't feel much in control of my own fate, but I was more so now than I had been in the past. First my parents, then a tyrant king, and finally… Well, I wasn't sure what would come next. What would I do after King Conall was off the throne? I always imagined I would simply go home to Riverstone, but then what? Could I live quietly again after what I'd seen and done here?

"What will happen to you once King Conall is overthrown?" I asked before I could reconsider.

"It depends on whether I'm implicated I suppose. The new king might have me either arrested or pardoned."

"Who would that be, do you think?"

"My hope is the people will determine that."

"Would you go back to Ilano?" The thought made me unexpectedly sad. Risteard was a true friend, and the thought of saying goodbye was distressing.

"That depends," he said.

"On what?"

"On whether or not I have a reason to stay."

"I think Aquila would be sad to leave," I said, hoping to lighten the mood. "She does love the mountain."

"She does," he agreed, smiling.

"What do you think of the new Lady Sharp and her husband?" I rose to browse the cramped shelves, feeling the need to change the subject before delving further into an emotional topic.

"Lord Sharp is generally well respected, and I think his demeanor suits his bride."

"Really? I never would have guessed the match. He's rich, to be sure, but he's so old and unattractive."

"I never took you to be so superficial," he grinned.

"*I'm* not! *She* is!"

"Lord Sharp is a good choice for a woman like her. He's wealthy, as you said, and often busy. Which means he'll dote on her and be home very rarely."

"Leaving her to live as she pleases."

"Exactly. A woman like her plans for everything."

"And doesn't allow something as trivial as a marriage to get in the way of her pleasure."

"You speak as if you know something of it."

"She was talking to the ladies, and I overheard. She doesn't intend to remain faithful to Lord Sharp."

"I would say I'm not surprised, but that would be ungentlemanly. I would also add that his Lordship will repay the courtesy, but again…"

I shook a finger at him in mock disapproval. "That would be most ungracious of you."

"They may not seem an obvious couple, but their manners suit one another."

My smile vanished. "Risteard." I came around the desk to stand before him. "Be careful there. I believe she still harbors some resentment toward you."

He nodded. "Lady Sharp does not forgive easily. You should be on your guard as well."

CHAPTER 40

The rains were fully upon us, and the downpours defining our days confined us indoors. Despite the lack of activities, life was anything but boring. Lady Sharp made it her personal mission to unite Miss Derville with Prince Brannon and drew Lord Sharp into her intrigues. I saw him with the prince often, acting like a concerned elder brother with a reassuring pat on the shoulder and attentive ear. He reported his progress to his wife, which she then passed onto the ladies. It was tedious, it was arduous, and I was sick of it. This business of whispering behind doors and careful maneuvering was wearing me thin, and my patience was exhausted. The prince would never convince himself that marrying Miss Derville was the right choice. He was selfish enough to deny her just to spite his sister.

Now I understood her insistence on this particular woman for her brother, I knew the princess would never allow Miss Derville to be replaced, and they would continue to go in circles until the prince relented and consented to this marriage. Even the king grew tired of the prince's indulgent nature and was pushing him to decide. When another month passed and winter was approaching with still no engagement, everyone's frustrations were palpable.

"Even the Shaw sisters could have secured engagements by now," Princess Caelyn muttered cruelly to Lady Sharp one evening.

I made every effort to avoid being alone with Lady Sharp during her stay, and thankfully she was too busy matchmaking to pay attention to me. But I feared the longer she stayed, the more likely my luck would run out. So far, I remained a spectator in this game. One evening when I saw the prince once again ignoring the ladies, I knew I could no longer stand idly by.

"There's no reason the prince should slight Miss Derville," I explained to Risteard. "There must be an impediment. And the only reason must be him holding out hope for someone else."

"You mean the Praed girl?" he clarified.

"Noraa, yes."

"He was ordered to sever all ties with her," Risteard reminded me.

"Is there any proof of this?"

"He was escorted to Thistledon to end the attachment. He spoke to Lord Wyrwyk under close observation and was permitted to speak to the girl privately. We only have his word he used the time to end the relationship."

"He could have told her anything. If he had a note from her that she no longer wanted him, do you think he would finally accept Miss Derville?"

"If he felt there was no reason to pine for her, then I believe he would move forward. Brannon does not dwell on the past. How do you propose we orchestrate such a letter? Can you forge her hand?"

"I haven't seen a sample of Noraa's hand in years. The prince would be able to detect the fraud."

"Then what did you have in mind?"

"I need to go to Thistledon to speak to Noraa in person."

"How were you imagining you'd do that? Does the princess often grant you leave?"

"No," I said irritably. "I'd have to sneak out. I would need several hours."

"The roads are horrendous."

"I could ride."

Risteard leaned forward, his chin resting in his hand as he considered the plan. "How would you escape the castle unnoticed?"

"I could leave when I'm supposed to be cleaning the mews."

"Who would clean them in your place?"

"Would you be willing to volunteer?"

"Oh, no! If you're leaving the castle on this dangerous errand, I'm coming with you."

"Fine."

"I'll also have a note sent to the princess informing her you were needed to fill in for a sick stable hand. That should buy you the time you need. I know someone I can trust who will not ask questions."

"Ask him soon." I turned to leave. "I'm leaving tomorrow."

Water dripped from my hood while I stood in the rain waiting for Risteard. I was in sight of the stables, ready to sneak in and steal a mount while he distracted the groom. I wrapped my new woolen cloak, a 'gift' from the princess to avoid another winter illness, more securely around myself.

He was late, and I was annoyed. What was taking so long? Was the man taking my place at the mews being uncooperative? A twig snapping made me jump, and Risteard's tap on my shoulder nearly made me scream. He raised a finger to his lips.

"What are you doing?" I whispered. "You're supposed to be distracting the groom."

"No need," he said. "Come."

I followed him to the stables and the groom emerged with two horses saddled for travel. Risteard placed a few coins in the groom's outstretched hand and then beckoned me forward. I mounted silently and waited for Risteard to join me.

"You could have said we merely needed to bribe him," I teased when we were alone.

"It wasn't a bribe," Risteard corrected. "It was a thank you."

"Did you *thank* the man now cleaning the mews?"

"I did."

"Good. Shall we?"

"Lead on."

I kicked my horse into an easy trot to test the terrain and warm up the animal's dormant muscles. Risteard rode beside me, and we travelled off the mountain in companionable silence and into the valley.

The movement of the horse beneath me was like a lullaby, and I swayed to its soothing motion and urged the animal faster. I felt its feet tuck under its body to canter, and even the rain painfully hitting my face could not erase the smile that bloomed. I imagine it is what some people must feel when seeing a lover after a long absence--a swell of affection and happiness that makes you believe you can fly.

Risteard followed my lead, matching my pace and direction. I knew the way to Thistledon as well as Riverstone and steered my horse north out of Market Town. The rain drove most of the vendors indoors, but a few braved the weather. I caught the scent of fish stew, and my mouth watered. Fish stew was a favorite of Ula's and mine on days like this, but there was no time to stop.

The road was thick with mud, but we quickly left it to take shortcuts through estate grounds. Risteard kept a watchful eye in case we were spotted, but I knew the best places to ride to avoid being seen. Soon, the terrain shifted from soggy pasture and farmland to rocky, and I slowed my horse to a walk.

"That was a bit risky, don't you think?" Risteard said.

I wiped mud off my face and grinned. "Wasn't it great?"

He shook his head, but there was amusement in his eyes.

"We'll reach the crossing soon," I said. "Thistledon isn't far from the other side."

"Other side?"

"Of the Rhyvor."

His eyes widened and I swear he paled. "We're crossing the river?"

"You're not afraid, are you?"

The color rushed back into his cheeks tenfold. "Is it safe for the horses?"

"Have faith, Risteard." It was unfair how much fun it was to tease him. "No one's been lost yet."

The first bridge built to cross the Rhyvor on Wyrwyk lands had barely been wide enough to accommodate a single horse and cart. Decades later, the bridge was widened so a carriage could pass. That was almost two hundred years ago. Made of stone mined from the Heyshey Mountain Range far to the north, the bridge was sturdier than it appeared. That's what I tried to explain to Risteard when he saw it for the first time.

"Absolutely not," he said.

I grabbed his reins when he tried to turn around.

"Trust me. It'll be fine. I'll ride behind you if it makes you feel better. There'll be plenty of room."

He urged his horse a few steps closer and studied the distance. I rolled my eyes when he dismounted to take a closer look at the supports. It was a waste of time, but I knew he couldn't be rushed.

"Satisfied?" I asked when he was back in the saddle.

"Not at all. It looks slippery."

"It was built for traction. It does snow here after all." When he continued to eye the bridge dubiously, I said, "This must have been why Thistledon was left alone. None of your knights were brave enough to cross the scariest bridge in all of Praed."

His head snapped up and he glared. Got him. I suppressed a smile when he tentatively led his horse onto the bridge. He gestured for me to follow when he deemed it safe.

On the other side of the bridge, rocky banks gave way to lush grassland, and we were able to pick up speed. Thistledon lands encompassed the westernmost edge of the Sessyl Forest. Trees thrust into the sky like spears, their leaves heavy with rain. I tilted my head back and opened my mouth to catch droplets of water.

"You have a water flask," Risteard said.

"This is more fun."

I glimpsed turrets rising out of the trees and slowed my horse, leading it to the front gate. An elderly man approached and asked us to state our business.

"I wish to speak to his Lordship Wyrwyk immediately," I said with great importance. "We have been travelling through inclement weather expressly to see him."

"Is he expecting you?" the old man asked. He shivered and I noticed a tinge of blue on his lips.

"Good, sir," I said with a smile. "Let us not keep you out in this weather any longer. Open the gate and allow us to enter. We can discuss our business indoors and save us all from illness."

Reluctantly, the man opened the gate, and we rode into Thistledon. The building looked just as I remembered: sandy stone with four turrets and an impressive wall of vegetation growing up the sides. There were subtle changes. The garden was not as well tended. The front door needed polishing, and the steps were covered with dead leaves. The moment my feet touched the ground, the old man was in front of me beckoning us inside. I followed with my chin raised as Mother taught me, Risteard close behind.

"Now," the old man said as the doors closed behind us. "What is your bus---"

"What's going on down there, Vokay?" a voice yelled from inside the house. From the shadows, the master of Thistledon appeared, and the elderly man bowed apologetically.

"Very sorry you were disturbed, my lord---"

"Laria?" Lord Wyrwyk asked when he was close enough to recognize me. I nodded, and he rushed forward to pull me into a tight embrace.

"Thom," I said as I extricated myself from him. "No time for pleasantries. We have something very important to discuss."

"Don't just stand there!" Lord Wyrwyk admonished Vokay. "Lady Audrey is in need of a warm fire and a hot drink." The old man's eyes widened, and he hurried off to the kitchens.

"You should not have told him who I was," I said. "Besides, I'm no Lady of Riverstone."

"Whether you live there or not, you're still Laria Audrey of Riverstone. Come. To my study."

Risteard and I followed him, but when we entered his private domain, he nearly closed the door in the knight's face.

"Does he really need to be here?" Lord Wyrwyk asked suspiciously. Risteard's sword hand twitched, and I sensed the prospect of a fight. I assured Lord Wyrwyk the black knight could be trusted.

Lord Wyrwyk begrudgingly relented and beckoned me to sit. I waved away his request and bluntly asked, "Has the prince been making regular visits here?" By the reddening of his Lordship's cheeks, I already knew the answer.

"I couldn't deny him entry. He's the crown prince!"

"Were you aware of his attentions to Noraa?"

"I had my suspicions."

"Did she encourage him?"

"I couldn't say. I wasn't with them every second."

"Don't play coy with me, Thom. Has Noraa changed so much that she's no longer the shy child I grew up knowing?"

"What exactly are you implying, Laria?"

"I think you know."

"You think I instigated the match?" he asked angrily. "Maybe even sanctioned it?"

"I think you're very smart, Thom," I said with an eerie calm that even frightened myself. "And I don't blame you for ensuring a positive outcome for Thistledon by aligning yourself with me *and* the royal family. But how could you use your own sister so crudely?"

"It was her idea!" he yelled before checking himself. "She was worried about what might happen should your little revolution prove fruitless."

"So, she offered her virginity in exchange for protection?"

Lord Wyrwyk paled. "She did what?"

"Didn't you know?" I asked lightly. "What else did she have the prince could want?"

"I thought she'd charmed him into a proposal," Lord Wyrwyk said numbly as he fell into a chair.

"Noraa is a very sweet girl," I said, squeezing his shoulder in sympathy. "But you and I both know she is incapable of charming anyone, especially the prince. She would be too terrified."

"Your words are cruel, Laria," he said, burying his face in his hands.

"Did you accept money for your silence?"

"Yes."

"And then the prince and Noraa spoke in private?"

"They did." He looked up at me, and I felt sorry for his despair.

"I must speak with her," I implored.

"She's in her room," he said hollowly.

"Do not punish her harshly. She did all of this for you."

"Did she?"

"You told me yourself you would do anything to keep Thistledon. Noraa was merely doing her part, I'm sure."

"I find myself in need of rest." He rose, bowed, and bid me farewell.

I grabbed his arm and froze him with my most practiced icy glare.

"If you betray me," I warned. "No connection of ours will save you." I released him roughly and preceded him out the door. Behind me, I could hear his hesitant footsteps follow, then stop when Risteard blocked his path.

"You know who I am?" I heard Risteard say in a low voice.

"I do, sir," Lord Wyrwyk answered.

"If you speak of this meeting to anyone, I will hear of it."

I stifled a smile as Lord Wyrwyk beat a hasty retreat, and I led Risteard up the stairs to Noraa's room. I knocked, and a fragile voice bid me enter. I'm not sure whom she expected, but it certainly was not the drenched, ginger-haired woman and her tall, dark-haired companion. She stepped back, clutching a thin hand to her chest. I walked boldly up to her, ignoring her startled expression.

"Do you recognize me?" I asked. She nodded. "Events are unfolding and you are interfering with them. It means freedom for Praed. Answer me truthfully, Noraa. Does the prince have reason to hope for an alliance with you?"

She turned away and her skin turned pink.

"Please, don't speak to me so harshly. I was only doing my duty," she said.

I leaned close and clutched her wrist. "Was it your duty to lure the prince into your arms?"

Risteard cleared his throat, and I released her, but the anger did not leave my face.

"I didn't know what else to do," she whined. "Thom was insistent that I enchant His Highness, but I didn't know how. I don't know how to talk to people, let alone men. Especially a *royal* man." Tears shimmered in her eyes, and my heart softened.

"When he came to end the relationship," I began in a more sensitive tone, "did you release him from his promise?"

"I did!" she cried. "But I had to tell him the truth. How could I not?"

"What truth?" I asked, and I felt the blood drain from my face.

"I cannot be certain yet, but I think…" she hesitated and glanced at Risteard.

"You may be assured of that man's secrecy," I said. I waved toward him, and he stepped away to give us privacy.

"I think," Noraa whispered. "I think I may be carrying the prince's child."

My heart seized. My voice was not strong enough to leave my mouth, so my jaw opened and closed several times without making a sound. Risteard sensed my distress and came forward, but I held a hand up to stop him.

"You are not certain?" I asked.

"I've felt ill lately and very tired. Please don't tell Thom."

"Have you had your monthly courses?"

"Not yet."

"How long has it been?"

"A few weeks? But so much has been happening I just haven't noticed."

I strode over to the small writing desk in the room and placed a piece of paper and quill in the center of it. Without question, Noraa sat before it and looked at me expectantly.

"You will write to His Highness and tell him you were mistaken. There is no child. Do you understand?" She nodded, took up the quill, and wrote. I paced behind her, waiting several minutes until the scratching stopped and she declared it had been done. I perused the letter and satisfied with its contents, I laid a hand on Noraa's trembling shoulder and squeezed reassuringly.

"If there is a child, Noraa, you will be taken care of, I promise. The greatest service I can do is to save you from a life chained to that man."

"He seemed so kind," she sobbed.

"And I'm relieved he was gentle with you, but not all women have been so lucky." She continued to cry loudly, and I placed my hand on her head and gently stroked her hair.

"You have been very brave, Noraa, and have done more for Praed than many greater than yourself."

"What will Thom say?" she wailed.

"If your brother gives you any trouble," I said. "He shall answer to me."

I galloped away from the house, not caring about the rain or the slippery grass that might send my horse crashing to the ground. I ignored Risteard's shouting when I barreled across the bridge and rode hard until Thistledon was a memory and the castle loomed in front of us. Sweat lathered the horse's neck and its breathing was harsh, so I pulled it to a halt to rest. I became aware of my shaking legs and hands. I clenched my thighs to keep myself steady, and when my eyes squeezed shut tears slipped down my cheeks. I hated the way the nobles spoke down to the lower classes, and I treated Lord Wyrwyk and Noraa the same way, with threats and anger. It didn't matter that I worked for the benefit of Praed. If I couldn't secure their loyalty through honest means, how could I expect them to trust and follow me?

Risteard's presence stilled my troubled thoughts. I opened my eyes and saw him staring at me with worry.

"Are you all right?" he asked.

I expressed my concerns, and he waved away my actions as necessary for the cause.

"That cold-hearted woman back there was not me," I said. "I don't want to be feared."

"People will follow those that display strength. That's what you showed me today. It's what Lord Wyrwyk and his sister responded to."

"Along with a healthy dose of threats," I muttered.

"You can apologize later if you deem it necessary. As you told your friend, there is no time for pleasantries."

I took a deep breath. "Let's get back quickly," I said. "Too much time has passed already."

Risteard grabbed my reins to stop me, but before I could protest, my words froze under the intensity of his piercing gaze.

"Don't bring yourself low by feeling ashamed," he said sternly. "You were perfectly justified to act as you did under the circumstances."

"Perhaps," I said. "And they might respect me in time, but I shall be loath to live without feeling the effects of my own cruelty. The day when I no longer consider the feelings of others will be the day I cease to be worthy to walk this world."

"No one empathizes as you do, and that's commendable," Risteard said, gripping my shoulder. "But don't ever let me hear you speak of you leaving this world because you feel you don't deserve to be here. This world is barely tolerable as it is. It would be desolate without you." He looked at me strangely, then kicked his horse into a gallop and rode ahead of me to the castle.

CHAPTER 41

Not a day goes by that I am not amazed at the fickleness of men. Days after Noraa's letter was placed in Prince Brannon's hands, he acted like the lady never existed. Now free from obligation, he was able to divert his attention to other ladies. I must admit I found his commitment and faithfulness to Noraa when he thought she carried his child refreshing, but I had no doubt this was a passing phase and he would return to his true nature after the novelty wore off. Lady Sharp was especially pleased with the change in him and credited the transformation entirely to her own making. She watched Prince Brannon and Miss Derville from a distance with a self-satisfied smile. The princess was equally pleased, and I'm sure she already had the seamstresses ready to begin making wedding gowns.

"Lord Sharp and I prefer to return to Ilano before the snow falls," Lady Sharp whispered to the princess while they observed Prince Brannon leaning close to Miss Derville while she painted in the archway of the courtyard. "But we would be willing to extend our stay if it meant an invitation to an impending wedding."

"Of course, you must stay!" Princess Caelyn whispered. "Now Brannon has gotten over himself, I expect he'll offer Miss Derville his hand any day now. And I have you and his Lordship to thank for it." The princess interlocked her elbow with Lady Sharp and the two tittered in satisfaction. I frowned. I had hoped success would mean the end of Lady Sharp's visit.

"Not everyone is as pleased with these developments as we, it seems," Lady Sharp's silken voice spoke low near my ear.

Horse manure. I allowed my disappointment to show on my face. I resisted the urge to slap myself in the forehead for being so stupid.

She turned my face toward her so I could read her lips and asked, "Do you not approve of the match, or do you abhor public displays of affection in general?"

"I made it clear she was not to engage in any untoward behavior," the princess explained. "If her fear of retribution led to her despising relationships in general, then so be it."

"Such a pity for a young woman to never know desire. How can you be so cruel, Caelyn?"

"You would prefer my lady-in-waiting to be the whore of the castle?"

"No, of course not," Lady Sharp said. "Have you thought about what you might do with her once *you're* married?"

"The same, I imagine."

"You should consider her worth as an offering to a potential suitor. She does have a distinguished lineage in Praed after all."

The princess sneered, "Potential suitor indeed."

"You don't think someone might ally with her to enter court? Or make a trade?"

"Perhaps if she were not so hideous. No respectable Ilano would take a freckled, ginger-haired bride. Let alone one that cannot hear or speak. She might be considered a curiosity, but what man wants that for a wife?"

"You haven't noticed anyone paying any particular attention to her?"

"Jervell used to torment her for his own amusement." A flicker of sadness crossed Princess Caelyn's features and then just as quickly dissipated.

"If you covered her hair and powdered her face, she wouldn't look nearly so offensive. You should consider it, Caelyn. Having a young lady in your entourage that is pleasant to look at could be beneficial."

"For luring in unsuspecting suitors?"

"A pretty woman is a useful tool for maneuvering gentlemen."

"As we are all well aware."

"If nothing else, you can use her as a pawn to manipulate Risteard." My heart seized at Lady Sharp's words, but I managed to keep my expression neutral.

"What do you mean?" the princess asked in confusion.

"Haven't you noticed how protective he is of her?"

"Oh, that." The princess waved away any hidden implications. "That's because she's my lady-in-waiting. He's under orders. You know how dutiful he can be."

"Are you certain duty is all he feels toward her?"

"You know I have no affection for my cousin," the princess said darkly. "But you insult my family by suggesting there is a relationship between them. Besides, Risteard is too righteous to defile a young woman, especially my lady-in-waiting. He would consider it dishonorable."

"He shows no interest in defiling anyone. I did wish he would break his celibacy for me, but I found him as stubborn as ever."

"Save yourself the trouble, I beg you," the princess said. "No man's pleasures are worth making a spectacle of yourself."

"We shall agree to disagree on that score," Lady Sharp smiled wickedly. Their attention returned to the prince and Miss Derville, who were packing up the lady's supplies to retreat inside as rain began to fall.

"Let's concentrate on one conquest at a time, shall we?" the princess said as we followed the couple into the castle.

While Prince Brannon resumed his attention to Miss Derville, the rest of the castle busied themselves in anticipation for an engagement. Lavish dinners were planned followed by entertainment that might throw the couple together. The king invited Miss Derville to his table, and the prince was excused from his regular duties so he could concentrate fully on the lady. Honestly, all the fuss was getting ridiculous. Yes, it was important the prince marry for several reasons, but shutting down the castle to focus solely on their courtship was crossing the line.

I was certainly not above meddling in their affairs, but once their relationship was back on track, I had the decency to leave them alone and let nature take its course. Miss Derville accepted the attention with her usual grace and poise, whereas I would have been an absolute mess. Thank goodness I never had to worry about such things.

Apparently, I wasn't the only person who felt some distance was in order. Lady Sharp, astute as she was in these matters, commented to the princess one afternoon how difficult it must be for the couple to never have a moment alone.

"They need a respite," Lady Sharp mused. "An escape from the pressures of the court. Do you know where they could go to find sanctuary?"

The princess pondered the question for a moment, and then suddenly glanced at me.

"I know of a place," she said.

With King Conall's blessing and hopes for a positive outcome, a party was formed to leave the castle and overwinter at an estate in the valley. The party would include Miss Derville, Princess Caelyn, Prince Brannon, and Lord and Lady Sharp. The king insisted on a heavy show of knights to protect his precious children and their guests, a concession Princess Caelyn reluctantly agreed to. Torrential morning rains gave way to icy nights, and by the time the ladies were shown into their carriage, the first snowflakes touched the earth.

A cold breeze caressed my face where I sat in an open gig that also held the last of the noble luggage. I wiggled my toes in my boots that were too tight after I'd grown several inches over the past two years. I rubbed my threadbare gloved hands vigorously together to restore warmth to my frigid skin. Knights surrounded the caravan with birds aloft, watching the horizon for danger. I watched the landscape as we travelled and would have recognized the route were I blindfolded.

Toward Riverstone.

I knew the moment Lady Sharp asked for a place to retreat and Princess Caelyn looked at me. I saw in her eyes she remembered coming to Riverstone her first winter, that isolated place in the valley where she'd had a house to herself. A place where the temperatures were mild and the sun broke through the gray clouds. She would never admit it, but she enjoyed her time at Riverstone. It offered her everything she needed to hasten an engagement.

"Did you know where we were going this time?" I heard Risteard ask. I rose from the little nest I made for myself between trunks and peered over the side of the gig. I glanced ahead at the carriage carrying the ladies then back at him. He rode very close, clad in a long, black woolen coat and black gloves. His head was bare, and the wind tossed his dark locks like a mother playing with her child's hair. His beard was once again full, and I resisted the urge to say it made him look older. Besides, his face was probably much warmer than mine right now.

"I had an inkling," I responded.

"Does this please or depress you?"

"I haven't seen it since the last time we wintered there. I'm excited but afraid of how it may have changed."

"I'm certain it's much cleaner. They may have even refurbished the library."

"That would mean the world to me. I haven't been inside an actual library since Jervell Kade destroyed the one at Praed Castle. I noticed King Conall never went out of his way to repair and restock it."

"It's not his priority."

I looked around at our party, mentally counting heads.

"I don't know if Riverstone can handle these many guests. Some of you will have to share."

"Will the princess use that as an excuse to room Brannon and Miss Derville together?"

"Not even the princess would do such a scandalous thing. But everyone will be snug together. There will be no escaping each other's company. If the prince has not proposed by the end of winter, it will not be for lack of trying on Princess Caelyn and Lady Sharp's part."

"Because simply forcing one another into each other's presence should be enough to secure an engagement?" Risteard said dryly.

"It is with these people. There is no real affection here. Only maneuvering and power plays. Still, if the prince has the chance to really get to know Miss Derville, he may discover at least enough sympathy to erase any objections he may have."

"I'm sure Brannon has no qualms about Miss Derville as a wife on a personal level," Risteard said. "His reluctance stems from a general disregard for marriage entirely."

"But he knows he has no choice, so why drag this out?"

"His own amusement? He's been accused of baser feelings."

"Well, for Miss Derville's sake, I wish he'd stop leading her around in circles. The poor girl deserves a solid decision."

"I agree. I hope this winter proves beneficial for her."

I glanced past Risteard to the outskirts of the Riverstone estate. The house rose out of the snow like a beacon welcoming us home, and the changes wrought over the last two years were immediately obvious. The stables had been rebuilt and now included an attachment of mews. Some trees had been pruned while others were missing, and the climbing vines that encircled the front pillars since I was a child were stripped away. The banners of the Elejick royal family flanked the entrance, along with a statue of an eagle looming over the doorway. My cheeks burned with anger at the defilement of my house, and I couldn't hide the flash of hatred in my eyes.

"There's nothing you can do about it," Risteard whispered. "At least the house still stands." I shook my head to clear my thoughts and kept my eyes down while I worked. I knew he was right, but I wasn't in the mood to be placated.

The guests were gathered in the front hall when we entered carrying a heavy trunk between us. It was much cleaner than the last time. The dust and cobwebs were gone, and the area was well lit. The debris from the aftermath of the conquest had been removed and the broken furniture replaced. All evidence of my family was gone, as if we had never existed here. In the place of our family heirlooms and crests were those of the Elejick family, yet another reminder the past was truly in the past. The servants were lined in the hall as before, but now there were several more, and as before they were led by the caretaker, Eugen.

"What a charming place!" Miss Derville said.

"Indeed," Lady Sharp said. She glanced at me as if shocked I could hail from such a distinguished home.

"It's definitely improved since my last visit," the princess said.

"It's small," Lord Sharp said rudely.

"I don't know," Miss Derville said, admiring the woodwork. "It's certainly not as large as your estate in Ilano, but it's impressive as a family home."

"Maybe a Praed family," Lord Sharp mumbled before venturing further into the house, no doubt to find more things to disapprove of.

"Your Highnesses," Eugen greeted with a low bow. "What an honor to receive you again. I hope you will find your stay comfortable. Don't hesitate to call on me for anything you might need."

"Have you prepared the same room for me?" the princess asked.

"Yes, my lady. And my lord Prince Brannon will be in the master's rooms. The young lady's room will be on the same floor, and Lord and Lady Sharp will be housed on the third floor."

Probably in the tower.

I was proved correct when I was forced to deliver the last of Lady Sharp's luggage to my former room. The bed still had the coverings Risteard adorned them with on my sixteenth birthday, but the rest of the room was refurbished in the Ilano style. *Enjoy sleeping in a bed once occupied by a servant*, I snickered to myself.

"Oh, pardon me," Lady Sharp said graciously. She stepped forward, forcing me back into the room. "This must be very difficult for you, having us all take your family's place in your home. Who did this room belong to?"

I stared at her, not willing to respond.

"Well, the princess told me she's in your mother's rooms, and the prince obviously has your father's. So, either this or the smaller room downstairs was yours, though as the eldest, I'm sure you did not possess such a modest space. You should be honored to have your rooms occupied by a true Lady." She smiled and walked the length of the room, inspecting the stonework and lavish tapestries placed there expressly for her visit. She looked out the window at the new stables but didn't appear impressed. The built-in bookcases that once held volumes of books now contained trinkets and mementos symbolizing Ilano. The maids placed Lady Sharp's perfumes and grooming supplies on a large vanity, a new addition to the room. She paused at the bed and ran her hand over the coverlet.

"Interesting choice," she said to herself. "We'll have to order new bedding. The latest fashion," Lady Sharp told her maid. "This will not suit a lady of my standing."

I rolled my eyes and quietly backed toward the doorway.

When she noticed me trying to leave, she raised her hand and called, "You're not leaving already?"

I motioned that I had work to do.

She sighed. "Go on then." She waved me away, disappointed her fun was ruined.

Dinners at the palace were usually boisterous affairs that often became so loud one could barely think with course after course of rich foods and the steady flow of cider. In contrast, the evening meal gatherings at Riverstone were intimate. The food was plentiful yet simple, with complex tastes and aromas reminding me of the meals I ate as a girl. They retained the cook who'd served the Audreys and the recipes were the same. The nobles complained about the flavors, but with her characteristic sweetness, Miss Derville commented it was always good to try new things.

"We could pretend we're traveling abroad," Miss Derville suggested. "We are in another country after all."

"I commend your enthusiasm, Mwiryn," Lady Sharp said. "We should all try to be as optimistic. Don't you think, Your Highness?"

"Indeed," the prince answered. "Miss Derville can turn even the direst situation into an adventure." He smiled warmly at the lady, who blushed demurely.

"More cider!" Lord Sharp ordered. "To wash this vile meal from my mouth!"

I hope you choke on that vileness, your Lordship.

Lady Sharp ignored her husband's rudeness. "Speaking of adventure, what do you all say to an outing tomorrow? I would very much like to see the famous Rhyvor for myself."

"One river is much like another," the princess said.

"Don't be so dull, Caelyn," Lady Sharp said. "If the weather is favorable, I would very much enjoy exploring the grounds."

"If you insist, Eveene," the princess said.

"How exciting!" Miss Derville clapped her hands. "It's been so long since we've had a good walk. It rains quite a bit here, doesn't it?"

"An intolerable amount, I would say!" Lord Sharp said.

I speculated the damp aggravated his Lordship's rheumatism.

After dinner, the men retreated to the gentlemen's room to indulge in glasses of thick liquor while the ladies retired to the drawing room.

When my family lived here, Father would join us if there were no guests, and we listened to Ula's piano playing while Mother embroidered and I read. Father sipped kumis and watched Mother, admired Ula's performance, and completely ignored me. Mother and Father talked amongst themselves, and eventually Ula played something for me to dance goofily to and make her laugh. Mother rolled her eyes and muttered disparaging remarks on my parentage, and Father stared at me in disappointment while I spun clumsily around the room, encouraged by the laughter that made Ula collapse to the floor. Ula's opinion was the only one that mattered, and I ignored Mother's pleas to comport myself. Looking back, I really hadn't been fair to my poor mother, who tried so admirably to turn me into a lady despite my resistance. I didn't regret holding true to who I was, but I wished I hadn't been quite as obstinate.

The drawing room was laid out with a piano in the corner and several comfortable chairs arranged near an enormous fireplace. A side table flanked by elaborate sconces held a selection of cakes and refreshments. The decor was designed in the Ilano style, with bold floral patterns and colors reflecting the fruit from which much of that country's prosperity arose. The ladies arranged themselves on the sofa before the roaring fire, placing before themselves plates of treats and glasses of dessert wine. My eyes drifted shut once or twice as the ladies droned on about Ilano fashions and the relationships of people they knew back home. The day had been exhausting and all I wanted was to collapse onto the small cot awaiting me in the library. But based on the ladies' animated chatter, they were nowhere near ready for bed.

Miss Derville sipped daintily from a crystal glass. "I just wish Nela could find someone. She seems so lonely and would make such a dedicated wife."

"The most dedicated wife is one who is grateful for any man they can get," the princess said. "Whoever proposes marriage to Nela will have the most loyal wife in Ilano." She and Lady Sharp laughed wickedly. Miss Derville shook her head but made no comment.

"The prince has shown you a marked increase in attention, Mwiryn," Lady Sharp said.

"We are extremely pleased he's come to his senses," Princess Caelyn added. "And he will see your constancy as a trait he will appreciate more over time."

"I don't know if I'm made for this sort of thing," Miss Derville lamented. "Either of you would have secured a proposal by now. What am I doing wrong?"

"Nothing, dear girl," Lady Sharp said. "You are sweet, kind, and beautiful. But if you would like advice on how to hasten a commitment…" Lady Sharp arched an eyebrow.

The princess shifted in her seat and gave Lady Sharp a dark glare, unnoticed by Lady Sharp, but I was suddenly very awake.

Miss Derville cast a quick glance at the princess. "Well, I suppose it wouldn't hurt to listen to your advice even if I choose not to follow it."

"Of course, you must do whatever you think is right," Lady Sharp said.

"An engagement would mean so much to our people," Miss Derville continued. "I should consider what's best for Ilano as well as myself."

"Precisely!" Lady Sharp said. "You have the true heart of a princess, Mwiryn. You're always thinking about the greater good."

"So, what do you suggest I do?"

"Yes, Eveene," Princess Caelyn said. "Please educate Mwiryn."

Lady Sharp seemed puzzled at the princess' tone, but when no explanation or apology was forthcoming, she proceeded.

"Men are simple creatures," Lady Sharp began. "They do not respond to hints. Playing hard to get works for a time, but if there is no reward, the man will lose interest. They can be persistent, but also extremely lazy if there is no pay off. Once you have their attention, you must continue to entice him if you are to keep it."

"How do I do that?"

"You can start simply. Take his arm when you walk. Touch his hand when you reach for something. Stand close enough so he can smell your perfume. His anticipation for what may come next will keep him interested."

"What do I do when he grows bored of this?"

"A strategically placed kiss on the cheek would be a good start."

"Eveene! I couldn't!"

"You intend to be his wife, Mwiryn. A kiss means nothing compared to what your duties will be then."

Miss Derville turned a shade of red matching the wine she sipped nervously. Her hands trembled so visibly I feared she'd spill.

I felt sorry for her. She was clearly innocent in her knowledge of men, unlike Lady Sharp. Mine wasn't much better, but I'd seen enough from the shadows to know men liked touching. Miss Derville would have to overcome her shyness to have any chance of wooing the prince, whose experience vastly exceeded hers.

"Do you think," Miss Derville whispered through pale lips. "Do you think he'll expect me to allow certain liberties before we're married?"

"Undoubtedly," the princess replied dryly.

"That upstart from Praed was able to secure a promise from him in exchange for her favors," Lady Sharp said. "And she is nothing to you."

Miss Derville straightened and spoke firmly. "I won't offer up my virginity in exchange for a marriage proposal. That is a prize reserved only for a husband."

Lady Sharp smiled in approval. "A smarter stance to take, in my opinion."

The gentlemen entered the room, ending the intimate conversation and turning the discussion to more mundane subjects. I was growing tired of the monotony of my life, of waiting in the shadows. Were I Laria of Riverstone, I could move about the house as I pleased, escaping to the library or my own room.

When the princess was about to climb under the covers, she grabbed my wrist and fixed me with a burning stare. I raised my candle to better see her face, and she spoke in a low voice.

"I need you to do something," she said. "You'll have some idle hours to pass here. I want you to watch Prince Brannon and Miss Derville. Report on their every move."

I held out my hands as if to ask, 'How?' and she told me to improvise.

"I must know everything," she continued. "Every conversation, every look, every touch." She was so persistent I agreed, though admittedly I had no choice.

The princess never asked me to become involved in anything so personal. I suspected she was motivated by jealousy and some perverse need to know about Miss Derville's seduction of the prince. I wasn't thrilled about the prospect of watching them, but at least I wouldn't be plagued by boredom. When I finally fell into bed, the hour was very late, but my mind was abuzz with the promise I had been forced to give.

CHAPTER 42

Fresh snow blanketed the landscape on the morning of the planned excursion to the Rhyvor. Seeing the layer of white now several inches deep, the princess elected to remain indoors. A nudge of the elbow convinced Lady Sharp to do the same, which was all the convincing her husband required to spend the day lounging in the gentlemen's room. Miss Derville would have joined her companions indoors, but she was encouraged to go on with the prince since the sight of the infamous Rhyvor on such a lovely winter morning was not one to be missed. I don't think Miss Derville, nor the prince were ignorant of their motives in sending them out alone, but to their credit they said nothing and wrapped themselves in layers of fur-lined wool for the icy temperatures.

"We shouldn't require such a large entourage," the prince told Risteard while surveying the four men ready to venture out to protect them. "We are out in the middle of nowhere after all. But," he said with a raised hand to halt the anticipated protest, "if you insist on following along, I won't stop you. Just keep your men at a respectable distance."

The prince and Miss Derville were not three paces out the door with their trailing protectors when the princess seized my arm and ordered me to follow.

"At a respectable distance," she said. "You can read lips from afar, I trust?" I nodded, and she shooed me out into the cold.

I tracked the steps left in the snow, and it became apparent the prince had no idea where he was going. The footsteps led in the opposite direction of the river, so I hurried forward, my feet crunching in the fresh snow. Delicate flakes began to fall, tiny pinpricks of ice that stung when they hit my already pink cheeks. I saw the cluster of people in front of me, gathered around in obvious confusion. I could hear the prince arguing with Risteard about the location of the Rhyvor, and I wasted no time getting this party moving in the right direction. I marched up to the prince, made a motion of moving water, and confidently pointed toward the river.

Miss Derville smiled. "The river must be that way."

"Undoubtedly," the prince grumbled. He took the lady's arm and shuffled off, waving at the men to keep their distance. When he was out of earshot, the men chuckled quietly at the prince's obstinance until Risteard fixed them with a hard stare.

"Don't let them get too far ahead," Risteard ordered, and the men obeyed, hurrying through the haze to catch up.

Risteard and I followed silently, and the small flakes grew into large tufts falling quietly upon the ground to build up the already deep snowbanks. A thin layer formed on our shoulders and Risteard's hair, still bare in the winter chill. We reached the bank of the Rhyvor and looked at the water below. The prince and Miss Derville were there, watching the water move lazily over rocks and through ice built up along the banks while the bodyguards surveyed the horizon. In a few spots, the river was narrow enough that when the winter was particularly cold, it would freeze over. I used to test the ice by carefully walking across. Several times, it was not thick enough to support my weight, and the ice would break, sending me into the frigid water. Thankfully, it was barely to my knees at that time of year, so I only managed to ruin a dress and a pair of boots.

The snow fell thick and heavy now, and I could barely see through the curtain of white. The air was still and calm, the world so eerily silent I could almost hear each snowflake touch the ground. The voices of the prince and Miss Derville reached us faintly through the haze. I would have to venture closer to have anything to report to the princess. I stole a few moments of indulgence, closing my eyes and tipping my face so snowflakes tickled my cheeks.

"Did the princess send you out here to spy?" Risteard asked.

I kept my eyes shut. "Yes."

"She will be pleased you're taking your job seriously."

I opened one eye and noticed his smirk. I sighed and agreed I should probably move closer.

"In a moment," Risteard said. "They don't appear to be talking right now anyway."

I gazed upward and stuck out my tongue to catch the falling snowflakes.

An amused chuckle rumbled low in Risteard's chest.

"What?" I grinned.

"You," he responded, shaking his head.

"Do you think I'm childish?"

"Sometimes," he smiled. "But not in a bad way."

My tongue caught another snowflake. "Have you ever tried it?"

He shook his head.

"What exactly did you do as a child?"

"We don't have snow in Ilano."

"Try," I said. "Just tip your head back and hold out your tongue to catch the flakes. They're refreshing!" I demonstrated.

He eyed me doubtfully, then looked around to see if anyone was watching.

It was a funny thing to see--a fierce, bearded man catching snowflakes like a child. I watched him bend and sway to direct them into his mouth, and I smiled at this tender moment, taking a second to enjoy the little pleasures in life. He snapped his jaws shut and smiled triumphantly, his eyelashes and beard glittering with melting snow.

"Well?" I said.

"Come on," he said gesturing toward the couple walking arm in arm along the river. A smile played at the corner of his mouth, but it vanished by the time we were near enough to hear their conversation, Risteard once again the menacing black knight.

"I do hope you're enjoying your stay, Miss Derville," the prince was saying. "I know it hasn't been easy, and I fear I may be to blame for any distress you may have experienced."

"Oh, don't trouble yourself, Your Highness," Miss Derville said. "I can't blame you if you developed feelings for someone else."

"It was a foolish inclination," the prince said bitterly. "The lady coerced me, and I should have known better. There are many ladies who try to capture themselves a crown and care nothing for me."

"That must be very stressful for you, never knowing who your true friends are," Miss Derville said. She squeezed his arm and leaned closer, pressing the side of her body against the prince.

"You're the only person to remain wholly unchanged through the years," the prince said. "You're as constant as the stars."

I rolled my eyes. Stars move, you idiot.

"It's very kind of you to say so, Your Highness."

"Miss Derville. Mwiryn," the prince said. He stopped to face her and took both her hands and pressed them to his chest. "You and I both know what is expected of us, why we are here alone, do we not?"

"Yes," Miss Derville said, blushing and avoiding his gaze.

"It would be ungentlemanly of me to lead you on further without some assurance I will not treat you as abominably as I did a few months ago. It also wouldn't be fair of me to keep you here if I have no intention of entering into an engagement."

"No, it would not. I confess, Your Highness, I've been very confused these past few months. I only desire a straight answer to a plain question. Do you mean to marry me?"

Risteard and I stood still and waited for the prince's response. I could argue we were just as invested in the marriage as Miss Derville, and the prince's answer would determine the course of everything we planned.

"My dear Miss Derville, of all the women in Ilano, none would please me more than you as my wife, but I cannot enter into an engagement at this time. My reasons are personal, and mainly selfish, I admit, but it would not be fair to you to propose and then ask you to wait further until we're married."

She glanced down. "I understand." She spoke so quietly I could barely hear.

"Don't take this as a rejection. If you will grant me patience, I will make you a promise that I will propose."

"When?" she asked.

"I cannot say for sure, but hopefully in the spring. Can you wait for me until then?"

"Of course, Your Highness."

"Let us keep this conversation to ourselves for now. After all, if we are to become man and wife someday, we must allow each other secrets, don't you agree?"

"Yes, Your Highness."

"If it pleases you, you may call me Brannon when we're alone."

"If you wish… Brannon."

They resumed their walk, and I looked up at Risteard. We both knew the prince would only postpone an engagement for some nefarious purpose the princess most likely knew nothing about. How many webs of intrigue were spun in this tangle of lies?

I did my best to report what I'd seen and heard between the prince and Miss Derville over the next several days, but the princess grew frustrated at my inability to convey everything into gestures and pantomime. In the end, she resorted to asking yes or no questions, mainly the same ones repeatedly: "Has the prince proposed?" or "Have they kissed?" To these the answer was always 'no,' to which the princess would respond with a mixture of annoyance and relief. Her own feelings toward Miss Derville left the princess in a confusion of emotions. She wanted her to marry the prince, but on the other hand she was reluctant to share. I pitied her situation, having someone you love so close without being allowed to be together.

A blizzard confined the occupants of Riverstone for many days, which stretched into weeks. I had never seen a winter so brutal, and my thoughts turned to those without roofs over their heads or food to fill their bellies. How many new graves would be dug in the spring?

The guests did their best to entertain themselves during their forced imprisonment--as Lord Sharp described it--but the ladies only knew so many piano pieces and games until their accomplishments were exhausted. If there was kumis, the men were satisfied to idle away the days, but the ladies were clearly growing bored. I was confused as to why this could be since they rarely did anything but paint and embroider most of the time anyway. I started leaving books in the drawing room thinking at least one of the ladies would pick one up to read, but I was disappointed.

"What sort of crafts do your people do on days like this?" Miss Derville asked me one day, her hand resting on my arm. Behind her, the princess scowled, and I carefully pulled away. I mimicked riding a horse, and she wondered how we could ride in such weather. I shook my head, mimed riding again, and then gestured to my imaginary horse.

"Oh!" she exclaimed. "You do horse crafts?" I nodded. "Can we try, Caelyn?"

"If it pleases you, but I have little hope you'll enjoy yourself," the princess responded bitterly.

"I'm willing to entertain the notion," Lady Sharp said. "What do we need?" I held up my finger to indicate they should wait, then rushed to the stables.

I trudged through the snow, keeping my head down against the harsh wind, and ducked through the stable doors. It was warm inside, and I inhaled the sweet smell of hay and musty odor of horse I so cherished. Glass lamps were placed strategically down the length of the stable, casting light and a comforting warmth throughout the building. A guard and stable hand stood respectfully as I entered, and I dipped my head briefly in acknowledgement before walking down the aisle and entering a stall.

"Shhhh," I soothed the startled occupant. The young animal stared at me with its big brown eyes, ears pricked forward. It inhaled my scent, decided I wasn't worth getting further excited over, and resumed eating. I ran my hand along its body back toward its haunches, grabbed a lock of tail, and cut it with my dagger. I repeated this several times with more horses until I reached the stall housing Risteard's big black gelding.

"I don't suppose Risteard will appreciate me cutting a piece of your tail off," I whispered. The great beast stuck its head over the stall and buried its nose against my cap. I laughed as the animal blew out a great puff of air, blowing the cap off and messing up my hair in the process. I giggled, remembering how Amore used to do the same. She nuzzled my hair until all the pins became dislodged and Mother declared the result suitable for a family of rats. Thinking of my beloved horse sent a pang through my heart, and I rubbed my hand against the soft muzzle of the black horse and pushed it gently away. I looked down the long aisleway and saw the guard and stable hand were too absorbed in their own conversation to notice me, so I quietly ducked into the horse's stall.

"I thought the pain would go away," I whispered. The horse blew its nose at me, and I laughed, wiping the moisture from my face. "I miss this," I said. "I used to talk to Amore all the time. She always knew just what to say." An ear twitched, and then he shook his head, whipping his long mane about his head. I reached up to fix it and tangled my fingers into the long locks. I found comfort in the dark mane, burying my face against the great beast's neck and filling my lungs with his earthy smell. I listened to the munching horses, the low murmur of the grooms' conversation, and the rhythmic clomping of shifting hooves.

"I don't know what I'm doing," I continued. "Everything seemed so clear before, but I feel like I keep going around in circles. I'm afraid I'll never be free." My voice cracked, and I wept into the soft mane that matched the color of his master's hair. "What if I let him down?" I cried. "He's counting on me. So many people are counting on me! What if they're making a mistake?"

The stall latch clicked behind me, and I spun around. There he was, as if materialized out of thin air, my fellow conspirator, Risteard. I wasn't sure how much he heard, but it was enough to elicit the concerned furrow of his brow.

"Did he give you an answer?" he whispered.

"No," I sniffed, wiping the tears from my face. "Horses are fantastic listeners, but terrible conversationalists."

Risteard stroked the animal's head in response to its enthusiastic nudging and gave it a few firm pats.

"May I?" he asked.

"May you what?" I cocked my head.

"Answer for him?"

"I suppose if you know what he would say…"

"I do. He would say you're worrying unnecessarily. Even if we fail, there is no mistaking the faith being placed in you. Even if you did nothing else, your courage alone is an inspiration. Never underestimate your worth in this world."

"I just feel like I'm not accomplishing anything right now."

"That's not your fault. These types of maneuverings take time."

"I'm getting so tired of this."

"I know."

"It must be worse for you. They're your family after all."

Risteard said nothing. I used the opportunity to collect myself enough to go back into the house without looking like a blithering mess.

"If you ever need to talk to someone who'll answer, I'm always available," he said.

"I know," I told him. "But sometimes you just want to be listened to without a response."

"I can do that, too."

"Can you?" I was skeptical.

"If you tell me not to."

"Liar. You can't help it. It's in your nature to want to fix everything."

"Like a typical knight?" he smirked.

"You're anything but typical," I blurted out, then flushed with embarrassment. I brushed past him mumbling that I needed to get back to the house. He called out for me to wait, and I paused but did not look back.

"He wanted you to know," he said, speaking for his horse again. "You've never disappointed me." A smile crept over my face, and my chest swelled with pride.

I heard a few comments from the ladies about the length of my absence but ignored them and set to laying out strands of tail. The ladies watched with interest while I placed different colors together and began weaving them as Ula and I once did as children. One of my most prized possessions was a bracelet I made with Amore's tail interwoven with my own hair. I regretted the loss of this trinket more than anything else I owned.

Miss Derville was my most dedicated student while the princess and Lady Sharp indulged in the pastime for her sake. The princess quickly abandoned her project to practice at the piano, and Lady Sharp left hers once her husband and the prince joined them in the afternoon.

"What a lovely thing you're making, Miss Derville," the prince said.

"The lady-in-waiting showed me. It's a Praed craft," Miss Derville said.

"A perfectly destructive waste of a decent horse's tail if you ask me," Lord Sharp said.

No one did, sir.

"Oh, don't be so dramatic, my dear," Lady Sharp admonished her husband. He made no response and tension filled the air. I glanced up casually, and noticed Lord Sharp staring at me

"I've never seen it 'uncapped,' so to speak," Lord Sharp said, scrutinizing me. "It's quite a shock to see such an unusual color on display so brazenly."

Sweat broke out on my forehead when I realized I'd never retrieved my cap after the horse blew it off my head.

"Your Highness," his Lordship called to the princess, "might I have permission to touch your lady-in-waiting's hair? I'm curious if it feels normal."

"Suit yourself," the princess said without stopping her playing. "Wash your hands afterwards."

I watched Lady Sharp's reaction when her husband stroked my long ginger hair, inspecting the texture and even smelling it. If one could be struck dead by a look alone, I would be cold in the grave. I tried to pull away, but Lord Sharp held tight, and he leaned close to inspect my roots.

"I wonder," he whispered inches from my ear, "if the hair between your legs matches those on top of your head."

I remained still. He moved in front of my face and met my eyes.

"Does anyone else in your family have red hair?"

I shook my head.

"Interesting." He released me and sauntered toward the side bar.

Lady Sharp, however, did not match her husband's casual demeanor. She glared at me for a few minutes more, then asked to speak with him privately. They did not return to the drawing room, and I overheard the servants whispering about the loud argument between the Lord and Lady that lasted for several hours. They reappeared at dinner, but based on Lady Sharp's dark expression, the quarrel was far from over.

Ula's birthday passed, but Miss Derville gave me a great idea for a gift. I harvested several more locks of dark brown horse tail and braided it intricately with strands of my own hair. The bright copper color contrasted beautifully with the horse tail, and I was pleased with the results. I showed it to Risteard, and he said my sister was certain to like the gift.

"I wanted to make one for myself, but I've taken enough chunks of everyone's horse I'm afraid if I take any more there might be some retaliation. Or there will be a barn full of tailless horses," I laughed.

"You can use some of my horse's if you wish. I noticed you haven't so far," he said.

"If anyone was going to be upset about me defacing their animal, I figured it would be you. I wanted to avoid a fight."

"I hope you don't consider me so unapproachable you were uncomfortable asking."

I rolled my eyes. "No. Well, no more than a venomous snake coiled to strike."

"Very funny. You have my permission to use my horse's tail to make yourself a braid," he said.

I took several locks before he could change his mind.

I was in the library crafting a bracelet from the black strands of tail and my own hair one evening when I heard the door open and shut. Expecting to hear the distinct sound of Risteard's boots, I paid no attention to the interruption. However, what followed the soft click of the door latch was not heavy stomping, but rather the dainty tapping of a woman's stride. I jumped from the make-shift bed, expecting Princess Caelyn, but the figure that emerged from the darkness of the bookcases was not the princess. It was Lady Sharp. She paused momentarily, surprised I noticed her enter, and I mentally kicked myself for responding to the sound I supposedly couldn't hear.

"Were you expecting a visitor?" Lady Sharp asked.

I shook my head, and she advanced toward me.

"What have you got there?" She indicated the hand behind my back.

In the split second it took for me to turn my head to follow her gaze and remove the braid from behind my back, I was struck against the temple. I stumbled backwards. A sharp pain spread across my skull, and I struggled to regain my footing and fumbled for the dagger at my side. Vaguely, I heard the door open and close again, then the heavy footsteps of a man, whom I hoped was Risteard. I looked up as Lady Sharp held a candlestick high overhead.

"Enough!" a man's voice shouted. It was not Risteard. Lord Sharp appeared behind his wife, and she lowered the weapon. "We don't need to kill the girl."

Lady Sharp fixed me with an angry glare and tried to push me onto the bed. I kicked out and she took several steps away.

"How dare you strike out at me!" she hissed. She rushed forward, but her husband restrained her by the arm.

"You are entirely too quick to temper, my dear. Let's just get what we came for," Lord Sharp said.

Oh, no you won't! I reached inside my dress for the dagger.

"Watch out!" Lady Sharp yelled when I swung forward, blade in hand. Lord Sharp struck me again with the candlestick, dropping me to the ground and sending the dagger spinning across the floor. I tried to crawl toward it, but my vision blurred, and my muscles wouldn't cooperate.

"Cheeky bitch," Lord Sharp grumbled. The candlestick hit the floor, and in the next instant Lord Sharp picked me up. I fought against him, but my limbs felt numb. He threw me face down on the bed, ground his knee into my back, and pinned my wrists against my sides. I wiggled back and forth, trying to free myself.

"Hold still," Lady Sharp commanded, grabbing my hair. I twisted and bucked, and she angrily pushed my face into the pillow. "Keep struggling if you don't wish to live through this," she hissed.

With both hands, she gathered all my hair together, held it tightly in her fist, and out of the corner of my eye, I saw her pull a knife from her waist. I started resisting again, but Lord Sharp pressed his weight into me. She started slicing just above my scalp. The blade sawed back and forth, and my hair pulled away from my head. After an eternity the cutting stopped, and Lady Sharp sat up with the entirety of my hair clutched in her fist. Lord Sharp released me, but my eyes remained transfixed on my ginger locks.

"Do you really think this will fetch a good price?" Lady Sharp asked her husband.

"There's a market for everything, my dear. Such an unusual shade will doubtless be of interest to a wigmaker at the very least."

"The princess will be displeased we disfigured her lady-in-waiting."

"According to your information, she felt the girl's disfiguration was the hair itself. We've simply relieved her of it. Besides, she can keep her head covered."

"Her face may bruise."

"She'll heal. Let's go. We're finished here."

Their footsteps receded and disappeared with the closing of the library door. I raised a trembling hand to my head and ran my fingers from my forehead to the abrupt termination of my once long hair. The ginger color brought me nothing but ridicule, and yet I felt its loss more acutely than even Riverstone. Tears flowed in cascades down my cheeks, and I buried my face in the pillow to muffle the wailing emanating from the depths of my soul. It was just hair, I tried to tell myself, but I couldn't stop the waves of despair overcoming me. I cried until I couldn't breathe and my eyes dried, and still I continued to cry.

The sorrow of my loss overcame the pain, but my body could no longer ignore the throbbing at my temple and the top of my head, and it enveloped me in darkness until I lost consciousness.

The next morning, I lifted myself unsteadily from the bed. Judging by the sunlight streaming from the window on the east wall, the hour was late, and if I didn't hurry the princess would notice my absence. Tentatively, I touched the top of my head and felt a large lump, and at my temple dried blood crusted in my hair. I trudged to the washbasin and splashed cold water on my face and cleaned the blood from the side of my head. I dressed and donned my boots in a daze, letting my body take control of my movements. Finally, I pulled a cap tightly over my head, resisting the urge to touch my hair. I still felt the heaviness of the previous length, and I knew if I shattered that fantasy I would break down and not be able to work. I carried out my morning routine in the same absent state, staring blankly ahead. Normally, I would smile at the staff, but today I couldn't muster the strength, and I turned my back on their concerned looks.

I could have shown the princess what Lord and Lady Sharp had done, but to what end? For all I knew, they had her full blessing. Even if they had not, the princess hated me and took pleasure in my humiliation. I wasn't about to give her the satisfaction of seeing me in this vulnerable state and give her fodder for further torture. Nor could I tell Risteard, not only due to my embarrassment, but he would challenge his Lordship to a duel or something on principle. I didn't have the energy to have an argument about the futility of such a venture.

The rest of my day passed in a blur as I performed my regular chores by rote. Lady Sharp pretended nothing happened, secure in the knowledge I would keep quiet about what transpired the night before. Princess Caelyn noticed nothing amiss in my behavior, and luckily I didn't see Risteard at all, otherwise he would have detected the alteration in my mood. I was in no mood to explain my aloofness and desperately wanted to go to bed and curl myself into a pathetic ball of misery.

When my day was blissfully over, I dragged myself into the library, stripped off my dress, and pulled on my nightgown. When I was about to climb under my blanket, I noticed the scabbard lying next to the bed and remembered my dagger. I dropped to my hands and knees to hunt for it. I looked along the wall and under bookcases and tables then expanded the search and scoured the entire library. After searching the room thoroughly, I sat on my bed, empty handed and filled with dread.

The dagger was gone.

CHAPTER 43

I recovered from the hair trauma and moved on to the bigger problem looming over me--my missing dagger. I suspected either Lord or Lady Sharp took it and were waiting for a chance to reveal it to Princess Caelyn and get me in trouble. Or they were hanging onto it for insurance so I wouldn't rat them out about my hair. Whatever their reasons, their possession of the weapon meant they had control over me, and that made me sick to my stomach.

For days, I did not reveal to Risteard what they'd done to me, but I couldn't hide the loss of my weapon. The last thing I needed was a lecture, but there was no avoiding it. I chose to approach him with the news while he visited Aquila since the chance of him being in a favorable mood was higher.

The mews at Riverstone were arranged like the stables with several cages of varying sizes on each side of an aisle-way and lit with the same type of lamps. The building was therefore quite warm compared to the outdoors, ensuring the birds were comfortable. The expanse of hallway was suitable to exercise the birds when the weather was not favorable, and that's where I found Risteard on a blustery morning. I left the princess to her breakfast minutes earlier, and I knew I wouldn't have long until she required my services again. I cracked the door and peered inside as a blur of black flashed across my vision and landed heavily on Risteard's arm. Aquila spread her wings and shook her head in satisfaction before swallowing a piece of meat. When she caught sight of me, she cocked her head and chattered and squawked as if we were old friends catching up. She flapped excitedly at my approach.

"She's missed you," Risteard said.

I put my hand on her breast and stroked her dark feathers. "You'll see more of me once we're back at the castle." I turned to Risteard. "I need to talk to you. It's important."

He nodded and stepped past me to secure Aquila back in her cage. She settled on her perch intent on the remains of her breakfast.

"What's wrong?" he asked.

I wasted no time. "My dagger. It's missing."

"Missing? How?"

I looked down at my feet, chewed on my lower lip, and tried to think of an explanation that didn't require a retelling of everything that happened.

The words gushed out of me. "I think either Lord or Lady Sharp took it."

"What makes you think that?"

"They knew I had it."

Anger crept into his tone. "How? What aren't you telling me?"

I swallowed the lump building in my throat. "A few nights ago, they came into my room and… attacked me."

"What? Why didn't you tell me? What happened?" His hands clenched into fists.

"I didn't tell you for this very reason!" I held up my hands to halt his advance toward the door. I hadn't told him everything and already he was prepared to start a fight.

He stopped and stared at me for a few seconds, his expression dark. He took a few deep breaths and stepped away from the door.

"Go on," he said.

The story unfolded from my lips. As I spoke his skin flushed with rising anger. I explained how the dagger dropped from my hands when Lord Sharp hit me over the head, and then skipped to the next evening when I realized it was gone.

"I'm not sure at what point they took it, but it has to be one of them."

"What happened after you fell? Were you unconscious until the next morning?"

"No," I said evasively.

"Did he…" His voice trailed off, his meaning unsaid.

I shook my head vehemently. "No."

"Then why were they there? Nothing else happened?"

"Stop interrogating me!"

"We promised each other honesty," he reminded me with an edge to his voice.

My throat tightened and I resisted the urge to sob. I couldn't tell him. It was too humiliating. I reached up and dragged the cap off my head, squeezing my eyes shut so I couldn't see his expression. I heard a sharp intake of breath.

"I'm hideous!" I wailed.

"Has the princess seen this?" he asked.

"No!" My eyes flew open. "And I don't want her to! Please don't say anything or challenge Lord Sharp to a duel!"

"Are you sure? This should not go unpunished." I felt certain if I would have asked it of him, Risteard would have gladly plunged a sword into Lord Sharp's heart, but the indignity of my short hair was the least of our problems.

"I'm asking you not to. Please. We have more important things to worry about, like my dagger. I pulled it on a Lord and Lady of Ilano. You know it doesn't matter what they were doing to me. If they tell the princess, she'll have me hanged."

Risteard clenched and unclenched his fists several times as he struggled against his instinct to defend my shorn locks.

"Fine." He looked at my worried face and his features relaxed, then he reached out and inspected a few of the uneven strands of hair.

I held back my emotions while he continued to silently study me, until a tear escaped down my cheek.

"It's not… so bad."

I laughed and crammed the cap back on my head. "My mother would faint if she saw me."

"I'll take care of the dagger." He indicated my hair. "I think I know someone who can fix this."

I gave him a skeptical look before he took my hand and led me back to the house.

Outside the door to the drawing room, Risteard asked me to wait before going inside. I paced the length of the hallway until the door opened and Risteard appeared with Miss Derville.

"Can we go someplace private?" Risteard asked Miss Derville. She looked at me, no doubt noticed my reddened cheeks and startled expression, and smiled sweetly.

"Come to my room," she said.

We followed her upstairs to what was previously Ula's room. Like the others in the house, this room was cleaned and furnished with a new bed, chaise, vanity, and chest of drawers. A tapestry of an orchard adorned one wall, and on another was a portrait of an old man with a black eagle.

She closed the door behind us. "Is something the matter?"

Risteard beckoned me to take off my cap. I hesitated, but between his encouragement and Miss Derville's kind expression, I relented.

"Oh!" Miss Derville gasped as my ruined appearance was revealed. "What happened?"

"Can you fix it?" Risteard asked.

"Well…" Miss Derville mused as she looked closer at the varying lengths of my hair. "I think I can even everything out in any case. Who knows? Short hair on women may become the new fashion. You're simply ahead of everyone." She led me to the chair at her vanity and pulled out a pair of scissors.

"Go on," she shooed Risteard. "Leave the ladies to their beauty treatment."

Risteard bowed and left me alone so Miss Derville could salvage what was left of my hair. She worked silently, occasionally meeting my eye in the mirror and smiling.

"It will be quite short, I'm afraid," she said. "But it will grow back evenly, and the length will be the same." She stepped back for a moment to inspect her work, then went on. "I've always liked your hair color. It reminds me of a sunset."

I smiled, grateful for her kindness. She moved behind me as she worked, musing out loud to herself.

"I feel sorry for you sometimes," she said. "It must be very difficult for you being in this house as a servant instead of a host. I can't imagine what your people are going through. You're like prisoners in your own home." She paused and became lost in her own thoughts. "I suppose that's how many wives feel." Outwardly, I had no reaction, but my heart sank as she mused on the disadvantages of marriage. "When I was a little girl, I imagined marrying a man I loved very much and living happily forever." She took a few unsteady breaths and continued, "I know I must marry to please my family, and I will do so without hesitation, but I wish I was free to make my own choices in life. You will probably find some nice stable boy to marry, or a valet, and be happy with him while I will live in misery with my crown of gold."

Honestly, I empathized with her plight, but I couldn't bring myself to feel completely sorry for her. After all, the marriage she dwelt on would make her a princess. How many other women destined for an arranged union could say the same? Yes, her husband would be a scoundrel, but living in a castle with the wealth of a nation certainly made up for any philandering she suffered through.

She leaned over my shoulder and met my eye in the mirror. She smiled like we were old friends gossiping over tea.

"So, then," she said. "Do you have a beau?"

I cocked my head and wondered if she had lost her mind, but she interpreted this as me not understanding.

"You know, a special man in your life?" she clarified.

I shook my head.

She sighed, "Oh, right. Caelyn forbids it. Well, I don't suppose you have a *secret* lover?"

Again, I denied a relationship, and she laughed.

"No," she said, straightening. "With Caelyn as your mistress, you wouldn't dare, would you?"

I sulked while she continued to trim my ruined hair. She wondered aloud what happened but didn't ask me directly. She once again began to muse about her situation, and I was about ready to get up and walk out when she made an agonizing comment.

"It would be easier, I think, to reconcile marriage if I wasn't so attached to someone else."

I knew she meant the princess, and though she was no favorite of mine, I did feel a pang to think she must conceal her identity to secure her future. I was acting in much the same way, and the commonality bonded me to her infinitesimally.

"There!" She held a hand mirror up so I could see my entire scalp. She watched me expectantly while I inspected my short style, and the longer I stared, the more nervous she became.

"Well? I'm not the best at this sort of thing, but I did try my best. I think it complements the shape of your face. You have such lovely cheekbones. And those striking green eyes!"

The corner of my mouth twitched. I regretted the heartless things I thought about her marriage to the prince. She had no obligation to help me, and yet she had without question. I nodded my thanks and gave her a genuine smile.

"You are very pretty," she said wistfully. "Despite what everyone says, you've grown into a beautiful young woman. I'm sorry if someone was cruel to you. No woman deserves that." I abruptly left the room before she could see my tears.

The morning blizzard gave way to a sun-filled afternoon, yet the occupants of Riverstone were content to gather around a fire and play cards while indulging in glass after glass of kumis. Inevitably, the ladies' cheeks flushed, and the men began to sway as drink turned them into senseless idiots. Gauging their level of intoxication, I wagered I could escape and remain unnoticed for an hour at least.

I inched out of the room and sneaked down the hallway to the front door unnoticed. The crunching of my boots in the snow was the only sound that accompanied me as I ran down the valley to the banks of the Rhyvor. I sunk to my knees to catch my breath, each puff coming out in a white plume around my face. In my haste to leave, I forgot my coat and gloves, and as the warmth of my exertion faded, the chill crept into my skin. I rubbed my arms and leaned over to peer at my reflection in the meandering water. It was hazy, but at this time of year, the water was slow and still in some places. I pulled the cap from my head and looked at my hair. Miss Derville fixed it quite well, I thought, evening out the choppy ends so it didn't appear I'd lost my hair in some tragic farming accident.

Footsteps approached--Risteard's by their cadence. His reflection joined mine, his face distorted in the rippling river. He sat in the snow next to me and very gallantly wrapped me in his heavy wool coat.

"Thank you," I said absently. "I forgot mine."

He inspected my hair. "Miss Derville did a good job."

"Yes."

"It'll grow back."

"I know."

"What is it then? Are you worried about the dagger? I have a plan."

I met his eye. "Tell me."

"I don't believe Lord Sharp would trouble himself to enter your room again. He got what he came for. Lady Sharp, however..."

"Received no reward for her troubles."

"Right. She's never been fond of you---"

"To put it lightly," I snorted.

"She would risk going back for the dagger if it meant leverage over you."

"So, how do we get it back?"

He avoided my gaze. "If I distract her, could you get into her room and search for it?"

"Distract her how?" I asked. My spine tingled, raising the hairs on the back of my neck.

"I'm sure I can think of a way."

"No!" The echo of my voice carried across the river. I cast a furtive look around, but we were alone. "Don't you dare," I hissed. "Don't compromise your integrity for a stupid dagger."

"You said it yourself. If she shows it to the princess and tells her you threatened her with it, you'll be hanged. Especially if the prince catches wind of this. He's kept his mouth shut so far, but if Lord and Lady Sharp expose you, he'll have no qualms doing the same. A little integrity is a small price to pay for your life."

"There has to be another way." My stomach twisted in knots. I racked my brain, thinking about Lady Sharp and how devious she was. "What if you beat her at her own game?"

"What do you mean?"

"I mean, pretend you're on her side."

"Go on."

"Ask to speak with her in confidence. Tell her you have suspicions you don't feel comfortable bringing to the princess without proof. If you pretend you're looking for evidence of some treachery, won't she produce the knife?"

"What will stop her from going to the princess herself?"

"Tell her you're collecting evidence but need something really big to tighten the noose, so to speak. Make some comment about how grateful you'd be to the person who produces such evidence. She'll trip over herself to give it to you if she *thinks* you'll express your gratitude to her."

"It might work."

"Anything is better than the alternative."

His mouth twitched, and he stifled a laugh. "In this case, I would agree with you."

"I've been thinking about Miss Derville," I said, abruptly changing the subject. "Do you think she'll be all right? If, or rather when, she marries the prince, I mean?"

"Do you have fears about her safety?"

"Not exactly. I don't believe the princess would place her in danger. And she certainly will not want for anything. But she did voice fears about living like a prisoner in misery."

"A fact I'm certain she's come to terms with since she hasn't left Praed by now," Risteard said. "You can't protect everyone any more than I can. She's a grown woman who has chosen her path fully aware of the consequences. It isn't fair that many women must sacrifice happiness for an advantageous marriage, but it doesn't have to signal the end of her life. She may find herself lonely, but she won't be alone. Caelyn will never cease to be her companion. And if the marriage is graced with children, she'll have fulfillment in her duties as a mother."

"She would make a good mother," I murmured. "But what happens to her when King Conall is off the throne?"

"Brannon may no longer be a prince, but he won't be destitute. The family retains a vast estate in Ilano. They'll live comfortably there."

"I wonder what the prince is waiting for," I mused. "If he intends to propose, why the delay?"

"I don't know. And if the princess is just as frustrated, she doesn't know either, which makes me believe he has his own agenda."

"What a mess." We walked back to the house in silence, and I handed Risteard back his coat once we reached the front door.

"You're very introspective lately," Risteard observed. "Is there anything else on your mind you want to talk about?"

"Just trying to figure some things out. Nothing important."

"Maybe I can help."

"Maybe. I'll let you know."

We parted ways, and I made my way back to the drawing room. Everyone was still there, but the card game was over. They moved on to charades, and the spectacle of watching several intoxicated adults act out scenes was enough to bring an amused grin to my face. I'd been feeling morose lately but had been unable to pinpoint the cause. There was no shortage of disturbing events to dwell on over the past two and a half years, but I sensed something else plagued my inner thoughts. I continued to watch the ladies giggle and the men fall over themselves and resolved to push these unnamed thoughts aside, keep them at the back of my mind, dormant until the time came when I had the strength to face them.

CHAPTER 44

A few days later, Risteard reported Lady Sharp was all too eager to produce my dagger in anticipation of satisfying her desires. She was an intelligent woman, but she was quite predictable and easily motivated by flattery and vanity. When Risteard implored her for help, she placed the dagger directly in his hands, her eyes flashing at the prospect of sealing my fate and eager for a romp in Risteard's bed. At least, that's how I pictured her. Of course, Risteard spoke much more diplomatically. He thanked her, asked her to keep the exchange to herself, and promptly left. Knowing Risteard, there was probably a healthy dose of threats before he walked away because Lady Sharp would have ensured her information was given to the princess, and if time passed without me dangling from a rope, she would raise a fuss. I don't know what he said to secure her silence, but she avoided me for the duration at Riverstone.

The relative peace of the remainder of winter was tainted by my certainty it would not last. I lived in constant fear that something awful would happen, and I would slip into a depression over the unfairness of my situation.

The prince and Miss Derville acted engaged, though the words were yet to be said. They held hands, whispered in each other's ears, and sat together. Lady Sharp's pleasure was palpable, and she showed her husband extra affection in the form of obsequious cheek kisses and perching on his knee to read letters over his shoulder. The princess appeared as stoic as ever, though the blatant displays of affection surrounding her must have been hard to bear, especially since one of them was Mwiryn. She bore their behavior with grace, expressing her joy to Miss Derville at her conquest.

Seeing the couples paw at each other was irritating, but the sight no longer filled me with the disgust I previously experienced at such displays. I could not name the feelings I had now--maybe a mixture of curiosity and embarrassment.

I kept the princess from discovering my newly shorn locks, and avoiding her wrath was a further relief. For all I knew, she appreciated my dedication in keeping my head covered. Eventually, the shock of my appearance dissipated, and I was able to look in a mirror without feeling a rush of anger and remorse. I even considered showing Mother just for the thrill of seeing her expression.

This devilish thought brought a tiny smile to my face, and it was then Risteard approached where I stood a distance from the Rhyvor watching the party venture among the rocks. The snow was melting with the warmth of spring. Soon, trunks would be packed, and everyone would return to the castle. These were our last days at Riverstone and having to say goodbye left me more glum than usual.

"It's been a while since I've seen that," Risteard said quietly.

"What?" I asked.

"Your smile."

My face fell and I turned away. "Not much to smile about these days."

"Things are certainly not as bad as they could be."

"True."

He made no response, and we observed the young knight I had seen on several occasions assisting the princess when she slipped on a rock. I nearly burst out laughing when he casually looked over his shoulder to see if Risteard took note of his gallantry.

"Olim!" Risteard called out. The knight dashed over ready for orders.

"Yes, sir."

"The time is drawing near for us to return to the castle. There is much for me to do before then."

"Understood. What do you want me to do?"

"Stay here with the others and keep an eye on their highnesses and their guests. You're in charge, so if any harm comes to them, you'll answer for it."

The knight puffed out his chest with pride, but his eyes showed a flicker of uncertainty.

"I'll serve them with my life, Sir Risteard," he said.

"Good." He turned me to face him. "You'll need to start arranging the packing of the ladies' things. Come with me and we'll get started."

I nodded and headed back to the house. Risteard dismissed the young knight.

When Risteard caught up to me, he clutched my elbow and directed me away from the front entrance.

"Where are we going?" I asked.

"Stables," he answered tersely. I didn't resist as we sloshed through melting snow and entered the warmth of the building, and I breathed in the familiar aromas.

"Sir?" the stable master said.

"Saddle my horse please," Risteard said. "And one for the lady."

"Of course, sir." The man bowed, and I could tell this was an odd request, but to his credit the man asked no questions. We waited outside, and shortly the stable master led Risteard's black gelding and a sturdy bay from the stables. I didn't know what Risteard planned, but if it involved a ride, I wasn't going to question him. I raised a foot to the stirrup, but Risteard stopped me and turned on the stable master.

"This is a sidesaddle," he pointed out.

"Yes, sir?" The stable master's confusion was evident.

"Sorry, I should have clarified. Please exchange this for a regular saddle." Again, the stable master complied, and at last I was permitted to climb into the saddle. Once Risteard was atop his own horse, he instructed the stable master to inspect the tack in preparation for everyone to travel back to the castle. Without waiting for a reply, he aimed his mount toward the valley and beckoned me to follow.

Once we had trotted a safe distance from the house, I asked where we were going.

"For a ride."

"Just for fun?" I asked.

"That's the idea."

I dug my heels into my horse's sides, and took off across the valley, white with receding snow. My horse's hooves skittered briefly as he gained speed, but his long strides were sure, and we raced over the soggy ground, kicking up moist earth and cold snow. My legs became wet, and my face streaked with tears from the wind blowing against my cheeks. All my troubles faded into the blackness of my blank thoughts, replaced with the joy of flying across the valley. I raced over the hills and down across a vast plain toward my secret spot, a pool fed by a stream feeding into the river. Here I used to swim naked during the hot summer months. At the rocky outcropping I slowed, maneuvered my horse down the slope to the pool, and dismounted. The waterfall was a mere trickle at this time of year, and the pool was probably no deeper than my waist. I gave no thought to Risteard, who had yet to reach me, as I dropped to the ground and pulled off my boots. I flung them aside, followed by my coat and cap, and finally I shrugged out of my frock. Clad only in my underclothes, I waded into the icy water.

The shock travelled from my toes directly to my chattering teeth, but I continued deeper, giving my body little chance to acclimate. Vaguely, I heard hoofbeats above the waterfall, a sharp call, and then hoofbeats coming closer toward the water. I stood in the middle of the pool now. I closed my eyes and filled my lungs, held my breath, and sat down, plunging my entire body. I came back up immediately, a shrill cry escaping my shivering lips.

"What are you doing?" Risteard yelled. "You'll freeze to death!"

He dragged me to shore and wrapped my coat around my shoulders followed by his own. He sat me on a log and cleared a spot on the ground. I watched him rummage in his saddle bags and then collect several branches. He knelt and started laying a fire in the space he'd made. I was not surprised he had everything at the ready. An ember glowed in the kindling, and he added the wood.

I shook my head. "They'll be too wet."

"Nonsense. It's dry enough."

I watched him try to coax a fire from damp sticks. My eyes roamed over him as he sat hunched over, and I noticed he hadn't even removed his boots when he went into the water after me. Miraculously, a flicker of flames emerged from the moist wood, mostly fueled by Risteard's tenacity. Satisfied the fire would not go out, he grabbed my hands and placed them directly over the flames, then shuffled close and began rubbing my back and shoulders. I remained quiet, not feeling the cold, but rather a soothing peace.

"Thank you. I needed that."

"I didn't intend for you to drown yourself," he muttered.

"I wasn't." My fingers danced over the fire. "I used to come here all the time. I knew it wouldn't be deep, but I needed to feel the water. There have been so many thoughts swirling around my head. Feeling the wind on my face and the shock of that cold water hitting my skin is the only thing to quiet them."

"I'm glad," he said. He continued rubbing my arms. "I hoped a ride would help cheer you up, but I didn't expect an impromptu swim."

I laughed softly, but the euphoria was fading, and I became more aware of the chill in my skin. I leaned toward Risteard, shivering more violently, and he wrapped his arms around me and pulled me to his chest.

"Next time you need to clear your mind in a pool of water, do it in the summer." He spoke close to my ear, his warm breath tickling my cheek. All I wore underneath the coats was my thin underclothes, now clinging revealingly to my body. I was aware of every inch of skin, like feeling coming back after being numb. A wave of heat followed, setting my cheeks aflame. I sat up, scooted away, and wrapped the coats tightly around me.

"I think I'm dry enough to put my dress back on," I said nervously. He retrieved it from where it rested on my boots. I wrenched it from his hands and took several steps away. He turned his back to give me privacy and I pulled the frock on over my underclothes that were decidedly not dry enough. I struggled for longer than necessary, but finally I was decent again.

"Here," I said, holding out Risteard's coat. He hesitated, and I placed it over his shoulder, unwilling to have a conversation about how I needed it more. Reluctantly, he donned the heavy wool greatcoat and I kicked wet earth over the fire. Wordlessly, we both mounted our horses and headed back to the house. I gained some clarity of mind with this little adventure, and my spirits were lifted, but I couldn't bring myself to meet Risteard's eye, even after we returned the horses to the stable.

"Thank you again." I stared at my boots. He placed a finger against my chin and lifted my face so I would look at him.

"Are you well? Truly?"

"I'm not feeling quite myself lately," I admitted. "I'm sure I'll return to normal once we're back at the castle."

"You'd think being at home here again would do that."

"This isn't my home anymore." I gazed at the house. "It's merely the place I'm from. I'm still looking for where I belong."

"Is that what's been bothering you? You don't feel you belong anywhere?"

"Anywhere," I said absently. "Or to anyone." My brow furrowed and I blinked rapidly. What did I mean by that? I looked back at Risteard, and he was staring at me strangely. My skin burned, and without another word I rushed to the library and sank into a miserable pit of shame. With any luck, we'd return to the castle soon and leave the memories of this peculiar winter behind.

CHAPTER 45

The final days at Riverstone were a flurry of activity. Everyone was in an uplifted mood, all smiles and hopes for a promising spring. Most of the snow had vanished, replaced by the first shoots of green grass. The chill in the air was gone, and the warm temperatures coaxed the group outdoors while the last of the luggage was hauled into the carriages. Everyone ventured to the banks of the Rhyvor one last time, the water now rising with the melting of the snow. The prince and Miss Derville walked arm in arm with the princess and Lady Sharp close behind while Lord Sharp, already deep in his cups, sat on a large stone periodically checking his timepiece. A few knights milled about looking just as bored, leaving only young Olim to keep watch. Risteard was readying the horses, so I was alone with my thoughts, trailing my fingers in the icy water. Otters would soon emerge from their dens, kits in tow, in search of fish. Birds would skim the surface catching insects and gather twigs and grass for nests. I used to find them in the stalls pulling tufts of hair off the horses' backs. Blooming wildflowers brought bees, and my mouth watered thinking of honey. Spring meant life in the valley, and it was my favorite time of year to be outside.

My reverie was broken when Lady Sharp sat next to me and watched my fingers gliding with the quickening current. I hoped she'd leave if I did not acknowledge her, but apparently she chose this moment to break her blessed avoidance of me. She tapped me on the shoulder to get my attention, but I shuffled away and ignored her. Undeterred, she grabbed my shoulder and spun me around.

"How dare you ignore me!" she huffed. She glanced around, a flicker of fear on her pale features.

I stared at her, my jaw set.

"Don't look at me like that," she whispered. "It wasn't my idea. I know you can't understand the relationship between man and wife, but when your husband makes demands, there is no denying him."

My expression didn't change. I didn't believe her explanation. Lady Sharp was a strong, independent woman. She could not convince me she acted against her will.

"I wonder what goes on in that brain of yours," she mused while we stared at one another. "I once thought you were a simpleton, and that Risteard protected you because of your diminished capacity. But if that were the case, he never would've given you his dagger."

My eyes widened, and she smiled. "Of course, I knew it was his. I found his initials carved into the pommel. They're small, but they're there. I suspected you had stolen it, but when he approached me about finding evidence against you, and then completely changed his manner once I placed it in his hands, I knew immediately he gave it to you. Don't worry. His threats against me will secure my silence. That brute knows all the secrets in Ilano," she said bitterly. "I just don't understand. Why does he care so much about you?"

Without taking my eyes from hers, I stood, holding her gaze for a few moments before walking away. I would not allow her to unsettle me or sabotage my friendship with Risteard. I heard her rise behind me, but she said nothing, nor did she follow. Thankfully, she reverted to avoiding me for the rest of the morning.

I chose once again to walk the last few miles to the castle, enjoying the sunshine and the smell of fresh grass and moist earth. The young knight, Olim, came back a few times to check on me, but aside from those brief moments, I was alone. I relished the solitude and used the opportunity to think about the upcoming engagement. The kingdom would undoubtedly rejoice, and the king would declare a celebration that, if the prince's birthday was any indication, would span several weeks. Preoccupied with the engagement and wedding plans, the entire castle would be distracted. It was the perfect opportunity for an uprising. I would call on all my supporters, and Risteard would call on his, and this whole nightmare would end. It was a fluffy fantasy where everything ended my way with the king stepping aside merely out of intimidation with our show of force, but it was entertaining to daydream such an outcome. My thoughts drifted from one subject to another, a jumble of confusion I struggled to understand.

My uncertainty remained when we rode to the front entrance of Praed Castle and an awaiting king and queen. The king embraced his children as if they had been parted for years, and the queen graciously extended her hand for them to kiss. I watched the king lead the queen inside, followed by the prince with Miss Derville on his arm, the princess with her unwavering gaze on her, and Lord and Lady Sharp, their heads pressed closely together. I felt a tightening in my chest watching them walk into the castle. I was tired of not understanding my own feelings, and I resolved to identify the reason so I could conquer them and move forward.

Not surprisingly, the king held a feast to welcome his children home. If he was as devoted to his family in private as he acted publicly, even I would adore him. This dinner was like any other in Praed Castle: a cacophony of noise redolent with the aromas of fine foods and lubricated by the steady flow of cider. But tonight, I looked upon the guests differently. I watched, hoping to find some clue to my morose moods. I'm not sure why I thought the answer would lie with the throngs of people laughing as they ate, jesting and praising each other in turn. My eyes fell on Lady Sharp smiling sweetly across the table at her husband, and for a second I believed her performance as a devoted wife. I watched their exchange, repressing a smile when he placed a morsel of food in her mouth followed by her appreciative grin and flash of eyes. She turned and spoke to a lady at her right, and from my vantage, I saw Lord Sharp reach under the table and run his hand along the thigh of the woman on his left. Instead of the slap he deserved, the lady's color rose, and her eyes slid sideways to meet Lord Sharp's gaze. Her smile was one of promise. I stepped away, disgusted.

The prince's behavior toward Miss Derville changed once they returned to the castle, much to the distress of the lady and Princess Caelyn. Where once they were constant companions, they now sat apart. Miss Derville looked on solemnly as the prince flirted with other women and drank heavily with the king, once again the boisterous scoundrel.

Meandering around the room, I watched the same story unfold. No relationship was sacred. Husbands waved away wives and lovers secretly held hands under the table. My mother and father may not have had a blissful marriage, but theirs was more honest than any I saw here under the Elejick rule. I came back to the head table where Miss Derville and the princess were in animated conversation. I heard snippets here and there about wedding clothes. Despite the prince's lack of interest, they still hoped for a marriage.

What woman wishes for any of this? At that moment, I had an epiphany. My jaw dropped when I realized all around me were such horrid representatives of human behavior it was no wonder I abhorred the thought of men and the prospect of love. How could I long for something if the only examples I had were so ugly? So close to eighteen and to have such a negative view of something that was supposed to be pure and wonderful. It was depressing.

I had no hope of marriage or love, no expectations I would even be allowed such privileges. But the unfairness of it struck me harder than anticipated. For months a thought gnawed at me, something I couldn't name, a feeling I didn't understand. But as I stood silent amid the chaos of an Elejick family celebration, I discovered one more freedom stripped away: the ability to feel love and to be loved in return.

For days I tried to reconcile my depressing thoughts, to come to terms with the sad reality of being a servant devoid of free will. But no matter what platitudes I used to soothe myself, my dark mood persisted. Finally, I realized I could not vanquish my inner turmoil alone. There was one way I could think of to turn my perception around. My stomach churned imagining the consequences, but I needed another perspective. No one in the castle could help me but Risteard, and it took several more days until I had the courage to face him with a most unusual proposition.

Late in the evening, long after the princess was asleep, I knew Risteard would be using the last glow of a fire to read in his study. Before I lost my nerve, I opened the door, making no attempt to be silent. Even if I crept in on tiptoe, he would know I was there--the curse of an ever-vigilant knight. He sat in front of the hearth, embers twinkling in the dwindling firelight. He didn't stir, but I had no doubt he was listening. My mouth opened to speak, but the words caught in my throat. I closed my eyes and inhaled, trying to calm my nerves. I chastised myself for being such a coward. This was ridiculous. There was no reason to be so hesitant. Here was Risteard sitting in front of me, my friend of almost three years. We talked all the time. Why was this any different?

"Can I ask you something?" my voice trembled slightly, but I couldn't understand why. I rubbed my hands together that were inexplicably cold despite the warmth of the room.

"Of course," he said without looking up from his book.

I took another steadying breath. "Remember when you told me about the difference between what happens in the Trophy Room and how things are when people are in love?" The words came out in a rush, and he finally looked at me, though his eyes were concealed in darkness.

"I remember." He set his book aside and straightened.

"The only...affection...I've seen between men and women repulsed me. Every kind gesture hides some terrible secret or dishonesty. And that day with the prince..." My voice drifted away, and Risteard rose to stand over me protectively. "It's all right," I assured him, my hand outstretched. "Please, I need to get this out." I couldn't look up, afraid that if I saw his expression and tried to decipher his reactions I would falter and lose my nerve. "It's just...what if I never feel the desire to...kiss someone? What if I'm not capable of falling in love because of what I've seen and experienced? I don't even know if I'd want to."

"I can't answer those questions for you, but it would be a travesty to allow those poor examples to taint your views." His voice was soft, different than I'd ever heard it, but I still couldn't make eye contact.

"But it *is* tainted," I argued. "All I know of these things I've learned from my life here, and it's sick and harsh and remorseless." Tears welled in my eyes, but I kept them from falling. "I have nothing good to compare it to. How can I want something I've never experienced?"

Unexpectedly, Risteard reached out and ran a hand down the side of my cheek, cupped my chin, and lifted my face so our eyes could finally meet.

"What do you want me to do?"

He watched me, his expression patient and kind, but his words held a strange undertone and his chest rose and fell quickly. If I lost my resolve now, I would be too embarrassed to try again. I swallowed, gathering my courage, ignored the tightening of my throat, and forced the words past my quivering lips.

"I want you to kiss me," I whispered. Then more confidently I added, "Nicely. Please."

Eyes normally cerulean blue turned black. I held my breath, waiting for a response, worried I had crossed a line.

"Are you sure?"

"Yes." I answered quickly before I changed my mind. I trusted Risteard. I knew he wouldn't hurt me, and I knew he would stop if I asked. I needed this, to know for certain if all this kissing business was worth getting upset over. If nothing else, at least I would have this one instance of affection borne of friendship and not fear or lust.

He trailed his thumb along my bottom lip, and my eyes squeezed shut as I puckered in anticipation, demonstrating my complete lack of experience in this situation. He chuckled softly.

"Open your eyes," he commanded.

"Why?" I asked peeking out of one eye.

"How are you going to recognize a kindly kiss if you don't see it coming?"

I laughed and some of the tension drained from my body. Then he lowered his face to mine.

I'm not quite sure what I expected. To remain indifferent? To be repulsed? For nothing to change? One fact was certain: none of those things were true. Our lips touched, softly, barely making contact before he drew away, leaving me strangely bereft. He hovered inches from my face, breathing against my mouth. I opened my eyes, only then realizing they slipped shut. We looked at each other, unmoving, our breaths mixing in the silence between us.

"What do you want me to do?" The sound of his husky voice warmed my skin.

This time, there was no hesitation. "Don't stop."

Risteard's mouth crashed into mine, his lips tenderly moving against my skin. I blushed, saying I didn't know how to kiss him back.

"Whatever you want," he breathed. "If it feels good, it's right." My eyes slid shut again, and I abandoned all coherent thought and simply listened to my body.

His hands held my head steady, and I absorbed the feeling of his mouth exploring mine. His lips were firm yet gentle, the only discomfort the slight scratch of his beard on my chin. Without thinking, I bit into his lower lip, then ran my tongue along the indentations left by my teeth. A guttural sound I'd never heard before emanated from his throat, something between a growl and a purr. He wrapped his arms around my back and pulled me close while his tongue darted out against my lips. My mouth opened of its own accord and his tongue slid against mine, hot and wet and inviting. The last time I witnessed someone kiss like this, I nearly lost my stomach. But this was not like the sloppy mess I'd seen.

Risteard did not cram his tongue halfway down my throat or lick my face like a dog. His touch was tender, his tongue dancing against mine then retreating into his own mouth, leaving me wanting more until my tongue would seek *his* mouth, our movements complimenting each other. My hands moved up his chest and crossed behind his neck, pressing me fully against him. This was my first kiss, but my body responded as if it had been starving, deprived of something I had no idea it craved. A moan rang in my ears, and I was shocked to realize it came from me. The sound triggered a groan in my companion, and he continued to kiss me, revealing the true meaning of passion.

I broke the kiss, not because I was finished, but for lack of oxygen. While I caught my breath, Risteard trailed kisses along my jaw, down my neck, and across my collarbone. My head lolled to the side to give him access, my eyes remaining closed, reveling in the feel of his soft lips and tickling beard on my skin. His hands stroked upward, caressing my waist, but when they brushed against the sides of my breasts, my eyes flew open and I pushed him away, suddenly startled and unsure. He stood before me, breathing in short, ragged gasps.

"I wouldn't have gone further," he said.

"I know." I felt shy and looked away.

"Laria---"

"I have to go." I left the room without a second glance. He didn't follow, for which I was equal parts grateful and disappointed.

Later, while I lay in bed replaying the scene in my head, I realized that was the first time I'd ever heard him say my name.

CHAPTER 46

For weeks, I did not seek Risteard out, speak to him, or even look at him. To his credit, he acted completely normal and didn't pressure me into an unwanted confidence. I did everything I could to avoid him, and he didn't place himself in my path. He was absent from all social gatherings. I appreciated him giving me space, but I was a little disappointed he seemed unaffected by what happened.

There was no one to confide in and sort out this mess. Ula would be angry on principle. Risteard was the only other person I talked to, and he was obviously out of the question. I needed someone who would listen and offer advice. I needed my mother.

Though I saw her often in the queen's rooms, it wasn't easy to speak to her alone. A few times when we gathered for lunch, I placed myself near her, but she always avoided my attempts to draw her into conversation.

One evening the queen held a special reading at the request of the princess, probably spurred by the lack of engagement announcement. The queen asked my mother to prepare the herbs gathered earlier for the occasion, and when she left, I gestured I would assist her and followed.

My mother was arranging various dried plants in the queen's greenhouse when I found her. The air was thick with the scent of flowers and herbs used for both cooking and conjuring visions. Plants hung in clusters from the ceiling as they dried, and several pots were filled with flowering buds and plump green shoots. I stepped forward to help Mother tie a bunch of grey-green leaves together, but she pulled away and glared at me.

"What are you doing?" she whispered. "If they see us together, we'll be punished."

"Relax, Mother. We won't be gone long. I need to talk to you."

"Now? Laria, if you want to gossip, this isn't the time."

"No!" I hissed, slamming my hands down. "I need to *talk*. It's important." I held her gaze, and she relented.

"You have as long as it takes for me to finish." She busied herself with the herbs and with the same tone she'd use if she were asking me to pass the salt said, "Are you with child?"

"No!" I replied, a little too loudly. I lowered my voice. "Of course not."

"But it is about a man?"

"Yes." My voice quivered. "I've kissed a man."

"And?" she prompted.

"And I'm not sure what to do."

"Is kissing all that happened?"

"Yes."

"You're almost eighteen years old, Laria. This isn't something worth bothering about." She finished her task and prepared to leave.

"How did you know you wanted to marry Father?" I blurted out.

She froze and turned to look at me.

"Though I'm pleased you've changed your attitude toward men, marriage is not an option for you at present."

I didn't respond, and she sighed and placed the basket of herbs back on the table.

"What made you decide to marry him?" I repeated.

"You," she said bluntly. I was shocked into silence. "I knew Maccus would be a good provider and father to my children. He was already in the king's favor, so his position in society was ideal."

"Was he my father?" I asked, afraid of the answer.

"Of course, he was!" she exclaimed. "What do you take me for? Really, Laria. Your imagination is truly insufferable sometimes."

"Did you love my father?" I asked.

"In my own way." Her eyes misted as she remembered. "He was handsome and made me feel young and beautiful. I was faithful to your father for fifteen years. That's my definition of love."

I nodded and stared dejectedly at the floor. Her intensity softened when a tear trickled down my cheek.

"My dear girl." She brushed the tear away. "You've grown into a woman at last. I only wish we still lived in a world where you were free to be with this man. But you are not free, so you must forget him, and concentrate on staying alive."

"Yes, Mother," I whispered.

"Enough now. Collect yourself so we can go back inside without looking suspicious."

I shook my head and dried my eyes before returning to the queen's rooms to hear Princess Caelyn's inane questions and Her Majesty's vague answers. I tried to concentrate since the marriage affected me too, but my thoughts drifted to Mother and what she just confessed, to Risteard and his ardent kisses. I felt the heat rising in my face, and it required all my resolve to banish these thoughts from my head. We could not go on like this forever. If all went well, the prince would soon marry Miss Derville. We needed to work together to bring about change. We couldn't do what was necessary with this uncertainty and awkwardness hanging over our heads.

That night, I lay in bed rehearsing the speech I wanted to deliver to Risteard. I still couldn't name the feelings I was experiencing, but I did know I missed him, not as someone to talk to because I was lonely, but for himself. This last month had been awful being so near and yet so far away from him. I missed his companionship, the way he forced me to think, the way his hands turned pages in the candlelight. I missed the sound of his voice, its masculine timbre. He always seemed to know exactly what to say to cheer my mood, and when to say nothing at all. My entire life I had been independent, rarely seeking the company of others. Besides Ula, I never needed anyone. Now, lying in bed worried I had destroyed our friendship, I admitted I needed Risteard. I was willing to do anything to make amends and get back to where we were before I opened my big, stupid mouth. I only hoped I wasn't too late.

The eve of my eighteenth birthday dawned with me experiencing more trepidation than the first morning I awoke as a servant. My hands shook through my morning routine, spilling water all over the floor as I washed my face. I tripped on my way to the kitchens and skinned my knee, and I pulled the princess's hair brushing out the tangles.

"What's wrong with you?" The princess rubbed her head. "Be careful or I'll rip *your* hair out!" She would be in for a surprise. I'd wrapped my head in a thick scarf since Lady Sharp cut off my hair, and the fabric gave the illusion I still had waves of ginger hair beneath it. I bowed low in apology. By the time I stuck a pin in her and pulled her corset too tight, she was eager to be rid of me.

"Go see to your chores and if you know what's good for you, you won't be so absentminded when you return," she said.

With the cessation of rain, the ground became drier, and dust plumed around me as I plodded toward the mews. I still hadn't settled on what I was going to say when I confronted Risteard, but I had to decide soon. The uncertainty was tortuous. Each mew I cleaned was occupied by an eagle I subjected to my musings, and I practiced on a few to hear the words out loud. None seemed impressed.

"Who asked you anyway?" I snarled at one eagle that defecated at the conclusion of my speech.

I was still mumbling about the uppity birds when I opened the door to Aquila's mew and discovered it was empty. I set the rake against the wall and steadied myself against the door frame. If she was gone, I knew where Risteard was, and there was no more avoiding him. My limbs were heavy when I shuffled out of the mew toward the stand of trees. Beyond them, Risteard would be flying Aquila at the cliffside, and there would be no escaping the overdue conversation.

Each step through the trees, my hands shook harder and my knees grew weaker. He had to know I was coming because between my clumsy steps and harsh breathing, I was loud enough to wake the dead. Yet as I broke through the trees, he stood with his back turned, not bothering to face me while I walked toward him. Aquila's feathers puffed out and she called to me, but still he did not move nor speak. My heart fell to realize how horrible of a mistake I had made.

"I came to apologize," I said, my voice small and hoarse. "I placed you in an awkward position, and that wasn't fair. I shouldn't have asked you to indulge my curiosity. I knew you would do anything I asked of you, and I took advantage of our friendship, and for that I'm truly sorry. Can you forgive me?" I hated the pleading tone, but if I had to beg on my knees I would have.

He turned around, a puzzled expression on his face, and I almost didn't recognize him. His face appeared thinner, drawn, tired. Perhaps the last month had been just as miserable for him as it had for me.

"You're asking *me* to forgive *you*?"

"Uh...yes. Please, Risteard. Your friendship means everything to me, and I couldn't bear it if I ruined it."

His expression was unreadable, not the blank face he usually wore, but something different. He looked pained, and I couldn't imagine what to say to fix the distance between us.

"I cannot forgive you," he said and held up his hand when I opened my mouth to protest. "You've done nothing that warrants forgiveness. You asked for a favor in good faith, and if there was any pain that resulted, then the fault is mine." His voice broke on the last word, and he brushed past me back toward the mews.

I chased after him, worried there was still a breech needing to be mended. He returned Aquila to her cage, then turned to me, and my breath caught at the look of defeat on his face.

"Go back to your work." He turned away.

"Wait," I insisted. "Please. Tell me I haven't lost your friendship."

He stared at me for several seconds, weighing his next words, then nodded to himself, resolved in whatever he was preparing to tell me.

"If friendship is what you want of me, then I promise you will always have it. But I have to confess I no longer wish for you to be my friend."

My mouth fell open, and I learned the shattering meaning of the term 'heartbroken.' I was so devastated I almost missed his next words.

"I want you to be my wife."

I had prepared to argue, but the words froze in my throat. I blinked and shook my head, thinking I misheard him.

"What?" I asked.

"Will you marry me, Laria?"

The sound of my name from his lips stirred something deep in my belly, and I felt dizzy. I pressed my hand to my forehead and gazed up at Risteard in disbelief.

"You want to marry me? Why?"

A short laugh erupted from him, though I didn't find the question very funny.

"Because I love you, impossible woman." He smiled now, the sunlight illuminating his blue eyes. The smile faded when I stared at him.

"You don't have to answer now," he said quietly.

"It wouldn't be fair to make you wait." I took a deep breath and watched his smile fade. I could tell he was trying to hide his disappointment.

"I never imagined something so simple as a kiss could change things so drastically," I began. "When we didn't speak afterward, it was because I was so embarrassed about making a fool out of myself, and then I was afraid to talk to you because I thought I'd lost you. You have become one of the most important people in my life and I couldn't handle it if something I'd done so impulsively changed that. I was so absorbed in the aftermath I barely gave a thought to the kiss itself."

He looked away, his expression blank.

"Or...to the fact I wanted you to do it again."

He looked up, startled.

"I've never hidden the fact that I haven't wanted the same things other women want, and I suppose in a way that's still true. But I also never expected to be standing before a man telling me he loves me and believing him because he knows me better than anyone, and yet he's still brave enough to make such a confession."

Risteard listened in complete stillness, his only movement the steady rise and fall of his chest.

I stared back, remembering something Ula once said. "If you want to know the honest answer to a question, ask yourself out loud and then whatever comes into your head immediately afterward is the truth." Right now, Risteard was asking the question, and in that one brilliant moment, everything became clear.

"Yes," I exhaled, feeling a smile form on my lips.

"What?"

"I believe you asked me a question. My answer is *yes*." Before I finished speaking, I was in his arms. He held me tightly, lifting me off the ground, and I laughed when he spun me around. Still held aloft, I pulled away, pressed my forehead to his, and watched a lone tear trickle down his cheek. I'd never seen him cry, and I was nearly undone. But he was smiling, and my happiness reflected his.

"I love you, too," I said shyly, and if I thought his smile couldn't get any broader, I was wrong. He kissed me then, punctuating each touch of his lips with whispered affections. At last I felt whole, I felt like I belonged, and I felt like I had come home.

CHAPTER 47

We agreed to keep the engagement a secret, but we debated on waiting to marry until after the uprising. Risteard told me there was no rush, and when I was ready, I could name the date. I knew his assurances were purely for my benefit, and I appreciated his delicacy. I met his statement with a firm resolution of my own.

"You'd better be prepared," I said. "I intend for us to marry as soon as I have a dress." This obviously pleased him, and I immediately ventured into the workroom to speak to Ula.

We'd been engaged several hours, and the euphoria was on par with the elation I felt galloping over the valley on Amore. If I was being honest, nothing ever made me so happy. I wished there was a word that could properly describe the emotions running through my veins, but the only one that kept coming to mind was that tiny adjective--happy. I tried to smother the smile on my face, but the corners of my mouth curved upward despite my efforts. The glee accompanied me as I raced through the workroom, heedless of the dressmaker's shouting.

"Watch what you're doin'!" she yelled as I ran toward Ula's corner. "Mind the fabrics! Nothing the princess wants is that urgent!"

I ignored her, my eyes on Ula.

"Laria?" she asked. "What's going on?" I pushed her into the corner and looked around to make sure no one was listening.

"What's got into you?" she whispered.

"Ula, I need you to make me a dress," I said, the silly grin plastered to my face.

"A dress," she said suspiciously. "Another simple frock, or is the princess finally going to allow you a wardrobe fit for a lady-in-waiting?"

"Neither. I need something special." Excitement had me bouncing on the balls of my feet.

"What's the occasion?"

"A wedding."

"Has the prince finally proposed?" she gasped. "We've heard rumors, but nothing for certain. Do you know when the wedding will take place?"

"No! It's not for the prince's wedding. It's for mine!" I waited for Ula's reaction, but she stared at me as if I'd grown antlers.

"I don't understand. Is this a joke?"

"No," I told her, annoyance seeping into my voice. "I need a wedding gown. I trust you to make it wonderful."

"You're getting married?"

"Yes, I am. The least you can do is believe me, Ula. Would I lie about something so important?"

"When did you get engaged?" she asked, her head tilted and brow furrowed.

"This morning," I beamed.

"Who is he?"

My smile faltered. "I can't tell you but trust me when I say you don't have to worry."

"Too late." Ula's lips pursed and one of her eyebrows arched, mimicking the way Mother looked at us when she suspected we were lying. Well, when *I* was telling falsehoods.

"Ula," I placed my hands on her shoulders. "I'm sorry I can't tell you, but I will in time. Please, can you make me a dress?"

"Do you love him?" Worry furrowed her brow.

"Yes," I breathed. I could hear the passion in my voice. This was enough to satisfy my tenderhearted sister. I hugged her, and we shared a giggle when she told me to hold out my arms so she could measure me. The scene was nearly perfect, as if we were normal women excited over wedding preparations and not servants stealing a special moment.

"How long do you think it will take?" I asked while Ula wrote down the last measurement.

"Are you in a hurry?" Ula asked, her eyes travelling to my stomach.

"Ula!" My hands flew to my belly. "It's not like that. Shame on you!"

"Sorry." She blushed furiously. "I didn't mean to imply that's why you're getting married."

"Well, it's not."

"But." Ula shifted shyly and would not look at me. "Have you...?"

I had to remember Ula was becoming a young woman, and unlike me blossomed early. Where I had been oblivious, she was curious about relations between men and women.

"No," I said, my color rising. "We've kissed. That's all."

"What's it like?"

"Not what I expected. It actually feels really nice." My face grew hotter, and Ula's eyes wider, but it was refreshing to be able to talk to my sister about something other than our miserable situation.

"When's the date?" she asked.

"We'll marry when the dress is finished."

"Then I'll work on it every chance I get and see my sister married before month's end."

For someone who abhorred public displays of affection, I had no qualms engaging in such activities myself. I thought of nothing but Risteard for the remainder of the day, and even the princess' dubious glare was not enough to erase my smile. She hated to see me happy, but I didn't care. She could drag me from the room, tie me to a post, and flog me again, and my spirits would not fall. I had not seen my betrothed since I left him to commission a dress from Ula, and I hoped to see him at the evening meal.

Princess Caelyn stood before her full-length mirror and inspected herself after I completed the task of preparing her for dinner. Her eyes drifted to my reflection behind her, and noticing my wistful expression, narrowed. Before I could react, she spun around and slapped me hard across the face, throwing me off balance. I fell to my hands and knees and gave her a questioning look.

"Wipe that smile off your face! What could you possibly have to be happy about?" she screamed. Her face was red, and I was truly fearful. I considered drawing my dagger, but I suspected if faced with a physical attack, it was better to bear it than risk losing it again. The princess was formidable, but she wasn't strong, and any beating delivered by her personally wouldn't be severe.

When no beating was forthcoming, I raised myself from the floor and resumed my duties. Unbeknownst to me, my scarf had gone askew when she struck me, and the new angle showed something was amiss with my once plentiful hair.

"What's this?" She wrenched the garment from my head. My short hair sent the princess into shock.

Once she had found her voice again she asked, "Did you do this?"

I shook my head, and she demanded to know who had. I couldn't tell her, and I tried to shrug it off as if it didn't matter. But the princess disagreed.

"As if it's not enough to be cursed with a lady-in-waiting with ginger hair, now she looks like a boy!" She threw the scarf at me and stalked away. I gathered the material and was about to wind it around my head, when the hurried footsteps of the princess drew my attention. I looked up just before a cane smashed the side of my face. I tasted blood, and the princess grabbed my hair and pulled my face up so I could read her lips.

"If you want to look like a boy, then you'll take a beating like one." She released me and proceeded to strike me with the pent-up frustration festering for months. I could have easily taken the weapon, but I endured the beating, knowing she would tire soon and leave me to pick myself up off the floor.

I heard a snap, and the cane broke in two across my back, signaling the end of the punishment. The princess tossed the remaining piece aside, exhausted. She looked at herself in the vanity, then commanded me to fix her hair since it had become undone during the 'unpleasantness.' I pushed myself off the floor and did as I was told.

"Fix yourself before accompanying me to dinner," she ordered. With a final flourish, she left the room, leaving me to make myself presentable.

My shoulders and upper back ached, but I didn't think anything was broken. I inspected my face and saw a bruise was already forming from my left temple to my cheek and I would most likely have a black eye. The blood came from my teeth cutting the inside of my lip, but none were loose or chipped. I applied some of the princess' powder, not for her sake, but for Risteard's. I feared if he saw what she had done, the princess' life would be in danger, and I didn't wish to see him hanged so soon after our betrothal.

I sought him out at dinner, but he was absent for most of the meal. When the final course was served, my stomach tingled, and I sensed I was being watched. I looked toward Risteard's usual spot, and there he was. To anyone else, he appeared his normal stoic self, staring placidly at his surroundings. But I knew better. His expression might be neutral, but his eyes burned with life. I turned away, fearing if I held his gaze any longer, I might burst into flames. A smile played at my mouth, but I bit down on the wound on my lip to suppress it. I kept my right side facing him for the remainder of dinner and rushed out with the princess when she retired with the ladies. I maintained my composure while she conversed with her friends late into the evening and incurred no more of her wrath.

"I'm glad to see you've learned your lesson," she said when I helped her into bed. "Make no mistake: you're here to serve, not to please yourself." She waved a hand toward the door. Before I left, I glared at her back. If you only knew, Princess, how much pleasure I hope to glean from this life.

I left her room imagining the look on her face if she found out about my engagement, when a voice from the shadows scared me out of my skin.

"You look quite pleased with yourself."

The low, seductive, voice sent a shiver down my spine. But it was not a trill of fear. I turned to Risteard, my chin raised, the devilish smile still playing at my lips.

"I just find myself incredibly hilarious," I said.

"Come to my study."

His tone brooked no opposition, and I followed without protest. My smile faded and concern took hold. Did something happen?

He opened the door to the study, and I hurried inside, but before I could ask what was wrong, his mouth covered mine, and I was swept up in the sensation of his desperate kiss. The pain of my wound was unnoticeable as our lips moved together, but I broke away so I could breathe and laughed when he continued to kiss and nuzzle my neck.

"Did you miss me?" My joviality disappeared when Risteard pressed a hand against my upper back, and I couldn't suppress the hiss of pain that escaped my lips.

"I'm sorry," Risteard said, pulling away.

"It's all right," I assured him, breathing through the pain.

"What's wrong?"

There was no sense in keeping the truth from him. We always prided ourselves on the honesty of our relationship, and now we were to be married, that honesty was more important than ever.

"The princess discovered my new hairstyle," I confessed before wiping off the powder and standing in the firelight. The bruise had blossomed and my face throbbed. Risteard touched the wound with the tips of his fingers, his expression murderous.

"Where else?" I pointed to my back, and he eased open my frock to look. My skin flushed with the forwardness of his actions. He released the fabric, laying his hand lightly against me, then he stalked toward the door.

"No!" I threw myself in front of him. I winced when my back pressed against the door, but I did not obey his command to step aside.

"She can't get away with that!"

"Yes, she can!" I signaled we should quiet our voices.

He stared at me angrily, and I guessed he was considering forcing me away from the door.

"Don't you dare," I warned in my most menacing voice.

"I can't just stand by and allow her to beat my wife!"

"We're not married yet," I said calmly.

His anger remained, but I sensed his temper fading.

"If she knew, you would be under my protection."

"You know we can't tell anyone," I said. "It would expose us to accusations of treachery. And they would be right."

I could see the war rage within him, between wanting to do what was right and doing what was smart. He sighed heavily and took several steps back. I pushed away from the door, unsure what form of comfort he might find acceptable. In the past, I would simply be present, but now everything inside me screamed to hold him. He didn't like to be touched, but with me he had been affectionate, and often offered physical comfort even in friendship. I decided to take the risk and pressed myself against his chest, wrapping my arms around him. My eyes squeezed shut as I laid my ear against his heart and listened to the slowing rhythm. His arms came around me, cradling me to avoid hurting my back.

"It won't be like this forever," I whispered.

He placed a kiss on the top of my head. I smiled and relaxed further into his embrace.

"Where were you all day?" I asked.

"I'll tell you tomorrow."

I could tell by his tone he was keeping something from me. I pulled away and looked up at him with one eyebrow raised. I was relieved to see he was smiling.

"Should I be worried?"

He answered my eyebrow with one of his own complete with a mischievous grin.

"You'll see. Tomorrow."

The next morning, so early not even the chickens were awake, Risteard woke me with a soft knocking at my door. If I didn't love him so much, I would have killed him. I opened the door after wrapping myself in my coat, my eyes mere slits, and peered up at his beaming face.

"No normal human being is that happy this early in the morning," I grumbled.

"Get dressed," he said. "Quickly."

I mumbled and closed the door in his face. I considered crawling back into bed, but he was persistent. I chose to dress as opposed to being dragged out in my nightgown. I reemerged, finishing wrapping my headscarf, and he nearly yanked my arm out of the socket when he grabbed my hand and pulled me through the castle.

"What's the hurry?"

He dragged me into the chill morning air.

"You wanted to know where I was yesterday?" He was still smiling like an idiot.

"Yes," I said cautiously.

He stopped so abruptly, I almost ran into him. "Close your eyes."

"Are you always this chipper in the morning? Because if you are, we're going to have a problem if we don't lay down some ground rules about waking me up too early."

"Close them," he said again.

Sighing, I complied. I felt his breath at my ear, and he whispered, "I promise when we're married, I'll let you sleep in as long as you wish," before leading me once more by the hand. I blushed violently and tried to concentrate on my footing to keep the ensuing thoughts from entering my brain.

"All right." He stopped me, took a deep breath, and said, "Open your eyes."

I eagerly obeyed and standing before me was the most beautiful dappled gray mare I had ever seen. She was tall, well-muscled, and her kind eyes were staring at me, her ears pricked forward. An elderly man held her lead rope, and I glanced at him nervously, then at Risteard.

"It's all right," he assured me. "Efram is loyal to my father. He can be trusted." I nodded, then turned my attention back to the horse. She bobbed her head and shook her mane, and I breathed in the sweet scent of her.

"I tried to find a mare like you had," Risteard said, filling the silence nervously. "But I didn't want you to think I was replacing her. I want you to make new memories with this horse."

"She's mine?" I whispered.

"If you'll have her," Risteard said. "Oh." He took the lead and presented it to me as he dropped to one knee. "I present you with a horse and a promise that I will not touch you unless I have your permission." I recalled a long-ago conversation when I said the only token of affection I would accept from a suitor would be a horse and a promise such as Risteard had just issued. I launched myself into his arms and hugged him fiercely.

"Stop being so generous," I whispered.

"Never," he whispered back. "You deserve every bit of it and more."

I looked away, suddenly shy and unable to speak. I absently brushed my fingers behind an ear as if my hair was still long enough to tame an errant strand, a faint smile playing along my lips. Avoiding Risteard's intense gaze, I walked over to my new horse and stroked her soft muzzle, then blew air into her nose so she would become familiar with my scent.

"Does she have a name?" I asked.

"You'll have to give her one."

I ran my hand down her forelock as I contemplated, my eyes locked with the soulful stare of the mare. In her eyes I saw memories of my childhood, and the chance to heal. Amore had died in flames and from her ashes rose rebellion. There was a chance *this* mare would carry me on a battlefield. Together, we could bring freedom to Praed.

"Promise," I said. "Her name is Promise."

"Do you wish to ride her, my lady?" the old man, Efram, asked.

I looked at the man in surprise. The title 'my lady' had not been directed at me in years. I smiled and nodded. He moved toward the stables for a saddle, but I stopped him.

"A leg up, if you please." He nodded in approval and assisted me onto the mare's back. I grabbed a handful of mane and looked down at Risteard.

"Thank you," I said to him, hoping he could see all the appreciation and love I felt.

"Happy birthday," he said.

I rode Promise down the mountain and across blooming wildflowers. Until Risteard had wished me a good day, I had completely forgotten today was my eighteenth birthday. As I moved with my new mare, I had hope for the year ahead, a feeling I had not experienced since I watched our stables burn to the ground.

A week after I turned eighteen, the engagement between Prince Brannon and Miss Mwiryn Derville was officially announced.
Two days later, King Conall became violently ill.

CHAPTER 48

Between the prince's engagement and the king's illness, Praed Castle was tossed into utter chaos. Whispers circulated about the coincidence of the events, a suspicion I shared. Rumors spread that the king had been secretly unwell for months, and he'd grown to suspect an attempt would be made on his life. The fear, it was whispered, had driven him mad. The king appeared well enough upon our return from Riverstone and every night since, but who knew what happened behind closed doors? Only the king's most trusted advisors, his physician, and his children were permitted access to the sick bed. The princess visited him in private several times and always emerged dabbing her eyes, but I suspected her concern was an act.

My suspicion of the princess' involvement was fueled by a meeting with the prince after it became clear the king wasn't experiencing an ordinary sickness.

The princess seethed the moment Prince Brannon entered her rooms. "You idiot! Why are you so intent on ruining everything?"

Prince Brannon folded his arms and said he didn't have to answer to her, that she may be a princess, but she was still his little sister. The sound of her slap was shocking, and I flinched. A red welt formed on his cheek in the silence that followed.

"I got tired of waiting," he snapped.

"You were tired?" She squeezed the words through clenched teeth. "*You* are the one who insisted on waiting to be married. *You* kept putting off an engagement. I've been waiting years for you to grow up and take some responsibility. And now we've finally taken a step forward, you've taken ten backward."

He thrust a finger at her. "This was *your* plan. I took the initiative to move forward. I thought it would please you."

She pinched the bridge of her nose. "It wasn't time yet. You were supposed to wait for Arlen and Crane to bend the council. We won't have enough support without them."

"I don't see a problem," the prince said. "We're both getting what we want. The difference is I'm actually doing something while you sit here and have your hair brushed."

"How dare you!" She grabbed a heavy glass vial from her vanity and threw it at him. It barely missed his head, and she screamed at him to get out.

"Like it or not, Caelyn, we're in this together." He slammed the door, shaking a portrait loose and crashing to the floor. The princess screamed in frustration and threw several more bottles, then demanded I clean the mess.

When I met Risteard in his study, I burst through the door and announced, "I think Prince Brannon has poisoned the king!" before Risteard had risen halfway out of his chair.

"What makes you think that?" He resumed his seat.

I sat across from him. "Don't *you* think so?"

"I have my suspicions, but no evidence."

"He fought with the princess this afternoon. She was furious, saying he was going to ruin everything."

"Did he admit to poisoning the king?"

"Well…" I hesitated. "Not in so many words, but it was implied."

"That's not enough," he sighed, clearly disappointed.

"It would be my word against theirs anyway," I said.

"Unfortunately."

"She mentioned her friends in the council again. Arlen and Crane?"

"They're careful, but they've commented on the king's health under the guise of genuine concern. Now that he's indisposed, they've openly cast doubt on Conall's ability to rule."

"Bold."

"I'd call it desperate. It sounds like they're being rushed by the prince's actions."

"Does the doctor suspect anything?"

"Certainly, but he has no proof either. The king's symptoms are so vague he's not sure what's causing his illness. If it wasn't for the duration, he would suspect a simple seasonal sickness."

"What sort of symptoms?"

"Headaches, vomiting, stomach pains, exhaustion--anyone might complain of these things. They could also be symptoms of poisoning, but so far the doctor hasn't been able to find a cause."

"Does the doctor think he'll survive?"

"The king has been relatively healthy until now. He has a good chance."

"Are the council members listening to Arlen and Crane?"

"They'll continue to support the king if he can overcome his delusions."

"What do you mean?"

He folded his hands and explained. "For the last several days, his anxiety has reached drastic proportions. He's convinced someone is trying to kill him, and he trusts no one, not even his own cook. He even employed a food taster."

I leaned back in my chair, shaking my head. "I heard he suffered from some form of lunacy or melancholia. But the princess didn't believe it and was so adamant I wasn't sure."

"She didn't know. He sequestered himself and wouldn't even speak to Brannon and Caelyn."

"How could Brannon poison the king if he wasn't allowed to see him?" I wondered aloud.

"He must have an accomplice in the kitchens."

"But the taster would have fallen ill. Has he?"

He shook his head. "He must have found another way."

I felt him watching me, and I racked my brain thinking of an explanation that placed the murder weapon in Prince Brannon's hands. I suppose I shouldn't sentence the king to death quite yet. Something was missing... I ran my hands through my hair and growled in frustration.

"There's no use driving yourself mad, my darling," he said. "We have to focus on what this means for us."

"If the king dies, we send for our people?"

"It would be prudent to alert them before that happens. Brannon insists on expediting his marriage to Miss Derville. The combination of a wedding and dying king is the perfect recipe for rebellion. The kingdom will be distracted, confused, and in mourning. We couldn't ask for a better opportunity."

I gathered paper and ink. Excitement throbbed through me as I readied my quill. "What should I say?" My heart was pounding, sweat broke out at my temples, and my face flushed in nervous excitement. For years I waited for this moment, for the day when I would avenge my family and secure my freedom. My hand trembled over the paper, waiting to unleash the words that would spark a revolution.

I met Risteard's eye across the desk, and it struck me how strange life can be. Three years ago, I never would have imagined the man who dragged me from my room would be helping me overthrow the king who commanded it, much less that I would soon be marrying him. Though he was looking at me, his thoughts were far away, contemplating our next move.

"It will take time for my supporters in Ilano to mobilize," he said. "I'll write that they should prepare to travel here, but I want you to wait. If the king recovers, there will still be a wedding, but our timeline will be pushed back. If you alert your people now, there's a chance either someone will talk or one of the king's spies will discover the plot. When the time comes to signal the Ilanos to move, that will be the best opportunity for you to do the same in Praed."

"Oh." My voice dripped with disappointment. I put the quill aside and stared at it, watching the ink drip from the nib.

Risteard rose and came around the desk to kneel before me.

"It's difficult to be patient when we're so close." He held my hands. "But with the king ill, Brannon has declared himself the Prince Regent and is acting in his stead. Conall's distrust is nothing to his. If he's truly involved in a plot to kill his father, Brannon will be watching the castle and everything that goes on closely. An influx of letters, no matter how carefully I arrange their sending, will certainly draw his suspicions. Furthermore..." He released my hands and stood, his head lowered. "I think it would be wise if we didn't meet quite so often."

"Why?" My voice was the barest of squeaks.

"Brannon no doubt has informants everywhere. If they notice you coming to my study, it will give him a reason to interrogate us because there is no reason for you to be here. It would be safer for you to remain near Caelyn and play the supportive lady-in-waiting as much as possible."

"I understand." It was true, but I didn't like it. He took my hand again and pressed a kiss to my palm. I laid it against his cheek and ran my fingers through his beard before withdrawing and walking to the door. He stepped in front of me to open it and paused with his hand poised on the handle. I stared at it, collecting myself as I waited. I had a vague recollection of being in this position before, a distant memory.

"It's because I love you so fiercely," he said.

I looked up. "What do you mean?"

"That's why we should be careful and not see each other so often. I don't think I can hide it much longer."

He continued to stare, and I watched his expression crumble and realized how difficult it was for him to maintain his usual composure. My lips parted and my breathing quickened, a response to the unabashed passion in his eyes as he looked at me.

"I understand." I tried to turn away, but his intense gaze held me in place. His face inched toward mine, then hesitated, twisting away in frustration.

"What's wrong?"

"We shouldn't."

"Why?"

"Because I'm afraid I won't be able to stop once we start."

"Oh," I smiled, pleased yet shy. I blushed and looked away.

He turned and struggled to regain his indifference. Before he was completely lost, I raised myself up on tiptoe and placed a quick kiss on his cheek, then pushed him away so I could open the door myself.

My steps echoed in the empty hallway, and I resisted the urge to look back. I feared if I did, I wouldn't be able to stop either.

Heeding Risteard's advice, I kept close to Princess Caelyn over the next several days. Prince Brannon indeed declared himself regent, ruling Praed while his father remained confined to his bed. The princess insisted on being present for council meetings. For the first time, I was privy to what happened behind the massive doors. The king's condition was always the opening topic, but soon the discussion focused on the business of running a country. I'd never cared about politics, but the last few years opened my mind. The council consisted of around forty men of varying age--diplomats, nobles, and knights. I learned about crimes requiring trials, crop yields, and the business of taxes. A new Lord Protector was appointed following the death of Jervell Kade, and judging by his letters, he was sadly unprepared. The Praed council therefore directed all Ilano policies. Because there was much for the council to do, meetings lasted hours. The prince's attention often wandered, but the princess took diligent notes. Later, I would read them hoping for clues, but they were detailed accounts of the issues with her own ideas on how to solve them. I admired her ambition, but most of her solutions involved violence.

I looked around the long table at the polished men. At first, I'd only recognized a few faces, but after several meetings, I could name half the council members. Only one man was Praedan, a concession the king made after the winter celebration. He never spoke and voted with the majority every time.

I closely watched Crane and Arlen, who Risteard pointed out was the tall man I'd seen the princess acknowledge months ago when she stormed into council to expose Prince Brannon's affair with Noraa. They sat far apart from her and each other. None of them so much as glanced at the others.

One day during council the prince announced his wedding would take place by month's end. This was met with silent stares, the council members uneasy such a decision would be made in the king's absence.

"With all due respect, Your Highness," one man spoke up. "Don't you think a wedding celebration at this time would be...inappropriate...considering the king's illness?"

"I do not," the prince said. "What better way to raise the people's spirits?"

"The king should be in attendance at the marriage of the prince," another pointed out. "How can this marriage take place without him?"

The questions were beginning to anger the prince noticeably. Surprisingly, he kept his temper in check.

"The king fares quite poorly," the prince said sourly. "It is also *his* spirits I wish to uplift. The doctor informs me his condition is extremely grave. A wedding will give him a reason to rally."

The men exchanged uneasy glances. Merely whispering about the possibility of the king passing could be considered treason. The prince had practically declared he was dying and the marriage would save him. It was a bold declaration, and I'm certain the men knew if they continued disallowing the prince his wedding, they were essentially denying the king's recovery. In essence, any man who spoke against the plan could be accused of wishing the king dead. It was a manipulative move. Surprising for a dunce-headed prince. I glanced at Risteard to gauge his reaction, but he remained impassive, staring ahead without meeting anyone's eyes.

The princess spoke up. "Though this is perhaps not the most ideal of circumstances for planning a wedding, Prince Brannon has a point that now may, in fact, be the best time. The king may need a reason yet to conquer this illness. If not for the Prince Regent, we should at least consider the proposal for the sake of His Majesty and the queen, who suffers greatly during this difficult time."

Well met, Princess, and very clever. The men looked uncomfortable, shifting in their seats and looking uneasily at each other.

"Risteard," a white-haired council member who had remained silent thus far asked. "What is your opinion?"

"*His* opinion?" the prince thundered. "*I* am your Prince Regent! It is my opinion and orders you follow. Not his!"

"With all due respect, Your Highness," the old man said calmly. "I wish to hear what the First Knight has to say."

"He is no longer the First Knight!" Prince Brannon pounded his fist on the table. "While the king is confined to bed, there is no First Knight!" Even Princess Caelyn stared at the prince, stunned at this outburst.

I swallowed, feeling my throat suddenly dry.

Risteard locked eyes with the prince. "As long as the king lives, there is a First Knight. And until I draw a last breath, that man will be me."

The prince paled, but his defiance remained.

"I trust we can count on your continued service should the worst happen?" the prince asked shakily.

"We all hope for the return of the king's health," Risteard said. "But should King Conall succumb, you can be assured I will serve whoever inherits the crown."

The prince relaxed, and I heard the princess exhale.

"To answer your question," Risteard addressed the old man. "I believe we should do whatever we can to bring King Conall comfort. If the prince feels his much-anticipated marriage is what the king requires to expedite his recovery, then who are we to deny him?"

"Well, there you have it, gentlemen," the old man said. "It appears there will be an Ilano wedding at Praed Castle."

The princess withdrew to her room to embroider, but the sewing lay abandoned in her lap, and her gaze focused blankly on the flickering firelight of the hearth. I worked clumsily on my own skills. Slowly, she turned her head and watched me try making the stitches small and neat, my tongue peeking out from between my lips. Wordlessly, she covered my hands with hers, then directed my fingers in the correct movement to make a neater stitch. Satisfied I would follow her directions, she pulled away.

"You embroider like a child," she said. "As if you always have better things to do."

Her introspective mood was unsettling, but there was no time to wonder. The door opened, and the prince came in, sat on the settee next to the princess, and watched the fire without speaking. She sat stiffly beside him, her back straight and her lips pursed, clearly still angry. The prince laid a hand lightly over hers where they rested, folded tightly in her lap.

"Thank you," the prince said. "I know we do not always agree, but we cannot lose sight of our goal." The princess relaxed, and the prince removed his hand.

"You cannot leave me in the dark," she said. "No more acting without consulting me. Promise?"

"I promise."

She eyed him askance.

"I won't!"

"When will the wedding take place?" she asked.

"I've pushed for the end of the week, but I'm told that's too soon."

"It is," she agreed. "Better to have at least a month or two to plan."

"Two months is too long."

"Any sooner will raise suspicions. Besides, we cannot possibly have an acceptable dress made for Mwiryn in less time."

The prince rolled his eyes and returned his attention to the fire.

"Fine."

"Mother is holding a special session so we may send our good thoughts out into the ether to help heal Father."

"Will you be attending?"

The princess' jaw dropped. "Of course. *Everyone* will. Including you if you have the slightest trace of intelligence."

"Because it will look suspicious if I don't?"

"Exactly. Be careful, Brannon. Now is not the time to act foolishly."

"Have you been to see Father lately?"

"Yes. He's gone mad, I think. When he's not complaining about his head, he's raving that someone has poisoned him."

His eyes shifted to the door while he fidgeted with the hem of his doublet. "Do you think he's said this to others?"

"So, what if he has? Who would believe his ravings?"

"I hope you're right, but what if someone does and they investigate?"

"What would they find?" she asked pointedly.

"Nothing."

"Then there's no need to worry, is there?"

"I have some reservations about Risteard." The hairs on the back of my neck stood up and my skin broke out in gooseflesh. With great trepidation, I leaned closer to catch every word about my betrothed.

"Risteard is the least of our problems," the princess assured him. "You heard him. He will remain loyal to the crown regardless of who wears it."

"But what if that person is me? You know he's always hated me."

"If anyone can put aside their personal feelings in order to serve the greater good, it's our cousin. He's dutiful to a fault. And he would not tarnish his father's name by denouncing your claim to the throne."

"Perhaps, but he still makes me nervous."

"Don't do anything stupid," she warned. "It would certainly draw suspicion if the First Knight suddenly fell ill so soon after the king."

The pounding in my heart faltered and my breath caught in my throat. I bristled at the casual way they discussed poisoning Risteard.

"I will do nothing now, but we need to consider the threat he poses in the future," the prince said.

"I agree Risteard is a threat to us and our plans," the princess conceded. "But we will need his protection in the coming months. Once he is no longer useful, we will revisit this discussion. But we must be careful. He has the support of many Ilano nobles, and if something happens to him, we'll lose them. And he may not be the brightest of knights, but he is very strong, and you are not."

I held back a secretive smile. The prince and princess still underestimated Risteard and this would be their downfall.

"Very well, dear sister," the prince sighed.

"I will see you at Mother's session?" the princess inquired.

"Yes, yes, of course," the prince waved over his shoulder as he left.

She took up her embroidery. "He better not do anything stupid," the princess muttered to herself.

Such an act would not be in *his* best interest, but it would serve mine splendidly.

The Queen's Royal Rooms were crowded with well-wishers dabbing at their eyes and wringing their hands concerned over the health of the king. The scents of incense and pungent herbs permeated the room. There were too many people to form the usual circle like they did in the morning session, so they sat on the floor like children waiting to hear a story. The princess sat in the front, ever the anxious daughter, and next to her sat Prince Brannon, trying to squeeze a single tear from his eye.

"The king suffers," the queen began, "But my children have also the burden of watching their father toil in this sickness. For all their sakes, we gather here to send our positive thoughts to that invisible realm surrounding us so that they may heal our beloved king and soothe his children." She lowered her head, and the attendants mimicked her actions.

I looked around at their bowed heads, wondering how many wished the king well and how many had simply shown up for the spectacle.

"Dear King Conall," the queen called out. "Our strong and fair leader. You have brought us wealth and prosperity and with your mighty army extended our kingdom so that we may fulfill your vision of a great empire. This illness has brought you low, but you are a fighter. Feel our energy so that you may make it your own and defeat this foe."

The queen continued to name off King Conall's virtues as reasons why he shouldn't die, and my attention wandered to Mother sitting calmly behind the queen. She stared vacantly ahead, and I wondered about her life since leaving Riverstone. I knew nothing of her day-to-day routine as the queen's attendant, but she appeared thinner and older every time I saw her. I resented that she never made any attempt to speak to me, and that she had become angry and irrational. I convinced myself she had given up, that she accepted her fate. But the last time I spoke to her, I caught a glimpse of the mother I had known, and I realized her complacency was a form of self-preservation. I became a deaf-mute to hide who I really was, while Mother became a vacant shell. I hoped when this was over, she would find herself again and become the woman I once knew. And needed.

Mother looked up and met my eye. We regarded each other silently, our expressions neutral, and I remembered what Risteard had said about not being able to hide his feelings for me. Perhaps this explained why Mother avoided me--so no one would see how much she loved me and how helpless she felt being unable to express it. No doubt she also felt a great deal of frustration over her inability to do anything about our current situation.

Don't worry, Mother, I am taking care of us.

A flicker of a smile and softening of her features flashed across her face, as if my thoughts had been sent to my mother's ears. Just as quickly her expression returned to indifference, and she looked away. This time, I did not feel resentment or anger. At last, I felt I understood my mother and hoped I would fulfill my promise and make her proud.

With the blessing of the royal council, wedding preparations began immediately. Invitations were sent to honored guests, and I wondered how many were also to receive a summons of a different sort from Risteard. The princess took charge of the menu and decorations, and I was constantly delivering messages to the cook and sending for several merchants who specialized in banners, flowers, candle making, and script writing. In Ilano, I learned, the marriage proceedings were recorded in a book read to future generations describing the splendor, the vows, and the ceremony in detail complete with illustrations. It was a beautiful idea, but also another excuse to run me completely ragged in a struggle to find someone in Praed worthy enough for such a task. Miss Derville, though excited with all the activity, had very little to do with the planning at the princess' insistence.

"Your job is to look beautiful," the princess told her when Miss Derville expressed interest in helping. "Leave everything else to me and don't stress yourself."

She sent for the dressmaker and Ula to take Miss Derville's measurements, and the five of us were gathered in the princess' rooms one afternoon for the important task. Ula was carefully taking notes while the dressmaker called out the inches of Miss Derville's bust, waist, arms, and thighs while the lady stood awkwardly in a simple shift. The princess had a long list of demands for the dress itself from the length of the sleeves to the color to the type of fabric.

The princess sighed. "How long will this take?"

"The measurin' or the sewin'?"

"The dress of course," the princess sneered, glaring at the older woman through narrowed eyes.

"Your Highness has ordered a very fancy gown. It could take months," the dressmaker said. Ula scribbled down the woman's instructions.

"Months!" the princess said.

"If the lady wishes for somethin' else, we may be able to move up that time."

"It doesn't have to be so elaborate, Caelyn," Miss Derville said. "It's only a dress."

"A woman only wears a wedding dress once," the princess argued. "I want you to look perfect. You will make the dress I described," the princess ordered. "And you will have it completed in one month. I don't care if your girls must work day and night. This is for the prince's bride after all."

The dressmaker's face reddened, but she held her tongue and bowed her head. She nodded towards the door, and Ula hurried behind. I rushed to open the door for them, earning me a stern nod in thanks from the dressmaker and a brief squeeze of the hand from Ula. Before I could give her a glare, I felt the contours of a small piece of paper. I glanced at the princess, but she was cinching Miss Derville into her dress and prattling on about flowers. I opened the note and read Ula's secret message:

Come tonight. I have something for you.

I crumpled the paper in my trembling hands, casually walked to the hearth, and fed another log into the flames. I bent down to adjust the embers with the fire iron and tossed the note in the flames. The edges of the paper curled as they were set ablaze, and I did not look away until it was reduced to ashes. Behind me, the princess discussed the selection of meats for the wedding feast including venison, goose, and roasted boar. Miss Derville voiced a desire for broiled fish from the Rhyvor as a nod to Praed culture.

"I don't know why you bother," the princess muttered.

"There will be Praed nobles there," Miss Derville reasoned. "I want them to feel I'm their princess, too."

I admired her consideration, but the princess was less than impressed.

"That's very thoughtful of you, Mwiryn, but the point of conquering these people is to convert them to our ways, not live in harmony with them."

"Perhaps if we treat them with respect," Miss Derville said boldly, "they'll be less resistant to change." She and the princess regarded each other silently, one angry and the other impassive. My eyes darted from one to the other.

"Very well," the princess said coldly. She scratched out a note and placed it in my hand for the cooks. I required no further incentive to leave, a smile threatening to break free in celebration of Miss Derville's triumph.

CHAPTER 49

Every creak of the floor set my nerves on edge when I crept down the hallway to the top of the stairs leading to the workroom. In the back of my mind, I thought about Prince Brannon's suspicions and worried he had spies lurking at every turn. I took several steps, stopped, listened, and made sure I wasn't followed before braving another step. This resulted in an excruciatingly long journey, and by the time I started down the stone staircase, I hoped Ula hadn't given up on me.

The workroom was dark, and I walked with hands outstretched to keep from running into tables and chairs. I maneuvered around the room, calling out quietly for Ula, and feeling with every passing moment that I was too late. Suddenly, I saw a light in the farthest corner of the room, and Ula's face appeared. I moved quicker with the aid of the meager candlelight.

"Ula!" I threw my arms around her.

"I was worried you couldn't get away."

"I was being careful so I wouldn't be followed."

"Were you?" she asked, her eyes wide.

"Not that I'm aware of, but you can't be too careful these days." I grinned. "You said you had something for me?"

She smiled and pulled out a form covered in a plain canvas sheet from the corner of her workspace. She laid a hand upon it and told me to close my eyes. I heard the flutter of fabric, then she instructed me to look. I opened my eyes and gasped.

The gown was pure white, crafted in soft linen across the form-fitting bodice intricately decorated in delicate flowers embroidered to resemble the wildflowers that surrounded Riverstone. Straps mimicking petals ran up the shoulders and crossed in the back. A gap between the sleeves and straps exposed bare skin. The long fabric of the sleeves was translucent and parted just above the wrist to billow in waves to the ground. Below the corseted waist, the dress plumed outward slightly in several layers. She explained as the dress moved, the train resembled the flow of water, like the Rhyvor. Carefully, I rubbed a piece of fabric between my fingers and enjoyed the feel of the softness next to my skin.

"I don't know what to say," I finally said, my voice thick with emotion. "How did you finish it so fast?"

"I'll only work day and night for the princess if she orders it," Ula said. "But for you, I did it gladly."

"Oh, Ula." Tears filled my eyes. I hugged her again and told her I didn't deserve to have her as a sister.

"Don't be silly, Laria. You've been the best sister anyone could hope for. It's the least I can do to repay you for everything you've done for me. I only wish I could see you marry in it."

"Me, too," I said.

"Will you try it on for me?"

"Of course!" I released her and pulled off my frock, taking my scarf with it. Ula gasped at the sight of my hair.

"Don't ask," I said. She helped me into the gown, tightened the laces, and stepped back to get a good look at me. I stood before her, self-conscious while she studied me.

"You look so beautiful I could cry," she said.

I covered my chest. "I feel a little naked with all this skin exposed."

"At last you've developed a figure to fit into it," she teased. I gave her a good-natured poke and wished I had a mirror to see myself in.

"You'll just have to take my word for it. You're absolutely stunning."

"You're making me blush," I said. "I should take it off now. It's late."

She helped me out of the dress, folded it, and wrapped it in a bundle.

I clutched it to my chest and grinned so broadly my face ached. "Thank you again, Ula. It's wonderful."

"I want to know every detail of the wedding."

"I promise." It was difficult to leave her after such a moment. We rarely had a chance to be alone, and with all the current drama, who knew when we would see each other again.

With that thought in mind, I hurried back and hugged her tightly, then left the workroom before she could see me cry.

The next evening, I dared exposure once more to venture to Risteard's study. Once again, I inched slowly along the wall, stopping every few feet to listen. I felt ridiculous and probably looked like an idiot, but I made it to Risteard's door positive I wasn't followed. The barest flicker of light could be seen under the door, and I knocked softly before stepping inside.

We had not spoken privately in weeks, since the day Risteard said our clandestine meetings must end. He stood behind his desk, his eyes betraying the exhaustion he struggled to hide. I kept to my side, the expanse of the desk keeping us apart. For several seconds we stood silently, both content to be together once again.

"I have two things to tell you," I said.

"Go on," he said in that impassive tone I missed dreadfully.

"You were right about the prince," I said, trying to match his indifference. "He's dangerous. I don't believe you have to fear him now, but he may make an attempt on your life in the future."

"Has he said those exact words?"

"He said he doesn't trust you and considers you a threat to his plans. The princess convinced him to spare you. For now."

"I'm not surprised Brannon harbors a wish to be rid of me."

I knew he spoke so coldly in order to maintain his composure, but it still stung to be standing before the man I loved and hear him converse so dispassionately.

"What else?" he prompted.

I felt rushed, like he was trying to be rid of me. Despite the way he spoke, I couldn't help the tiny smile that crept along my mouth.

"I know you've been very busy, but I hope you can spare a thought or two for us. I have a dress. So, when it's most convenient, you may name the date of our wedding."

Risteard's expression softened, and I finally glimpsed the side of him I so cherished, the side that was mine. He nodded, a slight smile on his lips. Satisfied, I turned to leave.

"Wait," he said.

I looked back. He came around the desk, took my hand, and placed upon it a tender kiss. I pressed my forehead against his and inhaled his masculine scent. I wanted to kiss him, but I resisted, and finally dragged myself away.

I lay awake with a mixture of anticipation and fear trilling in my chest. I never pictured myself as a wife, and I wondered if I was ready. Everything was happening so quickly, and though that was my choice, I worried I'd made a mistake rushing into the marriage. I did not regret saying *yes* to Risteard. I loved him and wanted to marry him. But the timing felt wrong. So much was happening in the castle between the king's illness and Prince Brannon's wedding. How could we possibly hope to get away with this? On the other hand, it was probably the best time to elope. Who would notice if I disappeared for the night provided I was back to attend the princess in the morning?

I closed my eyes and took several cleansing breaths to steady my galloping pulse. I saw Risteard's face in my mind and imagined looking up at him while wearing that beautiful white dress tucked safely away in my little chest. Did I want to wait to see the look in his eyes when he saw me in it for the first time? I knew he would if I asked, but did I *want* to? The answer came to me immediately, like the last time I asked myself such an important question: no. I wanted to marry Risteard almost as much as I wanted to see the fall of King Conall, and I didn't want to wait. I fell into a deep sleep, my dreams no longer filled with the sounds of dying horses and crackling flames. Now, I dream of riding a gray horse, of the impending summer, and a flowing white gown.

Princess Caelyn's incessant planning and arduous tasks that had to be performed to her demanding specifications completely exhausted Miss Derville. The strain showed. She no longer sat with the perfect posture I admired but slumped forward. Her hair was styled elaborately but was no longer lustrous, and several strands blew free. I felt sorry for the poor woman. She had always been kind and deserved to revel in the excitement of her impending wedding, even though she was marrying a monster. If the princess really cared about her friend, she wouldn't put her through this turmoil.

One evening when the ladies were gathered after dinner, Miss Derville listened attentively while the princess discussed the wedding breakfast. Guests were already arriving, some I recognized from the princess' birthday two years prior. Each had opinions about color schemes and the fabrics for her dress.

"Lace is the most desirable trim for a wedding gown," Miss Sonisa Murchad interjected. I remembered her as dry, emotionless, and practical. She hadn't changed.

The princess sneered. "Yes, it is--if you want to be perfectly gauche. No one uses lace on wedding gowns anymore, Sonisa."

Listening to their arguments made me grateful to be eloping.

After leaving Riverstone, Lord and Lady Sharp returned to Ilano at his Lordship's insistence because he could no longer stand the "rugged savageness" of Praed. Her Ladyship was dispatched and asked to return once the wedding date was decided. Now she sat among the ladies, sans husband.

"Now, ladies, can't you see your bickering is exhausting the bride?" Lady Sharp said. "She needs to be glowing for her special day!" She petted Miss Derville as if she were a cat.

"It's very sweet of everyone to give advice," Miss Derville said, "but it would be nice to talk about something else for a while."

"What would you like to discuss?" the princess asked. "The menu? Decorations? I've sent for an Ilano illustrator for your wedding tome."

"I mean I would like to talk about something other than the wedding. I would love to hear how you've been since we last spoke, Sonisa." Miss Derville looked at the surprised lady, hoping to divert attention from herself. The princess crossed her arms and pouted.

"There really is not much to tell," Miss Murchad said. "Father has begun entering into negotiations for my hand---"

The princess snorted.

Miss Murchad lazily rubbed the side of her nose. "He expects me to be comfortably settled by next spring."

"How romantic," Lady Sharp muttered before taking another bite of sweet cakes.

The gentlemen joined us then, much to the relief of the ladies who wore expressions of painful boredom at any topic other than Miss Derville's impending nuptials.

Risteard was among them. He rarely participated in the ritual after-dinner fraternizing with the men, and it was even more unusual to see him with the ladies. He found such gatherings to be tedious. He either wanted to keep an eye on the prince or the prince didn't trust Risteard out of his sight.

I kept myself from stealing glances at my betrothed. Mostly. I was rather proud of myself for keeping my feelings in check and maintaining a passive expression, even when I caught him staring at me from across the room. We did not speak, and every moment was torture.

Miss Derville retired early, claiming a headache, no doubt brought on by these ladies and their nonsense. After Miss Derville left, the motivation to continue the conversation went with her, and the ladies turned their minds to idle gossip while the men drank glass after glass of port.

I was carrying a tray of empty glasses when I felt something against my foot and I stumbled, sending the tray clattering to the floor. I landed on a rug, preventing the glasses from shattering.

"Clumsy fool!" the princess shouted. The roomful of people paused and stared at me. The princess stalked over and lifted my chin. "Watch what you're doing, or you'll be spending the night in the dungeon. I won't have you breaking dishes at Miss Derville's wedding. Clean up this mess immediately." She pushed me aside, and out of the corner of my eye, Lady Sharp hid a quick smile behind her hand. She tripped me. A flush of anger flared up my neck.

A hand covered mine when I reached for a glass, and I looked up into Risteard's stern face. His expression revealed he was also struggling to control his temper. I took a deep breath and let it out slowly, hoping he would mimic my actions. Reluctantly, he relaxed the tension in his face and huffed. I found my eyes drifting to his mouth and my lips parted. His eyes darkened again, and I almost forgot we were in a room full of people.

I busied myself with cleaning up the mess to hide the blush that spread over my cheeks. Risteard assisted me while I held the tray, and as he placed the last glass upon it, he locked eyes and held my gaze, then he dropped a folded piece of paper inside the glass. I turned away and heard Lady Sharp comment on how charitable Risteard was helping the poor servant girl.

I brought the dishes to the sideboard for the housekeeper to remove and struggled to regain some composure before removing Risteard's note. A quick glance confirmed everyone had lost interest. My hands shook when I read the short missive.

Study. Tonight.

How I would be able to function the rest of the night I didn't know, but the task was made easier when I turned and saw Risteard was gone. I'd have gone mad if I'd had to pass the evening pretending I was not waiting anxiously to run off and meet him. I might have slipped a sleeping draught into Her Highness' goblet, but the last thing the castle needed was another poisoner.

The princess finally indicated she was ready for bed, and I had to press my hands together to hide the trembling. Lady Sharp rose with her, and I bit my tongue to keep from screaming.

"Have you considered the honeymoon?" Lady Sharp said.

Princess Caelyn reared back as if to dodge a blow, and my arms flew out to catch her. She pushed me away and said, "I beg your pardon?"

"Mwiryn's honeymoon? It would be nice if they could go to Ilano, but I don't suppose it's the best time to travel."

The princess shook her head and started walking to her room. "No. No."

I almost felt bad for finding her discomfort amusing. Almost.

"She deserves a beautiful night," Lady Sharp continued. "A break from the castle, time to themselves. What every new bride wants."

"Uh huh."

"She can't conceive a son if she isn't relaxed."

The princess turned away and covered her mouth. Lady Sharp rambled on, unaware of the effect of her words.

"I have the perfect idea. Why don't we bring Ilano to Praed?"

"What?" The princess' voice was weak, but I could hear her confusion.

If they turned around, they would see my mouth frozen open as I silently asked the same question.

Lady Sharp's smile widened and she pushed the princess' door open.

"You sit. I'll talk."

While I prepared the princess for bed, Lady Sharp unleashed a flood of words detailing her plans. I had a headache by the time she finished.

The princess rubbed her temples. "You've thought about this a lot."

"I've found the perfect place. A friend of Lord Sharp's has agreed to put his estate at our disposal. An Ilano noble with an Ilano cook and Ilano servants. How wonderful would it be to be attended by proper ladies in waiting." She paused, and she and the princess looked at me disdainfully.

I guess that means I'm not invited.

"I thought we could prepare it as a surprise," Lady Sharp continued, "but wouldn't it be wonderful if we took Mwiryn away for a few days *before* the wedding? She's so tired, and her complexion will never recover if she doesn't get some rest."

The princess exhaled loudly through her nose and her fingernails dug into the vanity. I stilled, gripping the hairbrush, afraid she was about to explode.

"I think that's an inspired idea," she said.

My limbs went numb and I nearly dropped the brush. Lady Sharp clapped excitedly.

"We'll settle everything tomorrow. Mwiryn will be so happy!" Lady Sharp swept out of the room while I watched the princess' downturned face in the mirror.

"I'll make sure of it," she whispered. She shook her head and waved me away. I watched her climb into bed and hide under the covers before slipping out of the room and rushing to Risteard's study.

I threw open the door without knocking, halting Risteard before the hearth.

"Sorry," I gasped, catching my breath. "I thought she would never go to sleep." I stilled under the intensity of his stare. His eyes were dark, the flames dancing over the contours of his jaw, his hand gripping the mantle. I swallowed and wrung my hands.

"What's wrong?" I whispered.

He released a breath, lowered his gaze, and said, "Nothing." His voice was strained, weakening my limbs as worry spread through me.

"Liar." I tried to smile, but I lacked the strength.

"The king is worse," he said.

I trembled. "I don't know what to say to that. I hate him, but there's this tug at my heart that feels suspiciously like pity."

The corner of his mouth curved. "You can't deny your compassion."

"I don't want it to be known that I have feelings."

He looked at me, his smile reaching his eyes. "I won't tell."

In unison, we stepped toward each other. We paused, waiting. Then we stepped closer again, and I laughed.

"What happens now?" I asked.

"We take another step closer and try not to get too carried away," he said.

I blushed. "I meant about the king."

"The doctor made a list of ingredients he needs to make a special medicine. He won't say what it's for, but I suspect he knows what's ailing the king and is keeping quiet in case he's wrong." He reached inside his doublet, pulled out a piece of paper, and handed it to me.

I ran my finger down the list of plants and--*gulp*--animal parts, pointing out where the ones I recognized could be found. I got to the end and paused.

I tapped my finger on the gibberish words. "What language is this?"

"Ancient Ilano. It's the language of the scholars. It's only used by diplomats now."

"What does it mean?"

"Roughly translated, it means 'hinged-shelled water meat.'"

I raised an eyebrow dubiously. "All right. Creative." I looked back at the list, wrinkling my nose. "I've never seen anything like that in the Rhyvor."

"I've never heard of them either, so I asked the doctor. He said they can be found along coastlines." He strode to his desk and shuffled some papers, then waved me over.

I looked down at a map of Praed, simply drawn, with estate names circled. Risteard had been keeping track of our allies.

He pointed to the edge of the Sessyl Forest where it met the Temar Sea. "This seems the most promising place to look."

I chewed at my bottom lip. I'd grown up hearing stories about the cursed Sessyl Forest. Though my family had never been superstitious, they warned Ula and me to stay away, citing hundreds of years of tumultuous history. I rubbed my arms and shivered.

"Did you volunteer or did Prince Brannon order it to get you out of the way?"

"A little of both." He met my gaze and his eyes narrowed. "What are you afraid of?"

"The forest isn't safe."

"How do you mean?"

I sighed and sat down. "When Praed was young, people from the east settled in the forest. They were called the Sessyl Mystics. Mother didn't tell me much about them, but I think they had similar beliefs to Queen Shaeli. At first, they were considered harmless. They even sold their wares in Market Town. But when people started dying from a mysterious illness, the Mystics were blamed." I glanced at the map, then covered the forest with my hand. "The people were scared. A third of the population died in a short amount of time. The king ordered the Mystics burned out and then outlawed religious teachings. Since then, every attempt at settling the area failed, even the establishment of a port."

"I thought you didn't believe in superstitious nonsense?"

I glared at him. "I don't. I even disobeyed Mother and sneaked into the forest with Ula. It seemed perfectly normal--trees, flowers, grass, birds chirping. But it didn't *feel* normal. It felt...heavy. It was hard to breathe, like something pressed against my chest, and even when I stole a breath, the air was too thin. Ula said she felt like we were being watched. I haven't been there since."

"Well, I'll have to risk the ire of vengeful spirits. I'll probably be gone for a few days."

My heart sank, but then I remembered Lady Sharp's plan.

"Lady Sharp and the princess are planning on taking Miss Derville on a holiday. I gathered the princess won't require my services. If we're lucky, I'll be left alone at the same time you leave on your errand." I watched Risteard's face as the words sunk in, and I could practically hear him formulating a plan.

"Once Brannon hears of this, he'll push them to leave right away for his own reprieve." He placed his hand over mine. "I'll arrange everything. Be ready to leave when I send for you."

I beamed, feeling my stomach flutter. Then my smile faltered when a thought occurred to me.

"Did--were--are you planning on me going to the Sessyl Forest with you?"

He smiled, his eyes mischievous, and I pursed my lips. I shook my head. He nodded. I crossed my arms and glared. He placed his hands on his hips and arched an eyebrow, a challenge.

"Fine," I huffed. I wasn't thrilled about the prospect of slogging through a creepy forest, but if it meant being able to marry him, I'd take the trade.

I pinched my nose to block out the disgusting odor wafting out of the Trophy Room. The princess and I stood in the doorway, her arms folded and her chin raised as she surveyed the mess.

"I'll enjoy not seeing you behind my shoulder, especially now." The princess paused to focus on my head. "But I can't have you wallowing in leisure while I'm gone. In addition to cleaning the mews, I've decided this room could use a good...tidying up." She smiled smugly.

I looked around the room, dismayed. The rugs were soiled, dust covered every surface, and cobwebs draped from the stuffed animals. Clothes were scattered across settees and a few articles hung from armor. Servants passed behind us without stopping. Every sensible human being avoided this room. Sweat broke out on my brow and I felt queasy. I gave her a pleading look, but she shook her head.

"I suggest washing your hands thoroughly when you're done," she said. She sniffed and strode away.

My eyes traveled from the ceiling, along the walls, and across the floor. This was a massive undertaking that could take days, days I didn't have. I fell against the doorway and slid to the floor, burying my head in my hands. The ladies were leaving tomorrow and would return by week's end. That left little time for Risteard and I to marry and travel to and from the western coast of the Temar Sea. The princess assigned a task that would take forever to complete, and she knew it. I pounded my fists on the floor and clenched my teeth to keep from screaming.

A hand touched my shoulder, startling me so violently I slammed my head into the doorframe.

It was Ailis' mother. I'd seen her in passing, but since her daughter's death, she'd kept her eyes lowered and didn't speak.

"Sorry to scare you," she said, smiling gently. "I couldn't help overhearing." She glanced into the Trophy Room and her nostrils flared. "It's horrible the way she treats you."

I squeezed her hand and smiled feebly, shrugging my shoulders as if to say it doesn't matter.

"We'll help you," she said, gesturing behind her. I looked down the hall and saw two servants lingering in the shadows. "We'll start tonight and you can join us as soon as she leaves. We'll have this room…" She searched for the word with a wave of her hand. "Habitable. In no time. I'd hate for you to spend the whole time she's gone in this filth."

I smiled, placed a hand over my heart, and nodded in thanks.

"For Ailis," she said. "For everything you did for her."

Eight hours. Eight hours of scrubbing, wiping, and sweeping. Eight hours and multiple buckets of water, loads of garbage, and soiled rags. Even after Ailis' mother, Edde, and the other servants worked well into the night, it still took us eight hours to clean the Trophy Room. When we were finished, I wouldn't call it habitable, but it didn't smell as bad.

I scrubbed my hands until they were raw, dumped the dirty water, and then scrubbed again. I dug grime out from under my fingernails and tried not to guess what it was. I swallowed bile every time I thought about the mysterious stains, the sticky residues, and discarded clothing. We threw them all away, knowing we'd never find the owners.

Edde met me in the kitchens and the cook presented me with a delicious meat pie for supper. I listened to their gossip while I ate. No one liked King Conall, but the prince and princess weren't exactly favorites, either. There was general relief at having the princess and her friends out of the castle for a few days.

"I got a few extra winks of sleep this morning since I didn't have to make Her Highness' special breakfast," the cook said. "Just some simple vittles for the road and safe journey." She chuckled and chewed on a piece of jerky.

Upstairs, Princess Caelyn was working to gather supporters, but downstairs, the odds were in *my* favor. If I listened long enough, how many more secrets could I learn? When the princess was in the castle, I was attached to her like a dog on a leash. Now that she was leaving, I was given a chance to roam unchained.

"If the prince spent more time makin' sure the fields of Praed were tended rather than his own, we wouldn't be paying double for half full sacks." The cook punctuated her rant with the rhythmic pounding of a wooden spoon.

I chewed thoughtfully, barely tasting the food. If something wasn't done about Prince Brannon, Praed might starve. But what *could* be done?

I was sopping up the last of the juices with a piece of bread when a footman came in. He leaned over and whispered in the cook's ear. She pointed at me, and I froze.

"Make sure you keep eye contact," the cook said. "She's deaf, so she has to read your lips."

The footman brought his face so close to mine I had to lean back.

"Your presence is required in the princess' room. It seems you left it untidy when she left this morning," the footman said loudly.

"Deaf means she can't hear, you dolt! And now *we* can't, either," the cook said.

The footman blushed. "Apologies." His eyes darted to me, and I dutifully rose and followed him out.

I stalked down the halls, nails digging into my palms, face heated. Princess Caelyn's room had been perfectly orderly when she left, but she was devious enough to have someone come in and make a mess just to spite me. I threw open the door, the *bang* reverberating in the empty room, and paced around. I slowed, then stopped. I turned in a circle. Nothing was out of place. The bed was made, the vanity orderly, and the hearth clean. I looked closer, opening drawers and peering under furniture. Nothing amiss. I wandered over to the vanity. The hairbrush was slightly askew.

Well, call the council and put me on trial.

I straightened the brush and revealed the corner of a piece of paper. I slid it out and opened the folded note.

Stables. Now.

Two simple words, yet they meant my whole life was about to change. I ran to my room, retrieved the wrapped bundle from my chest, pulled on my coat and boots, and then dashed to the stables. I was wary of every snapping twig and rustling branch. The front of the building was illuminated by the soft light of the afternoon, revealing a figure pacing back and forth. I moved close enough to verify it was Risteard. I called out, and he looked up mid-stride. I stepped out of the bushes and saw our horses were already saddled.

Risteard pulled me into his strong embrace. "We have to hurry. They're waiting."

"Who's waiting?" I asked. I tied my bundle to the saddle and mounted Promise. "Where are we going?"

"You'll see when we get there."

I asked no more questions, and Risteard took off at a gallop down the mountain. We journeyed further, past the marketplace and village, past small farms, and past a few of the remaining valley estates. The pale dusk lingered in the sky to light our way. We rode for hours, stopping only once to rest the horses when the sun finally dipped below the horizon. I didn't ask where we were going. I would have known even if it was pitch dark.

Riverstone.

CHAPTER 50

It was obvious we were expected when we arrived at the front entrance. Every window was alight, and a groom stepped forward to take our horses. I dismounted nervously, clutching the precious bundle. The princess had been the hostess the last few times we were here. Yes, many of the original servants were still employed, but I thought the steward was one of her people.

Risteard took my hand to lead me inside.

I hesitated. "What are we doing here? We'll be caught."

"No. These are your people," he said.

"Not all of them! What about the steward? What's his name...Eugen?"

"He's one of mine."

"How can you be sure?"

"Who do you think brought him here?" I blinked and stepped back. Risteard was certainly full of surprises.

I allowed him to lead me inside, and when the doors opened, Riverstone once again became the welcoming, warm house it used to be.

The entrance hall was bright and warm, and the smell of freshly baked bread filled my nose. My shoulders relaxed and warmth bloomed in my chest. The princess' banners were gone, replaced by those of Risteard's family as well as my own. I placed a hand over my heart and stared at the Audrey crest, a sword flanked by a horse on one side and a circle of fish on the other, until the edges blurred.

Eugen stepped forward, bowed, and welcomed us back to Riverstone.

"I hope you will find everything suitable to your specifications, Sir Risteard," he said.

I reluctantly turned away from the banners, but the faces of the servants were out of focus. From behind him, an older woman inched toward us. I squinted, but her features remained fuzzy. I rubbed my eyes. Finally, she could no longer contain herself, and she rushed forward with her arms outstretched.

"Laria!" she called out, and the instant I heard her distinctive voice, I knew who it was.

"Morgan!" I cried. We embraced, tears tracing the lines of her face.

"I never thought I'd see you again!" she exclaimed between sobs. She pulled away and inspected me from head to toe. "You've grown into such a lady! I always told your mother you would eventually. 'Just be patient,' I told her. 'Laria always does things her own way.' And now look at you." She caressed my face and smiled fondly. Her gaze shifted to the man standing silently behind me, and her expression hardened. "I suppose you're the groom."

"Yes." I pulled Risteard forward and introduced them. "Morgan has been with my family for years."

"Nigh on twenty years," she said. She wrapped an arm around me possessively. "I've known this girl since the day she was born, and since her father, rest his soul, nor her mother could be here today, I suppose I'm the closest to family she has." She scanned Risteard from head to foot with a critical eye. "So...that being said, it's my duty to determine whether you're a fit match for a Lady of Riverstone."

"It's a little late for that, Morgan," I said.

She shot me a narrow glare. "How late?"

My gaze darted to Risteard, then lowered as flames spread over my face. "Not that late."

"I know I'm a stranger to you," Risteard said. "But I have earned Laria's trust and affections. I promise I will endeavor to deserve her."

"Well said, I suppose," Morgan said. "So, as you're a knight you can offer her protection?"

"Yes."

"And comfort? I know she's been living as a servant these three years, but that was not the life she was born to. Can you give her that?"

"Yes."

"A man of few words." She whispered to me, "I like that."

This was the closest to her approval Risteard could hope for.

"Well then, come on young lady. Let's make you a bride." She smiled and linked her arm with mine. I glanced over my shoulder at Risteard. Eugen stood beside him, smiling.

"You should ready yourself as well, sir," the butler said.

Risteard's voice cut through the bustle of servants. "Everything is in order?"

"Everything as you said, sir. No need to trouble yourself. Go on now. We don't want to keep the lady waiting." I smiled at the easy manner of the butler as he spoke to my taciturn knight.

Morgan led me to my mother's rooms, still decorated in the lavish style of the princess. My gaze travelled across the space, pausing to remember objects that once filled it. I shuddered, hugged myself, and meandered around the room. I ran my fingers along the mantle. Mother displayed portraits of family there, but now it was empty. I wandered into the bedchamber, trailing a hand over the new furniture and resisting the urge to knock the Ilano trinkets onto the floor. I picked up a perfume bottle and inhaled the scent. The odor hit me like a bouquet of flowers being shoved up my nose. I drew back, trying to shake off the aroma, huffing through my nose. I gripped the bottle in my shaking hand, ready to throw it. Liquid sloshed onto the floor, soaking the rug. I lowered my hand and allowed the rest of the perfume to spill. My shoulders sagged, and I dropped the bottle. Morgan was kind enough to allow me a moment to reflect, but her patience waned like it always did when she tried to wait out my daydreaming.

"Come on, Laria, let's get you out of those clothes. A hot bath's drawn, and it should be perfect now." Morgan stripped off the thin layers I wore, pursing her lips at the state of my garb, but she graciously held her tongue. When all that remained was my thin shift, she led me to the enormous copper tub the princess herself bathed in numerous times. I dipped my fingers into the water and inhaled the steam that carried the subtle aroma of wildflowers and mint. The temperature was perfect.

"Hurry up then," she urged, and before I could stop her, she pulled the scarf off my head and gasped. Her hands flew to her mouth.

I ducked my head under my arms. "Don't ask me what happened," I pleaded.

"It's not much to work with." She wiped an eye. "But we'll manage something. In you go." She helped me pull my shift over my head, and then I lowered myself into my first hot bath in years. I laid my head back, closed my eyes, and let the soreness and tension drain from my body.

"I wish you had more time to loll about in there, but we've got things to do!" Morgan said as she scrubbed my body. "You certainly developed a fine figure," she noted, more to herself than to me. "Who would have thought it?"

She soaped what remained of my hair.

"Morgan? May I ask you something?"

"You can. Hopefully it's a question I can answer."

"There's no one else I can really talk to." My voice wavered, and I cleared my throat to cover my nervousness.

"I suspect not," she paused briefly and studied my downturned face. When I lacked the courage to continue, she prompted, "Is this about tonight? After the ceremony?" I nodded and heat flushed over my skin. She finished washing my body and then held a towel out for me to step into. Once my skin was dry, she produced clean underclothes and motioned for me to sit down at the vanity.

"I suppose you know the basics?" she asked.

I nodded, and she brushed out my hair, puckering her lips as she studied the short strands.

"Well, what else do you want to know?"

"Does it hurt?" I asked quietly.

"It can, to be honest with you, but not for long." She saw my wide-eyed expression in the mirror and sighed. "Laria, I do wish your mother were here, but I feel if she were, she would tell you to do your duty as a wife and not complain. And it would anger me because that's not how she felt at all. She adored your father, and they were mad for each other. I suppose it's a mother's duty not to tell her daughter how wonderful lovemaking can be. At least until *after* she's married." She winked, and I relaxed slightly. "If your husband is a decent man, the pain will be minimal, and it's only the first time. Some women bleed, but not very much."

"I don't know what to do," I whispered.

"Women have been doing this for hundreds of years, Laria. It's in your blood. Your body will help you."

"Morgan?"

"Yes?" She became distracted while weaving tiny plaits in my short hair.

"What you said downstairs, about being the closest I have to family? Well, since Mother isn't here, will you walk me down the aisle and present me to Risteard?" She stopped. She chewed on her bottom lip and her nose turned red. I worried she was about to cry, but she contained her tears.

"Do you love this man, Laria?"

My throat tightened and went dry. I rubbed my chest, trying to relieve the sudden ache.

"He is the other half of my soul," I said.

"Then I will. I wish she was here to do the honors, but I will happily stand in her stead. I only wish your father were here to perform the ceremony."

We lapsed into a comfortable silence while she styled my shorn locks into intricate braids that crossed the top of my head and joined a tangle of twisted strands in the back. She then placed fresh wildflowers within the knots and braids, turning my hair into the valley in summer. The fragrance of the flowers took me back to my childhood and memories of Amore. I choked back my memories and commanded myself to put those events where they belong, in the past. This was the time to make new memories with Promise, the gray mare, and my soon-to-be husband.

Morgan stepped back to examine her finished work. "Now," she said. "Let's see the dress!"

I grinned, bounced over to the bundle, and unfolded the beautiful gown. Morgan gasped and ran her fingers reverently over the embroidered flowers.

"Ula made it," I told her.

Morgan gave a knowing look. "She's always been an amazing talent."

I stepped into the dress, and she cinched me up tightly, leaving just enough room for the wedding feast.

"Are you ready?"

She turned me around slowly, and I stared at my reflection in a full-length mirror, stunned at the woman looking back.

"Is that me?" I whispered.

"You're a vision," Morgan said.

"Can you hold something for me?" I reached into the bundle.

"Anything for the bride."

I placed a gift for Risteard in her hands, and she stared at it for several seconds without speaking. I reached up to tug on a strand of hair, but my fingers grabbed empty air. Her eyes misted over, and she tucked the trinket into a pocket. Then she squeezed my shoulders, turned me toward the door, and ushered me into my future.

There was no question it was Risteard who had designated the library as the place we would exchange our vows. Historically, marriages at Riverstone were conducted outside or in the picture gallery. The library held special meaning for us both, and it touched my heart that this is where we would be joined as husband and wife.

I stood outside with Morgan, clutching her arm while we waited to be summoned. I shuffled my feet and shifted restlessly until Eugen poked his head out and asked if I was ready. I nodded enthusiastically and he opened the door wide. Had it not been for Morgan's steady hand and sure steps, I probably would have tripped and fallen on my face.

Bookcases towered on either side of us, flanked with floor candelabras directing our path to the enormous stone fireplace. All the servants stood to witness, their faces bright with excitement. A roaring fire further illuminated the room and standing before it was Efram, the older man who had presented Promise to me. To his left stood Risteard, dressed handsomely in a black doublet, tall black boots, a black half cloak, and a chain of office with his family's crest on a pendant. His sword was sheathed in its scabbard at his hip, and I pictured a dagger hidden in his boot. He looked at me so tenderly it took my breath away.

We walked up to him, and Morgan paused, giving Risteard a stern look.

"Sir," she said. "I present to you a Lady of Riverstone. Do you promise to safeguard her from harm, support her in her endeavors, and bring honor to her family name?"

"I do," he answered. Morgan nodded, kissed my cheek, and placed my hands in his.

I smiled up at Risteard, and he squeezed my hands. Efram spoke about the tradition of marriage, the reasons men and women decided to form alliances, and other platitudes I did not hear. In that room, there was only Risteard and me, and that was enough.

"Risteard Elejick of the Black Eagle," Efram intoned. "Will you take this woman, Laria Audrey of Riverstone as your wife? To cherish her in faithfulness and love until you draw your last breath?"

"I will," Risteard answered.

"And do you, Laria Audrey of Riverstone, take Risteard Elejick of the Black Eagle into your household as your husband? To honor his name in support and love until you draw your last breath?"

I wanted to make a joke. The fact I didn't is evidence of my growth as a human being.

"I will," I said.

Efram passed something to Risteard, and he placed a silver ring on the third finger of my left hand.

"Laria," he said. "I give you this ring as a symbol of my unending devotion to you. It will connect me to your heart and show the world we belong together."

Weddings in Praed generally did not involve the exchange of rings during the ceremony. It was a beautiful gesture, but it left me feeling awkward.

"Sorry, I don't have one for you. But I do have something else." I waved Morgan forward. "I planned on giving this to you later, but now seems appropriate." Morgan handed me the small trinket I made for a wedding present.

I revealed a carefully woven bracelet finished with leather and tied it around his wrist. "It's braided from my hair and the hair from your gelding's tail." He inspected the bracelet and the copper strands glimmered among the black of the horse tail.

"You don't have to wear it after today if you don't want to," I whispered.

"On the contrary," he whispered back. "I don't intend to go a day without it."

Efram continued. "You have both taken a vow which cannot be broken. And like a letter, your vow must be sealed, not just with words, but by your first kiss as husband and wife."

Risteard required no further prompting. The instant the words left Efram's mouth, I was in his arms, and he was kissing me with all the passion restrained over the past weeks. Applause and cheers rose from the servants gathered around us, but I barely heard them over the rush of blood in my ears. I pressed my forehead against his, my body lifted off the ground by his strong embrace. There was nothing we could do but grin at one another, and exchange brief kisses. He lowered me to the ground, trailed his fingers along my cheek, and ran his thumb over my bottom lip.

"Come on, come on, then!" Morgan's voice broke the spell. "The kitchen worked hard to make a magnificent feast, and it would be a shame for it to go to waste."

I laughed, and Risteard intertwined his fingers with mine and led me from the library. I entered the dining room no longer Laria Audrey, but as Laria Elejick, bearing the name shared by my greatest enemy and my greatest love.

The cook had indeed arranged a delicious feast complete with all my favorite dishes of fresh fruit, bread, mare's milk cheese, fish from the Rhyvor, and the tiny, clawed creatures that only come out at night and taste amazing with butter. The last stores of my father's equi was served alongside kumis and mint water. Musicians played all the traditional Praed songs, and I enjoyed watching the servants dance and feast with us. It was easier to break a yearling to saddle than it was to get Risteard to dance, but a few glasses of equi proved sufficient encouragement.

"I don't know any of the steps," he argued when I tugged at his arm.

"That's all right, I'm terrible at them! It'll make everyone laugh," I said, my cheeks bright from the excitement and kumis.

"I don't like to be laughed at," he said sourly.

"You should have thought of that before you married me." I pulled the best serious face I could muster. A corner of his mouth turned upward, and I knew I had him.

We danced horrifically, him because he didn't know the steps and me because I had no rhythm, but we enjoyed every minute of it.

I gave no thought to the hour, but Morgan was conscious of how late it had become. She tapped me on the shoulder and informed me it was time to turn in for the night before I collapsed. Faced with the prospect of the marriage bed, I was rendered instantly sober. She led me away from Risteard, but not before whispering for him to wait a few minutes. I blushed from my scalp to my chest and didn't have the courage to look him in the eye before going upstairs.

To my surprise, Morgan did not lead me back to Mother's rooms. We climbed to the third floor and entered my old room. I recalled how it appeared when Lady Sharp stayed there, the gaudy colors and the tapestries with scenes of Ilano, the bookcases empty. Now, the walls were nearly bare, but candlelight flickered from the stones jutting out of the walls. Books filled the once empty cases, and the bed was tastefully adorned. The vanity was still there, and over the back of the chair was the nightgown I brought, another of Ula's creations.

"It's beautiful," I breathed. Morgan sat me at the vanity and removed pins and flowers from my hair. She loosened my stays and helped me out of my dress before pulling the nightgown over my head.

"There now," she said and patted my cheek like she did when I was a child.

"Thank you for all of this, Morgan." I hugged her, relishing the warmth of familiarity. A soft knocking ended the embrace, and we looked toward the door.

"Enjoy this night, Laria," she said. "There's no need to be nervous. I think he might like you."

I stifled a laugh when she winked, then she opened the door.

"Sir," Morgan said respectfully as she curtseyed. Risteard bowed, stepped aside, and Morgan left without a second glance.

I stood in my nightgown fidgeting when Risteard came into the room and softly closed the door. My thoughts were a jumbled mess of ridiculousness I could not turn off. What if I made a mistake? What if my body didn't please him? What if I wasn't good enough?

"You don't have to be nervous," he said, misinterpreting my restlessness. "If you would prefer…" he faltered, and I shook my head.

"I'm not nervous," I assured him. "It's just…I don't want to disappoint you."

"You could never disappoint me. It's *me* who should ensure *you're* not disappointed."

He hadn't moved since coming into the room, and I felt an overwhelming ache over the distance between us. I rushed into his arms. Our lips met in a frenzy of kisses. His hands roamed over my back, along my waist, and the top of my backside. My fingers tangled in his hair then travelled to his chest, shakily unlacing his doublet. When it was loose enough, Risteard paused briefly to pull it over his head followed closely by his undertunic, and I was given my first glimpse of his naked torso. My hands roamed over the expanse of muscle across his upper chest and shoulders, noting several scars and a sparse covering of dark hair. While I explored, he busied himself kissing down my neck and I felt his tongue lap at the base of my throat. My breaths were shallow, and I moaned softly, which seemed to increase his fervor. A hand moved up my side and he ran his finger along the neckline, stopping at the laces, tiny scraps of fabric that meant the difference between fully clothed and laid bare. He looked into my eyes, silently asking permission. Wordlessly, I pulled the laces loose, and with the barest shrug, the thin material slipped down to pool at my feet. His eyes flickered intently over my body, and I suddenly felt self-conscious. Before I could cover myself, his finger resumed its wanderings, tracing my collarbone and gently running down between my breasts.

"So beautiful," he murmured. I was in his arms again, our kisses full of love and promise. Effortlessly, he scooped me into the air and carried me to the bed, gently laying me amid the soft coverings. I didn't feel afraid or nervous. I felt cherished.

That night, I learned an important lesson. Morgan was right. Lovemaking was in my blood.

CHAPTER 51

Mornings were never easy for me, but none were more difficult to face than the dawn of my first day as a wife. The sun was low in the sky, and warm rays filtered through the windows. I lay content, wrapped in a downy comforter with my head on a soft pillow. A strong arm was draped protectively across my stomach, pressing me against a warm body. My eyes opened briefly, but I squeezed them shut against the glare and rubbed them with my fingertips. The movement disturbed Risteard, who shifted in sleep and pulled me closer. His warm breath caressed my ear as he brushed kisses along the side of my face. I sighed and stretched languidly.

"Good morning," Risteard said in a heavy, sleep-laden voice.

"It isn't morning yet," I groaned and buried my face in the pillow.

Risteard chuckled. "Come on. We have a long way to go and need to get back before Caelyn is forced to brush her own hair."

I rolled over to look up into Risteard's face gazing down at me with adoration. I traced the line of his jaw, his soft beard tickling my fingertips.

"You married me," I whispered, smiling.

"I did." He covered my body with his and kissed me, hard and urgently. I wrapped my arms around him, grasping his muscled shoulders, and returned his kiss with equal fervor. My skin tingled with every touch of his hands in my hair and on my face. Lower and lower along the length of my body to my thigh. The heat from his body set me aflame, a burn that couldn't be cooled by the sweat trickling down my skin. He kissed me deeper as his hand slid up my thigh and cupped the back of my knee, lifting my leg. My breathing quickened and my stomach fluttered in anticipation.

A soft knocking interrupted. Risteard growled.

"Cover your ears," he told me. He yelled at the unfortunate soul on the other side of the door, "What is it?"

If my ears hadn't been covered, I would have been rendered deaf.

"I beg your pardon, sir, but you told me to wake you should you still be abed at this hour."

I recognized the voice as Eugen's. Risteard sighed in resignation.

"Thank you. We'll be down shortly."

"Very good, sir." Eugen's footsteps retreated, and Risteard and I looked at each other with disappointment.

"How long will it take for them to prepare breakfast?" I trailed a finger through Risteard's chest hair.

"Not long enough."

Catching him off guard, I threw him off me onto his back and sat astride him.

"What sort of knight doesn't enjoy a challenge?" I claimed his mouth with mine. For someone who was so worried about the time, he put up no resistance.

I nearly drove my fist into the wall when the knocking sounded again. This time it was me who yelled, "What do you want?"

Morgan's stern voice spoke through the door. "My lady, it's time to dress."

I covered my mouth to stifle a giggle.

"You can't come in," I said with little composure. "Risteard's still in here, and he's quite indecent." I burst into laughter, falling against Risteard's chest. He wrapped his arms around me and laughed just as heartily.

Poor Morgan huffed and knocked even louder.

"My lady…" Her tone brooked no argument.

I recognized the tone from my childhood. That and Risteard's resigned expression signaled the end of my fun.

"One moment," I called out.

Risteard extricated himself from my embrace. I lay back against the pillows, disappointed that once we left this place, stark reality would return, and I worried we might not be able to recapture this moment.

Risteard dressed himself and resumed his taciturn knight expression. He noticed my morose disposition and knelt by the bed, taking my hands and kissing them gently.

I blinked away tears. "I don't want to leave."

"Nor do I. But we must."

I nodded. He pressed his forehead to mine and advised me to dress with haste so we could break our fast together before leaving. He marched to the door and opened it to Morgan looking particularly cross. He inclined his head and bid her to enter before closing the door behind him.

"Hurry up, then," Morgan ordered.

She lumbered toward the wash basin carrying a jug of hot water. I leapt from the bed to help her, and we poured the steaming liquid into the basin. She handed me a large washcloth and said, "This one is for your face and arms." She placed a smaller one next to the basin and told me it was for…private areas. I blushed fiercely.

"How are you feeling this morning, my dear?"

"Good." I pulled on my underclothes.

Morgan laid out the day's clothing on the bed. "Not so full of questions as you were last night it seems, hmm?" she cast a glance over her shoulder.

I chuckled. "All of my questions have been answered."

"I'm glad of it."

In typical Morgan fashion, she ensured I was not late to breakfast.

While Risteard ate like he'd been starving for three months, my plate sat virtually untouched. I'd remember I was supposed to eat, take a bite, then become lost in thought. After breakfast, we were supposed to travel through the Sessyl Forest, but as time ticked by, I wondered if my path led somewhere else. The thought of spending several days with Risteard alone filled me with shudders of pleasure, but what if someone noticed my long absence and reported it to the princess? Who was cleaning the mews while I was gone? I voiced my concerns, and Risteard spoke succinctly between bites.

"They won't. A friend," he said.

"How could no one notice?"

"Do you think they did before?"

"The servants did." I picked at my food, my fork squealing against the plate. I looked up when I realized he'd stopped eating. He stared at me for a few moments, then set down his fork and sat back.

"Go on," he said.

"I've been thinking." I took a deep breath. "That I should stay behind at the castle."

"They're just stories---"

"No." I slammed a fist against the table, rattling the dishes and startling the servants bustling about the room. "I'm not scared of the forest. I want to go with you." My voice cracked, and I swallowed a lump in my throat.

He rested his hand on mine and gently stroked my whitened knuckles. I relaxed and his grip tightened.

"If I stay in the castle without the princess watching me," I continued, "I could learn things from the servants. And as an unnoticed servant." I shot him a glare. "I could freely move about the castle and listen at doors. It's possible even the council members will let something slip."

I tugged the short hairs at the base of my neck while he considered the change in plans. He frowned at the table, shoulders sagged. I'd never seen him look so defeated. I opened my mouth, but I couldn't form words. I lowered my head and tried not to cry.

"You're right." His voice was barely a whisper.

I looked up, but he didn't.

"It's..." I took a shuddering breath. "It's not that I don't want to."

"I know. We don't have the luxury of our own holiday." He pushed away from the table and stood.

I rose slowly, wringing my hands. "I'm---"

He held up a hand to stop me, then extended it toward me. I took it, and he pulled me into his arms. My tension eased as I melted into his embrace.

"I'll take you back to the castle, then leave for the coast," he said.

"That's so much time out of your way."

"I'm not letting you go back by yourself. It's a long journey and could be dangerous, especially for a woman alone."

I snickered. "How chivalrous of you."

His hold tightened. "My motives have nothing to do with being a knight. You're my wife, and I won't lose you."

I smiled and nestled against his chest. But we didn't have time to linger in each other's arms. We soon parted, but the warmth didn't fade even when we climbed into our saddles. The servants were lined up outside to bid us goodbye like they used to when I was a girl. The cook passed Risteard a satchel of food for the journey, and Morgan stepped forward and beckoned me to lean close.

"Here," she whispered. She placed a small jar in my hand.

"What's it for?" I whispered back.

She gestured between my legs. "The parts that'll be sore later." She shook her head, her lips pursed, and rolled her eyes. "Riding all the way back to the castle. And you a newlywed."

I'm shocked the blush that spread over my face didn't set me on fire. I shoved the salve into a pocket and mumbled, "Thanks."

I took one last long look at the house, my gaze pausing at each stone, each window, and each face smiling up at me. Then I looked at Risteard. He raised an eyebrow, and I nodded. We kicked our horses forward and once again said goodbye to Riverstone.

The closer we came to Praed Castle the more my heart felt wrenched in two. Leaving Riverstone behind when it had become home again was devastating. The days ahead were going to be difficult, and in the aftermath of overthrowing King Conall, no one knew what sacrifices would be made. I did not wish to think of failure, but I wasn't a fool. If King Conall's forces successfully defended his rule, the punishment would be severe. Riverstone could be razed, and I could be hanged. And if Risteard survived the battle, he would be hanged alongside me. I looked back, keeping Riverstone in sight until it faded in the distance, hoping it wasn't the last time I'd see it.

My dark mood persisted when we reached the stables and handed our reins to a confused stable master. Risteard placed a sizable number of coins in his hand, and any questions he might have had were forgotten.

My gaze drifted toward the castle, then returned to Risteard. Both of us were reluctant to part. He planned on staying the night and leaving early the next morning. This would be the last time we'd see each other for almost a week. But it would be too risky to embrace now, so we just stared at one another, lost in thought.

"I'd better go," I whispered, taking a step away. He took my arm, and I froze. I felt his warm breath against my ear, and my heart quickened.

"Come to me tonight."

I steadily met his ardent stare.

"That could be dangerous. What if we're seen?"

"I'm willing to risk it if you are."

I raised an eyebrow. "Don't you have an early start tomorrow?"

A laugh escaped him before he clamped his mouth shut.

"I'm too much of a gentleman to respond to that the way I want to," he said.

I bit my lip to stifle a laugh and lowered my eyes to regain composure.

"All right," I said. "I'll come to you."

He released me, and I steeled my face into the expressionless mask I learned by watching him. I took off my ring and tucked it within the bundle of clothes, wishing I could wear it in public for all to see. Perhaps someday, but for now, our love must remain a secret.

That night, I lay next to Risteard in his bed, the sheets cool against my heated skin. I brushed hair off my damp brow and sighed.

"You'll have to cross the old bridge onto Wyrwyk lands," I said. "There's no other place to cross the Rhyvor. Follow the river west until you reach a stream. On the other side is the Sessyl Forest. It'll probably take you a few days to reach the coast."

I continued detailing the route Risteard already knew, but he let me talk. His fingers tickled a path along my collarbone, between my breasts, to my navel and back again. I placed a hand over his to still his movements.

"You shouldn't go alone," I said.

"I can manage." His voice was slurred, and I turned to face him. His eyes were closed.

"I know." I swallowed and squeezed his hand. "But I swear if you're not back in a week, I'm coming after you. And I know how you feel about a woman travelling alone."

A puff of air blew across my skin, and he smiled. Then his breathing became deep and steady, and I knew he was asleep. I snuggled closer and fought against sleep for as long as I could, not wanting to let him out of my sight. But the exhaustion of the last two days was too much, and I lost the battle.

I reached across the bed and clutched sheets. I sat up, and the light of dawn illuminated the empty space where Risteard once slept. I wrapped the covers around me and numbly slipped from the bed and looked out the window. The mountain was bathed in orange and blue hues, and I stood there until the sun brightened the sky. There was no princess to serve, no breakfast to order, no hair to brush but my own. I slowly turned to survey the room. I wanted to be angry at Risteard for leaving without waking me but understood it would have been harder to say goodbye.

I dressed in a daze, made the bed, and prepared myself to face the day with an indifferent expression. Before I left the room, a gleam caught my eye. Propped against the settee was my sheathed dagger. I ran my hand over the worn leather and polished hilt, then tucked it safely within my frock. It was a message from Risteard to be safe. I smiled, inhaled the scent of the room, and raised my chin. I strode out, arms swinging, ready to bring down a monarchy.

CHAPTER 52

I wrapped my arms around my stomach to muffle the rumbling on my way to the kitchens. The smell of fresh bread intensified my hunger, making my mouth water. Between the smacking of my lips and the grumbling of my stomach, the cook was alerted to my presence. She was rolling dough and paused to toss me a heel of bread and gestured to a plate of hard cheese. She wiped a hand down her cheek, leaving a trail of flour, and sang under her breath as she resumed her work.

I shoved the food in my mouth, stuffing my cheeks, and headed out the back door. A chill wind buffeted my face, but the sky was clear. I ate the last of the cheese and marched to the mews, determined to act normally. But when I reached Aquila's and found it empty, my knees buckled and I sank to the floor.

"Keep it together, Laria," I whispered. I closed my eyes and concentrated on breathing slow and evenly. "The last thing you need is to turn into a sniveling mess."

I managed to make it through cleaning the mews without weeping. Mostly. I blame the dry straw.

I shut the door to the shed and prepared to hustle back to the castle when I remembered there was no reason to hurry. I relaxed and spread my arms to absorb the sunshine. With the princess gone, I was beholden to no one. No schedule, no running around, no beatings, no worries. I sighed and returned to the castle. Yes, the princess was gone, but there was still much to do.

I found Edde coming from the laundry burdened with a heavy load of bedding. I grabbed half, and she was able to peer over the top.

"Oh, thank you, dear," she said. Her cheeks were red and puffed up. She waddled down the hallway chatting about her various ailments, and every few steps I'd take another sheet off her pile. By the time we reached the bedrooms, I carried most of the burden.

A pair of young servant girls hurried up to us, heads bowed, hands clasped, and faces flushed. Edde narrowed her eyes at them.

"About time you two showed up," she said. "Had to be helped by Her Highness' lady-in-waiting."

In unison, their heads snapped up and the color drained from their faces.

"Go on," Edde said.

The girls relieved me of the bedding and curtsied at me. I waved away the gesture, placed my hands over my chest, and nodded enthusiastically.

"You're lucky she's happy to help," Edde said. "Get to work." She shook her head at their retreating backs and muttered under her breath.

I put a hand on her shoulder, gestured toward the girls, and tilted my head inquisitively.

"A pair of empty-headed flibbertigibbets is who they are," she said. Though she had an annoyed tone, she was smiling. "But they're sweet girls. Fara and Mae. Sisters if you didn't notice."

She jerked her head and I followed her down the hall to a bedroom. The room was paneled in dark wood and sparsely furnished. On the dresser was a hairbrush and a basin. A screen was beside it covered in a woodland scene. I guessed we were in a man's room. I quickly scanned the room looking for clues to the owner's identity. A writing desk was tucked under a window next to the fireplace, but it would look odd if I wandered over to snoop in front of Edde. Instead, I helped her strip the rumpled sheets off the bed and remake it with the clean linen, still warm from being pressed.

"Thank you, dear." She squeezed my arm. "I'm sure you're busy."

I shook my head, pointed at myself, then her.

"I would 'preciate the help." She was breathing hard and steadying herself on the bedpost. The poor woman was about to faint after a few minutes of work. "Come on," she panted, beckoning me to follow.

I glanced once more at the writing desk. To have any chance of learning something useful, I needed to be in these rooms alone.

I spent the afternoon doing Edde's chores, allowing the older woman to rest and ramble. Like everyone else, she believed I was deaf, but that didn't stop her from talking non-stop. She told stories of her youth, about Ailis--which was difficult to hear without betraying I could understand, and the other servants. I think she missed the company.

I learned Fara and Mae were orphaned during the conquest of Praed, their parents used to work in the castle, and they were obsessed with knights. Thankfully, neither were violated like Ailis, though not for lack of effort.

"Those two flounce around handsome faces like cats on the prowl," Edde said. "If only their parents were here. I do my best, but nothing puts children in line like a father's hand."

I shuddered, then covered it by shaking water out of a sponge.

"Couldn't have them sweeping the barracks anymore. One of them was likely to run off with a soldier. They pouted but makin' 'em tend to the council chambers has kept them out of trouble."

I dined with the servants in the kitchen. Unlike the raucous meals upstairs in the Great Hall, the mood around the table was relaxed, like a family dinner. Steam rose from stewed vegetables, and loaves of bread and butter were passed around the table. To my delight, fish from the Rhyvor were served whole with fresh herbs. This was a traditional Praed meal. I looked at the people around the table and felt certain they were all Praedans.

"I'm not switchin' roles with you, and that's that," a man said around a mouthful of food. He flicked a crumb off his pristine burgundy tunic. I'd seen him in passing and recognized the streak of gray in his brown hair.

"Please, Jonas," the man sitting beside him said. His blonde hair was in disarray and his color high. He leaned forward and reached to grasp his friend's hand, but the other man jerked away.

"Not what you were expecting?" Jonas said. "I thought serving the prince was going to open doors. 'I'll be serving the king in no time,' you said."

I dropped my bread and blinked in surprise. The young man sitting across from me was Prince Brannon's valet. The last time I saw him was in the Riverstone parlor, his golden hair gleaming and his smooth skin glowing with pride. Right before he tried to kiss me, and I attacked him like a rabid squirrel. Life with the prince had left his complexion sallow and he fidgeted incessantly.

"I can't stand these late nights," the valet said. "It's gotten worse since the princess left. I cleaned vomit out of his shoes yesterday. His *shoes*! And don't even get me started on the stains."

I swallowed my food hard to keep from gagging.

Jonas lit a pipe, filling the room with acrid smoke. I covered my mouth, and the head of staff issued him a stern reprimand. He was ignored.

"We're all trying to get by," Jonas said, blowing smoke in the valet's face. "If you're lucky, you'll be serving a king before you know it. Like you wanted." He flicked ashes onto the floor. "It just won't be King Conall."

"Stop it, fool," Edde hissed. She looked around, then focused on Jonas. "If one of his spies hears you, it's treason."

Jonas shrugged, then nodded, and no more was said of King Conall's eventual demise.

I focused on the valet and the voices of the other servants faded. He ate frantically, shoveling forkfuls of food into his mouth faster than he could chew. He cleared his plate, wiped his mouth, and pushed away from the table. I popped out of my chair and blocked him from leaving.

"Excuse me," he said, and tried to brush past me.

I stepped in front of him.

He looked at me for the first time, his mouth opened to issue an angry retort. But it died on his lips, and his jaw dropped when he recognized me. He gripped my shoulder, and I instinctively slapped his hand away.

"I know you," he said. Tears filled his eyes. Actual tears.

I smiled and patted him on the arm.

"You and I, we have it the hardest," he said. He tipped his head toward the other servants. "They don't understand."

I nodded.

He extended his hand. "Can we start over? I'm Godfrey."

I eyed his outstretched hand. As the prince's valet, Godfrey could be a powerful ally, a window into the prince's private life. I shook his hand with a wobbly smile.

"My father served with yours," he said, his voice cracking.

I raised my chin and gripped his hand harder. His eyes searched mine, and I pushed all of my resolve into my steady gaze. Finally, his features relaxed and he released my hand.

I watched him ascend the dark stairs into the upper castle, aware his evening in service to the crown would be unpleasant. I felt guilty for never considering him as an ally before, but if I was careful, Godfrey could reveal all the prince's secrets.

Alone in my bed, I burrowed deeper in the blanket and tried not to think about Risteard. I tried not to think about him when I rubbed my chilled feet together for warmth. I tried not to think about him when I rolled over and grabbed empty space. And I definitely didn't think of him when I shimmied over to nestle against him and hit my face on the wall.

I might have mumbled curses at him when I checked my nose for breaks.

I laid back and stared at the ceiling. I considered sleeping in Risteard's room but didn't want to risk being seen. The walls of my tiny room pressed in on me, the darkness stifling. I'd never minded being alone. Preferred it, actually. Life certainly had a funny way of proving me wrong.

I proudly kept myself from crying but the effort cost me several hours of sleep.

In the morning, I submerged my hands in the icy water of the washbasin and kept them there until they were numb, then pressed my fingers to my puffy eyes. If I had a mirror, I would probably be horrified at my reflection. I rubbed my temples and tried remembering what I was supposed to do that day. But the only thought breaking through the sleep-deprived haze was, "Go back to bed." Very helpful.

I sighed and dropped my hands, hitting the side of the basin and spilling water everywhere. I pursed my lips and counted ten breaths before opening my eyes. I stared at the puddle spreading on the floor and couldn't bring myself to care.

"It'll dry," I muttered before heading to the kitchens for breakfast.

Godfrey smiled when I took my seat at the table. I smiled back, a little wider than was necessary to show him how friendly I am. I may have overdone it because he moved to sit next to me.

"It's horrible how the princess keeps you locked away," he said.

I leaned back and placed a hand against his shoulder. Why did people think they had to talk three inches from my face to be understood?

"Sorry," he said. His cheeks were pink, his eyes bright, and his hair and clothing were tidy. By the evening, I expected he'd be a complete mess.

I smiled politely and accepted a bowl of sop.

"We hate how she treats you like an animal," he continued. "You, the daughter of Maccus Audrey."

He lifted his bowl and drank it like a cup of tea, then wiped his chin with his sleeve. I held my spoon in my fingertips and sipped a dainty portion. The longer I ate like a proper lady, the deeper his cheeks reddened. I daintily patted my lips with a napkin to hide my smirk, then placed a hand over my heart and bowed my head in thanks for his concerns.

"So, um, did you lose your hearing and voice during the war?"

I felt the blood drain from my face. Like a fool, I hadn't anticipated feigning disability with someone who knew my family. Numbly, I nodded.

"We've all lost so much." He swallowed and looked away.

Please don't cry. I didn't know how to comfort him, a man I'd cruelly rejected in the past. How did one comfort a man as his equal? Should I punch him? Nah. Instead, I grabbed his shoulder and gave it a little shake.

Thankfully, he collected himself and hid his embarrassment by shoving bread in his mouth.

Across from us, Fara and Mae lamented over their broken hearts.

"It isn't fair," Fara said. She threw down her spoon and crossed her arms. "It's unbearable here. Why shouldn't we have some amusement?"

"It might seem harmless to flirt with the soldiers, but you can't be too careful," Edde said patiently.

Fara hugged herself and bowed her head, but not before I saw her face flush. Everyone must have known about poor Ailis.

"If we work together, we'll be safe," Mae said. She glanced at Fara. "We won't do anything dangerous."

"Just being a woman in this castle is dangerous," one of the maids said before stabbing her fork into a sausage.

The two sisters picked at their food in silence. I looked at Edde finishing her food and wondered how she could be so calm.

"She's not wrong," Godfrey muttered. He lifted a glass to his lips and it clanked against his teeth. I watched him try to avoid spilling the contents as it vibrated in his hand, then carefully place it on the table.

I rested a hand on his arm and softened my features to look sympathetic. He grabbed my hand and smiled, but it didn't reach his eyes. He squeezed my fingers in his clammy grip when I tried to pull away. His face was pale, sweat glistened on his brow, and he fidgeted in his chair.

"They're destroying Praed," he said. "I wish everything could go back to the way it was." He pushed away from the table and rushed from the room.

I used to wish for the same thing, but now I wanted something more. I wanted King Conall and his family gone, but I didn't want to go back to living under selfish kings obsessed with glory and fathers constantly leaving for war. If Risteard and I were successful, I hoped the people would crown a king who would bring prosperity back to Praed. But I also hoped he would be a fair king, an enlightened king.

Nothing would change without taking risks. I looked at Fara and Mae pouting across the table. Today, they were tasked with delivering firewood to the rooms of the council members. The day before, I'd volunteered to clean the barracks. I knew what I had to do.

I kept a close eye on Fara and Mae to the detriment of my meal. I'd only managed a few bites before they rose to see to their work. I pushed my plate aside and chased after, tugging on Fara's sleeve when I caught up. I gestured to myself, mimed carrying a heavy load, and pointed to her. She tilted her head and stared at me blankly. I pointed to her, pretended to sweep, and marched like a soldier.

Fara looked at her sister and said, "I don't get it."

I tried again to mime a reversal of our duties, growing more and more frustrated when they didn't get it. Finally, I shooed them forward and followed them to the woodpile. I grabbed a log out of Fara's hands and pretended to place it in a hearth. Then I pointed to them and gestured toward the barracks.

"Oh!" Mae exclaimed. "She wants to trade chores."

"You're supposed to clean the barracks?" Fara's eyes glittered in anticipation. I nodded.

The sisters looked at each other, the color rising in their cheeks. Wide grins spread across their faces and they nodded enthusiastically. I stepped aside, and they hurried off toward the barracks.

I gathered an armload of logs and hoped they'd keep their word and stay safe. I felt guilty for potentially putting them in harm's way, but desperate times…

I went straight to the bedroom I'd helped Edde in the day before. Thankfully, it was empty. After dropping the logs near the hearth, I hurried to the writing desk and started rummaging through drawers. I scanned the addresses, noting they were all from Ilano, and all sent to Councilman Armen Ferrys. I chewed my lower lip while I tried to remember him. I glanced around the room but didn't see any clues. I looked in the nightstand and found a jar of sharp smelling salve. Next to the washbasin was a brush with strands of gray hair stuck in the bristles. Armen Ferrys must be the eldest council member.

Listening for approaching footsteps, I quickly read through the letters. They detailed news from his estate--apple yields, illnesses, and repairs. The general feeling was that the current Lord Protector's incompetence was bleeding the country dry. Taxes rose while a drought made production fall. Unrest rippled through the household. I picked up another letter and discovered it was from a councilman serving in the Ilano capital. He didn't say anything blatantly treasonous, but he was evidently frustrated that the council met for hours and nothing was resolved. When, he wanted to know, would they hear from King Conall?

I lowered the letter. Did the people in Ilano not know of the king's illness? Surely someone would have told them, even through rumors.

After carefully replacing the letters, I left to deliver more firewood. I visited several rooms, all empty, and all worthless. Discouraged, I shuffled into a suite of rooms without knocking.

"Relax. It's only a servant," a low, gravelly voice said.

I lowered the logs so I could see and almost dropped them. In the dark recess of the room, Councilman Arlen reclined in a plush chair, his arms dangling over the sides. Across from him, Councilman Crane reluctantly removed his hand from inside his doublet.

"Come on, then. Get on with it and leave," Arlen said.

"She can't hear you, silly," Crane said with a smug grin. He wiggled into the cushions of his chair and chuckled.

Arlen sighed, rolled his eyes, and waved me toward the fireplace. I gripped the logs and hoped they couldn't see me trembling. I knelt next to the cold hearth and shakily stacked the wood.

"As I was saying," Crane said, "Prince Brannon may appear decent enough in council, but behind closed doors, he's completely wild since Princess---"

"Don't you think we should continue this conversation later?" Arlen interrupted.

"I told you." Crane paused and sipped an amber liquid from a small glass. "She can't hear us."

"How can you be so sure?"

"I can't. But I know for sure she's mute."

"How?"

"Because she didn't scream when Brannon tried to rape her."

I bit my tongue to keep from gasping aloud. I resumed stacking the logs and peered at the men. Arlen studied his steepled fingers while Crane brushed imaginary dirt off his impeccable clothing. I looked away before I was spotted staring. Did the princess tell him? Or Jervell Kade? Who else knew?

"Brannon is a fool, but he isn't blind. And unfortunately, *he* can hear quite well," Arlen said. "We cannot speak out against him or King Conall in public."

"Agreed. We have to be discreet." Crane watched the liquor swirling in his glass, his eyebrows raised and his mouth quirked.

Arlen tapped his fingers together. "What did you have in mind?"

I could hear his annoyance. I stood and wiped my hands down the front of my dress. They watched me, and I gestured to the hearth and pretended to light a fire.

"Not necessary," Arlen said with a dismissive wave.

I curtsied and prolonged my journey to the door by straightening tapestries and arranging furniture.

"The most easily swayed of the council frequent the Trophy Room. If one were to whisper in their ears in their vulnerable states..." Crane's voice trailed off.

I busied myself dusting a picture frame and watched the men. Crane was picking at the armrest while Arlen glared, his hands clasped so tightly they shook.

"You hate the Trophy Room," Arlen said.

Crane lazily lifted his head. "We all have to make sacrifices."

"Indeed."

I tiptoed to the door and quietly slipped out, listening as I slowly closed it.

"Keep playing the game. And remember it's just a game," Crane said. His toothy grin split his face unnervingly.

A game with too many players. It looked like my next destination was the Trophy Room. If those men make a mess after we spent hours cleaning it, I'm putting castor oil in their cider.

CHAPTER 53

The next morning while the prince was in council, I delivered fresh linens to the rooms of the councilmen. Fara and Mae kept our role reversal the day before secret and enthusiastically agreed to do it again. I don't think Edde was ignorant of our deception, but she didn't interfere so long as the sisters stayed out of trouble. I knew her forbearance wouldn't last, so I planned to use my time wisely.

The first room I visited was where I stumbled upon Arlen and Crane. I listened at the door, then peaked inside when I didn't hear voices. The room was dark, like before, but the chairs were empty. I crept inside and waited for my eyes to adjust. It was a modest sitting room, a fireplace on one side and a desk with bookcases on the other. At the back of the room was a door. I searched the desk, but found only blank sheets of paper. I wasn't surprised. I pressed my ear to the door. Silence. Slowly, I pushed down the door handle, wincing when the latch disengaged. I held my breath, listening. Silence. The hinges creaked when I pushed open the door, but no one came out of the darkness. I slipped inside.

Light filtered in from a window tucked into an alcove, illuminating a large bed carved from dark wood and draped in green bedding. The bed dominated the space, leaving barely enough room for a chest, settee, and dresser. I tried opening the chest, but it was locked. Under the window was a small writing desk, but my search there turned up nothing. I checked the dresser, carefully lifting the neatly pressed and folded clothing. Nothing. I tugged a lock of my short hair in frustration.

"If I was a part of a conspiracy," I whispered aloud, "where would I hide the evidence?"

I'd burn it.

I hurried back into the anteroom and knelt in front of the hearth. I checked to make sure it was cold then started digging. I moved the remnants of wood aside and ran my finger through the ashes. A gray plume made me cough and stung my eyes, but I kept looking. Desperate, I plunged my hands into the ashes and felt around, blinking away tears. My fingers brushed against paper, and I bit my lip to stifle a giggle.

In my blackened hand was a scrap of burned paper with small, neat handwriting.

I heard footsteps in the corridor and shoved the paper in my apron pocket. My heart pounding, I grabbed the linens as they came closer. The footsteps were moving quickly, heavily, coming closer. Breathing shallowly, I pressed up against the door and waited.

The footsteps stopped right outside. I held my breath and listened to the creaking floorboards under shifting weight. Someone scratched at the door, and I clamped a hand over my mouth to keep from shrieking. They scratched again, more urgently, and the door shuddered with the weight of a body falling against it. I tightened my hand and squeezed my eyes shut. It felt like hours passed, but finally the weight shifted and a letter slid out from under the door and glided across the floor.

The footsteps retreated down the hall, and I released a *whoosh* of air. I waited a few minutes before picking up the letter. It was not addressed. The paper was thin and soft--expensive. The wax seal was stamped with a sword piercing some kind of fruit. I brought the letter to my nose and detected a subtle floral scent.

I sighed and dropped the letter. Sorting out these clues would have to wait until Risteard returned. I'd stayed busy to keep from missing him, and the rush of longing hit me like a dagger to the heart. I left the room rubbing my chest and wondering what *he* would do next.

He'd always placed securing allies as a top priority.

So let's get ourselves more allies.

I found Godfrey rushing around the lower levels of the castle tossing clothes needing mending to the seamstress. She held it out between her thumb and index finger grumbling that she didn't get paid enough. Godfrey ignored her and tucked into a corner with the prince's boots to polish them.

I stood over him and tapped on the top of his head. His eyes snapped up and he jumped back.

"You scared me," he said, relaxing. "I can't talk now. Prince Brannon wants all of his boots shining before council is over." He bent over and scrubbed caked mud off a boot, paying careful attention to the stitching.

I looked around Godfrey's feet at the pile of boots. I hunkered next to him, grabbed a cloth, and started scrubbing. He paused, opened his mouth to protest, then decided this was too much work for one person.

"Thank you," he said. "The prince has been spending a lot of time outside at the mews and stables. Between you and me, I think he's doing more than just training."

I don't doubt it. I bent over the boots in my hands.

"I'm constantly cleaning dirt and grass stains off his clothing. Mostly the knees of his breeches if truth be told."

I blushed and wondered if he would speak so freely if he knew I could hear.

"I honestly thought the king's illness would force him to grow up, but he's just as bad if not worse. At least when the princess was here, he was more discreet.

I hope his marriage tempers him, otherwise he'll have a string of bastards all through Praed."

Godfrey wasn't telling me anything I didn't already suspect, but it was nice to be proven right.

He prattled on as we worked, and when the last pair of boots were shining, I helped him carry them upstairs. I'd never been in the prince's rooms--the princess was too concerned about cleanliness to go there--so I was filled with trepidation. Godfrey had no such qualms and boldly walked into the anteroom. I only had a chance for a brief perusal before we headed into the bedroom, but I noted it wasn't as elaborately decorated as I was expecting. A portrait of the king and queen was the only wall hanging. A desk sat under the window and on the opposite wall two bookcases--mostly empty. The absence of chairs and tables confirmed the prince didn't use this room for entertaining.

We passed under an archway into the bedroom and I stopped at the threshold. My jaw dropped when I took in the lush carpets and lavishly draped canopy bed, all the color of fresh blood. Before the fireplace was a settee large enough for two people to sleep on, and in an alcove behind drawn-back curtains was an enormous bathtub. Candles lined the mantle and dressers. The walls were adorned with tapestries depicting beautiful women dancing among flowers. My cheeks grew hot when I looked closer and realized the women were naked.

Godfrey took the boots out of my hands and fastidiously lined them up on the floor of a closet beneath shelves of perfectly folded doublets. While he made sure the toes were even, I explored the room. Though the bed was neatly made and the surfaces devoid of dust, I avoided touching anything. You'd have to be pretty naive not to know what goes on in here.

I wandered over to the writing desk and glanced over my shoulder at Godfrey. Seeing he was still preoccupied with organizing the prince's closet, I shuffled through the messy stack of papers. I read a few of the letters and tossed them aside in disgust. They were all from admirers and filled with flowery nonsense. I opened the drawers and found more love notes. I resisted the urge to slam them closed in frustration. I should have known I wouldn't find anything useful in this idiot's room.

I jumped three feet in the air and my hand flew to my concealed dagger when a hand touched my shoulder. Godfrey stepped back, hands raised, an apologetic look on his face. He's lucky I had the presence of mind not to stab first and ask questions later.

Godfrey's gaze shifted to the desk, and my heart beat faster. I adopted a casual stance and coolly looked around the room, hoping he didn't suspect I was snooping. He picked up a few of the letters and perused the contents, then looked at me.

"He may seem simple, but he's ambitious," he said. "Don't let him fool you. He's dangerous."

I pressed my lips in a firm line and felt my chin tremble.

His eyes narrowed. "He visits the princess in her rooms a lot. I don't suppose you know anything?"

I raised an eyebrow and pointed at him. Do *you* know anything?

He glanced around and ran a hand through his hair.

"He orders me around, but that's all. He doesn't talk about anything important."

I shrugged. Godfrey might not have any inside information, but he'd been helpful nonetheless. There was one more place to search, and the thought made my stomach churn.

Between missing Risteard and dreading the next day, I slept fitfully. I could feel the servants' eyes on me at breakfast, and I was glad I didn't have a mirror to see how awful I must have looked. Edde asked if I was all right, and I knew she wasn't convinced by my enthusiastic nod. She eyed me narrowly and watched me closely as I finished my food and hastily left the kitchens. I didn't have time for questions and couldn't risk her stopping me.

Godfrey said the prince paid more attention to his attire on his days off from the council. Based on the meticulous preparations the day before and Godfrey's tardiness to breakfast, I knew there was no council today. I shivered in the drafty corridor, ducked into a doorway, and waited. Several servants passed carrying trays of sweets, goblets, and decanters. I picked out a lagging older gentleman and stepped out of the shadows.

"Oh," he gasped.

I grabbed the tray to keep it from toppling.

"I didn't see you," he said. The slight exertion left him breathless. This would be easier than I thought.

Smiling, I pulled the tray from his weak grasp.

"Oh, no, that's not necessary," he said, though he didn't reach for the tray.

I gestured that I would carry it, and he stared after the rest of the servants. I could see him wrestling with his conscience. I took a few steps back, nodding encouragingly. His shoulders relaxed, and he inclined his head.

"Thank you, young lady. Don't stay in there. Set the tray on a table and leave."

The goblets vibrated noisily the closer we came to the Trophy Room. I gripped the tray tightly and willed myself not to drop anything. The servants filed inside, striding purposefully. I took a deep breath and followed.

A gray haze stung my eyes and burned my nose. A sickly sweet smoke filled my lungs. I set the tray on a nearby table before I dropped it and doubled over coughing until my throat was raw. I braced against the wall as my vision blurred and my head felt dizzy. Vaguely, I heard laughing, the sound muffled and distorted. A figure loomed over me and slapped me on the back.

"Easy there, girl."

I sluggishly rubbed my eyes and looked up. A man I almost recognized smiled down at me. His shoulders were broad and his skin deeply tanned. A soldier or knight perhaps? His simple green tunic hung open, revealing a mass of dark hair. He steadied me when I wavered, and I didn't have the strength to pull away.

"Better sit down," he said. He led me to a group of men and women lounging on the floor around a...vase? Planter? I wasn't sure, but straight pieces projected from the base and smoke drifted out the top. A man leaned over and put his mouth on one of the projections and inhaled, then fell back, smoke trailing from his lips.

The man pushed down on my shoulders and my legs folded underneath me. A grizzled man pulled a lady onto his lap while lazily looking me up and down.

"Who's your new friend, Ned?" he asked.

"A lady, Jeb. Surprised you don't recognize her." The big man, Ned, sat beside me, his thighs touching mine. I inched away, and the lady next to me giggled behind her hand.

The grizzled man, Jeb, squinted and leaned closer. Then his eyes widened, and he burst into laughter so violently the lady fell off his lap.

"Well done, Ned," he said.

I scooted out of the circle, but Ned braced a hand against my back and gestured toward the strange, smoking object.

"Be our guest, m'lady. It will help you relax," he said.

I shook my head, smiling to soften the blow.

He shrugged and inhaled himself. His eyes closed and he blew out a puff of pungent smoke. I tried to retreat, but he fell back and blocked me with his body. I tucked my knees against my chest and wrapped my arms around them to avoid touching anyone.

"Whadaya think, lads?" Ned said, his words pouring out of his mouth like honey on a cold day. "Is it better to serve King Conall or Prince Brannon?"

"Having more fun with the prince," Jeb said.

"Less drills," another man added.

"Tha's because Sir Risteard's gone," Ned said with a dismissive wave.

"More fun without him," Jeb said.

"Bored without him," another said. His head rested on his fist and he picked at a loose thread. Bored, indeed.

"Soft without him," one of the ladies said. She giggled and pinched one of the men's upper arms. He grabbed her waist and rolled on top of her.

"Who's soft?" he growled.

I scrambled over the top of Ned, flipping backwards when he tried to wrap an arm around me. I crawled away and wedged between suits of armor until the fog cleared from my mind and I could breathe without fire engulfing my chest. I peered out and studied the mass of people. Men were clustered in groups waving goblets while they talked. Others were entangled with women on couches or against walls. On the far wall near the fireplace a group of councilmen sipped amber liquor from sparkling glasses.

I leaned against the wall. I wouldn't learn anything if I hid in the shadows. You're a married woman, Laria. You can handle walking past people kissing and touching each other. I gathered my courage and boldly stepped into the room, picking up a tray to look busy. Dodging writhing bodies and waving arms, I listened to fragments of conversation. There wasn't much to learn from the men entwined in women's arms, nor those who were playing cards. My focus was on the councilmen. I moved my way across the room, holding the tray high. Someone bumped into me, and I nearly dropped it. I put my hand out to keep my balance and recoiled when I encountered skin. A woman stared at me over her shoulder, her red lips curved into a seductive smile. She wore nothing but a chemise, and I'd inadvertently touched her bare backside. My skin flushed from neck to hairline.

"Why have you stopped?" A face appeared from underneath the woman. I hoped the seizing in my chest signaled my imminent death.

Prince Brannon.

Our eyes met, and he paled. Another woman I hadn't noticed groaned in protest. I narrowed my eyes. For someone who was supposedly eager to marry, he wasn't acting like a devoted groom. I disapproved, and he knew it. Fear flickered over his features, probably because he worried I'd report his behavior to the princess.

He pushed the ladies away, ignoring their pouts, and swung his legs off the divan.

"Sorry, ladies, I just remembered I asked to be dealt in the next hand," he said.

I turned away, scowling, while he fixed his breeches and pulled on an undershirt. I didn't expect Prince Brannon to become celibate after announcing his engagement, but he could've shown some discretion.

I resumed making my way toward the councilmen. I recognized Crane's casual ease and distinctive tones. He swirled his drink, never taking a sip, a crooked smile frozen on his lips. When I got closer, I could hear their hushed conversation.

"I understand what you're saying, Crane, but Conall is still the king." The white-haired councilman's glass clattered against a side table in his unsteady hand. It was Armen Ferrys, I was sure of it.

"We all wish good health for King Conall, but what sort of state will he be in when he recovers?" I glanced at the councilman who spoke and tried to remember his name. He was old enough to be my father but younger than Ferrys. Kenter--that was it.

"Prince Brannon has promised me land and titles in exchange for my loyalty. King Conall never offered me either."

Probably because he was Raff Demas, barely twenty and only on the council because he was the prince's friend since childhood. He also had an attractive sister.

The men ignored me, so I watched Crane as I filled empty glasses. His expression didn't change as he listened to the old men cling to their loyalty and the young ones bend to promises of riches. They argued amongst themselves, and still Crane fixated on the play of flames reflecting off his glass. A shiver climbed up my spine and sweat covered my palms. I tried to move, but my hand remained suspended between table and tray. Slowly, Crane raised the glass to his lips and took a small sip.

"I feel your confusion, gentlemen," Crane said. His dark eyes fixed on each face, his lower lip pouting slightly. "But last I checked, it was your sons and fathers that conquered Praed, not King Conall. Where are they now?"

The men stared at him, still and silent.

"Yes, you have lands. Maybe." He locked eyes with each councilman who resided in the castle. "But shouldn't you have more power, more say in how this new kingdom should be run, especially since your family spilled blood for it?" He took another sip and licked his lips. "Who do you think will listen, an old man or a young boy?"

The men were looking at each other, so I'm sure they didn't see my jaw drop and quickly snap shut. Crane was openly speaking against King Conall where anyone could hear. He was either extremely confident or gravely stupid.

The older men still seemed uneasy, but the younger leaned back in their chairs with smug smiles. One by one, the others bowed their heads in resignation, except Armen Ferrys.

"What are you waiting for, Armen?" Crane asked.

"A king worth fighting for," he said. He looked so sad I almost reached out to comfort him.

I want that, too, sir. If Risteard and I are successful, you can choose him.

CHAPTER 54

The entirety of the castle, from lowliest kitchen maid to the queen, stood on the steps to welcome the princess and her friends home. The prince stood at the forefront, pretending to be as eager as expected. The circles under his eyes and his constant massaging of his temples suggested he wasn't looking forward to his sister's return.

Morning sunshine coaxed mist from the road, lending an ethereal quality to their arrival. I'm sure Queen Shaeli would appreciate it if she could see. I stood beside her, an honor bestowed upon me as Her Highness' lady-in-waiting. In the three years I'd served the crown, I'd never been this close to her. She was smaller than she'd appeared in the sessions in her room. Though she was dressed in a magnificent purple gown and crown of gold, she looked frail, like the weight of the crown hunched her back. She held her chin high, her milky eyes staring in the direction of the road. I watched her closely, and when relief relaxed her features, I knew the princess' carriage would soon appear.

The ladies swept out of the carriages like exotic birds eager to display their feathers. I admit, they looked well, especially Miss Derville and Princess Caelyn. They looked refreshed, rested, their cheeks flushed with laughter.

The princess rushed into the queen's arms, whispering, "It's all right. I'm back. We'll fix everything."

The queen took her daughter's face in her hands and ran her slender fingers across her brow.

"Your brother needs taming," she said.

The princess' features darkened. "He always does." Her eyes shifted to me, and her shoulders slumped. "It was so nice to be attended to by proper ladies."

The other ladies approached to greet the queen, except Lady Sharp. Her dark eyes missed nothing, and *I* didn't miss them darting around the crowd.

"The First Knight was too busy to greet us?" she said.

"He's on a special mission for the king," the queen said. "He is due to return this evening."

My heart thudded to a stop, then beat faster than galloping hooves. If they noticed my flushed face, they didn't remark upon it.

Throughout the day, the princess cast a few disparaging glances my way, but my impassive features gave her no reason to suspect I was anticipating Risteard's return. It took all my willpower to keep my expression neutral, especially when my gaze drifted out the windows. The princess and her friends were blissful after their respite, and even Miss Derville was happy to discuss wedding plans. I didn't hear a word of it over the sound of my heart pounding in anticipation of my husband's embrace.

The princess was extra demanding at dinner. Apparently, Ilano servants are not only better at dressing, styling hair, and being entertaining, they also know what you want before you do. I *obviously* should have known she needed a refill of wine. I *obviously* should have known she was finished with her first course after one bite. And *obviously* I should know she no longer cares for fish. *Obviously* if I was from Ilano I would know these things.

She was obviously asking for me to slip castor oil in her morning tea.

Annoyance consumed me. I stared at the back of her head, fists clenched, face burning. I'd enjoyed my respite, too, and resented once again being shackled. Suddenly, the hairs on the back of my neck and arms prickled. Every inch of my skin came alive. I could feel someone watching me. Slowly, I scanned the Great Hall and spotted him.

Risteard.

When I stared into his intense blue eyes, I recalled the touch of his hands on my face, my back, and the feeling of them skimming across my stomach and backside, the tingling in my breasts. I shifted uncomfortably with unbidden thoughts of his kisses. I squeezed my eyes shut and silently recited passages of books and the names of trees.

My sleeve was shaken violently, and my eyes flew open to see the irritated face of the princess looking up at me.

"Are you ill?" she asked.

I shook my head.

She raised her glass for me to fill, but her expression did not change. When her attention was distracted, I released a heavy sigh. The day had been interminable, and as time ticked into the late evening, I was a wreck.

The ladies' tedious conversation tested my patience further. Never had I been so fed up with their gossip, so disgusted with the belittling comments and backhanded compliments. When my family used to visit the castle, ladies gathered and carried on in a similar way, and I never gave it a second thought. Now, I felt the impact of their cruelty, and I hoped with a drastic change, a new, more positive society would evolve.

"I suppose one does not get to choose her sister-in-law," Lady Sharp was saying. "But there is no reason to expect a close acquaintance is required. She is so desperate to be friends, but how can I be friends with someone whose husband is in trade?"

That was enough. Casually, I rose and moved to sit under the glow of a candle for my embroidery. Their voices faded, though I could still hear snippets. I blocked them out with thoughts of my own, full of eagerness of the princess' retiring for the night so mine could begin.

She may not have noticed a change in me, but the princess certainly couldn't miss how eagerly I prepared her for bed. I practically ripped the clothes off her, rushed a brush through her hair, and nearly pushed her into bed. She stumbled through the routine in confused silence, but when I started to leave without being dismissed, she gave me a stern shake and commanded me to stop.

"What has possessed you?" she said, her face inches from mine.

I stared at her blankly while she searched my eyes.

"I don't know what it is," she said. "But something is different about you." Her eyes met mine, and I boldly stared back.

"There will be much to do over the next month," she told me. "I expect you to be here early for instructions. No dawdling during the day, either. As soon as you're finished with the mews, come straight back to me. The prince, with all of our support, will be married at month's end." She dismissed me, and it took all my restraint to keep from running out of the room.

I did not go straight to Risteard's room, but to my own. I waited there, pacing in my nightgown, to ensure the princess was asleep before I crept down the hall. I detected a note of suspicion in her eye, and the last thing I needed was for her to catch me roaming around at night. It was very late when I peeked toward her room. No light shone from beneath the door, so I wrapped myself in a coat and sneaked through the corridor barefoot.

I crept silently in the darkness, my heart thudding in my chest, hurrying past closed doors and empty rooms. I froze when I heard voices, and from underneath the door in front of me I saw flickering light. I tiptoed closer and pressed my ear against it, and from within I heard a distinctly feminine voice.

"Come now, we had a deal," I recognized the sound of Lady Sharp's giggle followed by the swish of fabric and a deep groan. "Talk first. You tell me what I want to know, and I'll give you this." A soft thud followed, and by the sound I guessed it was Lady Sharp's gown hitting the floor. I swallowed and continued to listen.

"I already told you," a man said. "Only a trusted few are allowed to see the king."

I didn't recognize his voice, but by his clipped tones, I suspected he was a knight.

"Which trusted few?" Lady Sharp insisted.

"The doctor, the royal family, a select few council members, and the First Knight."

"Risteard?"

"Yes. And no one else. He's guarded day and night. Now give me what you promised!"

There was a scuffle, and Lady Sharp commanded the man to wait for one more question.

"I understand there's a chance the king's illness is not natural. Who is suspected?"

"No one in particular and everyone," the man said with an edge of irritation. "Nothing goes on in the castle that's not seen by the king's spies. Everyone is followed, everyone is watched."

"Including the First Knight?"

"Everyone!" he exclaimed. "Any more questions?"

"Mmm, come here. Come get your reward," she said.

I moved away leaving sounds of Lady Sharp's adultery to my imagination.

I was troubled by the time I reached Risteard's door and absently grazed it with my knuckles. Lady Sharp was clearly still interested in Risteard and his movements, but why was she asking about the king? Did she suspect Risteard had something to do with his illness? Or was she simply sticking her nose where it didn't belong? The door opened, interrupting my wanderings, and I was pulled into the room so forcefully I nearly toppled over. Risteard wrapped me in his arms and claimed my mouth in a desperate kiss before I could speak, but my jumble of thoughts prevented me from enjoying the moment.

"Wait," I managed to squeak out. He had stripped down while waiting for me and was clad only in his breeches. I forgot my concerns when I touched his bare chest, warm and strong against my palms.

"What is it?" His voice was heavy with desire. He pushed the coat off my shoulders and kissed his way down my neck and shoulders.

I shook my head and pushed him further off me.

"Something's wrong." I knew these words would get his attention. He stilled, his eyes dark and jaw clenched.

"Tell me."

"I overheard Lady Sharp just now. She's asking questions about you and the king. Whomever she was talking to said there are spies everywhere and they're even watching *you*. If we thought we should be careful before, now I fear we must reconsider this meeting."

"You're already here," he pointed out.

"Well, then maybe after tonight we shouldn't meet." It broke my heart to say it, but I didn't want to risk being discovered.

"Unacceptable," he said.

"Risteard, what if someone sees me come here?"

"Were you followed tonight?"

"No. At least, I don't think so. But you're being watched according to what I heard."

"No, I'm not."

"How can you be sure?"

"Because the spies in this castle are clumsy. I would notice them. And if I did, they wouldn't dare continue."

"You think you're so terrifying?" I felt myself beginning to relax.

"I worked very hard to appear so."

"You don't scare me." I ran my hands up his chest to tangle in his hair, pulled his head down, and brushed his lips with mine, barely touching. It became apparent my husband was not interested in being gentle, and he crushed me against his body and kissed me, our teeth clacking together as our passion escalated. From that moment to when we lay exhausted and satisfied on the bed was a blur of flying clothes, sweat, and heavy breathing, and it struck me how diverse the practice of lovemaking could be.

I thought about the days ahead. The prince's wedding was in a month and would signal the rise of our revolution. Risteard's people would mobilize, and I would write to mine and give them the purpose they'd been waiting for. I looked at my sleeping husband and wondered about his stressful life. He raised an army with his uncle to overthrow Praed only to turn around and form an alliance with me to usurp him. He played the loyal knight daily, protecting the king and his family while at night he consorted with his secret ally. He played a dangerous game as the cold-hearted villain, never letting his guard down, while around him people lived happy, carefree lives. We both were forced to hide who we really were, but soon we would be free to be together without restraint. Or we would die trying.

Gingerly, I shook him awake, overcome with the sorrowful feeling that I might soon lose him, and this time when I grazed my lips across his, he responded with the gentleness I desired.

"Was it very terrifying? Did you see any ghosts?" I asked Risteard the following evening. I went to his study after the princess retired with the honest intention of telling him everything I'd learned while he was gone. But the moment the door closed, his lips were on mine. In the blink of an eye, he swept his arms across the desk, sending papers and books crashing to the floor.

That night I learned Risteard's desk is wide enough for two people to lie on.

I leaned over and frowned at the spreading ink stain on the floor while he laughed at my question. I wasn't going to clean that up.

"No ghosts," he said. "A lot of trees. I did find some ruins. I made some rubbings." His brow furrowed and he looked around our bodies, then met my eyes. "They were on the desk."

I laughed and nestled against his chest. "Did you find what you were looking for?"

"Yes." His breath was warm against my ear and he tightened his hold.

"I meant on the coast."

"Yes. I gave everything to the doctor. He said he should have something ready in a few days." He placed soft kisses on my knuckles, my palm, moving down my hand. "What did you do while I was gone?"

"I made friends with the servants and snooped in the rooms of the councilmen."

He stilled, his lips against my pulse. "And?"

"To sum up, the younger councilmen are easily swayed. They follow Prince Brannon because he throws rewards at them. The older ones are more loyal, but I think they'll bend toward whoever's stronger. I didn't find anything useful in Brannon's room---"

"You went to Brannon's room?"

I rolled my eyes. "Calm down. I was helping his valet put away boots. Anyway, all he had was a bunch of love letters, but in *Crane's* room---"

"I'm never leaving you alone again."

"I found the scrap of a letter he tried to burn." I shifted and glanced down at the coat I was currently laying on. "It's under me."

He sighed and rolled out of my arms. I sat up, wrapping his greatcoat around my chest as I watched him dress.

"Time to get to work?" I asked.

He leaned over the desk so close I closed my eyes in anticipation of his kiss. But instead of the feeling of his warm lips, I was wrenched forward and cold when he snatched his coat away.

"Hey!" I jumped off the desk and pulled on my frock. "Some gentleman you are."

I showed him the paper and he studied the handwriting in the firelight.

"Do you recognize it?"

He shook his head. "It might be Arlen's."

"All I can make out is 'no' and 'crown.' Can you tell what those words say?" I pointed to the tiny words I'd tried to decipher.

He studied the paper closely, his lips moving as he worked through the possibilities. I chewed a thumbnail anxiously while I waited.

"For all time," he said in a soft, quiet tone.

"What do you think it means?"

He lowered the paper and stared into the flames. "I don't know."

"Someone slipped a letter under his door while I was there. I should have stolen it."

"No. That would have been dangerous, especially if he tore through the castle looking for it."

"There wasn't any writing on it, but the paper was expensive and smelled like flowers. Could it have been from a lover?"

"Maybe."

I squeezed his arm and whispered, "Back to work?"
"Yes." He caressed my cheek and smiled faintly. "There's much to be done."
The honeymoon was over.

CHAPTER 55

For a week Risteard and I conducted our marriage with no one suspecting. I passed the days normally with the added tasks of dashing around the castle with instructions from the princess. The impending wedding distracted the castle, so barely a word was spoken regarding the health of the king. As the date drew near, the princess became more tense, and I did everything she asked with haste, conscious that if I slipped it would give her reason to relieve her tension by punishing me.

"The dressmaker is almost finished with your wedding gown," the princess said to Miss Derville as she and her ladies were arranging flowers. "The craftsmanship better be worth the wait."

"I'm sure it will be lovely," Miss Derville said with little enthusiasm.

"I don't know why you've been moping around, especially after our holiday," the princess said harshly. "You're close to getting everything you wanted." The other ladies looked from the princess to Miss Derville in shock. She had never spoken to her friend in such a manner. I suspected the strain of having to watch Miss Derville marry her brother was making the princess heartsick, but the others were not aware of this secret.

"I appreciate everything you're doing," Miss Derville said.

"Have you noticed," Lady Sharp spoke lightly to break the tension, "that a change has come over your lady-in-waiting?" My heart sank and I'm sure the color drained from my cheeks, but I did not move or change my expression.

"Yes," Miss Derville said, her shoulders relaxing and color rising. "She doesn't look at the floor anymore."

"Not when she's sitting nor walking," Lady Sharp agreed. "Have you noticed, Princess?"

"There is something different about her, but I haven't been able to put my finger on it," she said.

I felt her eyes burning into my skin.

"She seems more confident, like she's finally grown into a woman," Miss Derville said. "I think she's become quite pretty actually."

Oh, no.

"Pretty?" Princess Caelyn snarled. "You think that creature is *pretty*? You must be blinded by your impending nuptials, Mwiryn. There's nothing remotely attractive about that skinny, freckled, ginger-haired freak!" A few snickers emanated from the ladies, and the princess continued, "She's practically useless to me. For three years, she's been attending me, and you would think there'd have been an improvement in manners. She's proven time and again she's still a savage. And don't give me that look, Mwiryn. It's not as if she can hear me."

"And if she could?"

The challenge in Miss Derville's voice rippled through the ladies. They lowered their eyes and were so still I'm sure they stopped breathing.

"I would tell her exactly what I think of her."

"You shouldn't be so unkind to her, Caelyn. She's served you faithfully without complaint even though the circumstances of her coming here were very grave."

Princess Caelyn stood abruptly and shouted, "Who are you to tell me what to do? What makes you so sympathetic to her? Her supposed beauty?" She stalked over to me, her eyes ablaze, and ripped the scarf from my head. She pointed at my short hair. "There. Still find her pretty?"

Lady Sharp shifted uncomfortably and wouldn't meet my eye while the other ladies stared open-mouthed. It was certainly an entertaining afternoon for them.

Miss Derville's hands flew to her mouth. "What happened? Oh, Caelyn, how dreadful!" Miss Derville proved herself a fine actress. I caught her eye briefly, but she stared at me with believable shock. Nothing betrayed her prior knowledge of my condition.

I reached for the scarf, but the princess pulled it away.

"No," she said to my face. "You'll go without covering your head from now on." She resumed her seat at the table, mumbling, "Not so pretty anymore," under her breath.

From then on, I received curious and shocked stares wherever I went. I bore the attention with as much dignity as I could muster, holding my head high as Mother taught me. My grace in the face of embarrassment angered the princess further, though I couldn't know how much. She had always hated me, treated me abominably for the past three years despite my 'faithful' service. Her spite and jealousy knew no bounds, and if she felt threatened by Miss Derville's praise, then I was in trouble.

One night, as I brushed the princess' hair and avoided her dark stare, I saw her hand move to a drawer in the vanity. Without taking her eyes off me, she slipped her hand inside…

The door to her room flew open and the prince strode in, his face dark with stubble. His hair was in disarray and his eyes red.

"What is the meaning of this?" the princess shouted. I stood aside while the prince paced around the room in obvious agitation, stopping now and then to warm his hands at the fire.

"Father."

The princess paled. "He's…dead?"

"No. I've just spoken to the physician. He was relieved to report that His Majesty is recovering."

"No." The princess lowered herself onto the settee and stared into the flames.

"I don't understand." The prince groaned and dug his fingers through his hair.

"You made this mess!" the princess said. "You fix it!"

"I'll have to postpone the wedding."

"You wouldn't dare!"

"I would. I am."

"You can't! So much work has been done already."

"Don't be so dramatic. There's no harm in having more time to make everything perfect." He paused and looked at me strangely. "I'm postponing the wedding until further notice. We hoped the festivities would cheer the king, and it has. Now we must focus on his recovery."

The princess eyed him, her nostrils flaring.

"Caelyn?"

"Yes," she said. "The king must be our first priority."

"Good." And just as quickly as he appeared, he left the princess' room.

Stunned by the news, the princess remained seated. I watched her nervously, my brain buzzing. Hesitantly, I reached out and touched her shoulder. She recoiled violently, fixing me with a vile expression.

"Don't you ever touch me!" she hissed. She grabbed the brush from my hand and struck me across the face with it. The impact threw me off balance, but I maintained my footing and met her gaze. Her brow furrowed as we locked eyes, and her color deepened as every second passed.

She struck me again and screamed, "Stop looking at me!"

I did not relent, meeting her glare boldly. She pushed me aside and reached into the drawer of her vanity. She spun to face me holding a knife she obviously had no practice handling.

"Get out," she ordered as she jabbed it in my direction. "Or I'll cut your pretty face to shreds."

Though confident I could overpower her should she attack me, I complied. I'd escaped without injury, but tomorrow I might not be so lucky.

I knew I should wait before sneaking off to Risteard's room, but the news from Prince Brannon was urgent and I didn't want to waste time. The moment the princess' door slammed behind me, I scurried through the corridors, sticking to the shadows and pausing every few steps, alert for spies. I made one last glance down the dark hallway at Risteard's door, then entered without knocking.

"I have important news," I blurted out before he could pull me into his embrace. "Have you heard? About the king?"

"Tell me."

"The prince said he's recovering. Apparently, he just heard this from the doctor. Princess Caelyn was stricken dumb, then she was furious! Did you know?"

Risteard couldn't speak for several seconds, and I could tell his mind was spinning frantically.

"What else?" he asked.

"The prince is going to postpone the wedding to concentrate on helping His Majesty heal."

"Of course, he is," Risteard growled. He began pacing the length of the room.

"Why? It doesn't make sense. You said yourself it's favorable for him to have a wife. He was so anxious to marry when he thought the king would die. What difference does it make if the king lives? His inheritance is secure regardless."

He stopped and stared at me, his eyes bright and cheeks flushed. "Unless it isn't."

"You think...the king was intending to disinherit him?"

"It would explain his rush to marry while he lay dying. Brannon could declare himself king, and with a bride beside him as a queen, there is little chance he would be denied."

"But if the king lives, there's no sense in marrying Miss Derville if he's passed over."

"Precisely."

"The princess wants the marriage, too. She wants it badly." I paused, thinking about her possible motives. "Who do you think the king will name as his successor?"

"Caelyn seems the obvious choice."

"Do you think she knew?"

His breathing quickened as the pieces suddenly fell into place.

"The queen," he whispered. "She could have told Caelyn what was going to happen."

I rolled my eyes. "I don't believe in her 'visions' nonsense."

"The king could have confided in her and then she passed it off as a vision," he reasoned.

"Why would the king pass over his own son?"

"Have you met Brannon?"

"Notwithstanding his excellent personality, intelligence, and humility. It never seemed to bother the king."

"Outwardly, no. Conall is no fool. Brannon would bleed both countries dry indulging his own whims."

"Why push him to marry her friend?" It didn't make sense. If the princess wanted Miss Derville close, why marry her to the prince if she knew he wouldn't be king? A thought occurred to me then.

"Risteard," I ventured. "What would happen to the prince if the princess was named queen?"

"He would go back to Ilano, I imagine."

"And do what?"

He shrugged. "He would most likely be placed into office to appease him."

"Perhaps made Lord Protector?"

"What are you thinking?"

"I think the princess knew all along the king would not make Prince Brannon king, but she made him believe he would. She's been manipulating the prince into thinking they were overthrowing their father together, but secretly she was arranging a marriage so when she was made queen, her best friend and lover would be the wife of the Lord Protector. I am convinced the prince would not last long in this world after ascending to that position. Then Queen Caelyn and Lord Protector Mwiryn would effectively rule Praed and Ilano together."

"Very clever. Do you think Miss Derville is aware of the particulars?"

"It's clear she's in on a scheme to become queen and be close to the princess, but I doubt she's aware of the plot to kill the prince. Just based on what I know of her, I don't think she would be a party to murder."

"I agree. I also don't think Caelyn would remain in Praed if she were to become the queen."

"No, she wouldn't. She did mention to Miss Derville that things wouldn't be like this forever. You think she meant living here?"

"Among other things."

I chewed my thumbnail. "Jervell Kade was part of this plan. What did he have to gain by losing his power as Lord Protector?"

"He was Caelyn's closest ally. Being at the queen's right hand holds more power than Lord Protector."

"How could I not see it before!" I slammed my fist against the wall and turned to watch the flames dance in the hearth. "All the pieces fit. It was so obvious the prince and princess wanted their father dead and Caelyn was scheming behind her brother's back. Whenever the queen referred to 'their' plans, she meant her and the princess the whole time."

"What happened?" Risteard touched the side of my face. A welt formed where the princess struck me twice.

"It's nothing," I said, brushing his hand aside. "We have bigger problems to worry about than the princess' tantrums." I could feel his anger, but he restrained his fury.

"I've already been in contact with my people," he said. "This development will set us back, but I think you should prepare your friends. We can still use the wedding as our opportunity to strike."

"All right."

"It's almost over," he assured me.

"Every time I think that's true, something happens to dash those hopes," I said.

Risteard placed his hand under my chin and made me face him.

"I know how you feel, but as long as we're still in this world, there's hope."

I nodded and buried my head against his chest. He enveloped me in his strong arms, and I sighed.

"Can you just hold me tonight?" I asked. "And nothing else?"

"Whatever you wish, my lady," he whispered against my hair. "I am yours to command."

CHAPTER 56

King Conall's health gradually returned, and the prince announced the wedding would be postponed until the king was able to preside over the ceremony. The princess' irritability reached epic proportions with this declaration, but Miss Derville seemed relieved at the reprieve. For several days, only the physician could see the king to administer healing draughts and monitor his progress. The prince tried to see his father many times, but was denied, leaving him frustrated that he couldn't fix the problem he created. He visited the princess' rooms often, each time delivering the disappointing news. Every time the princess unleashed her temper, hitting me with whatever was available whether it was her fist or a hairbrush. The bruises were becoming difficult to hide. Every new injury sparked a fury in Risteard, and it took all my strength to restrain his wrath.

When the king felt well enough, he held a small council, to which the princess was not invited. She sat with the queen while the council met, restless and petulant.

"It isn't fair," she complained. "I have just as much right to be there as Brannon."

"Patience, my dear," the queen soothed. "Trust in the king's decisions."

"I'm tired of *waiting* for things to happen. If I were a man---"

"If you were a man, I would fear for the kingdom."

"You think I'm ruthless?"

"I think your femininity allows you to think clearly when you would otherwise act irrationally."

Unexpectedly, the princess grabbed the queen's hand and spoke in a low voice.

"Has he said anything to you about an announcement?" she asked.

"He has not." The queen spoke so quietly I could barely hear.

The princess sighed, and if I wasn't mistaken, tears welled in her eyes.

"I'm getting tired of this," the princess said.

"The end is coming soon. I can feel it. Patience, my dear."

Prince Brannon entered the queen's chambers, cast a sly look at Princess Caelyn, and kissed his mother's hand.

"You will be happy to know Father looks quite well," he told the queen.

"Praise Artur for that," the queen said.

"Father's very interested in the plans for the wedding, Caelyn. He's requested you visit him this evening."

"I'll be happy to," the princess said.

I was troubled. Between the king's miraculous recovery and the strange looks passing between the prince and princess, something was wrong. They spoke no more of the meeting, and I was on edge the rest of the day, wondering.

Later, I stole a few moments to drop in on Risteard in his study. By the thunderous look on his face and the state of the room, I concluded the council meeting did not go well.

"What's wrong?" I called out as a shelf of books and artifacts were swept to the floor in a crash of glass and leather bindings. Risteard braced himself against the bookcase and wouldn't look at me. Not a good sign. I stepped forward to pick up the mess.

"Leave it!"

He hadn't spoken to me this way in years. My hands shook, and I backed away from him to sit in my chair.

"Is this about the council meeting?" I'd never seen him lose his temper like this before, and I worried about pushing him. But I had to know.

"Yes," he growled.

"Tell me," I said calmly.

He sighed heavily and turned to me, dark hatred in his eyes, cheeks red, and temples throbbing.

"The king may be able to lift himself out of bed, but his mind is weak. He'll listen to anyone who suggests a plot against his life, even his thick-headed walking erection of a son."

I startled at the vulgar language I'd never heard from him. I didn't pretend men didn't speak this way, but Risteard always presented himself as a gentlemanly knight.

"What happened?" I said.

"The king is sending me away."

"What?" I managed to say through trembling lips.

"The king is sending me away. Ostensibly to further our interests in outlying countries before travelling through Ilano and back to Praed. But I suspect the prince's concerns about the trustworthiness of the king's council influenced the decision. I'm not the only one being sent on a fool's errand."

"For how long?"

He cast his eyes downward and muttered, "A year."

"A year?" I gasped, my vision starting to blur. "You cannot!"

"I know. Trust me I'm trying to get out of it, but the king isn't exactly in his right mind."

"Where is he sending you?"

"Countries where we've historically had good relations. The king would like me to negotiate trade routes."

"But you're horrible with people!" I blurted out.

He gave a wry smile. "I can be diplomatic when I want to be." He crossed his arms over his chest, defeat etched in his face.

"What are you not telling me?" I asked.

"One of my duties in Ilano, aside from interviewing possible candidates for Lord Protector..." His color rose in embarrassment. "Is to meet with a woman whom King Conall has arranged as a potential bride."

My rigid expression said it all, but Risteard didn't notice.

"His presumption is insulting." He paced back and forth. "He has no authority over any marriage of mine."

"What did you say?"

"I told him we'd discuss the matter more in private. The last thing I wanted was Prince Brannon's face gloating at me while I argued."

"Risteard," I said with more serenity than I felt. "You cannot leave me for a whole year."

He knelt and squeezed my hands tightly.

"I won't," he promised. "I will fight this. And if he does not yield, I will venture no further than Ilano for the purpose of organizing our forces."

I struggled to understand what I'd just heard. I leaned forward and propped myself against Risteard's forehead.

"Will you take care of Aquila while I'm gone?" he asked.

"Me?" I exclaimed in surprise. "Won't you take her with you?"

"No. I'll be travelling hard. She may not be able to watch over you in the castle but release her outside and she'll defend you if you find yourself threatened."

I nodded, and he took my face in his hands. He brought his lips close to mine then waited, giving me the opportunity to pull away or complete the kiss. I sealed his mouth with mine.

I know my husband. I know he was true to his word and fought fiercely to keep himself in Praed. But the king was obstinate, and his paranoia coupled with his staunch refusal to back down meant Risteard would be leaving Praed. By the king's command, he was ordered to reinforce the stability that waned with the king's absence. My devastation was palpable. I drew stares from the princess and her friends when going about my duties, face flushed and puffy. The closer his departure drew, the more distant I became, building a wall to protect me from the pain of losing him. I did not visit his room for days and knew by the look in his eyes when we passed in the daylight this hurt him, but I had to prepare myself, steel myself.

The king recovered enough to join the castle for dinner on Risteard's last evening. I was shocked at his changed appearance. Where once there stood a muscular, brutish man there was now a shadow. His hair had turned from the darkest brown to the whitest snow, and his eyes were dull. I worried he would drop the goblet of cider he held aloft or the slightest whisper would send him toppling to the ground.

"Gentlemen, knights, and ladies." His voice no longer projected with the same commanding timbre. "It brings great pleasure to these infirmed bones to see your faces and hear of the well wishes that brought me back. It is a testament to the strength of Ilano and your king." A wave of applause was followed by the king's gracious bid for silence.

"I am delighted beyond words that my son has been able to make such a wonderful choice of bride during my convalescence. It is my honor, Miss Derville, to welcome you into our family and to personally join you to Prince Brannon in marriage." Another round of cheers, and I almost rolled my eyes out of my skull.

"Our kingdom is growing, and I have looked into the future and seen our boundaries are limited only by our courage to explore. To that end, I have dispatched several of my most trusted advisors to points around the continent. Among them I send my beloved First Knight, Risteard, as a token of my goodwill and hope."

Murmurs circulated at this news, and I stole a glance at Risteard. His stoic demeanor masked hidden wrath.

"Let us raise a glass," the king continued, "to our brave travelers, most especially my nephew, Risteard! He journeys on the morrow with our hopes and wishes for safe travels!"

The attention Risteard so loathed followed this ingratiating toast. I worried the next person that slapped his shoulder in congratulations and good luck would meet a gruesome end.

"So Risteard is to leave us then?" Lady Sharp whispered to the princess.

"Indeed," she said.

"Has he fallen out with the king?"

The princess glanced around the room. "I think the king has finally realized whom he should be listening to."

Risteard did not join the ladies with the other gentlemen after dinner, though I wasn't surprised. My stomach was in knots all afternoon, and I hoped to see him so my nerves might be settled. Outwardly I was composed while internally it was a struggle not to vomit. I sat apart from the ladies, concentrating on each stitch I embroidered, wishing the task would take my mind off the fact that tonight would be the last Risteard and I spent together for some time. My tongue peeked out of the corner of my mouth as it often did when I was deep in thought.

"A cute little tease," said an unfamiliar voice close by. "I'd like to feel that pink tongue lapping at my lips."

I froze and stole a glance to the side. Two knights stood near, one of them Olim, Risteard's young protégé.

"Reminds me of a cat," Olim said.

"A cat?" the crude knight sneered. "*Are* you a man, sir?"

"Last I checked. I figured you would agree since any further discussion of the lady's attributes may draw the ire of the princess. That lady is her personal maid." He brushed away a stray lock of blonde curls. The other knight straightened and moved away.

Later, I became aware of a figure hovering over me, and I expected to see the lascivious knight from earlier. But when I looked up, Lady Sharp stared down at me with a friendly smile.

"You've improved," she said, bending over to examine my work. An obvious lie intended to bring her face close to mine, and to indicate I was wise to her intentions, I set the sewing aside and met her gaze steadily, as if to say, 'Let's dispense with the pleasantries and get to the point.'

"You've certainly improved in confidence," she said in a low voice. "You must be devastated tonight after hearing the news about your protector's departure. What are you to do without him?"

My jaw tightened, but I kept my features impassive.

"Once he's gone," she continued, "there will be no one to uphold the threats placed against me."

My heart fluttered, and I felt the weight of the dagger at my hip. I left my seat and attended to the princess' empty glass. I vowed if Lady Sharp put her hands on me again, I'll slit her throat. The dark glares I directed toward her the rest of the evening managed to convey my thoughts, and she had the common sense to leave me alone thereafter.

The princess was in a delightfully pleasant mood, prompted by her glee over the imminent departure of her meddling cousin. Her animosity toward Risteard was no secret, neither was her pleasure at seeing him leave Praed. She laughed and mingled well into the evening, giving her attention to eager knights and sycophantic ladies. My eyes grew heavy when she continued to exhibit herself well past her usual bedtime, and I swayed against the wall. She finally indicated she would turn in, much to the disappointment of a gentleman suitor, which was no doubt her intention.

I'd never seen the princess so pleased with herself, so openly joyful as she danced into her room. She hummed brightly while I loosened her stays, and she tossed her gown into my face with her foot. She laughed at my displeasure and twirled to the chair at her vanity. My fingers itched toward my hip, and it took all my self-discipline to keep from plunging my dagger into her back. The princess sighed, and I tamed the errant tangles of her hair while she played with a ribbon.

"Everything will be so much easier once Risteard's gone," the princess said to herself. "He's become much too inquisitive for his own good. At last, everything will fall into place." I swallowed hard and soon finished the evening tasks.

I closed the door quietly, proud of myself for not smothering the princess' satisfied smile under a pillow. I turned to see Risteard lurking in the corridor. He did not speak, but by his expression I knew he intended for me to follow. I shivered as he led me to his room, my stomach clenching. The moment his door closed, he addressed me with a hollow voice.

"Did you intend to avoid me until I left? Were you even going to say goodbye?"

I crumpled in on myself, clutching my aching chest. I couldn't speak through the tightness of my throat. Risteard gathered me into his arms and rocked me gently while I sobbed.

"I can't leave wondering if you still love me."

"What?" I asked incredulously. "How could you even think such a thing?"

"I didn't know what to think," he said, and I could see the pain in his eyes. "You stopped coming to me after I told you I was leaving. I thought you were angry in the least, or that your disappointment changed your feelings for me."

"I thought..." I took a deep breath. "I thought it would make your leaving easier if I stayed away."

"Has it?"

"No, I've been miserable."

Risteard laid his hands against my face and dried my tears with his thumbs.

"Do you still love me?" he asked, a trace of desperation in his tone.

I wrapped my arms around his neck and kissed him with all the reserved passion and loneliness built up inside me from the last few days, pressing my body against his. He met my kiss with equal ferocity, his fingers gripping my hair so tightly it hurt. Our mouths sought solace in the other, kissing so hard our lips bruised, our tongues wet and frantic. My arms slid down his shoulders, and I grabbed the fabric of his shirt and pushed him toward the bed. He fell backwards when his knees hit the edge of the mattress, and I used the moment of separation to rip my frock and shift off and toss them aside. He shrugged out of his shirt, and I climbed up his torso to once again claim his mouth with mine.

I lay curled against Risteard's chest, his arms wrapped possessively around me, and our bodies glimmering with sweat. He tickled my upper arm, his fingers trailing up and down my skin. I nuzzled closer, tucking my head under his chin.

"Does that answer your question?" I asked.

"Vaguely."

I heard the smile in his voice, but I wanted to leave him in no doubt. I propped myself to look into his eyes.

"Nothing in this world could make me stop loving you."

He nodded, his face serene, and he tucked me back against his body.

"Don't...don't test that."

I laughed as his tickling fingers travelled down my sides. "Stop! Stop!" I pleaded.

He ceased instantly and mumbled something about me being saucy.

After tonight, I didn't know when we would see each other again, and we didn't discuss it. Tonight was for us to enjoy. Tomorrow would be the start of heartache, and there was plenty of time for that.

Early the next morning from the princess' window, I watched him ride away from Praed Castle. She stood beside me, a satisfied smirk plastered on her face. While I was watching my heart depart from this place, she was waving goodbye to a nuisance. She turned her back to the window and flounced to the vanity. I conducted my day in a daze, performing my tasks by rote. The close of the evening fell on me like waking from a dream, my mind hazy and confused about where I was. I barely ate, and I lay lonely in my cold bed, quiet tears soaking my pillow. I felt an overwhelming sense of emptiness and despair. I was truly alone, and I was helpless to further our interests. I could not send secret messages to my people, and I could not spy on the king. All I could do was wait, listen where I could, and try not to lose hope.

CHAPTER 57

Weeks blurred by in a whirl of routines and an undercurrent of intrigue. The princess conducted herself as the devoted daughter, socializing with guests and visiting with the king while he continued to regain his health. I hadn't seen her so energetic in ages, and her exuberance influenced those around her. Miss Derville's lovely complexion returned, and she seemed more relaxed and livelier. Lady Sharp tittered and gossiped, as did their other friends who continued to infiltrate Praed. The prince was his jovial self, and the camaraderie between him and the king returned during the evening meals that were once again boisterous and gluttonous affairs. The queen resumed her 'vision' sessions, which the princess attended faithfully. I didn't bother looking in my mother's direction, but I sensed her studying me, no doubt noting my pallor and vacant eyes. Regardless, she made no attempt to communicate with me and we continued as strangers.

True to my word, I kept Aquila company when I was able. Her demeanor changed after Risteard left, and she seemed as lost as I was. I wished I was strong enough to exercise her, but I did arrange for her to be brought into the yard on sunny days so she could stretch her wings. She called out to me whenever I entered her enclosure, her head tilting from side to side.

"No, he hasn't come home," I would say, and she seemed to understand my meaning. I stroked her soft feathers and fed her morsels while speaking low, encouraging words like I'd seen Risteard do many times before.

"I miss him, too," I whispered, swallowing my tears.

When I had time to spare, I would visit Promise. The stable master recognized me very well at this point, and he would smile and give me a report on the gray mare.

"She's a good eater," he said, "but she is desperate for exercise."

I pointed a finger at him and smiled.

"I would be honored to take her for a ride." He laid a hand over his heart and bowed to me.

I entered the stall with an arsenal of brushes and began the relaxing task of grooming her soft coat to shining perfection.

"How are you this fine afternoon?" I asked. She nickered and stomped a foot. "I know," I laughed. "I'm restless, too. I wish we could go for a gallop, but I'm afraid we're stall bound until… that changes." I pressed my face against her mane and breathed in her earthy smell. "Oh, Promise," I whispered. "What if he doesn't come back?" It broke my heart to voice this fear, but I couldn't pretend it wasn't a possibility. Did I have the strength to go on without him and finish what we started?

The royal marriage became foremost on the king's mind despite the prince's attempts to distract him. Preparations resumed with renewed vigor, and the date was set much too soon for the prince's taste.

"These are my last days of freedom," he grumbled to the princess a few nights before the wedding.

"Stop whining," she said. "You knew this day was coming. You may as well get it over with."

"I just don't see why he's rushing me. He should be focusing on his recovery."

"It gives him something to do besides lie in bed. How would you feel if you had been sick for months and then finally have something to do? You would cling to your wedding plans, too."

"Indeed." He narrowed his eyes suspiciously.

"Besides." She looked pointedly at the prince. "A wedding celebration will be a welcome distraction."

"Especially with so many people around. One could easily be persuaded to let their guard down, perhaps."

"Exactly." A smile spread over her lips.

Deaf as I was, their implications were obvious.

The morning of the prince's wedding, I was already exhausted. The night before, the princess stayed up late into the night organizing final details and weaving a band of flowers for Miss Derville's hair. My head barely hit the pillow when I was ordered to rise and deliver messages to the kitchens with last minute changes to the menu and instructions for the bridal breakfast. Afterwards, I descended into the workroom to collect dresses and trains, a task which took several trips to accomplish. I almost toppled over going up and down those stairs so many times. The princess had a dress for breakfast, luncheon, the afternoon parade through town to show off the couple, the wedding itself, and the reception. For that day only, I was released from cleaning the mews to attend to the princess, but it was hardly a reprieve.

By the time I was dressing the princess in a luxurious riding gown of dark violet, my feet were sore, I had a headache, and all I wanted was to sleep. My fingers fumbled with the ridiculous number of buttons up the back of her dress, and I could hear her growing frustration with how long it was taking.

"Come *on*!" she said. "I cannot be late!"

She wasn't, of course, since she had put me to task hours before she was required to saddle up. I made sure the princess was comfortable and handed her the bundle of dried flowers she sniffed to keep herself from becoming sick from the offensive smell of the horse, then moved to the back of the line where my own mount waited. I smiled when the stable master presented me with Promise, and I ran my hand down her face and stroked her soft nose.

"I don't recognize that animal," I heard the prince say. I tensed, and he came close to inspect Promise. The stable master bowed and complimented His Highness on his notice of such a fine horse.

"Oh, I just happened to see it at a glance as I walked by," the prince said distractedly. "A mare?"

The stable master nodded.

"She is a fine animal. Has the king recently acquired her?"

"I beg your pardon, Your Highness, but she does not belong to the king," the stable master said, darting me a quick glance.

"Oh? Who else would own such an animal?"

"Sir Risteard, my lord."

The prince's features darkened at the name, and I quickly mounted to avoid his glare.

"Risteard isn't in Praed anymore," the prince said. "Get rid of her."

The color drained from my cheeks, but the stable master remained calm.

"I would were it your horse to do as you pleased with, but as it belongs to Sir Risteard and he left me explicit instructions for her, I cannot."

"Why is that woman riding her if you have such careful instructions? He cannot know you are allowing a servant upon her well-bred back."

"Who rides her is up to my discretion," the stable master said. "The lady may be a servant, but as a child of Praed, she is well versed in how to handle such a creature."

I hid a smile while the prince stalked away, and though I admired and appreciated the stable master's words, I feared they would seal his fate.

The wedding of Prince Brannon and Mwiryn Derville was a magnificent affair. Miss Derville's gown was lavish, with a train stretching the length of the aisle. The prince wore a shining red tunic with his family's crest boldly displayed on a sash across his chest. They were married in the ebbing sunlight of the inner courtyard, the king presiding over the couple. The ceremony was drawn out, with pomp and ridiculous circumstance so over the top I couldn't have been the only one to notice. I fell asleep once or twice, I confess, but at my position far in the back with the servants, no one was aware or cared. I felt a twinge of sadness in my heart when I witnessed the prince place a ring on Miss Derville's finger, wishing I could wear my own precious band.

An uproar of cheers and clapping awoke me from my latest doze, and I watched the newlyweds exit the courtyard to receive well wishes and dine in the Great Hall. Beautiful floral arrangements adorned the room and tables were piled high with meats and sweets. Cider flowed freely, and the toasts of congratulations and advice for the couple's life ahead were offered well into the night. Music played throughout the meal and dancing commenced as guests dabbed at their faces and prepared to work off their full bellies. I stayed along the perimeter of the room, watching for the princess to signal she required my services. I filled glass after glass, until it became apparent she would soon forget her own name. I served her watered-down cider thereafter. She didn't notice.

The crowded room made me dizzy and overly warm, and I braced myself against a table more than once to keep from passing out. After this night was over, I hoped to return to my normal routine, including my normal bedtime and normal time to wake. I'd never felt so drained, as if all the blood had left my muscles. My mind was dull, my thoughts sluggish, to such an extent I didn't realize I was being watched.

Fingers dug painfully into my arm, and I was dragged into an alcove. I whirled on the culprit, my hand reaching for my dagger, when I saw the person's face and stilled.

"Mother," I whispered. "What are you doing?"

She stared at me intently, studying my face and body.

"Laria..."

My mother's tone was very serious, and my mind flashed to Ula.

"Is Ula all right?"

"As far as I'm aware. It's *you* I'm worried about."

"Me? What do you mean?"

"I've seen that look before. I've had it, and many other women have as well."

"What look is that, Mother? Exhaustion?"

"This is no time for jokes, Laria. Tell me truthfully: when was your last monthly courses?"

My jaw dropped.

"Wh-what? Why would you ask that? I'm not---"

"Are you certain?" she demanded. "Is it impossible?"

My cheeks burned, and in a small voice I said, "No."

She closed her eyes and massaged her temples, a clear sign of her disappointment coupled with aggravation.

"How could you be so foolish?"

"It's not what you're thinking," I argued. "I have not dishonored you."

"You have lain with a man?" she asked bluntly, so there was no chance of a misunderstanding.

"I have lain with my husband." I spoke in a steady, clear tone. Now it was her turn to look shocked.

"Your *husband?* Laria, what were you *thinking?* I can't even imagine what punishment you'll receive if you're found out!"

"I'm not going to be found out. Am I?"

"You know if the queen becomes suspicious and demands an answer, I cannot lie."

"Then let's not give her a reason to wonder."

"Who is he?"

"I cannot tell you. I cannot!"

She opened her mouth to argue.

"For many reasons. And if the queen asks you questions, you can honestly say you don't know." I leaned against the wall, closing my eyes as my head throbbed.

"Is it the man you talked to me about before?" she asked, almost kindly.

I nodded.

"When were you married?"

"Two months ago." A time not long ago, but so much had happened since then.

"Does anyone know?"

"A few people. Ula knows. Only that I was getting married, though, not the name of the groom. She made my dress."

"It must have been lovely then."

"It was." Wistful memories tugged at my heart and a smile quivered on my lips.

"Where were you married?"

"Riverstone." I glanced at her. I could tell she was trying to compose herself.

"I ask again. Do you recall when you last had your monthly?"

"Before the wedding--the last time I can remember anyway. It's possible I simply didn't notice."

"You didn't notice blood coming from between your legs for four days?"

At times, my mother could be truly annoying.

"I cannot be pregnant," I insisted, my eyes welling with unshed tears. "Not now."

"We cannot control these things, Laria. You take after the women of my family. We are very fertile."

"It's possible I'm not," I continued. "I've been under a lot of stress lately." I looked at Mother hopefully, but she didn't seem convinced.

"We have to think rationally, Laria. I have access to the queen's gardens. I will make you a tonic and we'll take care of this."

I was incredulous. "Excuse me?"

"You said yourself you cannot afford to have a child now. The best thing to do would be to terminate this pregnancy. You can have another when it's more prudent to do so."

I was shocked beyond the ability to form words. I understood why she suggested such a desperate course, but this child, if there was one, could possibly be all I had left of Risteard were we to never meet again.

"I can't do that," I whispered.

"You can't keep this a secret forever. What will you do when it starts to show? My belly was swelling by four months! That's not too far away, Laria."

"I know you're trying to help, but I will not do what you suggest." I was no longer able to handle this conversation and turned to leave.

She caught hold of my sleeve, and when I met her eye, I was astonished to find tenderness there.

"Will you take better care of yourself then? You're so pale."

I nodded, and my mother released me. She gave me the barest of smiles, and I retreated before I lost my resolve.

I spent the rest of the evening in denial. My mother was wrong. She *had* to be. It was too soon for me to be with child--our marriage was brand new. I sat down and racked my brain, trying to remember for certain when I'd last had my monthly courses. I could recall needing sanitary rags just prior to the wedding, and after that, not at all. It had to be the stress and the lack of nourishment postponing my courses. I decided I would wait another week before making an absolute determination either way. Until then, I heeded my mother's advice, and snuck extra morsels of food until my appetite was satiated.

CHAPTER 58

Surprising no one but a fool, shortly after the wedding between Prince Brannon and Miss Derville, King Conall suddenly and unexpectedly died. He went to bed complaining of stomach pains and fearing a relapse called for his doctor. Before the physician arrived, the king slipped into a coma and soon thereafter passed beyond the veil. The guests who attended the wedding had returned to Ilano, and the castle was settling into old routines when the king passed, and now everything was turned upside down again. Black shrouds were draped over the windows and the court was clothed similarly. The queen sequestered herself in her rooms to begin her mourning and did not receive visitors. The princess played the inconsolable daughter, placing her hand on her breast and declaring how grateful she was that he lived to see his son marry. The prince wasted no time declaring himself regent, and because he was married and the obvious choice, he was certain the council would quickly crown him king.

It had only been ten days since the wedding.

According to Ilano tradition, King Conall was dressed in formal garb, wrapped in the banner of his people, placed upon a funeral pyre, and set aflame just as the sun set on the third day following his death. Gathered to witness the ceremony were his family as well as his trusted council and friends. The next morning, his ashes were gathered and sent by a special emissary to his estate in Ilano to be interred with his ancestors. I wished King Conall farewell on his journey and hoped to never hear his name spoken again.

Based on my new morning ritual of vomiting profusely followed by a ravenous appetite, it was impossible to deny Mother was right: I was with child. There was no way to inform Risteard, and even if I could, I wouldn't have. He had enough to worry about without this complication to distract him. I managed to sneak extra rations of food from the kitchen, avoided overexerting myself when cleaning the mews, and slept soundly every night. The most eventful summer of my life was coming to an end. The rainy season and winter meant colder temperatures and an excuse to bundle myself in extra layers to hide my growing belly. I still didn't have a plan for the birth, or what I would do with the child afterwards. Everything depended on whether Risteard came home and our success taking back the country.

A few weeks later, a semblance of normalcy returned to the castle. Princess Caelyn's wardrobe resumed its colorful hues, but the queen announced she would mourn for the requisite length of time--one year--for a widowed queen. The council, feeling the pressure of a kingdom without a king, ruled Prince Brannon would ascend the throne and be crowned before the rains came. The prince was beside himself with joy and immediately ordered lavish preparations for the ceremony. Shocking.

I had never witnessed a coronation. King Llewlyn was king years before I was born and King Conall stole the throne, which required little formality. I felt ill at the prospect of seeing the crown passed to such a horrible man, a fine change from the usual feelings of nausea I dealt with daily. The prince was to be crowned in the inner courtyard, unless the rains came early, in which case the Great Hall was marked as the best place. The coronation would be as private an affair as one could have with such an extravagant king.

Every day, I expected to see Risteard ride up the mountainside leading an army to prevent it. I watched every morning for a month, pretending to be watching for dark clouds that would threaten the ceremony. And every night I went to bed disappointed. My morning nausea had subsided, but the hunger increased, and I worried I wouldn't be able to keep up with my body's demands in the coming months, nor hide the aches in my lower back. I rolled over and stretched, feeling my tight muscles loosen, and rested my hands on the slight swell of my belly. I hadn't felt the baby move yet, but I recently started showing, and I knew soon I would have to work diligently to hide my precious secret.

The morning of the coronation promised to be warm and blue, and though I was busier than ever, my mind was full of Risteard. Surely, he would come. Perhaps at the last moment like a hero in a novel. But he did not ride into Praed like a conquering knight with banners flying. And when Queen Shaeli placed the crown upon Prince Brannon's head and declared him henceforth 'King' Brannon without so much as a trumpet blast to signal my husband's arrival, I knew he would not be returning to Praed. It was perhaps what I feared--the last time we were together would have to sustain me for the rest of my life. The queen removed her own crown and placed it on Miss Derville's head. In the span of a few minutes, Praed had a new king and queen.

After her brother was pronounced king, Princess Caelyn insisted on attending every council meeting. Her voice was often the most persuasive of all, and soon King Brannon was holding private sessions with just the princess where they would decide policies before approaching the council for approval. Many of the elder members did not care for this arrangement, but the new king was proving himself more of a tyrant than the last one, and eventually the council members stopped trying to voice their opinions for fear of banishment. Queen Mwiryn also attended these meetings but remained silent. Her beauty hadn't faded, but her eyes grew dull over time, and I worried she would soon become a hollow shell under the strain.

The princess had never been so content, and her appearance improved considerably. She had always been pretty and well dressed, but her happiness brightened her eyes and brought color to her cheeks. It was a stark contrast to her dear friend, and I wondered if they still had a secret relationship. Now that Brannon was king and clearly in her way, what was her plan?

Nights fell earlier, and I spent my days going about my usual routine and hoping no one observed my sullen mood. It had been two months since Risteard left Praed, and every day without him tore at my heart. I found comfort in my one-sided conversations with Aquila and my stolen moments with Promise, whose mane was often damp from my tears. My body was changing rapidly, and I wore loose-fitting frocks and a large apron to hide my growing body and swollen breasts. The aching in my skin and sore muscles was wearing on my nerves, and I had to restrain my temper daily. I was fortunate the princess was too absorbed in her own affairs to notice the subtle changes. I shuddered to think what would happen if she discovered my secret.

The ladies met often in the afternoons to entertain themselves while the king occupied himself with so-called "matters of state," which meant indulging in his own pleasures. The princess maintained that nothing was amiss, but poor Queen Mwiryn fidgeted and sighed miserably.

"You're playing atrociously," Princess Caelyn scolded her good-naturedly when Queen Mwiryn lost yet another hand of cards.

"I'm sorry," Queen Mwiryn said flatly. "I suppose I'm just not in the mood today."

"What's troubling you, my dear? You look positively set down."

"I didn't expect to be put aside so quickly. That's all."

The princess gave her a pitying look. "Now, enough of that. We both knew this was going to happen. It's how men are. You are still the queen no matter what trollop he cavorts with."

"Why must he cavort at all?" she whined. "Am I not enough for him? I give myself to him whenever he wishes."

"One woman is never enough for a man." The princess dealt another hand. "You mustn't take his behavior as a personal affront."

"This isn't what I expected marriage to be," Queen Mwiryn said somberly.

"It won't be like this forever," Princess Caelyn promised and reached across the table to squeeze her hand. My ears perked up at this, and I shifted slightly to listen.

"I half hoped I would find happiness in marriage."

The princess pulled away and fixed her friend with an angry stare.

"It's nothing against you, my dear," the queen amended hastily. "But I did hope I would at least find some pleasure in it. Though I could not do what must be done if I had any affection for my husband, could I?"

"No, you could not," the princess agreed.

Queen Mwiryn lapsed back into silence, and they played another round of cards, which she lost soundly.

"You know what you need?" the princess said brightly. "A party. Something simple and fun, just as you like."

A smile played at the queen's lips.

"You would like that, wouldn't you?" the princess prompted.

The queen nodded shyly, and the princess giggled and took her hands. "Wonderful! We'll serve all your favorite foods and have music and dancing. We can all have new dresses made. All of us! Even her!" the princess exclaimed, pointing at me. I pretended not to notice, but encouraged by the queen's giggles, the princess glided over, grabbed my arm, and pulled me to my feet.

"She is a lady-in-waiting after all," the princess said, twirling me around. The queen laughed, and the princess pulled me close and danced me around the room.

"She'll certainly require something more suitable if she's to be my partner!"

The princess had never been so exuberant, and under any other circumstances, I would find this transformation refreshing. But every second I spent near her made me more and more uncomfortable. She spun me under her arm and flung me away, then wrenched me close. I collided into her and let out a "whoosh" of air as my belly bore the brunt of the impact. The blithe expression vanished, replaced by a puzzled tilt of the head and narrowed eyes.

A few seconds passed without a word from the princess.

"Caelyn?" Queen Mwiryn said. "Is something wrong?"

The princess stepped away, her eyes never leaving mine. I maintained a stony expression, and our stalemate made the queen uneasy. She came to stand next to the princess and tugged at her sleeve.

"What's happened?" the queen whispered.

"Take it off," the princess ordered.

"I beg your pardon?" the queen said.

"Her." The princess pointed at me. "Take off your frock."

I shook my head. Before I could blink, the princess lunged.

"Caelyn, *stop*!" the queen pleaded.

But the princess was in a frenzy and wrestled me to the floor. She clawed at the neckline of my frock and tore at the straps of my apron. I brought a knee up against her chest and pushed her off. She landed on her backside hard, further igniting her anger. The queen tried to hold her back, begging her to explain herself. But the princess could not form words much less control her temper.

While they were distracted, I reached inside my frock and withdrew my dagger. Such an act could sentence me to death, but I would risk it to protect my unborn child. The queen turned white when she saw the blade, and the princess turned red.

"Guards!" the princess shouted.

Several guards burst into the room, swords drawn. I kept my eye on the princess. She ordered the men to disarm me. A hand clamped on my shoulder, and I whirled around to face the knight who dared remove my weapon.

"Come on." It was the young knight, Olim, sympathy in his eyes. "Give it over and we'll figure this out. Don't make things worse."

I hesitated. I didn't want to hand over the blade, but I understood the practicality of his words. Regretfully, I placed the dagger in his outstretched hand.

"Now take it off!" the princess demanded.

"Your Highness?" Olim asked in confusion.

"I want her to remove her frock. Relieve her of it."

"I don't think---"

"I'm not asking you to think. Do it."

When Olim stood his ground, another knight shouldered him aside and obliged the princess. He ripped the apron off my body as if it were made of paper, then tore my frock down a seam until it was in tattered rags at my feet. I stood before them clad only in my underclothes humiliated and quivering with rage.

"What have you done?" the princess hissed while pointing at my exposed protruding belly. The knights were quiet, and the queen stared in shock. I raised my chin defiantly.

"Take this whore," the princess seethed through gritted teeth, "and throw her in the dungeon. You will be presented to the king tomorrow morning. Take the time to reflect on your indiscretion and how you will defend your honor."

I put up little resistance to being escorted into the bowels of the castle and tossed in a cell. I hit the cold, hard stone on my hands and knees, pain radiating through my body. I crawled to the wall and propped myself against it as the iron door slammed shut. Footsteps receded, taking with them the last of the candlelight. When the heavy wooden door of the dungeon closed heavily, I was enveloped in total darkness. There were no sounds save for my steady breathing and the occasional dripping of water. I crossed my arms over my belly and rested my forehead against my raised knees. It didn't matter what response I gave in the morning. The king would surely sentence me to death at Princess Caelyn's insistence. She had always hated me, and now was her chance for revenge. Sobs overcame me, and I cried until my chest burned and my throat was sore before falling asleep in pitch blackness.

The creak of an opening door followed by heavy footsteps woke me from a tormented sleep. I raised my head to see a guard holding a candle aloft. He tossed a piece of bread at me through the bars. I stiffly inched my way forward to settle my grumbling stomach on the meager nourishment. The guard watched me while I ate, then he opened the barred door and roughly pulled me to my feet. My legs buckled underneath me, all feeling lost after sleeping on the hard ground. He pulled me up and practically dragged me up the steps. He paraded me down the hallway, the eyes of curious servants and early risers watching. I was conscious of my disheveled appearance, dirty underclothes, and sleep-tossed hair, but I strode toward the council chambers with my head held high. I had nothing to be ashamed of, and I made everyone else in the castle aware of this fact.

The guard pushed open the doors to reveal only three people in the room. Generally, a trial included all council members, but it was clear the princess intended to prosecute this crime expeditiously and as quietly as possible. The king sat upon a throne on a raised dais, the queen beside him on her own throne with the princess standing at her left. The guard planted me several feet away from them and forced me to bow before leaving the room.

"I wouldn't have believed it had I not seen it myself," King Brannon mused, looking me up and down. "Well, out with it. Who is responsible for your current condition?"

I made no effort to reply and stared blankly. The princess waved to draw my attention and I turned to her.

"Your king has asked you a question," she said angrily. "Answer him as best you can, and you may be given mercy."

A lie, of course. I shook my head slowly. Her face flushed, and I turned away.

The king stood and took a few steps toward me, giving me his best empathetic gaze, his attempt at appearing a fatherly liege.

"Has someone harmed you?" he asked.

I gave no reaction.

"Taken you by force? Seduced you? Made promises he clearly had no intention of keeping?"

"I'm mostly shocked someone was desperate enough to take out his pleasures on her," the princess said.

The king shifted awkwardly and turned away to hide his reddened face. I clamped my lips to keep from sneering. Desperate, indeed. The king was quite familiar with the concept. Out of the corner of my eye, I watched the princess lean closer to the queen and whisper loudly in her ear.

"A truly despicable man, I'm guessing. A cripple? A bastard dropped on his head as an infant? Maybe a blind man?"

The queen's cheeks flushed the same shade as her husband's.

"Maybe she has a lover," the queen said in a tiny, nervous voice.

The princess threw back her head and laughed. The king joined her, and once more composed, turned to me with a leering smile.

"I'm sure word of your imprisonment has spread. And yet, you stand alone. Perhaps a public beating will flush him out. Would you care for a stroll through the castle…naked?"

Sweat broke out over my heated skin. I shivered when a bead of moisture trickled down my back.

"He's just as guilty as you. There is no sense protecting him when he obviously won't help you."

Behind me, the doors opened, and tramping boots echoed in the chamber. My heart seized and I held my breath. The princess and King Brannon paled.

Even if I were blind, I would know those footfalls. A man loomed beside me, and I feared my quaking knees would give out. I risked a sidelong glance to confirm his identity.

Risteard.

CHAPTER 59

"Risteard," King Brannon said. He reached for the armrest, missed, and stumbled. He wiped his hands on the front of his doublet and smoothed out his hair. "Back so soon?"

Risteard stared directly at him without offering me the slightest glance. I desperately wanted him to look at me.

"When did you arrive?" The king tried to maintain a conversational tone but the nervous tremor was evident.

"Just now."

"Did you hear about the death of my father? And my coronation?"

"That's why I'm here. I was informed on my arrival that a young woman was on trial." He looked around the room briefly. "Interesting that there is no council here to conduct such a trial."

"This is a private, family matter," the princess said. "We saw no need to involve the council in such a trial."

"It must be something very particular if you felt the need to toss your own lady-in-waiting in the dungeon," Risteard said.

If the king was aware of the undercurrent of anger in Risteard's tone, he made no indication.

"She has dishonored me and her position in this household irreparably," the princess said. "Show him." She waved a hand at me.

I didn't move, my eyes fixed on Risteard.

The princess sighed in exasperation and told Risteard to make me show him the reason for my presence here.

He looked at me, and my heart swelled.

His expression softened, and he gently bid me to show him. This wasn't the way I wanted to tell him. I looked down at my arms wrapped protectively around my midsection, and I struggled to contain my tears, but despite my best efforts, I could not. I squeezed my eyes tightly before sliding my arms apart to reveal the bulge of my belly. I heard his intake of breath and gathered the courage to steal a glance at his expression. He was staring intently at my stomach, clearly aware of the significance. His jaw clenched, and he turned a murderous glare at the three gathered in front of us.

The king shrugged and raised his hands helplessly. "She refuses to tell us who is responsible for her condition."

"She can't be seen in such a state," the princess added. "What would people think?"

"What were you planning on doing with her?" Risteard's tone was dangerously low, but only I seemed to realize how close he was to losing his temper.

"She must be punished, of course," the princess said lightly. "Regardless of how she ended up in this condition, she should have been careful. A sound lashing is in order, perhaps a lengthy stay in the dungeon." The princess prattled on, oblivious to the rising color in Risteard's face. "She cannot be allowed to carry the child to term, obviously. I'll have Mother make a tonic, or we can simply beat it out of her."

I sucked a sharp breath through my teeth and trembled with rage. I could feel Risteard's anger reaching the breaking point, and yet the king and princess *still* did not notice. The only person remotely aware that something was amiss was Queen Mwiryn, whose furrowed brow signaled uncertainty at Risteard's reaction.

"It's regrettable." The king shook his head, feigning sympathy. "We expect a certain level of civility in those that serve in our household. Especially in one who has been shown so much mercy over the years."

"Your Majesty," the queen said quietly. She rested a hand on his arm, her eyes fixed on Risteard.

The king ignored his wife and the storm brewing in the First Knight's eyes and blathered on. "We cannot allow a defiled woman to serve our princess. It would be a disgrace to Ilano and our family. If she were a victim and sought restitution and forgiveness that would be a different matter, but her complete lack of cooperation leads me to believe she is just as responsible for her current situation."

"Your Grace…" the queen warned again.

He brushed away her hand and continued. "The child must be destroyed for certain. How embarrassing to have her walking around with a bastard growing in her belly? But perhaps we should also ensure she's incapable of producing children in the future?" He looked to the princess for her agreement.

It took all my self-control to keep from flying at him and clawing his face.

"Brannon, *stop*." The queen spoke sternly and gripped his arm. She looked pointedly at Risteard. The king and princess followed her gaze, puzzled at Risteard's angry expression.

"You threw a pregnant woman who has served you faithfully for years into the dungeons because you feared your own disgrace?" Risteard said.

The princess moved her mouth to speak, but no words came out.

"And what would you do to the man responsible?"

There was no answer.

"I claim this child," Risteard said boldly, and I nearly fainted. He took my hand in his. "And this woman. As my wife."

The expressions on King Brannon's and Princess Caelyn's faces were breathtaking. They paled and their jaws dropped in astonishment. Queen Mwiryn looked from one to the other and back at us, her sympathy and sadness evident.

"When?" the king sputtered.

"We were married four months ago." Risteard's ominous stare never left the king's face. "She is therefore under my protection and has committed no offense against you." His voice dropped, and he spoke through gritted teeth. "You have threatened the life of my unborn child and bodily harm toward my wife. That was a mistake."

The queen and princess turned their shocked faces to the stunned and frightened king.

"This trial is over." Risteard turned toward the door, pulling me along behind him. I could barely breathe as I stumbled out of the council chambers.

A small group of knights led by Olim approached Risteard when we burst into the corridor, and Olim's confused expression would have been endearing if not for the dangerous situation we faced. The king's angry roar of Risteard's name echoed behind us, and I could no longer maintain my composure. My knees buckled and I sank to the floor. Risteard gathered me in his arms and carried me down the corridor.

Olim struggled to keep up with us. "Sir Risteard, please tell us what's going on!"

Risteard stopped at the door to his chambers, and the young knight obliged him by opening it. Risteard led the men inside, and they hovered curiously by the door while I was placed gently on the bed.

"Are you hurt?" Risteard asked.

I shook my head, and he turned to face his men.

Olim shifted with uncertainty. "Sir?" His gaze flickering from me to the black knight towering above me.

"Knights," Risteard spoke in a commanding voice, "I have just declared war on the king."

Their eyes widened, and I slipped my hand in his and squeezed tightly.

"You have a choice. Remain loyal to him or to me. If you choose to stand beside the king, I will not hold it against you, but you must leave now or be branded a traitor."

Olim looked steadily from knight to knight standing behind him. Without hesitation, he turned to Risteard and said, "We stand with you."

"You," Risteard indicated to the men closest to the door. "Gather anyone else who feels the same."

They nodded and hurried off.

"Olim," Risteard began, and the young knight straightened. "This woman is my wife."

Olim placed a hand over his heart and said, "Then I will protect her life with my own."

Risteard nodded and moved toward the door without a backward glance. I gripped his hand, pulling him back. The look he gave me was tinged with annoyance, piquing my own ire.

"Where do you think you're going?" I asked. Olim's swift intake of breath when he heard me speak for the first time distracted Risteard, but a tug on his hand brought his attention back.

"It's beginning," he said.

"Then I'm coming with you." I shifted off the bed.

"No!" he said sharply and placed a restraining hand on my shoulder. I brushed it away and pulled my other hand from his grasp.

"I need to warn my people," I insisted.

He sighed, unable to deny my words. "Olim, the lady has an important mission. While she carries out her business, she is not to leave your sight. Understood?" He shrugged off his greatcoat and wrapped it around me.

"Yes, sir."

Risteard and I had only seconds to convey everything we wanted to express. His mouth opened and closed, then he briefly touched my cheek.

"We'll talk later," I said with more conviction than I felt.

He nodded.

In the next moment, he was gone, and I hoped we would be afforded that chance.

Olim looked at me expectantly, and I snapped out of my reverie and raced from the room. He stayed close as I ran down the corridors without a care who saw me, ignoring the curious onlookers and protests when I bumped into someone. I almost slipped down the stone steps to the workroom, but I waved off Olim's attempts to assist me. I burst into the room and dodged exclamations of surprise from the stern dressmaker.

"What's the meaning---" the words stuck in the dressmaker's throat when she saw Olim. All work ceased, and everyone's eyes turned to me rushing toward Ula.

"Ula!" I exclaimed. "I need your help!"

"Laria, what's going on?" She studied my disheveled appearance: dirty face, tousled hair, bare feet, and oversized greatcoat. "Are you all right?"

"There's no time to explain everything." I grabbed her shoulders. "Listen, you must leave the castle. Don't ask questions," I ordered before she had a chance to open her mouth. "Go into Praed. Visit every house and bid others to do the same. Give them a message: Laria of Riverstone is asking them to keep their promise."

"Laria…?"

I turned my back on Ula and addressed the gaping expressions of the ladies.

"If you're happy with your current situation," I called out, "then remain where you are. But if you're anxious for change, join us." I looked back at Ula, whose surprise and confusion had rendered her speechless. I spoke loudly so the whole room could hear. "Go into Praed. Tell them a revolution has begun and bid others to spread the message."

"Laria, I don't understand," Ula whispered.

"Do you trust me?" Time was running out.

"Of course."

"Then do as I ask." I left the room, hoping someone would listen.

Coming out of the stairway, it became obvious word had spread there was a threat to the king. People rushed frantically in the hallways, locking themselves in their rooms and stopping each other to ask what was happening. Using the chaos as cover, Olim and I slipped by and made our way through the castle. I wished I could warn Mother, but her proximity to the dowager queen made that too risky.

Voices fraught with anxiety arose from the kitchens, and I entered the room to see questioning faces. Word had indeed spread fast, and even the servants were not safe from the turmoil. They all looked at me in shock, and a hushed silence settled over the room.

"Ladies," I projected. Gasps arose and hands flew to mouths when they heard me speak for the first time in over three years. "If you've ever hoped for change, now is the time to make it for yourselves. Either remain here under King Brannon's tyrannical rule, or travel into Praed to alert your families that freedom is within your grasp. I cannot promise victory, and if we lose, you may live out your days in the dungeon or hang from a rope, but you will do so knowing you left nothing to fate, and that you took your life into your own hands." I moved past them to the back door, and my chest swelled with pride when they abandoned their stations and followed.

The ladies from the kitchens ran down the mountain while I surveyed the helter-skelter. Men were running toward the mews and the stables, either to defend the king or to support Risteard. Ladies who had been enjoying an early morning turn in the gardens were hastening back inside, their faces white with terror.

"I wonder what the king has told them," I mused out loud.

"Something to paint Risteard in a rather grim light, I imagine," Olim said.

"Risteard," I whispered. I whirled on Olim and demanded, "Take me to him. Now."

Olim headed around the outside of the castle, and I nearly ran to keep up. Then I saw the reason for all the haste and panic. Knights spilled out of the barracks and gathered in formation with shields raised and swords drawn blocking the front entrance to Praed Castle. My heart sank, thinking the king's forces were preparing to attack. Then it dawned on me the knights were facing the castle, not defending it. Risteard strode to the front of the line, sword drawn, inspecting his men. Olim gasped, and I looked up at his shocked face. I followed his gaze down the mountain and saw soldiers in garb I didn't recognize.

"Who are they?" I asked.

"They're from Ilano. Risteard brought an army with him. He came prepared," Olim said.

Boldly, I stepped forward, passing the line of knights. A few watched me, but most were disciplined enough to keep their eyes forward. Risteard froze when he saw me, and I sensed a reprimand at the tip of his tongue, but he was intelligent enough to keep quiet.

The front of the castle was packed with people in neat rows, standing for hours without moving. The sun shone directly overhead, and I shielded my eyes from the glare reflecting off the knights' armor. Banners rippled lazily in the breeze, and I counted the different crests in amazement. Between the Praed Castle knights, soldiers, and the forces from Ilano, there were hundreds of houses represented here. Risteard's eyes remained fixed on the castle doors, and though I tried to remain as stoic as him, my feet ached and my stomach rumbled.

After another hour passed without anything happening besides my legs cramping and my hunger reaching the breaking point, I broke the silence.

"What are we waiting for?" I asked.

On cue, the doors to the castle opened, and a small contingent of guards preceded King Brannon, Queen Mwiryn, and Princess Caelyn. Risteard tensed but gave no orders when the king approached with hands raised in supplication.

"Are you offering your surrender?" Risteard asked.

The king was not amused.

"Hardly," he said, lowering his hands. "This is madness, Risteard. You cannot honestly think you'll get away with this."

Risteard looked over his shoulder, met the king's eyes with an eyebrow raised, and waited. The king took a moment to observe the battle-ready knights and the Ilano soldiers behind them.

"This is treason!" the princess hissed. "You think a few knights and traitorous soldiers will save you?" Her face paled, and her eyes moved over our heads and beyond the knights. Risteard and I turned to see a plume of dust traveling up the mountain. Knights moved aside for Risteard and me to see. From the dirty cloud at the crest of the mountain, voices and men emerged.

"It's Praed," I whispered, gripping Risteard's arm.

Risteard turned and marched with confidence toward the king, who took several nervous steps back. We stopped a few feet in front of him, close enough to see the sweat running down his temple.

"It appears you have no support here, Brannon," Risteard said.

"We don't need them," the princess told her brother. But he was less a fool than I thought.

"No, Risteard is right," the king said. "I cannot defend myself against such an army."

The princess' face flushed and she beat her fists against her thighs. The queen's eyes darted from face to face while she fidgeted nervously.

He straightened and thrust out his chest. "Therefore, I invoke the Law of Bern under the Right of Succession."

My jaw dropped, not only at his declaration, but in shock that he'd studied our history enough to know our laws. The Right of Succession laid out the rules of ascendency, and the Law of Bern stated a king could be challenged by a high lord or knight in single combat. King Bern had ruled Praed briefly six centuries ago, and when he was overthrown, it started a tradition of in-country fighting for the throne. King Brannon changed the roles to suit him, but the rules were the same--two men fight until one is dead.

"Brannon don't be stupid!" the princess said.

The king raised a hand to stop her protests.

"What do you say, Risteard? No armies, no eagles. Just the two of us, as you've always wanted."

I watched the king warily, suspecting he had a wicked plan.

"Name the weapon," Risteard said.

My heart plummeted into my stomach and my mouth went dry.

"You idiot!" the princess exclaimed.

The king ignored her. "Swords."

"When and where?" Risteard asked.

I clutched his arm.

"Inner courtyard. One hour."

"So be it," Risteard said.

The king nodded and stalked toward the castle with the princess tailing him, her protestations fading.

I turned to Risteard. "What have you done?" A tear slipped down my cheek and dropped to the earth. The people of Praed mingled with the soldiers from Ilano, and several came closer still. I'm sure if I looked, I would recognize them, but I had eyes only for Risteard.

"There's no chance of Brannon beating me in single combat," Risteard said with a dismissive wave before turning to his men. I grabbed his arm and forced him to face me.

"And he obviously knows that!" I cried. "Don't you find his challenge in the least bit suspicious?"

"I find everything suspicious," he said, his face inches from mine. "That's why I'm still alive."

"Your overconfidence is comforting, but it may yet be the death of you."

We glared at each other, conscious only of our heated exchange. My words drove his temper to the boiling point, but I would have done or said anything to keep from losing him.

"My lady?" a voice spoke from the crowd.

Risteard and I turned to see Morgan's worried face. Without a word, he towed me toward her and practically tossed me into her arms.

"Keep her out of trouble," he ordered and marched away.

"How dare you!" I yelled after him, tears trailing down my soiled cheeks. The soldiers and knights looked away and shuffled awkwardly, but I didn't care. "You left me here for months, waiting miserably, and now the day we've been working for is finally here and you expect me to sit back and do nothing?"

He slowly turned around, and though his features were placid, his eyes glistened.

"Yes," he said.

I wiped a hand across my face and stepped closer to look straight into his face. "Why are you pushing me away?"

"I can't---" he struggled to speak, and at last I saw my husband again, and I understood.

"Oh, my poor knight." I cupped his cheek with my hand. "You're not going to lose me. But you can't expect me to stand aside. That isn't the woman you married."

"Did you know?" He cast a quick glance at my belly. "Before I left?"

I shook my head. "Not till...after. Weeks after." I pressed my forehead against his. "I'm not leaving your side."

"If this ends badly," he said, "please promise me you'll flee." He moved a hand toward me, then thought the better of it.

"I will," I promised.

"I need to prepare," he said, once again the steadfast knight. "I'll see you in the courtyard."

I nodded and he walked away, his trusted knights following. I felt Morgan's hands rubbing my shoulders, and I sank against her. It was then I noticed our exchange had been observed by someone other than our people.

My pulse stumbled when I spied Queen Mwiryn staring at me, her angelic face regarding me with, dare I believe it, envy? She opened her mouth but closed it again without speaking. Any moment, I expected her to hurry off to reveal my secret to the king, but like me, she remained transfixed. Her guards tried to escort her away, but she was frozen in place.

"Come, my dear," Morgan said. "Let's get you changed."

I dragged my attention away from the queen. "I can't. All my clothes are in my room, and I can't go back in the castle."

"Let me help you," the queen said, surprising both Morgan and me. "I can bring you out one of my gowns. It might be a little long, but it may still fit your... shape."

Morgan turned to me. "What does she mean by that?" I didn't answer. I stared at the queen and tried to decide if I could trust her offer.

"Why?" I asked simply.

"Please." Her cheeks flushed and a wobbly smile teetered on her lips. "It's the least I can do. You cannot meet your destiny dressed like that."

"Meet me at the stables," I said. "Quickly." I headed in that direction before I reconsidered. Morgan hurried to keep up, and she was out of breath by the time I pushed open the stable doors and startled the stable master. He was relieved to see it was me.

"You're not the first to come here," he said. "Many have saddled their horses and fled. Would you like yours?" I shook my head.

"Laria," Morgan gasped. "I know you don't have time to explain everything, but you have to tell me something."

"Risteard and I have raised a rebellion," I explained as we walked the length of the aisleway. The stable master blinked in surprise when he heard but said nothing.

"I could see that with my own eyes," she said with annoyance. "Why would the queen help you?"

I stopped at Promise's stall. "I don't know." I stroked the horse's nose.

"I won't pry," Morgan said gently. "But if there's something you want to talk about, I'm here to listen."

"If Risteard doesn't survive," I choked on the words, "will you help me escape?"

"All of Praed will help you, my dear."

"He has to survive," I said. "I cannot live without him."

"You lived without him for most of your life, Laria. You will learn to be alone again. If you must."

"But I won't be alone." I gripped a handful of Promise's mane and buried my face in the soft strands. Morgan understood and quietly took my hand clutching the greatcoat. I relaxed, and she removed the garment and placed a protective arm across my swollen belly.

"Oh, Laria," she whispered. "Don't worry yourself. If you're made a widow today, you will be taken care of. Both of you." I collapsed against her and unleashed the pent-up exhaustion, fury, and despair. She held me tightly, stroking my head and back, and whispered endearments.

We heard a breathless, "Your Majesty, wait," and looked to see the queen flanked by two ladies-in-waiting marching toward us. She carried a gown bundled in her arms. She cleared her throat and waved away the ladies.

"Here," she said quickly, holding the dress outstretched. "The time is nigh."

I took the garment from her hands and hesitated, wondering whether to thank her. By her expression, I knew she had questions. I had some of my own, but there was no time. With a short nod, she left with her entourage and I ducked into a stall to change. Morgan helped me step into the moss green gown and pulled my laces tight, but with room to breathe. I splashed water from a trough onto my face, much to Morgan's chagrin, smoothed back my hair, and left the stall. I nearly tripped over the long hem and gathered much of the fabric in my arms before rushing from the stables.

One hour. Sixty minutes. No matter how you broke it down, time was time. I entered the courtyard, Morgan scurrying to catch up, and scanned the crowd. At one end, the king stood with his queen and sister beside him. The queen's cheeks were red and her ladies were panting. They must have ran to get here in time. It seemed very few people had chosen Brannon's side, but there were more than I expected. Knights and soldiers from Ilano stood around the perimeter, and people from Praed looked down at us from among the ramparts. And standing formidably dressed completely in black among his faithful knights was Risteard.

Morgan came up beside me breathing hard. I held my chin high and proudly marched through the courtyard. I felt everyone stare, but I didn't stumble on my way to Risteard's side.

The king, the queen at his arm, and the princess walked forward. Risteard placed a hand at the small of my back, and together, we met the trio in the middle of the courtyard. The princess glared at me so fiercely I could read what she planned to do if she got her hands on me. I stared back defiantly, further igniting her fury.

"I assume we can forgo the customary search for hidden weapons?" the king said smugly.

"Can we?" Risteard asked.

The king narrowed his eyes. "You should learn to hold your tongue."

"Likewise. We're not here to talk, are we?"

"It was never your strong suit anyway," the king said.

Risteard led me away without another word. He paused when the king continued to taunt him.

"What do you think we should do with her, Caelyn, after she's made a widow?"

"Whatever you wish, Your Majesty. Your pleasures will be hers to serve," the princess said.

Risteard's fingers dug painfully into my back. I lay a restraining hand against his chest and whispered he should ignore them. The impending fight was purpose enough for Risteard to avoid provocation. He would have his revenge soon enough.

"Fellow countrymen, knights, and ladies," the princess said. She turned to us and let her eyes roam over the people of Praed. "Traitors, whores, and deceived people of Praed. The king has allowed this man a chance to defeat him in single combat in order to spare your lives. He will have no help from an army nor his eagle. He must fight to the death. If he wins, no punishment shall befall him. If he loses, all who support him will suffer." She stared menacingly at me and at the knights circled around Risteard.

"I hope you find honor in what you've done," she addressed Risteard. "Like a typical man, you've followed your *urges* instead of your head. If you denounce this woman as the reason for this madness, you will be spared."

Risteard stared back coldly.

"So be it." The princess beckoned the men forward, and they faced off with her between them. "Remember. Swords only." The moment she stepped away, swords were unsheathed, and the first spark of their meeting echoed in the vastness of the crowded courtyard.

I knew little of the art of swordsmanship. Father never bothered to teach me since I was the wrong gender, and my undercroft lessons with Risteard covered only the basics of knifework. The movements of the blades as they arced through the air was hypnotic, but I cringed at every clash and rasp of metal on metal. Waning sunlight reflected off the blades, blinding me with flashes of light. Their footwork was fluid and graceful, their feet dancing with each lunge and riposte.

The king grimaced, and his brow was red and damp, while Risteard appeared calm. If I didn't know any better, I would swear he was drawing this out for his own amusement. All eyes were fixed on the combatants, their faces tense. My gaze drifted to the queen where she sat on her throne, watching intently. I glanced to her right and felt like I'd been punched in the stomach.

The princess had disappeared.

CHAPTER 60

I scanned the multitude of faces focused on the duelists, frantically hoping to see Princess Caelyn. Nothing. I walked the perimeter of the courtyard calmly, angling for a better look at the crowd. Still no evidence of the princess. I panicked. There was no chance of signaling Risteard without distracting him from the fight. Swords continued to clash, and I sensed the king beginning to tire. His thrusts were less forceful, and his deflections took more effort. I couldn't shake a feeling of dread. Risteard's sword came down hard on the king's, but Brannon gritted his teeth and fought back, pushing with all his strength. His sword slashed across Risteard's arm, and he stumbled.

I ran. Not to flee from Risteard's inevitable defeat, but to save him. I ran hard, driven by fear and love. I struggled with the extra length of dress, and my bare feet were bruised from the bite of sharp rocks. Sweat trickled down my back and forehead. I ran out of the castle, past the cages housing the falcons, noting the one for Gyonessa, Princess Caelyn's falcon, was empty. I ran through the yard to the eagle mews, grabbed one of the doors, and wrenched it open. Aquila gave me a curious look, and I took a deep, shaky breath and gasped, "He needs you." I stepped away from the door and she was out in a flash of black feathers. She circled my head once, then settled on the roof of her house, looking at me expectantly.

Exhausted, I gathered enough momentum to propel myself back to the castle with Aquila's shadow overhead. I staggered into the courtyard and leaned against a wall to catch my breath. At the edge of my vision, I detected a blur of feathers, followed by a sharp, high-pitched shriek. A flicker of confusion crossed Risteard's face before he was set upon by flapping wings and grasping talons. There were shocked screams from the crowd and a triumphant sneer from the king. The falcon flew away, leaving Risteard on his hands and knees, blood flowing from wounds on his shoulder and face. The king was panting, bearing his own wounds, but he still held his sword. Risteard's lay in the dirt.

I tried to scream, but my lungs failed me. Another shriek filled the air, and the princess' falcon went on the attack again, covering Risteard's eyes. The king pulled back his arm, pointed his sword at Risteard's chest, and thrust.

A call reverberated and a black mass swooped upon Risteard an instant before the king's sword struck. Aquila's great talons ripped into the falcon, and she tore its head off with her massive orange beak. I heard a distant anguished cry, but the king continued his attack, and I couldn't look away. The king's blade tasted blood, but it was not Risteard's. It sank into Aquila's soft feathers, penetrating her breast. The great bird flapped her wings nobly, and the king pulled the blade free, his face drained and fixed upon her in horror. She dropped to the ground, and with the king momentarily distracted, Risteard rose, his sword reclaimed.

The king dropped his sword and backed away, but today the knight would show no mercy. In one bold thrust, he drove his sword upwards through the king's abdomen, impaling him just below the ribs. Blood sputtered from King Brannon's mouth when he tried to speak. Risteard raised his blade so they were eye to eye and watched Brannon's life drain away until he hung limp and bloody on the sword. With a turn of his wrist, Risteard tipped the blade down, and the body slid to the ground. Silence ruled the courtyard and I felt certain everyone could hear the ragged gasps of my breathing. Drained of his stamina, Risteard slumped next to Aquila's still form.

It took my last remaining strength to walk the short distance between us and stand over where he sat overlooking his beloved eagle's body. Carefully, I placed a hand on his shoulder, and he slowly looked up. Blood oozed from several scratches across his face. I lowered myself to my knees and wrapped my arms around him. I held his head tightly against my breasts, my fingers clutched in his hair. I braced for tears or anguished cries, but he did neither. He pulled away, and I used my sleeve to wipe the sweat from his brow and the blood from his eyes. His gaze drifted down my torso, and he gently laid a hand on my swollen belly. He sighed contentedly.

"I love you," he rasped. "Both of you."

The princess stormed into the courtyard, eyes wild, red-rimmed, and furious.

She pointed at Risteard. "Murderer!" she screamed.

I scrambled to my feet while Risteard rose with deliberate slowness beside me.

"You used an eagle to murder our king," she said. "Arrest him!" A few of the king's supporters shifted but thought better of it.

"You broke the rules first," Risteard said. "Or was it not your falcon Aquila ripped in two?"

"Bastard!" she shrieked. "I'll have you killed for this! Everyone in Ilano will hear of how you betrayed and murdered the king. You will both be hanged for your treachery!"

"Careful," I told the princess. I would hold the look on her face when she heard me speak for the first time in my heart forever.

With that one word, she went white and threw her arms out when she swayed unsteadily.

I stared boldly. "I would be mindful of how you report what happened here today. I know *all* your secrets."

Her head shook in disbelief.

I hoped she understood my meaning. I'm certain every conversation she had in my presence passed through her mind. She fled the courtyard.

"She won't get far," Risteard said.

"I know." My joy faded when Queen Mwiryn came forward and looked down at her dead husband. I pitied her lost expression and wondered what would become of her now. Slowly, she sank toward his body, and I expected her to plant a kiss on his forehead or touch his cheek, but instead she slid the crown off his head, ran her fingers over the jeweled surface, and stepped over him as if he were a pile of refuse.

"The king is dead," she called out to the crowd, holding the crown high. "By the Law of Bern, I proclaim Risteard Elejick king. All those who support him, say 'yea'!"

The courtyard erupted in deafening cheers. Risteard gripped me hard. The knights applauded and stamped their feet, and the old council members raised their hands in agreement. The queen turned her regal gaze on Risteard and offered him the crown.

"You don't have to," she said. "But there is no one more worthy."

Risteard and I looked at each other, his eyes silently seeking my opinion. This was not the outcome we anticipated. After overthrowing the king, we expected the council and the people to elect a suitable king. It appeared they had, and Risteard was the man they chose. Brannon had invoked the Law of Bern after all.

I agreed with Queen Mwiryn. My husband would make a fair and honest king. My eyes told him this was his decision, but I would stand by him. He smiled back, then knelt before the queen. She placed the crown on his head and bid him to rise.

"By the power of the royal house of Elejick, I crown you King Risteard of Ilano and Praed," the queen declared. I covered my ears when the courtyard broke into a roar of cheering and songs, their joy uplifting as they embraced and clapped. The queen then looked at me and removed her own crown, and my smile faded.

"A king requires a queen," she said. "May I?"

It was my turn to look to Risteard for guidance. Of course, she would want to make me queen if Risteard was king, but I hadn't considered this when I encouraged him to take the crown. I had no business being queen--I was clumsy, awkward, opinionated, snarky, and could barely be trusted to run a household let alone a country. Mwiryn was the epitome of the perfect queen--beautiful, poised, graceful, and kind. Did she really want to give up her power to me? She gestured toward me with the crown, smiling without reservation.

My fear must have been obvious. Risteard touched my cheek and said, "Stop what you're thinking. You don't have to, but don't say *no* because you think you're incapable. You have proven beyond a doubt you were born to accomplish the extraordinary."

My attention drifted to the jeweled crown glittering in the last rays of the afternoon sun. Praed had a long history of overthrows, betrayals, and greed to secure power. Did I want to be part of that violent tradition? My gaze wandered to Brannon's body lying in a pool of blood. Change had to start somewhere.

I accepted the crown, believing with Risteard by my side, there was no limit to what we could achieve. When I arose no longer Laria of Riverstone but as Queen Laria, the people of Praed were especially exultant. Their cries became deafening when Risteard pulled me close and kissed me for the first time in two months. I thought I'd be too shy to display affections publicly, but nothing deterred me from that passionate embrace and the promise it held.

The princess didn't make it very far. She was arrested in Market Town and later brought in chains to the council chambers. Risteard and I sat on our thrones, the members of the council and several knights surrounding the room. Her captivity did little to erase the rage from her face or teach her humility. Her mother, the former queen of Praed, was brought in as well, but only as a witness. There was no point in punishing the old woman, who had used her gift to avenge her daughter. I'd bluntly asked about her motives during the search for the princess, and what she told me was appalling.

"My husband wronged her," she said.

I snorted. "I find that hard to believe. King Conall bent to her every whim."

"In recompense for his mistakes."

She explained that Caelyn was sent away as a young woman to a doctor who could cure her 'unnatural proclivities.' What Shaeli described was nothing short of torture. I laid a hand on her shoulder when I couldn't hear anymore.

"You understand," Shaeli continued, "what a mother will do for her child."

I decided Shaeli would be sent back to Ilano accompanied by Mwiryn, the new dowager queen.

Risteard's wounds healed, the scratches on his face fading while a few red marks remained to soon become scars, one extending from his forehead just past the corner of his left eye and the other just below his right eye down his cheek. I told him it would make him more menacing, which he did not appreciate, but then I remarked it also gave him a roguish look which I found most attractive, and he accepted his new face. The sword cut to his right arm was minor but required several stitches. He refused to wear a sling. Baby.

Despite the former princess' obvious loathing of the current situation, she had enough intelligence to give Risteard and me the respect due our status. She curtseyed respectably, and kept her head bowed until she was addressed.

"This council is divided on how to proceed with you," Risteard said. "Some are calling for your death." The princess shifted nervously. "Others have taken pity and are asking for mercy. Which do you feel you deserve, knowing the part you played in several suspicious events?"

The princess looked at Risteard coldly. "I deserve whatever you feel is *fair...*Your *Majesty,*" she spoke as if the words tasted spoiled.

"On the contrary, your fate is not in my hands. It's in your queen's." He casually extended a hand toward where I sat on his left.

Caelyn's furious gaze drifted to me, and I relished the fear on her face. I smiled magnanimously and waited for her to defend herself.

"There's no point in trying to plead my case." She spoke with a tremor in her voice. "You know everything I've done, and I know you'll show me no mercy. I expect you'll sentence me to death? Well, get on with it then."

I'd considered it. When I thought of everything she'd done to me, I knew she deserved it. But death was an easy escape for her. Mostly, I didn't want my first act as queen to be ordering the death of the former princess. Revenge wasn't the example I wanted to set. Sure, I wanted to command the removal of her lying, evil tongue, but such an extreme punishment wouldn't endear me to the people.

"Oh, no." I shook my head. "I intend for you to live a long life knowing what you've done and that despite your efforts to break me, you did not succeed." She flinched under my scrutiny. "You've lost, Caelyn, and I want you to remember that until the day you die an old woman alone and miserable. I do not sentence you to death. I sentence you to the life you bestowed upon me, a life of servitude." Her eyes widened and her face flushed. The sentence was such an insult to her sensibilities she would have gladly chosen the noose.

"I should have killed you when I had the chance," she hissed. Knights seized her immediately.

"Yes. You should have."

She struggled with the knights leading her away, but I held up a hand to stop them.

"One more thing. I cannot have you spreading aspersions about me or lying about what happened here. From this day forward, you will take a vow of silence. If it's reported that you break this vow, you'll answer to the council and hope they'll be merciful. Perhaps you may learn that listening can be more beneficial than running your mouth." She screamed for her mother, and the lady stepped forward, reaching for her daughter.

"Mother," Caelyn sobbed. "Why didn't you warn me this would happen? Why didn't you tell me my own servant would ruin us?"

"It was not the woman," the old queen explained. "The child inside her was your downfall."

Caelyn shrieked and was dragged from the room, the door closing on the final sound I would ever hear from her.

Risteard squeezed my hand and asked, "Are you sure?"

"Yes," I asserted. "I want her to live with her failures."

"The people will appreciate your mercy."

"She may not feel her punishment is entirely merciful."

"Sometimes doing what is right means making difficult and heartbreaking decisions, but that doesn't make it less honorable."

"You would know. You always do what is right."

"Only to make up for all the wrongs I've committed."

"How does my honorable king feel about seeking reparations?"

His brow furrowed in confusion, and I could no longer look him in the eye. I focused on the hand resting comfortably against my belly and idly twirled the silver band on my third finger.

He leaned close and lowered his voice. "Are you thinking of someone specific?"

I nodded.

"Someone who has committed grievous offenses toward you?"

I nodded again.

"Though it would please me greatly to see Lady Sharp pay for her behavior, as your king I must advise against any violence."

A part of me felt betrayed, but I held my temper in the room full of people.

"She was horrible to me," I said. "How can she be allowed to go without consequences?"

"She *and* Lord Sharp will certainly live in fear once they learn of your coronation," he pointed out.

I considered this, imagining Lady Sharp's face when she heard of our triumph. If there was justice, she would fall into an apoplectic fit.

"Bide your time," Risteard said. "There are more important matters to attend to here."

I closed my eyes, took a cleansing breath, and nodded.

Risteard assisted me out of my chair. We walked out onto the front steps of Praed Castle and officially presented ourselves as the new king and queen amid cheers and smiling faces, both Praedans and Ilanis gathered in the hopes of a truly united kingdom.

I retired early, too exhausted to endure another moment of celebration. Risteard was duty bound to continue into the night, an imposition to his taciturn disposition. He wasn't pleased when I told him I was going to bed.

"If I have to smile and accept fealty from every simpering noble, why shouldn't you?" he asked sourly.

"Because I'm tired."

"I'm the one who was stabbed."

"I'm growing a person." It was a low blow, but I had no shame in playing the pregnancy excuse. It had the intended effect.

Risteard's expression softened. He wished me goodnight and promised not to disturb me when he came to bed.

A few ladies were assigned to attend to me, a few whom I recognized, but I did not require a horde of ladies to watch over me every second, and I ended up dismissing most of them. I allowed two to stay behind and help me undress and prepare for bed, Edde and Ula, whom I insisted be my lady-in-waiting.

A knock sounded at the door. Edde went to answer, muttering about the lateness of the hour and how in her day the queen remained undisturbed once she'd retired. She spoke to someone, then approached me in repressed exasperation.

"I'm sorry to disturb you, Your Majesty," Edde said. "But Lady Audrey requests an audience with you."

Mother.

"Of course." I rose with as much grace as my nerves would allow. Ula looked at me, but I shook my head and dismissed her. Mother entered the room and studied my short hair.

"I have only seen you from a distance this last day and a half. I thought you had styled your hair to look short. It suits you. I think." I didn't respond, waiting for her to collect her thoughts. She paced around the room, her eyes alighting on my gown and the crown on its pedestal.

"My daughter a queen," she mused. "I never imagined…never thought you of all people…"

"…could have possibly achieved so much?"

"Exactly."

I could tell it shamed her to say so. "Nor did I."

"I never thought to prepare you for such a day. How remiss I have been as your mother."

"I should have paid more attention to my embroidery. I'll certainly make a fool of myself now."

She smiled, and I was relieved to see she understood and indulged my humor.

"Mother," I said seriously. "I do not wish for you to serve me. I want you to simply remain my mother. I want you to return to Riverstone and resume your position as Lady there."

For the first time, I saw my mother's eyes mist with tears.

"I would like that," she said. She took a deep breath and shrugged the emotions away. Her expression grew serious and she said, "I don't know which was the greater shock: seeing my daughter crowned queen or discovering the identity of her secret husband."

I raised my chin defiantly as she continued.

"Why, Laria? The man who aided the murder of your father, who dragged you from your bed in the middle of the night and forced you to watch our stables burn. A monster!"

"I'm sorry that's all you've seen of him. I can assure you he is no monster."

"Was it you who uncaged the eagle?"

I nodded.

"You saved his life. And I saw your embrace after you were crowned. You have a true affection for him."

"Yes, I do. I hope you will try to get to know him, for my sake at least."

"And for the sake of my grandchild," she said as she reverently laid her hands on my belly. "You're showing well, as I did."

She was smiling, and I felt proud that I had pleased her for the first time in my life.

"Have you felt it move yet?" she asked.

"No." Suddenly worried, I asked, "Should I have?"

"Not necessarily. It's your first, after all. It may be another month before you feel the quickening."

I placed my hands over my mother's, and we looked at each other as two equal women, united in mutual respect and our love for the child within my womb.

CHAPTER 61

Two days after Risteard and I were crowned, I was pacing in my antechamber, wringing my hands. Ula watched with increasing worry, but I waved off her attempts to settle me into a chair. Today would be our first official council meeting, but that wasn't the only reason for my distress. I'd summoned Mwiryn.

My head was full of questions. Why did she help me? How did she feel about Caelyn's punishment? Why did she conspire with Caelyn and Brannon? Did she already regret giving me her crown?

There was a knock at the door, and I jumped with a startled cry. Ula raised an eyebrow, and I looked away to avoid her stare.

"Come in," Ula called.

I drew my shoulders back when Mwiryn swept into the room accompanied by her ladies. Her eyes were bright, cheeks pink, and hair glossy. Though she wore black, she didn't appear mournful. She dropped a low curtsey.

"No. You don't have to do that," I said.

She looked up in surprise, then smiled.

"I don't think I'll ever get used to the sound of your voice," she said.

I beckoned her to stand. "You'll tire of it quickly. I have a lot of questions."

"Go on."

I glanced at Ula. She was concentrating on embroidering, but I could tell she was listening. How much did I want her to know? Mwiryn followed my gaze.

"We both know what's happened, so there's no need to open old wounds. I suppose you're mostly curious about why I went along with it?" she said.

"Yes." I indicated the settee, and we sat across from each other. She smoothed her hands down her dress, and the firelight reflected off her wedding band. It caught her eye, and she fiddled with it, turning the band over and over.

"I just wanted us to be together," she said.

I leaned closer to hear better.

"She wasn't always so angry," she continued. "She used to be happy. As children, we spent hours in the orchards, climbing trees, playing games, filling our stomachs with apples..." She slid the ring off her finger. "Then Conall sent her away. She was gone for months, and no one would tell me where. When she returned, I wasn't allowed to see her for weeks. When they finally let me, I was shocked at the change in her. She was thin and pale, and so angry. I asked her what happened, and she told me I didn't want to know. I wish I hadn't forced her to tell me."

I covered her hand with mine. "You don't have to go on. Shaeli told me."

Her shoulders sagged. "I don't know how a father could treat his daughter so horribly. I was scared I'd be next, so I left and didn't see her again for a long time. I missed her terribly, but I also feared they'd succeeded, and she didn't love me anymore. But I was wrong. She came to me one night, telling me nothing had changed. Well, something *had* changed. I didn't see it then, but she'd been consumed by her anger. When her father announced his intention to attack Praed and become king, her mother had a vision. Caelyn believed she was destined to destroy him. She drew me and Brannon into the plot. He joined out of greed, and I because I loved her and hoped revenge would heal her soul."

"Did you know she intended to kill Brannon?"

She shook her head. "She told me once Conall was dead, Brannon and I would be king and queen and she would be my lady-in-waiting."

"She wanted to be queen herself. I'm convinced she was going to make you Lord Protector and the two of you would rule from Ilano."

"Perhaps. She hated it here. I never understood why." She took a deep breath. "It wasn't until she attacked you and threw you in the dungeon that I realized how bloodthirsty she'd become. The woman I loved was gone."

"I'm sorry."

"I had to do whatever it took to keep Brannon and Caelyn off the throne, even if it meant becoming a murderer myself."

I furrowed my brow. "What?"

"When King Risteard surrounded the castle, Brannon panicked. He wanted to surrender, but Caelyn wanted to fight. I didn't want a war, for innocent people to die because of them. So, I told him about the Law of Bern. He dismissed it, knowing he couldn't defeat Risteard one-on-one, but I appealed to his ego. He thought about it, then agreed."

"He planned to cheat."

"Knowing Brannon, I'm sure of it. I promise I didn't know. I just wanted Risteard to win."

"Did you plan on giving him the crown when he did?"

She spread her hands wide. "According to the Law of Bern, the victor wins the crown. Risteard and I were never close, but I knew him to be an honorable man. Like his father before him, he was respected in Ilano. Anyone would be a better king than Brannon, but I felt Risteard would give us our best chance."

"What about you? Why did you give me the crown?"

"Would you have wanted me to rule alongside your husband?" The side of her mouth quirked in a wry smile.

"I trust both of you. You would have kept your relationship purely political."

"Thank you. The truth is, I never wanted to be queen. I wanted Caelyn and I to be together. Without her, I've lost all my ambition." Her lips quivered in a forced smile.

"I hope her punishment hasn't upset you too much."

"You could have sentenced her to death, and you would have been justified. I thank you for sparing her."

I didn't want to distress her, nor did I wish to waste my breath talking about Brannon and Caelyn. Both of us needed a change of subject.

"By rights, Conall's lands and holdings are yours. I hope you'll be comfortable there."

"Thank you, but I'll be returning to my family home."

"Why? After putting up with being Brannon's wife, you've earned a life of your own."

She laughed, a brief, sweet sound, and shook her head.

"I wish to put the past behind me," she said. "I can't do that if I'm the mistress of Fionchar."

"Very well." I tried not to betray how irritable her decision made me, though I understood her reasoning. "We'll find someone to lease the estate. I insist the rent be paid to *you*." I raised my hand to halt her protest. "Please. For my own conscience if not for yours."

"As you wish, Your Majesty."

"If it'll make you feel better, we'll tax it heavily."

She smiled. "It would. Thank you, Your Majesty."

"I don't know if I'll ever get used to that."

"I think you'll make a great queen. You already have experience with patience."

Ula coughed to cover a laugh. I stared daggers at her, but she ignored me.

"I'll endeavor to deserve the honor. I would hate to disappoint you. This was your doing after all."

"No. It was yours. I knew Risteard would win, not because of his skill, but because he had *you* to fight for. And he had you to fight for *him*. Do you see? I didn't just want Risteard to be king. I wanted *you* as my queen."

"Are you ready?" Risteard asked.

I stared at his hand poised over the door of the council chambers. My hands were clasped to hide their trembling, and the churning in my stomach had nothing to do with the child. I was wary of civil discussion with Ilanos, worried they believed me a savage, as Caelyn had. It was wrong of me to allow a few people to define a nation, but I remained uneasy.

"Open the door," I said before I completely lost my nerve.

The councilmen rose and knocked their knuckles against the tables in welcome. I scanned the room and noted some men were less enthusiastic than others. Not everyone was happy with the new arrangement. It was going to get worse before it got better.

I lowered myself into my chair and Risteard gestured for silence.

"Be seated," he said.

The room echoed with the scraping of chairs and rustling of papers. Risteard and I planned this meeting carefully. We were going to make changes many of the councilmen wouldn't like. The younger men could be bought, but the older men had honor. We needed all of them on our side.

"Gentlemen," Risteard said. "We know it's been difficult for you with all of the uncertainty and upheaval this past year. Your loyalty to the crown has been commendable."

I watched a few men shift and bit the inside of my lip to keep from smiling.

"We all want stability and prosperity. But we can no longer consider these things exclusive to Ilano."

Their eyes turned to me. I raised my chin and stared back.

"We are two countries united under one crown, formed not by war, but marriage."

He looked at me and I couldn't help smiling.

"In order for Praed and Ilano to prosper, we must work together. Build on our strengths, promote trade, and be treated equally."

A few nodded, but otherwise the room was still.

"We know things will be rough at first while we learn to work together, but if we're patient, we'll become the strongest country on the continent." He spread out the notes we'd spent half the night writing.

The men leaned forward, and I studied their faces. My eyes alighted on Armen Ferrys beaming at Risteard like a proud father. I smiled. I knew I liked him.

Risteard cleared his throat. "Our first order will be to pay recompense to Praed lords who lost their lands. We have a list of those still living. Their homes will be returned to them."

The council erupted in anger. I sat back, noting the men who protested the loudest, while Risteard glared. The back of his neck turned red and his hand curled into a fist. I squeezed this thigh under the table. The last thing we needed was Risteard losing his temper. I folded my hands and rose, hoping I looked graceful. The protests ceased.

"I understand your anger, my lords. No one wants to be forced from their home." I paused, and they had the decency to look ashamed. "We don't intend to leave you homeless. If you will allow His Majesty the courtesy of listening, he will explain." I sat back down.

Some of the younger councilmen grumbled, but Risteard was able to continue without further interruption. Our plan was simple. Confiscated lands would be returned to the closest living relative. If there was none, the Ilano lord may retain the land. An Ilano lord who must give up his Praed estate could return to Ilano or build a new estate on Praed land gifted by the crown. We knew this decision would cause the greatest debate, and it was hours before the men were settled enough to accept it. We moved on to the proposal for a new Lord Protector, which the council welcomed since none of them cared for the incompetent oaf currently in office. Risteard elected his friend and loyal ally Efram Ekhane. The council agreed.

The last item on our agenda for this first meeting was to announce the addition of Praed lords to the council. There was a ripple of discontent, but no outright objections.

There was so much more to do, but we were pleased with this first meeting. However, there were two men whose notable absence weighed on my thoughts. Arlen and Crane were confined to their rooms while Risteard and I debated on what to do with them. Regardless of how we felt about King Conall, these men committed treason. Their large spy network and intelligence meant they could also be powerful allies. Risteard suggested we offer a pardon in exchange for their service, but men who served because of fear were as dangerous as snakes about to be trampled. I wanted them on our side, but I wanted it to be their choice. I wanted their loyalty.

Instead of summoning Arlen and Crane to the throne room, I decided it would be less intimidating to meet privately. The last time I was in Crane's rooms, I was terrified of being discovered. Now, I strolled casually around the room, making the men wait while I studied the tapestry, the bookcase, and the desk. Arlen's fingers rapped against the armrest, but a sharp glare from Risteard stilled them. Crane reclined in his chair and inspected his nails. I wandered to the hearth and stared into the flames.

"You've no doubt heard of Caelyn's exile?" Risteard said.

"Yes," Arlen said. He glanced at Crane, but he continued to look bored. "We appreciate your mercy but wonder what your majesties intend for us."

I silently left the hearth and sank into a lush chair next to Risteard.

"That depends on how you picture your future," Risteard said. "You committed treason, yet you're still alive. Why do you think that is?"

"You need us," Arlen said, a smug smile on his face. "So, what are you offering?"

I felt Risteard's eyes on me, but I focused on Crane. He not only remained silent, but he wouldn't look at us. He reminded me of a child biding their time until an elderly relative left.

"To offer your lives in exchange for compliance seems contrived, don't you think?" Risteard said.

Arlen smiled. "Nothing less would suffice. With all due respect, Your Majesty, we can't be bought. If you wish to sentence us to death for our crimes, so be it."

I could hear Risteard's frustration building, but we'd prepared for this.

"For all time," I said.

Crane finally looked up, his dark eyes fixated on me. Arlen glanced at him, then quickly looked away.

"What does it mean?" I asked.

The crackle of flames filled the silence as Crane and I stared at each other. His color rose and his fingers dug into the armrests. I leaned forward, pushing all my sympathy into my eyes, and laid a hand over his. He tensed under my touch, but he didn't pull away.

"There will be no punishment," I said. "Not for those who fight for justice. For peace. You are safe here."

Crane and Arlen's eyes locked, and for several seconds, they engaged in a conversation only they could hear. Risteard's fingers brushed down my face, but my gaze didn't falter from the two men.

Arlen turned to us, his features drawn. "If we return to Ilano, we're nothing. If we stay, will we continue to serve the council?"

"Yes," Risteard said.

"Then we'll stay," Crane said. He leaned back and folded his hands in his lap. "To serve your majesties however you wish."

"We are in need of men with vision," I said. "To help our countries move forward."

"We are at your disposal, Your Majesty," Arlen said. His voice was hoarse and sweat glistened on his brow. Was he relieved or afraid?

Risteard stood. "Gentlemen, your confinement is at an end. You're free to move about the castle. We'll see you in council tomorrow." I took his offered elbow and we left Arlen and Crane alone.

Later I asked, "Do you think it worked?"

"Did you mean it? Are they safe?" Risteard said.

"Of course."

"They believed you. It worked."

Arlen and Crane attended every council meeting thereafter as we worked to rebuild. A surprising number of Ilano chose to stay, and the population of Praed increased. This led to the construction of a larger market, resumption of the horse breeding trade, and overall surge in prosperity. Ilano and Praed exported goods across the border, strengthening our reliance on each other. Subsidies were granted to farmers, resulting in a surge of crops. For the first time in three years, Praed families were profiting alongside Ilanos.

I felt the gravity of our victory fully when I visited Thistledon to personally invite Thom to sit on the new council. He took me to the stables barely able to repress a smile and led me to a stall. Inside, a gorgeous ebony mare perked her ears, hay dangling from her mouth.

Thom placed his hand against her belly. "Feel here," he said.

I ran a hand over her glossy coat. Her stomach gurgled, but I felt nothing else. I raised an eyebrow.

"We bred her last week. The first ebony foal in three years," he said.

I smiled, my vision blurred, and hugged him.

Praed wasn't going to return to normal. It was going to be better.

EPILOGUE

The graceful gait I worked so diligently to perfect gradually devolved into an awkward waddle with the increase in my waistline. The discomfort I experienced was secondary to how grateful I felt to be alive and carrying the child I came so close to losing. Risteard not only proved himself a fully capable king, but a devoted husband. I looked out at the falling snow, recalling the first time I felt the child move. I was sitting with Ula reading stories when I suddenly felt a flutter, as if hundreds of bubbles were popping inside me. I clutched my belly and gasped, frightening Ula to pieces. The feeling continued, and against my hand there was the tiniest push. I dismissed Ula's panic and told her to get Risteard immediately. She'd never ran so fast, even though she was still very afraid of him. He burst into the room minutes later, and without a word, I placed his hand against my belly. He waited--a rare show of patience--but nothing happened. I frowned, and just when I was about to release his hand, the fluttering happened again, followed by what I guessed was kicking that Risteard could now feel. He hugged me, and we laughed and cried together.

The child was large enough now I could watch it dancing underneath my stomach, and I would lie for hours wondering what it could possibly find amusing in that dark and confined space. Risteard came to check on me one afternoon to discover me laughing hysterically at my own notion that I was growing an acrobat and the child would cartwheel out of my womb. He didn't find the fantasy so hilarious, but he did find the strange movements of my belly entrancing. Once, I was certain I could feel the outline of the child's foot, and I made Risteard feel it to confirm. I expected him to laugh, but his eyes misted and he asked in a sweet, awed tone:

"Is that really a foot?"

I nodded.

He smiled. "I can feel it."

I wanted to say something like, 'What did you think was growing in there?' but he looked so innocent I couldn't bring myself to spoil the moment. I forgot that while he was experiencing every moment he could, he wasn't carrying the child himself, didn't feel every kick and movement or have his bladder squished constantly. These moments were few and therefore precious to him. He laid his face against my belly, and I smiled, running my fingers through his hair, feeling I couldn't possibly love him more.

The time of my confinement was nearing, but I refused to be 'confined.' Risteard knew better than to argue, but Mother, who had travelled from Riverstone to stay for the birth, was adamant I at least keep to my rooms.

"You don't want to be in the middle of a council meeting or in the Great Hall and have your waters break in front of everyone, do you?"

"It would certainly give them something to talk about," I said. To keep the peace, I agreed to my mother's request. I didn't care for company much these days anyway.

The impending birth was a few weeks away, and I was all too willing to heed my mother's advice and rest myself while winter settled over Praed. A fire roared in the hearth, and I sat in a cushioned chair while Mother tried to teach me how to sew swaddling clothes. I should have been comfortable, but my expansive belly made it difficult to find a favorable position to sit, and I was constantly shifting and stretching my aching back.

"You need to make the stitches neater and closer together, Your Majesty. Otherwise, the fabric will tear," Mother said.

I rubbed my sore sides. "How many times do I have to tell you? You don't have to address me so formally when it's just us." 'Us' meaning me, Mother, Ula, and a few ladies busy minding their own business.

"You are the queen, Laria, and I want to show respect for your title," Mother answered.

"Show me some respect as your daughter and hand me that pillow." She looked at me oddly but did as I asked. I stuffed the pillow behind my back.

"Are you discomforted?" Mother asked.

"Ugh, obviously! I'm the size of a horse." I felt a sharp pain in my side again, and I changed position in the chair to help relieve the strain.

"Are you having pains?" She set her embroidery aside. Ula looked up to attend the conversation.

"Yes. In my ass. Stop asking so many questions!" An excruciating pain spread from my spine to my abdomen. I doubled over and cried out, clutching my stomach.

Mother calmly singled out one of the ladies. "You. Send for the midwife. The queen's labor has begun."

"It's too soon," I squeaked out between bouts of pain.

"Clearly it's not," she said. "Help me, Ula." Together, my mother and sister lifted me by my forearms, half carried me to my bedchamber, and stripped me down to my underclothes. I was pacing around the room, feeling perfectly fine, when the midwife entered accompanied by a familiar face.

"Seline?"

"Your Majesty," she curtseyed.

"So, you've become a midwife?"

"Still in training, Your Grace."

"We have been through much together. Please call me Laria."

"Come, Laria." Seline indicated the bed. "The midwife Fryda, would like to examine you and see how you're coming along."

"She's wasting her time, I'm afraid. I'm not in labor."

The midwife examined me, which was incredibly awkward in front of my mother and sister. She peeked over the top of my nightgown.

"Whether you believe it or not," Fryda said. "You're having this baby today." Proving her point, a sharp pain took my breath away.

Seline took my arm. "Come on. Let's take a walk." She led me around the room, talking me through the pain and rubbing my back. At one point, while I was practically screaming in pain, I realized the man responsible was nowhere in sight.

"Where's Risteard?" I growled. "I want him to see what he's done to me." Mother, Fryda, and Seline hid smiles, and I nearly screamed.

"Ula," Mother said.

My sister perked up, ready to help.

"Go tell the king the queen's labor pains have started."

Her face was pallid, but she rushed from the room.

I was an embarrassing mess. One moment I was angry and resentful and the next I was crying and sentimental. The pains were coming closer and closer together, and I inexplicably gained more respect for my mother for bearing this more than once.

After an eternity, Ula burst into the room and announced the king was waiting outside the door. I moved toward it, but Mother stopped me.

"This isn't a place for men," she said.

"He was there for the conception," I said. "Why not the aftermath?"

Mother didn't bat an eyelash. "Men are perfectly capable of handling the making of a child. But they don't have the stomach for the birthing."

"It's true," Fryda said. "Even the strongest men faint when they see their woman bear a child."

I swayed when I walked toward the door and pressed myself against its cool surface.

"Risteard," I called.

"Laria!" His voice was muffled through the thick wood. "Are you all right?"

What a stupid question.

"They said you can't come in," I said, and another pain wracked my body.

"What do *you* want?" he asked, and I could almost feel the heat from his hands where I pressed mine against the door.

I gritted my teeth. "I don't want you to see me like this."

"I've seen you in worse states."

I smiled and glanced at Mother, but she shook her head.

"I'll have them send for you when the child's born." A tear trickled down my face, then intense pain stabbed through my belly, nearly bringing me to my knees.

Seline supported me while leading me to the bed, and Fryda assessed my progress.

"Soon, Your Majesty," she said.

Soon came in what felt like hours of pain and agony. Several times I wanted to slap Mother to upset her composure. I wanted to curse at Fryda every time she wanted to 'check me.' And I wanted to scratch the serene smile off Seline's face.

I had walked miles around the room when Fryda instructed Ula to brace me against the bedpost.

"It's time," Fryda said. "On the next pain, bear down."

"What does that even mean?" I grunted through a particularly sharp pain.

"Push," she said shortly. "The child is ready to be born." On cue, a flood of liquid poured from between my legs. At this point in the evening, my entire insides could have fallen out and I wouldn't have cared.

The room faded, and I pushed down with every pain, my teeth clenched, and my eyes closed tightly. My mother tried to encourage me, but the sound of her voice gave me a headache, and I rudely told her to shut her mouth.

"I see the head!" Fryda said. "Get her on the bed."

Seline and Mother helped me lie down. Ula dabbed my forehead with a damp cloth, and the cool dampness felt refreshing on my hot skin.

"Now is not the time to rest, Your Majesty," Fryda said. "Push!" I could feel my energy draining with each effort, but I tapped into my reserves, gritted my teeth, and pushed.

"The head is out! You're doing beautifully, Your Majesty!" Every update of progress from Fryda gave me the extra strength I needed to continue, and I clutched Ula's hand hard for strength to bring the child into the world.

"Small pushes now," Fryda advised. "The shoulders are coming." I did as she asked, ignoring my mother's added comments.

"Easy now," Fryda said. "Take a break, Your Majesty. The next few pushes and the child will be born."

I opened my eyes, and the blurred face of Ula came slowly into focus.

"I can't do this anymore," I told her.

"Yes, you can," Mother said. "You've conquered worse than this."

"Remember when you were trying to teach Amore to jump logs?" Ula asked. "She kept shying away and more than once you were pitched to the ground. You never gave up, even when you were exhausted and bruised. You were too stubborn and determined to give up then. You can't give up now. You're so close."

Bolstered by my sister's words, I pushed hard. Pain raced up my spine, and I screamed.

A tiny cry echoed in the room and I collapsed against the pillows. The high-pitched voices of the women around me mingled until they became one. I felt the urge to bury my face in a pillow to drown them out. My eyes fluttered open when I heard the raspy cry of a babe, and all other sounds ceased to exist. I reached my arms out, and a small, warm bundle was placed on my chest. Everything around me became insignificant when I gazed wearily into a little pink face, wide eyes looking curiously at me while tiny fingers clenched and unclenched.

"What is it?" Mother asked.

"A boy," Fryda beamed. "A fine, healthy boy."

"Look at his tiny fingers!" Ula squealed.

"A little prince," Mother smiled. "Well done, my girl."

I could not take my eyes off him, his beautiful face, even to acknowledge my mother. I never believed in the fairy tale notion of love at first sight until I looked into the hazy blue eyes of my son.

I floated in a dream. "Ula, tell the king he may come in now. I'm sure he's anxious."

Ula left to open the door, but I could not tear my eyes from the tiny infant. When I heard Risteard's heavy footsteps, I looked up.

"Come," Mother said to Ula. "Let's give them some privacy." The midwife followed, leaving Seline to finish cleaning the room.

"Come here," I beckoned Risteard, holding out my hand. "Come meet your son."

"My son?" He smiled dreamily and sat next to me on the bed.

"I'll give you some time alone," Seline said. "I'll return shortly to show you how to feed him."

"Thank you."

"You did beautifully," she said. "You were made to have children."

Our son held Risteard's finger in his tiny fist, and I sighed when my husband placed a gentle kiss on his soft skin.

"Would you like to hold him?"

Risteard looked worried, but I placed the precious bundle securely in his arms.

"I've been thinking of a name," I said while stroking the fine hair of the baby's head, reveling in the feathery softness.

Risteard made a noncommittal noise and continued to admire our son.

"How would you feel if we called him Alyx?"

Risteard swallowed audibly, and I feared I made a mistake in suggesting we name our son after his grandfather. But the glint in Risteard's eyes when he looked at me said otherwise.

"I would like that," he whispered. He leaned forward and kissed me softly, and I felt a rush of emotion that nearly made me weep.

Alyx began to fuss, which progressed to a wail. Seline returned and said it was time for him to feed. Risteard gently placed him in my arms, and Seline stared at him expectantly.

"What's wrong?" I asked.

"Forgive me, Laria, but the husband is not usually present for the feedings," Seline said.

I looked at Risteard then said, "He's seen my breast before. If he doesn't want to be here, that's one thing, but he's going to see me feed our child eventually."

Her gaze flicked to Risteard, and his stony response was enough to convince her to proceed. She opened the front of my nightgown and instructed me on how to help my son latch to my breast.

"How will I know when he's finished?" I asked.

"He'll stop," she said practically. "He'll most likely feed every few hours around the clock." She hesitated, looking shyly at her feet. "Many noblewomen and queens choose to have a wet nurse---"

"I will feed him myself."

"I figured you would. I just wanted to offer." She smiled, looking as tired as I felt, and left us alone again.

Risteard and I watched our son feed from my breast in silence, both of us running a finger along his impossibly soft skin. Risteard nuzzled my neck and trailed delicate kisses from the line of my jaw to my collarbone.

"I think I must warn you," I said.

"Of what?"

"I expect you to give me at least a half dozen children."

"A half dozen?" he repeated with a half-smile.

"At least," I clarified.

His grin broadened. "Whatever you wish, Your Majesty. I am yours to command."

ACKNOWLEDGMENTS

I once had a teacher who said my poetry made him green with envy. I had a veterinarian tell me I had a real talent. It is to them I extend my appreciation. And it is to my mother I extend my thanks, for she exhausted her carpus tendons writing frantically as I dictated stories as a small child and typed until the wee hours the hand written book I wrote at 16 so that I could see my words on paper. Every one of you are why I am here today.

To my amazing editor, Ron, who forced me to question all my life decisions and made Laria's story what it is today. Your advice was worth its weight in gold. Buckle up for the next book, good sir.

Special shout out to my beta reader, Krista, who is always eager to point out my flaws.

My beautiful cover is by Violet Design. Thank you for putting up with all my nitpicking, Rena! I can't wait to work on our next project together.

This book would never have made it to page without the support and encouragement of my wonderful husband, Rick. Chapter by chapter, you've been there to urge me forward and I cannot thank you enough. Let's go have an adventure!

ABOUT THE AUTHOR

Mandy received her B.S. in Zoology from Washington State University and an A.S. in Veterinary Technology from St. Petersburg College. Clearly, her life goals were not geared toward a career as an author. She is a Certified Veterinary Technician specializing in small animals on the Oregon Coast. When she's not saving lives, she's weaving tales of strong women using their intelligence to pursue incandescent happy endings. The Rise of Riverstone has been a labor of love and is the debut novel in her Daughters of Riverstone series. She lives on the Washington coast with her husband and their four children as well as a menagerie of pets. Besides leaning uncomfortably over a computer screen, Mandy enjoys camping and hiking with her family, reading, and wearing out her dogs on the beach.

www.ingramcontent.com/pod-product-compliance
Lightning Source LLC
Chambersburg PA
CBHW021239200726
48288CB00014B/80